ACQUAINTED WITH THE NIGHT

I have stood still and stopped the sound of feet
When far away an interrupted cry
Came over houses from another street

But not to call me back or say good-by;
And further still at an unearthly height
One luminary clock against the sky

Proclaimed the time was neither wrong nor right.
I have been one acquainted with the night.

'Acquainted with the Night'
ROBERT FROST (1874–1963)

ACQUAINTED WITH THE NIGHT

Edited by
Barbara Roden and Christopher Roden

Ash-Tree Press
Ashcroft, British Columbia
2004

First published 2004
by Ash-Tree Press
P.O. Box 1360
Ashcroft, British Columbia
Canada V0K 1A0
www.ash-tree.bc.ca/ashtreecurrent.html

ISBN: 1-55310-075-1 (Limited Edition)
ISBN: 1-55310-076-X (Paperback)

This edition © Ash-Tree Press 2004
All stories © the individual authors 2004
Introduction © Barbara and Christopher Roden 2004
Cover artwork © Jason van Hollander 2004

All rights reserved. No part of this publication may be reproduced, stored in a retrieval system, or transmitted, in any form or by any means, electronic, mechanical, photocopying, recording, and/or otherwise, without the prior permission of the publishers.

Ash-Tree Press makes every effort to obtain permission for the use of copyright material. Any errors or omissions in attribution of copyright are entirely unintentional. If notified, the publisher will be pleased to make any necessary correction at the earliest opportunity.

Typesetting and design by Ash-Tree Press
Printed and bound in Canada by Morriss Printing Ltd, Victoria, B.C.

CONTENTS

Introduction	vii
Mark P. Henderson	
Rope Trick	3
Don Tumasonis	
A Pace of Change	19
Simon Bestwick	
Beneath the Sun	38
Brian Showers	
The Old Tailor and the Gaunt Man	42
Joseph A. Ezzo	
Vado Mori	54
Ramsey Campbell	
Breaking Up	70
Barbara Roden	
Northwest Passage	80
Gary McMahon	
Out On a Limb	105
Edward Pearce	
Jenny Gray's House	113
Reggie Oliver	
The Devil's Number	130
Melanie Tem	
Visits	136
Adam Golaski	
Weird Furka	149
Jessica Amanda Salmonson	
The Weeping Manse	170

Chico Kidd
    Salvage   176

Joel Lane
    Beyond the River   199

Peter Bell
    Only Sleeping   209

Cathy Sahu
    You Should Have to Live with Yourself   228

John Whitbourn
    The Sunken Garden   244

Edward P. Crandall
    Survivors   252

Steve Rasnic Tem
    Inside William James   266

Steve Duffy
    Someone Across the Way   272

Rick Kennett
    The Cross Talk   291

Paul Finch
    The Belfries   294

John Pelan
    Crazy Little Thing Called Love   318

Stephen Volk
    Three Fingers, One Thumb   326

Glen Hirshberg
    Safety Clowns   330

Christopher Harman
    The Listener   351

    Biographical Notes   363

Introduction

IN HIS REVIEW OF *Shadows and Silence* (2000), our previous volume of new weird and supernatural fiction, Stefan Dziemianowicz wrote: 'Its contributors have all clearly been nurtured on classic weird fiction, but their efforts are hardly the familiar or derivative writing that might have been expected. The quality and diversity of their contributions suggests that the basic principles that informed the landmarks of weird fiction continue to instruct writers of today, and that the lessons they teach never grow outdated or irrelevant.'

What is important, of course, is that writers, however steeped in tradition they are, should continue to strive for new ways of invoking the frisson that we seek in our supernatural fiction. We may feel that a certain plot has a familiar feel to it, but a good writer of spooky stories will be able to find an original, modern, or inventive twist sufficient to convince us that the story isn't familiar after all. The 'spooky' tale remains a work in progress—it continues to develop in the same way that the world around us is changing all the time. It is as possible to conjure up a chill from shadows lurking in a dim corner of a room lit by electricity as it was when rooms were lit by gas lamps; and as possible to find horrors in a modern urban scene as in the gas-lit squalor of Whitechapel.

For *Acquainted With the Night* we have brought together the work of twenty-seven modern practitioners who all clearly know their craft, and who are able to conjure up chills and horrors in locations as far apart as a Dolomite peak and a remote valley in the Canadian interior, and as diverse as a brand new housing estate in rural Britain and a razzamatazz American theme park.

May your reading be a suitably chilling experience.

BARBARA RODEN
CHRISTOPHER RODEN
ASHCROFT
NOVEMBER MMIV

ACQUAINTED WITH THE NIGHT

Rope Trick

Mark P. Henderson

Dear Suzie,
Soaked, famished, pissed off with Assynt, rain, Roger, and all other dreary prospects. Got some Durness limestone (section for microfossils—some hope!) and a few bits of gneiss etc. Rowland's as philosophical as ever but he can't plead a case for the Highlands any longer. Home Wednesday, D.V.—get your knickers off.
Love,
Pete

Dear Conrad,
Laxford Bridge is a name on our map signifying nothing in immediate experience. Whether the packed countour lines correspond to real-world mountains, as alleged, a ten-day season of mists and hellish fruitlessness has not revealed. I can testify to the region's reputation for rain, midges, and high petrol prices. Book dinner for Szabo's 8 p.m. Wednesday and remind Camilla I'll collect her at 7.15.
Regards,
Rowland

Dear Mother,
Wilderness, especially without views, makes me crave civilisation; shameful, but neither Shelley nor Swinburne had to suffer Rowland's endless cigars and Latin quotations or Pete's adrenaline highs and tendency to bang rocks together. I put it down to experience—one I shan't repeat. I have very few pictures; the weather's been too unkind.
Best wishes,
Roger

MARK P. HENDERSON

THREE POSTCARDS SLID INTO THE BOX with a faint hollow thud; Peter Brent had almost expected a splash. He shook the rain from his hair and beard and climbed back into the driver's seat. Roger Vance, half-buried among the overspill of luggage on the back seat, wiped his spectacles; the damp map on his knee looked cramped. Brent started the engine and the BMW faded into the unending drizzle. Their watches indicated mid-afternoon; the light indicated no time at all.

'At least we can't mistake the road, since there's only one,' commented Rawlinson. He had adjusted the passenger seat to his comfort.

'Until Lairg,' amended Vance.

Brent offered no remark. The long glaciated valley between harsh ancient hills could permit of only one route, hugging the loch-side. Further east, where the rock was younger and more yielding, there would be a choice of roads. Landform would always be the primary determinant of human activity.

'Impossible to maintain a centralised system of government or law here before the advent of modern communications,' mused Rawlinson. 'One understands the survival of the clan system.'

'Personally,' said Vance, 'I can't understand the survival of anything here, except waterfowl and midges.' He shifted amongst the luggage. The camera strap slid down his shoulder.

'Okay, Roger, the weather's been lousy,' snapped Brent. 'Let's drop it. You don't win 'em all.'

'*Non semper vincis*,' smiled Rawlinson. 'Possible motto for the MacDonalds, I suppose. Though doubtless my geography's inaccurate.'

'Out by a hundred miles or so, Rowland,' agreed Brent.

'Case of mass euthanasia, if they had to stand this bloody climate,' moaned Vance.

The valley widened, the mist vanished, and the sky cleared. The occupants of the BMW cried a cynical greeting to sudden warm sunlight; they were driving through wide-open green——

'Hang on, this isn't right.' Vance squinted at the map. 'What was that about not being able to mistake the road?'

A brief silence hung.

'Who was navigating?' sneered Brent. 'Taken you just half an hour to get us to Sussex.'

'I told you you drove too fast.'

'Sussex minus all signs of human habitation,' interrupted Rawlinson. 'Certainly green and pleasant, but the vista terminates in cloud-capped mountains, suggesting that we remain in the Highlands.'

'This map's bloody inaccurate,' frowned Vance. 'We should still be in that narrow valley. Glen. There's nothing like this.'

'Rowland's inaccurate as well. Again,' added Brent. 'I spy a house.'

Large, white-harled, set back from the road amid a stand of native trees. It was quite alone; not another building in sight.

The engine cut out. Brent swore and guided the idling vehicle into the roadside. Rawlinson lit a cigar.

'What's wrong, Pete?' inquired Vance.

Brent took a deep breath and with studied patience replied, 'The car's stopped.' He unlocked the bonnet, leapt out of the moribund BMW, and thrust the upper part of his body into the maw of the engine housing. Rawlinson stepped on to the verge. Vance struggled after him, brandishing the map.

'Look, Rowland, it's just not here. Not this plain, not the house.'

'The map represents the map-maker's perception,' replied Rawlinson, 'not ours. Do you agree that we stand in warm early evening sunlight in a quiet green place close to a large white house?'

'Yes, but——'

'Those are our sense data. Maps are second-hand knowledge. Which do we believe?' Rawlinson inhaled cigar smoke and released it again slowly.

'Of course, but the discrepancy——'

'Is of no consequence, unless we're sharing an illusion.'

'I'm sure we're not,' agreed Vance, 'but let's have evidence anyway.' He opened his camera case and began to photograph the landscape.

'We already have evidence,' said Rawlinson, pointing towards his eyes, 'though I agree a permanent record——'

'I need the tool kit,' announced Brent. 'Probably the electrics.'

He was wrong. The ignition seemed faultless. The battery was fully charged. The tank was half full and the fuel system in good order. Brent shook his head.

'Let's ask at the house and ring the AA. I can't find anything wrong. She just won't start again.'

Fifty metres to the house gates, another fifty of drive.

'The map's not altogether wrong,' commented Rawlinson softly. 'So far as I saw, the road didn't fork.'

'It didn't,' confirmed Brent.

'But if it's the only road,' murmured Vance, 'how come there's been no traffic either way for the past three-quarters of an hour?'

Nobody answered. The gravel of the drive was raked and weedless, the lawns immaculate, the flower beds lovingly tended. There was no one around but themselves. No sound but the gravel beneath their boots.

'No telephone wires,' resumed Vance.

'Underground?' wondered Rawlinson.

Brent gave a sharp bark of laughter. 'This country? This distance?'

'There's money here,' returned Rawlinson, 'and it's isolated. They're almost certain to have a means of communication. And transport.'

Everything was clean, freshly minted. The drive curved to the front of the house. Two steps up to the covered portico. Rawlinson pressed the button beside the door and a bell sounded faintly in the depths of the house.

No response.

'Just our bleeding luck,' growled Brent. 'They're shopping. Or on holiday.'

'Visiting the neighbours?' Vance's voice was a touch tremulous.

'Leaving the door open,' added Rawlinson. He pushed the door and it swung wide with only a slight creak. 'Well . . . since there's no one at home, and we only need to make a short phone call, and the telephone is almost certainly in the hall, where all respectable telephones live. . . .'

'Rowland, we can't just walk into . . .'

'We have a problem, Roger. Not an emergency, true; but if you were the absent owner, would you object to stranded travellers using your phone?'

'Maybe not, but I don't like to . . .'

'Think Kant, Roger. Categorical imperative.' Rawlinson crushed out his cigar, disfiguring the edge of the upper step.

Brent pushed past his companions into the house.

'Lots of hall, not a phone in sight,' he announced.

The others followed him slowly. The hall was half-panelled; embossed wallpaper in its upper reaches; moulded plaster cornices. A mounted stag's head.

'Wonder how fast *that* was going when it hit the wall?'

Rawlinson tapped on a door on the left and pushed it open. He sniffed.

'They're not far away,' he decided.

The others entered the room in his wake; a library. Rawlinson touched the back and seat of the black leather wing-chair.

'Warm.' He sniffed again. 'Chanel Number 5. Common, according to Camilla.' He picked a long strand of red hair from the chair-back and displayed it. Then he called loudly, making the others jump: 'Hell-o?'

No answer.

'Back garden,' suggested Brent.

'Possibly. Let's go and see.'

Rawlinson took a step towards the French windows and then, reconsidering, led the way back into the hall; an owner in the garden would be angry at strangers coming through rather than around the house. Two paces beyond the library door he stopped dead. Standing at the far end of the hall was a small, slight Asiatic man in an immaculate white suit. His face was impassive, his age impossible to estimate. He had not been there before, all three were sure. Despite the gloom they would have seen the white suit.

Rawlinson found his voice first.

'We're sorry to intrude, but our car has broken down and we want to ask use of your telephone. We rang the bell. There was no answer, but the door was open. . . .'

ROPE TRICK

The Indian watched steadily, unreadably; no reaction, no movement. No hostility but no welcome. No understanding?

'Do you have a telephone, and please may we use it?'

No response. Rawlinson mimed the acts of lifting a handset and dialling. Still no reaction.

'Let's check the garden,' muttered Vance.

Brent spoke slowly and loudly. 'Is this your house? Or is the owner here?' Still no movement, no word. 'The red-haired lady?' added Brent.

The silence hung. There was no clock in the hall.

Whether the last question had evoked it, or some internal debate had concluded, the Indian finally moved: two steps right, still facing them; a bow, left arm horizontally extended. The invitation was clear. The trio advanced slowly. A dim carpeted passage to their left was politely guarded by the silent Asian. To their right, where the extended hand ushered them, a staircase; light oak banisters, carved newel post, the whole lit through a cupola by the westering sun. It was plain but well-proportioned. ('But you could say the same about Tina Turner,' thought Brent, 'except for the cupola.') Vance's eyes appreciated the curve of the staircase and the etchings of Highland scenery on the walls.

The three men climbed the stairs.

Apart from the usual appointments, the first bedroom contained Vance's suitcase. The walls were decorated with enlarged panoramic photographs of the area, the full sequence of pictures encircling the four walls, interrupted only by the door and the wardrobe and complemented by the living view through the window. In the second bedroom, Brent's suitcase and rucksack lay on the floor in front of a display cabinet filled with geological specimens: rock crystal, dog's tooth calcite and Iceland spar, a feldspar bearing (presumably) malachite, and another striped with bands of galena. (No—on closer inspection, the second feldspar was actually barytes.) On the bedside table of Rawlinson's room was a leather-bound volume of Virgil and a cloth-bound edition of Juvenal's *Satires*, together with a paperback copy of Hume's *Inquiry into Human Understanding*. His window overlooked the back garden, which was defended on all sides by the trees. There was a decorative maze and a sundial, perfectly maintained. But the nearest approximations to human occupancy were a statue of an eighteenth century Irish bishop and another of Pan. Rawlinson opened the Virgil and immediately heard Brent's voice on the landing.

'Look, pal, this is generous, but we're not asking to stay.' His tone had the bluster of mild anxiety. 'All we want is to ring the AA.'

Rawlinson stepped out of his room. The Indian, inscrutable as ever, was facing Brent. Vance was sidling towards them, looking worried.

'Let's be logical, Pete,' said Rawlinson firmly. 'Unless we get a lift, we can't go anywhere till the car's repaired. It's evening, so it would be silly to walk, and anyway we've all the luggage. Our friend here realises this but either

7

cannot, or for some presumably good reason will not, answer us, and none of us can speak any language of the Subcontinent. So he's inviting us to stay to await someone who can help us. We have evidence for at least one Caucasian resident: red hair. I suggest we accept this Asiatic offer of Highland hospitality with good grace.' He smiled warmly at the Indian, who responded with a slight bow.

'How did he get our stuff up here?' muttered Vance. 'There wasn't time.'

'Others. Servants.' Brent shrugged. 'Car isn't locked.'

'But so quickly, and without our seeing him? Them?' persisted Vance.

'It's the best hypothesis,' soothed Rawlinson. 'Good servants are invisible. I think Pete's probably right. The house and grounds couldn't be maintained to this standard without a coterie of servants, or at least many willing hands.'

'And they know our tastes. How?' Vance pointed to the rock samples in Brent's display cabinet. 'Those photos on my wall are top-quality work.'

'We're probably not difficult to read: one with a geological hammer, one with a camera.... Anyway, with three differently appointed guest rooms, there's a one-in-six chance of our being allocated appropriately.'

'Right. Three factorial. I fancy a shower,' announced Brent. He strode along the landing. The shower room, containing three fresh towels, was identifiable through its open door. 'Don't want to stay, Roger?' he bellowed, pulling off his boots.

'It's unsettling. Too good to be true,' replied Vance.

'But comfortable,' returned Rawlinson.

'No use, Roger, Rowland wants to meet the redhead. Nice change from Camilla, eh, Rowland?' yelled Brent.

Rawlinson almost replied but closed his mouth again. There was a noise of rushing water and lusty inaccurate singing. The Indian had slipped away again, unnoticed.

'The landscape and weather are surprising, Roger, and the inconsistency with the map is more so,' Rawlinson conceded, 'but we seem to be in hospitable hands, and this surely beats having to sleep outside or in the car with rain-soaked belongings.'

'We're being treated as though we were expected.'

'Good hospitality has that effect.'

'Isolation. No other houses in sight, or on the photos on the wall. No 'phone. No car that I've seen. Only one mute occupant of a house that must take dozens to maintain. No traffic on the roads——'

'None that we've seen or heard,' amended Rawlinson.

'My window overlooks the road. Nothing. No animals in the fields, no farm tracks, no sign of forestry or peat-cutting——'

'Well, if this is the only house——'

'Why is it the only house, in countryside like this?'

'The Highlands are depopulated,' shrugged Rawlinson. 'Our so far invisible host is probably a recluse, but knows how to look after guests. As for the traffic—consider the weather everywhere but here. No one wants to travel in persistent rain.'

'But where is everyone? Owner, servants?' persisted Vance.

'The longer we stay, the likelier we are to see them. Meanwhile, let's follow Pete's excellent example; shower and change.'

Half an hour later the Indian reappeared. Rawlinson was combing his wet hair, the grey at his temples disguised. Polite gestures led them downstairs and along the dim carpeted corridor to the dining-room. The table was set for three. A cold consommé was followed by a fish mousse, then veal escalopes, and lemon sorbet and cheeses; a Sancerre, an unusual Provençal red, port to finish. The Indian served throughout, silently. And at the end he conducted them to a drawing-room, served coffee, provided brandy, offered Rawlinson a cigar and lit it, and effaced himself with a slight bow.

'Some hotel. I could get used to this,' muttered Brent, pouring the brandy.

'Hotel with an apparent staff of one?' queried Vance. 'I think it's weird, Pete. Rowland doesn't seem to agree.'

'I do. Nice rooms, great meal, but it's weird,' affirmed Brent. 'I mean—where's your redhead? That seat was warm from contact with a body, right? She'd been there until almost the moment we arrived. So where did she go, and why hasn't she come back?'

'You're going beyond the evidence,' said Rawlinson. 'But most likely she went out through the French windows. She has her own reasons for not wanting to meet us, at least not yet.'

'What reasons? Virgin?' leered Brent. 'What are you saying, maestro? She heard us tinkering with a dead BMW, instructed Gandhi in the details of our care and maintenance, tiptoed into the garden, and is still hiding out there, with no supper?'

'It's a big house,' replied Rawlinson. 'Perhaps she's in one of the rooms we haven't visited, making it a breach of manners for us to explore. Anyway, this is useless speculation. Let's decide what we do, in the absence of telephone, transport, passers-by, or any available English-speaking resident.'

'I'm all for that. Action,' agreed Brent.

Outside, the long not-dark of the Highland night deepened imperceptibly. A flying beetle struck the window. The sound was startling but normal.

'Get out as soon as possible,' said Vance hollowly.

'Which in practice means tomorrow morning. Next question: how?'

Brent stared at Rawlinson. 'Maybe you're more like me than I thought, Rowland. I expected you to need a full explanation before you considered action. Personally, I think you only find things out by trying, and either succeeding or failing. The details can be resolved later.'

'If "intelligence" signifies anything at all, it's the ability to make correct decisions on the basis of inadequate or incomplete data,' said Rawlinson. 'So . . .?'

'Walk,' said Brent. 'One road, no forks, so we'll get somewhere. We'll head towards Lairg and try to hitch a lift.'

'Why not back up the road we know?' asked Rawlinson.

'Better to head for more inhabited country,' replied Brent. 'All plans assuming the owner doesn't return in the meantime and whisk us off to Lairg in the Rolls.'

'We've yet to see the Rolls. Or, as you pointed out, the owner. Unless our Asian friend is the owner. But there's at least one other person around, as our friend's hair is not long or red and I detect no trace of Chanel about him.' Rawlinson looked closely at Brent. 'You sound definite, Pete, but you're not certain.'

Brent frowned. 'We should also stay here, so's we can explain things to the owner and not land Gandhi in the shit for housing and feeding us. He might have done it all off his own bat. Also, do we just abandon car and luggage to persons we don't know?'

'Why not two of us go and one stay?' suggested Vance. 'Or one go and——'

'I'm not sure,' murmured Rawlinson. '*In unitate sanitas*. What do you think, Pete?'

Brent frowned again. 'Roger's right,' he said at length. 'If we all go it'll look ungracious, even if we leave a note to explain, but one person staying can do the necessary. Two should walk, so if a lift comes, one can go with it while the other comes back here to . . .'

'That's fine, but the problem's deeper than you're admitting,' interrupted Vance. 'You're both expecting rational explanations and outcomes, either by examining the data or by taking action and judging the consequences. Right? Well, I think the presumption's false. The situation's inherently irrational. I mean . . .'

'A situation can't be irrational, Roger,' explained Rawlinson. 'People are rational or otherwise. Situations can be subjected to rational analysis but they don't have rational status in themselves.'

'All right, pedant. I mean the situation isn't amenable to rational analysis.'

'That's logically impossible,' argued Rawlinson. 'We only apprehend situations through our sense data. All sense data can be accounted for by rational theories, because rational theories are derived exclusively from sense data. Therefore there can't be a situation that's not amenable to rational analysis. Otherwise, we can apprehend a situation by means other than sensation, or else theory exists apart from data, both of which are self-contradictory positions.'

'To say that there's no theory apart from data denies metaphysics, and the denial is metaphysical in itself,' countered Vance. 'And we *can* apprehend situations by other means, at least complementary to sensation, and . . .'

'Oh, for God's sake!' Brent swallowed his brandy in disgust. 'Your artistic bleeding sensitivity picks up nuances that ordinary mortals like Rowland and me are too coarse-grained to apprehend. This is real life, Roger, not poetry.'

'Is it, Pete? How can you be sure that what we're in is real, not an illusion?'

'Well,' said Rawlinson calmly, 'we can't, ultimately. But if it's real then we'll solve our problem by thinking and behaving rationally, and if it's an illusion—which is doubtful, because we all seem to be sharing it—then it's potentially dangerous only if it makes us act, or think, irrationally.'

Vance gave up. Brent was growing angry, Rawlinson keeping the peace. At least some of the regularities of ordinary experience survived.

'You two walk,' he said. 'I'll stay. Pete's an obvious choice because he could walk to Lairg without breaking stride. And if I go with him I'll fall behind and we'll fall out.'

'Sure?' asked Rawlinson.

'Certain,' said Vance brightly. 'I'll take photos of the house and garden so we can show everybody when we get home. And there's plenty to read in the library.'

'No telly, though,' grumbled Brent. 'Not even a radio.'

'I know,' agreed Rawlinson. 'And nothing personal. No family photos, no day-to-day things left where they'd be readily to hand. Even with servants . . .' He shrugged.

'Quite,' nodded Vance emphatically. Then he added: 'Shouldn't we have another shot at starting the car first thing tomorrow, before anybody sets off walking?'

'Waste of sodding time,' growled Brent. 'I'll have a go, but it's hopeless. And if it's pissing down again, I'm staying here and some other sucker can walk to Lairg.'

During the night Rawlinson was awakened by a distant roll of thunder. He lay wondering whether the sound had been part of a dream. Above the drumming in his ears he thought he heard from afar the stampeding of hooves and trotters and paws and the screaming of terrified animals, and after it a sound like cold laughter. He rose and opened the window, but all was quiet and still. The north-eastern sky shone like silver in firelight, and a three-quarter moon picked out the maze and the statues in the garden. He went back to bed and slept.

Brent dreamed of Suzie. Not unusual; but she seemed anxious and confused, neither hearing nor seeing him, repeating over and again: 'Pete? Pete, where are you?' Increasingly frustrated, he yelled 'I'm here, you daft cow!' and awoke angry and tense. The bed was comfortable, the air clean and mild. It was some time before he slept again.

Vance dreamed that he was a camera, or maybe the film exposing frame by frame, or maybe the developing fluid. As the prints were drying he saw that he had taken a self-portrait. When he awoke he was trying to remember how holograms were made. Then it was morning. The sun was east of north-east, climbing above the trees that framed the garden. The shadows were sharp and clear. He rose and washed and dressed and went downstairs to the dining-room. Brent was wolfing down kippers and slurping tea.

'Morning, Pete. Rowland not up yet?'

'Lightly breakfasted and retired to the library,' replied Brent through a mouthful of kipper. 'Said something like *veritas hominis in libris suis est*.'

'Any sign of the missing owner?'

'*Nyet*. And before you ask, I've tried the car, which shows as much sign of life as Nefertiti. At least the weather's still fine.'

Vance helped himself to tea and cereal. The Indian materialized, silently as ever, and cleared the dishes. Rawlinson entered, yawning and stretching, and performed an elaborate mime of sandwich-making. The Indian watched him, bowed, and retired.

'Any insights?' asked Vance.

'Eclectic.' Rawlinson rubbed his eyes. 'Classics, science fiction, poetry in various languages, works of various religions, geography, history, astrology, biographies (mainly nineteenth century), travelogues, collections of local folk-tales, a Highland flora and geology. But nothing to indicate individual personality or taste. No names on flyleaves, no hand-written notes, not even a bookmark. No typewriter, no PC.'

'And no redhead?'

'No, Pete, no redhead.'

'Should suit you, Rowland, this lack of personalisation. A truly objective reality,' remarked Vance.

'To the contrary. The marking of possessions and territory is normal human behaviour. This is anomalous. Doubtless the explanation will come.' Rawlinson lit a cigar and continued: 'Are we agreed? Proceed according to plan?'

'You two go, I stay,' confirmed Vance. A little of his tea spilled into the saucer.

'Right. We'll make up a couple of flasks, take map, compass, rain-gear, basic first aid kit, and—with luck—sandwiches.' Rawlinson tapped his cigar on an ashtray with a picture of Andromeda in the glazing.

Brent ran upstairs for his rucksack. The Indian reappeared with a plastic box full of sandwiches, which he presented with his customary slight bow. Fifteen minutes later the two walkers strode out of the gate and along the road. Brent administered a perfunctory kick to the car as they passed.

For half a mile they walked in silence. Then:

'This is all wrong, Rowland.'

'What in particular, Pete?'

'A beautiful house and garden in the middle of nowhere, no telly, no radio, no car, no phone, and one mute Paki as resident. A red-haired female occupant who disappears the moment we arrive and won't show herself again. Everything laid on for us according to personal taste. Any rational hypotheses, maestro?'

'Only speculation. We don't have enough secure data.'

'Okay, speculate.'

'A red-haired lady of sophisticated taste and cultured lifestyle suffers an accident in which she is disfigured. She becomes a recluse, retiring with her wealth to the remotest place she can find and severing all connections with the world, save for one mute companion. She chooses to know nothing of her fellow-creatures and will not allow them to know about her. Nevertheless, she maintains a tradition of hospitality, gaining insight into the needs and tastes of individuals from their appearance, behaviour, and possessions. She makes any chance guest welcome and comfortable, but will not permit them to see her, or perhaps—if she can so arrange it—even to suspect her presence.'

Brent made a sceptical noise in his throat. He began: 'I had this lousy dream last night . . .', broke off, and kicked a loose stone at the roadside. The stone described a flattish parabola and vanished in the grass verge. The two men walked on. A hundred paces later, Brent said: 'It's not just the house and the isolation and the catering. It's this whole landscape. It shouldn't be here. Rowland, stop a minute and look.'

They stopped. Brent drew out his compass and map and went on: 'Look, I checked the odometer in the car. We're here.' He jabbed his finger at a point on the map where the packed contour lines paralleled the roadside to the north and the loch waters widened to the south. 'Now look around. Miles of gently undulating grazing land, grazed by nothing. And I mean, miles.'

'Difficult to judge distances. There's mist around the horizon, three hundred and sixty degrees, with a hint of hills. Is it two miles away or twenty?'

'It shouldn't be *any* miles.'

'All right, Pete. The map's inaccurate.'

'Inaccurate? Hah! No map's been that inaccurate since about 1450. And you want to know something else?'

'I feel sure you're about to tell me,' replied Rawlinson.

Brent stooped at the roadside and gathered up another piece of rock.

'See this? It's native, not from road-building, and see this fossil coral? Carboniferous limestone. There's no rock nearly as young as that in this part of Scotland.'

'There was limestone at Durness,' objected Rawlinson. 'Smoo Cave . . .'

'Precambrian, and not fossiliferous,' snapped Brent.

'So when you get back to the department, you'll have the pleasure of correcting both the standard texts and the OS surveyors,' remarked Rawlinson. 'You have direct evidence. And Roger's taken photographs.'

'You might think I'm daft, Rowland, but I'm worried about having left him alone,' muttered Brent, adjusting his rucksack and striding forward again. The way before them was as straight as a Roman road, completely deserted.

'He's a big boy,' said Rawlinson.

'Maybe.' Brent checked his compass. 'Still exactly east-south-east,' he murmured. Then, more loudly: 'Another thing. This road is totally empty. I mean, no traffic. That's unaccountable.'

'Since it seems to be a fact about the world, it's hardly unaccountable. The area's unpopulated, and apart from this surprising oasis of summer, there's persistent rain, discouraging tourists. One would expect traffic to be extremely light.'

'But non-existent?'

'Merely an extreme form of extreme lightness.'

After a moment, Brent observed: 'You know, Rowland, you're so damned reasonable there's no reasoning with you. Do you mean none of this worries you?'

'No, Pete.'

'No you don't mean it, or no you're not worried?'

'I'm worried.'

The admission gave Brent a bigger jolt than he'd bargained for.

'What about, mostly?' he asked quietly.

'If my hypothesis were correct, which it can't be because it doesn't allow for the care and maintenance of the house and grounds, the red-headed recluse would have become personally involved with her possessions. They would bear her name or the stamp of her personality. If I were right about the error on the map, or the geology, why has no one reported it? This is Britain, not the Arctic waste. As for light traffic, this is the only road between east and west for very many miles. The population's low but it isn't zero. My explanations are inadequate, and inadequate explanations worry me.' Rawlinson was silent for a dozen paces or so, and then added: 'So we need better explanations. I rely on your method—action, to wit walking out of the situation.'

The road went straight on, east-south-east. The sun moved over them and to the right. It shone on their shoulders and then on the rucksack. The two men stopped to eat. The sandwiches contained not only cucumber and tomato, but also smoked salmon. The tea in the flasks was somewhat stewed. They packed away their flasks and followed the road east-south-east. The hills and mist seemed no closer.

The sun was on their left shoulder blades when Brent at last descried a house ahead of them. It was on the left of the road, nestling in a small stand of trees.

'And there's someone there,' he announced, relief tangible in his voice. 'There's a car outside.'

'Yes, I see it,' agreed Rawlinson. A hundred paces later, he slowed his steps and added: 'Pete, that car looks familiar. So does the house.'

Brent stopped dead. There was a moment's stunned silence and then a succession of screamed obscenities. Rawlinson waited for him to finish.

'Let's check the compass,' he suggested quietly.

They were heading east-south-east.

'Right,' snarled Brent, 'so we've circumnavigated the globe in seven hours without getting our feet wet.' There was perspiration on his brow but he was resolutely not shaking.

Rawlinson stared at the house and the immobile BMW for a long moment and said nothing. The silence was total. The tableau, two men in a motionless landscape, had a timeless quality.

'Have you noticed, there are no birds?' inquired Brent. His voice was quite neutral.

'Obviously we *have* travelled in a circle.' Rawlinson spoke at last, softly and hesitantly. 'So two surprising events have synergised. At least two. First, the road did branch, twice if not more. We took one branch and it led us round to rejoin the same road miles to the west—that was the second branch, the rejoining.'

'A few problems there,' countered Brent calmly. 'One, the road didn't branch, or we'd have noticed. Two, road systems don't go in circles, unless a village has been bypassed, and there wasn't a village. Three, the road's been as straight as a failed lawyer all day, as far as the eye could see. Four, we've been heading in the same compass direction....'

'That's the second surprising event,' nodded Rawlinson. 'This is your field, Pete, but if the rocks here are Carboniferous, surely they could include magnetite? If we've passed over magnetite, our compass could have ...'

'Plausible if unlikely, Rowland. But if that's what happened, how come the sun's not been on our left, or in our faces, at any point since this morning?'

The quiet debate ended. Rawlinson eyed his companion stonily.

'I suspect that once we work out the truth, its simplicity will embarrass us. For the time being, we don't have it. So rather than torment ourselves with speculation, I suggest we return to the house, shower, discover whether Roger's made contact with someone who can speak, and see what's for supper.'

He walked forward again towards the house, his pace steady. Brent sighed, squared his shoulders, and followed.

Still the quiet drive, the flower beds, the bell unanswered, the door opening at a touch. Still the lack of visible human occupancy. Rawlinson glanced into the library and then walked down the hall, up the stairs, and into his room. He sat wearily on the bed and took off his boots. Taking a shower was an effort, but he felt partly refreshed afterwards. He took care over dressing for supper; the civilized ritual calmed him. Brent came in, towelling his hair, as Rawlinson was adjusting his tie. Brent was casual and clean; sandals, no socks.

'Let's go down.' Rawlinson gave the mirror a farewell glance.

Inside the dining-room they stopped again, staring. The table was laid for two.

'Roger seems to have eaten already. Have you seen him?' Rawlinson's throat felt constricted.

'No,' answered Brent. 'I'll check outside.'

'I'll check his room.'

Brent glanced in the library again, went out through the French windows, and ran to and fro—back garden, front garden—calling 'Roger! Roger, where are you?' He ran to the car: unoccupied. He ran back into the garden and shinned up a sycamore tree and snagged his jersey. The view from the upper branches revealed nothing animate. He slid down to the lawn again and went back indoors.

'Rowland?' he shouted.

'Dining-room.' Rawlinson's voice sounded strained over the intervening distance. Brent navigated towards it. Rawlinson was standing by the window, sherry in hand, staring at the statues in the back garden. He turned as Brent entered and asked, 'Any sign?'

'*Nyet*. I gather you haven't.'

'It might be good news,' said Rawlinson, calmly and carefully. 'All his belongings have gone. So probably he *did* meet the owner, who conveyed him and his luggage to Lairg or somewhere. Therefore the road did branch, or they'd have passed us at some point.'

He sipped his sherry. Brent breathed steadily for a moment and then said, 'It won't wash, Rowland. That's not what happened and you know it.'

'I can't think of a plausible alternative. The room's been cleared. Better a weak explanation than none at all. But I admit two difficulties.'

'Which particular two have you in mind?'

'I'd have expected him to leave a note for us, but I haven't found one and I've looked in what I think are all the likely places. And those big photographs that were on his wall have gone as well. All of them. Possibly the owner knew his professional interest and made him a present of them.'

'Oh, yeah, the owner's an Arab with long red hair. What do we do now?'

'Wait for them to return,' said Rawlinson, 'and in the meantime, eat.'

As soon as the word was spoken the Indian entered, pushing a small wooden trolley laden with food, and began to serve the soup. Rawlinson asked him, with accompanying mime:

'There were three of us, now there are two. Where is Mr Vance?'

A look of polite incomprehension.

'Has Mr Vance gone to Lairg with the owner?'

A smile and a bow, which might or might not have been affirmation. Brent lost his temper. Seizing the white jacket by the lapels he jerked the diminutive Indian off his feet and roared, his face some six inches from his victim's:

'You understand all right, you little bastard. Tell us where Roger's gone or I'll smash every bone in your body!'

The Indian made no attempt to defend or disengage himself, or to speak.

He stared Brent quietly in the eyes. Rawlinson put a calming hand on his companion's shoulder and spoke softly. Brent lowered his victim to the carpet and released him. The Indian smoothed his lapels and went on serving soup.

'Sit down, Pete,' ordered Rawlinson gently. 'Let's have the first course.'

It was another excellent meal. The two men exchanged steaks; Brent had been given the rarer one. They didn't linger over port, but went to the drawing-room for coffee and brandy. Once again, Rawlinson accepted the proffered cigar and allowed the Indian to light it for him.

'This will be quite a story to tell our grandchildren,' he observed when the silent Asian had retired.

Brent was in no mood to talk. He paced the room and conversation waned. In the end he marched out to search the house from top to bottom, only to return ten minutes later with a story of locked doors and silence and no axe to smash the locks. Both men were mentally and physically exhausted. They went early to bed and, against expectation, slept.

Rawlinson awoke a little after seven and took his time over washing and dressing. He went down to the dining-room at about twenty-five to eight. The table was laid for one.

He ran upstairs and knocked on Brent's door. Hearing nothing, he entered the room. The bed was unoccupied and neatly made. The display cabinet with the geological samples was no longer there. Nor were Brent's suitcase or rucksack. Nor was Brent.

Rawlinson swallowed. His mouth was dry. He licked his lips and tried to order his thoughts. He squared his shoulders and marched downstairs, not hurrying. He walked to the front door, down the drive to the gate, seeing no one.

The car was gone.

He felt panic rising and fought it down angrily. Panic was treason. No wonder it made him angry. His anger gave him control.

'Of course. Pete rose early, tried the car again, and *mirabile dictu* it started. Rather than risk its relapse into immobility, he set off without awakening me. . . .'

(But packed all his gear and tidied his room?)

'All right, good point. So, assuming that we would be departing early today, one way or another, he rose early, packed his belongings, and took them to the car. While he was there he tried the ignition, and *mirabile dictum* . . .'

(So why didn't you hear it start and drive away?)

'Easy. I was asleep at the back of the house.'

(What became of the display cabinet? If Pete left the house so quietly, how did the Indian know he'd gone so he only need set one breakfast place? Why hasn't Roger come back with the mythical owner?)

'Whoever's been looking after us is very well-informed and efficient, hence the display cabinet and the breakfast place. As for Roger's non-return, I can think of a dozen explanations. . . .'

(Such as?)

'First, maybe he has returned. Absence of breakfast place is the only contrary evidence. I'll go back indoors and look.'

He did so. Vance had not returned. There was no note from him. Or from Brent.

'What I need,' mused Rawlinson, 'is to relax with a cigar, and to think logically.'

He went to the library, sat in the wing-chair, lit a cigar, and inhaled. The peaceful view through the French windows was conducive to calm. He sat, and smoked, and looked, and thought.

The door-bell rang, but as usual no one answered it. After a few moments, it opened tentatively. On the doorstep, peering into the gloom of the hall, were three young women.

'Just our damned luck,' snapped the first of them. 'Nobody in.'

'Well,' observed the second, 'since the door's open and the telephone's presumably in the hall, we're hardly likely to be charged with breaking and entering.'

'Eleanor, we can't just walk into . . .'

'Would you mind if stranded strangers entered your house to make a quick phone-call, Mary?'

'Maybe not, but . . .'

'Do as you'd be done by,' returned the tall woman addressed as Eleanor.

The first speaker pushed past her, strode into the hall, and looked around. Eleanor followed, then Mary. Eleanor's long Titian hair glowed in the dim light.

'Some hall, but I don't see a phone,' said the first.

Eleanor walked to the library door, tapped gently on it, opened it, and sniffed.

'Someone was here recently,' she announced. 'You can smell his cigar.'

A moment later she added:

'Very recently. The chair's still warm.'

A Pace of Change

Don Tumasonis

'THE PROCESS OF PROGRESS from point A to B, involves for the mountaineer the lifting of one foot, and placing it in front of the other. That this is done mainly in the vertical makes no difference to the thesis. At times, necessarily, this progression is perverted by the difficulty of the terrain; then subterfuge, involving backtracking or sideways motion, and various other contortion, is applied.

'Nevertheless, generally speaking, movement remains as described. Within those mechanical limits, an infinite variety of individual permutation is possible. We can for example think of sliding; or the bold step forward (taken without hesitation); the manoeuvre called *smearing*, whereby the synthetic and grippy sole or side of the boot, in these days of high technological materials, is applied at almost any of its points against the rock, and relied upon, through pressure, for whatever friction it is worth.

'And then there is the reliable *hesitant thrust*, familiar to all of us here, when we—not fully committed to a move, and without the need to lunge forth in a desperate effort to compensate for our previous literal *misstep*—shyly go forward, somewhat in the manner of a bather approaching bath water of unknown, but potentially scalding, temperature.

'Of course, this last represents a luxury, a choice provided to us when on solid dry rock, giving good purchase, with birds parliamenting in the sky, a blue heaven above, and a stance wide and comfortable enough to allow us this leisurely form of decision. Every climber's dream,' Eggleston said, puffing at his pipe. And then, after a short pause, he tantalizingly added, 'Of course, it is not always given to us to have that option.'

A short silence ensued. Moore non-committally fed another split section of pine to the blaze warming the darkening room, the sudden addition illuminating his swarthy jaw and dark head, whilst bearded and balding MacLong, our token Scot and—although he will not volunteer it—AC member, silently busied himself with coiling a section of rope, checking for signs of abrasion and imbedded small splinters of stone that could damage the synthetic kern. I warmed my stockinged feet by the fire, and with the certitude of the just, come upon me after a long day on the snow and rock, poured myself another dram of the local, unblended without ice, thank you, waiting for Alex, our Professor, to resume. We all knew our Eggleston, and were wondering what was to come next.

Finally, he continued. 'I mentioned all this just to underline what all of us already know: one step, in mountaineering, can make all the difference.'

He looked around, almost in challenge, to each of us in turn. No one gainsaid his statement; no one bothered to naïvely ask what *difference* was being talked about. *That* we all knew without asking, every one of us having lost one or more friends to various mountain accidents over the years. Danger goes with the activity; if it wasn't there in some form, none of us, I believe, would bother.

He went on: 'It being early in the autumn, I suppose it is the right time to tell you about my mother's grandfather's last climb, which took place in the Dolomites about this same season, more than a hundred years back. The tale came to me through mum's dad quite some while ago, in the form of a hand-written memoir written for him by his father.'

This was news to us: MacLong looked over at me while the fire crackled away, and I looked over to Moore, who only lifted a black eyebrow discreetly. We had all known about Eggleston's grandfather Digby, the hero of several minor epics in the Alps during the '20s, when he was a well-respected amateur of the rope. That a great-grandfather had been involved in even more ancient days of climbing glory had escaped us until now.

After a pregnant pause, Alex continued: 'Digby found the story so striking when his father told it to him years ago, that he asked old Archibald to write it down after the telling, not wanting to forget any detail. It was well enough that he did so: Archibald Derwent joined the Great Majority the spring thereafter, while Digby was at University, departing this world in 1914. With the events of those times, many details would have otherwise likely escaped Digby's memory. Grandfather handed the account—annotated with a few details in his own hand from about the time of writing—to me shortly before his own death at the age of eighty-three, and I recollect having read through it with some avidity, only to put it away, half-remembered.

'While recently going through some papers of mine, I came across the tale, which I had not seen for decades. The first half of Archie's memoir had over the years been chewed through by mice, randomly holed and nibbled so that a good deal of it was gone. Enough remained, fortunately, for me to reconstruct it in memory; I now recall that first part well enough to give it fair justice, I think. The finish to the story, however, I will read to you directly from the undamaged part of the manuscript that I happen to have with me. It was stored in another place, mouse impervious. These are the combined narratives I propose to relate tonight.'

Hearing this, I settled even more comfortably in my seat, as did my other companions in theirs, banter and carping about the day's missed holds and scraped hands forgotten in anticipation of the tale about to be told.

Seeing us ready and primed, as it were, Alex started off.

'The British have been involved in the Dolomites since the early days; in fact they were the first ones in: John Ball climbed the first big summit in the 1850s. It didn't take long before things warmed up, and more climbers came. In a few years, most of the major peaks were bagged, astounding when you consider the equipment and techniques they had available back then.

'What it meant was that latecomers, like Archibald Derwent, my maternal great-grandfather, were left with the crumbs—the unclimbed minor summits out on the area's periphery, and, increasingly, the more difficult rock routes on those tops already conquered.

'In the late summer of 1884, just out of university, he set forth with a couple of friends—Arthur Bramley, a student of divinity, and Henry Dawes, who was following the path of Hippocrates—for the Venetian Alps of the South Tyrol, in search of good companionship, invigorating air and exercise, new landscapes, and fresh climbs, with the chance—who knows?—of getting some obscure arête named after one of them.

'Parts of what we now call the Dolomites, you must remember, were still at the time pretty far off the beaten track. The fraternity of alpinists had of course made some inroads over the past decade or two, but ordinary tourism and permanent hostelries were only starting to be sparsely established. The region could still, by today's standards, be considered relatively primitive and remote, and the friends could yet count on being the pioneers—on rock, at least—of the little-visited valleys and villages themselves.

'They had with them a cicerone, whom they had hired on the recommendation of a near acquaintance. This seasoned guide, a bluff native of Valais named Hermann Zeltener, was a veteran of many climbing campaigns, not only of the area but also of his native southern Switzerland.

'Unlike many of his fellows, for whom the art of leading clients up the mountain was nothing more than a paid chore to fill the pocket while satisfying the inexplicable whims of rich foreigners with outrageous notions, he had taken the idea of mountaineering to his heart. Rather than follow the easy way of some tame *voie normale*, he actively sought out the difficult routes and new variations, and as a consequence was much sought after by younger patrons from Germany and Britain. Again, the guide was unusual in his extreme competence at rock-work, distinguishing him from his Swiss compatriots, who, more at ease on ice and snow, seldom transgressed into the realm of their Dolomite peers.

'Crossing the Brenner by rail from Innsbruck, then posting on, the clients, having met up with their guide and new associate in Cortina in late July, started on some of the more well-known climbs near there and in the Ampezzo area, doing Sorapis and Antelao, before going on to peaks around the Drei Zinnen.

'Early on, their guide and mentor hinted that if the group did well on the more frequented routes, there was a chance, weather permitting, of continuing on to some of the lesser-known districts, which were just starting to open up to the hardier breed of mountaineer. He had, according to Derwent, on several occasions strongly implied that new territory could be won, to everybody's great fame and fortune.

'That was enough to inspire the three friends. They complemented each other well, Bramley being extrovert and very steady in tight spots, with red-haired Dawes possessed of great physical courage and boldness. My own great-grandfather Archibald was an intellectual technician on rock, who could size up a route, and make it "go". He had, I was told, a particularly good sense of balance. Remember that, as I go on.

'Under the tutelage of their experienced guide, themselves surfeited with the stamina and audacity of youth, they went through the summits with style. They needed as much, given the unnerving sheerness of the huge faces they were storming. The Dolomites, as you all know, have given to the word *verticality* its definition.'

This was a polite courtesy to we others, as only MacLong had even seen those fantastic mountains, myself and Moore being more ice and snow men, inclined in our travels towards less technical peaks.

'Zeltener, without having said as much, wanted to make sure that his young patrons could handle the effects of peering down some of the most awful abysses known to man. Quite a few climbers going to the district, more used to pitches of a few hundred feet, give or take, are awed by the absolute perpendicularity of the extreme faces, not a few of which overhang, and, after a token attempt or two, return home.

'Even today, with modern gear and aid, visitors take a week or more to build up enough nerve to confront the incredible exposure between their toes, before going on to the truly intimidating cliffs and their drops. Just imagine what it must have been like back when there were no carabiners to hold a rope, nor pitons and the like to guard a fall, but only skill and moral courage making the difference between yourself and your extinction.

'Once he was sure of them, and thought them ready, Zeltener suggested during their third week that they consider moving camp to the lesser known westerly groups, where virgin territory was more likely to be found. Accordingly, a few days later, with the possibility of fresh summits and their names in some future issue of the *Alpine Journal*, the four moved on, setting up in a small village further to the west.

'Whether what subsequently happened was on the edge of the main group, or across the valley in the Brenta area, Digby was never able to worm out of his father. That worthy did not even tell him which language was spoken there; purposely, Digby thought, obscuring the details of its location. The only feature he precisely described was a south-facing valley.

'When, shortly after their arrival, Zeltener proposed a new route on the south face of some as yet unspecified peak above the valley, Archibald and his friends had not the slightest hint that the guide's suggestion involved anything other than the lure of a fresh ascent. The man had shown himself a steady, open type, a dab hand on the rope, absolutely cold and nerveless in the most impossible situations. There was no reason to suspect him of any other motive than giving his clients their money's worth, so no question was made of his intent.

'Nonetheless, having arranged with a peasant family for lodging, the three friends could not help but observe from a window while settling in that Zeltener, outside on the path, was engaged in vehement discussion with their host, a stocky half-shaven man with short blond hair. At first they thought it was merely bargaining, to better the price for their accommodation. But as the two men continued, with their guide pointing to a peak up the valley, and the purse-lipped peasant, his hand on Zeltener's shoulder, pointing to another, it dawned on them that perhaps the local man was trying to divert their leader from some objective. In the end, Zeltener merely turned away and went in, while his host looked after him, shaking his head.

'That the countryman had seemed discouraging was perhaps not to be unexpected. Mountain peasants are known for their superstitions. It may have been that some local legend accounted for the lively discussion—until it was climbed, for example, the Matterhorn was thought to have harboured a city of demons at its top. Maybe there was some similar rural folklore regarding certain summits in the near vicinity.

'Whatever the matter, Zeltener remained tight-lipped; the house-owner did not allude to it at the breaking of the bread. After a friendly evening at the table of their host and his large family, with the previous controversy seemingly forgotten, and the household's simple but ample rustic fare inside them—there was no inn or hotel in the village—the four went to bed early, so as to have sufficient time for their next day's climb. It was imperative that a start before dawn be made, with the descent not much later than noon, since Dolomite weather breaks in the afternoon, with storms common after midday throughout the year.

'The friends could scarcely sleep, in anticipation of the glorious excitement that awaited them on all sides. Here there were magnificent rocks; the isolated spires and broken massifs so characteristic of the area, that, piercing the alps above the valley, and lifting their needles transfused with fiery light to the heavens, were enough to evoke awe and wonder in the heart of any true lover of the hills. With dreams of conquest flying about in their minds, they one by one finally drifted off to a sound sleep.

'Up and out in the dark, early next morning, it was not before they were well along their trail that Zeltener revealed their objective in the first morning light, with a dramatic flourish of his cap.

'Now the peak that the guide had pointed out for their first objective was a typical Dolomite monster of pale and colourful layered stone, with one huge face thrusting high towards the skies like a jagged petrified palisade; a thousand feet and more of mostly horrendous blankness, threaded through here and there by fissures going almost, but not quite, to the top. It must have been this same spire he had indicated the day before, during his discussion with their peasant host.

'The friends, for their lives, could not but wonder how they would attain its summit, so featureless and impossible did the mountain's façade appear, with any cracks that might form an upward passageway giving out some hundreds of feet from the goal. Yet with Bramley joking behind him, and Dawes placidly following, and my ancestor as end-man, Zeltener stolidly led the way, unconcerned, almost as if the approach had been known to the Swiss previously.

'The air was cool, the sun not having yet risen, as they made their way in shadow up the characteristic rocky slopes, the heritage of eons of those rock falls for which the friable slabs of some of the Dolomites are known. As they drew closer, they saw, as is often the case, that what had appeared impossible from a distance gave, upon closer examination, signs of being in the realm of the feasible after all.

'Archibald said later to my grandfather that he had a feeling of foreboding; there was something about the mountain that Zeltener had chosen that flushed Derwent with a sense of faint dread. He held his counsel, not wanting to upset the others, who had enough to think about.

'At the foot of the climb, already high up, they divided the gear they had between them, leaving behind their walking boots and knapsacks. They then tied together for the ascent, one pair to each of the two ropes, Zeltener leading the way with Bramley.

'Brave men! Consider what they were attempting, and the meagre tools they had to do it. Inadequate footwear—probably canvas shoes with rope bottoms, twisted long hemp lines that would break if subjected to any not overly large strain, no technical aids, no helmets or safety harnesses. . . .'

Alex left his words hanging, and I thought I saw at least Moore faintly shudder.

'It was apparent that the route attempted would follow up a series of long splits in the perpendicular rock, where a skilled climber could make his way through, and coming to some fairly safe place or platform could then guard his fellow up with the rope. It was here that Zeltener convinced my great-grandfather of his supreme nerve and skill, as if he needed any more proof after the weeks they had been together. Taking advantage of the slightest protrusions, almost imaginary nubbins of rock, he jammed and elbowed his way upward like a steeplejack, until the rope hanging from his waist ran out. Plugged into a crack, he saw his fellows up, aiding when necessary the team of Derwent and Dawes, repeating the process rope length after rope length, until the little group was high above the valley floor, in their sensational situation, like flies lightly depending from a ceiling.

'They were so concentrated on their perilous position that, Archibald said, there was no time for other than thinking out the next move, and guarding one's position so one did not slip. A couple of hours into the climb, and more than halfway up, however, going out of one crack system, there were discovered two platforms—if small shelves giving just about enough room to sit on while dangling your feet over eternity could be dignified as such. With one ledge about five feet above the other, together they provided a resting place, where the party could catch their collective breath, and admire their stupendous placement, high above the valley, with the sunlight streaming in from the east.

'A pebble, Archie said, would, if dropped, have fallen right to the deck, a thousand feet or more straight down. He was pondering that, half-listening to the imperturbable Bramley telling the classic story about the vicar and the hare. Then, in the middle of his friend's rattling on, he had an odd feeling suddenly come over him, as if he were being watched. It was not your ordinary "third man on the rope" phenomenon that you find in every other climbing autobiography these days.

'The feeling was so strong that he gave a small involuntary start, and, looking around, saw Dawes with his red beard staring back at him. Archibald immediately felt that, whatever it was, Dawes had sensed it too, and that his staring was the sign of his mutual comprehension they had experienced the same thing. Neither of them brought this to the attention of the others, perhaps so as not to create apprehension, which can run through a small group and lead to fear, the handmaid of irrational panic.

'Looking about him, however, Archibald saw nothing. He did trace what he thought might have been a glimmer of unusual alertness—for want of a better word—on the part of their guide, but at the time he wrote it off as a figment of his own unease.

'Their rest complete, the little group climbed upward, following a leftward trend chosen by their leader, which did not look promising at all. After a few difficult pitches, they mounted a large block wedged into the crack near its high end. Its flat upper surface was the first place they could all assemble together during the entire climb thus far.'

At this point, Eggleston stopped for a moment, and, plucking up a sheaf of paper, indicated that he would from then on read from the surviving pages of the new-found manuscript. He continued, in Archibald's own words:

'As Hermann, standing, gathered the rope into neat loops, the usually taciturn Dawes, looking about him, remarked, "Well, chaps, I reckon that's as far as she goes today," to which we, his fellows could only nod assent.

'The crack system had run out—there was no possibility of continuing upward along our chosen line, there being no further crannies to follow. Even more remarkably, the rock above was devoid of any handholds of use, being polished to smoothness by weathering and the eons-long bombardment of rock from the crumbling summit crest. The difficulty above us was probably higher in degree than anything yet attempted at that time: it would require years before those bold enough would, with better technique and equipment, try anything of the sort. And the face of the rock immediately to either side was, for all practical purpose, blank.

'Zeltener, listening to our developing consensus, nodded sagely, with a gleam in his eye. Then, after passing the coiled rope over his right shoulder, so it crossed his chest and rested partly on one hip, he intoned ponderously, "Now the young gentlemen will have their adventure of the day—an unclimbed mountain, and their names in the book!"

'Bramley, thinking that our guide meant somehow to continue following the same line, was looking up about the same time as I, towards the flat summit only a few hundred feet above us now, trying to make some sense of the guide's statement.

'Then Arthur said, unexpectedly, "You'd better forget the *unclimbed* part of it, Hermann—there's someone already beat us to it—you can see him up there now!"

'He was right—for a very small space of time, high above, what seemed the head and torso of a figure leaned out over the edge of the summit ridge, as if to regard our party below. The movement had been so quick that only Bramley and myself had seen it. Zeltener, looking up with Dawes, frowned, and wondered aloud whether my companion might not have imagined some stone formation shaped by the wind to be a fellow climber.

'Bramley avowed the actuality of what he said he had spotted; he looked to me for support, which plea I studiously ignored, preferring to keep my own counsel about this odd apparition. The interval had been so short, it was hard to tell what I had seen. I had an odd sensation nonetheless, that my view had been somehow momentarily magnified, bringing the distant figure close. The impression was of something either dark green and black, or brown; bald and thin, with ropy, twisty arms, that looked somehow dry and rubbery. This was, as said, the impression of a moment, and rather than add to the building unease, I held my tongue, preferring that the descent be made in company not distressed.

'Still shaking his head, Zeltener elucidated his previous statement, momentarily interrupted by Bramley's observation of the figure.

'"I repeat, the gentlemen think the day's climb is at an end. But I say, the adventure is only beginning. I mean we shall take the summit—look! There!" Saying this, he pointed along the blank wall, a bit above chest height, inviting our gaze away from the wall above, and directing our vision towards the left.

'It was Dawes who first comprehended what was meant, then myself, and finally Bramley. The wall there was not truly smooth and without relief; to the left ran a very thin edge of rock, more or less flat and level. This continued about fifty yards until it met another crack system that, from our vantage, seemed to go straight to the top.

'That ledge was in fact the remaining portion of a slightly protuberant layer of harder stone which, fractured across its middle perhaps ages back, had lost its upper half, leaving the lower part still adhered.

'This remaining piece of rock, stuck to the face like a giant thin wedge of cheese point down, seemed but loosely attached: at the juncture where its inches-wide top met with the main wall, a hairline running the whole length of the narrow shelf showed that someday, sooner or later, this veneer would peel off, following the upper half that now lay broken in the scree far below. It could happen tomorrow, or in ten thousand years, but it was sure to go.

'With all these thoughts running through our minds, I would have supposed my friends had already discounted the possibility of continuing.

'Zeltener searched our eyes, eagerly awaiting our opinions; I mentally rejected the proposed "stroll" out of hand. It was clear, looking at this little *variation*, that nowhere along its detestable length was much broader than the width of an adult foot. Also, there was a small but perceptible downward tilt to that same narrow mantle, towards its outer edge, echoed by a slight overhanging tendency of the wall along which one would be plastered, if foolhardy enough to try the route.

'That same wall, always pushing the victim slightly outward, towards the abyss, was smoothly weathered; there seemed to be nothing more than a nubbin or two to provide any handhold whatsoever for the entire fifty yards.

'And were anyone idiot enough to try this, one thing was very clear: that there could be no use of the rope. The slightest drag at either end would be enough to upset the delicate balance of any of a party attached, and send them tumbling through eternity, down the enormous drop below.

'I thought this all very self-evident for my fellows; it was, then, with great surprise that I heard Bramley murmuring, encouraged by little nods of the smiling Zeltener, come out and say, almost to himself, "Yes, I believe by Jove, it could go. Yes, I say!" Dawes was nodding too, albeit more cautiously. By the time I had recovered my tongue, it was too late—the Swiss was already engaged in an "interesting manoeuvre" to gain the minuscule shelf, shinning up a small buttress, legs locked around it like a monkey, thereafter to ease first his left foot, then the other, onto the barely existent way.

'I watched, mouth gaping, as he squeezed along, glued against the face, one heel caressed by open air. He was followed in short order by my two companions; each giving for some reason a grunt of exclamation as they gained their purchase. Without thinking overmuch on the significance of this, I followed *en suite*, leaving the extra rope behind in obedience to the shouted instruction of the guide.

'Clamping myself around the little column, and having tightly swarmed the requisite yard upward, I, while swinging left to attain the precarious ledge, received my first shock: I saw before me, carved in the rock, a very odd symbol, a sort of cuneiform cross.'

At this point, Eggleston broke off his reading of the manuscript, and passed to us a sheet of paper bearing the sketch of a sign, the approximate likeness of which I have appended here, saying that it had been drawn by his great-grandfather in response to Digby's own request for a representation. It appeared thus:

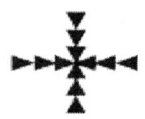

Having shown this to us, Eggleston continued with the manuscript of Derwent's climb:

'*This* was obviously the cause of the mutters of surprise from my friends. Notably, Zeltener was unmoved by this incredible sign of someone's having preceded us. Who, or what, could possibly have been responsible for this engraving, and for what purpose had its design been cut at this lofty point?

'At the time, however, I had little capacity to give more than a passing glimpse to the very strange device before me. My awareness was very much more concentrated on my situation, where one false step could dislodge me from my precarious position, to send me hurtling downward, into the endless depth.

'Movement forward was accomplished in the following fashion: tight up against the rock, with my right cheek hard against it, my left arm stretched forward and the other trailing, and scrabbling for whatever adhesion might be gained. My left foot led, parallel to the length of the tiny shelf, whilst my other foot faced inward at a right angle, heel over the brink, supported by nothing more than air.

'I was able to see the progress of Bramley and Dawes ahead of me; both were far along, and the guide, minutes ahead, had already gained the relative safety of the other side. Not once did I look down to examine my sensational stance. To look down, and experience the slightest vertigo, would have been death.

'Fortunately, the face was not quite as blank as first inspection made it seem; there were a few tiny protrusions and knobs along the way, that enabled one to rest from the terrific pressure built up in the calf muscles. These small protuberances were in fact fossils imbedded in the matrix of rock, as is common in the Dolomites. What was not common was their ugliness. I have never discovered of what species they were members, but I know that had it not been for the situation I found myself in, I would have been loath otherwise to touch the things. Had it not been for the brief respites they provided, I wonder if the traverse would have been possible at all.

'Exercising the utmost care, I inched and shuffled along, freely perspiring from my face, until at last the goal was almost reached: another widening of the ledge, with room enough for three of us, with a fourth jammed into the fissure above. A veritable congress-hall, compared to what we had been on!

'A final slide forward, and I was through! But while my companions were congratulating me, and Zeltener, satisfied of my having come safely across, was already roped up and leading upward on the first of the last pitches, my eye came to rest on a thin, vertical plate of stone, thinly attached at its base to the rock. It was about the size of a dinner dish, and on it was incised a symbol matching the one at the other end of the traverse!

'The whole exercise was beginning to take on proportions of unreality, but there was no time to ponder now the implications of these incredibly placed figures. Tying on to the rope end, I admired the view until a tug from Dawes above signalled me to ascend.

'Not many minutes later, with the steepness easing slightly nearer the summit, we emerged upon the top. Jubilation and shouts of glee were the order of the day, as we waved our hats looking down at the village, which seemed so far away that one could almost cover the view of it with the little finger of an outstretched arm.

'The summit platform was a large flat ridge of about thirty yards in length, by about eight wide, free of snow and comfortable enough to lie down on and stretch out. There was no trace of anyone about; if there had been anybody, they were gone now. The whole thing was odd, given what we had sensed or seen on the way up.

'Still wondering, we quickly built a little cairn out of the loose stones, taking care to insert a bottle with our calling cards inside. Using our rude monument as a back rest, I was soon after lighting my pipe, admiring the inconceivable view, when Dawes settled in beside me. Majesty. We wordlessly watched the grand vista before us awhile, content in silent companionship, when I noticed, at the far end of the mesa-like top, our guide on his knees, intently lifting rocks as if looking for something buried, and Bramley on his way over to him. That Zeltener was perhaps digging up rocks to set up a second cairn was, I remember, my unconcerned thought.

'As we watched our friend kneel down next to Zeltener, Dawes made mention of the deceptiveness of the eyes; how one's sight could play tricks when agitated or tired; he discreetly did not add "frightened". I was not so sure, and I think he was trying to convince himself that all was well, in spite of several signals to the contrary we had received throughout our climb. We, I recall, briefly discussed the *outré* crosses, wondering how they had been chiselled, and to what purpose.

'Loud exclamations from our comrades at the other end of the ridge made us break off our meandering speculations and join them. Reaching the two, we were astounded to see that what I had taken to be an outcrop of rock was a broken angle of hand-built wall. Were that not enough, the material was of flat moulded brick, of indeterminate age, with some shards of pottery scattered around the ruin. Before I could form any theory of what might be involved, Zeltener let go with a cry of triumph, pulling out of the loose rock of the ridge, with Bramley helping him, some artefact that had been evidently long buried there. Further digging revealed several more such things, which although indubitably ancient and likely to be of great value, I found so revolting, of such a disgusting nature, that I will not bother to describe them here.

'The others had fewer qualms; I was especially surprised by Bramley, who, as a future man of the cloth, would be the last one you'd expect to admire, let alone touch, such miserable obscenities.

'I morosely turned aside whilst the others stuffed their pockets with their booty, all the while thinking that our guide had somehow known of this treasure, and that our expedition had more of the planned, and less of the impromptu, about it than I had at first imagined.

'Upon our starting back after an hour or more on top of the world, Zeltener insisted on our reversing the same route we had taken going up. I think all we others had banked on going down by some easier course; anything rather than face that hazardous dance on the edge of the void that had stretched our moral and physical resources to the breaking point not two hours past. I had in truth begun examining the drop on all sides, to see if any lighter prospect for descent was available, thinking I would go it alone, rather than face again what we had been through. Alas, nothing obvious presented itself, and with Zeltener's almost overbearing insistence that we take our original way back, I reluctantly agreed to his plan.

'Going down, our positions were reversed, myself leading, Dawes following, Bramley next, with our guide last of all. Through judicious use of the rope, we were all soon down the fissure, and gathered at the near end of the horrendous traverse.

'Now, there is something to bear in mind when you consider our return journey: most of us are right-handed (as were we four). That means there is a bias, however slight, regarding one's balance, when placed into a position like the one we were about to essay. Simply stated, it is easier to achieve a forced manoeuvre of the type we were about to do, when leading with the left side, as we did going up.

'To move in the same way to the right affects us so that we feel, even if only infinitesimally, less at ease with the exercise. It is almost like a slight pressure being lightly exerted on the alpinist by a single finger; not enough to matter in most circumstances—but this was decidedly not what could be called "most circumstances". The left-handed, by the way, experience the same sensation when doing this, except, of course, in reverse.

'In short, this was going to be worse. I heard Bramley softly say a prayer. Dawes just shook his head. Thinking myself of a more practical bent, I took out a very thin metal flask of Cognac brandy, as all true mountaineers have with them, and having offered it, with the others abstaining, I took a quick pull.

'Then I set out, keeping my eyes straight ahead, looking only at the goal, marked by the other weird cross at the end of the lofty passage. I was nonetheless very aware of the horrible vast space beneath; that if I slipped, I would fall forever. The brandy helped me to block out this last thought as much as I was able. To dwell too long on it would be fatal. No doubt, as they eased onto the ledge after me, the others were thinking similar thoughts, except perhaps the ironed-nerved Swiss, who was last in line.

'It is still difficult for me to think about those minutes, with the very faint pressure of the outward-leaning rock against my breast as I edged forward. At the same time, I was so tight against the wall that there could not have been an atom of space between myself and it. It was a question of close, but not too close. I could not stop for fear of getting a cramp, with its inevitable result. All too slowly, I reached a point not much more than seven or eight yards from the terminal cross and buttress, and salvation. A wisp of euphoria welled up within me; all too soon, as it turned out.

'Because, at that same moment, our guide must have started onto the thin shelf which by now was supporting the rest of us, making our cautious way across. A sound of rock cracking, then falling, clattering against the stony face behind and below us, a curse in German from the lips of Zeltener, and the words "*das Kreuz!* . . ." froze me, and I suppose the others, in place.

'On the feather-thin edge of maintaining my equilibrium or falling, unable to turn around to observe, I guessed that the guide had used the convenient engraved stone as a handhold; fragile, it had broken off, and had been pitched out into the void when the startled Zeltener released it. I dared not look around to confirm this, if I were to keep my balance. Some moments passed, and I had started to recover. Bramley, first to react, shouted in concern, "Hermann, are you safe?"

'To his query, there came a sudden shriek, and the dreadful sound of someone falling, equipment and loose ends shattering on rock. I almost fell, and would have, I believe, had it not been for the brandy I had taken. I was petrified nonetheless, and stood fast, when forward motion was more imperative than ever.

'After what seemed a lifetime, Bramley shouted out "Hermann has fallen! My God!"

'And then, with a choked voice, almost screaming, he called "Dawes, Derwent, move ahead *quickly*, for the love of God!" I needed no further prodding, and although stunned by our disaster, in fewer seconds than I thought possible had reached a spot only about four yards from safety. It was then that I heard the sound of what could only have been a second falling body, thumping downwards until only silence reigned.

'A moment after, penetrating that silence, there came another sound I could not identify; but were I to liken it to anything, it seemed to resemble slightly the loud noise of a massive dried-out ivy branch, being dragged across some rough surface.

'Throat dry, unable to speak or swallow, I then became vaguely aware of heavy breathing close behind. It was Dawes, who had somehow nimbly danced along until he was right upon me. Softly, I am sure so as not to wreck my already shattered courage, he begged, in a hoarse voice not much stronger than a whisper, "Archie, old boy, please, I say *please* get a leg on! There's something——" and his words stopped, cut abruptly off, right then.

'I *knew* he was gone. His disappearance was worse than that of the others, *since there was no sound of falling*. I was by now trembling, on the verge of losing my grip entirely, but at the same time, I had almost reached the cross, with the buttress just inches past that.

'Mist was rolling up from the depths in a momentary cloud-like surge; while I moved towards my hold on the buttress, I heard very close to me a terrifying and ghastly sound, which I will never forget, as long as I inhabit this mortal world. It was the plant-like rasping, now magnified, with other smaller sounds interspersed—dripping as of hot grease, tiny poppings, noises like gutta-percha being ripped upon stretching, accompanied by the unbearable smell of animal and vegetable rot.

'There are times when a single action, a small gesture, a solitary movement, makes all the difference. This was one of them. I knew it. There was, however, the slightest problem—I was frozen by fear—I could not move!

'The smell of rotting flesh grew strong, the stench so penetrating that I began to gag. At the same time, that horrid rustling, those infernal noises like blisters bursting, increased by degree. My left hand was stretched out behind me; my choice was to stay in place and meet my unknown fate; to leap and end it all; or—and this was the hardest—to exercise my will, make a supreme effort, and, against all inclination, take that forward pace.

'With all these thoughts rattling around in my fear-soaked brain, I at that moment felt just the whisper of movement touch the edge of my left hand, and a searing jolt ran up it, as if kissed by a hot coal. It was then that all thinking stopped, and my body took over. Looking ahead, I saw myself moving my foot, without volition, a single step, past the odd cross.

'And everything stopped with that single stride. The sounds, the smell, my fear.

'Now a machine, no longer thinking, I somehow slid slowly down the small protruding column, legs wrapped on either side, gaining the small platform below, as the waves of fog boiled rapidly up, obscuring the setting of the tragedy entirely. There I collapsed, wracked with heaving convulsions from a cramp deep within me. Whatever had been behind me was gone on my having passed by the cross; when the chill vapours had cleared a few minutes later, as such fogs may in these valleys, I was alone. There was no trace of anyone, or anything, on the ledge above me.

'Of the nightmarish descent there is little remembered, and little to say. Had I not had the extra rope left at the wedged-in block, I doubt I would be alive today. At the absolute limit of my mental and bodily resources, I only remember a never-ending struggle. At times, it seemed that I had left my own body, and was calmly regarding my puny efforts with amusement, wondering why I bothered to fight on at all.

'I hardly recall, that evening, touching the ground at the rockfall embracing the tower's foot. So dulled was I, I showed no surprise whatever when a party of villagers met me, and carried me down, myself accepting without question this singular coincidence as part of the natural order of things, before consciousness suddenly fled.'

'I awoke a full day and a half later, in a feather bed at the home of the same peasant with whom we had lodged, carefree and innocent of impending disaster, two nights before. It gradually was explained to me by a visitor, the schoolmaster, who spoke rough French, that he had, the afternoon of the accident, as possessor of the single telescope in the village, first observed our presence on the summit, a feat that had astounded him and the other villagers, since the *Cima*, or peak, was thought to be impossible of ascent.

'Every few minutes thereafter he watched our further movements; once the descent had begun, he stayed at his station, surveying the train of events that followed, until the mist had thrown its encompassing opaque shadow. When it had cleared, seeing me starting down, he raised the alarum, assembling the men who rescued me.

'Further questioning from myself drew forth a brief, curt description of the sequence of the tragedy, as seen from far below. The teacher had seen us begin our perilous shuffle across the face of the tower, with myself in front, and the others in the order I have described. He was adamant that Zeltener was on the frightening traverse. This was quite unexpected, since I had surmised his fall to have been the result of overbalancing, when the plate with the cross had come off in his hand.

'The schoolmaster was insistent that this was not the case; that Zeltener, having recovered his balance, was well on his way when a *fifth figure* appeared behind him. The man was not to be persuaded that there were only four of us on the crossing. Obstinate regarding this, he furthermore claimed that this fifth presence had gained upon our guide, and *nudged or pushed him off*! Before the poor teacher had recovered, the figure advanced. Describing this, the man blushed, since it seemed to him that whoever or whatever it was, it was changing shape as it perambulated.

'With my prodding, he claimed that when he first observed it through the imperfect optics of his glass, the thing looked almost like a man-sized starfish walking on two twisted limbs. By the time it had reached poor Bramley, the shape had seemingly grown two or three more arms or branches, the body at the same time becoming more compact.

'But nearing dear, unfortunate Dawes—who, I now realise, had done everything to keep me from panic—it waxed into something completely anamorphic, a darkness of blurred edges. Instead of dislodging my remaining companion, it *enveloped* him. This last, the schoolmaster admitted, was an impression, since the mist swirled up then, eclipsing the scene for the next few minutes. When the view was clear again, he saw me already started down alone.

'This fantastic story left me completely agitated, and I am afraid I fainted, losing consciousness once more. I slept profoundly, and was the next day only hobbling about. Entreating the schoolmaster to do all within his means to recover the mortal remains of my poor friends, I was told that was impossible. Asked why, he replied that a thorough search had been made at the foot of the fatal precipice, and no bodies had been found. When I expressed my incredulity concerning that intelligence, I was reassured of its truth.

'Furthermore, he told me that no one in the valley had expected otherwise; the sweep of the peak's lower slopes had been made as a matter of form, to satisfy the district authorities when the necessary report was made. Some local belief, in defiance of Newton, was at work here—that what went up did not necessarily come down.

'Dissatisfied, I, when better in limb, though not in spirit, undertook a survey of my own, but contrary to my expectations, found not even a trace of my vanished companions.

'I left, but before doing so, cornered the teacher a last time, with the view of getting something more out of him. The man, by the way, had a reputation for sobriety and honesty, so I was in the end forced to take him at his word.

'When pressed, he reluctantly mentioned a sort of edict of the Church, standing for immemorial time, which forbade the dwellers of the valley even to linger in the vicinity of the place, which was associated with some unspecified evil presence or events. He would not go into detail, only making it clear that it had taken great courage for the succouring group who found me at the mountain's foot to have come so far. He stated that I had been extremely lucky to have come out of the affair alive. Others, and not just our party, had not been so fortunate.

'The only information I could pry from him was a half-admission that Herr Zeltener had perhaps been to the valley at some earlier time, speaking at length to some village elders then living. More I could not get out of him.

'By way of a final word: University friends of the presumed deceased, next season, went to the valley as a group in search of some evidence that might have explained the unbelievable series of events I have related. I stayed back, still too rattled to accompany them. I had already given up climbing, and have not been on the rope since.

'They found no more than did I; but the infamous shelf, that deadly edge of rock on which the three met their fate, had in the springtide—as a result, no doubt, of the freezing and expansion of ice in the crack behind it—exfoliated from the cliff face, crashing one afternoon to the base of the tall tower, adding to the loose rocks built up over the years in their myriad thousands. That particular variant of the climb, of which we were the sole executors, could never be repeated.'

Eggleston finished, and the rest of us were silent for a while. I remember pouring myself another drink, while Eggleston filled his pipe anew, and MacLong kept fiddling with ropes and equipment, as he had throughout the telling of the tale.

It was Moore, stirring the embers of the fire with a stick, who finally broke the stillness.

'So it was the cross, you think, that saved your grandad's pa.'

'One can assume nothing else. The symbol must have contained some talismanic power, or, I suppose if one were sceptical, it was a warning to something, not to approach any further. It was the accidental removal of one of these marks that allowed the destroyer of Archie's friends to venture onto the ledge, from which it had, until then, been prohibited. At least, I assume that Zeltener would never wilfully have displaced the protective icon...'

Moore nodded, and continued poking at the coals.

Our normally taciturn Scot, MacLong, added then a surprising comment: 'I ken those signs. Coolidge, in one of his scarcer monographs, the one with the notice of his climbing aunt, gives—buried in an appendix—the locations of one hundred and eighteen of them, all high up in the mountains. The Basle Museum has one on display, and the tiny exhibition in Zermatt has another, kept out of sight in the cellar.'

'I think I know the book: *The Alps in Folklore, Legend, and Myth,* 1906,' I chimed in, giving pedantry free rein. Privately, I could not remember having seen the section under discussion in the edition I had perused years back.

'They are amazing things,' Eggleston continued. 'They seem to be pre-Christian, dating back to the Bronze Age, perhaps before. They appear always to be associated with some perilous passage, set up as signs of warning, or protection, or both. That early man was already, thousands of years ago, capable of astounding feats of escalation is well-known: explorers of cave systems high up in the Pyrenees have reported evidence of our primitive ancestors, inside grottoes with openings accessible only by climbs of the Fifth Grade. Plus,' he added.

'And that's not the only mystery surrounding these strange signs. . . .' Here, he hesitated momentarily, as if for effect.

'All of you sitting here are without question familiar with that rare and famous book of Wherry's, *Alpine Notes and the Climber's Foot*?'

'1896,' Moore could not but help add, while the other two sagely nodded heads. Reading about climbing, next to climbing itself, remains the favourite activity of the fraternity, and most mountaineers are very well-informed regarding the history and background of their sport. The title was, however, unknown to me.

'Good,' intoned Eggleston. 'Now you know that splendid tome is filled with photographs of climbers' feet, positioned variously, to demonstrate proper movement when on rock. I happen to have with me now a copy of that venerable work'—and here he reached over to a nearby table, where lay a nondescript book bound in green cloth, which, picking up, he opened to a page already marked.

'Wherry used the feet of several well-known climbers and mountaineers for his subjects. Please take a close look at the plate before you.'

With that he passed the volume to me. I could make nothing of it except for an exceptionally ugly bare foot, attached to a squatting figure whose face was not shown, and who was wearing a tweed jacket, jodphurs or plus fours, and a ribbed stocking on the other foot.

Moore, who I noticed in the meanwhile had discreetly drawn a pair of slippers over the bare feet he had been warming at the fire, took the book from my hands, and looked it over, saying nothing, before passing it to MacLong.

MacLong immediately, upon seeing the photographic illustration, arched his eyebrows in surprise, before giving the work back to Eggleston.

I could bear it no longer, in the face of all this, and blurted out, 'For God's sake, what *is* it that everyone else has seen, that I have not?'

'Look again, laddie, hard,' was the Scot's comment as I grabbed the volume back. Then I saw it. A very faint trace—scarcely obvious, but there nonetheless—of the cross that Eggleston had shown to us, was just visible on the top of the big toe in the picture.

'I have it,' said Eggleston somewhat pontifically, 'on the best authority that the anonymous foot is that of a pioneer climber who disappeared about one hundred years ago in the Karakoram, *after* having lost that toe in a freak accident involving two penny-farthings in a country lane in Somerset.'

While I chewed that over, Moore joined in, almost as if reluctantly: 'A close friend, a medical doctor who climbs, told me in confidence that the most famous of all modern climbers, Bertold Gessner, had, before the sad loss of his toes on Ra'um Dhudl IV, a similar or identical tattoo on one foot.'

I was on the verge of spluttering, hearing this. The implications were deep, almost too profound to be comprehended. Looking round at the solemn faces before me, I finally exclaimed, 'But what of the bodies of Archibald's friends? I assume they disappeared into the snow, into some hole in the ice. Haven't they popped out of the glacier by now?'

Here I had in mind not particularly the Iceman, but rather other incidents, where people who vanished into crevasses surfaced decades later, still intact in their icy youth, whilst people alive when these unfortunates were killed had aged physically far past their eternally young and frozen former companions. Ask any Swiss.

'Ah,' said Eggleston, shaking his head sadly. 'The Dolomites have very few glaciers, and none of any real size. In the case of Archibald's companions, that would have made no difference, since he stated to Digby categorically that the vale where the tragedy took place faced south. There was no, and never had been any, glacier there at all.'

I could only shake my head, speechless as I was for once.

As I silently sipped my third for the night, Eggleston could not refrain from adding a coda: 'You know, there was *one thing* I didn't mention, told me by my grandfather about all this. It was simply that Archibald, on the outer edge of his left hand, just below the smallest finger, had a small spot lacking pigmentation. No matter how dark the rest of his hand might be of a summer, that one patch remained bone pale, like a burn mark. Whenever Da asked him about it, he would change the subject, ignoring the question.'

As there was absolutely nothing I could say to this, and the dark was encroaching, and a new day of hours of exercise was ahead of us, I bade goodnight to the others, and, still muttering to myself, went to bed, mentally reviewing the locations of the tattoo parlours in the town where I lived.

A hard-core climber takes all precautions necessary, and that is a fact.

Beneath the Sun

Simon Bestwick

I T WAS THE SUMMER after my mother died. My father and I had moved out of our old house and to another, more memory-free, on the outer edges of suburbia, bordering on the countryside. If you walked far enough, you were lost in the green hills and woodlands of Cheshire, without even a farmer or upper-class moron—a species common in Cheshire then and still, and sadly showing no signs of extinction—to break the solitude.

That was what I needed. The atmosphere in the house was almost unbearable at this point. Grieving, in retrospect, is a process we all handle in different ways and by different means. My father's was to withdraw into his work. Mine? To wander off. To go places where my brain didn't work anymore, because there were trees and flowers and birds and hills and streams to lose all awareness in. The house suited us both. It allowed my father to make his withdrawal absolute, and it enabled me to walk away. Silences ached like wounds between us and I often thought that if I didn't come back from one of my early-morning or early-evening rambles through the woodland, it would take him about a week to notice.

I had no friends—we'd moved too far away from our old home for there to be a hope of my retaining them. So I walked alone through the woods and came back later and later. Soon I took to taking a packed lunch with me. Other times I didn't even bother with that.

The particular morning I want to tell you about was no different from any other. I was at this time twelve years of age. I went out and walked into the woods. I stood in the front doorway before going and listened to my father pounding the typewriter keys—he still regarded computers as the tool of the devil—for a few moments before leaving. I slammed the door hard. If I'd hoped for a response, I didn't get it.

Something of my numbness cracked around me that day and sobs hitched in my chest as I walked. The sunlight, sky, and heat-dried yellow grass blurred together, then faded into the warm dark green, black, and brown of the woodland.

I don't know exactly where it happened. When my crying fit subsided, I couldn't tell where I'd ended up. I was on a hillside, and at its foot the pines were thick. They were the first conifers I'd seen in the area surrounding my house. I wondered how far I'd travelled. I looked up at the sky, trying to gauge east and west and north and south. The sun was close to its zenith, at any rate, and burning hot. There were clouds, but well in the distance. I felt parched and dry.

I walked down the slope instead, towards the cool piney shade promised by the trees. Mum had used to hang one of those little pine air fresheners in the family car. Dad didn't. Perhaps the memory of them was painful to him, or perhaps he just kept forgetting.

I could smell the pines as I walked, and thought of my mother. I hadn't dared do so in a long time. It occurred to me that I needn't worry about bawling here. There was no one around, nobody to see or hear. But nothing came out then. Nothing has since. That morning was the last time ever. I can't cry now. I don't know why that should be. I've never understood it.

The pines were cool and their smell was my mother's. That felt good. Then I emerged from their shelter into a broad yellow field.

I walked. The field was wild and thickly overgrown, snarled with brambles and wild tall grass. A dead black tree loomed up ahead and cast a spill of shadow over the yellow stalks. I kept walking, in its general direction. There was nowhere else to go.

Then I tripped on something and went sprawling. My eyes stung. They might have been tears, but not the kind I can't cry now. I looked and found I'd tripped over a stone. Closer inspection showed it to be the broken remains of a slab. There was worn lettering on it; a name, and dates.

On my hands and knees in the long grass, I saw there were more of them, strewn about. I was lucky to have fallen only once. Most of them were only modest headstones, but here and there was a stone cross and, tumbled on her side, the remains, worn and lichened and pitted, of a stone angel.

Something moved the grasses nearby. I looked, but only glimpsed some loping shadow. Within seconds, I couldn't even be sure that it wasn't just the wind rustling at the dry hollow stems.

I stood and walked more slowly and carefully, the way you always do when you've seen what lies beneath the surface you're presented with at first. I moved towards the dark tree. A cricket somewhere nearby let out its relentless chirupping whirr.

They were under the tree.

At first I thought they were more stones, large ones; they were grey and pitted-looking, lumpy and unfinished and rough-surfaced. There were patches on them that resembled lichen in the baking summer heat. Then I began to notice things about them; there was a mottled, moist texture to them that argued against rock, that argued instead the flesh of something that wasn't meant to be in the sunlight, or spent a long time out of it. And they smelt—a bit like a tramp who hasn't washed in a long time, though there was something else it took me a moment to place—the way some pieces of chicken my father had bought had smelled after being left out too long. I felt myself gagging and clapped a hand over my mouth.

There was something else, too. They were moving.

There were, I think, about five or six of them. They had hands and feet and heads. I don't know if they used to be men and women—maybe back when they were alive—or if they were something else entirely. But they were tussling over something on the ground, in the centre of them. It was red, or a lot of it was; the pieces they picked up and lifted to their thankfully unseen faces to tear at were, at least. Flies were buzzing. The crickets had fallen silent but the flies seemed very loud. I couldn't believe I hadn't heard them before. It was burning hot. My lips and mouth were dry. They always had been. I felt giddy. I tried to breathe deeply, but breathed in the smell that was coming off them and again almost threw up. I clamped my hands back over my mouth. I didn't want them to see me. I didn't want them to know I was there. I backed slowly away, slowly and quietly, not daring to look away but tense over where each footfall might come down, in case some dry dead thing snapped to alert the feasters.

It didn't. But instead I trod on something hard and unyielding—I think it was another fragment of gravestone—that gave underfoot and buckled my ankle over. A scream at the sudden shocking insult of the pain tore out of me at the same time as my leg collapsed. I missed hitting my head on the stone angel by inches. I made a fumbling effort to stand, but even as I tried to put weight on my hurt ankle a spear of pain turned bone and muscle to liquid and I fell again.

But I could hear the crash and swish of things moving through the field towards me, large and ungainly and clumsy, of broad heavy hands swatting the grasses aside. I tried to drag myself away, wriggling like a snake, but they were too fast. There was no outpacing them. I saw their silhouettes looming around me and circling, like shadows on a bamboo screen.

As they closed in on me, they blotted out the sun. It was directly above and they made shadows of themselves against it. They smelt worse than ever. I glimpsed a part of one of them. There was an open sore on its flesh with flies crawling over it. I still couldn't see much of their faces as they bent over me. Just grey. Their eyes and mouths were red.

I was babbling—blubbering—something by this point, over and over again. I can't really remember it now, except for two words. *Not me. Not me.*

The stench, the heat, the fear—one or all of those and I passed out. When I woke up, the shadows were stretching out along the field, trailing through the grasses like weeds in the river, drawn out by the pull of the current.

I was alone, and there was no sign of anything grey and moving. I picked myself up and put some weight on my twisted ankle. It twinged but this time my leg held me up.

I made my way back to the hillside. From up there, with the height and thickness of the pines, the field was invisible, as if it had never been.

It was easier than I thought, finding my way to the familiar paths that would take me home. Perhaps I clicked into some kind of automatic pilot as I began to tell myself that what I'd seen that morning wasn't real, couldn't be real, that it was just some hot fever dream. I wanted to believe it so it wasn't hard. It was getting windy by then, and a bit cold; the sky was greying over. A dull dark mottled grey, like stone, or something else.

I almost ran—as close to it as my bad leg would let me—down the woodland path that led to my house. When I stumbled out, I stopped. I knew Dad didn't like company—that was why we'd moved out here—so I couldn't understand why there were so many cars parked outside. And a white van, or at least what looked like one. But then I saw the little yellow-black strips of tape fencing off the house from me, the men in black uniforms around it, the red stripe around the body of the van, and the blue light on top of it.

Mrs Green was there—she was our nearest neighbour. When she saw me she let out a cry and pointed. The policemen ran over to me. 'Come on son,' I heard one of them say. 'Come on.'

'Where's my dad?' I asked.

'Come on.'

'Poor little mite . . .' I heard Mrs Green saying. The rest was sniffles and lost in the slam of the police car door.

The sky was all grey now. A policeman started the engine. He was talking to me soothingly but I didn't listen.

Not me. I'd lie awake thinking that, over the aching but tearless nights that followed. *Not me.*

Someone else, anyone else, but not me.

Of course, I don't know what I might have said, much less why they should have listened to it. If listen they did. If they were there at all. A fever dream. I tell myself that. Most of the time I believe it. Most nights.

The Old Tailor and the Gaunt Man

Brian Showers

THE OLD MAN'S KNEES ACHED with age as he knelt on the worm-riddled ground at the side of his wife's grave. He carefully picked away the twigs and fallen leaves, but the October wind, not in the mood to be argued with, kept blowing them back. 'If I don't look after you, who will?' Another fierce gust of wind rushed across the crumbling and overgrown graveyard, dragging the breath from the old man's throat. He did what he could to brace himself with the thinning threads of his jacket, but bundling himself against the wind was useless. The disrepair crept in on all sides.

'I'm sorry,' he said to the grave in a low, low voice. 'I haven't had as much business as we used to. I'm afraid I can't even afford flowers today.'

The old man sighed. 'Styles change and people don't have an interest in hand-tailored suits anymore. They want suits made cheap and fast by buzzing and blinking machines. Where's the warmth and craft in a machine?' The old man's words froze in the air as they left his mouth, 'I'm obsolete. I simply can't compete. Just the other day a client left, dear, he left laughing at me. I showed him my finest garments, but he wasn't interested.' The old man closed his eyes. 'There's no room left in the world for an old tailor like myself; no one left to appreciate what these old hands can do. And they used to make such beautiful suits.' The old tailor looked down at the calluses on his fingertips and the spots on his hands: 'I wish I had one more chance to make another suit before I pass on.'

As the old tailor spoke the October wind howled and the graveyard unearthed a haunted moan. The setting sun elongated the shadow of a cat as it

THE OLD TAILOR AND THE GAUNT MAN

trotted along the side of the church. The old tailor rarely stayed in the graveyard past sunset. Few townspeople did. The old tailor shivered, though not from the chill.

'I promise you, my dear, flowers will be second only to a morsel of food on my plate. And if I can't earn that, then I'll be joining you soon enough.'

As the old tailor rose to his feet he was startled to find himself looking into the eyes of the black cat perched on the roughly hewn top of the adjacent tombstone. The fiery sunset smeared a feline shadow across the grave in front of the cat's tombstone-throne. The black cat looked at the old tailor with its ears perked and a knowing expression. He gave the cat a nervous nod before hastily picking his way through the dead and the overgrown brambles, homewards. He was expecting a visitor tonight.

The church bell tolled six o'clock as he approached the cemetery's iron gates.

The old tailor's shoes clacked along the cobblestones of the empty streets as he walked back to his shop. The twilight streets were empty, save for a few straggling shopkeepers who had just closed up for the night. Sleepy shades were drawn over the windows of the bookstore and the bank, while stray dogs and tomcats sniffed the back alley behind the butcher's shop for their dinners. By half past six, families were eating their evening meals together. The village streets after sunset became as silent and lifeless as the graveyard.

The rattling of the key into the keyhole of the shop rattled the old tailor's memory. He remembered, once upon a time, when he was greeted with the warmth of a fire, the smell of freshly baked bread, and the loving embrace of his wife. But those days were nothing more than fragments of memories boxed away in the back of his elderly mind.

The old tailor paused before the doorway. He always remembered to scrape the mud off his shoes. It used to be that he'd always forget, making a mess of the floor and provoking his wife's wrath. If only he could forget to scrape his shoes, just once, he thought, maybe she would be there again beyond the threshold.

Slowly, he opened the door, but was met only by darkness and a cold draught. Nothing. He kicked his shoes against the boot scrape, knocking clumps of graveyard mud from his soles, and went inside. He started a fire in the hearth and ate a small meal of bread, butter, and cheese before settling down to some mending. His visitor would arrive soon.

The echo of the church bells tolled half past seven. There was a firm rapping on the shop door. The old tailor put down his needle and thread and stared vacantly into the fire. Then came the growling voice; barely kept at bay by the thick, wooden door:

'Open up, old man, I know you're in there.'

The old tailor got to his feet as quickly as his old bones allowed. William Cruttwell banged on the door again. 'Just a minute!' The old tailor looked out through the glass window hoping it wouldn't be whom he expected. He unbolted the door and let the simmering volcano, his landlord, into the shop.

William Cruttwell, Jr., who had inherited the family business from his father, had ferocious red hair, and the temper of a hungry dog. He was much taller than the old tailor, who barely stood as tall as the sag of the landlord's lowest chin. He reminded the old tailor of a swollen child who'd been fed too generously year after year; and this child was still hungry. Cruttwell stood, huffing and puffing, in the doorway.

'Blast this weather.' He relit the extinguished cigarette pinched between his teeth.

'M–Mr Cruttwell, how n–nice to see you. Please come in. I just put the kettle on for tea. Have a seat and——'

'Not this time, old man,' growled Cruttwell, 'I'm here to collect the money. It's due on the fifteenth of the month and it's already the seventeenth. You've been late too many times in the past.' William Cruttwell wiped the sweat from his forehead with a crisp, white linen handkerchief.

'I–I'm sorry, Billy, I merely——' The old tailor stopped. Dust was suddenly swept off the boxes in his head and he unpacked his memories of young Billy Cruttwell. He remembered the energetic spirit in the boy's eyes and how he used to hide behind his father's legs when his father came to collect rent. Billy never cursed October. But that youth, since his father's death, had burned away, leaving nothing but a smouldering man whose heart incinerated the old tailor's smile. 'I'm sorry, Mr Cruttwell, I forgot.'

The landlord's face and neck turned as red as a kerosene jack-o-lantern, and the anger in his eyes glowed like the tip of his cigarette. He erupted: 'You don't have it? You're late again.'

'I apologise, Mr Cruttwell. I'll have the rent soon. Business is slow—I'm earning all I can with these mending jobs, but I'm just not getting any orders for new suits these days.'

'Ha!' snorted Cruttwell, wiping his forehead again, and shooting smoke through his nose. 'You're getting on, old man. Times have changed. No one wants to wait around while you make a new suit.'

'But the quality of the suits I used to make——' stuttered the old tailor. Cruttwell cut him off.

'Face it, old man. You're outdated. An antique. You should retire. Then I could get a real business in here that makes real money.' Bits of cigarette ash fell to the floor. 'Father was foolish to offer you such a long and lenient contract.'

'But Mr Cruttwell, your father was my friend. If it weren't for him I never would have been able to get my business started. I'm indebted to your family. If you can find it in your heart, Mr Cruttwell, to give me a fortnight, I give you my word this will never happen again.'

The old tailor held his breath as Cruttwell searched for his heart.

'Look, old man, I'm not my father and I'm not your friend. I'm a businessman. You have two weeks to come up with the money'—he dropped the butt of the dead cigarette to the floor—'or you'll be out with the cats'—and lit a fresh one.

'You're very kind, Mr Cruttwell,' said the old tailor as he stared at the discarded butt on his shop floor. He swallowed hard. 'Thank you.'

The landlord turned on his heel and waddled out the door, slamming it behind him. The old tailor watched through the window as Cruttwell disappeared down the empty street. Cigarette smoke still hung heavy in the air, choking the room.

The church bell tolled eight o'clock.

The old tailor settled down into his chair and picked up his needle and thread. 'I used to make such beautiful suits,' he thought to himself. 'Perhaps the boy's right. There's not a man alive who requires my services anymore. Maybe I'm just too old. Lord knows I only have a few years left.'

The old tailor laboured into the night. After a time, his eyelids grew heavy and he drifted off into a deep sleep. The church bell tolled away the hours as they crept past.

The church bell tolled quarter to eleven, waking the old tailor from his slumber. The garment he was working on had fallen from his hands. The fire was now a pile of red, hot embers, and what was once a candle at the end of the table was little more than a frozen puddle of wax. He cursed himself for falling asleep with so much work left to do. He picked up the garment from the floor and started mending in the light of a fresh candle.

Outside, in the lifeless streets, the wind's strength grew. It rattled the panes, played on the rooftop, and tapped the tree branches against the window.

Tap, tap, tap.

'I must remember to trim back those branches. One of these evenings a strong gale will send one of them right through my window. I can barely afford food, let alone a broken window.'

The old tailor continued his work, quietly humming a song to the empty room. As he worked, a chill wormed its way into the shop, down the chimney, through the keyhole, and between the loose window panes. It wasn't long before the wind rose and the branches tapped again.

Tap, tap, tap.

This time a curious notion struck the old tailor: 'Billy had that tree cut down nearly five years ago. If it's not the tree, what in the name of God could be making that tapping noise?' The old tailor shivered a bit and tried to stir up the fire for more heat. The noise came again.

Tap, tap, tap.

The old man put down his work and slowly got up from his chair.

Tap, tap, tap.

'It couldn't possibly be a tree that's not even there,' the old tailor mused as he made his way to the door. 'Unless it's a ghost tree,' he laughed to himself uneasily, 'but it can't be that either, seeing as I don't believe in ghostly trees.' His eyes darted nervously about the room, probing the shadows. His workshop took on a sinister midnight life. The moonlight streamed through the shop window and into the store, illuminating, and seemingly animating, the mannequins and draped fabrics.

The church bell started to toll midnight.

Dong, dong, dong . . .

Tap, tap, tap came the sound again. The old tailor peered out through the window into the moon-bathed street. It was empty. 'What could be making that noise?'

As if carried by the wind, the large, shadowy mass of a black cat leapt up onto the windowsill. The old tailor's heart attempted to take flight from its seat. The black cat put one of its paws against the windowpane.

. . . dong, dong, dong . . .

'Y–you gave me quite a fright, puss!' stammered the shaken tailor. He looked at the black cat more closely. 'Did we meet earlier today in the graveyard? That was you, wasn't it?' The black cat mouthed a meow from the other side of the glass. 'How would you like to come in for a saucer of milk and keep me company for a while, puss?'

Another pantomime meow.

. . . dong, dong, dong . . .

The cat leapt down from the window sill and the old tailor unbolted the front door. It burst open effortlessly with the fury of the wind; the night exhaled into the tailor's shop, blowing out the candle on the table. The black cat, possessed by the night's breath, ran past the old tailor's legs and into the darkness of the shop. The old tailor watched as the cat's shadow passed in front of the embers of the dying fire and then disappeared along with the cat.

. . . dong, dong, dong!

The old tailor turned to look back at the gaping door.

The scent of mould and unwholesome damp invaded the small shop and the old tailor's nostrils. Standing, silhouetted by the moon's light, in the doorway was the most peculiar form the old tailor had ever set eyes on. In the veil of darkness and half-blinding cataracts, the old tailor was barely able to make out the shape of what looked like a scarecrow from one of the neighbouring cornfields. The old tailor, frozen with fear, leaned against a chair to steady himself. After an endless age of divining the figure's features across the blustery gulf between them, the gaunt man conjured a thin and hollow voice from his cavernous throat.

'I did not mean to frighten you . . . that much.' He was barely audible over the whistling wind. 'I saw a light in your window. Other than the moonlight, it is the only light on in the street. I assume you are open for business?'

THE OLD TAILOR AND THE GAUNT MAN

The old tailor, still shaken, peered into the gaunt man's dark face. 'I–I'm afraid I'm n–not. It's quite late and I was j–just up finishing off a bit of work.'

The gaunt man cut in with the precision of a bat's wing. 'I am here for your services. It is whispered that you are a man of skill and talent.'

'I'm afraid you'll have to come back during the day,' the old tailor finally managed. 'I'm an old man and it's very late. I'm afraid your mending will have to wait until tomorrow.'

The gaunt man took two long strides into the shop. 'It is not mending that I am here for. I am in need of a new suit, and I am told you are a haberdasher of talent who makes garments of an antique quality.'

The old tailor saw something, like a shiny black button, scurry across the gaunt man's shoulder. 'A n–new suit did you s–say?'

'My name is Mortimer Quickly,' said the gaunt man in a low hiss. 'You will make a new suit for me, and I shall reimburse you for your efforts.'

The old tailor's mind leapt at the name. For a brief moment he recognised it from long ago, but that moment dissipated at the sudden prospect of a customer. 'Y–yes, please come inside.' He had forgotten that it was past the witching hour as he ushered the gaunt man into his shop.

The gaunt man, moving from the darkness of midnight into the shadows of the shop, remained eclipsed. The old tailor lit a fresh candle and stirred life into the dying embers of the fire in hope of dispelling the draught. 'What kind of suit are you interested in?'

'I want a suit of quality,' the gaunt man answered, 'one that will last me as long as my current suit has.' He took a seat in the corner by the fireplace and the black cat jumped into his lap. 'My current suit has served me for quite some time, but, like most things material, it has started to'—he paused and stroked the cat—'deteriorate.'

'I hope I can make a suit to your liking, Mr Quickly, though it's been a few years since I've tailored a proper suit.' The old tailor studied the gaunt man's frame through the shadows.

'A skill like yours is not easily lost or forgotten,' replied the gaunt man. As the flames flickered and licked away patches of darkness, the old tailor began to make out the other's features. The gaunt man's words came from between tight, bloodless lips and teeth that resembled the yellowed keys of an old piano. Cobweb strands of hair decorated his chalk-white pate, and hung long and unkempt, just shy of his narrow shoulders. The hand he stroked the cat with was crowned with withered fingers as thin as twigs, that were decorated with long, chipped nails. 'I have complete faith in you.' The old tailor could not see the gaunt man's eyes, but he felt the whites of whatever dwelled within those sunken caves.

'I–I'll need to take your measurements.' The old tailor motioned the gaunt man to the dressing screen with a trembling hand.

'If you'll just hand your old suit over to me,' said the old tailor. The gaunt man shuffled through the shadows, wheezing dust from his lungs as he made his way to the dressing screen. He began to disrobe.

'Do you mind if I ask you why you were out walking at such an hour? After all, most shops are open during the daytime,' ventured the old tailor.

A moment passed before the gaunt man answered.

'I am,' he began, 'of an advanced age. I find the dry night air preserves me. It is for this reason that I mostly walk the nights of October; perfect for stretching my old bones out beneath the moon.' The gaunt man flung his trousers over the top of the dressing screen; they slapped the side with a cloud of dust billowing from the empty legs.

As the gaunt man disrobed, the old tailor looked over the discarded remains of the old suit in the candlelight. The suit looked as though it had been shut up in some long-forgotten cellar. It was covered from cuff to cuff in a fine dust, and throughout were deposits of encrusted soil and tiny gnawed holes. Strands of cobwebs criss-crossed the lapels, holding the suit together along with dried moths' wings. On the inside of the breast the old tailor found a small label sewn into the lining.

'This suit,' said the old tailor with astonishment, 'it was made by my old master, Arthur Trimmings!'

'Is that so?' replied the gaunt man from somewhere behind the dressing screen.

'Yes, I was apprenticed to him when I was a young boy. That was right after my father passed on. Mr Trimmings took me in even though he was nearing retirement. This suit must be very old!' The gaunt man coughed and wheezed from behind the screen. 'Mr Trimmings is buried up near the church, isn't he?' wondered the old tailor aloud.

'Yes, the suit is very old. It has served me for my whole life and more,' replied the gaunt man. He stepped out from behind the dressing screen in his undergarments.

The gaunt man was even thinner without the bulk of his clothing around him. He stepped into the light of the fire for the old tailor to measure him. The old tailor trembled as the fire flickered and shadows played over the gaunt man's body. His arms stretched from his torso like cracks in ice. There seemed to be no muscle to support his emaciated structure. His taut skin showed every round and angle in the skeleton buried beneath. A skull grinned coldly at the old tailor from under the gaunt man's surface. The old tailor felt the nervousness creep up his spine to the base of his neck and into his own skull. He quickly completed the measurements and jotted them in his notebook while the gaunt man returned his ancient frame to his tattered wrappings.

'I'll have the suit done in a fortnight, kind sir,' said the old tailor.

'So it is agreed. I shall return to your shop on All Hallows Eve to collect my new suit,' replied the gaunt man, now fully dressed.

'Y–yes sir, I'll make the finest suit you've ever set eyes on.'

THE OLD TAILOR AND THE GAUNT MAN

The gaunt man made his way to the door. He paused there, his skeleton silhouetted through parchment skin in the moonlight. The black cat darted out of the shadows to the gaunt man's feet. The gaunt man clacked his bony teeth at the old tailor in a dry, hideous smile before he nodded once and disappeared, silently, down the dark street.

Dong!

The old church bell tolled one o'clock in the morning.

During the next two weeks the old tailor gave little thought to his peculiar client and the nocturnal call. Infused with new life, he effortlessly did some of his best stitching in years. The old tailor soon got into the habit of working on the suit into the evening; often times past midnight and right up until the church bell tolled the dawn hours.

On certain nights he was visited by the strange shadow cat, which would always appear at dusk and sit with him until just before dawn.

After a fortnight of snipping and stitching, the old tailor completed the suit for the gaunt man. It was one of the finest suits he'd ever tailored. 'I'm sure Mr Quickly will be most pleased with this,' he thought to himself. 'I've put the experience of my whole life into it.'

The sun slowly went down on the evening of the thirty-first. Bales of corn stalks and hanging gourds still decorated the streets from the day's festival. Before going to bed, the villagers set fresh sweets on their front doorsteps. This, as tradition went, would ward off any unexpected or unwanted callers. Tonight was the night that the dead became restless.

The church bell tolled six o'clock.

The old tailor sat down to a dinner of bread and cheese. 'Tomorrow I'll have a proper dinner,' he thought to himself, as he admired the suit hanging on the mannequin. 'And, my dear, you shall have your flowers!' he added.

The church bell tolled seven o'clock as the old tailor sat down to start his mending work for the evening. It wasn't long before he started to doze in his chair, needle and cloth slowly falling from his hands. The flames cringed and the fire slowly asphyxiated. The old tailor didn't wake up until he was stirred by the rustling of the wind.

Tap, tap, tap.

He quickly propped himself straight and rubbed his eyes. *I'd almost forgotten!* he thought to himself. 'Just a moment!' He rose from the chair, put on his glasses, and made his way to the door. He peered through the window into the pitch-black night. Nothing. 'It must have been the wind,' he said aloud. He laughed an uncertain laugh to himself, and turned back to his mending. His mind wandered briefly to the old tree that once stood in front of his shop.

Tap, tap, tap.

'Now surely that can't be the wind!' He turned back around, unlocked the door, and threw it wide open. Standing there before him was the skeletal form of the gaunt man. His body, though thin, seemed to block the entire doorway.

'I understand your nervousness on the thirty-first. All Hallows Eve. Not a night to be out.' Popping a sweet into his mouth, the gaunt man smiled wickedly and crossed the threshold. 'One of my favourite nights,' he added darkly. 'Have you got my suit ready?'

'Of course,' whispered the old tailor. The two old men crossed the room to the mannequin; the black cat darted in to lead them.

'It is marvellous,' said the gaunt man as he inspected the craftsmanship. 'I shall try it on immediately,' he added, popping another sweet into his mouth.

The old tailor removed the suit from the mannequin and handed it to the gaunt man behind the dressing screen. Questions and apprehensions began to form in the old tailor's head.

'May I ask you a question?' ventured the old tailor.

'Yes,' replied the gaunt man curtly.

'I've never seen you around the village. Do you live in the area?'

'A long time ago, yes'—the gaunt man paused as though amused by something—'but not anymore. I now dwell in the shadow of the old church.'

The old tailor considered this before saying, 'I go up there every Sunday to visit my wife. I can't say I recall seeing any cottages near there.'

'I live on the church's grounds,' replied the gaunt man coldly.

'Do you tend the grounds?'

'In a manner of speaking . . . yes.'

'It must get lonely living up there, always surrounded by death,' said the tailor, his apprehension returning.

The gaunt man stepped out from behind the screen dressed in his new suit. He looked at the old tailor and spoke, the black pits of his eyes smouldering. 'Death puts an end to life . . . not living.' His breath smelled of sugar. 'I do not get lonely. The dead speak, you know, but only to those who lie still . . . and listen very closely. Even the beating of one's heart is much too loud, and drowns out their voices.'

'I'm afraid I don't believe in ghosts,' the old tailor laughed nervously.

'That is a pity,' replied the gaunt man solemnly. 'October nights may be the last bastion of superstition. Apparitions are not yet obsolete. There is still enough faith for dark things to walk the night. Faith . . . sometimes . . . must be re-learned.'

The old tailor gazed deep into the hollows of the gaunt man's eyes. From within their inky black recesses, the old tailor saw why children quiver in the dark, and why they know, for certain, what lies hidden there. Eternity passed between the old tailor and the even older gaunt man. The old tailor stood there in the store amidst scraps of cloth and strands of thread, his hands hanging numbly at his sides.

THE OLD TAILOR AND THE GAUNT MAN

The gaunt man turned to look at himself in a mirror. He stretched his arms in the sleeves and looked proudly down the trousers to the tips of his shoes. A ghost of a smile appeared on his lips. 'You are easily as skilled as our own Mr Trimmings. The suit fits perfectly.'

'You're welcome,' was all the old tailor could say.

'Care for a sweet?' said the gaunt man as he ate another. The black cat rubbed itself against his legs.

The old tailor shook his head in silence.

'You should be paid for your work.'

The old tailor nodded helplessly.

The gaunt man reached his spidery fingers into the pockets of his new suit. Like a magician, he produced two copper coins from the empty pocket and flashed them in front of the old tailor's eyes. 'This suit and these two copper coins are all my worldly possessions.' He held the two coins in the light of the fire, then snatched the old tailor's wrist in an icy claw and drew it towards him. The frosty grip burned, though the old tailor somehow managed to turn his palm upwards, as if to offer the gaunt man the rest of *his* worldly possessions.

The gaunt man leaned forward so that their noses almost touched, and spoke. 'This is all the payment I have. It will suffice.'

The old tailor felt the heavy coldness of the two copper coins as they dropped into his palm. 'Thank you,' he said quietly, still hypnotised by the depths of the gaunt man's eyes; nostrils inhaling his sweet, frozen breath.

'There is one more thing you can do for me,' the gaunt man added. 'I have many . . . associates, all of whom are in need of new suits. I will recommend your services to them.'

Another 'Thank you' was all the old tailor could muster.

'You are indeed welcome,' said the gaunt man as he moved towards the door. He paused in the threshold. 'And I guarantee you the custom of my associates. You may have faith in *that*.' The gaunt man's lips parted and his skull grinned at the old tailor one last time before he walked down the cobblestone street; the black cat trotted not far behind.

The old tailor felt weak, though relieved. His wrist still throbbed with pain. Briefly, in the candlelight, he looked down into his palm at the two copper coins. They felt unnaturally heavy. He tried to laugh nervously to himself, but could only manage a partial sob. He deposited the coins on the table. The old tailor rubbed his eyes, feeling in them the effects of two weeks' worth of pre-dawn work.

Lying on the floor were the remains of the gaunt man's tattered suit. The old tailor didn't stop to look twice when he saw something squirm and flutter within the suit's crumpled folds. He quickly picked it up and cast it into the fire.

Dong, dong, dong . . .

In the distance, the church bell tolled midnight.

The next morning the old tailor awoke in the morning sun, refreshed with life. Dismissing from his mind the cold imprint left by the previous night, he started to ready himself for visiting his wife's grave. He dressed and prepared to venture out into the first day of November: All Saint's Day. When he sat down to eat, he noticed the two copper coins on the table. They stared up at him, two antique eyes that reflected the gaunt man's peculiar midnight request.

The old tailor didn't recognise the copper coins at all. 'They must be old.' So old that the old tailor doubted that they had any value at all. 'Still, I ought to try,' he thought, as he put the copper coins into his pocket. 'I can take them to the antiques dealer down the street.' He put on his coat and went out into the bright morning, heading towards the antiques shop.

The bell above the shop door tinkled as the old tailor entered. The shop was piled high with dusty African woodwork and Persian rugs that were rolled up tight with mildew. In the centre of the exotic treasure pile stood Mr Stacks with a wide and wrinkled smile on his face.

'How good to see you again!' Mr Stacks greeted the old tailor with a vaguely foreign accent. 'How is your luck with business these days?'

'Good morning, Mr Stacks. I think it may be doing better, thank you. I've brought something for you too look at.' The old tailor dug into the depths of his pocket for the two copper coins. His stomach dropped as his fingertips touched their coldness. He let them fall into Mr Stacks' open palm with relief. 'Do you think they are of any value?'

Mr Stacks hefted them in his hand, puzzled by their unnatural weight, before raising them in the dusty sunlight for a better look.

'Ah, these are very odd indeed. Very old. I don't recognise them, but I suspect they are older than you or I would expect. I think I could fetch quite a price for them.'

Despite their cool heaviness in his hand and the peculiar apprehension in his stomach, Mr Stacks bought the two copper coins from the old tailor for much more than the old tailor expected.

'I could live on this for a year!' thought the old tailor. 'Good day to you Mr Stacks!' He left the antiques shop for Mr Cruttwell's office, invigorated.

In the antiques shop, Mr Stacks shivered.

Cruttwell's office was an inferno, dense with smoke from the lit cigarette in the ashtray and the hundreds before it. William Cruttwell, Jr. was snoozing in a chair that creaked under the weight of his every snore. The old tailor dropped the rent, waking up the landlord as the coins hit the desk. Cruttwell embarrassedly regained what composure he could.

'I assume you'll be moving out within the week?'

'I–I'd like to stay, if it's all right,' said the old tailor. 'It seems my business has found a new life. Here's the rent I owe you'—Cruttwell's face and neck turned a bright pink—'as well as the rent for the next two months.' Crutwell flushed a deep red. 'Rent will be the least of my worries now.' He left the office, leaving the enraged William Cruttwell, Jr. to count his money in the punishing heat of his office.

The old tailor stopped at the flower shop and bought a beautiful bouquet for his wife before continuing on to the churchyard.

He picked his way through the plots until he found his wife's grave. Kneeling down in the grass, he felt the remainder of the morning dew soak into the knees of his trousers. Gently putting the flowers on his wife's grave, he spoke. 'You see, my dear, I always keep my word.' He felt her smile, approvingly, through the pine lid and six feet of earth. He said a quiet prayer before standing to leave. That was when he saw it.

Blood drained from his face, then his arms, then his legs, leaving him as cold as death, feet planted immobile on the ground. He swayed back and forth, knees trembling. In all the years visiting his wife's grave he never bothered to read the name on the moss-covered stone next to hers. Engraved in the cold stone, over a century old, were the words:

> In sacred memory of
> Mortimer Quickly
> b. 20 March 1692
> d. 31 October 1802

The old tailor was frozen to the spot like a dead weight. It was only after a single, endless moment that his senses sparked mercifully back to life.

Hurriedly, and ill at ease, he picked a single flower from his wife's bouquet and placed it on the gaunt man's resting place. The old tailor hastily stumbled homewards through the field of hundreds of tombstones. A black cat stalked the far off hedge near the cemetery wall.

That night, the old tailor sat down to what was a modest meal to some, but was a feast to him. After his dinner, he sat for a long time warming himself in front of the fire and reading a book. Gradually his chair became overwhelmingly comfortable. The book slowly slipped from his hands as he dozed off into a restful sleep.

And the old tailor would have rested peacefully all night in front of that fire, in his comfortable chair, in his very own shop, if it had not been for the tolling of the church bell at midnight, followed by a gentle *tap-tap-tapping* at his shop door.

Vado Mori

Joseph A. Ezzo

I said to my soul, be still, and wait without hope
For hope would be hope for the wrong thing.
T. S. Eliot, 'East Coker'

THE *FESTSCHRIFT* HAD GONE EXCELLENTLY. Tom Willoughby had done an exemplary job setting up the programme and providing top-drawer facilities at his university for the presentations. The weather had cooperated, featuring brilliant sunshine and mild evenings during that first week of April. Afterwards the reception and supper were hallmarks of class and good cheer. The old professor's hand had been shaken countless times by colleagues, his cheek pecked repeatedly by respectful women, and before the night grew too late Tom Willoughby was able to whisk the old man away to his house, accompanied by three other of the professor's first wave of protégés, for brandy and conversation into the wee hours of the morning.

They sat around a comfortable fire in Tom's living-room, sipping outstanding brandy and reliving those exciting days, more than a quarter-century before, when the four of them—Willoughby, Carolyn Reilly, Brett Jarvis, and Julian Goode—had studied under Professor Jerrod on their way to doctorates and university positions.

'It's so nice to be here, with you four,' the old man said, for perhaps the twentieth time that evening. 'So wonderful to be together this one . . . er, this time.'

By and by the conversation lulled, and Tom Willoughby could not help but feel the evening was destined to end very soon. Not wanting this to happen just yet, he racked his brain for a fresh direction for the proceedings. 'Tell me, Jerrod,' he mused, getting everyone's attention, 'how do you plan to amuse yourself come retirement?'

The old man seemed to ponder this quite intently for a bit. 'Probably in the same fashion as I have been of late, Tom. You see, when you get to be my age, when you know your days are numbered, you spend a lot of time in reflection. Did I make the right decisions about what I wanted to study? Did I do my research properly, or could I have done better? Did I train my students as well as I really could have, or was I lax on occasion? Have I lived my life in a meaningful way? Finally, I suppose, do I understand what is real in this life, and what is not? Is there truly, finally, something we can confidently call reality? Is it what is in our minds, is it what we experience, is it what we can observe and measure in the empirical, corporeal world, or is it some intricate and indecipherable fusion of those sources, as well as others of which we are aware, and still many more of which we are not?'

'The wisdom of age, that kind of thing,' Tom Willoughby considered.

Carolyn Reilly chuckled, then looked chagrined. 'Is that what we have to look forward to? Contemplating such questions?'

Absently Jerrod caressed his brandy snifter. 'You see, I've never told any of you this. You all know I earned my doctorate at Yale, but you don't know that I had nearly completed my studies for the Ph.D. elsewhere.'

'In history?' Tom Willoughby asked.

'Well, of course. No, I originally matriculated at Buchanan, a small university in Queens that was quite a fashionable place to study history back in the fifties. But my interest did not lie in Mediaeval Europe, as has been my focus of research for nearly half a century now.'

'Really?' Brett Jarvis entered the conversation. 'What was it?'

'I was going to be a Civil War historian.'

Murmurs of astonishment emanated from the lips of the four protégés. 'That's quite an astounding leap, from the Civil War to Mediaeval Europe,' Tom Willoughby remarked, speaking for the group. 'How on earth did that happen?'

'Or, another question would be, why did you leave Buchanan?' Carolyn Reilly asked. 'To pursue Mediaeval studies instead of the Civil War?'

Jerrod nodded, as if he had not quite looked at the issue from that perspective. 'Ostensibly, you could say so. But the fact is, I had no choice. I had to leave and find another university. I certainly didn't have to abandon Civil War history; the change to Mediaeval history was a consequence of the experience that expedited my departure from Buchanan. I'm not entirely sure why, when I applied to Yale, I claimed that my interest was in Mediaeval Europe. I guess it became so, as a result of what happened to me at Buchanan, a strange obsession, a calling from a direction and source I could not exactly identify.'

After a slight, pensive pause and a sip of brandy, he added, as if by way of coda, 'Now that I think about it, I've never disclosed the full story to anyone.'

'Certainly you can't leave us in the dark now, given this mysterious build-up,' Carolyn Reilly offered.

'Is the story appropriate for a night around the fire with old friends?' Tom Willoughby added.

Jerrod chuckled, then coughed, cleared his throat. 'Perhaps it would be more appropriate if we were camping in the woods, or spending the night in an old, deserted house. I doubt I've ever said much to anyone about it.'

Julian Goode, always the most reserved (and perhaps the most talented) of the quartet, chose now to speak. 'Why do I have the impression there is something very painful in this experience of yours?'

Jerrod regarded them all briefly, then looked at his brandy snifter. 'Well, the short answer to "why" is that the department at Buchanan—for all intents and purposes—imploded. I really had no choice, if I wanted to finish.'

'"Imploded." An interesting word,' Tom Willoughby noted. 'Not even in existence when you were a student, eh?'

Jerrod attempted to laugh, but coughed several times instead, rather violently. '*Touché*, Tom. But . . . that's the best description of it.'

'So,' Julian Goode asked, 'do you feel it worthwhile to recall it all and tell us?'

The old man rubbed his goateed chin. 'I can't say for sure, but it's strange. The events that led to the department's collapse are still so clear in my mind I wonder if I haven't invented them. I mean it happened, but have I reinvented the facts to justify my own actions? Especially of . . . oh, forget about that. You know, sometimes fabrication can be so much more powerful than memory of actual fact. And well . . . strange thing is, although I'm pretty certain that I've never told anyone the tale, it's stayed in my mind all these years. But not in any kind of dormant fashion, quite the opposite. It's grown and twisted and turned, demanded my attention, and I've embellished it with details I could not possibly know.' He paused, then set down his snifter and extracted pipe and tobacco pouch from the inside pocket of his jacket. He unzipped the pouch, then looked up at Tom Willoughby. 'Do you mind, Tom?'

Now in fact Tom Willoughby was quite against smoking in his house, but he waved at the old man. 'Whatever makes you comfortable.'

After the old professor had filled his pipe, Tom produced a taper from the fire and lit it for him. Jerrod puffed pensively, sat back, took up his refilled snifter. 'Very well, then, it's settled. The story involves the bizarre triangulation of three professors—Messrs Laidlaw, Dalton, and Gaunt—and a wet-behind-the-ears graduate student who thought he wanted to study the Civil War. . . .'

* * * * *

My mentor, Duncan Laidlaw, was three years away from mandatory retirement, and had spent thirty-four years teaching at Buchanan. He had moved into the office that he currently inhabited twenty-six years before. So it would not surprise anyone to learn that during the last quarter-century he had witnessed, within the rather cramped confines of the room, his share of unusual, even bizarre, encounters. Therefore, the one presented him by Orlando Dalton on that grey November morning, when rain spat on the office windows and wind rattled the glass with annoying vigour, was not something that could be labelled as wholly unique.

Dalton, a generation younger than Laidlaw, was a scrawny, balding, sickly looking fellow who smiled rarely and socialized with members of the faculty even less. He walked with a slight limp, shoulders stooped, face set in a disagreeable grimace. He had a number of eccentricities that caused no small source of discomfort among students, office staff, and a fair number of the faculty. For example, he had unusually large black eyes that he would fix intensely on whomever he was addressing. He never touched books with bare hands, but always wore white cotton gloves, even when handling brand-new or inexpensive volumes. He kept several pairs of such gloves in conspicuous locations in his office, so that should anyone enter and wish to consult one of his books, they understood the protocol immediately. Three years earlier, when a student breached this protocol, in full view of Dalton, the latter demanded, first of the department chair, then the dean, then the university president, to have the student expelled. He was an ardent Roman Catholic, and as Buchanan was a private school that catered largely to wealthy Jewish Manhattanites, his religious pretences, often worn on his sleeve, offended no small number of people. He further unsettled people with his insistent formality of addressing everyone as either 'Mr' or 'Miss'. At first it was thought that he was attempting to show refinement, possibly even a trace of aristocracy in his bloodline; later, people associated with the department (graduate students, mainly) decided that he was so misanthropic he merely lacked the skill to learn anyone's given name.

Laidlaw set aside a bundle of sheets and smiled. 'Morning, Orlando. What's the good word?'

Dalton took a seat opposite the old professor and raised his head. 'Mr Gaunt is trying to kill me,' he said between heavy breaths.

Laidlaw's eyes widened, and he shook his head slightly, as if something had come loose inside and required readjustment. 'Our esteemed departmental chair, newly arrived from Columbia? I haven't got the impression he was all that bad. A little full of himself, naturally, but then those in the university game with political aspirations are generally not lacking in ego. But . . . sorry for being flippant, Orlando. I gather I'm not supposed to take you literally. What is he doing, swamping the junior faculty with administrative and committee responsibilities? He's not making you sit on divisional, is he?'

Dalton did not take his eyes off Laidlaw. 'Understand me clearly, Mr Laidlaw. Mr Gaunt is trying to kill me. Or rather, I have not put it quite properly.

He has come for me. As in . . . how do you want me to explain? Corporeal death.'

Laidlaw traced his finger over the top sheet in the bundle before him. Dalton was certainly not the most emotionally stable professor, and faculty rivalries and turf wars in a given department were *de rigeur* in academia. There had been cases, a decade or so earlier, when the department had nearly imploded, with faculty suing each other, *et cetera*. Before he could muster a reply, Dalton was speaking again. 'Are you aware that Mr Gaunt has two sons? And do you know their professions? One of them is a classical musician, performs in a small symphony orchestra in the Midwest. Plays the flute. The other is a carpenter, some type of master craftsman who constructs all kinds of fancy furniture and what not.'

'I was vaguely aware of his sons, but what does this——'

'Well, I suppose that could be written off as a coincidence. It bothered me for a while. The flute-player and the carpenter. I tried not to think too much of it, until I could take no more of Mr Gaunt's manner.'

'Manner?' Laidlaw was growing increasingly confused, and was starting to conjure up some excuse for why he needed to leave his office for a time.

'Yes. You know how he treats me here. You're well aware. Just yesterday I had a short meeting with him.' Dalton produced a small tape recorder from the pocket of his jacket. 'Here, listen.'

> GAUNT: I'm just not sure I can take your research seriously. And your behaviour around students!
>
> DALTON: Do you find a problem with that, Mr Gaunt?
>
> GAUNT (laughing sarcastically): Do I! Good God, man, you strut around here as though it's the turn of the century, with your silly mannerisms and your phony formal speech.
>
> DALTON: I don't find your comments particularly professional, Mr Gaunt.
>
> GAUNT: Oh, please, spare me. Before we discuss these matters in greater detail—and I assure you, we will—I want you to take serious stock of yourself as a professional, you understand? As a teacher and as a scholar. Next time we meet, I expect you to explain to me why your research is of any significance whatsoever, and if I don't see an improvement in your overall behaviour around here—particularly towards students—well, suffice it to say you'll have a fair bit of explaining to do on that front as well. And now, *Mis-ter* Dalton, I have a lot on my plate at the moment, if you'll——

Dalton shut off the tape recorder. 'I think you get the general drift.'

'Certainly it's critical, but hardly condemnatory,' Laidlaw remarked. 'Or necessarily a case of mistreatment.'

'Mr Laidlaw, you're familiar with the tradition of the *danse macabre*, of course.'

Laidlaw laughed. 'Come now, Orlando, if you'd asked me this question forty years ago, when I was preparing for my qualifying exams, I could give you an adequate answer. But I'm along in years, set in my ways. I'm a Civil War historian, you know that. Just before you came in I was reading through the thesis draft of one of my students, dealing with Nathan Bedford Forrest and his men at Dover Landing. This is the stuff I know. Mediaeval traditions aren't my forte, nor have I given them much of a thought, truth be told, in a very long time. You are our resident expert on such matters.'

'Granted, but—and hear me out on this—if one were to take a typical passage from a *danse macabre*, where the text exists, either from the fresco panels or from manuscripts, and translate the dialogue of Death, particularly towards those in respectable positions, into modern English, it might sound very much like Mr Gaunt's vituperative comments towards me.'

'Vituperative? A bit of an exaggeration, I think.'

'Perhaps. Well, please consider this. At the Church of St Mary's, in Lubeck, Germany, there is a depiction of *danse macabre*. Eight panels. The first panel depicts a cleric with a rendition of Death on either side of him: a skeleton wrapped in a white shroud. One skeleton is playing the flute, the other is carrying a coffin. At the top of each panel is text of Death tormenting his victims. Sarcastic, uncaring, harsh in his language towards everyone, regardless of their class, rank, vocation, sex, ages. This is one of the best-known examples of the *danse macabre*. However, there is a much lesser known one that was enshrined on the wall of the cloister of St Genevieve in Paris. The cloister no longer exists, but a few manuscripts remain from it, including drawings of a few of the panels. In one Death torments a learned man, whom he accuses of having been too wrapped up in the pursuit of knowledge to pay sufficient homage to God. The first panel also was rendered in the drawings. It shows two Death-figures surrounding a cleric. One of them plays a flute, the other uses tools to build a coffin. Still think this is all just a coincidence, Mr Laidlaw?'

Laidlaw was beginning to feel annoyed, and was trying to resist the temptation to condescend to the younger professor. 'So, are you telling me then that our new department chair, Anthony Gaunt, who arrived here from Columbia last year to run this show, is Death himself?'

Dalton shot Laidlaw a nasty look, one that Laidlaw sensed was filled with contempt. 'No, I don't. Not quite as you put it. But we're all mortal, Mr Laidlaw. And Death comes for all of us when he decides it is time. Death has now come for me. In the guise of Mr Gaunt. Not you, not anyone else. Only I am in mortal danger. Need I remind you of Mr Gaunt's physical appearance?'

'Tall, very slender, pale, a bit unhealthy in some respects; so?'

'There are two principal depictions of Death in the *danse macabre* artworks. The most common is a skeleton, but some of the older depictions—and the St Genevieve panels are among the oldest known—Death appears as a pale, emaciated human. Need I remind you of the name of Mr Gaunt's wife?'

Laidlaw was becoming nonplussed. 'Jennifer, I believe.'

'Quite. The English equivalent of Genevieve. Do you want to insist that this is all coincidence? I've studied the themes and images of the *danse macabre* for nearly two decades, and I can assure you that the possibility of Death using this motif to claim a victim, especially one not ready, is a real one. If you observe the *danse macabre* panels, you will never see an old man on his deathbed being led away; no, only healthy individuals recognizing that they have been cruelly deprived of many precious years. Good day.' With that, Dalton replaced the tape recorder in his pocket and left the office, closing the door quietly behind him.

Laidlaw turned and looked out the window, where the rain continued to pelt the glass. Such an incredibly dreary day, he decided. 'I suppose if you're going to go mad,' he murmured, 'today is about as good a day as you can get to do it.'

I, of course, was not privy to this conversation, but pieced it together later from what Laidlaw told me, and what I figured must have gone on, given how things played themselves out. What is strange is that not long after this conversation took place, I happened to pass by Professor Gaunt's office one morning, quite early, actually, and noticed that the door was ajar and sounds of an animated conversation issued from within. Do not ask me why, but I slowed my pace as I reached the door, just to satisfy my curiosity. I glanced in long enough to see the back of Orlando Dalton's head as he gestured furiously before the department chair. During my moment at the door, Gaunt did not speak, but sat grinning at his young colleague. I remember how his eyes, although steel black, seemed huge and aflame, how his teeth looked more like those of a vicious predator than a man. I also remember how my blood ran cold, how gooseflesh covered me from head to toe, and how I hightailed it away from there ASAP, vowing never to cross one Professor Lucius Gaunt.

My direct involvement in the Dalton-Gaunt-Laidlaw triangulation began shortly thereafter. One afternoon, just as Laidlaw and I were finishing a discussion about the floating hospitals that plied the Cumberland River near Nashville during the Civil War, he asked if I knew anything about Mediaeval traditions.

I felt like I was back at my oral preliminary examinations for a moment. 'I vaguely learned a few things last year in Professor Dalton's class,' I murmured, a bit embarrassed. 'But I certainly couldn't tell you much off the top of my head.'

'No, no, that's fine,' he replied reassuringly. 'But I do need your help. Please don't ask what this is all about just yet, but would you do a little library work for me, see what you can scrounge up on the *danse macabre*, the Mediaeval tradition of the dance of death? I know we have an expert in the department in this area, but I would rather you didn't consult him on this. Not just yet.'

Naturally this came as a most unusual request by my advisor, but at the time I was sort of on the bubble, as they now say. I was close to convincing

Laidlaw that I was a competent student and would write a more than adequate thesis under him, but I had not yet moved into his inner circle of protégés. In other words, I needed to impress him more. 'I'll be happy to,' I responded without delay. 'I'll get on it tonight, I promise.'

Well, he seemed very pleased with me, even mumbling something about how he was sure I would do a fine job, get him exactly what he needed. It did not dawn on me until I had left his office just how strange this request was. Why send a student when he could consult with Dalton? Or why not just send a student to Dalton? Either way it would save a lot of time and effort. Fortunately, I suppose you could say, I was still just naïve enough back then not to think the business through too thoroughly. I was happy to have been offered such an assignment from my advisor, and was determined to succeed beyond his expectations.

Apparently Dalton had confided his fears only in Duncan Laidlaw. Why, no one will ever know, but after this initial meeting, we all began to notice the change in Dalton. He became even more reserved, more moody, certainly quirkier. On the door of his office he tacked up several holy cards of religious scenes. He could be heard mumbling prayers as he slogged through the departmental corridors. As for me, I duly did my work for Laidlaw, with the help of a couple of librarians, and got my hands on about everything I could find in English. Since I could read Spanish, I likewise found what I could in that language, and wrote out translations. Needless to say, my own research and progress came to a screeching halt, and I admit I started to become morbidly fascinated by the grisly metaphor inherent in the *danse macabre*. Laidlaw seemed grateful for my efforts, but I noticed that he too was growing more moody, as if under undue stress. I was politic enough not to ask questions, but just did as I was told. Rather like what T. S. Eliot once wrote: 'For us, there is only the trying,/The rest is not our business.'

One of the strangest things in this whole business occurred shortly before Thanksgiving. Laidlaw called me into his office, and at once I noticed, on the desk before him, a considerable stack of material I had fetched for him.

'Jerrod,' he said in an authoritative voice, 'please go to Dr Dalton's office and tell him I wish to confer with him at once.'

I did as I was told. When I delivered the message, Dalton nodded almost fatalistically, and like some kind of automaton got up from his desk and accompanied me back to Laidlaw's office. The odd thing was that, no sooner had we got there, I leading the way, Laidlaw instructed Dalton to close the door, and began talking immediately. I still do not know if he was aware that I was in his office; trapped as I felt I was, I eased back against one of his bookshelves and tried to look as inconspicuous as possible.

'Orlando, this is getting out of hand,' Laidlaw announced, again in his voice of authority, 'and today it is my intention to put your morbid fears to rest once and for all. I will do so by pointing out the flaws in your logic, therefore challenging an intelligent, logical scholar like yourself to cast aside such beliefs. Are you prepared to listen to what I have to say?'

'I am, Mr Laidlaw,' Dalton answered rather mechanically.

'Very well. First point: the *danse macabre* is a Mediaeval tradition that has long since died out. It has not been employed for nearly four centuries. Second point: it is a metaphor commemorating death, and most frequently exists as a painted or etched fresco on the walls of a church, chapel, convent, or cloister. Most often these depictions seem to be associated with plagues and epidemics, with the destruction of large portions of a community's population. Third point: the image of Death, therefore, as pale person or skeleton, is not literal, and he calls many, not one. Fourth point: do you presume to have me believe that Death walks among the living at present in the form of Lucius Gaunt? Gaunt is a man who can be fixed in time; surely Death cannot. Gaunt is a scholar and teacher of known reputation. Gaunt is a specialist in the social history of southern Americans who had left the States after the Civil War and relocated to Brazil. He has written the definitive history on the topic, actually. I ask you then: given these facts, how can you possibly believe in this personification of Death and of your imminent demise?'

Dalton seemed puzzled, as if Laidlaw had been speaking an unintelligible language. 'Your points are excellent, Mr Laidlaw. Eminently logical. All I can tell you by way of reply is that before meeting Mr Gaunt, I would have agreed wholeheartedly with you about the *danse macabre* as metaphor.'

Laidlaw looked quite rueful. 'What do you mean, man?' he cried out.

'I doubt I can explain myself well in a logical fashion. Only that the years of studying the *danse macabre* have convinced me that these panels are indeed a glimpse of death just before one dies. And that death comes to people in many forms. Death is a trickster, Mr Laidlaw. A cruel, tormenting heckler. I believe he comes for everyone in a unique fashion. In my case, he has chosen my particular field of study as the medium.'

'And why only you, and not us, as the panels depict?'

'Maybe . . . maybe he *is* coming for all of us. Maybe I am only the first. Or . . . the only one who recognizes him for what he is.'

I felt my blood run cold at this last comment, and at the same time Laidlaw smote his forehead with the palm of his head. 'Look, Orlando, please do something for me. You don't look well, and this business is grinding you down. This is not an issue of logic to you, but of metaphysics, not intellectual but spiritual. You're a devout Catholic, a churchgoing man. Consult the priest at your parish church. He can help in that realm. Please do that.' Then Laidlaw sighed, and absently began to rub his forehead where he had belted it. 'Thank you for stopping by, Orlando,' he said quietly. 'Good luck.'

I left the office with Dalton, with no idea where I was going, what I was doing, or anything else. Laidlaw noticed my departure no more than he had my presence during this meeting. I recall that my spirits were lifted only by the reality that it was around four in the afternoon. I left the department and walked four blocks to the closest bar, and eased my pounding sense of confusion and fear with a double whisky.

The university recessed for Thanksgiving, and when we returned, Orlando Dalton's demise seemed to intensify. Now his physical appearance was clearly affected. He looked as if he had stopped eating or bathing, and he could be identified as approaching before coming into view by a nasty, hacking cough. He still managed to teach his classes, but seemed to be in need of a respirator by the end of his lectures. During the first week back I found a note in my departmental mailbox. It was handwritten and unsigned, and read 'Find out for me the significance of those religious cards on Dalton's door. As soon as possible.' I shook my head at the thought of how strange things were becoming in my life, but I knew I had to pursue this and come up with an answer. I went to Dalton's door and studied the cards as well as I could, trying to construct mental pictures of their appearances.

The only place I could think to start was a Catholic Church. The following Sunday morning, I bicycled over to St Matthew's, the nearest one I could find, to see if anyone there could help. There was a small gift shop in the church annex, where a few people were milling about after Mass. The place sold all manner of things of which I was wholly unfamiliar, but when I saw a couple of rows of holy cards near the main counter, I decided to have a look. I tried to be discreet, and was looking askance at the cards from a bit of a distance when an elderly woman working behind the counter caught my eye and asked me, in a very kind voice, if she could help me.

'I am interested in . . . these,' I blurted rather stupidly, pointing to the cards.

Still smiling, she nodded. 'Of course. They're very popular.' She turned and pulled down three or four and placed them on the counter, then repeated the gesture. The fates decided to smile down on me that day, for I immediately recognized at least two as being identical to those on Dalton's door. I picked one up. On the front was a reproduction of a painting of a man in a tunic, on his knees and praying. A halo encircled his head. I turned it over and noticed there was information about something or other.

The woman was nodding. 'Good choice. That's St Jude.'

'Why is . . . what is . . . important about St Jude?' I asked rather feebly.

'He demonstrated great faith in his life, and taught us to maintain our faith even under the most difficult situations. Many people pray to him for this reason.' Then she looked a bit embarrassed, and added, 'And also, because he is the patron saint of lost causes.'

Dalton, it appeared, was on his way to taking his obsession to the highest level. Fortunately the cards were quite inexpensive. I bought three of them, thanked her, and went on my way.

First thing the following morning I brought the holy cards in to Laidlaw and reported my findings. He cursed under his breath, then ran a hand through his hair. 'The crazy bastard is really playing this full throttle, isn't he?' he said, staring at the ceiling of his office. 'Maybe it's time I sat down with Professor Gaunt and apprised him of the situation.' He looked sharply at me then, as if he had not intended me to hear these words, and with a curt gesture excused me.

As you all know, and can attest to with fond memories, December is a frenzied time for a graduate student, so I was glad that Laidlaw did not call on me for some days to probe more into the *danse macabre* or related matters. I had two major term papers to finish and final exams to prepare for, which back in those days were three hours long and comprehensive. When I did find a note in my departmental mailbox from Laidlaw, I shrugged with frustration, but, to my surprise, it was merely an invitation to a New Year's Eve party he was holding at his house.

A week before Christmas I took my last exam and then went to Laidlaw's office to turn in a term paper. I had a bag packed and a train ticket in the pocket of my jacket, and was heading home to Pennsylvania for the holidays. I could have dropped the paper off in his mailbox, but wanted to give it to him personally so I could thank him for the party invitation and let him know I would be there. His office door was closed, which was unusual, since he was holding office hours at the time, so I knocked and then entered. Laidlaw was on the telephone.

I shall never forget the haggard, anxious expression on his face, nor the words he uttered, apparently in near desperation, just as I crossed the threshold: 'And he told me, "Yes, he's exactly right. He knows who I am, but what can he do about it?" Then he laughed like a madman."' Laidlaw looked up and saw me, and—well, if looks could kill, you all would have had a different graduate advisor, I can promise you that. I have never seen such intensity on a man's face before, certainly not Duncan Laidlaw's. I sensed he was about to do something terribly risky, terribly irrational, and consequently my whole cosy world of graduate studies was about to come crashing down around my ears. He jabbed a finger in the air at me, and I beat a hasty retreat out of his office, dropped the term paper off in his mailbox, and caught the train for home and Christmas.

The holidays should have been a blessing for me. We had a nice Christmas Eve snowfall, my parents were enjoying good health, and they seemed particularly pleased to have me home this time around. But I spent my time brooding, wondering to whom Laidlaw had been speaking, and how much he now believed of Dalton's bizarre obsession. Whenever I thought of Gaunt, I got chills, and dismissed him from my mind. A number of times I thought that if I changed my travel plans and headed back to Buchanan after the New Year, thereby missing Laidlaw's New Year's Eve party (after all, I had not committed myself to going), I might feel much better and enjoy the holiday season more. But there I was, at dawn on New Year's Eve, hugging my mother and shaking my father's hand at the Lancaster train station, and plying the rails back to Queens.

By late afternoon I was back in my apartment, and decided to hike over to the department to see if grades had been posted (as mine had not yet arrived in the mail). With the university in recess everything was closed and locked up, but I had a key to the building and let myself in. The heat had been turned off for the break and it was menacingly cold in there. No one else was about. I climbed the two flights of stairs to our department and went to the doors of various professors' offices to check on grades. Back then, a professor was allowed to post grades coded by a student's identification number. I intentionally avoided Laidlaw's office until the last, and when I got there, I found that not only were grades from his courses posted on his door, but that there was a letter of some kind tacked there as well. It was addressed to Laidlaw, and I immediately recognized Orlando Dalton's handwriting. I thought about leaving it there, and not mentioning it to Laidlaw that night at his party, but I tore it off the door and stuffed it into my overcoat, justifying my actions by telling myself that I was involved in all of this.

I did not read the note, but carried it to Professor Laidlaw's house that evening. Fortunately he lived not terribly far from where I did, because that New Year's Eve was particularly brutal, and my only means of conveyance for that distance, due to extreme penury, was my antiquated bicycle. He greeted me at the door like an old friend.

'Jerrod!' he chortled, offering his hand, 'thank you so much for coming. I have several friends here from other departments at Buchanan, and I'm anxious to show off my prize pupil to them. Get their goat, make them green with envy, that sort of thing. Please come in. Let me take your coat, and please enjoy yourself.'

The party was fairly lively, actually, and I found that I was the only one of Laidlaw's students present. In fact, I was the only graduate student from our department. There were a couple of professors from our department there, but neither Dalton nor Gaunt. Somehow this did not surprise me, and I did experience considerable relief as a result. It was still quite a ways before midnight when I saw Laidlaw slip off into his kitchen to refresh the eggnog bowl. I hurried after him, explaining about the note. My news did not faze him in the least. He nodded, sighed, set his jaw, and asked for it. He opened it and read it without outward reaction, then absently handed it back to me. The note read:

> Mr Laidlaw,
> Quite unfortunately, I have forgotten the very basic treatment of Death towards his victim in the *danse macabre*. He torments them, heckles them, and delights in tricking them. Exactly what Mr Gaunt has done to me, I now realize. I am riddled with a particularly violent fever right now, and I doubt I'll survive more than a few more days. It is all I can do to keep my pen steady as I write this. I mentioned to you before about the *danse macabre* at St Genevieve in Paris. Well, St Genevieve is the patron saint of

fever. In other words, those suffering from fever pray to her. How typical a ploy for Death to use! He takes those things we hold dear and desecrates them so effortlessly! He takes our strength and turns it into a parlour-room jest. He all but gave me this information, and I missed it completely. And now, you still don't believe? Then hear me out, here is the *coup d'grâce*: the feast day of St Genevieve is January 3rd. I trust this will be the day of my passing. When Death comes for you, be on much better guard than I have been. Of course, it's not likely to help you any. Goodbye, sir, it has been a pleasure serving at Buchanan with you.

The day following New Year's I received a telephone call from Professor Laidlaw early in the morning, asking me if I could meet him at the department. I assented and pedalled down there as quickly as I could. He looked pale and exhausted when we reached the floor of the department, and we went directly to Dalton's office. On the door of the office was found a notice, written in calligraphy:

This is the *VADO MORI* of Orlando Clinton Dalton (b.1914), to wit—

What strange and brutal anguish does
My wretched being now render;
To be called so early, so unfinished
In this life I now must surrender.

Before my Maker, I say you now,
This lack of justice is appalling.
I curse you, Gaunt, and your tormenting ways
That my days now end is galling.

'What is "*Vado Mori*"? Laidlaw mumbled; to himself I am quite sure, but since I had come across it in my research for him, I threw in my two cents, sounding more like a poorly written encyclopaedia than anything else.

'"I prepare myself for death." Apparently this was a Medieval tradition that predated the *danse macabre*. The association between the two is uncertain, although some historians feel the *Vado Mori* was the direct antecedent to the *danse macabre*. I think Professor Dalton has published on this, and is a strong advocate of this school of thought. The motif was written in poetic verse and originally consisted of a prologue, which describes the inevitability of death, followed by the complaints of a number of characters for whom death is imminent. The complaints were composed of two verses per character. In later versions the prologue was dropped as the number of characters increased.'

'Well, Goddammit,' Laidlaw said. Without another word, he turned and walked away, more despondent than I had ever seen him. I remember thinking how badly I wanted to get out of that place.

We never saw Dalton again.

* * * * *

The old man glanced down at his watch, sighed, and shook his head very slightly. 'Well after midnight, it seems,' he murmured, apparently more to himself than to anyone else. 'Which makes it April seventh.'

'Is that it?' Tom Willoughby asked. The others had their eyes fixed on the old man.

Jerrod looked up at Tom and seemed genuinely confused for a few seconds, then shook his head again, more emphatically. 'In terms of the story? Pretty much so. Well, after more than two weeks we finally had a glimpse inside Dalton's office, and in fact it had been completely cleared out. Rumours began circulating that the university had sent a couple of custodians in there late at night to remove all his belongings. Then rumours started about Harriet Seiner, a flirtatious, heartbreaker of a co-ed—excuse the term, Carolyn—but what we called a vamp back then. Rumours that perhaps she was more than a student in one of Dalton's classes. Her father was a very powerful man, it seemed. Harriet did not return to school for the spring semester and was likewise not seen again around Buchanan.'

'But the others?' Tom Willoughby asked. 'Gaunt and Laidlaw. I thought they were part of the implosion as well.'

Jerrod sighed through his pipe, then shook his head as if to free himself of something painful. 'Duncan Laidlaw was never the same after those few weeks. He let his research slide and spent more and more time studying the *danse macabre* phenomenon. I saw him rarely during spring term, and then only when I'd receive a note from him asking me to fetch him various tomes from the library. Books in French, German, even Hungarian—languages I was certain he could not read, but all of them had references in them to the *danse macabre*. The few glimpses of his office I had—well, I still shudder when those images come to mind. He had begun decorating the walls with garish drawings of skeletons and corpses, images I had seen in the books that I brought him. He was sixty-seven and, by April, looked ninety. He stopped attending his classes, stopped answering the telephone, eventually ceased coming to the university at all. I never saw or spoke to him after that, but heard that he had to be institutionalized for the remainder of his life, which apparently was not very long at all.'

'And Gaunt?'

'Gaunt.' Jerrod expelled the name as if spitting out poison. 'He left after the spring term. Seems he had a clause in his contract that he could leave after a year if he didn't like the job, as well as a deal with Columbia to take him back. He returned there, and I went off to Yale.' Jerrod puffed his pipe, then slid it from his lips to sip his brandy. 'Such exquisite brandy, Tom. You are indeed a man of rare elegance and taste.'

'As always, Jerrod, you're too kind,' Tom murmured. Then, in a louder voice, he asked, 'So, Gaunt left, you left, and that was the end of all of it, finally?'

Jerrod scratched the side of his face with the bit of his pipe. 'I'm sure it was. Some strange thing happened a few years later, but . . . well, maybe I'm just grasping at straws.'

'Do tell,' Carolyn Reilly enthused.

'Well, it seems there was a strange situation down in Nashville, in the history department at Vanderbilt. Allegedly a professor committed suicide, and another went mad. Within a few months of each other. I learned years later, from someone who witnessed it, that in fact the department had a visiting professor that year. One Professor Lucius Gaunt of Columbia.'

Silence followed.

'Is he . . . still around?'

Jerrod shook his head absently. 'Apparently he left the country after that year. Took a position at a university in Brazil, and, so far as anyone knows, he has never returned to the United States.'

The conversation ebbed for some minutes before eventually becoming quite animated once more, highlighted by Tom Willoughby calling for a toast.

'To our mentor, Jerrod,' he said. 'May you live and prosper for a hundred years or more!'

'Hear, hear!' the others shouted happily.

Jerrod raised his glass and smiled, and put it to his lips as did the others; but did not drink.

No, he could not tell them. Nor *would* he tell them. Why disillusion them here at the very end, give them over to thinking that he had become senile? This was a night to enjoy, to celebrate. No more talk about Laidlaw, Dalton, Gaunt, *danse macabre*, and such things. No reason to mention the cloister of St John Baptist de la Salle in the town of Mont-de-Marsan in Gascogne. Or of its recently discovered *danse macabre* in an old vault beneath the chapel. And what a strange anomaly it was, being the most recent *danse macabre* known, done impeccably in the Mediaeval style, yet its execution dating to the last decade of the nineteenth century. Conjured up out of thin air, almost, as if to provide an old historian of Mediaeval Europe with one final scholarly puzzle to solve.

His name was not Gaunt anymore, but he had joined the faculty of Jerrod's department as a visiting professor in the fall. The pale, thin, drawn face was unmistakable, the spitting image of what was found on the wall of the cloister chapel. Just before attending the *Festschrift*, Jerrod had tacked a small bit of verse to his office door.

Suddenly the old man coughed loudly, spilling his brandy. Before anyone could react he coughed again, more violently, and lost control of his pipe. Tom and Carolyn were at his side at once, but the seizure that gripped him became worse, and in seconds his face turned a hideous reddish-purple, and his eyes rolled up into his head.

'I'll call the paramedics,' Tom said, trying to keep his voice steady. Julian and Brett had crowded in, trying to offer their mentor some relief.

With a furious rush Jerrod bolted out of his chair and staggered towards the fireplace. As three sets of arms reached to steady him, he turned and bellowed, 'St John Baptist de la Salle is the patron saint of teachers. Feast day is April seventh. In the fourth panel Death is leading him away—I mean leading a teacher away—and in the fifth——' He gagged, fell against the wall next to the fireplace, coughing savagely. He pushed the flailing arms away, and clawed at the brick and mortar of the wall. 'The fifth . . . immediately following . . . four students . . . two on each arm . . . I'm so sorry. . . .' He managed to straighten up, the colour now completely drained from his face. Hands that clutched his found a dry, rigid cold so intense that gasps echoed all around. 'My dear ones! My wonderful friends! Do not hope! There is no hope! Only prepare! Prepare!' Then he crashed to the floor, as cold as a stone.

Breaking Up

Ramsey Campbell

As KERRY GLANCED THROUGH the display window at the street that was bony with frozen snow, a mobile rang. 'Will that be him?' Harvey said.

At first she wasn't certain it was hers—more than one of the thousands of phones they sold might play that disco tune—and then she realised the sound was muffled by her handbag on the counter. It stayed a little indistinct when she slipped the phone out of the bag. She read the displayed number and terminated the call. 'Not him,' Harvey said, as if she needed to be told.

'Just a customer,' she almost said, remembering how Russell had waited for her to be free so that he could ask whether she thought he was too old for a mobile. 'Just someone I used to know,' she said.

'Never a stalker, is it? Would you like me to stick with you till Jason picks you up?'

'I'm sure he would have rung if he wasn't nearly here.'

'I'd be happy to, all the same. Then if he doesn't show up I could run you wherever you like.'

She suspected the manager had somewhere that he liked in mind. His hair was dyed a shade too black, and a sunbed and a gym also kept up his appearance, but his jowls were starting to bag his age. 'I thought you had someone to go home to,' she said.

'Nowt wrong with being friendly as well, is there?'

'I normally am, I think.' His voice had taken on some of the edge he used for second warnings to staff, and she didn't want to be alone with that either. She gave her scarf another turn around her throat and tugged her gloves on before picking up her bag. 'You lock up,' she said. 'I'll be fine.'

The first thing she saw on stepping outside was her breath. The cold set about making a mask of her face at once. Along both sides of the deserted street the shop windows were dusty with frost, glass cases in an abandoned museum. The pale mounds with which the glittering pavements were heaped seemed to glow from within. A wind from somewhere even colder sent a shiver through her, which lent Harvey an excuse to look concerned as he withdrew the key from the door. 'Really, I could——'

'Really, don't.' She was about to put some distance between them when her mobile intervened. As soon as she extracted it she was able to say 'This is him.'

She keyed the phone but didn't speak until Harvey made for the car park, skidding as he reached the alley between the shops and righting himself with a penguinish flap of his arms. She heard his walled-in curse at a second tumble as she said 'Where are you?'

'I'm bloody——' Jason paused to reclaim some of his temper. 'I was on my way,' he complained.

'Aren't you still?'

'Would I be talking to you if I was? You know what I think of these clowns that talk on their phones while they're driving.'

'Not the ones that sell them, I hope.'

'There ought to be a law that says you have to tell your customers how to use them. You know that's what I think. Save it, all right? I don't need an argument just now.'

She could miss Russell's politeness after all. 'You still haven't told me where you are.'

'Some bloody place in the middle of nowhere. I've come off the road.'

'Are you lost, do you mean?'

'Off the side. In a bloody snowdrift and a ditch. I'm waiting for a tow.'

'You sound as if you're blaming me.'

'I wouldn't have been going so fast if you didn't get in a panic whenever I'm a minute late.'

'Hold on, I don't panic. I haven't been panicking now.'

'A huff, then. You make me feel I've let you down and it's a major insult even if you don't say anything.'

'Well, please don't feel obliged to meet me tonight.'

'You're doing it now. I don't know if I can,' Jason added, less apologetically than she thought the conversation warranted. 'I'll let you know what's happening.'

'Don't put yourself to any extra trouble. I'm going home.'

'I'll call you there, then.'

She didn't quite advise him not to bother. She broke the connection and was stowing the phone when it stirred, a vibration muffled by her glove. As the disco melody began to tick she blinked at the digits through the whitish glow with which a streetlamp coated the display. It was Russell's number.

For an instant she was tempted to agree to dinner at a restaurant or a chat over drinks, except that he would end up pleading gently for more, every plea primed with the expectation of refusal. She might have given him the option of leaving a message, but she wanted to deal more decisively with him than she had with Jason. 'Kerry,' she said, turning along the path between the huddled mounds.

'Russell.'

He sounded uncertain, presumably of her response. 'I can see that,' she told him.

'Can you?'

She took his surprise as a joke not much less feeble than he was making his voice. 'On the call display,' she explained nonetheless.

'You're up on these things, not like us oldsters. That's why I came to you.'

'Haven't you charged your battery?' she said or, if she was honest, hoped. 'You're starting to break up.'

'Oh, don't say that.' His voice surged, hissing and fragmenting in her ear, then subsided. 'What would do that? Would the cold?'

'This much might. Why were you calling, Russell? I'm outside and I don't want mine to die on me.'

'Mustn't.' He might have been talking to himself until he said 'I think it's even colder up here.'

Kerry's gaze was drawn beyond the shops to the darker streets that climbed increasingly steeply to the glimmering ridge a thousand feet above the town. 'Where's that?' she felt required to ask.

'Home.'

She had no more idea where he lived than she had let him have about her; she'd found him a little too eager for that information. 'Then I should do something about it,' she said.

'Oh, will you? I knew you'd still be kind. Anything you feel you can. Just come and see me if you like.'

'I'm sorry, Russell, but it's over. You must know that.' Kerry hadn't finished when she heard a rattle and a sprinkling of static that put her in mind of a shower of ice. 'Are you still there?' she said and, convinced of the opposite, shut the mobile in her handbag.

She'd reached the end of the shops without encountering a solitary person. She might as well have called in sick like several of her colleagues; the shop had hardly seen a customer all week, and none in the last three hours despite staying open late. Kerry heard the distant clatter of a garage door, and somewhere else uphill a woman was shouting to a child or a dog. Whatever the name was, it seemed to shatter on the sharpness of the air. The low moan that had occupied the pauses in Russell's speech must have been the note of Harvey's car as it laboured up into the dark.

Since the pavements of the first road homewards had been turned into slides by children or less wilfully by adults, she kept to the middle of the road. The light of the floppy-capped streetlamps fell short of her path, and it was only by treading gingerly on it that she established which of the blackness was ice. All the windows of the cars parked on both sides of the slope were either encased in frost or spread with the local newspaper, every visible page of which mentioned someone's death. The windows of the staggered houses were hermetically curtained even if dark, and Kerry felt as though the entire town apart from her was hiding from the weather. She'd tramped as far as the lowest crossroad when her phone began to clamour.

Was it wearing out, or had it caught a chill? Once she managed to fumble it out of her bag she was unable to read the faltering digits in the greenish window. She halted on the intersection, pinning down the hour hand of her shadow and a less distinct minute one while she located the key with a clumsy finger. 'On the way?' she said.

'I think you are.'

Before he spoke she knew he wasn't Jason, from a rush of static like an effort to breathe. 'Russell, can you please stop. I'm expecting a call.'

'Anyone but me.' For as long as it took him to say this he seemed hardly even to be talking to himself. 'I wasn't asking what you think,' he said.

To begin with he always had; it had been much of his appeal. 'Don't you care about that now?' she was disappointed enough to retort.

'Didn't mean that. Don't confuse me,' he protested so harshly that his voice grew almost shapeless. 'I meant all I want is for us to see each other.'

'I told you once, Russell. I'm sorry if it was rude of me not to answer all your messages, but you did leave a lot after I kept telling you I couldn't meet you. And now I've told you it's over.'

'Don't say that.' His voice sounded close to disintegrating altogether. 'Once more is all I ask. You can see me at least.'

'Find someone else, Russell. I'm sure you will. You deserve someone more——'

'More my own age?' he said, not so much interrupting as filling the pause. 'There's nobody. I only know your number.'

Perhaps he'd stored none except hers. Empty roads loomed on both sides of her vision, and she was aware of another at her back. She was making for the street ahead and trying to find words that would be as civil as final when he spoke. 'If it's something I said, please say. Just remember I've never met anyone like you.'

He'd ended up repeating that too often and too intensely, along with exhorting her not to waste herself on her job or on such of her friends as he'd met, but his insistence on introducing himself as her uncle had been worst of all. It had started as a joke, then turned into a plea for her not just to contradict him but to reassure him that everyone knew he was teasing. Although striving to hearten him exhausted her, she made a last effort. 'You will,' she said. 'You'll meet someone better, you'll see. Now I'm——'

'Never.' Before she could tell him not to be silly he said 'No time.'

'Look, Russell, is something really wrong? Because if there is you should call——'

'I just need you. You're coming. I can hear.'

Kerry closed her fingers around the mobile and strained her ears until they ached with more than the temperature. The phone muttered in her fist—she even seemed to feel it wriggling feebly—but she couldn't hear him in any of the houses. He must be pretending to locate her, unless he was deluding himself. When the crushed voice stopped trying to slip through her fingers she returned the mobile to her bag. She quickened her pace uphill, and a whitish figure peered around a hulking gatepost at her. The token face had fallen askew on its way to leaving the head.

At least half a dozen other snowmen were lying in wait as she toiled up the road. She was in danger of feeling surrounded by them and very little else, as if the townsfolk had been replaced with frozen snow. Of course she was simply nervous that the glazed silence might be interrupted by the shrilling of her phone, but the knowledge didn't help. At least there was a pub across the intersection at the top of the slope she was conquering. Even if she didn't go in, its presence would be company for her. The drinkers beyond the lit windows must be keeping their voices down; perhaps just a few would have ventured out of their houses on a night like this. She was sure that she was hearing muted conversation until she stepped onto the level crossroad and saw that ice had transformed the windows into marble slabs. Their light was borrowed from the nearest streetlamp.

Now that she was denied the chance she couldn't avoid realising she would have liked to be among people if she received another call. She could only make for home as fast as was safe. The rest of the route was yet steeper, and she crossed to the pavement, which consisted of giant steps with a railing to help her climb.

Despite her glove, the rail felt like a handful of ice. To her right, lumps of snow had been gouged out of the crests of the hedges for snowballs or by someone's desperate clutch. Beyond the hedges on both sides of the road, pale figures no more shapely than a child's first drawing appeared to mark her progress. She might almost have fancied they were watching her, even those that had least with which to do so. When a phone jangled, she was near to imagining that it related to a dim hunched shape with the sloughed remains of a face. The sound was in the house belonging to the snowman. She hauled herself past it in a rage at her nerves. It fell silent, and her phone rang.

She snatched it out so furiously that she was barely able to keep hold of it. A few indecipherable scraps of digits like traces of a fossil glimpsed through moss were visible in the window. She poked the key and clapped the mobile to her face. 'Who's there?'

'Don't go too fast. Don't hurt yourself.'

'I'm not going to.' This wasn't enough of a retort or a challenge. 'You can't see me,' she said, in case that made Russell betray he could.

'I don't need to. We've got a rapport, you and I.' If that seemed to bring his voice closer, she wasn't about to let it persuade her of anything; he must be holding the mouthpiece against his lips to blur his words so much. Before she could deny his claim he said 'We aren't as different as some people like to think.'

By people, did he mean her? She shouldn't care; if she kept him talking, perhaps she could locate him. She hung her bag on her left arm and gripped the railing as she forged uphill. 'Why are you saying that?' she had to ask.

'We both stayed where our roots are, didn't we? We never sought our future elsewhere.'

'I stayed for my parents.'

'So did I.'

Could they still be alive? Kerry doubted it, given how much older than she'd taken him to be he'd finally owned up to being. 'I thought you were going to write some more books about the countryside,' she said.

'That was the plan.'

'Why, have you given up?'

'I wouldn't be talking to you if I had.'

This sounded more like a plea than she welcomed. 'You don't need me, Russell. You were writing long before we met.'

A whisper of restlessness made her think she'd scored a point until he said 'Why did you start going out with me?'

His voice was disintegrating so much that she could hardly detect the tone, never mind the relevance. 'Because you asked me,' she said, and didn't add 'Because you kept asking.'

'You took pity on me, you mean. Couldn't you again?'

'No, Russell, because you had class. Can't you have some now?'

'There isn't much to me any more.'

'You know that isn't true. You write books people want to read. I've seen them all over the place.'

'If we're finished, so are they.'

Was he saying anything that came into his head? As she clambered up the next step, through a tree's sparkling shadow that felt like the threat of being buried under an avalanche, she said 'I don't believe you mean that. You must have got over me by now. It's been months.'

'Is that all? I can't tell.'

Was this another bid for sympathy? Presumably it was the transmission rather than his voice that sounded near to shivering to pieces, but it dismayed her. 'Russell, if you're truly feeling so bad you ought to call——'

At once the phone was dead as ice. If he'd given up pestering her, she would let that be enough. She fumbled the mobile into her bag and flexed her stiff fingers before entrusting the bag to them. A dozen clutches at the rail, and twice as many paces as there were slippery steps, brought her to her road.

It stretched left, iced with light under three streetlamps partly masked with snow. The scene might have been embedded in the amber of the night sky. Perhaps it was the silence that rendered it unreal as a Christmas card. The house where she lived was part of the emptiness, since the couple on the ground floor had gone abroad for the winter. She would be happy just to switch on the fires and draw the curtains and have nothing else that she absolutely had to do, she vowed, and was heading left when her mobile came to life.

It could have been Jason, but when she succeeded in wielding the phone her voice felt cold and heavy as the spiked caps of the roofs. 'Yes,' she said.

'Not far now.'

Russell's voice made her feel as if his lips were trying to keep their shape against her ear. 'So tell me where,' she said.

'Up here.'

Suppose he was unable to be any more specific and nervous of admitting it? 'Just talk as you walk. I'll hear you,' she gathered he was saying despite shedding several consonants.

She couldn't leave the situation unresolved. If he needed help, she ought to find out where to send it. She turned away from her house and grasped the uphill railing. 'Just talk,' he repeated, though the first word almost dissolved into a hiss.

This street was even steeper. She had to keep hold of the rail, though her gloved hand ached with its iciness. At the end of every pace the handbag on her wrist blundered like a blind but affectionate creature against her hip. Beyond their plots of white the houses appeared to be holding themselves still for fear of inundation by the burdens on their roofs. A wind like the essence of the frozen dark groped at her face as though searching for the bones. She licked her stiff lips to release her voice. 'What do you want to talk about?'

'Can't you think of anything?'

His voice must be shivering with static, not with panic. 'The weather,' she said, less than wholly as a joke.

'About us. Times we had together.' The silence that ensued might have signified exhaustion or a wordless plea until he said 'When we went dancing. I did enjoy myself, you know.'

It had been the beginning of their end. Once he'd finished shouting above the disco uproar that he was her uncle, he'd set about dancing with a violence that seemed designed to compete with everyone else in the room. She could almost see the thin figure jigging and jerking as if he'd borrowed all the artificial vigour of the strobe light, his sleeves and trousers flapping like flags in a gale. When he'd panted to a standstill he had subsided into a chair and watched her dance, his eyes flickering with resignation that might have concealed a plea. Now she could have hoped he would ask anything other than 'Didn't you?'

'I'm remembering. I don't do everything aloud.'

'Don't you want to talk about it?'

'I thought it didn't matter what I talk about as long as I keep talking.'

'It doesn't,' he might have finished saying if his voice hadn't collapsed into a flood of static.

In a moment the phone was lifeless. A wind drifted down from the white ridge that was gnawing the black sky. The gust lingered behind a hedge to disturb a newspaper or a bank of loose snow—something white that whispered, at any rate. As the wind fastened on her, Kerry shivered and nearly dropped the mobile, which had twitched in her hand. That was a preamble to playing the tune she might have heard at the disco with Russell. 'I'm here,' she told the blank phone.

'I know. You're outside.'

The house beyond the gate to her right seemed to advance from the rank, although it was no taller or thinner than any of its neighbours. A few sets of footprints smudged by last week's brief false thaw led to a front door unconcerned with any colour. The house was beetle-browed with icicles, and as far as she could see, it was unlit. 'Well, are you going to let me in?' she said.

'Sorry.' He sounded worse than that. 'If you could find your own way,' he said, dropping several consonants.

Kerry fumbled to thumb the key and then to snap her bag shut on the mobile. As she ventured up the path she felt as if the ill-defined prints were directing her course. If he didn't answer the doorbell she would certainly phone for help. She planted one foot on the doorstep bloated with snow and poked the bellpush in the middle of the door. It rattled more than rang, and at once the door swung inwards.

Light fanned along the hall in time to catch the white mass that swelled into her face. Could the house be colder than the street? The enervated glow through the puffy branches of a tree revealed half of the hall, the lower reaches of a staircase, two open doorways with a light switch between them. On her way to the switch a shiver overwhelmed her. She thought this and her glove were hindering her fingers until she saw that the switch wouldn't budge because it was encased in ice.

She was distracted by the notion that the house was somehow less defined than it ought to be. She peered into the rooms on either side of the switch and saw why. The first would be a sitting-room, the second for dining, but the furniture was close to unidentifiable. Though the windows were shut now, they had been open to the blizzard; the rooms and their contents were deep in snow. As she gazed at the dim pallid heaps, which barely referred to the shapes of a chair and a table and sideboard, Russell said 'Up here.'

She mustn't have switched off her mobile. His muffled voice was more fragmented than ever, and quite devoid of consonants. She wanted to finish whatever needed to be done, and so she hurried upstairs almost fast enough to outdistance a shiver, gripping the banister that felt cold and slippery enough for metal. 'Where?' she called.

She gained the upper floor without hearing any answer. All the doors off the landing were open. While the bathroom appeared to be clear of snow, icicles glimmered beneath the taps. Next was a room so cold that its darkness put her in mind of black ice. Around the door she caught sight of the foot of a bed. She was hoping that he didn't plan to entice her in that direction when his crumbling voice said 'Not there, here.'

That could only apply to one room. As she stepped over the threshold she saw the town draped in pallor under a sky of brass flawed with stars. Russell's desk must overlook the view, but the desk was buried in a snowdrift. All the same, a form was slumped or crouched in the snowbound chair in front of it. Kerry hurried forward, angry as much as dismayed. 'Russell, what have you——'

She was falling towards the chair. She regained her footing barely in time not to clutch at the chair and swing it around or worse. Whatever she'd slipped on, it wasn't ice. She blinked at the floor and tried not to believe what she was seeing. It was scattered with paper—with pages. The empty objects scattered among them were bindings, and she recognised the covers. He'd torn up all his books.

Had he done it for her to find? She wasn't going to feel guilty, but her eyes grew wet and unfocused as she leaned over the chair. 'Russell, what did you think——'

She almost planted an unwary hand on the object in the chair for support as she began to make it out. She could only assume he'd ensured for some reason that he couldn't sit at his desk. He'd built his version of a snowman, which was near to collapsing. The lump on top contained more holes than a head should, while the body had thawed and refrozen into such contortions it reminded her of a dead spider. The items like pale glistening sticks that appeared to be exposed here and there must be ice. She started to blink before deciding that she'd seen enough. She turned away hastily and picked her way over the waste of paper.

There was only the bedroom now. She was tempted to walk past and out of the house, but she was too anxious for him. She would have worried about anybody in the state of which she'd seen so much evidence. She pushed the door wide and strode into the room. 'Russell, I've had——'

She didn't even manage to utter all of that. For a moment—far too brief—she thought he'd wrapped a heavy quilt around him as he sat propped up against the pillows on the bed under the open window. It was snow, which filled his open mouth. His eyes were doughy wads. He looked no thinner than when she'd last seen him—and then she understood that he owed much of his substance to snow. The little she could distinguish of him was naked, and was that a withered icicle protruding from his fist between his legs? She was trying desperately to grasp how recently he must have lost the power of speech when she heard him. 'Not that,' he said.

Though each word was in shreds, the voice wasn't on her mobile. She didn't know where it was, and so she almost couldn't move. A shudder helped release her, and she staggered out of the frozen room. 'Don't go,' Russell said.

His voice was emerging from one of the rooms, and not only his voice. She was nearly at the stairs when whatever was behind her touched the back of her neck. Its grasp was so icy that although it almost instantly disintegrated, the feeling of it lingered like a brand. She would have fallen headlong if she hadn't seized the banister. She fled downstairs and along the unlit hall, and heard a whisper at her back that might have been an attempt to speak or the best her pursuer could do in the way of footsteps. She groped at the latch and dragged the door open and slammed it behind her so hard that it dislodged snow from the roof. She skidded along the path and slithered downhill, clinging to the rail, as fast as carelessness would take her. She wasn't out of sight of Russell's house when her mobile rang.

She had to force herself to halt and dig in her handbag, though the sound of any of her friends would be reassuring. She couldn't identify the unfinished digits that appeared to be struggling into view. 'Jason,' she almost hoped aloud, but the dogged incomplete voice wasn't his. 'You tried,' it said. 'My turn.'

Northwest Passage

Barbara Roden

How then am I so different from the first men through this way?
Like them I left a settled life, I threw it all away
To seek a Northwest Passage at the call of many men
To find there but the road back home again.

Stan Rogers, 'Northwest Passage'

THEY VARY IN DETAIL, the stories, but the broad outline is the same. Someone—hiker, hunter, tourist—goes missing, or is reported overdue, and there is an appeal to the public for information; the police become involved, and search and rescue teams, and there are interviews with friends and relatives, and statements by increasingly grim-faced officials, as the days tick by and hope begins to crack and waver and fade, like colour leaching out of a picture left too long in a window. Then there is the official calling off of the search, and gradually the story fades from sight, leaving family and friends with questions, an endless round of what ifs and how coulds and where dids pursuing each other like restless children.

Occasionally there is a coda, weeks or months or years later, when another hiker or hunter or tourist—more skilled, or perhaps more fortunate—stumbles across evidence and carries the news back, prompting a small piece in the 'In Brief' section of the *Vancouver Sun* which is skimmed over by urban readers safe in a place of straight lines and clearly delineated routes. They gaze at the expanse of Stanley Park on their daily commute, and wonder how a person could vanish so easily in a landscape so seemingly benign.

Peggy Malone does not wonder this, nor does she ask herself any questions.

She suspects she already knows the answers, and it is safer to keep the questions which prompt them locked away. Sometimes, though, they arise unbidden: when outside her window the breeze rustles the leaves of the maple, the one she asked the Strata Council to cut down, or the wind chimes three doors down are set ringing. Then the questions come back, eagerly, like a dog left on its own too long, and she turns on the television—not the radio, she rarely listens to that now—and turns on the lights and tries, for a time, to forget.

The road was, as back roads in the Interior go, a good one: Len had always ensured that it was graded regularly. Peggy, bumping her way up it in the Jeep, added 'get road seen to' to her mental checklist of things to do. She could not let it go another summer; next spring's meltwater would eat away even further at the dirt and rocks, and her sixty-three year old bones could do without the added wear and tear.

She followed the twists and turns of the road, threading her way through stands of cottonwood and birch and Ponderosa pine. Here and there the bright yellow of an arrowleaf balsam root flashed into sight beneath the trees, enjoying a brief moment of glory before withering and dying, leaving the silver-grey leaves as the only evidence of its passing. Overhead the sky was clear blue, but the breeze, when she pulled the Jeep in front of the cabin, was cool, a reminder that spring, not summer, held sway.

Peggy opened the rear of the Jeep and began unloading bags of supplies, which seemed, as always, to have proliferated during the drive. There was nothing to be done about it, however; the nearest town was an hour away, and she had long since learned that it was better to err on the side of too much than too little. Even though she was only buying for one now, the old habits died hard, and she usually managed to avoid making the journey more than once every two weeks or so.

She loaded the last of the milk into the fridge, which, like the other appliances and some of the lights, ran off propane; the light switch on the wall near the door had been installed by Len in a fit of whimsy when the cabin was being built, and served no useful purpose, as electricity did not extend up the valley from the highway some miles distant. The radio was battery operated, but seldom used: reception was poor during the day and sporadic at night, with stations alternately competing with each other and then fading away into a buzz of static. Kerosene lanterns and a generator could be used in an emergency, and an airtight fireplace kept the cabin more than warm enough in spring and fall. In winter she stayed with a nephew and his family on Vancouver Island; Len's brother's son, Paul, a good, steady lad who had given up urging his aunt to make the move to the Island permanent when he saw that it did no good. She would move when she was ready, Peggy always replied; she would know when the time came, and as long as she was able to drive and look after herself she was happy with the way things were.

Supplies unloaded, she set the kettle to boiling. A cup of tea would be just the thing, before she went out and did some gardening. It was not gardening in the sense that any of her acquaintances on the Island would understand it, with their immaculate, English-style flowerbeds and neatly edged, emerald green lawns which would not have looked out of place on a golf course; she called it that out of habit. She had learned, early on, that this land was tolerant of imposition only up to a point, and for some years her gardening had been confined to planting a few annuals—marigolds did well—in pots and hanging baskets.

Of course, she now had the grass to cut, and there were the paths to work on. It was Len who had suggested them, the summer before he had died, while watching her struggle to keep the sagebrush and wild grass at bay. The cabin was built on a natural bench, which overlooked the thickly treed valley, and was in turn overlooked by hills, rising relentlessly above until they lost themselves in the mountains behind. On three sides of the cabin the grassland stretched away to the trees, and Peggy had fought with it, trying, with her lawn and her flowers, to impose some sense of order on the landscape. She had resisted the idea of the paths at first, feeling that it would be giving in; but about what, and to whom, she could not have said. Still, she had started them for Len, who had taken comfort, that last summer, in watching her going about her normal tasks, and then she had continued them, partly because she felt she owed it to Len, and partly to fill the hours.

The paths now wound through a large part of the grassy area around the cabin. They were edged with rocks, and there were forks and intersections, and it was possible to walk them for some time without doubling back on oneself; not unlike, thought Peggy, one of those low mazes in which people were meant to think contemplative thoughts as they followed the path. She was not much given to contemplation herself, but keeping the existing paths free of weeds occupied her hands, and she supposed vaguely that it was good for her mind as well.

Now she stood looking at the paths, wondering whether she should do some weeding or check the mower and make sure it was in working order. It might have seized up over the winter; if so, then a good dose of WD-40 should take care of matters. She knew precisely where the tin was—Peggy knew precisely where everything in the cabin was—and was just turning towards the shed where the mower was stored when she heard the unmistakable sound of a vehicle coming up the road.

It was such an unusual sound that she stopped in her tracks and turned to face the gate, which hung open on its support, the only break in the fence of slender pine logs which encircled the property and served to keep out the cattle which occasionally wandered past. The road did not lead anywhere except to the cabin, and visitors were few and far between, for the simple reason that there was almost no one in the area to pay a visit. Peggy stood, waiting expectantly, and after a few moments a ramshackle Volkswagen van swung round the curve and started up the slight incline which levelled off fifty yards inside the gate, not far from the front of the cabin where her own Jeep was parked.

It pulled to a halt just inside the gate, and Peggy watched it. There were two people in the front seat, and for a minute no one made a move to get out; she got the impression that there was an argument going on. Then the passenger door opened, and a boy emerged, waving a tentative hand at her. She nodded her head, and the boy said something to the driver. Again Peggy got the impression that there was a disagreement of some sort; then the driver's door opened slowly, and another boy emerged.

She would have been a fool not to feel a slight sense of apprehension, and Peggy was not a fool. But she prided herself on being able to assess a situation quickly and accurately, and she did not feel any sense of threat. So she stood and waited as they approached her, taking in their appearance: one tall and fair-haired, the other shorter and dark; both in their early twenties, with longish hair and rumpled clothing and a general impression of needing a good square meal or two, but nothing that made her wish that the .202 she kept inside the cabin was close to hand.

The pair stopped a few feet from her, and the fair-haired boy spoke first.

'Hi. We, uh, we were just passing by, and we thought . . .' He trailed off, as if appreciating that 'just passing by' was not something easily done in the area. There was a pause. Then he continued, 'We heard your Jeep, and were kinda surprised; we didn't think anyone lived up here. So we thought that . . . well, that we'd come by and see who was here, and . . .'

The trickle of words stopped again, and the boy shrugged, helplessly, as if making an appeal. It was clear the other boy was not about to come to his aid, so Peggy picked up the thread.

'Margaret Malone,' she said, moving forward, her hand extended. 'Call me Peggy.'

The fair-haired boy smiled hesitantly, and stuck out his own hand. 'Hiya, Peggy. I'm John Carlisle, but everyone calls me Jack.'

'Nice to meet you, Jack.' Peggy turned to Jack's companion and looked at him evenly. 'And you are . . .?'

There was a pause, as if the boy was weighing the effect of not answering. Jack nudged him, and he said in a low voice, 'Robert. Robert Parker.'

Something about the way he said it discouraged any thoughts of Bob or Robbie. The conversation ground to a halt again, and once more Peggy took the initiative.

'So, you two boys students?' she asked pleasantly. Jack shook his head and said, 'No, why d'you ask?' at the same moment that Robert said sullenly, 'We're not boys.'

Peggy took a moment to reply. 'To answer you first,' she said finally, nodding towards Jack, 'we sometimes get students up here, from UBC or SFU, studying insects or infestation patterns, so it seemed likely. And to reply to your comment, Robert,' she said, looking him directly in the eye, 'when you get to my age you start to look at anyone under a certain age as being a boy; I didn't intend it as an insult. If I want to insult someone I don't leave them in any doubt.'

Jack gave a sudden smile, which twitched across his face and was gone in an instant. Robert glared at him.

'If you don't mind my asking, what brings you to this neck of the woods? Seems kind of an out of the way spot for two . . . people . . . of your age, especially this time of year.'

Nothing.

Really, thought Peggy, *was my generation as inarticulate as this when we were young? You'd think they'd never spoken to anyone else before.*

Again it was Jack who broke the silence.

'We're just, well, travelling around, you know? Taking some time out, doing something different, that kind of thing.' Seeing the look in Peggy's eyes, he added, 'We just wanted to go somewhere we wouldn't be bumping into people, somewhere we could do what we wanted. We've been up here for a few weeks now, staying in an old place we found over there.' He pointed an arm in an easterly direction. 'It was falling to pieces,' he added, as if he was apologising. 'No one's lived there for ages, we figured it'd be okay.'

Peggy held up a hand. 'No problem as far as I'm concerned, if it's the place I think you mean. Used to be a prospector's cabin, but no one's used it for years. You're welcome to it. Last time I hiked over that way was some time ago, and it was a real handyman's special then. You must have done a lot of work to get it fixed up so that you could live in it.'

Jack shrugged. 'Yeah, but we're used to that. Lots of stuff lying around we could use.'

'What do you do about food?'

'We stocked up in town; and there's an old woodstove in the cabin. We don't need a lot; we're used to roughing it.'

Peggy eyed them both. 'Seems to me you could do with something more than just roughing it in the food line for a couple of days.'

'We do okay.' It was Robert who spoke, as if challenging Peggy. 'We do just fine. We don't want any help.'

'I wasn't offering any, just making a comment. Last time I checked it was still a free country.'

'Yeah, course it is,' Jack said quickly. He glanced at Robert and shook his head; a small gesture, but Peggy noticed it. 'Anyway, we heard your Jeep; we were kinda surprised to see someone living up here. We figured it was only a summer place.'

'No, I'm up here spring through fall,' said Peggy. 'Afraid you're stuck with me as your nearest neighbour. Don't worry, I don't play the electric guitar or throw loud parties.'

It was a small joke, but Jack smiled again, as if he appreciated Peggy's attempt to lighten the mood. Robert nodded his head in the direction of the van, and Jack's smile vanished.

'Well, we've got to get going,' he said obediently. 'Nice meeting you, Peggy.'

'Nice meeting you two,' she said. 'If you need anything . . .'

'Thanks, that's really kind of you,' said Jack. He seemed about to add something, but Robert cut in.

'Can't think we'll need any help,' he said curtly. 'C'mon, Jack. Lots to do.'

'Yeah, right, lots to do. Thanks again, though, Peggy. See you around.'

'Probably. It's a big country, but a small world.'

'Hey, that's good.' Jack smiled. 'Big country, small world.'

Robert, who had already climbed into the driver's seat, honked the horn, and Jack turned almost guiltily towards the van. The passenger door had hardly closed before Robert was turning the van around. Jack waved as they passed, and Peggy waved back, but Robert kept his eyes on the road and his hands on the wheel. Within moments they were through the gate, and the curve of the road had swallowed them up.

Over the next few days Peggy replayed this encounter in her head, trying to put her finger on what bothered her. Yes, Robert had been rude—well, brusque, at least—but then a lot of young people were, these days; some old people, too. Their story about wanting to see something different; that wasn't unusual, exactly, but Peggy could think of quite a few places which were different but which didn't involve fixing up a dilapidated shack in the middle of nowhere. Yet Jack had said they'd done that sort of thing before, so it was obviously nothing new for them.

Were they runaways? That might explain why they came to check out who was in the cabin. But if they were running away from someone, they would hardly have driven right up to her front door. Drugs crossed her mind; it was almost impossible to pick up the paper or turn on the news without hearing about another marijuana grow-op being raided by police. Most of them were in the city or up the Fraser Valley, but she had heard about such places in the country, too; and didn't they grow marijuana openly in some rural spots, far away from the prying eyes of the police and neighbours? That might explain why Jack had looked so nervous . . . but, when she recalled the conversation, and the way Jack had looked at his friend, she realised that he was not nervous on his own account, he was nervous for, or about, Robert, who had seemed not in the least bit nervous for, or about, anything. He had merely been extremely uncomfortable, as if being in the proximity of someone other than Jack, even for five minutes, made him want to escape. What had Jack said? They wanted to go somewhere they wouldn't be bumping into people.

Robert must have had a shock when he saw me here, thought Peggy. *Bet I was the last thing he expected—or wanted—to run into.*

She did not see the pair again for almost three weeks. Once she saw their van at the side of the road as she drove out towards the highway and town, but there was no sign of Jack or Robert, and on another occasion she thought she saw the pair of them far up on the hillside above her, but the sun was in her eyes and she couldn't be sure. She thought once or twice about hiking over to their cabin, which was two miles or so away. There had been a decent trail over there at one time, which she and Len had often walked; but the days were getting hotter, and her legs weren't what they once were, and when she reflected on her likely reception she decided she was better off staying put. If they wanted anything, or needed any help, they knew where to find her.

It was late morning, and Peggy had been clearing a new path. A wind had been gusting out of the northwest; when she stopped work and looked up the hill she could see it before she heard or felt it, sweeping through the trees, bearing down on her, carrying the scent of pine and upland meadows before rushing past and down the hill, setting the wind chimes by the front door tinkling, branches bending and swinging before it as if an unseen giant had passed. Sometimes a smaller eddy seemed to linger behind, puffing up dust on the paths, swirling round and about like something trapped and lost and trying to escape. But Peggy did not think of it like this; at least not then. Those thoughts did not come until later.

She straightened up, one hand flat against her lower back, stretching, and it was then that she saw the boy standing at the edge of the property, by the mouth of the trail leading to the prospector's cabin. She had no idea how long he had been standing there, but she realised that he must have been waiting for her to notice him before he came closer, for as soon as he knew he had been spotted he headed in her direction.

'Hello there,' she said. 'Jack, isn't it? Haven't seen you for a while; I was beginning to wonder if you'd moved on.'

'No, we're still here.' He gave a little laugh. 'Kind of obvious, I guess.'

'A bit. Your friend with you?'

'No.'

'I'm not surprised. He didn't seem the dropping-in type.'

'No.' Jack seemed to feel that something more was needed. 'He was a bit pissed off when he found someone was living here. He thought we had the place to ourselves, you see, no one around for miles.'

'He likes his solitude, then.'

'You could say that.'

'Still, it's not as if I'm on your doorstep,' said Peggy reasonably, 'or, to be strictly accurate, that you're on mine. If your friend doesn't want to run into anyone, he's picked as good a spot as any.'

'Yeah, that's what I've been telling him, but I think we'll be heading out before the end of the summer.'

'Because of me?'

'Well, no; I mean, sort of, but that's not the whole reason. Robert'—he paused, looking for words—'Robert likes to keep on moving. Restless, I guess you could say. He's always been like that; always wants to see what's over the next hill, around the next corner, always figures there's somewhere better out there.'

'Better than what?'

Jack shrugged. 'I don't know. He gets somewhere, and he seems happy enough for a while, and then, just when I think "Right, this is it, this is the place he's been looking for", off he goes again.'

'Do you always go with him?'

'Yeah, usually. We've known each other a long time, since elementary school. His family moved from back east and we wound up in the same grade three class.'

'Where was that?'

'Down in Vancouver. Point Grey.'

Peggy nodded. Point Grey usually, but not always, meant money, respectability, expectations. She could see Robert, from what little she knew of him, being from, but not of, that world. Jack, though, looked like Point Grey, and she wondered how he had found himself caught up in Robert's orbit.

'He's always been my best friend,' the boy said, as if reading her thoughts. 'We hung out together. I mean, I had other friends, but Robert just had me. It didn't bother him, though. If he wanted to do something and I couldn't, he'd just go off on his own, no problem. It's like he always knew I'd be there when he needed me.'

'Has he always liked the outdoor life?'

Jack nodded. 'Yeah, he's always been happiest when he's outside.' He shook his head. 'I remember this one time I got him to go along with a group of us who were going camping for the weekend. We were all eleven, twelve; our parents didn't mind, they figured there were enough of us that we'd be safe.' He paused, remembering. 'We rode our bikes from Point Grey out to Sea Island; you know, behind the airport.' Peggy nodded. 'There used to be a big subdivision out there, years ago, but then they were going to build another runway and the houses got . . . what's the word . . . expropriated, and torn down, and then nothing happened, and it all got pretty wild, the gardens and trees and everything.

'Well, we all had the usual shit . . . I mean stuff; dinky pup tents and old sleeping bags and things, and chocolate bars and pop, but not Robert. He had a tarp, and a plastic sheet, and a blanket, matches, a compass, trail mix, bottled water; he even had an axe. You'd've thought he was on a military exercise, or one of those survival weekends, instead of in the suburbs. We goofed around, and ate, and told stories, and then we crawled into our tents, all except Robert. He'd built a fire, and a lean-to out of branches and the tarp, and he said he'd stay where he was, even when it started to rain. Rain in Vancouver: who'd think it?

'Anyway, when morning came round, we were a pretty miserable bunch of kids; the tents had leaked, and our sleeping bags were soaked, and we'd eaten almost everything we'd brought. And there was Robert, dry as a bone, making a fire out of wood he'd put under cover the night before, with food and water to spare. Made us all look like a bunch of idiots.'

'Sounds like a good person to have around you in a place like this.'

'Yeah, you could say that.' He scuffed the toe of one foot against the dirt, watching puffs of dust swirl up into the air.

'So where is he this morning?'

Jack stopped scuffing and looked up at Peggy. 'He went off a couple of hours ago; said he needed to get away for a while, be on his own. He gets like that sometimes. I hung around for a bit by myself and then . . .' His look was almost pleading. 'It just got so quiet, you know? You don't realise how quiet it is 'til you're by yourself. Robert doesn't mind; sometimes I think he'd rather be by himself all the time, that he wouldn't even notice if I never came back.'

Peggy tried to think of something to say. Jack went back to scuffing the dirt, and a breeze picked up the cloud of dust, swirling it in the direction of the paths. Jack followed the cloud with his eyes, and seemed to notice the paths through the grass for the first time.

'Hey, that's pretty cool.' He took a couple of steps forward, and she could see his head moving as he followed the curves of the paths with his eyes. 'Bet it would look neat from overhead, like in one of those old Hollywood musicals.'

Peggy had not recognized the tension in the situation until it was gone; its sudden disappearance left her feeling slightly off-balance, like an actor momentarily surprised by the unexpected ad-lib of someone else on stage. Jack was still gazing out over the paths.

'Must've taken a long time to do this,' he said. 'What's it for?'

'Nothing, really.' Peggy moved forward so that she was standing beside him. 'It was my husband's idea; he said he got tired of watching me trying to control the brush, that I should work with it, not against it.'

If you can't beat 'em, join 'em, she heard Len's voice say. *And looking at all that*—he had waved his hand towards the expanse of scrub and the hills beyond— *I don't think you're ever going to beat 'em, Peg.*

'If you can't beat them, join them,' said Jack, and Peggy started slightly and looked sideways at him. 'That's how I feel about Robert sometimes. Can I take a closer look?'

'Go ahead.' Peggy looked at her watch. 'I'm going to go and make some lunch; nothing fancy, just sandwiches and some fruit, but if you want to stay then you're more than welcome.'

'Could I?' he asked eagerly. 'I'd really like that. Our cooking's pretty . . . basic.'

Peggy, noting Jack's pinched face and pale complexion, could believe it. 'I'll go and rustle something up; come in when you're ready.'

She stood at the kitchen counter, letting her hands move through the familiar motions of spreading butter and mayonnaise, slicing tomatoes and cucumber, while in her head she went over the conversation with Jack. There were undercurrents she could not fathom, depths she could not chart. She had thought of them as two boys from the city playing at wilderness life, and Jack's words had not dismissed this as a possibility; but there was something else going on, she was sure of it. Were they lovers? Had they had a fight? That could be it, but she did not think so. She could not connect the dark, intense figure she had seen three weeks ago with something as essentially banal as a lovers' tiff.

Through the window she could see Jack moving slowly along one of the paths, his head down as if deep in concentration. He stopped, seemingly aware of her gaze upon him, but instead of turning towards the cabin he looked up at the hillside above, intently, his head cocked a little to one side as if he had heard something. Peggy followed his gaze, but could see nothing on the bare slope, or in the air above; certainly nothing that would inspire such rapt attention.

She stacked the sandwiches on a plate, then sliced some cheese and put it, with some crackers and grapes, on another plate. She wondered what to offer as a drink. Beer would have been the obvious choice, but she had none. Milk or orange juice; or perhaps he'd like a cup of coffee or tea afterwards. . . .

Still pondering beverage choices, she put the plates on the table, then went to the door. Jack had not altered his position; he seemed transfixed by something up on the hill. Peggy looked again, sure that he was watching an animal, but there was nothing to be seen.

She called his name, and he turned to her with a startled look on his face, as if he could not quite remember who she was or how he had got there. Then he shook his head slightly and trotted towards her, like a dog who has heard the rattle of the can opener and knows his supper is ready.

'Sorry it's nothing more elegant,' said Peggy, pointing to the table, 'but help yourself. Don't be shy.'

She soon realized that her words were unnecessary. Jack fell on the meal as if he had not eaten in days, and for some minutes the only sound was him asking if he could have another sandwich. Peggy got up twice to refill his milk glass before finally placing the jug on the table so he could help himself, and watched as the cheese and cracker supply dwindled. Finally Jack drained his glass and sighed contentedly.

'Thanks, Peggy, that was great, really. Didn't know how hungry I was until I saw the food. Guess I wouldn't win any awards for politeness.'

Peggy laughed. 'That's okay. It's been a long time since I saw someone eat something I'd made with that much pleasure. I'm sorry it wasn't anything more substantial.'

Jack looked at his watch. 'Geez, is that the time? I better be going; Robert'll be back soon, he'll wonder where I am, and I'll bet you've got things to do.'

'Don't worry, my time's my own. Nice watch.'

Jack smiled proudly, and held up his wrist so Peggy could see it better. Silver glinted at her. 'Swiss Army. My parents gave it to me when I graduated. Keeps perfect time.' He sat back in his chair and looked around the cabin. 'You live here by yourself? You said something about your husband. Is he . . .?' He stopped, unsure how to continue the sentence to its natural conclusion, so Peggy did it for him.

'. . . dead, yes. Four years ago. Cancer. It was pretty sudden; there was very little the doctors could do.'

'I'm sorry.'

'That's okay. You didn't know him. He went quite quickly, which is what he wanted. Len was never a great one for lingering.'

'So you live up here for most of the year on your own? That's pretty gutsy.'

Peggy could not recall having been called gutsy before. 'You think so?'

'Yeah, sure. I mean, this place is pretty isolated, and you're . . . well, you're not exactly young.' His face went pink. 'I don't mean that . . . it just must be tough, that's all, on your own. Don't you ever get lonely?'

'No, there's always something to do. I spend the winter with family on the Island; I get more than enough company then to see me through the rest of the year.'

Jack nodded. His eyes continued moving around the cabin, and he spotted the light switch. 'Hey, I didn't think you had power up here.'

'We don't. That's a bit of a joke, for visitors.'

'Bet you don't get too many of those.'

'You'd be right. My nephew and his family have been up a couple of times, but not for a while. He doesn't like it much up here; says it makes him uncomfortable. This sort of place isn't for everyone.'

Jack nodded. 'You've got that right.' He looked through the screen door towards the hillside and gestured with his head. 'You ever feel that something's up there watching you?'

Peggy considered. 'No, not really. An animal sometimes, maybe; but we don't get too many animals up there. Odd, really, you'd think it would be a natural place to spot them.' A memory came back to her; Paul, her nephew, on one of his rare visits, standing on the porch looking up at the hills. 'My nephew said once it reminded him of a horror movie his sons rented; *The Eyes on the Hill* or something.'

'*The Hills Have Eyes*,' Jack corrected automatically. 'Yeah, I've seen it.' He was silent for a moment. 'Do you believe that?'

'What—that the hills have eyes? No.'

'But don't you feel it?' he persisted. 'Like there's something there, watching, waiting, something really old and . . . I don't know, part of this place, guarding it, protecting it, looking for something?'

Peggy couldn't keep the astonishment out of her face and voice. 'No, I can honestly say I've never felt that at all.' She considered him. 'Is that what you think?'

'I don't know.' He paused. 'There's just something weird about this spot. I mean, we've been in some out of the way places, Robert and me, but nowhere like this. I'll be kind of glad when he decides to move on. I hope it'll be soon.'

'I thought you wanted him to settle down somewhere.'

'Yeah, I do, but not here.'

'Why don't you leave? Robert seems able to fend for himself, and he appears to like this sort of life better than you do. Why do you stay with him?'

'I've always stayed with him.'

'But you said that he likes to go off on his own, that you don't think he'd notice if you didn't come back.'

Jack looked uncomfortable, like a witness caught by a clever lawyer. 'Oh, I just said that 'cause I was pissed off. He'd notice.'

'Is he your boyfriend? Is that why you stay?'

Jack looked shocked. 'God, no! It's nothing like that. It goes back a long way. . . . Remember I told you about that camping trip out to Sea Island? Well, when I went round to Robert's house to get him his mom was there, fussing, you know, the way moms do, and he was getting kind of impatient, and finally he just said "Bye, mom" really suddenly and went to get his bike, and his mom turned to me and said "Look after him." Which was kind of a weird thing to say, 'cause I was only eleven, and Robert wasn't the kind of kid who you'd think needed looking after—well, we found that out next day. But I knew what she meant. She didn't mean he needed looking after 'cause he'd do something stupid, she meant that he needed someone to . . . bring him back, almost, make sure he didn't go off and just keep on going.'

'Is that why you stay with him? So he doesn't just keep on going?'

'I guess.' His smile was tinged with sadness. 'I'm not doing such a great job, am I?'

'You're a long way from Point Grey, if that's what you mean.'

'Yeah, and I can't see us making it back anytime soon. Robert wants to keep heading north, up to the Yukon, and then head east.'

'What on earth for?'

Jack shrugged. 'He does a lot of reading; he's got a box of books in the van, all about explorers and people who go off into the wilderness with just some matches and a rifle and a sack of flour and live off the land. I think that's what he wants to do; go up north and see what's there, see what he can do, what he can find. He loves reading about the Franklin expedition; you know, the one that disappeared when they were searching for the Northwest Passage, and no one knew for years what happened to them. I think he likes the idea of just vanishing, and no one knows where you are, and then you come out when you're ready, and tell people what you've found.'

'The Franklin expedition didn't come out.'

'Robert figures he can do better than them.'

'Well then, you should break it to him that the Northwest Passage was found a long time ago, and tell him he should maybe stick closer to home.'

'He doesn't want to find the Northwest Passage; anyway, he says it doesn't really exist, there is no Northwest Passage, not like everyone thought back in Franklin's time.'

'And you'll go with him?'

'I suppose so.'

'You do have a choice, you know.'

'Yeah, like you said, it's a free country. But I kind of feel like I have to go with him, to . . .'

'Look after him?'

'I guess.' He shrugged. 'It's like there's something out there, waiting for him, and I have to make sure he comes back okay, otherwise he'd just keep on going, and he'd be like those Franklin guys, he'd never come out.'

The conversation was interrupted by the unmistakable sound of a vehicle coming up the road towards the cabin. Jack stood up so quickly his chair fell over.

'Shit, it's Robert.'

'Probably,' Peggy agreed drily. 'Don't worry, there's nothing criminal about having lunch with someone.'

'No, but . . . Robert can be . . . funny, weird, sometimes. Don't tell him what I said about looking after him, he'd be really pissed off.'

'Your secret is safe with me.'

They went out on to the porch and watched the van drive up. Robert climbed out and glared at Jack.

'Thought you'd be here,' he said, ignoring Peggy. 'C'mon, let's go.'

'Hello to you too,' said Peggy. 'You're a friendly sort, aren't you? In my day we'd have considered it bad manners to order a person out from under someone else's roof. Guess times have changed. Or are you just naturally rude?' Robert stared at her, but she gave him no chance to speak. 'Jack's here as my guest; he's had a good lunch, which I must say he needed, and you look like you could do with something decent inside you, whatever you might think. So you can either stay here and let me fix you some sandwiches, which I'm more than prepared to do if you're prepared to be civil, or you can climb back into your van and drive away, with or without Jack, but I think that's his decision to make, not yours. He found his way here by himself, and I'd guess he can find his way back if he decides to stay a bit longer.'

Robert started to say something; something not very pleasant, if the look that flashed across his face was anything to go by. Then he took a deep breath.

'Yeah, you're right. He can stay if he wants. No problem.' He turned towards the van.

'Wait a minute,' said Jack, moving off the porch. 'Don't go. Peggy said you could stay, she'll fix you some sandwiches. Don't be a jerk. You must be as hungry as me.'

'We've got food back at our place,' said Robert; but he slowed down. Jack turned and threw a pleading look back at Peggy. *What can I do?* was written on his face.

'Robert. *Robert.*' He stopped, but kept his back turned to Peggy. 'If you don't want to stay now, that's fine; maybe this isn't a good time, maybe you've got things to do, I don't know. But why don't you both come back over for supper? I've got some steaks in the fridge that need using up, and I can do salad and baked potatoes. Sound good?'

'What do you say, Robert?' said Jack eagerly. 'I'll come with you now, then we both come back later and have supper.'

Robert looked at Jack, then at Peggy. She put her hands in front of her, palms out, like a traffic policeman. 'No ulterior motive, no strings, just a chance to give you both a good meal and talk to someone other than myself. You'd be doing me a big favour, both of you.'

'Yeah,' said Robert finally, slowly, 'yeah, okay, supper would be great.'

'Fine! About six, then.'

Robert climbed in the driver's seat, and Jack mouthed *Thanks!* and gave a wave; the sun glinted off the face of his watch, making her blink. He got in the other side, and once more she watched as the van rattled out the gate and round the curve.

'I hope I've done the right thing,' she said aloud. 'Why can't things be simple?'

The afternoon drew on. Peggy did a bit more work on the paths, clearing some errant weeds. She straightened up at last, and glanced down across the valley below. It was her favourite view, particularly in the late afternoon sun, and she stood admiring it for a few moments, watching the play of light and shade across the trees. The wind, which had been playing fitfully about her all day, had at last died down, and everything was still and calm and clear.

Suddenly she turned and looked up behind her. She could have sworn that she heard someone call her name, but there was no one there; at least no one she could see. Still, the feeling persisted that someone was there; she felt eyes on her, watching.

The hills have eyes.

For the first time she realised how exposed she and the cabin were, and how small. Crazy, really, to think that something as essentially puny and inconsequential as a human could try to impose anything of himself on this land. How long had all this been here? How long would it endure after she was gone? *Work with it, not against it,* Len had said. *If you can't beat 'em, join 'em.* But how could you work with something, join with something, that you couldn't understand?

She shook her head. This was the sort of craziness that came from too much living alone. Maybe Paul was right; maybe it was time to start thinking about moving to the Island permanently.

Or maybe you just need a good hot meal said a voice inside her head. *Those boys will be here soon; better get going.* She took one last look at the hill, then turned towards the cabin. The wind chimes were ringing faintly as she passed, the only sound in the stillness.

Inside, she turned on the radio; for some reason which she did not want to analyze she found the silence oppressive. The signal was not strong, but the announcer's voice, promising 'your favourite good-time oldies', was better than nothing. She started the oven warming and wrapped half a dozen potatoes in foil, to the accompaniment of Simon and Garfunkel's 'The Sound of Silence', then started on the salad fixings: lettuce, cucumber, radishes, tomatoes, mushrooms. As she scraped the last of the mushrooms off the board and into the bowl, she glanced out the window, and saw a figure standing on one of the paths, looking back at the hillside. *Jack*, she thought to herself, recognizing the fair hair, and looked at her watch. It was ten past five. *They're early. Must be hungry.*

Simon and Garfunkel gave way to Buddy Holly and 'Peggy Sue'. The oven pinged, indicating it was up to temperature, and she bundled the potatoes into it. When she returned to the window, the figure was gone.

'C'mon in,' she called out, 'door's open, make yourselves at home.' She put the last of the sliced tomatoes on top of the salad, then realised no one had come in. 'Hello?' she called out. 'Anyone there?' Buddy Holly warbling about pretty Peggy Sue was the only reply.

Peggy went to the door and looked out. There was no one in sight. The van was not there, and it registered that she had not heard it come up the road. *It's such a nice night, maybe they walked.* She looked to her right, to where the trail they would have taken came out of the woods, but no one was there.

A squawk of static from the radio made her jump. For a moment there was only a low buzzing noise; then Buddy Holly came back on, fighting through the static, for she heard 'Peggy' repeated. Another burst of noise, then the signal came through more clearly; only now it was the Beatles, who were halfway through 'Help!'.

'Interference,' she muttered to herself. They often got overlapping channels at night; another station was crossing with the first one. She went outside and looked round the corner of the cabin, but there was no one in sight. When she went back in, 'Help!' was ending, and she heard the voice of the announcer.

'We've got more good-time oldies coming up after the break,' he said, and she realised the radio had been broadcasting the same station all along. They must have got their records, or CDs, or whatever they used now mixed-up, she decided.

She placed the salad on the table and got the steaks out of the fridge. She was beginning to trim the fat away from around the edges when the radio gave another burst of static, then faded away altogether. She flicked the on/off switch, and tried the tuner, but was unable to raise a signal. *Dead batteries*, she thought. *I only replaced them last week; honestly, they don't make things like* . . .

She broke off mid-thought at the sound of a voice calling her name. *Definitely not Buddy Holly this time*, she thought, and walked to the door, ready to call a greeting. What she saw made her freeze in the doorway.

Robert was running towards her across the grass; running wildly, carelessly, frantically even, as if something was on his tracks, calling out her name with all the breath he could muster. In a moment she shook off her fear and began crossing the yard towards him, meeting him near the back of her Jeep. He collapsed on the ground at her feet, and she knelt down beside him as he gasped for breath.

'Robert! Robert, what's wrong? What's happened?'

'Jack,' he gasped; 'Jack . . . he's gone . . . got to help me . . . just gone . . .'

'Gone! What do you mean? Gone where?'

He was still panting, and she saw that his face was white. He struggled to his knees and swung round so that he could look behind him, in the direction of the blank and staring hillside.

'Don't know . . . we were coming over here . . . walking . . . and then he was gone . . . didn't see him . . .'

'Right.' Peggy spoke crisply, calmly. 'Just take another deep breath . . . and another . . . that's it, that's better. Now then'—when his breathing had slowed somewhat—'you and Jack were walking over here—why didn't you come in the van?'

'It wouldn't start; battery's dead or something.'

'Okay, so you decided to walk, and Jack went on ahead, and you lost sight of him. Well, as mysteries go it's not a hard one; he's already here.'

Robert stared at her. 'What do you mean, he's already here?' he almost whispered.

'I saw him, over there.' Peggy pointed towards the paths. 'I looked out the window and there he was.'

'Where is he now?'

Peggy frowned. 'Well, I don't know; I went outside, but couldn't see him. I thought you'd both come early and were looking around.'

'What time was this?'

'Ten past five; I looked at my watch.'

'That's impossible,' said Robert flatly, in a voice tinged with despair. 'At ten past five he'd only just gone missing, and I was looking for him a mile from here. There's no way he could have got here that fast.'

Peggy felt as if something was spiralling out of control, and she made a grab at the first thing she could think of. 'How do you know exactly when he went missing?'

'I'd just looked at my watch, to see how we were doing for time; then he was gone.'

'Maybe there's something wrong with your watch.'

Robert shook his head. 'It keeps perfect time.' He looked down at his left wrist, and Peggy saw him go pale again.

'What the fuck . . .' he whispered, and Peggy bent her head to look.

The face of the digital watch was blank.

Robert began to shiver. 'What's going on?' he said, in a voice that was a long way from that of the sullen youth she had seen earlier. 'Where's Jack?'

'I don't know; but he can't have gone far. Did you two have a fight about something? Could that be why he went on ahead?'

'But he didn't go on ahead,' said Robert, in a voice that sounded perilously close to tears. 'That's just it. We were walking along, and he asked what time it was, and I looked at my watch—it was only for a couple of seconds, you know how long it takes to look at a watch—and then he was just . . . gone.'

'Could he have . . . I don't know . . . gone off the trail? Gone behind a tree?'

Robert looked at her blankly. 'Why would he do that?'

'I don't know!' Peggy took a deep breath. The boy was distraught enough, without her losing control as well. 'Playing a joke? Looking at something? Call of nature?'

He shook his head. 'No.'

'Think! Are you sure you didn't just miss him?'

'I'm positive. There wasn't time for him to go anywhere, not even if he ran like Donovan Bailey. I'd have seen him.'

'Okay.' Peggy thought for a moment. 'You say you were both a mile from here, at ten past five, which is the same time I looked outside and saw Jack here, at my cabin. I'd say that your watch battery was going then, and it wasn't giving you an accurate time, which is how Jack seemed to be in two places at once.'

Robert shook his head again. 'No.' He looked straight at Peggy. His breath was still ragged; he must have run the mile to her cabin. 'Jack's gone.' Then, more quietly, 'What am I going to do?'

Peggy got him inside the cabin and into an armchair, then went back out on the porch. The clock on the radio had died with the batteries, but her old wind-up wristwatch told her it was almost six. *Time for Jack and Robert to be arriving. . . .*

She called out 'Jack!' and the sound of her voice in the stillness startled her. She waited a moment, then called again, but the only reply was the tinkle of the wind chimes. She walked round the cabin, not really knowing why; Jack hadn't seemed the kind to play senseless tricks, and she didn't expect to see him, but still she looked, because it seemed the right—the only—thing to do.

She stood at the front of the cabin, looking down over the valley. All those trees; if someone wandered off into them they could disappear forever. She shivered, then shook her head. Jack hadn't disappeared; there had to be an explanation. He and Robert had had a fight; Jack had stormed off, and Robert was too embarrassed to tell her about it. Jack was probably back at their camp by now . . . but that didn't explain how he had been outside the cabin at ten past five. Unless he had come to the cabin as originally planned, then decided he couldn't face Robert, and gone back to their camp by road . . . no, it was all getting too complex. She took a deep breath and walked round the side of the cabin . . . and stopped short at the sight of a figure over on the paths.

Only it wasn't a figure, she realised a split second later; there was no one, nothing, there. She had imagined it, that was all; perhaps that's what she had done earlier, looked up and remembered the image of Jack standing there from before lunch. He hadn't been there at all; Robert was quite right. In which case . . .

'We need to go looking for Jack.'

Robert looked up at her as if he did not understand. Peggy resisted the urge to shake him.

'Did you hear me? I said we need to go look for Jack.'

'Shouldn't we . . . shouldn't we call the police?'

'Yes; but first we need to go looking for him.' She told him about her mistake with the figure. 'He was never here at all. So you must have missed him on the path. And he must be injured, or lost, or he'd be here now. So yes, we'll call the police when we get back. Even if we called them now, though, it would be almost dark before they could get here; they wouldn't be able to start a search until daybreak. We're here now; we have the best chance of finding him.'

She turned the oven off—*last thing I need now is to come back and find the place burned down*—then gathered together some supplies: two flashlights, a first aid kit, a couple of bottles of water, a sheath knife. She put them in a knapsack, which she handed to Robert. Then she went into her bedroom and got the .202 out from the back of the cupboard. The sight of it seemed to make Robert realise how serious the situation was.

'What do you need that for?'

'There's all sorts of animals out there, and a lot of them start to get active around this time of day. It's their country, not ours, but that doesn't mean I want to become a meal.'

'Do you know how to use it?'

Peggy stared at him levelly. 'It wouldn't be much use having it around if I couldn't use it. I'm not an Olympic marksman, but if it's within fifty yards of me I can hit it. Let's go.'

They headed out towards the trail, skirting the paths. A little gust of wind was eddying dust along one of them. Peggy was conscious of the hillside above them to their left, and could not shake off the sense that something was watching. What was it Jack had said? *Something there, watching, waiting, something really old . . . part of this place, guarding it, protecting it, looking for something.* No; she had to stop it, stop it now. Thoughts like that were no good. She needed to concentrate.

'Come on, Robert,' she called over her shoulder, 'let's go. We have a lot of ground to cover, and it'll be dark in another couple of hours. You better go first; it's been a while since I was last through here. Keep yelling Jack's name, and keep your eyes open.'

They started along the trail. It was fainter than Peggy remembered, but still distinguishable as such; more than clear enough to act as a guide, even for the most inexperienced eye. They took turns calling, and stared intently about them, looking from side to side, searching for any signs of Jack; but there was nothing, not a trace of his passage, not a hint that he was calling or signalling to them. They stopped every so often to listen, and to give them both a chance to rest; but they only lingered in one place, when Robert indicated that they were at the spot where he had last seen Jack.

'Here,' he said, pointing; 'I was standing here, and Jack was about fifteen feet in front of me, and then . . . he wasn't.'

Peggy looked around, trying to will some sign, some clue into being, but there was nothing that marked the spot out as any different to anywhere else they had passed. Birch and poplar and pines crowded round them, but not so thickly, she thought, that someone could disappear into them and be lost to sight in a matter of seconds. A breeze rustled the branches, and something skittered through the undergrowth; a squirrel, she thought, from the sound. They called, but there was no reply, and searched either side of the trail, but there was no sign of Jack. Without a word they continued on their way.

Robert was still in front, Peggy behind; the trail was not wide enough to allow more than single file passage. *Indian file.* The phrase from her childhood popped unbidden into Peggy's mind, along with the accompanying thought, *I suppose you can't call it that anymore, but Aboriginal file doesn't sound right. Or would it be Native file?* Natives . . . now what did that . . .

'Natives don't like that place.' Who had said that? Someone, years before, who she and Len had run into in town, someone who knew the area and was surprised when they told him where they lived. 'Natives don't like that place,' he had said. 'Never have. Don't know why; you can't pin 'em down. Used to be a prospector lived back in there, not far from where you are, I guess, and there was a feeling he was tempting . . . well, fate, I suppose, or the gods, or something. . . . What happened to him? He just up and left one day; disappeared. Some people figured he'd hit it lucky at last and had cleared out with his gold, others said it was cabin fever; whatever happened, it didn't do anything for the place's reputation.'

Why had she thought of that now, of all times? She shivered uncontrollably, and was glad that Robert was up ahead and couldn't see her. She hurried to close the distance between them; and although her breath was becoming more ragged, and the ache in her legs more pronounced, she did not stop again until they were at the cabin.

It was much as she remembered it; a low, crudely built structure of weathered pine logs, with a single door and one window in front, and a tin chimney pipe leaning out from the roof at an angle. There was no smoke from the chimney, no movement within or without; only the sound of the wind, and a far-off crow cawing hoarsely, and their own breath. The dying sun reflected off the one window, creating a momentary illusion of life, but neither one spoke. There was no need. Jack was not here.

They checked the cabin, just to be sure, and the van, sitting uselessly in front, and they called until they were hoarse, but they were merely going through the motions, and Peggy knew it. Robert tried the van again, but the battery was irrevocably dead. Still silent, they turned and headed back the way they had come.

They did not call out now, or search for signs; their one thought, albeit an unspoken one, was to get back to Peggy's before dark. The sun had dipped well below the hills now, and the shadows were lengthening fast, and Peggy found herself keeping her eyes on the trail ahead. Once she thought she heard movement in the trees to their right, and stopped, clutching Robert's arm; but it was only the wind. They continued on their silent way, and did not stop again.

They reached the cabin as the last of the light flickered and died in the western sky. Peggy ached in every joint and muscle in her body, but she lit the propane lamps and put water on to boil for coffee while Robert collapsed into a chair and put his head in his hands. Finally, when she could think of nothing else useful to do with her hands, Peggy sat down opposite him.

'Robert.' He looked up at her with tired eyes. 'Robert, it's time to phone the police. I'll do it, if you'd like.'

'Yeah, that'd be good. Thanks.'

She would not have thought that this was the same Robert she had seen earlier in the day. He seemed lost, diminished, and she realised with a start that Jack had been wrong, completely wrong, when he had told her that Robert wouldn't have minded if Jack had gone off and never come back. Something inside Robert compelled him, but Jack, she thought, had always been there, a link with the life he had left behind, and a way back to it. As long as Jack had been with him, Robert would have kept moving; now, without him, Peggy had the feeling that there'd be no Northwest Passage. She wished that Jack could know that, somehow.

She moved to the phone, an old-fashioned one with a dial. She picked up the receiver and listened for a moment, then jiggled the cradle two, three, four times, while the look on her face changed from puzzled to worried to frightened. She replaced the receiver.

'No dial tone.'

Robert stared at her. 'What do you mean, no dial tone?'

'Just what I said. The line must be down somewhere. We can't call out.'

'Great. Just fucking great.' Anger mixed with fear flashed across his face, and for a moment he looked like the Robert of old. 'What do we do now?'

'We have a cup of coffee and something to eat; then we get in my Jeep and drive to town and tell the police what's happened. After that it's in their hands.'

'Shouldn't we go now?'

'Frankly, until I get some coffee into me I won't be in a fit state to drive anywhere, and I'd be surprised if you're any different. And the police won't be able to start a search until morning; another half an hour or so isn't going to make much difference now.'

Robert looked at her bleakly. 'I guess not,' he said finally.

She busied herself with the ritual of making coffee. As she measured and poured, something caught her eye at the window, and she looked up automatically.

A face was staring in at her.

She gave a brief, choked cry, and dropped the teaspoon, which clattered on to the counter. It took her a moment to realise that what she saw was her own reflection, framed in the darkness of the window and what lay beyond. That was all it could be. There was no one out there.

But she had seen something at the window, out of the corner of her eye, before she looked up. No; it had been a reflection of something in the room. The cabin was brightly lit, and the windows were acting like mirrors.

From the front of the cabin the wind chimes rang.

Peggy was suddenly conscious of feeling exposed. The little cabin, lights streaming out the windows into the darkness, did not belong here; it was an intruder, and therefore a target. She turned to Robert.

'Close the curtains.'

'What?'

She pointed to the picture windows overlooking the valley. 'Leave the windows open, but close the curtains.'

He did as she asked, while Peggy reached for the blind cord by the kitchen window. The Venetian blinds rattled into place. *That's better*, she thought, and took the coffee in to the living-room.

They sat and sipped, both unconsciously seeking refuge in this ordinary, everyday act. There was silence between them, for there was nothing to be said, or nothing they wanted to say. The wind chimes were louder now, the only sound in the vast expanse around them. The only sound. . . .

A thought which had been at the back of Peggy's mind for some time came into focus then, and she looked up, listening intently. She placed her cup on the table in front of her so hard that coffee sloshed over the side. Robert looked up, startled.

'What . . .' he began, but Peggy held up her hand.

'Listen!' she whispered urgently. Robert looked at her, puzzled. 'What do you hear? Tell me. . . .'

Robert tried to concentrate. 'Nothing,' he said finally. 'Just that chiming noise, that's all. Why, did you hear something? Do you think it's . . .'

'*Listen*. We can hear the chimes, yes, but there's no wind in the trees; we should be able to hear it in the branches, shouldn't we? And the windows are open, but the curtains aren't moving, they're absolutely still. *So why can we hear the wind chimes, if there isn't a wind?*'

Robert stared at her for a moment, uncomprehending. Then he went pale.

'What are you saying?' he asked; but she saw in his eyes that he already knew the answer, or some of it; enough, anyway.

'I'm saying we have to leave,' said Peggy, startled by the firmness in her voice. 'Now. Don't bother about the lights. Let's *go*.'

She picked up her purse and keys from the shelf where they lay, and moved to the door. She did not want to go out there, did not want to leave the cabin, and it was only with a tremendous effort of will that she put her hand on the knob and pulled open the wooden door, letting a bright trail of light stream out over the rocky ground. She thought she saw something move at the far end of it, something tall and thin, but she did not, *would not* look, concentrating instead on walking to the driver's door of the Jeep with her eyes on the ground, walking, not running, she would not run. . . .

'Hey!' Robert's voice rang out behind her, and she turned to see him still on the porch, looking, not towards the Jeep, but towards the paths. She followed his gaze, and in the faint light cast by a three-quarter moon could just see a figure standing silent, twenty yards or so from them.

'Jack!' cried Robert, relief flooding his voice. He stepped off the porch and moved towards the figure. 'Hey, man, you had us worried! Where've you been? What happened?'

Peggy felt a trickle of ice down her back. 'Robert—Robert, come here,' she called out, fear making her voice tremble. 'Come here now; we have to go.'

He stopped and looked back at her. 'Can't you see?' he said, puzzled. 'It's Jack!' He turned back to the figure. 'C'mon, come inside, get something to eat, tell us what happened. You hurt?'

'Robert!' Peggy's voice cracked like a gunshot. 'That isn't Jack. Can't you see? *It isn't Jack.*'

'What do you mean? Of course it is! C'mon over here, man, let Peggy take a look at you, you're frightening her. . . .'

All the time Robert had been moving closer to the figure, which remained motionless and silent. Suddenly, when he was only ten feet away from it, he stopped, and she heard him give a strangled cry.

'What the . . . what are you? What's going on?' Then, higher, broken, like a child, 'Peggy, what's happening?' He seemed frozen, and Peggy thought for a moment that she would have to go to him, pull him forcibly to the Jeep, and realised that she could not go any closer to that figure. A warning shot, if she had thought to bring the rifle, might have broken the spell, but it was back in the cabin . . . She wrenched open the driver's door and leaned on the horn with all her might.

The sound made her jump, even though she was expecting it, and the effect on Robert was galvanic. He turned and began moving towards the Jeep in a stumbling, shambling run; as he got closer she could hear him sobbing between breaths, ragged, gasping sobs, and she was glad that she had not been close enough to see the figure clearly.

She had dropped the keys twice from fingers that suddenly felt like dry twigs. Now, on the third try, she slammed the key into the ignition and turned it. Nothing. She turned it again. No response. She tried to turn on the headlights, but there was no answering flare of brightness. The battery was dead, and she realised, deep down in a corner of her mind, that she should have expected this.

Robert turned to her, eyes glittering with panic. 'C'mon, get it started, let's go! What are you waiting for?'

'The battery's dead.' Her chest was heaving as she tried to bite down the panic welling up inside her. Robert began to moan, a low, keening sound, as Peggy forced her mind back. *Think, think,* she told herself. *There's a way to do this, you know there is, you just have to calm down, remember. . . .*

Len's voice sounded in her ear, so clearly that for a moment she thought he was beside her. 'It's not difficult,' she heard him say, 'as long as it's a standard; automatics are trickier.' And she remembered; she had asked him, once, what they'd do if the battery went dead, up here with no other car for miles. 'We make sure the battery doesn't go dead,' he'd said with laugh, but when she pressed him—she was serious, it could happen, what would they *do?*—he had replied cheerfully, 'Not a problem; just put the clutch in, put it in second, let gravity start to work, let out the clutch, and there you go, easy-peasy. Make sure the ignition's on, and just keep driving for a bit; as long as the engine doesn't stop you'll charge the battery back up.'

She had no intention of stopping once she got the engine started.

She took a deep breath. The Jeep was parked on the flat, with the downward slope beginning twenty feet away. She would need help.

'Robert.' He was still moaning, looking out the passenger window, and

Peggy risked a look too. The figure seemed closer. 'Robert! Listen to me!' Nothing. She reached out and shook him, and he turned to her, his eyes wide and scared. She hoped he could hear her.

'You need to get out and push the car,' she said, slowly and clearly. He started to say something, and she cut him short. 'Just do it, Robert. Do it now.'

'I can't get out, I can't, I don't . . .'

'You have to. You can do this, Robert, but you have to hurry. Just to the top of the slope. Twenty feet; then you can get back in.'

For a moment she thought that he was going to refuse; then, without a word, he opened his door and half-fell, half-scrambled out. Peggy turned the ignition on, pushed in the clutch, put the Jeep in second, and they began to roll, slowly at first, then faster, Robert pushing with all his strength.

It seemed to take hours to cover the short distance; then Peggy felt the car start to pick up momentum, and Robert jumped in, slamming the passenger door. She said under her breath, 'Work, please, work,' and let out the clutch.

For one brief, terrible second she thought that it wasn't going to work, that she had done something wrong, missed something out. Then the engine shuddered into life, and she switched on the headlights, and they were through the gate and round the curve, and the cabin had disappeared behind them, along with everything else that was waiting in the darkness.

They did not speak during the drive to town. Peggy concentrated on the road with a fierceness that made her head ache, glad she had something to think about other than what they had left, while Robert sat huddled down in his seat. She did not ask him what he had seen, and he did not volunteer any information. The only thing she said, as they drew near the police station, was 'Keep to the facts. That's all they want to hear. Nothing else. Do you understand?' And Robert, pale, shaking, had nodded.

They told their story, for the first of several times, and answered questions, together and separately. Peggy did not know exactly what they asked Robert; she gathered, from some of the questions directed at her, that he was under suspicion, although in the end nothing came of this.

Officialdom swung into action, clearly following the procedures and guidelines laid out for just such a situation. Appeals for help were made; search parties were sent out; a spotter plane was employed. There were more questions, although no more answers. Peggy sometimes wondered where they would fit all the pieces she had not told them: eddies of dust and the ringing of chimes on a windless day, someone (not Buddy Holly) calling her name, the figure they had seen outside the cabin, the battery failures, the phone going dead. She imagined the response if she told the police that they should examine local Native legends and the vanishing of a prospector years earlier, or that she had felt that the hillside was watching her, or that Jack had not disappeared at all, he was still there, watching too, that he had only been looking after Robert.

All the searches came to nothing; no further traces of Jack were found. A casual question to one of the volunteers elicited the information that the phone in the cabin was working perfectly. Peggy herself did not go back; no one expected a sixty-three year old woman to participate in the search, and everyone told her they understood why she preferred to stay in a hotel in town. They did not understand, of course, not at all, but Peggy did not try to explain.

Paul came up as soon as he could. He, too, was very understanding, although he was surprised at his aunt's decision to put the property on the market immediately. She was welcome to stay with him and the family for as long as she needed to, that went without saying; but wasn't she being a bit hasty? Yes, it had been a terrible, tragic event, but perhaps she should wait a bit, hold off making a decision . . . she didn't want to do something she would regret. . . .

But Peggy was insistent. If Paul would go with her while she collected some clothing and personal items, she would be grateful; she would arrange with a moving company for everything else to be packed up and put into storage until she had found somewhere to live. She had clearly made up her mind, and although he did not agree with her, Paul did not argue the point any further.

They went up early in the morning, the first day after the search had been called off. Peggy worked quickly, packing up the things she wanted to take with her, while Paul cleared out the food from the fridge and cupboards. When everything had been loaded into his SUV, he went round the cabin, making sure that everything was shut off and locked up, while Peggy waited outside.

Now, in the daylight, with the sun high overhead and birds wheeling against the blue of the sky, everything looked peaceful. A gentle wind ruffled the branches of the trees, and a piece of paper fluttered along—left by one of the searchers, no doubt. It blew across the grass, and landed in the middle of one of the pathways. Out of habit, she walked over to where it lay, picked it up, and put it in her pocket.

She looked up at the hills above her, then back at the cabin, realising that this was the same spot where she had seen . . . or thought she had seen . . . Jack on the afternoon he had disappeared. She shivered slightly, even though the day was hot, and started towards the SUV, anxious to be gone.

It was as she moved away that she saw it, a glint of something metallic at the edge of the path near her foot. She bent down and picked it up. A Swiss Army watch, silver. Although she knew what she would find, she looked at the face. The hands showed ten past five.

When Paul came out and locked the front door, his aunt was already in the SUV. She did not look back as they drove away.

Out On a Limb

Gary McMahon

'Most madness is overactive curiosity.'
Peter Mullan

MAWSON KICKED AN EMPTY DRINK CAN, sending it spinning in a flash of primary colour across the rocky ground. The sound it made was tinny and lonely in the morose northern landscape, and he pulled his fleece tighter around his lithe torso to keep out an imagined chill. He walked back over the scraggly, uneven ground to the hired four-wheel-drive, and took a pen and spiral-bound notepad from the cluttered glove compartment, then locked up the vehicle and turned to face the imposing presence that was the Daleside Institute.

The building glowered at him from beneath jutting eaves, its multi-paned windows watching without pity from deep shadow and refracting the pale daylight in sparks across the distance between them. If a structure could have a personality, then this was it; the place squatted like a huge spider upon densely packed layers of a past that some believed best forgotten.

Lighting up a cigarette, Mawson stared back at those leering windows, wondering what had really gone on behind the dirt-crusted glass; what horrors had been absorbed into the fabric of the structure, and passed down through deep foundations into the cold and uncaring earth.

His boss, McIntosh, had sent him here on what Mawson considered a fool's errand: to inspect a location for some lowbrow, low-budget British horror film that would no doubt languish unseen on video-store shelves for years, and file a report first thing Monday morning. According to McIntosh, it was another rung on the long ladder of success in the film industry, but as usual Mawson simply felt exploited. Sent packing on some crappy trip in the middle of the freezing northeast countryside, while the overbearing sweaty Scot manhandled his teenage secretary all weekend in a country hotel in Bedfordshire.

He approached the wrought iron gates and stamped out his cigarette with the heel of a brand new walking boot, feeling thirsty and pissed off. The last petrol station he'd passed had been about an hour ago, and he'd forgotten to buy bottled water; his throat felt like wool and he couldn't even gather any spit in his mouth. Popping a Wrigley's between chapped lips, he attempted to chew some moisture onto his swollen tongue. This harsh country climate was wreaking havoc with his insipid city-boy system, and all he wanted was to be back among the polluted by-products of his natural urban habitat.

The trees behind and to the left of him rustled and whispered like old women gossiping over a garden fence, as if commenting upon his thoughts; birds shrieked and wheeled in the murky air far above, oblivious of his passing beneath.

The Daleside was an old private asylum that had been closed down by the local health authorities in 1982. There had been hastily quashed talk of ritual abuse, funds siphoned off by the then owners, and various other bad deeds carried out since the place had first opened in the late 1800s. The current crop of patients had been placed in council-run halfway houses immediately after the closure, and then jettisoned off into an uncaring community. For years afterwards, the odd ex-patient would make his way back here, over the miles of bleak Northumbrian countryside, and wait outside the gates to be let in.

Back in 1990, a crew of builders who had been called in to demolish an unstable part of the ageing structure had found a bedraggled old man dressed in shredded newspapers, plastic carrier bags, and dirty strips of cardboard. The man had been so far gone that even decades of therapy would not have been able to summon him back; he'd lived for months in the crumbly cavities between the walls and beneath the wooden floors, talking to the dust and the rubble, eating rats and drinking stale standing water from potholes in the concrete basement floor.

Mawson had read all of this in the impressively detailed fact sheet provided by Hummingbird Productions, the group who employed him as a lowly factotum and who were supervising production of the film. They had carried out a desk study on the Daleside, and decided in their infinite wisdom that its air of crumbling institutionalism would be ideally suited to one or two key scare scenes that featured in the script. Plus, as an added bonus, they could shoot here for a nominal fee, as the council now owned the land and didn't seem to care what happened to it.

Mawson was way out of his depth up here in the sticks. He was a South London boy, born and bred, and the sight of any greenery other than the salad on his donner kebab come Friday night made him uneasy. He much preferred the relative safety and comfort of graffitied concrete flyovers, piss-stinking high-rise stairwells, and densely trafficked main streets. All this silence and tranquillity left him feeling stranded, with nowhere to retreat but within the profound emptiness of himself. Being alone in an alien environment unsettled him, forced him to confront his inadequacies; he was far more comfortable with the raucous and shallow banter of a large crowd.

Empty noise and sweeping gestures were Mawson's barriers, and without them he realised that there was not much more to him than the façade. He was unable to keep a girlfriend for longer than a few weeks, during which time his lack of any real depth bored them; friendship was a concept that eluded him, and he mixed only with social acquaintances and workmates. Indeed, whenever he was alone, he tended to feel swallowed up by loneliness, and always sought out the company of strangers to keep whatever gulf sat deep inside filled up with the banal.

A long time ago he had come to understand, and even accept, that there was simply nothing at his core; the centre of his being was bereft of anything even resembling a real personality, and he had tailored his lifestyle to suit. Sometimes, when he sat in the quiet darkness of his room in Brixton, he felt barely there at all: a mere memory of a person, a ghost. If he sat long enough, and still enough, he often imagined that he might just disappear altogether, fading like the image in a photograph left out in the sun.

Pushing shut the crooked, knock-kneed gates after him, he walked towards the imposing building. Its gable roofs and huge ground floor bay windows seemed to inspect him as he neared, waiting for him to make a move. He jotted the sensation down in his notebook, as he'd been requested to do; his report was to include all feelings evoked by the site, and any unusual features he found there.

Grey clouds scuttled overhead through a steely sky, the ceiling of which seemed to Mawson to be lowering towards him like the bottom of a huge lift down its shaft. Hazy sunlight did nothing but peek through those dense clouds, barely registering any heat on his skin. The daylight was murky, with a strange texture; shadows were flattened and the stark scenery around him seemed two-dimensional, like a painted matte shot in an old Hollywood film.

His lips seemed to dehydrate even further, stretching the sensitive flesh far too tight across his teeth. He was aware of the heavy gates behind him, and of the car beyond that. If for any reason he had to run for the vehicle, those sagging gates might prove an awkward obstacle to overcome, and he wished that he'd left them gaping wide.

The weak sun dipped down below roof level of the huge red-brick building as Mawson stepped feebly into its shadow. He felt as though he was being consumed by the darkness of the place, swallowed in some cavernous and depthless maw to be stored and then digested at a later date. The vague echoes of insane screams seemed to live in that darkness: held forever within the bricks and mortar by the bonds of past atrocities.

He jotted this latest conceit in his pad, scribbling quickly so as not to avert his gaze from the hunched features of the Daleside for too long. He didn't trust the place, and was acutely aware of how stupid his reaction was. But still, he kept his eyes upon the worn brick and warped timber edifice that towered before him like a living thing.

The weathered front door sat atop a short set of thick stone steps. Mawson had the key in his pocket, but felt wary of using it; it would be too familiar, too *habitual*. Besides, what if another crazed ex-inmate, by now well into his old age, was hiding in the shadows, monitoring him through those high, white-painted windows? He had told McIntosh that he didn't want to come here alone, but the big Scot had laughed off Mawson's concerns, calling him a soft southern sissy and ordering him out of the office, a fat finger pointed towards the shining glass door. Fat Highland swine! He was probably having his way with that cute little secretary by now, his big red outdoorsy face blowing up like a balloon in the throes of illicit passion. The man was everything that Mawson was not—gregarious, jovial, successful, *vital*—and on countless occasions he had shamelessly and passionately wished the Scotsman dead.

Mawson took out the large key, slipped it into the rust-red lock, and turned with both hands. There was a loud grating sound as the dormant mechanism was forced into life and the key eventually twisted in his grip. The door swung open as he shoved it with his shoulder, feeling stronger than he was and thirstier still as dust billowed out and around him, coating both the steps and the inside of his mouth. Into a fist he coughed up stringy clumps of something unpleasant; it stained his palm charcoal, and he squinted through the doorway into the misty dark.

Peering into the dim corridor that lay ahead like an invitation to uncertainty, he saw that the interior of the Daleside was in quite good repair; dirty, yes, but at least as safe as the county surveyor had promised him. He stepped inside, closing out the wan sunlight, and gathered his thoughts on the gloomy threshold.

The main entrance corridor had a large curved reception desk set against the wall off to his left; this led onto a wide staircase. There were two doors at the end, flanking the foot of the stairs. One of these wings led to a cavernous main hall, and the other to several consulting rooms, and, eventually, the basement level. The county surveyor had furnished him with a copy of the architectural plans, which he had studied over too-hot coffee and a stale pastry in a Little Chef near York. The Daleside had two wings (west and east) and four levels: the top two floors had been the patients' quarters, the ground floor lay spread out before him, cloaked in terminal twilight, and the basement crouched unseen in its own dark spaces below.

But the basement didn't interest him, not today. If the location looked promising, he would return with a team of technicians from Hummingbird Productions, and carry out a secondary scout. He pushed an admission of fear as far back in his mind as he could, refusing it entrance to his conscious thoughts, keeping it chained in the back brain, where such things belong. The basement had been where a lot of the alleged abuse had taken place. He knew that there were worn leather restraint straps and cramped concrete holding cells beneath his feet.

There was one particular horror story in his notes relating to the rumour that certain unreachable patients had been kept down in that basement for years, repeatedly subjected to arcane mediaeval-style torture devices that had been designed specifically for stretching limbs and for distorting bone and sinew into obscene and unnatural shapes; creating bodies that matched the warped minds they contained, and moulding them like so much clay. These poor deliberately deformed souls were then kept as pets, led around on dog leads, fed from bowls, taught tricks. Staff members and favoured patients would bury them in the grounds when they eventually died from their physical infirmities, and then select replacements from those whose minds were shattered so badly there was little chance of recovery.

The door creaked behind him, and he spun on his heels to confront the settling dust. The timber repeated the sound, and seemed to bulge infinitesimally in its frame: old materials expanding and contracting with the weather and temperature changes, nothing more. The door hadn't bulged at all; his heightened state of awareness had induced an optical illusion. Or this had been the result of some kind of MDMA residue that continued to spark in his neurons, a legacy of too many nights wasted in the capital's gaudy and vapid clubland, losing in the depths of chemical oblivion what little of him there was.

Turning back to the yawning staircase, he quickly ran through a mental itinerary: *Check out the main hall, then pop upstairs for a peek into some of the old patients' rooms, and back in the car before the sun starts to set. Right as rain; fine as wine; sorted.*

The thick screed of dust on the uneven patched floor parted before him like shallow water, leaving a trail. As he approached the reception desk, he didn't actually see something pale, thin, and twitching flop down behind the counter: just another illusion summoned by his highly-strung condition. *Calm down. Nothing to see here.* Bending at the waist, he strained over the filthy stained counter, airborne dust clogging his nostrils with the parched bland odours of decay and disuse. Nothing moved on the floor but insects: a line of cockroaches marching into a fungus-rimmed hole in the splintered skirting. As he raised his head, he was only barely aware of a similar skittering movement behind, moving away through the doorway that led to the basement.

Stop it! For fuck's sake, you haven't even seen the script yet, and this damn stupid horror flick is getting to you.

Back in the darkest of dark days of the Daleside's history, those hideous torture devices had been built, maintained, and utilised by the most infamous head of the institute, a Doctor Quill. The man had obviously been as insane as his charges, but his reign of enforced brutality and man-made deformity had lasted for two decades. In the end, before the credits rolled on his personal footnote in the history of this museum of human misery, the man's own private grotesquery had murdered him. Its members had fallen upon him in numbers, dragging his struggling body down to the hated basement level, and strapping him into his own infernal machines of bodily manipulation.

Breathing deeply, Mawson moved on. He thought of what that bully McIntosh's hysterical reaction would be when he returned to London after being scared off by his own bloody shadow. *Southern pansy. Big girl's blouse.* That mocking Scottish lilt and those accusing blue eyes beneath bushy black brows. God, how he hated the man. No. He was going to finish this. It was still daylight, and there was nothing to be afraid of but the past and the depths of his own emptiness.

Those builders had gutted the main hall thirteen years before, and all that remained of the vast room were the original timber floor and gaping holes and gouges in the walls where fittings had been ripped out to expose the skeleton of construction beneath. Splintered timber laths and fluffy explosions of insulation spewed from the rents in the fabric of the room, showing that the job had been left half done. Nobody seemed to know when the project would resume, and Mawson guessed that the local councillors didn't have a clue what to do with the place, brushing it under the carpet of bureaucracy in case the taxpayers started asking questions.

He scribbled a few comments in his pad, having recalled that he still held it, and then walked through the sprawling expanse of the hall towards the kitchens. Weak sunlight shone in thin diagonal lines through the smeared windows, refracting like lasers in the dusty air. There were faded footprints beneath the layer of virgin dust on the floor; faint evidence of feet that had walked here years ago, the last time anyone had entered the Daleside. The sight emphasised the fact that Mawson was alone, and he determined not to look. Even when some of the footprints seemed misshapen, as if the feet that had made them were malformed or twisted in some way.

The kitchens were huge and silent and foreboding, barely able to hold the memory of the clattering of pots and pans across the years. The workbenches were thick with old grease, and the ovens were huge and black, sitting low to the ground, like stocky, waiting figures. Mawson noted this in his pad, and walked quickly away, not even bothering to enter the deeply shadowed room.

When he returned to the foot of the stairs he felt that he had just missed someone climbing them. There were no fresh footprints on the dusty grey carpet, but there was a sense of something having just passed. A shadow flickered lambently at the half-landing, as if disappearing upwards to lose itself on the floors above. His badly chapped lips were now beginning to crack due to the dry air, and when he pursed them blood began to flow from his cupid's bow.

'Shit!' he said, and his echo bounced back at him far quicker than it should have, as if someone had repeated the word an instant after he'd said it. He refused to accept that he heard muted giggling from above as he put a foot on the first tread of the stair.

Something scurried across bare boards directly above his head—a rat, or yet more insects busily going about their business. Gritting his teeth to calm his overheated imaginings, he pushed on up the throat of the staircase, dismissing the sense of something small, bloated, and far too low to the ground following. As he turned the corner on to the half-landing, he again believed that he'd glimpsed something turn the corner ahead. When he reached the spot, he was upon the first floor landing, and was certain that there couldn't have been a crumpled, absurdly skinny figure standing there a second earlier, slowly pistoning spindly arms and legs.

Thick panelled doors stretched ahead of him on each side of the wide landing, and he knew that he'd have too look into at least one of them, if only to prove McIntosh wrong and to quieten the stir of echoes at his own core. He approached the first with trepidation, feeling watched and mocked and strangely welcomed. His hand jerked towards the handle, and something brushed against the door from the other side. The sound was like a scattering of tiny steel balls, or a skittering of plastic straws across a smooth, hard floor. Then he felt a long, abnormally slender hand press down on to his shoulder, and his legs and arms began to spasm. A mad voice whispered harshly into his ear, telling him of beatings and rapes and fabricated deformities, calling to something deep inside him that stirred and strained to respond from the aching void at his centre. At the periphery of his vision, from each end of the long landing, low-set figures with elongated extremities advanced on all fours through the shuddering of shadows and dust.

He closed his eyes and pushed backwards from the door, feeling an authoritative presence step away from him and hearing that same hushed voice murmur '*Fetch*' in sibilant tones. Without seeing, he ran for where he hoped the stairs would be, feeling rubbery hands and chitinous nails on his body and in his hair. Swallowing the scream that bulged in his throat, and ignoring the mad urge to turn and join whatever chased him, he stumbled onwards. Eyes still squeezed tightly shut against the churning dust and whatever else capered down with him like excited house pets, he bumped into peeling walls, tripped on the moth-eaten stair carpet, and headed down to the front door. Deformed and stunted figures ran at his side, jostling and ululating child-like songs of torment and anguish.

When at last he reached the door, he somehow managed to fumble it open. Other clumsy hands with overlong fingers flopped against his own, their touch like that of something that has spent far too long underwater. And those songs continued, keened by the weak and the wounded: grim nursery rhyme tunes of despair and anguish, of shame and regret. He resisted the urge to sing with them, thankful for the dust in his throat and the scabs that broke on his lips when he tried to join their cacophony.

Then he was out in the pale sunlight, and at last he allowed his eyes to open. In the sudden glare, as he turned to face the Daleside, he saw many evanescent forms with all too human faces tumbling and rolling in the hallway, gibbering silently and twitching their abnormally protracted appendages; vague, crab-like beings with screaming mouths and empty eyes, apparitions that were held together by the glue of dust and a yearning to be joined by another. Then the door closed slowly, blocking out whatever pathetic spectres performed hopelessly for his attention.

Running to the gate without pausing for breath, Mawson felt the Daleside flex like a muscle behind him, straining and shifting with the effort of restraining all that mad darkness within. He managed to tear open the gates, cringing at the baleful whine of rusty hinges that reminded him of another more tragic sound, and slammed himself against the bonnet of the car. His notebook was gone, lost in the mêlée, but he could buy a new one on the motorway and write down whatever the hell it would take to keep people far away from here.

His shaking hands located the car keys and unlocked the door. He sat behind the wheel and gunned the powerful engine, feeling a blind insanity leaking from between the bricks of the Daleside, questing for a way into the creases of his mind. Reversing down the hill, he knocked over a small barbed wire fence and a signpost saying 'KEEP OUT. DERELICT BUILDING', then almost careered off the road and into a ditch as he headed back the way he'd come.

Soon after that he joined the darkening motorway. And, finally able to get a grip on himself, he waited for whatever sat on the back seat to finish unfolding its painfully long limbs and reach for him, then lead him singing into the empty rooms of himself.

Jenny Gray's House

Edward Pearce

MY EXPERIENCE OF THE SUPERNATURAL? I don't suppose you'll believe it. Being a sceptic no longer, I realise that trying to convince others of the reality of such events is a waste of time. If you'd told me this story instead of vice versa, I don't doubt I would have found it genuinely interesting, but it's highly unlikely I'd have believed you.

There were two of us involved, but whilst we both had inexplicable experiences, we did not feel, hear, or see the same thing at the same time, which might be said to make us less than perfect witnesses. Michael had already been under stress for some time, and you could argue that this, overwork, and auto-suggestion are sufficient explanation on his part. The things that happened to me could be explained away in similar fashion; I'd allowed myself to get drawn in, been influenced by the atmosphere he'd unknowingly created, and undergone sympathetic hallucinations of my own.

I can appreciate that viewpoint, and so I don't talk about this very often, as I don't especially enjoy people doubting my mental balance, even if the kindest of motives are involved. Anyway, you can take it or leave it, I don't mind which. All I can do is pass on the story as it unfolded itself to me. It began with an e-mail:

> Dear Tom,
> Hello, how are you? Sorry to have been so lax about keeping in contact. I've been working hard at getting this place fit to live in, plus my regular work went through a hectic phase recently and time flew past without my noticing it.
>
> Do you fancy some country air? Round here is about as away from it all as you can get in middle England. It feels as though time has bypassed the place, which has both good and bad points. But if you want a break

from city life, I can recommend it. Besides, it must be a good two years since we last got together, which seems far too long.

I manage my work to suit myself, so can fit in with you easily enough. If you feel like coming up, your company would be greatly appreciated, for one reason and another which I won't trouble you with now.

I've been out and about a lot recently and the phone often doesn't get answered. No need to call—just mail to say when you're coming and I'll be ready. It's quite civilised here, and you can stay as long or as short as you like.

I hope all's well and you're continuing to enjoy a life of comfort. Once again, apologies for not being in touch for so long, but I have been meaning to for quite a while and have finally got round to it.

All the best, and I hope to see you soon.
Michael

It was nearer three years since we'd last met, and a good year since I'd heard anything from Michael. At school he'd been intellectual, rather intense, and somewhat apart from the crowd. He was fascinated by England's social history, customs, and folklore and had accumulated a good deal of knowledge on these matters. This and his intelligence and dry humour made him a good companion, and there was always something to talk about besides the world's immediate concerns. Over the years we'd stayed sporadically in touch, through university, careers, and marriages, and it had been an enduring friendship rather than a really close one. Then out of the blue Michael got divorced, which seemed to throw his life out of gear, and he became quite reclusive for a while. His occupation as a freelance technical author made that all too easy.

After a time he got back to something like his former self, but the experience had marked him, and on the increasingly rare occasions we met I noticed a worrying tendency to withdrawal. Then he left London for East Anglia, where he bought an old house on the edge of a village in the fen country.

Perhaps Michael was just being sociable, but it was a bit odd hearing from him out of the blue like this. The 'casual' wording of 'one reason and another' seemed to indicate a delicate matter to be discussed. Anyway, I was glad of the chance to see him again, and a break from London life appealed to me.

It wasn't difficult to arrange a day or two off work, and Anne, my wife, raised no objections. Thus it was that I was able to let my friend know I would be arriving shortly and, on a hot, bright day soon after this, I drove up to see him.

Michael lived about half an hour from Cambridge down the back country roads. This was my first visit to his new home, and I had no idea what to expect other than that he was renovating an old house on the edge of a fenland village. The journey from the end of the motorway was not difficult, and the roads were comparatively empty—as I believe they generally are thereabouts—giving me leisure to take in a landscape which varied little for mile upon mile. Flat fields as far as the eye could see, few hedges or trees, long straight stretches of road, drainage canals large and small, and a big, wide horizon conveying an unusual sense of space were its dominating features. Here and there an island or ridge rose above the surrounding landscape.

Upper Marwell, where Michael lived, was centred round a crossroads with a pub, a single small shop selling the bare necessities, and an undistinguished-looking church. The houses were the usual mix for those parts: modern bungalows, dull inter-war cottages, Victorian villas, and some much older ones. Following Michael's directions, I came to a driveway between tall conifers and at the end found a typical plastered East Anglian cottage, with a low profile and windows in the roof, of the seventeenth or eighteenth century, I thought. I parked up and walked over the gravel to the old grey oak front door.

It was opened by my friend, who was his same old casual, slightly untidy self. He seemed genuinely pleased to see me, and the warmth and normality of his welcome set my mind at rest somewhat. We shook hands and said the things you do, then I followed him through a narrow passageway into the front room. 'Oh yes, this is nice!' I instinctively exclaimed, and indeed it was. Old wooden beams jutted across the ceiling. There was a large fireplace lined with ancient stone. On the back wall was a tall, glass-fronted Victorian bookcase with a couple of smaller ones adjoining it. These would, I knew, be packed with volumes on a remarkable range of subjects, my friend being an avid reader who enjoyed knowledge for its own sake, the more obscure the better. I felt confident that he would already be digging into the history of this area.

A comfortable-looking sofa and a couple of old leather-covered armchairs, a corner cupboard, a chest of drawers, and a small table completed the furnishings. Pictures and small antiques were dotted about the room and an Oriental rug covered the red-tiled floor. It would have been hard to find a better embodiment of the small country retreat.

Michael smiled. 'Glad you like it! I'm quite pleased too, even if it did drain off a lot of my money and effort. Take a seat and I'll do some tea. I presume you want some, after that journey?' I did. I sat in an armchair and surveyed the room while Michael busied himself in the kitchen.

Later, he showed me round the house, with its numerous interesting and original features, and pointed out the results of renovations, work still in progress, and other things that needed doing. 'Fortunately they don't go in much for cellars round here. One thing the place doesn't have is damp, which seems a minor miracle for a cottage in the Fens.'

After seeing the house, I had to agree that everything was as it should be— Michael had always been a perfectionist for that sort of thing—and the overall effect was impressive. But I found myself qualifying my initial impression. There was something that jarred with me ever so slightly. I could find no reasonable grounds for this, but there it was. And I wasn't sure if he was right about there being no damp, either, as there seemed to be something of a musty undertone, though so faint I couldn't be certain. However, I kept these thoughts to myself.

Having shown me round, Michael suggested a stroll. 'That'll clear your head, and it's quite pleasant around the fields at the back.' After changing into stouter shoes we stepped out through the back door.

Behind the house was a neat, wide lawn. This led down to a stream running straight across the end of the garden. No doubt it was really only a drainage ditch, but the effect was very appealing. Michael pointed out where it had once been re-routed through a culvert, rejoining its original course after a few feet. 'That's very old work. Perhaps it went around something that's gone and nobody bothered to route it back. So I dug it out myself the other week, filled in the diversion, and there you are. I was a bit worried that some unsuspected problem might recur, but it seems fine. They went to quite a bit of trouble over it. Take a look.'

We walked over the stream by a grassy crossing and on a few yards to the left. The scars of the old channel were clearly visible, and there was a little hollow at each end of the now-isolated culvert. 'It's lined with brick inside, made to last,' he said, 'and look at those stones at the end.' In the nearer of the two hollows, the culvert was finished with a small dressed stone arch, consisting of two stones and a keystone, into which a plain cross was neatly cut. It was simple, but beautifully crafted, and clearly made to fit *in situ*. Michael echoed my thoughts: 'That obviously isn't reused masonry, and it's been done so nicely that it seemed wrong just to bury it. The other one's the same.'

We passed through the garden and onto a little track that curved around hedge and stubby trees and joined the edge of a vast field, from which a crop of wheat had recently been harvested. We walked slowly round the edge, relaxing as we did so into a conversation that might have been broken off last week, so easy was it to resume.

Did I say relaxing? Not quite, because though my friend was doing his best to hide it, I was aware that he was uneasy. I didn't ask why. There are rituals to be observed, and levels of conversation to be gone through, even with a close friend. I was beginning to be very curious, but I am a patient person and I knew I would find out in due course what the matter was, so I just left him to pick the right moment.

Passing orchard and then more farmland on our left, we eventually came to a corner of the field, and I turned to take in the view. We had come quite some distance from the house, which was now out of sight. A far-off, untidy row of hedge, trees, and rooftops marked the road along which the village lay.

The day had started off hot and was now scorching. The air shimmered, and the faraway line of the village seemed to waver. Then I saw that Michael was standing absolutely motionless and staring across the field, or perhaps into the middle of it. He seemed about to speak, checked himself, and then, somewhat abruptly and with what seemed an effort, walked on. There was nothing to be seen in the field or beyond it.

I pretended not to have noticed this, and shortly the conversation returned to its former ease. The walk took us back to the house via a circuitous route of allotments and more field and orchard.

The rest of the day was spent as you might expect of old friends meeting after a long break. After something to eat, a look around the village was called for, and here Michael's leaning towards antiquarian pursuits and local history was evident. I was surprised by how much he'd found out about the history of the village and the individual houses in it. In this way, we reached the village pub. Like so many others in the Fens, it promised more olde worlde character on the outside than it delivered when you got in, but was comfortable and hospitable enough. A couple of drinks later and it was as if the years had rolled back, and so the rest of the evening passed. Gradually I heard from my friend about how his marriage had gone wrong, the divorce, and his desire to start again in new surroundings. He still felt the after-effects deeply, but had determined to put it all behind him.

We returned to the house, sat around talking, and at a late hour retired to our respective rooms. I was tired out and slept soundly all night.

The following morning I drove out alone to look around the nearby market town, Wakeford, which had a slightly doleful atmosphere but possessed a remarkable number of attractive Georgian houses and a delightful museum. The houses brought to mind Michael's revelations of the previous day about those in the village, and then it struck me that he hadn't said anything about his own. After dinner that evening, sitting in the front room, I asked about the cottage.

'Yes, it's quite interesting'—this in a tone indicating the beginning of a story. 'It's from about seventeen hundred, and apart from one or two minor things, plus I've upgraded the kitchen, it's pretty much original.' Here he stopped again, and I asked if he knew anything about its previous occupants. 'Yes . . .' he hesitated, then went on purposefully. 'In the village it's known as Jenny Gray's House. It's a local story that a venomous old woman of that name once lived here. Of course they supposed she was a witch, and she certainly sounds like someone you'd prefer not to meet. She was said to be able to stare people to death. I've heard of witches' powers, but that was a new one on me. Apparently she disappeared one day when the villagers ganged up on her. No one seems to know exactly what happened, but she certainly was a real person and she's not buried in the churchyard.'

Michael stopped and gazed abstractedly through the window, where the late sun was casting a beautiful red-gold glow over the front garden.

'How did you find out about this?'

'After I'd been to The Kings Arms a couple of times people started talking to me. That's how I heard about the old woman. They also say she used to be seen in the area, all in black and with a horrible face of evil. I might have thought twice about buying the house if I'd known that, but I didn't, and anyway she hadn't been seen by anyone in living memory.'

'You say she was a real person. It sounds as if you've done some research of your own.'

He laughed tersely. 'With a story like that, even the dullest house-buyer would be interested. And you know what I'm like: a bit of historical detective work and I'm hooked. So I decided to find out what I could. When you went in the museum today you might have noticed the reference room. It's usual nowadays for local records to go to the county office, and I think most of them have, but they've got a very big collection of paperwork, and I suppose it's a question of space, so some of it's here.

'I had to convince the woman there that I had a bona fide interest in local history and wouldn't mishandle the papers or walk off with them, but I think she was pleased someone was taking an interest. After a couple of visits she just left me alone, which was like leaving a boy in a toyshop.

'The papers about Upper Marwell are the usual stuff except for one particular manuscript. Some Victorian gentleman decided to write a history of the village, and not only did he collect a lot of local lore and tales that would otherwise have been lost, but he seems to have had access to the papers and diaries of various private individuals. Very few of those are in the archive, and I suppose most of them are lost.

'I read it all through in the next few weeks, and apart from my own house, there was a whole lot about the others in the village, which is where I got those facts I bored you with yesterday.' I made a show of demurring which Michael brushed aside. 'Obviously it was my house I really wanted to know about. The compiler—sadly, he didn't put his name on the manuscript—quoted at some length from the diary of the vicar here in 1722, which is when the business I'm interested in took place. Unfortunately I couldn't photocopy the manuscript as it's a bit delicate, so I had to copy everything in longhand and transcribe it. Here it is.'

He went over to the tall bookcase, took some sheets of typescript from a drawer, and passed them to me. With a feeling of anticipation that was not altogether comfortable, I began reading. The account was as follows:

> Jenny Gray, an old woman who lived in a house at the eastern end of the village, was believed by the villagers to be a witch, and was rumoured to have been killed by a mob of them. The story appears to be partially, perhaps wholly, true. According to the Reverend Mr Anderson's diary, on the 22nd of June, 1722, an attempt was made to arraign her at the county court on a charge of witchcraft. Public opinion had shifted somewhat in recent decades, the last conviction in England having been achieved some years before and then without sentence of execution. It is, perhaps, unsurprising that the case was thrown out of court.
>
> Jenny Gray was disliked in Upper Marwell. She kept her own counsel, and when she did appear in public, which was seldom, regarded the other villagers with an expression of malignancy. The offence for which they had wished to see her tried was that of casting the evil eye upon a certain John

Parker, who had a dispute with her over some matter of boundary fences. Parker told his family and friends one day that Jenny Gray had stared him full in the face as he passed her house, with an expression of such wickedness as to force him there and then to stop walking and rest, with the sensation of having been struck to the heart, as he put it, at which Jenny Gray turned and went back into her house. Parker went home with a growing weakness and sense of injury, and the following day was unable to rise from his bed. Three days later he died, seemingly of heart failure, but local feeling was that Jenny Gray was responsible.

The Reverend Mr Anderson touches on some tales current in the village about this woman. She had no relatives in the area, arriving a few years previously from no one knew where; the house she occupied was made over to her in settlement of some questionable debt; she was wealthy, though no one knew how she came by her money; then again, she was a blackmailer, buying evidence of scandals from wicked persons and managing this information for her own ends; she was of a spiteful and unforgiving nature and never had a good word for anyone; she may even have committed murder at some time. After the dismissal of the case against her, Jenny Gray was seen to turn a vindictive stare on the principal witness against her, who shortly afterwards was taken ill, though with no lasting effects as it turned out. He was in any case a stout and ill-conditioned man, and it was a hot day.

There were stories of a gathering in the village that evening and of shuttered windows and a procession with burning torches down the village street. Mr Anderson was not present, having been called away, and laments his inability to stop what he was convinced was murder. Jenny Gray was not seen alive after that evening and her house was ransacked. The matter was looked into by a commission of enquiry from Wakeford, but silence within the village appears to have been complete, so that the truth may never be known, although we can perhaps guess at it.

Shortly thereafter, stories began that a terrifying apparition of Jenny Gray was being seen in the vicinity of her old home, which remained empty for some time after this. It was thought by the villagers that her spirit was intent upon revenge, and some action was taken by them, Mr Anderson notes, whereupon the stories ceased. The reverend gentleman indulges in one or two speculations as to how the ghost was 'laid', which I need not repeat here. Legend has it that Jenny Gray is still seen occasionally in these parts, usually in hot weather.

I looked up at Michael, who was watching for my reaction. 'How interesting,' I said. 'It's a bit specific to be pure hearsay, especially from the vicar, who was probably the best-educated man in the village in those days. I'm not entirely surprised at the story of the ghost—typical local superstition—though the business about hot weather is intriguing.'

'So you'd dismiss it as superstition?' asked Michael.

'Wouldn't you? Okay, personally I've never encountered anything supernatural, but I try to keep an open mind. Maybe something really is going on around us that we don't see, and now and again it breaks through and no one knows why. After all, how long ago did we find out about infra-red and ultraviolet? Perhaps ghosts do exist, but I reserve judgement, though I'd very much like to see one and make up my own mind.'

'Would you really want to?' asked Michael.

'Yes, I think so. If it was several hundred yards off in broad daylight and didn't come any closer, then I imagine I could cope with it. After all, how frightening could that be?'

He shuddered. 'Take it from me, you do not want that to happen. You have no idea of the effect it would have on you.'

Clearly this was the moment for it to come out into the open, whatever 'it' might be. 'Look, Mike,' I said, 'why don't you tell me what's bothering you? You obviously want to talk it over, and I promise I won't laugh at you. I can't promise not to be sceptical, but I can listen in a spirit of openness, and talking it out could make things clearer. Besides, two heads are better than one.'

Michael seemed both relieved and resigned. 'Yes,' he said, 'I *have* been wanting to tell you ever since you got here, but I wasn't sure how you'd take it. All right, here it is.

'It started a week or two back. I'd been working hard on the house, and my ordinary work had to be done too. I was pretty tired and this particular day I overdid it. I spent the morning flat out on an assignment, then I finished my work on the stream, and I ended up doing some painting in the house. I was busy from early in the morning till about eight at night, and it was hard concentrating followed by hard labour. I was just about clapped out—I had that light-headed, empty feeling you get after a long exertion when it's all a bit of an anticlimax. I didn't feel in the mood for watching TV, or going down the pub, and I was too tired to read. I felt a sort of revulsion for the house, and I had a "What am I doing out here by myself in the middle of nowhere? and what on Earth is the point of all this—of anything?" feeling. I was pretty low, and I just slumped in that chair'—he gestured at the one I was sitting in—'not thinking about anything very much, and I dozed off.

'I think I went into deep sleep quite quickly. You know when you wake up and then go off to sleep again—if you dream then, it's especially vivid. Well, this one was like that. I was reading an old leather book, and I knew there was something in it that was important to me, but I just couldn't see the text properly. It was in old fashioned handwriting, which always seemed to blur or turn into nonsense. I was trying and trying to make it out, and all the time I had this horrible mounting sense that if I couldn't then I was in real trouble. And then the anxiety grew into a massive surge like a tidal wave out of nowhere, and that's when I woke up with this awful start and found I was sitting bolt upright with my hands clenched, my mouth open, and sweat on my forehead. And my head was echoing with this tremendous bang, which sounded really close by. And then I got a shock, because when I'd sat down it was twilight outside, but when I woke up it was a quarter past one, and I thought I'd only been asleep a few minutes. I got up in a state close to panic and looked all round the house to see what the bang was, but I couldn't find anything, and I supposed I must have imagined it, or it was part of my dream.

'I was in no mood to go to bed. So I made tea with whisky and sat up in here, trying to read a book and take my mind off that horrible dream. I couldn't focus on the book at all, and I tried watching TV, but it jarred so much I had to turn it off. So I just sat, pretending to myself I was reading my book, and I sort of drifted off eventually.

'I'm not sure if I was asleep or not, but I thought I heard scratching sounds during the night, as if rats had got into the house. And I seemed to hear whispering, too, but next morning I wasn't sure about that. Anyway, I spent a miserable night, and I woke up about six-thirty in that chair, feeling bloody awful and with a stiff neck. I looked all round the house and I was quite certain there weren't any rats or mice about.

'Well, the weather was fine next day, and in the sunlight it all seemed trivial stuff magnified by the night, solitude, and a touch of depression from fatigue. I had plenty of jobs to get on with, and I was out and about a lot, but I made very sure I paced myself carefully that day and by the evening I'd dismissed it from my mind. The only strange thing that happened was in the kitchen—I was suddenly convinced someone was watching me, and not in a pleasant way either. I looked round pretty quickly, but there was nobody there and the feeling was gone. So after a while I didn't worry about that, and the rest of the evening and that night were quiet.

'The day after was a scorcher, much like yesterday, and I strolled out round the field on the route you and I went. The afternoon was at its height, nobody else was around, and everything felt quiet and sleepy in the heat. It was one of those days when the air goes like water and everything dances about. I'd got to the far corner, where I had that bit of a funny turn which you kindly pretended you hadn't seen. It was before they'd taken the wheat in, and I turned round to admire the sight of a field in its full ripeness. That's when I noticed something strange. There was a peculiar figure in the middle of it which hadn't been there a minute ago, but I couldn't see how anybody could get there without me seeing them or hearing them rustle through the wheat. I tried to puzzle out what was there, but it was just far enough away to be indistinct. It was all in black, with a white face and a hat of some sort, and something made me think it was a woman, though what would she be doing there? I thought it must be a scarecrow, after all. As I watched, it seemed to move, but surely that was just the air waving in the heat? No—the heat couldn't make it lift its arms above its head . . .

'There was something very wrong about that figure. There was a menacing air to it, directed at *me*, if you please, and then I'll swear it started to move in my direction. The hair literally stood up on the back of my neck, and all over my head for all I know. I had this feeling of absolute horror, a gut fear I've never known before, not just for my physical well-being but something far more deep-rooted. I don't mind telling you that I legged it as fast as I could. After about five minutes I couldn't go any further, but I felt safe, for the time being at any rate.'

As my friend talked I began to feel uneasy. I'd spent an untroubled night in his house, but the prospect of another one suddenly seemed less than inviting. As I think I've indicated, I had always regarded the supernatural with a robust scepticism, but I was getting this story at first hand, and it was plain that Michael was speaking the truth as he saw it. I've already mentioned the general misgivings I had on the first day, and I was now becoming aware of an unpleasant prickling sensation, as if someone close by were watching and listening. Michael didn't seem to notice this, so I did my best to ignore it. This was not easy: it was not specific enough to pin down but possessed a strange, insinuating quality; a distant but definite creeping feeling that I hadn't experienced before, and one that I felt far from comfortable with.

He went on: 'Even as I'm telling you this, it sounds ridiculous to my own ears, and I can't expect anyone else to believe it. I know what I saw, but I'm beginning to doubt my own senses. This was after I'd been to the museum and read the manuscript, and of course I'd got it in my mind by then that I knew who was behind it. It's crazy, I know. I'm not psychic or anything. I feel the way a healthy man might do if he got a pain one day and dismissed it, but then it wouldn't go away and got worse, and he gradually had to face the possibility that a bad thing was happening to him. Maybe there's an innocent explanation, but I have the sense that a bad thing is happening to me.'

It was difficult to know what to say to this. 'Has there been anything since then?' I asked.

'No, nothing.'

'All right. I've known you a long time, Michael, and I'm taking you seriously. As far as you're concerned, something is going on, and if it were me I'd feel the same. I don't believe you're going off the rails. You seem balanced to me; a bit stressed out, but nothing like enough to start hallucinating. I think we have to try to figure out a way to deal with this. Let's also say that as I'm coming to this afresh, perhaps that gives me an insight that you don't have. I just need a day or two to mull some things over.'

I paused. It had grown dark since we began talking. The front room, still hot from the day, was oppressive, and we went and stood outside, taking the air in the back garden. It was a beautiful evening, with just enough light left to show the bushes and trees behind in sharp silhouette. At the end of the lawn the unseen stream tinkled faintly.

We sat up for a while longer but said nothing more about Michael's object of dread, finding music and a game or two of chess to be more congenial companions. At about eleven-thirty we retired to our rooms. The worrying sensation I'd felt earlier was gone and I had a strangely confident lack of apprehension, at least as far as the coming night was concerned, which proved to be justified. I slept soon and well, and so, he told me at breakfast, did Michael.

I had to return to London that day, but I promised to return on the Saturday two days hence. I had an idea but was reluctant to discuss it with Michael before thinking it through, as I did not want to raise false hopes. Besides, the disturbances were limited in number, and nothing had happened since that first night and the following day, unless you count the feeling I'd had in the front room. Whatever it was seemed weak and undeveloped, and even if it were gaining strength, this was a slow process. I hoped I could leave things for a day or two without anything further happening.

I left London on Saturday morning with a spade, fork, and shovel in the car boot. I had spoken to Michael the day before, and all was well. The weather had turned very hot again, and the atmosphere was close and sticky. Today we would—I hoped—put an end to all this. What I had in mind would take a few hours and I wanted to get it all over with in one day, even though working would not be pleasant on a day like this.

Much to my surprise, when I arrived at Michael's house, at ten-thirty, there he was sitting in his car in his own driveway. It was a very different Michael, whose face showed the effects of sleeplessness and severe shock.

We went into the kitchen, sat down, and I got the story.

'It was yesterday evening, and I haven't slept since. I spent last night in a B & B in Wakeford. I hardly dare come into my own house now, though it's a good deal better with you here. My worst fears have come true, and I've got no idea what to do now.'

'Actually, I think I have,' I replied. 'But what happened to you?'

He drew breath sharply. 'I can hardly bear to recall it, let alone talk about it. I was in the front room, not thinking much about anything; in fact, my mind was just idling, and anything out of the ordinary was miles from my thoughts.

'I'd been reading the paper and was tackling the crossword in a casual sort of way, but it wasn't working out. It was a lovely evening and I had the window wide open. It was about eight-ish, and there was just the start of that grey edge to things that you get at the beginning of twilight, but there weren't any clouds and there was still plenty of light.

'I decided not to bother with the crossword. I chucked the paper on the table and vaguely wondered what to do next. Then I realised I felt chilly and a bit shivery, and I wondered if I was coming down with something, because it was still nice and warm outside and there wasn't any wind. Then I thought I must be getting flu, because I felt distinctly cold and very iffy indeed. So I went over to shut the window.

'You have to put your arm right out to haul the window in by the catch, because it opens flat against the wall. I pulled it to, but I didn't shut it, because I'd got a glimpse of something dark outside, by the wall on the left. My first impression was that some thoughtful person had dumped rubbish in bin liners outside my house, which would have been very annoying. So I pushed open the window again and put my head out.'

At this point Michael stopped talking, scratched his head abstractedly, shifted his feet under the table, and stared at the wall, as if trying to find something. I said nothing, just sat and waited for him to resume, which he did within a minute.

'Not three feet away was a tall, angular woman, standing stock still, looking at me in a way I never want to be looked at again. She was as real and three-dimensional as you are, and I took in every detail. She wore a long black dress gathered into folds and belted in the middle somehow, and there was a crumpled black mob cap pushed back on her head. Her clothes looked like they could do with a wash—they were stained and blotched here and there. She had creased, black leather shoes with what looked like wooden heels.'

Michael's hand was shaking, but he continued. 'I remember noticing slender, graceful hands, with no rings on them and dirt under the fingernails. She was old and lined, but hard-looking and full of life. The hair was iron grey, long and wavy, centre-parted, and gathered into a pigtail. The face and hands were greyish white. There was a long, straight nose, and thin lips slightly parted in a mocking expression. The teeth were showing and I could see a couple of bad ones. But the eyes! They were a frozen blue, with a look of horrible self-assurance, as if she knew she'd got you where she wanted. I can see why the villagers hated her.

'I couldn't believe what I was seeing—I still can't—and I couldn't look away. I knew straightaway it was the woman I'd seen in the cornfield. There was a choking, musty smell. It felt as if all the warmth and life were rushing away from me. I thought I was finished. Then she took a step forward, and that face'—he shuddered—'was just about eighteen inches from me. I think I must have called out or something. Anyway, I jerked back into the room, catching my head on the window frame. That must have knocked me out, and the next thing I knew I was lying on the floor with my head against the sofa. I suppose it cushioned my fall.

'I can only guess that the knock on my head broke the energy flow somehow. When I woke up I felt awful, but I knew that thing wasn't there any more. As soon as I'd got my senses back I went upstairs and packed for a night. Then I came back this morning, and here we are.'

I was silent. Michael went on: 'She'll be calling round again if she can. She wants revenge and she isn't particular who it's on.'

Michael's hands had stopped shaking, but he looked tired, desperate, and older. Now, leaning over the kitchen table, I told him what I thought had caused the trouble and how I thought we could end it. My deliberations during the past couple of days had confirmed my original thoughts about Jenny Gray's

JENNY GRAY'S HOUSE

interment, and he calmed down visibly as I explained this, listening intently and nodding here and there. In two minutes I had said all I needed to.

If you have heard of the folk belief about witches and running water, you will have already guessed the task which we began work on that morning. Began? Yes. It should have been finished by the early afternoon, but we were halted by an unpredicted development. The weather had been growing hotter and more oppressive as the morning went on, and the warm, dry conditions of recent weeks had left the ground hard and resistant, so that working was a good deal more difficult than I had anticipated. We had been busy for less than an hour under an overcast sky, not achieving very much, when Michael noticed dark clouds gathering in the east. Thereafter the day became rapidly darker, sounds fell flat, and rain could be smelt in the air. It was shortly before midday that the first drops fell. We carried on for about a minute, when the rain became fast and heavy and forced us indoors. 'Well, at least it will soften the ground up,' I remarked. 'We might as well have some lunch.'

It certainly softened the ground up. After about three hours, we began to wonder whether the rain was going to stop that day. The weather reports were not encouraging, and there seemed no way to avoid getting soaked to the skin if we were to finish what we were doing. So out we went, jackets on and Michael, at least, in boots.

Have you ever tried digging in heavy rain on a close day? You soon overheat, and it is impossible to work in anything but shirtsleeves. No matter, we would survive getting wet. This turned out to be the least of the problems. Slipping around in mud, trying to dig ground that had miraculously gone from dry to saturated, holes filling with water, earth sticking tenaciously to spades, and my shoes unable to keep any kind of grip—it was no use. After Michael had gone over once and I had done likewise three times—in other words, in less than ten minutes—we returned to the house, our clothing wet through and plastered in mud.

It was a gloomy evening, sitting in the front room. We had showered and changed, but I had no spare clothes with me and had to borrow some of Michael's, which were rather too small. Even if we had been in the mood for going out somewhere, I wouldn't willingly have left the house dressed like that.

I phoned home and told Anne I wouldn't be back that night. I could hardly leave Michael alone in that house after the things that had happened. Going to bed was not an inviting prospect, and it looked as though we were faced with an all-night vigil.

The rain stopped at around ten and Michael went out to inspect the state of our works. He returned despondent. 'Everything's pretty much flooded. I only hope it drains away overnight.' There wasn't much more to be said on the subject, and we made ourselves comfortable in that room where only yesterday my friend had had such a shock. It was a strange sort of night; neither of us wished to discuss those events, yet there they always were at the back of our minds, doing their best to make their way to the front, increasingly so as the night drew on.

We settled down into the leather armchairs, made a large pot of coffee, and got the Scrabble set out. This turned out to be quite a successful distraction, and in the cosy glow of a standard lamp, with good company and a couple of hard-fought games, I do believe that for a while both of us forgot the thing that had brought me here and which was the reason we were sitting up into the night.

Even under the best of circumstances, however, there is a limit to the number of games you can play. Having reached this, more talking followed, going over old ground, old times, and old faces, and neither of us was aware of the stillness of the night taking hold. Nothing was happening to indicate anything out of the ordinary in this pleasant rural home.

Our talk became quieter, with longer intervals between remarks. It was me who began yawning, and though I tried to suppress it, Michael caught it too. He looked at the clock. 'Ten to two. Here's a blanket. I don't know about you, but I'm going to see if I can get some sleep.'

He wrapped himself up and leaned back in the deep armchair, crooked his elbow on the arm of the chair, and rested his chin in a cupped hand. Pretty soon his breathing deepened, and after ten minutes I should have said he was asleep. The only sound was the ticking of the clock on the mantelpiece, and an occasional car in the distance.

I reflected idly on the situation. This was crazy, crazy! And yet here I was, allowing myself to be dictated to by it. Was I crazy too? Right now it didn't seem all that relevant. I let my eyes wander around the room, and the wooden beams, the furniture, the old pewter plates, and the rest of its contents sent me off on vague, innocuous trains of thought. Had he bought these things before or after coming here? After, probably; they fitted in too well. Not in the slick, professional way of an interior designer job, though. There was an air of slight amateurishness about it, and yet that was part of the charm. Wonder if he found all these things locally? In Cambridge, maybe, or perhaps at auction hereabouts? I think I must have yawned again, and I forget which way my thoughts drifted after that. . . .

I woke up feeling stiff, uncomfortable, disoriented. Where was I? Oh, yes, here. What time was it? My watch said twenty past three; that couldn't be right? Craning my neck (with some difficulty) to look at the clock on the mantelpiece, I saw that it was. Something had woken me; what was it? I was wide awake now, alert to some unknown yet strongly sensed danger. Opposite me, Michael was sound asleep in his chair and snoring slightly.

Then I heard it: the unmistakable creak of a footstep, and, after a moment, another, and another. Someone, or something, was coming down the stairs.

Perhaps you have heard people dismissing the idea of nocturnal footsteps in supposedly haunted houses. It's just the house settling, the boards contracting as the temperature changes. I've known people come out with that too. All I have to say is this: if you've ever heard them you will know, for an absolute certainty, the difference between stealthy footsteps at night and a house settling down, and you will be less than charitably inclined towards those who suggest otherwise. I know what I heard, and I felt the hairs on the back of my neck prickle and stand up. I was scared in a way that was quite new to me.

I leapt out of the chair and hit the switch by the door. Light flooded the room, and the footsteps stopped. With a sensation I cannot describe, I heard them again—this time hurrying *back up* the stairs, and I thought I also heard the echo of a low laugh from the top of the house. Then, abruptly, all was silent.

Michael stirred, and I quickly switched off the main light. A bleary face with sticking-up hair peered at me from the blanket. 'What is it? What's happening?'

'Nothing's happening,' I said in a quiet, calm tone that surprised me. 'There's nothing to worry about. Go back to sleep.'

Michael disappeared into his blanket. I lay back in my chair, heart pounding, trying to breathe normally. It was difficult. Was something still upstairs? Had I stopped it? I didn't know, but I was going to stay awake for the rest of the night if I could. The atmosphere in the room was still humid and heavy. Opening a window, though, was the last thing I felt like doing.

I did my best to remain awake, but I must have dozed off again, because I was awoken, this time by the rumbling of thunder not far off. The weather was ready to break again, so it seemed. How much rain would we have this time? I was annoyed that I had fallen asleep, and with some guilt, mixed with relief that nothing had happened, I tried to wake up properly. Michael was still slumbering, one arm thrown out over the arm of the chair. It was twenty to five. In a minute or two I would go into the kitchen and make a cup of tea.

The thunder sounded again, closer this time. How hot it was in the room! The light from the standard lamp, over by the fireplace, threw a bright arc on the floor below it, a gentle light on our chairs and the low table between us, and barely penetrated to the other corners of the room, the furthest of which was quite remarkably obscure. I peered into the darkness, which seemed unnaturally dense. I tried to make out what was in that corner, but could see nothing. Or was there some sort of shape? I strained to see; could the blackness there really be growing denser, darker? Surely it was, before my eyes!

Something was materialising in that corner. I sat rigid, mouth open, unable to move, speak, or do anything but stare. What my feelings were I will leave you to imagine—if you think you can. A tall, thin, dark figure was slowly taking shape. Partially formed, limbs undistinguishable from the body, a head could nevertheless be made out, though of the face nothing was visible. But—horror of horrors—a whitish hand—the right hand—could plainly be seen in front of the body, crooked into the shape of a claw and evidently trying to reach forwards.

I have often wondered what might have happened if this process had carried on to its conclusion. What could Jenny Gray have done to us? I have always heard it said that ghosts can't harm you, and in most cases I am sure that may be true, but the malevolence of the thing before me led me to doubt it in this case. She—it—was aware of what we meant to do, and it is my belief that she had summoned up all her energy to materialize herself and somehow put a stop to it.

At that moment lightning flashed outside. Even through the heavy curtains the room was brighter for an instant, and I was granted a glimpse of what was in the corner. I saw the right hand very clearly. The other hand had begun to form but was still far less distinct. A face, too, was starting to become visible. I am thankful to say that it was little more than a pale, formless splodge, though I did fancy I distinguished a chin and the beginnings of a nose.

The briefest moment after the flash, thunder crashed deafeningly, and within a few seconds the pattering of rain began. In a few seconds more the patter had become a rattle, then a downpour. Almost immediately the thing in the corner began to fade. First the left hand disappeared, then the face. The body seemed to melt back into the shadows, leaving only the right hand, still as clear as before and immobile in its claw shape, to hang there a short while longer before suddenly dissolving into snow, like a TV picture in unstable reception conditions, and vanishing altogether. All this may have taken twenty seconds. As the hand disappeared, there came the faint, immensely distant, but clear sound of a scream that chilled my soul. There was a note in it of another world which I could not—cannot—bear to think of.

The rainstorm was heavy but short. When the dawn came, I awoke Michael, who had slept peacefully through everything, and told him what had happened during the night. We were not long in returning to the garden and finishing the task we had begun the previous day. We were both aware—so we told each other later—of a sensation of being watched. It was the same low-level feeling I had experienced a few evenings previously, but with an added dimension of almost tangible anger and hatred. We kept talking to each other as we worked, about all sorts of trivia, just to keep our minds from wandering and stop anything unwelcome getting in. By ten o'clock all was finished, the tools were back in my car, and the sensation of being watched had departed.

I am glad to say that Michael still lives in the same house at Upper Marwell. The stream runs in its old crooked course, and the house has not been troubled since that weekend. We have visited him there two or three times, and his life seems to have taken a turn for the better. Strangely enough, the shock appears to have done him some good, and he has certainly snapped out of the morbid state of mind he was in when he first went to live there. Just the same, it took him a little while to get over the events I have described, and he would never dream of telling this little story to anyone else in the village. He also told me not long ago that the unexpected sight of a pile of bin bags can still make him feel quite sick. By and large, though, we've tended to avoid the subject of Jenny Gray.

There is one more peculiar thing about all this. There is no manuscript history of Upper Marwell to be found in the local museum, and the woman employed there claims to know nothing about it. Nor can Michael find the sheets of paper he showed me that night. He is sure they must be in the house somewhere and will turn up when he least expects it.

The Devil's Number

Reggie Oliver

THREE YEARS AGO I WAS in the Czech Republic at a place called Duchov researching for a biography of Casanova. The great eighteenth century adventurer spent the last years of his life in the castle of Dux (or Duchov) as librarian to Count Waldstein. It was there that he wrote his *Histoire de ma Vie*, the masterpiece of autobiography known to the world as the *Memoirs of Casanova*. Naturally I studied what original Casanova manuscripts remained at the castle, but I also decided to examine all the books in the library dating from Casanova's time. I was looking particularly for volumes which had once belonged to him. It was known that Casanova came to Dux with a substantial library of his own, and that these were almost certainly absorbed into the collection at Dux on his death.

It was a huge task, but full of interest. I discovered a number of volumes which had undoubtedly belonged to Casanova. Some had his usual signature, 'Casanova de Seingalt', scrawled in sepia ink over the title page; some even contained notes in his handwriting. Many of the books testified to his lifelong interest in the occult, and one in particular, a quarto edition of Aldo Sinesius's *De Conjuratione* (Antwerp, 1567), was very well thumbed and annotated. But imagine my excitement when, turning to the back cover, I found, inserted into a sort of pocket in the binding, a few sheets of manuscript paper unquestionably in Casanova's own hand.

It is the sort of discovery that every researcher dreams about. I was quite alone in the library. I could have put those pages into my briefcase there and then and walked out with them, though in fact I was not remotely tempted to do so. It was late in the afternoon; soon I would be turned out of the library by the curator and forced to drive the six miles back to my dreary hotel. I began to read frantically, making as I did so a rough translation. Here it is:

There have been many who professed knowledge of *ars goetica* [the magic art] but most of these were scoundrels and charlatans, and ignorant ones at that. The whole of Paris wondered at Saint-Germain, who professed to be two hundred years old and who claimed that no food passed his lips. I knew him at once for what he was, an impostor, for, as the saying goes, 'It takes one fox to smell another', and I have to say in all modesty that though the *soi-disant* Count de Saint-Germain imposed upon King Louis himself, I was the subtler fox and possessed a deeper knowledge of the occult arts.

I have in my life met few people with a knowledge of these things equal to mine, and only one with a deeper understanding. It came about during my time in Paris in this way.

On a November evening in the year 1762 I was sheltering from the rain in the doorway of the Café de la Régence. I did not wish to go in, for I was waiting for the carriage of the Marquise de M. to pass by. The Marquise was being most jealously watched over by the good Marquis and his spies, and the only way we could celebrate a mutual passion undetected was in my lady's coach on the way to the opera. Be that as it may. . . . I shall record my dealings with the Marquise de M. at some other time. As I was waiting I was approached by a tall thin figure of a man wearing a cloak. He began to engage me in conversation and, reluctant as I was—for my brain was seething with anticipations of my encounter with the Marquise—I responded with as much courtesy as I could muster.

Was I Monsieur de Casanova? I was. The gentleman apologised for thus forcing his company upon me, but he had heard my name mentioned in connection with a divination system using a cabalistic pyramid of numbers.

He wore a heavy tricorn hat laced with gold, and his face was further obscured by the shadow of the doorway, but I could tell that it was long and thin, the skin waxy and of a strange pallor. It was a face which seemed to lack all animation save for the eyes, which not only glittered but—I could have sworn—glowed in the darkness. His address was most courteous—clearly that of a gentleman—and he introduced himself as the Baron de Caulard; but though he spoke French with the fluency of a native, and an educated one at that, there was some indefinably alien element in his accent.

We were soon deep in conversation. His knowledge of every branch of the occult arts was astonishing. I had supposed that my numerical system of divination using a cabalistic pyramid was my own invention, but he pointed out that a very similar scheme had been devised by Ramon Lull in his *Ars Notoria* more than four centuries before, a fact which I have since verified. He suggested various improvements and amplifications to my method, which I later incorporated to very good effect. So absorbing was our conversation that I quite forgot about the rain, and almost about my exquisite Marquise de M.

Her coach arrived and stopped on the other side of the street, opposite the Café de la Régence. Hastily I invited the Baron to come to me the next day so that we could continue our discussion. He said that he was occupied during the day but asked if he might come the following night. I agreed and darted across the road to meet my inamorata. On reaching the coach I looked back, but the Baron was gone.

When I stepped into the coach I found my Marquise in a frenzy of excitement. By the soft glow of the lanterns in the carriage I could see that her pretty face was suffused with the blush of eager passion. As soon as the door was shut and the vehicle was in motion our fevered hands began to explore the tenderest and most intimate parts of each other's anatomies. Strangely enough, however—perhaps because my mind was still full of the Baron and his conversation—my desire failed to manifest itself in its usual physical way. I could see the disappointment in her face as her fingers found that the object of her longing was only partially awake. My distress was equal to hers, but with a supreme effort of mind I hurled all thoughts of the Baron aside. This was assisted by a sudden lurch of the carriage which threw the Marquise and her petticoats into the most divine confusion, so that I was able to catch a glimpse of . . . But I must give details of this episode elsewhere.

The following night I waited for the Baron with a mixture of eagerness and apprehension, for, though I had found his conversation unusually fascinating, there had been something repellent about the man. On a number of occasions during our first encounter he had put his face very close to mine in order to impress some point or other. I had found this peculiarly disquieting, especially when I felt his breath upon my cheek: it was as cold as ice.

I did not know when he would arrive, but I had my servant prepare a cold supper with a bottle of my best wine in the front upper chamber. I myself took up a book, half hoping that he would not come to me. I did not notice the passing of time, for the fire and the candlelight made me drowsy and the book, a volume of Ariosto, was one I knew almost by heart. Near midnight my senses were suddenly alerted into full consciousness. I listened but I heard no sound; nevertheless something drew me to the window and, looking down into the street, I saw a figure in a long cloak and a gold-laced tricorn hat. It was the Baron. Not wishing to rouse my servant, I went downstairs myself and opened the door to him.

He came into my house as if it was the most natural thing in the world to be thus welcomed. We sat down together, but he would take no food or drink. We talked of many things, on all of which he spoke with great knowledge and keen insight. On the wars against the Ottoman Turk he spoke with peculiar fervour, and described battles which had taken place two centuries ago in such lively detail that I almost believed he had been present at them. When we touched on the subject of magic he gave me a formula for winning at Faro, based on the so-called 'Devil's Number'. I have since used this formula on two occasions and won large sums as a result, but, as these successes were both immediately followed by periods of acute personal misfortune, I have never used it since.

Knowing no better at the time, I was most grateful to the Baron for the secrets he had revealed to me, and asked if I could show him any kindness in return. I expected some polite demur on this point, and was surprised when he expressed his desire for a reciprocal favour in the clearest possible terms.

'I understand,' he said, 'that you are acquainted with a Madame V. and that you are partners with her in a certain business venture.'

'You are very well informed,' I replied, in a tone of irony to which, however, he appeared not to be susceptible.

'I am told,' he went on, 'that the lady in question has a select clientele, acquired always by means of a personal introduction?' I nodded my assent. 'And that she is able to supply her clients with untainted goods, by which I mean young persons who are virgins?'

I acknowledged that this was true, and he accordingly demanded an introduction to Madame V. as his favour.

Readers of the *History of my Life* will be well acquainted with my many vices, but they will also know that the wanton debauchery of the innocent is not one of them. It yields little pleasure save that of cruelty and leaves behind nothing but remorse. I naturally knew that Madame V. catered for such depraved tastes as the Baron's, but I flattered myself that my association with her was purely commercial and therefore separated from some of the more vicious practices of her trade. For the first time I began to be ashamed of my connection with her. Nonetheless I agreed to help him, and no action in my entire life have I come to regret more bitterly.

The moment I had consented the Baron rose to his feet, making no secret of his eagerness to leave. We had talked for some hours and dawn was approaching. I asked if he would not stay and take some breakfast with me, but he refused, and I saw something like fear pass across those icily impassive features. Pausing only to secure an agreement that we should meet at the same time the following night, he was out of the room, down my stairs, and into the street like the wind. Looking from my window, I caught a glimpse of him as he ran away down the road with astonishing speed. With his cloak billowing out behind him he seemed almost to glide, like some monstrous bird of prey.

The following night, true to my word—though more out of some nameless fear than from honour—I took him with me to Madame V.'s establishment. Having effected the introduction, I left him there and never saw him again; but not long after I was forced to see the work he had done. . . . [There followed three lines in the manuscript which had been scored out by some heavy strokes of the pen and were therefore illegible, then the handwriting became more erratic and I could just make out the following:] . . . the girl was no more than thirteen years of age but as white as marble and somewhat withered, as if all the blood had been drained from her. Others were found in a similar condition, all protégées of Madame V. The long and the short of it was that some of the blame for these atrocious crimes fell upon me, and I was compelled in the end to take ship for England.

If the solemn dictates of Reason did not decree otherwise, I might believe that this self-styled Baron de Caulard—for naturally no such title ever existed in the register of nobility—was the very Devil himself. Certainly he had better claims than that charlatan Saint-Germain to have hidden powers and to know the secrets of the grave. And when I come to my own grave, as I fear I shall soon, may my Creator have mercy and not send me to the place from which this Baron surely came.

Here the manuscript ended. The fragment is of interest to the Casanova scholar in particular because it helps to explain why he abruptly left France for England in June 1763. Up till now this had been something of a mystery. Readers of his memoirs will know that it was from this ill-fated visit to our shores that Casanova dated the decline in his fortunes.

My excitement at the discovery of these papers was slightly dampened when I turned over the last page of the manuscript and found some writing in another, later hand. It ran as follows:

> Could this be D? Van Helsing's papers, published and unpublished, should confirm. A.S. 1898.

A.S. was undoubtedly the minor poet and critic Arthur Symons, thought by some to be the model for Max Beerbohm's Enoch Soames. Symons had visited Dux in 1898 and, while there, discovered two new chapters of Casanova's *Memoirs* as well as some letters. One can only speculate why he did not also release this fragment to the world. The reference to Van Helsing suggested to me that the 'D' in question was none other than Dracula, and my guess was corroborated by the fact that the Baron's name 'Caulard' was an anagram for Dracula. Students of the *Cabbala* will know the mystical significance of preserving one's identity by using the letters of one's name in a different order.

But I was baffled; I still am. Everyone knows that Dracula is the fictional creation of Bram Stoker, and yet here was his contemporary Arthur Symons pretending he was real. Symons, as far as I know, was never acquainted with Stoker, though they were both in London during the 1890s and had some mutual acquaintances. Symons's friends, though, were more exclusively literary. Symons admittedly suffered from mental illness later in life, but why should he forge a document so convincingly, then hide it away in the back of a book? I had no doubt at the time of the genuineness of the document. Perhaps this Caulard had nothing to do with 'Dracula', though everything seemed to point to it.

But this was not the only mystery. When I returned to the library at Dux the following day and took down again the quarto of Aldo Sinesius's *De Conjuratione* I could find no trace of the manuscript. The pocket in the back cover was there, but it was empty. Did I imagine it all? Did I spend several hours translating a document that existed only in my imagination? Had the manuscript been stolen, and if so why and how and by whom? These questions kept turning and turning in my head, so that any further work became impossible. How could I prove it existed? The scholars would laugh at me. How could I trust myself?

Eventually, my mind became so tormented by what had happened—or what had not happened—that I had to abandon my biography and return my advance to the publisher who had commissioned it. It was a terrible time, and for a few weeks I needed to be hospitalised. I am only just beginning to recover, but the cherished project of a definitive Casanova biography is now quite beyond me.

You, the reader, have only my word that the manuscript ever existed at all. I swear it did, but how can I prove it? I can only say what I believe I saw and read and wrote. I must leave it to you to puzzle it out. I am, as I say, baffled.

Visits

Melanie Tem

PAULA HAD BEEN DEAD a few months the first time I saw her widower alone. It was Paula who'd been my friend, and I hardly knew Dale; I hardly know him now, though he's told me things no one else ever has. My impression of him was positive, mostly because, after two marriages to men nowhere near her match and then a long, restless period of singlehood, Paula had finally found the person to spend the rest of her life with. Sadly, the rest of her life had turned out to be only a few years.

Paula and I had been friends for so long we'd forgotten how we'd met. We'd been close in a distant sort of way. Even when we'd lived in the same city, we hadn't seen each other much, and, after we'd both moved, our contact had been reduced to occasional phone calls since she didn't do e-mail. When we did communicate, though, we cut right to the chase: Dominic and I were usually having a really good time, when we weren't recovering from the consequences of having a really good time. She always had cancer in one form or another, breast or colon or ovarian, newly diagnosed or recently excised, responding or not to conventional or alternative treatment, once in a while in remission.

So when, some time after the fact, she'd let me know they'd found a mass in her lung, it had seemed to me like more of the same, part of who Paula was, like my latest DUI or Dominic's loss of another job. I didn't know she had brain cancer until the mass e-mail from Dale. I recognized none of the other names on the 'To' list. Because of both his mental state and my own, I had to read the message twice before I comprehended that Paula had died.

I couldn't say I missed her, exactly. She hadn't been part of my daily life. It was Dominic I missed. He'd gone sober, seriously this time, and I couldn't understand why. He was a stranger. We had nothing to talk about anymore. Though he wasn't dead, neither of us had left, and we still shared the same time and space, we were suddenly and inexplicably no longer sharing a life.

Still, Paula and I had had a real connection, and I missed knowing she was in this world. My 'if there's anything I can do . . .' message to Dale had been sincere but also safe, given that I wasn't likely to be someone he'd seek out. I didn't expect to hear back, but he replied right away, writing that it was very hard but he had a lot of support, he was okay, thanks for the good thoughts. Beyond that, we'd had no reason to keep in touch, and we didn't.

Then, when business would be taking me to the city where he lived, it seemed wrong to avoid him. When he didn't answer immediately, I was both disappointed and relieved. His reply showed up in my inbox the day before I left, and we agreed—with some trepidation on my part—that I'd call when I got in.

As it turned out, my schedule precluded anything more than brunch at the hotel restaurant on my last day in town. Even that now seemed too much. I couldn't imagine what we'd have to say to each other, since our only connection had been Paula—and that a flimsy one. By the time the day came, I was utterly out of sorts: close to dreading the appointment, glad the need to be at the airport two hours before the flight would provide a built-in limit, feeling mildly guilty about my attitude and mildly resentful about feeling guilty, and suspecting he was probably feeling much the same way. A drink or several would have helped but, resentfully, I resisted.

I'd have put off packing, to give myself another excuse for cutting the meeting short, but check-out time was ten o'clock. I paid the bill, wondering if the company comptroller would spot the excessive room service and bar charges, left my bags with the concierge, got a table, and ordered coffee. Despite my resistance to meeting him at all, not to mention a muzzy head from too many Tom Collinses and too little sleep, I'd made a point of being half an hour early, so I'd be settled and wide awake when he got there and he'd be the one looking for me.

In any other setting I wouldn't have known him, not because widowhood had changed him so much—though I would soon learn it had—but because I'd seen him so seldom and hadn't paid him much attention. His appearance was unremarkable; he looked like many another man of his age and ancestry—receding grey-brown hair, fair skin, pleasantly jowly face, a paunch which, from what Paula had told me, I doubted was a beer belly but which did droop over his belt. Even when I saw him come into the restaurant at the right time, I wasn't sure it was the right person.

He knew me, though. It's hard to tell about yourself, but I had the impression that if I'd changed any it was just more of the same: a few more pounds every year, a few more shades of auburn applied to my hair, a little more desperation as emptiness and ennui settled in. Rather than changing my appearance, I imagined, all of this would make me look more and more like myself. This was not a happy prospect.

'Beth!' he was already saying as he strode to my table, 'it's so good to see you again!' His voice broke, giving an edge to the standard greeting. Suddenly remembering that Dale was a hugger, I stood up and extended my hand in self-defence, but he ignored it and hugged me anyway, and I felt him trembling. Lowering himself into the chair across from me, he wiped his eyes and blew his nose on a green and white bandana. Something about this had the air of preparation—not exactly orchestration or contrivance, but habit—and it put me off.

He inquired how I was, and I said, 'Fine', and that was enough for him. I had no desire to tell him anything substantial about my life, certainly not about the disaster of my marriage, which was the most substantial thing. But I was a bit miffed not to have to employ any of my avoidance strategies.

The waiter came and we ordered—a hearty breakfast for me in anticipation of airline pretzels, a Danish and a Coke for him, a fresh pot of coffee. Then I had little choice but to ask, 'How are you, Dale? How are you getting along?'

The blue eyes Paula used to go on about, now bloodshot and jittery, filled with tears again. 'Terrible,' he admitted readily. 'God, Beth, I miss her.'

'I'm sure you do.' I felt bad not to know what else to say, but it quickly became apparent that what I said was irrelevant anyway. He had a story to tell and was going to tell it no matter what.

He leaned towards me and lowered his voice, but not very much. 'She haunts me, Beth.'

After a moment I started to say, stupidly, 'Well, I'm sure that's a normal——'

Emphatically, he shook his head. 'No, Beth, I mean literally. She haunts me. I betrayed her and she's making me pay.'

Inwardly I groaned. The last thing I wanted to sit through was a confession of marital infidelity, given my own adventures, as recently as last night, and especially given a few things I knew about Paula.

If he noticed my discomfort, he paid it no heed. Mercifully, he did wait to launch into his narrative until the waiter had brought our food and found things to fuss over even in Dale's minimalist order. When the chipper young man finally quit asking was everything all right and how was our food and could he get us anything else, and went away to badger some other hapless patrons, Dale took a gulp of coffee, chased it with a gulp of Coke, and announced in a surprisingly—not to say appallingly—clarion voice, 'I killed her.'

My skin crawled, mostly with embarrassment, and I glanced around at the other diners, hoping they were engrossed in their own conversations, many of which I could hear word-for-word without wanting to. But even then there was also a chill fascination. I didn't want to hear this story, and I was compelled to.

Dale fortified himself with another double shot of caffeine, hot then cold. I saw him try to make eye contact with me, but his gaze kept jerking away as if pulled, and more than once during the ensuing narrative I wouldn't be able to keep myself from glancing over my shoulder—where, of course, there was nothing more disquieting than the sedate mid-morning hubbub of this decidedly worldly establishment. Then he began with: 'Paula.'

The speaking of her name set off terrible, silent shudders. I didn't know about grief then. Although I'd already lost someone dear to me, I hadn't admitted it yet, and I was sceptical. No need for melodrama, I thought. Pull yourself together, I thought. Now, of course, I know how much self-control it took for him not to collapse into insanity.

If, in fact, he wasn't already insane. I'm still not sure.

When he was able to resume, he said her name again. '*Paula*—had cancer in one form or another as long as I knew her. As long as I loved her. And, oh, I did love her. I do. My love wasn't enough, but it was a great love.'

This naked declaration made me queasy and jealous. I busied myself trying to identify the hint of unexpected flavour in my pancakes. Almond, I decided. Very nice.

Dale was telling how he and Paula had met. It wasn't quite the same story she'd told me, but close enough that I didn't have to pay much attention. I was restive, not yet uneasy about making my flight but distracted by stray musings about the professional successes and personal pleasures of the past few days. But Paula had been my friend, and Dale was a good storyteller who'd obviously rehearsed his tale, if only in his own mind, until it was crafted for maximum effect. It didn't take long for me to be hooked. We both settled in as if planning to be there a while.

* * * * *

Paula had a bottle of wine chilling in the refrigerator, fresh fragrant flowers in a vase on the table, and smooth jazz on the CD player when Dale got home from work that afternoon. At first he thought they were celebrating something— one of the small everyday miracles Paula was so good at noting, the smell of the cats' fur in sunlight or the way it felt to just barely touch fingertips He also dared to hope they might be celebrating good news about her health—her body showed no signs of cancer, the recent bouts of lightheadedness meant nothing.

Then he saw her face. She was wearing the red silk caftan he'd just bought her for their twelfth anniversary, and he saw how it made her look both elegant and frail, accentuating her patchy dark hair, sharp wrists and cheekbones, luminous eyes.

She wrapped her arms around him. Her tall sinewy body felt substantial against him. He put his hand on the back of her head where no hair grew anymore and pressed her to him. 'What is it, my darling?'

She looked up at him and met his eyes. He saw tears and determination. 'I love you,' she said.

Terror-stricken, he couldn't find voice to say it back. Though he told her he loved her countless times before and after that moment, he would hold onto it as a betrayal of Paula, the first in a spiral which from that point on was out of control.

'Dale, I have stage IV brain cancer.'

With treatment, she told him while she sipped wine and he couldn't even hold his glass, she might have four to six months. Treatment, though, was radiation so strong and global she'd lose every physical and mental function before she died anyway. Without treatment, she'd lose every function, too, and sooner.

She watched him, her gaze the only steady thing about her. When she set her glass down, red wine splattered, which Dale wouldn't realize he'd noticed until the dark spots on the lace tablecloth made his stomach churn and his heart race and didn't come out in the wash. She stroked his cheek as she told him what he already knew: 'This is it, my love. I won't go through that. It's time for our plan.'

'No. Paula. Please. I can't.' He was sobbing.

She took his face in her hands, featherweight and with little strength left in them. He would never forgive himself for flinching. 'You promised,' Paula whispered.

Indeed, he had promised.

He'd been the one to bring in the mail the day the book had arrived, plain brown wrapper drawing his attention and giving him the creeps; it was addressed to them both. He left it for her to open and to tell him what it was for. 'Self-deliverance,' she read aloud from the cover. 'Practicalities. Assisted.'

They'd had surreal study sessions together, and it was obvious she'd pored over the book on her own. Barbiturates and alcohol, she decided, and a plastic bag to be sure. None of those ingredients would be hard to come by. She already knew her doctor would write the prescriptions, and she could still manage the liquor and grocery stores on her own.

He was horrified by the satisfaction in her manner, the settledness. Then he was ashamed to be angry with her in the little time they had left.

'I won't be gone,' she assured him, as if she knew. 'I'll still be with you. I'll just be in a different form. The spirit doesn't die.' He held onto that.

The tumours revealed by the brain scan were large and numerous. They must have been growing for some time before she'd had any symptoms. The splotchy images on the screen made Dale faint and dizzy, the thought of the malignancy spreading through the very brain of his beloved while he lived with her, slept with her, loved her.

Now it asserted itself hour by hour, minute by minute, before his very eyes and behind his back. Paula fell. She spoke words she didn't mean, gibberish she expected him to understand. She lost control of one bodily function after another, drooling, regurgitating food she couldn't swallow, streaming thick pungent urine and thin pungent stool. She got lost in their house. She got lost lying in their bed.

He didn't know how she determined that Tuesday to be the last day of her life, but except to whisper, 'No, please, not yet,' he couldn't dispute her decision. She couldn't walk at all now, or sit up unless he held her. Her gaze was somewhere else, until it would suddenly focus on him.

Her lips moved under his kiss. 'I love you. It's time. Tonight.'

They had waited a little too long, for Paula couldn't do any of the preparations herself. She lay in their bed. The movements of her arms, legs, head, arching back, and the noises she produced made him frantic because he couldn't interpret them. He kept pleading, 'What, sweetheart? Paula? What should I do?' and going back and forth to touch her, peer at her, press his ear to her mouth or her heart.

He dimmed the lights, lit the candles and the incense she'd set up, started the CDs she'd cued up. He checked to see that all the documents were on the table where she'd laid them, turned the phone ringers off. When he allowed himself to realize why he was doing all this, he was paralyzed, so the mantra he chanted silently and aloud was, 'For Paula. For my love. For Paula. For my love.'

As he was carrying in the laced vanilla pudding and the glass of vodka, Paula spoke clearly. 'Thank you, Dale. I'll always love you. Always.' Then she sat up, reached for the bottle ready on the bedside stand, and took the glass from him.

But it didn't work. Physically compromised and mentally well into oblivion or the next world, Paula botched it, and he had to help her. Using the plastic bag the way they'd practised together, Dale had to kill the love of his life. Under his hands, her body struggled a little, but it didn't take long.

* * * * *

With Paula now dead, I assumed the story was over. I let my breath out. Dale was crying and I was crying and we were clutching each other's hands across the table. My sorrow was for him and for my friend, who now seemed to have been more important to me than I'd realized. It was also for myself, for I doubted my husband or anybody else would commit such an astonishing act of love for me, or, what was worse, I for anyone else.

Seeing that I had about twenty minutes before I should catch the airport shuttle, I made to extricate my hand, but Dale tightened his grasp. 'She haunts me,' he whispered again. I could hardly hear him over the cheery din of the restaurant, and despite myself I leaned towards him. 'She always will. I killed her, Beth. I murdered her.'

Suddenly impatient, done with this, I pulled free. 'You did what she wanted you to do,' I protested.

He was shaking his head emphatically. 'Her spirit will never forgive me.'

I signalled for the check. 'Come on, Dale, do you really believe in spirits?'

'Of course I believe in spirits. Don't you?'

Where were intrusive waiters when you needed them? 'Ghosts, I mean. Do you really believe in hauntings and vengeful ghosts?'

'Oh,' he said, 'yes.'

Two rows over, our waiter was chatting up another table of diners. I tried and failed to catch his eye.

Dale said, 'I'll take you to the airport, Beth. Will you let me tell the rest of the story?'

What choice did I have? The waiter finally came by, beaming and gushing. Wishing for Irish coffee, I ordered another refill of the standard brew and settled back.

* * * * *

Paula began haunting her brand new widower before he'd even grasped that her spirit had departed, while he was still desperately chanting the words she'd written out and helped him memorize, before her body had cooled, well before he made the necessary phone calls on the list they'd compiled. She tried to strangle him.

It wasn't literally hands around his throat, of course, or a tool wielded by hands. Always long and thin and quick both to touch and to push away, her hands were now metaphorically skeletal and very soon would be literally so. They lay inert where he'd reverently placed them at her sides. It wasn't thumbs boring into his Adam's apple, fingers squeezing his windpipe, a garrote twisting, rope pulled tight. But breath and the possibility of breath were being forced out of him, and voicelessly he was being given to understand that this was revenge.

He tried to protest. 'But, Paula, darling, you said—it's what you—you made me promise——'

His throat all but closed. He coughed and clawed. Eventually the pressure eased, not because of anything he did or said. Small round bruises turned purple then green then yellow like beads around his neck.

As Paula had pre-arranged, the kind, capable young woman from the cremation place came and took the body away. Even though Dale knew full well, had practised knowing, that Paula no longer needed her body, the sight of it leaving the house on the gurney made him howl when it happened and shake when he told about it later. As soon as the van had driven off, Paula set the house on fire.

Senses dulled and survival instinct all but disengaged, Dale didn't at first recognize the smell and sting of smoke or that it mattered, and by the time he traced it to an unused room he hadn't been in for months, half a wall was blackened and the winter clothes stored in the closet were smouldering. He called 911 and went for water, trying to hurry, trying not to scream along with the sirens.

The fire department ruled the blaze to be 'of undetermined origin'. Unable to fathom the insurance claim forms, Dale just shut the door to the room as it was, one more element of a shrine.

Paula's assault escalated. She pushed him down a flight of steps, blew in his ears to obscure the light-rail train approaching until its whistle sent him stumbling backward off the tracks, poisoned his chicken salad sandwich—all the while whispering inside his head that he had murdered her and he would pay. After a while it was almost comical, in a terrifying sort of way.

He went back to work part-time. It was hard to hold in his head the importance of keeping the business afloat, of making a living, of keeping himself from homelessness and starvation. One afternoon, having lasted until about one o'clock, he managed after considerable fumbling to get the garage door open and the car into the garage—then remembered in dull succession that Paula wasn't home, Paula would never come home again, Paula was dead—and collapsed onto the steering wheel. When at last he thought to turn the ignition key with one hand and pull up on the door handle with the other, neither moved. He was trapped.

He tried again, and again, thinking this yet another instance of his having lost the ability to perform simple sequential tasks. Eventually his mind came into hyperacute focus, and he realized something other than his grief-induced befuddlement was preventing him from shutting off the engine or opening the car door. Then, because she was sitting beside him, sitting close beside him, he realized it was Paula. 'Paula.'

'Who do you think you are?' She wasn't physically there. She wasn't vocalizing. But her presence and her accusation were palpable. 'You think you're God?'

'You were suffering—you wouldn't have lived much longer——'

'You had no right to take even a minute of life away from me.'

'You wanted me to—you insisted——'

'You killed me. You murdered me. How could you do that, Dale? I thought you loved me.'

'Oh, God, Paula, I did love you. I do love you. It was an act of love. A terrible act—it was so hard——'

He felt her on him. His shoulders hurt from the weight of her, and his groin. She covered his nose and mouth and he couldn't breathe. Although he would have said he had no particular desire to go on living without her, he struggled to breathe, to fend her off. She was stronger than he was. When she let him go, it was because of her will, not his, and her absence was as terrible as her presence had been. 'You'll pay. You'll pay. You'll pay.' Her voice was like the baying of the neighbours' dog, like the ticking of the engine shut off now and cooling. The car door opened easily, and the garage door, and oxygen filled his lungs whether he wanted it to or not.

* * * * *

I was having trouble taking all this seriously, except as evidence of Dale's unbalanced state of mind. This was way more than I had bargained for. I did not want to be here.

Ostentatiously I looked at my watch, just as Dale blanched and leaned heavily against the wall. I felt obliged to ask, 'What's wrong? Are you all right?'

After a long pause, during which I became increasingly alarmed and annoyed, he said weakly, 'It's my heart. Every once in a while she attacks my heart.'

'It's a panic attack,' I informed him. 'Feels like a heart attack, but it's not.' I knew something about panic attacks.

He shook his head. 'It's Paula. She's going to kill me, Beth. An eye for an eye.'

I'd had enough. I gave Dale a cursory goodbye hug and left him sitting there. I paid the bill, cutting off the waiter in mid-gush, and was imperious with the concierge. I barely made my plane. I ordered a drink before I was even buckled in, and just the anticipation of it calmed me.

* * * * *

More than a year later I saw Dale again. I hadn't thought I ever would, but once again I found myself in his town for other reasons, and once again it would have seemed wrong not to call at least.

In that year, Dominic had stayed sober and, when I wouldn't follow suit, had left me. I couldn't forgive him for either betrayal. But I was trying to stop drinking, too, in hopes he would love me again.

I expected Dale's phone to be disconnected, the number assigned to someone else. But Dale answered on the first ring, and he didn't seem surprised to hear from me. There was nothing for it but to inquire how he was. 'She haunts me, Beth,' he whispered, and I covered the mouthpiece to groan aloud, scrambling to think of some way to get out of this. No such luck; he invited me to his house, saying with a bitter laugh that he didn't go out much.

I, on the other hand, could hardly do anything *but* go out. I'd moved three times since Dominic had left, and even so the very thought of staying home set my nerves on edge. I worked late, which had the added benefit of covering how slow I was these days at getting anything accomplished. I discovered the piano bar circuit and learned I could sing heartfelt songs about lost love even when I wasn't high. I travelled, and had returned to this city to see the man I'd met at that convention, who was not glad to see me.

The house was familiar, although I'd never been there. I swore I knew the cedar tree out front, the three slab steps up to the porch, the way it felt to stand there listening to the doorbell ring inside. When the door opened, a fragrance billowed out, not unpleasant but unsettling because it made me think *Paula*, and I couldn't imagine why. The ambient light when I walked in was *Paula*, and the sound of the space enclosed by first the front hall and then the living room where we sat. The house had a definite taste and feel, too, which could only be identified as *Paula*.

Once again, I would not have recognized Dale if I hadn't been expecting to see him. Except for the blue eyes, glittering now as if with fever, he looked nothing like the man who'd sat across the table in the hotel restaurant and confessed to the murder of his wife. He must have lost a hundred pounds. His head, face, arms were completely hairless. His skin was ashen, his flesh oddly sunken. 'Beth,' he rasped. 'Beth, it's so good to see you.'

'You, too, Dale.' We touched cheeks. His breath was fetid, his skin preternaturally soft. We were both unsteady on our feet, I assumed for different reasons, and we sat on a dusty couch. More out of weariness than decorum, I dispensed with niceties. 'Dale? Are you sick?'

'Cancer.'

'Oh, Jesus.' Thinking vaguely about environmental contamination of some sort, I wondered if I ought to flee this house that smelled, looked, even tasted of Paula.

'Paula's given me cancer.'

'Cancer's not contagious,' I couldn't help pointing out.

'Paula's given me cancer. Because I betrayed her. The cancer is how she haunts me now.'

I was having trouble following this and wishing savagely for a drink. 'Paula "gave" you cancer because you did what she made you promise to do and helped her die?'

His gaze darted and jumped, never lighting on me. 'Because I didn't. Because I promised and then I went back on my word.'

This was all too much for me. Queasy and in desperate need of a drink, I started to get to my feet, but he stopped me. The bones of his hands on my arm were sharp.

'Please. Beth. Hear me out. I have to tell somebody.'

Shamelessly, I demanded, 'Have you got any beer? Or wine?'

He managed to bring me half a bottle of wine, chilled, and an elegant though dusty wine glass. 'I hope it's still good. It's been in the refrigerator since the night Paula died. She used it for the pills.'

He was waiting for me to assent to another tale. I pushed the bottle and the glass away and exhaled. 'Okay,' I said. 'Okay, I'm listening.'

The story started out the same—wine in the refrigerator, flowers in the vase, smooth jazz in the background. By now I knew something about the soothing nature of repetition, even of terrible things, for I was still telling the story of how Dominic had left me in exactly the same words, with exactly the same pauses and emphases, every chance I got. Dale didn't seem aware that he was repeating himself, and in a way I was actually finding it comforting, so I settled back against the lumpy couch pillow and just let him tell it.

Once again, he dared to think they might be celebrating something. Once again, Paula held onto him to keep them both from flying away when she told him she had stage IV brain cancer and what it meant, and she wasn't going to go through it. Once again she reminded him of his promise to stay with her while she ended her own life, and to help her if she needed him to.

My attention wandered now and then to the need for a drink and the need not to succumb, and the refrain of his words pulled me along, without any real landmarks. So I was ambushed by the new thing he said, and I had to stop him and ask him to repeat. 'Wait. What did you just say? Sorry, I—you lost me.'

He started to fill my glass and I covered it with my hand. 'I failed her, Beth. I couldn't do it. I promised I'd help her if she needed it, and she did need it, and I couldn't do it. She'll never forgive me for that. I'll never forgive myself.'

There was a long pause. Finally I gave in. 'Okay, Dale,' I sighed. 'Tell me.'

* * * * *

Paula fell asleep before she had ingested all the pills. Breathing heavily and snoring loudly, she didn't mimic normal slumber, for Paula had always been a light sleeper, and quiet. It was all Dale could do to stay in the room. It was all he could do to allow himself to wish for it to be over, which meant wishing that the woman he loved would die.

The CD ended and silence filled the space where the horns and drums had been. This late at night the house had only small noises, appliances and clocks, the stray creak and sigh. Lightly holding Paula's hand, waiting for the moment when life would palpably flow out of it, Dale passed the time quietly weeping, keening at full voice, chanting and singing to her, focusing on his breath and hers.

More than three hours passed. The plastic bag with its tape and drawstring was ready for him, on the bedside table beside the empty pill bottles and wineglasses and Paula's letter to the authorities. Dale withdrew one hand from Paula's and laid it on the bag, but the plastic felt like loose skin and he couldn't bear to touch it. 'Paula?'

More than four hours passed. Something like delirium set upon Dale, and for a while he thought maybe she wouldn't die after all, maybe the drug-induced coma would turn out to have been restorative instead of lethal, and Paula would emerge, if not cured, at least in long remission.

Twice in that last hour Dale had left Paula's side, once to go to the bathroom and once to put on another CD, this one a delicate chant. Fervently hoping she would die while he was out of the room, fervidly berating himself for the wish, he returned to her bedside to the snorts and whistles and rattles that told him it wasn't over yet. A dawn bird piped close outside the window, and he knew he was going to betray her.

He called 911. 'My wife,' he gasped into the phone, 'has taken an overdose of sleeping pills. She's—she's still alive. She's still alive.'

He heard the sirens before he'd even hung up the receiver, and had just enough time to turn off the music, put the book at the back of the shelf in the back bedroom, and fold the plastic bag without the tape into its box again. Lights and noise invaded Paula's house. She did not wake up when they rolled her onto the stretcher. He stood and watched them take her away.

* * * * *

'They pumped her stomach,' he persisted in telling me, though by now I was feeling sick myself and definitely didn't need any more information. 'They put her on life support. I couldn't make the decision to pull the plug. How could I do that to the woman I loved? To Paula? She died anyway. I wasn't with her when she died. I'd gone to the cafeteria to grab some lunch, even though I couldn't eat more than a bite or two, and they paged me—but by the time I got back up to the floor she was gone.'

I hadn't realized I'd been holding my breath until now. I let it out. My chest hurt. All I could think of to say was, 'She didn't want that.'

'No,' he agreed miserably. 'She didn't want that.'

He was so distraught and I was so preoccupied with wanting a drink that it almost didn't seem worth the effort to point out the obvious. But some perverse sense of entitlement made me press. 'But last time you told me exactly the opposite. You told me you did kill her, and that's why she was haunting you.'

He was looking over my shoulder. I resisted as long as I could before I snapped my head around as if to catch someone in the act. No one was there.

Dale finally spoke. 'What's true,' he said, 'what's indisputable, is that Paula will haunt me until I pay for betraying her. That's all that matters.'

* * * * *

When I got back from that trip, Dominic was at the house, drunk and lonely. In my fantasies of this scene, I'd imagined I'd be sorely tempted by both him and booze; in fact, I wanted only him. But when he realized I was sober and would be staying that way, he pushed me aside and stumbled out the door, cursing me as a traitor. I haven't seen him since. He doesn't answer my calls or e-mails, and I don't know where he lives.

I haven't seen Dale, either, and I haven't made any attempt to contact him. Nor, I have to admit, do I think much about Paula anymore. Dominic, though, is never far from my thoughts; I keep thinking I see or hear or feel his presence, and I don't know what he wants. I don't know what he wants me to do.

Weird Furka

Adam Golaski

'Around Dodge City and the territory out west, there's just one way to handle the killers and the spoilers, and that's with the U.S. Marshall and the smell of . . . gunsmoke! *Gunsmoke*, starring William Conrad, is the transcribed story of the violence that moved west with young America. And the story of a man who moved with it. "I'm that man. Matt Dillon, United States Marshall. The first man they look for, and the last they wanna meet. It's a chancy job, and it makes a man watchful—and a little lonely."'
—Intro to *Gunsmoke*

'Count down for blast off. X-minus five . . . four . . . three . . . two—X-minus one—fire! From the far horizons of the unknown come transcribed tales of new dimensions in time and space. These are stories of the future, adventures in which you'll live in a million could be years on a thousand maybe worlds. The National Broadcasting Company, in cooperation with Street & Smith, publishers of *Astounding Science Fiction*, presents: *X-Minus One*!' —Intro to *X-Minus One*

'Quiet, please.' —Intro to *Quiet, Please*

KADE, A COMMERCIAL RADIO STATION in Furka, Montana, was moving in a few months from its current location, the 'Furkabick Hotel', as the DJs had dubbed it, to a new location with a greater broadcast range. The Furkabick Hotel was a three storey house, built during the copper rush. The house ceased to be a residence in the mid-thirties, and became KADE shortly after. The station had broadcast nearly continuously, with only short interludes of dead air. KADE broadcast country and bluegrass music and syndicated radio shows until the late 1950s/early '60s, when the last episodes of *The Lone Ranger*,

Have Gun, Will Travel, and *Gunsmoke* were aired. The station switched over to an all-country format, which it has remained, adding several politically conservative drive time talk shows in the early 1990s.

The only exception to this format was an ambient/electronic/experimental music show broadcast Monday mornings, from 1.00 to 4.00 a.m., a time-slot that failed to draw any advertising dollars. The show was created and hosted by Craig Watson, a friend of the owner's girlfriend. He lived in one of the few houses left in Furka, worked as a bartender, and occasionally manned the pumps at Manny's. Once KADE moved, and its range increased, and advertisers became interested, his show would be cancelled. He called his show 'Songs of Degrees'. Virtually no one listened. Craig liked the idea that a sleepless radio listener might roll the dial low and come upon his broadcast, drawn in by unfamiliar sounds.

Craig was usually the only person at the station when his show was broadcast. He loved the Furkabick Hotel, and thought it a shame that the station was abandoning the old house. One more step towards turning Furka into another Montana ghost town. The nature of what he broadcast left him with long stretches when he didn't have to man the boards—twenty-minute compositions of water dripping, of string instruments recorded inside vast underground caverns, of people's voices phased into a fold of noise, and phased back into a conversation. Besides, he didn't like to talk too much during the show's broadcast—he didn't want to explain; he wanted listeners to encounter, and take from their encounter what they might. During these long stretches he liked to wander through the empty house. Other than the studio itself, a long unused recording studio, an office and a front desk on the first floor, the Furkabick was still very much a house, replete with old furniture, paintings, and knick-knacks. He'd explored the top, second, and first floor very thoroughly; the only treasure he'd found was a volume of western themed poetry, which he brought into the studio and read while broadcasting, and occasionally read selections of to his listeners.

Craig decided, during the last months of his show, that he needed to explore the basement. He hadn't done so yet because the door to the basement was locked with an old padlock—one that fit a skeleton key in its face. On the first Sunday of October, with a single swing of a small sledge, he sent the padlock singing across the floor. He located it and hung it back on the latch. With a camping lantern in hand, he carefully picked his way down the wooden steps—nearly falling through on a rotted plank. After the nervousness of the moment passed, he thought, 'It'd be a long morning laying down there with a broken leg.' The air smelled of dust and mildew, and he sneezed more than once as he peered around the dark space.

The basement was nearly empty. The floor was hard-packed dirt, and wooden support pillars, with bark shredded like fur, ran in even rows from one end of the basement to the other. Bare wooden bookcases lined one wall. Just beyond the boiler and the oil tank, both red with rust, was a set of bunker doors, which he reasoned must be how the owner and the maintenance people got in and out to check the gauges and the fuse box. On the other end of the basement was a doorless doorway. Craig walked to it and shone the lantern inside. A bare room, with a cement floor, without windows, but with a very intriguing feature: a wooden trap door in the floor. Craig looked at his watch and ran back upstairs—careful to avoid the rotted step—to put on another CD. He sat in the warm studio—the only room with any heat at that hour—listened to the drone piece he'd put on, and contemplated the trap door. The basement had been enough to make him a little uncomfortable—the thought of opening the trap actually scared him a little. 'This is silly,' he said aloud. The track he was playing had another thirty minutes to it, so he went back down to the basement to finish his exploration.

The trap door was locked with another old padlock. It resisted several blows from the sledge, but the latch itself finally gave, cracking out of the wood of the door with such a noise that Craig jumped back, startled, afraid he'd disturbed some animal's nest. He glanced at his watch, calmed down a bit, and lifted the trap.

A strong odour rose up in a gust: a vinegary smell, mingled with the acid smell of old paper. A wooden ladder led into the sub-basement. Craig lay on his belly and hung his lantern down into the darkness. With the light suspended into the small space, the basement around him was pitch dark. To Craig's pleasure, the room was furnished with metal bookcases, and the bookcases were filled with records and boxes of reel-to-reel recordings and electrical equipment. Excitement filled him with a tingling sensation. He started to climb down into the room when he caught a glimpse of his watch. 'Damn,' he said, and ran back upstairs to the studio. He looked for the longest CD he had with him, put it on, and went back downstairs.

He knew that what was in the sub-basement belonged to KADE, but decided to carry as much of his find out to his truck anyhow, figuring that the owner had no idea any of it existed, and that he could return it during the chaos of the move. The job took two hours, and was a lot of hard lifting. The transcription disks, and the machine used to make them, were the crown jewel of his find, he knew it, but it cost him a lot of lower back pain; and had it fallen on top of him, as he pushed it out of the sub-basement, it could've crushed bones. Again he pictured himself on the floor, unable to move; but this time so deep in the basement he might never be found.

At 4.00 the morning DJ came in, looking exhausted, strung out, thermos of coffee opened and steaming. An hour later, the receptionist came. By then, Craig was in his bedroom, everything hauled in from his truck and lying on the floor around his bed. He looked at the equipment he'd brought home and thought, 'What possessed me to do that?' He laughed at himself: he thought of himself as daring when it came to ideas, but not as a man of action. Briefly, souring his amusement with himself, a panic came over him, a clammy mist which filled his head. Just for an instant. He slept soundly.

Craig worked at the bar that same night. After his show and before his shift he usually didn't do too much other than sleep and have a late lunch. On that Monday, when he woke, he had a strong desire to set up the equipment he'd found and go through the boxes of records but decided, after some deliberation, that he'd rather wait until he had a solid block of time. He ate at his kitchen counter and walked to the bar a little early.

Johnson, a sixty-year old regular, was the only patron.

'Craig,' he said, when Craig emerged from the kitchen, tying a knot in the back of the apron he wore around his waist.

'Johnson.' Craig thought Johnson was okay. Johnson drove a delivery truck, usually at night, and liked to make fun of Craig's show, which Johnson insisted he never listened to.

'I made it through ten minutes of your programme last night.'

'Yeah?'

'But only because I thought I'd tuned my radio wrong and had two channels crossed.' Johnson laughed at his own joke. Craig forced a smile.

'How are you doing, Johnson?'

'I'm fine, fine. If I wasn't married I'd be perfect.' Johnson laughed again. Wife jokes were also part of his routine with Craig. 'You look dreadful, though. Always do on Mondays.'

'The show kind of messes with my schedule.'

'I bet. When're you going to give that up? You don't get paid, do you?'

'I like doing the show. I like radio.' Craig started drying the wet glasses the dishwasher had brought out. He'd had this same conversation week after week. 'But it looks as if I won't be doing it much longer. Station's moving and they won't be taking me with them.'

'That's a damned shame. But I bet if we tune in at the same time as always, and nothin's on, it'll be like hearing your show.'

When Craig returned home from the bar he stripped off his clothes, which stank of cigarette smoke, showered, and put on clean clothes. He brewed a pot of coffee, brought the pot into his room, and set about sifting through his find, which, when Johnson wasn't talking, had been all he could think about. The first box was filled with 16-inch transcription disks, acetate coated glass. By Craig's reckoning, they were in fine condition—no crystallization of the acetate. The basement room must have been very dry and cool. The next box contained metal disks and a few made on cardboard. He was extremely excited; terrified, too, that he was now responsible for these fragile recordings. He unlatched a suitcase-sized box and was overjoyed to see that it was a transcription machine—possibly the very machine used to make the recordings. There was also a record player, capable of playing the transcription disks—able to switch from 80 to 70 RPMs—and an Ampex tape recorder—the earliest commercially available tape recorder. The third box he opened was filled with tape recordings, the fourth with more, and the fifth with another set of glass transcription disks. 'Good Lord,' he thought, 'if these machines still work, I'll be able to listen to all of this.' He bit his fist to control his excitement. He wished there was someone he could tell, someone who wouldn't spread the word all over Furka, resulting in Craig's having to return everything to KADE. He uncoiled the wire, plugged the record player into a socket, and clicked the power switch to the on position.

He fell asleep on the floor of his bedroom, listening to a scratchy recording of a local news broadcast made in 1942.

On Friday, after sitting at Manny's in case a car actually came, Craig went home and put on one of the cardboard transcription disks. In tinny mono, he heard what sounded like some of the ambient music he played on his show. This had him; he wondered if he was about to hear a very old experimental record. Perhaps he had discovered a lost composer. After a few grooves of the disk, though, the music faded, and a man introduced himself.

WEIRD FURKA
Transcript Number One
Broadcast July, 1947

MUSIC INTRO: Pipes being tapped, individually and faintly at first, then all at once, firmly, louder, and faster. Once a cacophony of sound has been created, tapping ceases, and sound fades.

ANNOUNCER: [A deep voice] Greetings, listeners. I wish to welcome you to a new kind of weird radio show. The strange stories you are about to hear are true, and told by the people who lived them. If you scoff at the idea that there is a world outside of our common perception, another world beyond our own, [whispered] *the supernatural world* [no longer whispered], then prepare to have your assumptions challenged; if you already believe such a world exists, then prepare to have your beliefs confirmed. [In a booming, reverberating voice] Welcome to *Weird Furka*!

HOST: Thank you for tuning in. Tonight, on our first in what I hope to be a long-lasting series of broadcasts documenting the weird happenings in our own Furka, I have a peculiar tale told by a housewife, Mrs Buzzard, who lives in a well-kept house on Broad Street. In an effort to distance this show from *dramatic* shows, and because the modern American housewife is busy all day long, I took KADE's top of the line portable recording device to Mrs Buzzard's kitchen to capture her weird story. What you're listening to is a live recording. [Sounds from the street] Mrs Buzzard, is it all right if we close the windows? It'll be better for the recording.

MRS BUZZARD: Certainly. It'll get pretty stuffy in here, though. I'm baking.

HOST: And it smells wonderful. But the noise from outside. [Sound of windows being closed. Sound of an oven door opened and closed] Thank you. You answered a letter I sent out saying that you had a strange story to tell. Is this something that happened to you?

MRS BUZZARD: [Sounding distant] I wrote it on the card that it happened to my sister.

HOST: I know, but for our listeners. And please speak in the direction of the microphone. So, this weird event happened to your sister?

MRS BUZZARD: Yes.

HOST: Please tell our listeners what happened, just like you told me on the card you sent. And please speak toward the microphone.

MRS BUZZARD: Is this better?

HOST: Much.

MRS BUZZARD: Well, my sister—her name's Clara—is it okay to use her name, or is this like *Dragnet*?

HOST: It's okay to use her name.

MRS BUZZARD: My sister Clara lost her husband, Sam, to a heart attack. A terrible thing. Of course we're all upset but especially Clara and her son. She was very depressed and cried a lot and had a hard time doing anything. I'd come over and our brother, Francis, would come over too. He fixed up her sink and made sure there was enough coal in the basement, the things Sam would normally do. Some times Francis would take Clara's son out to watch a ballgame, too.

Now, this may seem a little unusual, but Clara had two phones, one for the upstairs and one downstairs. You see, they had a very big house, so that way, if Clara was cleaning upstairs and a call came through, she didn't have to run down to the living-room.

HOST: Sure.

MRS BUZZARD: One day the upstairs phone rang. She told me she ran up the stairs without thinking about it and answered it. The person on the other end said that he was her husband, and wanted to let her know he was okay. Though the man on the other end of the line sounded like her husband, she was furious, of course, and in tears, and hung up.

Soon after Francis came by the house and found her at the kitchen table, crying. When he asked what was the matter she told him that she answered the phone upstairs and a prankster said he was her husband. She asked Francis, 'Just how cruel can you get?' Well Francis looked at her in a funny way and reminded her that the upstairs phone didn't work. You see, a little before Sam died, he'd started on a project in the upstairs hall and had taken out the phone jack.

HOST: Amazing. A call from the dead.

MRS BUZZARD: Well that isn't all. The next morning she was in the kitchen washing the dishes and a man walked by the house and she was sure it was her husband. Absolutely certain. She dropped a dish in the sink and chipped it. Before she could go outside to see if he really was her husband—after the call the night before she didn't know what might be true—her son came running into the kitchen. He looked extremely happy and in a rush—you know how children talk when they're excited—he told her that he was just outside playing and his dad walked up to him and smiled and told him that he's okay.

And that's the story.

HOST: Thank you very much Mrs Buzzard, for sharing with our audience that weird but true ghost story. [The sound quality changes a bit. The HOST is back in the studio] Thank you very much for tuning in. Tune in next week for another weird but true story.

ANNOUNCER: *Weird Furka* is a new kind of show, in which listeners hear the bizarre stories of their neighbours. If you've had a weird encounter with the supernatural, please contact KADE, c/o *Weird Furka* [address]. Tune in next week for another story that will shake you free of the everyday.

MUSIC EXTRO: Same as introductory music, but cut off by the recording.

By Sunday, Craig had found two other episodes of *Weird Furka*, all on the cardboard transcription disks. He decided that at some point during his show, he was going to air all three episodes. He put on a long modern classical piece, one with sounds similar to the intro music for *Weird Furka*. Sure that everyone was out of the station, he ran out to his car and carried the disks and the machine he needed to play them up into the studio. Unable to dub the show successfully, he decided he'd just lower the studio microphone and air the show that way; it was short, he would sit silently and listen. He faded out the classical piece as he started the record. The pipe-sounds came up, and then the announcer. There was something about the show that he found utterly compelling. He promised he'd do a little library research when he got the time; for now, he listened to the familiar broadcast: the sounds in Mrs Buzzard's kitchen, the announcer, who he was beginning to suspect was the host. He could smell what she was baking, feel the heat in her kitchen. He sat and watched the disk spin. He didn't move at all.

On Monday night the bar was nearly empty, except for a few regulars. Craig was stacking glasses. He jumped at the large smack of an open hand on the bar, and at the barking of his name.

'What the hell was that?' Johnson demanded.

'What the hell was what?' Craig ran a towel over a dry glass, as if he were polishing a stone.

'I turn on the radio and I hear a voice I thought I'd never hear again. I know the man's dead, so I could only assume my radio'd fell into another dimension or I was tuning in Hell.'

'You listened to my show last night?'

'Hell no. I never listen to your show. When I'm driving at that hour I turn the station to something that doesn't sound like a room full of children with busted musical instruments. But last night . . . were you responsible for bringing Frank Shokler back from the dead?'

'Frank Shokler?'

'The guy who did that show.'

'*Weird Furka.*'

'That's the show. *Weird Furka*. Damn weird all right. Worse 'n weird.'

'You know about the show?' Craig put down the glass and the towel and leaned forward.

'Give me a draught and I'll tell you if I know the show.'

Craig poured a draught, all the while looking at Johnson, waiting for the story. Johnson waited until he'd had a drink before he spoke.

'I used to listen to that show when it first came on. They used it for filler between Benny and *Gunsmoke*. I liked those shows, so I heard a few episodes of Frank's show.' He took another swig of his beer, wiped his mouth on the back of his hand, and proceeded. 'I didn't like that man at all. I tolerated that show for a while, but when it got really weird—when *he* got really weird—I tuned out. I'd turn off my radio for twenty minutes rather than listen. And I like a good creepy story from time to time. Hell, back then I probably had a *Vault of Evil* or some nonsense stuffed in my glove compartment. But Frank was a bastard, and then he got to be a frightening bastard and I was done with him. Where'd you find that shit?'

'I just dug it out of a library.'

'Oh yeah?' Johnson didn't look like he believed Craig, but didn't seem to care. 'What possessed you to play it on the air?'

'I thought . . . it's interesting. It's local. I thought my listeners might like it.'

'You ain't got listeners.'

Craig knew that was likely. That was one of the reasons why 'Songs of Degrees' wasn't going to move with the station. 'What do you know about Frank Shokler?'

'Not much. He was in my high school. Didn't play sports. Built a crystal set we'd listen to in shop. I wasn't friends with him. He went away after high school. When he came back, it wasn't long until he was recording interviews with every nutty housewife and derelict in town. Then he was gone again.'

When Johnson was finished with his beer, Craig poured another. 'On the house,' he said.

During the next week Craig set up the Ampex and started listening to the reel-to-reels. Again, local news, a few field recordings of live jazz shows, and an on the scene broadcast of a great forest fire. He also found what he had hoped he might: more episodes of *Weird Furka*. Craig had begun to eat all his meals in his bedroom. Dirty plates and bowls accumulated around the equipment in his room. He brought a hot plate in to heat soup. The rest of his house seemed large and silent, seemed to press down on Craig, so he'd shut the door of his bedroom when he listened.

He searched unsuccessfully online for any mention of the show or of Frank Shokler. Furka hadn't had a library for over a decade, so after a few hours at

Manny's—during which he did nothing more than raise the gas prices on the marquee and sweep out the shack that he sat in—Craig drove to the library in the next town over. He didn't find much there, either. On microfiche were radio listings which provided him with a way to date the episodes. He carefully copied out all the dates, then realized no episode titles were given, and there were no titles on the recordings he'd found; some of them were numbered, but he wasn't sure the radio listings started with the first episode. The show was on the air for less than a year. He uncovered a small article from an issue of the *Furka Weekly*, which talked about *Weird Furka* and Frank Shokler's death— in rather flip terms, Craig thought. The central theme of the piece was that Shokler's death was as strange as an episode of his own show. After making that comment, the article was vague about how he died, stating that 'It may have been a heart condition', and mentioning that he was found at the station. As an extension of the joke the article basically was, the reporter had tracked down two of the women Shokler had interviewed on the show: Mrs Buzzard and Mrs Drummond. Mrs Buzzard talked about how he was still around, 'in the air'. Mrs Drummond said about Shokler, 'He was a polite fellow. He was skinny. And when we talked—which was really only the once but I remember it like yesterday—he was very intense, as if he were trying to see around me. Or around what I was saying.'

WEIRD FURKA
Transcript Number Four
Broadcast August, 1947

MUSIC INTRO

ANNOUNCER: Greetings once again, dear listeners. The strange stories you are about to hear are true, and told by the people who lived them. If you scoff at the idea that there is a world outside of our common perception, another world beyond our own, *the supernatural world*, then prepare to have your assumptions challenged; if you already believe such a world exists, then prepare to have your beliefs confirmed. Welcome to *Weird Furka*!

HOST: Thank you for tuning in. I'm your host, Frank Shokler. Tonight's mysterious story is told to us by Mrs Drummond, who had kindly invited me into her homey living-room. As I've said before, in an effort to distance this show from *dramatic* shows, I took KADE's top of the line portable recording device out of the studio and into the supernatural fire, so to speak. Nothing is scripted. What you're listening to, as always, is a live recording.

    Mrs Drummond, you wrote to me and shared with me a most fascinating story. Will you be kind enough to enlighten our listening audience?

MRS DRUMMOND: [Nervously] Yes. Should I start?

HOST: Yes, Mrs Drummond, please begin.

MRS DRUMMOND: For a time, I lived in a house that was haunted. This was the first house my husband and I bought. We bought it for a song and I suppose that was in part due to the rumours. We liked the idea that there were ghosts and hoped to see one.

At least until we invited my brother to the house for a night. My brother was a serviceman in the first war and on leave, and was driving to see a girl—he married her, in '19. Anyway, at the time, my husband was on a strict medical diet and to support him I went on it too. We served my brother a meal we couldn't eat—I don't think my brother ever saw a meal without a potato! [laughs] We told him about our diet and then moved to the living-room and spent a quiet evening chatting. Around eleven, we all retired. We put my brother in the downstairs guest-room.

In the morning, over breakfast, my brother grinned at us and asked which one of us was it, breaking our diet and sneaking down to the kitchen? We both denied having gone down. He accused us again and my husband asked him why he was so sure. He told us that he heard footsteps in the kitchen. He said that, with all the activity in the kitchen, he figured one of us was preparing quite a feast. He also added that he was sure he was going to be invited to join, because his door opened, though no one came in.

Well I looked at my husband, and he nodded, and I said to my brother, 'You're so lucky. One of the reasons we bought this house was because it is rumoured to be haunted by the first homeowner's butler. The guest-room, in fact, was the butler's room. We haven't heard or seen anything ourselves, you're the first.' Unfortunately, this story really bothered my brother. I didn't see him again until my husband and I moved out here.

HOST: That's quite a story, Mrs Drummond. Did you or your husband ever see or hear the ghost?

MRS DRUMMOND: No, we never did. We were very disappointed. I guess we're heavy sleepers.

HOST: Thank you very much Mrs Drummond. [Sound changes, back in studio] I find it really quite amazing just how many people have had supernatural experiences in Furka. Until I sent out my letters asking for such stories—and if you didn't get a letter, feel free to write me directly at the station—I never would have guessed. There are enough interesting stories for this show to go on quite a while.

I've been wondering, these past weeks, if Furka is for some reason a place where the supernatural and the natural cross, an intersection to other dimensions, perhaps, and whether people—sensitive people—are occasionally granted glimpses. Alternatively, I've wondered if Furka isn't exceptional at all. That if I were to go into any town in Montana, or anywhere in the country for that matter, and ask people to share with me their supernatural tales, that just as many would have stories to tell. Perhaps if we recorded enough of these stories, we would gain an understanding of the mysterious, and perhaps a way to make contact with the other side. This is Frank Shokler, signing off.

ANNOUNCER: And that takes care of another episode of *Weird Furka*, a new kind of show, in which listeners hear the bizarre stories of their neighbours. If you've had a weird encounter with the supernatural, please contact KADE, c/o *Weird Furka* [address]. Tune in next week for another story that will shake you free of the everyday.

MUSIC EXTRO

With a little inventive wiring, Craig found that he could digitize the reel-to-reels, and burn them onto a CD. This made it a lot easier to bring the shows to the station.

Johnson caught Craig's eye from the bar-room door. For a moment, Craig thought Johnson was going to charge the bar. Craig backed up a little, wringing his washcloth through his hands.

'Why do you insist on playing that nonsense?' Johnson demanded.

'I thought you didn't listen.'

'I keep my radio on KADE for country. When I get in my truck it's on that station. I can't change it fast enough. But I hear what's on.'

'You shut it off then, don't you?'

'Yes, I shut it off. Damn right. But I know it's on the air. I can sense it. I don't like it.'

'Look, Johnson, what're you drinking?'

'What do you think?'

Craig poured out a glass of the local brew Johnson drank. Once he had a drink, Craig said, 'It's a harmless little show. It's quaint.'

'Frank Shokler wasn't harmless. The show reminds me of bad times.'

'He wasn't harmless?'

'I thought his show was gone. That he was gone. You'll stop airing it, right? Go back to that trash-compactor stuff you used to play, right?'

Craig grinned. 'I still play that trash-compactor stuff.'

'Well play it all the time.'

'I don't understand why you care.'

'You'll take it off, won't you?'

Craig felt courage swell up inside him, the same feeling of courage that had sent him crawling around the dark basement two weeks before. 'No, Johnson. I don't think that I will.'

'Then damn you, Craig.' He left the bar, his glass still more than half full.

Craig found, among the reel-to-reels, thirty recordings of *Weird Furka*, in addition to the three cardboard transcription disks. He didn't want to hear them all at once, he decided. He wanted to make them last as long as he could. So he listened to a few episodes over and over, lying on his bed or on the floor of his room. Sometimes he listened to one of the other recordings. He started to reuse plates rather than take the time to wash them. Sometimes he urinated into a cup instead of leaving his room to go to the bathroom.

He did a little more research into the media the shows were recorded on, and learned that it was extraordinary for the recordings to have survived the way they did. The acetate coating on the cardboard disk typically became brittle, the petroleum separated out of it, or crystals formed on the surface. The reel-to-reels also should have become brittle, or, if conditions were different, turned into a sort of glue. Recordings made as recently as the 1980s in professional recording studios were unstable. The media *Weird Furka* were recorded on, and the shows stored with it, were all like new. Burning what he could onto CD comforted him, guaranteeing, he believed, the longevity of the show; in the back of his mind, though, he was fairly sure that he didn't have to worry.

In the middle of the night he woke up. He sat up in bed and shouted 'Who?' and looked around quickly, trying to figure out where he was and—once that was established—why his room was in the state it was in. He recognized, barely, the recording equipment, but he didn't recall bringing in the dishes or the mugs or the hot plate. He was a neat person. He was disturbed by the smell—an unfamiliar, stale smell. And then a metal corner of the transcription machine glinted, and caught Craig's eye, and he was lost, and then asleep again.

The next Sunday, when he pulled up to the station, he stopped before getting out of his truck, because there was a large black dog standing near the station door. He watched it, illuminated in his headlights. The dog didn't move. He got out of the truck slowly, gathered his CDs from the passenger seat, and walked towards the front door. The dog followed Craig with a slow turn of its head. At the front door, Craig and the dog were side by side. He tried to suppress the terror he felt, sure the dog would pick up on his fear and jump at him; he didn't think he could even bear the dog barking. Once inside, the door shut behind him, he looked out at the dog. In turn, it watched him.

Up in the studio, Craig warned the DJ about the dog.

'Thanks for the heads up, Craig.'

'It was the strangest thing.'

'Dogs are like that, sometimes. Nothing to worry about, I'd imagine. He'll probably be gone by the time I leave.' The DJ sniffed at the air. 'Maybe he smelled food on you.'

'Oh, sorry.' Craig hadn't done any laundry in the past week. His clothes either smelled like cigarettes from the bar, or like the peanut butter sandwiches he'd been eating almost nightly.

'Don't sweat it. You got your first song ready?'

Craig handed him a CD. 'It's track seven.'

'OK.' The DJ cued it up. 'What is it?'

Craig described the piece; the DJ clearly wasn't interested.

'I've been listening to your show on my drive home. You gonna play any of those shows?'

Craig brightened. 'Yes, yes I am.'

'Where the hell'd they come from?'

'Oh, ah, a friend of mine.'

'He found 'em? They sound really old.'

'No, no, he makes them. He makes them sound old. It's amazing what you can do with a computer.'

The DJ nodded, but didn't appear to believe Craig's story at all. The DJ swung the microphone in front of his face, faded out his song, and said, 'That wraps it up for me, folks. Next up, "Songs of Degrees", with your host, Craig Watson. I don't know about you, but I find those little shows he plays to be more peculiar than the music he likes. Hope none of it gives y'all nightmares.' The DJ started up Craig's CD, and wished Craig a goodnight.

Craig could hardly stand listening to the music; he desperately wanted to get to *Weird Furka*, to hear Frank's voice. He knew he needed to space the shows out, though; they were very short, he'd only brought three, and he was on the air until 4.00 a.m.

When Craig left the studio, the dog was still outside. As Craig climbed into the cab of his truck he said to the dog, 'Goodnight, Harold.' The dog nodded, and walked off. What he had done didn't strike Craig as peculiar until he was in bed. When he remembered it, though, he opened his eyes wide in his dark room, and covered his open mouth. Before questions could emerge, such as why his room was in the state it was in, or why he felt so driven to play *Weird Furka* during his own show, a wet feeling came into his body, a smothering.

Craig found that his desire to hear the *Weird Furka* shows he hadn't listened to yet was greater than his wish to extend his pleasure. On Tuesday night he listened to every episode he had. The shows being as short as they were—ranging from five minutes to ten—he was able to listen to them all in a couple of hours. He left his house when he had to work at the bar, arriving a little late. When he got back home, he listened to them all once more. Three of the episodes, not including the first, featured stories told by Mrs Buzzard, who became less and less nervous with each show. At first Craig dismissed Mrs Buzzard as a crackpot and a ditz, but gradually he grew to love her voice, and the way she told a story, and the smells of her home, which he imagined he smelled while he listened, and which covered the rotten, sweaty smell of his bedroom. One episode struck Craig as a sort of turning point, a moment when *Weird Furka* changed and became something more than just a collection of local legends and personal anecdotes.

WEIRD FURKA

Transcript Number Seventeen

Broadcast October, 1947

MUSIC INTRO

HOST: Greetings once again. I'm your host, Frank Shokler. If you scoff at the idea that there is a world outside of our common perception, another world beyond our own, *the supernatural world*, then I hope to challenge your assumptions; if you already believe such a world exists, then I hope to confirm your beliefs; I hope to be welcomed into your brotherhood. This is *Weird Furka*!

Until now, I have presented the stories of your neighbours. I have recorded the stories in their homes, at their invitation. I think these stories have all been compelling. I considered myself to be among the unfortunate who had not directly experienced anything supernatural.

Perhaps because I have been in the presence of those who have, perhaps because of my recent steady contemplation of unusual phenomena, or a combination of both, I have recalled a story from my youth, an episode I had quite forgotten until earlier this week. The story came to my memory so vividly, and so suddenly, I doubted it was anything more than a dream. I thought about it, and thought about it, and realized that no, it wasn't a dream at all, but a memory that had been lost to me for some reason. Perhaps suppressed because of what it hinted at, suppressed by my own self in a misguided attempt to keep me grounded in the reality of the day-to-day. Hopefully you will extend to me the same faith you extend to those I've interviewed these past few months. Hopefully you will not chalk this up as a radio stunt or as filler. I assure you, I have many other stories from your neighbours that I will broadcast for you in the upcoming weeks. Please indulge me: upon rediscovering this episode of my youth, I felt an urgency to share it with you.

When I was a boy I used to take long walks in the woods. My parents didn't like that I did it, because they were afraid I'd be mauled by a bear or shot by a hunter. Still, I went. There were trails I knew and loved, because of particular trees or rocks or tiny pools of water in the stream that frogs and fish lived in.

One late afternoon I was climbing on a rock and I saw what I thought must be a firefly. It was a light which flashed for a moment a few feet off the ground. I looked for the light and in a moment I saw it again. I realized then that it wasn't a flashing light, like the light of a firefly, but only appeared to be, as my view of it was obscured intermittently by trees. The sky grew dimmer, the light seemed to grow brighter, and I was sure that it was moving closer to me.

Once I got close to the light—it was a fireball, hanging in the sky, like a Biblical sign—I felt no heat from it, but it was flame just the same. Once I got close, it started moving away from me. I followed it. At times it was difficult, and had I been an adult I don't think I could have got through the brambles and dense shrubbery it led me through.

The fireball and I came out of the woods to a field. Along the field ran a dirt road. A mile down was a tall house. The fireball rose and rose and then vanished. I stared at the spot in the sky where I'd last seen it for a while, before I looked back at the house. I thought maybe the fireball had wanted me to go to the house, but seeing that tall house out there, having been lead there by a fireball—it terrified me. When I thought about what might be inside that house—

I didn't think I'd ever see that house again. But I realize now, now that that memory has come back to me, that that house was KADE, a good fifteen years before there *were* radio stations in Montana.

It probably sounds as if I'm just making this up, taking up radio time because I don't have a real show, but I ask that you believe me, and I assume some of you good listeners will. This memory came to me like that fireball did when I was a boy; it emerged from behind a thicket of trees in my mind and made itself known as a bright, burning point. I am really unsure what this all means. Is it Furka? Could it be this converted house that I'm broadcasting from? What draws the supernatural world out of its invisible place and into our sphere, where our perceptions are so dominated by five drab senses? I leave you to think on that.

Next week *Weird Furka* will return in its customary format—I will be interviewing a Furka resident who has had a supernatural experience. What will make next week's episode unusual, is that that Furka resident is a twelve-year-old boy! Goodnight.

MUSIC EXTRO

Craig didn't do anything for a while after listening to episode seventeen for the third time in a row. He let the tape's leader flap as the reels spun around. He was on his back, surrounded by bowls and plates. Upon hearing episode seventeen the second time something had grown in his memory—just a little bit, enough for Craig to detect it. When he played the show again, the memory moved forward, just as the fireball had in Frank's story. That memory of Craig's, which moved forward in his mind, was of the same fireball, and how it had led Craig to the Furkabick Hotel. Sure, the owner's girlfriend, one night at the bar, had listened to Craig talk about his love of radio and had said she would speak with the owner about finding time for Craig to do his own show; sure she had given him directions to the station and told him when to go. But, overlapping those truths, was the truth that Craig had followed a cold fireball to KADE that had left him standing in front of that tall house wondering how he'd got there.

When Craig couldn't stand the enormous roar of his own circulatory system, he carefully put on the next reel, to listen to episode eighteen again. He was not excited to hear it, because it struck him as a step back from episode seventeen; he knew later episodes were more like episode seventeen, so his inclination was to skip ahead. Yet—he felt as if that would be disrespectful.

WEIRD FURKA
Transcript Number Eighteen
Broadcast October, 1947

MUSIC INTRO

ANNOUNCER: Greetings dedicated listeners. The strange stories you are about to hear are true, and told by the people who lived them. If you scoff at the idea that there is a world outside of our common perception, another world beyond our own, *the supernatural world*, then prepare to have your assumptions challenged; if you already believe such a world exists, then prepare to have your beliefs confirmed. Welcome to *Weird Furka*!

HOST: Thank you for tuning in. I hope last week's episode was not too off-putting. Tonight, we have a peculiar tale for you told—with permission from his parents—by a twelve-year-old boy named Jimmy. [transitional sounds] How are you today, Jimmy?

JIMMY: I'm fine, Mr Shokler.

HOST: Well, now, Jimmy, you and your parents sent me a very interesting letter about a mysterious experience you had. Would you care to tell our audience your story? And please speak into the microphone, son.

JIMMY: [Too close to the microphone] My parents and I just moved out here.

JIMMY'S MOTHER: [In the background] We moved to Cedar Grove less than a year ago.

JIMMY: [facing away from the microphone] Mom!

JIMMY'S MOTHER: Sorry.

HOST: No, it's okay. Jimmy, if your mother can add details to the story, our listeners will certainly appreciate it. That gives weight to the story.

JIMMY: Okay.

HOST: Please continue.

JIMMY: The neighbourhood is still being built, and it goes for blocks and blocks, and in some places, on the outermost points of the neighbourhood, the houses haven't been finished or aren't even built, they're just grassy lots. I like to play down there, even though my mom doesn't like me to go so far.

JIMMY'S MOTHER: I worry about animals coming out of the woods.

JIMMY: There are no animals. Except skunks and raccoons and deer.

JIMMY'S MOTHER: Well, I don't need my son getting sprayed by a skunk.

JIMMY: [laughs at this suggestion. His mother giggles] Anyway, I was down there among the unfinished houses—I like to play in them because you can climb on the frames and see out where the roof hasn't been put on yet. One of the houses, that a week earlier was totally unfinished and open, now looked finished. But I could see that the door was wide open, so I kind of thought maybe the house wasn't done yet, and I wanted to see the inside.

    I walked up to the door and hollered into the house if anyone was home. No one answered and besides, the hall was still unfinished wood and the walls were open where they were putting in light switches and plumbing. I walked in and down the hall. On my left were two doors—pocket doors—and I pushed them open. I couldn't believe it. The room behind the doors was completely finished. And I got a weird feeling from it.

HOST: What was that feeling, Jimmy?

JIMMY: That that room had been lived in for a long time. But that's impossible and I knew that. But the floor was polished and clean and there was a carpet—a bear rug, with the head still on it—and a big leather chair and a table and lots of bookcases with books. I went over to the bookcases and looked at the books and a lot of them were in different languages. They all looked old. Some of them were in English and one said that it was ghost stories, so I took it down to look at it and it was really beautiful and there were pictures in it. I figured that no one would miss it if I borrowed it for a while so I took it home with me.

When Mom saw what I had she asked where I'd got it from and she told me I had to return it right away.

HOST: Do you remember the name of the book?

JIMMY: No.

JIMMY'S MOTHER: I don't remember either. It might have just been called *Ghosts*. It was a beautiful old book, leather bound with gold leaf. We wrapped it in brown paper with a note so Jimmy could just leave it on the front steps and not go into the house again, that we thought, obviously, someone lived in.

JIMMY: Anyway, so the next morning after breakfast I go back down to where that house was. The door is still wide open. I look in thinking I'd just as well put the book back on the shelf if I could. The pocket doors were open, like I guess I left them, but the room was different. I walked down the hall and looked, and the room was as unfinished as the rest of the house.

Before I got spooked I went outside and looked at all the houses around that one to make sure I hadn't just made a mistake. But I'm telling you, I hadn't. Well, now I was pretty spooked and wanted to get out of there. I put the book in the hall near the doorway and took off. I haven't been down there since.

HOST: A vanishing room! Perhaps a room from another dimension, briefly sent to Cedar Grove to deliver a book to young Jimmy here. I want to thank Jimmy for his story, and his mother, Mrs Johnson, for helping.

[Sound quality changes, back in the studio]

HOST: Just a quick word to wrap up tonight's episode. I have been the subject of some local controversy. Seeing as this is a small town, I'm sure you know of what I speak. You must also know that the rumours aren't true, couldn't be. The people who spread these rumours are stupid, thick-headed people who do not understand—maybe can't understand—the nature of my work. I am building a library of the supernatural, *among other things*. These people who insist I ought to take a step back and learn how to live normally are people who don't understand that my discoveries originate from a solid base. I am a solid person, and only because of this am I able to attempt to reach into the invisible. There are other dimensions that can be reached, I know it; chances are, I won't discover these places, *but there is a chance that I will*. Please discount those who criticize me.

I hope you enjoyed tonight's broadcast.

ANNOUNCER: And that takes care of another episode of *Weird Furka*. If you've had a weird encounter with the supernatural, please contact KADE, c/o *Weird Furka* [address]. Tune in next week for another story that will shake you free of the everyday.

MUSIC EXTRO

Thursday afternoon, exhausted, Craig sat in front of the gas station, staring blankly at nothing. He jerked in his seat when he heard his name. Johnson walked from his truck towards Craig. Craig stood up, tense.

'Leave me alone, Johnson,' he said.

Johnson put up his hands. 'Give me another chance, Craig. Just hear me out.' He stopped walking, and stood about two yards from Craig. 'I'm sorry I told you to go to hell. You're a good kid, I'm sure of it. You've been serving me beer a long time. You just need to listen to some sense.'

'You've told me everything already.'

'No, no, I haven't. I didn't want to. Now, can I come over and sit down?'

Craig sat, and Johnson took this as an invitation. He took a chair off the porch and set it in front of Craig. 'Just give me a couple of minutes and maybe I can clear up why I got so angry when I heard those shows on the radio again.'

Before Johnson could speak, Craig came alert, and asked, 'What's your first name?'

Johnson grimaced.

'Is it James? Jim, Jimmy?'

'Use your head, son, I can't be little Jimmy Johnson. Frank and I were in high school together. But don't look so disappointed. Maybe if you ever got some sleep you would've figured it out: Jimmy's my nephew. Only son of my brother, David, God rest his soul. It's my brother who made me aware of what Frank was up to. He was screwing any housewife who'd let him. You've heard Mrs Buzzard on the air, right? She was a frequent guest, wasn't she? She thought Frank was handsome and interesting, unlike Mr Buzzard—a friend of mine, by the way. Now you see why he made those recordings when their husbands were at work.'

Craig fought a grin and asked, 'But with Jimmy there?'

'A mother can shoo a child out of the house. My brother was sure something had happened. Bed sheets all thrown about, Mabel—my brother's wife—out of it and exhausted. House in disarray.'

'And you're sure?'

'My brother was. Ended his marriage. I haven't seen my nephew or Mabel since. So, I just don't like the idea of Shokler getting memorialized or glorified or anything. That's why I got so angry. I shouldn't have. But I'm calm now.'

'That's good.'

'I'm just sorry I didn't just lay it all out for you—I can see why you were bull-headed—I'd'a been if someone'd walked into my bar and told me what to do. I'm glad we got that square.' Johnson seemed unsure what to do now that he'd explained himself to Craig. He said, 'If I were you, I'd get out of this town all together.'

'Why's that?'

'Look around you. The town is shrivelling up. When was the last time you pumped any gas?'

Craig tried to place in time the small, green pick-up that was the last vehicle he'd topped off. He shrugged.

'That's right. When I'm driving through this town I make sure I have plenty of gas, 'cause if I ran out here I'd be in the middle of nowhere. Montana has a way of squeezing little towns until they're dead, and this town is pushin' out its last wheeze. Once your station moves, you ought to. Go someplace where you might find a nice divorcée and make a life for yourself.'

'I'll give it some serious thought.'

Johnson clapped Craig on the shoulder, then took Craig's hand and shook it. 'You do that. Now I gotta hit the road.' He started towards his truck, stopped, and faced Craig. He pointed a finger and said, 'You take care of yourself.'

As Craig watched Johnson drive away, he grinned. Shokler's rant at the end of episode eighteen had meant little to him, so long out of context, but Johnson had unwittingly provided Craig with the missing history. He knew what Shokler had been accused of, and was certain the accusations were baseless. Sunday night, Craig would broadcast all the episodes of *Weird Furka*.

Craig spent Sunday afternoon making CD copies of the last episodes. As he recorded episode twenty-five, his attention was caught by Frank's mention of a dog. Frank told the audience that he had his dog, Harold, with him in the studio, and intended to bring his dog with him to the station from that point on. Craig thought the dog at the station the previous Sunday must have been Frank's—never did it occur to Craig that the dog he'd seen *couldn't* have been Frank's.

And that night the dog was there, standing guard at the door. Craig walked up to the dog and said, 'Hello, Harold.' He knelt beside the dog and patted him, as he would a familiar animal—then he stopped, pulled his hands back, and rubbed his forehead. For a moment he had no idea who the dog was, became terrified of it—and the dog growled. Blood rushed to his head—he could nearly see a cloud-like infusion fill an empty space in his mind—then he resumed petting the dog. When he stood, he held the door open for Harold in case he wanted to join Craig in the studio. The dog didn't move, and Craig knew he was standing guard as he had for Frank.

He didn't speak at all to the DJ when he stepped into the studio, though the DJ spoke to him, and set up Craig's show. The DJ said, 'Dog out there tonight?' And when Craig didn't answer, he said, 'I didn't see any dog there last time.' Then he left, and Craig started airing *Weird Furka*.

Craig felt happy—giddy. And when, a little past 2.00 a.m., Frank Shokler joined Craig in the studio, he almost took no notice, as if Shokler had been there all night. Longer, perhaps. The two of them listened to the radio. The episodes of *Weird Furka* had dissolved from the original interview format into Frank talking for ten to fifteen minutes about supernatural revelations he'd had. Occasionally, a dog barked, and Craig wasn't sure if he was hearing Harold outside or on the radio.

'I was wrong for so long,' Frank said. His voice was a clear baritone. Craig admired it as a good radio voice.

'Was there an announcer, or was that you, too?' Craig asked, without looking away from the boards.

Frank smiled and, lowering his voice, said, 'If you scoff at the idea that there is a world outside of our common perception, another world beyond our own, *the supernatural world*, then prepare to have your assumptions challenged; if you already believe such a world exists, then prepare to have your beliefs confirmed.'

Craig clapped.

'Nothing else was faked, though, unless some of those housewives I interviewed were making stories up to pass the hours. I imagine that went on a little. Some of the women, though'—Frank grinned—'were very serious and touched, I think, by what took hold of me.'

Craig turned in his chair and looked at Frank. In the other chair, by microphone two, was a man-like figure, dressed in a white dress shirt, sleeves held up by cloth bands, a pair of brown, wool trousers, suspenders, and two-tone, white and brown shoes. The skin of the thing in the clothes was like moist black cloth. Between the weave, it shone. Craig gasped. Just beyond the thing was Craig's book of poetry; he focused on that as he switched on his microphone, drew it close to his lips, and whispered, 'Someone, please help me.'

Frank said, 'And what is taking hold of you, too.'

Craig turned back to the board, and stared at the counter as it counted down the minutes left of the episode of *Weird Furka* he was broadcasting. Gradually, he looked away from the LED light numbers and at Frank again; he couldn't not look at Frank.

'It took me a long time,' Frank said, 'to realize that Furka wasn't the nexus of the—shall we say *weird?*—but that the nexus was me.' Frank shrugged, sort of—at least, that's how Craig interpreted the gesture with which Frank capped his statement. Frank said, 'You should put on some of that music you like.'

Craig found the way Frank's mouth moved to be horrible; like bubbling molasses. Craig was dimly aware that the last episode of *Weird Furka* had been broadcast. Without thought, he took a record from the CD case he'd brought. It was the album he thought sounded like the opening music of Frank's show.

Frank's face rippled. 'Johnson has come to rescue you,' he said.

Craig knew Johnson's arrival did not mean he should have hope. He knew—almost as if he was outside watching—that Harold had leapt onto Johnson as soon as Johnson stepped out of his truck. Johnson would be found the next morning, dead air broadcasting from his truck's speakers. The papers would declare that he'd been 'mauled by a wild animal', though there would be no animal tracks to be found near Johnson's body.

Frank said, 'You should gather up all those records.' Frank indicated the burned CDs with a wave of his arm. Craig began to gather them, his will gone; gone since he climbed into the sub-basement of the Furkabick Hotel three weeks before.

'Good.' Again, Frank's face rippled. 'You should've turned that heating plate off when you left your house last. A fire has started already, fuelled by your own filth.'

And acetate and celluloid, Craig knew. Frank stood up and started out of the studio. Craig followed, the episodes of *Weird Furka* cradled in his arm. They walked through the empty house, to the basement door. The lock that Craig had broken still hung like a loose tooth from its latch.

The basement was dry and dark. In it, all that was visible to Craig was the white of Frank's shirt and the band of white on Frank's shoes. Craig followed, and whimpered.

'It's not so bad,' Frank said. 'It's not so lonely as you've been. Why, there's Mrs Buzzard, who's most pleasant, and Mrs Johnson.' Frank stepped into the small room at the far end of the cellar and bent over to open the sub-basement trap door. 'After you.'

Craig saw, as he'd seen Johnson mauled and his house in flames, a young boy, up far later than he was supposed to be, recording Craig's final broadcast. Craig got down on his knees, then dropped hard on his butt. He swung his legs over the lip of the sub-basement. Looking down, Craig saw a small point of light. He knew Frank stood over him, but also knew Frank was patient. The point of light grew; his eyes ached as his pupils shrunk to compensate for the ever-growing brightness below. The light, a ball of fire the size of a human head, was cold. The light was there for no more than a handful of seconds—when it vanished, Craig was blinded by the green-yellow circles burned onto his retinas. CD case held tight against his breast, he let his own weight pull him over the edge and dropped into the hole. Frank followed, carefully climbing down the ladder, pulling the trap door shut behind them.

For Conrad and Louise

The Weeping Manse

Legend of a Georgetown Murder

Jessica Amanda Salmonson

HENRY GLEASON, A SEATTLE ART DEALER, encountered the house by fortuitous accident. He'd made a wrong turn onto a back street on a narrow hillside in the old Georgetown district on the southern fringe of the city of Seattle. There rose before him a majestic ruin, the beleaguered hulk of a formerly stately Victorian mansion.

It had been left to ruin for at least a decade, and must have been but marginally maintained for considerably longer than that. Paint curled upon the shingles; windows were broken or boarded up. The yard had become a littered, weedy meadow. The porch was so decayed, one might climb the stairs to the front door only at peril, which risk the young art dealer soon brooked.

Peering through broken windows, he observed an interior badly vandalized, walls spray-painted with obscene slogans and gang symbols, floors strewn with trash, empty liquor bottles, empty tins.

Yet to an art dealer's aesthetic eye, the house and property constituted a diamond in the rough, requiring a loving hand to affect the restoration of erstwhile majesty. He at once imagined transforming the main floor into a splendid art gallery, with the spacious upper storey rooms serving as private residence.

As luck would have it, the place had been for sale for quite some while. Before long, having first paid an independent housing inspector to find out that the mansion was not suffering from wood rot, carpenter ants, or any irreversible problem, he and some of his furniture were moved into his marvellous purchase. Henry found himself veritably 'camping out' on the main floor.

THE WEEPING MANSE

His first day in the house was one of planning, sketching in a rag-paper notebook, and taking notes on what would be the first essential stages of a long-term restoration. He realized his task was daunting, yet looked forward to every stage of transforming the neglected manse.

The main floor, at least, was habitable, in a rugged sort of way, and he was not sorry to have given up the lease on his Queen Ann Hill apartment at the opposite end of the city.

Late in the evening, tired from the day's exertions, he retired to bed. The noises of an old house are always many and quaintly spooky, though that night began peacefully and quietly enough, but for the occasional creak of rafter and soft murmuring under the eaves.

Then, without warning, a woman's voice cried out in a panic, 'No! No! No!'

Henry sat bolt upright. An intense coldness enveloped his body. Had he been dreaming? Was he dreaming now? The chill crept further up his spine as he heard the pleading woman cry out a man's name. He looked at the ceiling over his bed, which seemed apt to burst downward upon him from the violent activity in an upper storey room.

Abruptly, with a final scream, the struggle ended. Then soft weeping came along the hallways and down the stairs and up the walls to the ceiling. In a few moments, the whole of the house seemed to be alive with a harrowing, doleful whimper.

Throughout that night, Henry stayed in his bed, refusing to answer the call of nature, let alone reply to the crying pleas of the house.

He had been far too frightened to set forth into the unfurnished rooms of the upper floor. Yet when daylight lit his bedroom, he felt he had been foolish, that it had after all been a dream. He told himself the dream's realistic effect had been heightened by the mood of the old dark house. In the wakeful mundane world, with bright sunlight slanting through bevelled glass and lighting dusty particles, he knew surely there were no such things as ghosts.

Despite that it had been a markedly convincing experience, he realized, upon reflection in broad of day, that he could not possibly have heard furniture shifting or objects thrown about in the room above—*for there was no furniture in that room to be thrown about.*

He investigated the second floor corner bedroom, chiding himself the whole while. The dingy windows, dirty casings, faded yellow wallpaper curling loose in spots, even the strange dark stain upon the hardwood floor, all seemed perfectly innocuous.

And yet . . . the approach of his second night in the house filled him with apprehension.

When he turned in for the night, he tossed and turned restlessly, his sense of foreboding unshakable. At 12.30 a.m., the shocking sounds came once more from the upstairs corner bedroom. If anything, they were louder and more certain than the night before, and he absolutely knew he was fully awake.

As he listened to the unfolding events, he pictured the battle between a woman and her lover, the furniture thrown about and shoved aside as she tried to evade him. He listened to her pleas for mercy, followed by a blood-curdling scream that told of injury. Then the woman, wounded and dying—as she must have died so many nights during so many cold forlorn years—filled every room of the house with her pitiable whimperings.

Oddly enough, the new owner of the haunted manse was abruptly emptied of fear. The weeping entity drew from him a profoundly empathetic sadness. To think anyone or anything was so utterably alone and afraid as the mansion's ghost! He wondered: could it be possible, that he might in some way assist a suffering soul?

When the impossible has undeniably intruded upon one's life, the whole of one's philosophy can change. A week before he had known that such things as ghosts and UFOs and Sasquatches populated the provinces of the superstitious, the credulous, or the insane.

Even now Henry did still wonder if he were losing his sense of reason. How could he be certain he had not become delusional? He wholeheartedly believed what he would recently have scoffed at, had it been laid out to him by even the most reliable of witnesses.

He knew to his very core that the house was reliving some traumatic event from out of its past. Yet he needed a corroborative, independent witness of the audio re-enactments, as assurance he was indeed in his right mind, and had not in fact merely joined the ranks of the aforementioned credulous or insane.

He asked a couple of artists, one from Sequim, the other from Anacortes, to visit Seattle and stay over with him in Georgetown. He wanted their opinions on certain planned renovations, he truthfully claimed, but gave no advance warning of the ghostly re-enactments he had been experiencing.

Two young men arrived, eager to see the much vaunted ruin, even if the invitation did come to them on short notice. Glad of the company, Henry and his friends stayed up late, losing track of time, speaking of the changes and repairs the house required, of art and cinema and the better restaurants and coffeehouses in town, and of other shared interests.

Before they knew it, it was 12.30, and there came, from the upstairs corner bedroom, the crash of non-existent furniture, the life and death struggle, the cries of 'No! No, Manny! Oh, Manny, why?' followed by the collapse of a body.

Then once more the house was weeping, every wall, every staircase, every hallway and room. The grief-stricken and frightened sobbing came upward from the floors, downward from the ceiling, as tangible as rainfall.

The looks on his friends' faces conveyed to Henry with abject clarity that they were hearing the same things he had heard on each night spent in that house. They went absolutely pale, stunned into silence, looking to their host for explanation. They must have thought he was perpetrating a grim prank, for he had a look of joy, knowing for the first time, with unutterable certainty, that he had been experiencing a thing that was both at odds with rational possibility, yet objective and real, and not the fault of a premature senility or a tumour pressing at one's brain.

'It happens every night at twelve-thirty,' he remarked with unusual casualness, as the whimpering of the house died away in choking sobs. 'I didn't warn you because I thought maybe it was in my mind. Now I can say quite certainly that when I bought this house, I bought a ghost into the bargain.'

'You jest,' said one of his friends nervously, trying to laugh. 'You've hidden stereo speakers in the walls.'

'By no means do I jest. Come, I'll show you the haunted room. I invite you to search the whole house—it's fairly austere at the moment, and any hidden sound equipment would be quickly revealed. If you can find any evidence of a hoax, I welcome it; but the depth of emotion in that weeping, my friends, is not easily invented.'

They swiftly took up the challenge and set forth upon an exuberant quest. They found no evidence of trickery. Only in the haunted room itself was there a lingering chill in one corner. This alone provided evidence of secrets of the Beyond.

The proud possessor of the haunted house visited the realtor, demanding to know the history of the house. The real estate salesman was reluctant to admit any knowledge. But, finding that the art dealer was not seeking a way out of his bargain, and had every intention of restoring the old house, the agent loosened up. Reluctantly, he admitted there were many reports of strange sensations and occurrences associated with the house. The previous owners were adamant that the place was haunted, and this was why it had remained empty so many years.

'They claimed to have heard muffled struggles and a weeping voice that cried "Manny!"' the agent admitted. 'Apparently a series of terrified owners sold the house as long ago as 1910, each telling much the same story.'

After his interview with the real estate agent, Henry visited the downtown library looking for information about old houses. He learned that Georgetown was originally called Duwamish and had formerly been Indian land outside the boundaries of pioneer Seattle. In time a few Victorian houses sprang up, surrounding themselves with farmed land. The area was plotted out for development in the 1890s by Julius Horton, and renamed after his son George. In the years that followed, the farmlands were developed variously for housing and industry. It became an independent working class town, linked to Seattle by streetcar, until it was absorbed by the expanding city. The few remaining Victorian houses all had chequered histories with legends attached.

Henry returned to the mansion without trepidation, for he was by now as fascinated by the ghost as he was with the august manse. He had no desire to part with either. The ghost's weeping was so tragic, he could not believe her dangerous. He wanted to know who she was, why she died. Besides his archival research, he spoke to elderly neighbours, and finally sought the advice of a prominent Northwest ghost hunter, Penelope Pettiweather.

From Penelope he learned that the 'ghostly re-enactment' was a classic kind of haunting. Just such re-enactments, she said, had been reported in all parts of the world. These recurring events almost always centred around a terrible crime. The spirits of the participants were compelled, after death, to perform the tragedy again and again. It may occur nightly, or upon the anniversary of the crime, or upon rare occasions when triggered by the presence of a 'similar' personality. One way or another, the ghosts of a past tragedy appeared as in a tableau, restaging their most terrible moments—moments that were frequently their last.

It seemed a hellish fate and smacked of Purgatory. If so, Henry hoped that for those spirits it was a temporary doom, as Purgatory was supposed not to be the final dwelling of our souls. A century is a small thing in contrast to eternity, so perhaps an eternal bliss awaited the victim of the crime, after an allotted period of repetitious horror.

By degrees, Henry gleaned from here and there imperfect bits of the story. His interest in the affair seemed to have quietened the suffering in the house. The re-enactments continued nightly, but with less severity, and Henry thought he heard, in the increasingly muffled sounds of the weeping, some slight edge of hope creeping in after despair. This inclined him to the belief that his presence, and his investigative endeavours, were in some manner beneficial to the lingering spirit.

The real break in his research came one day in the library as he strained his eyes over a collection of yellowed news clippings regarding the Georgetown neighbourhood.

He found her in a narrow, faded column of type on brittle newsprint. In 1899, the Georgetown mansion had been a brothel. The upstairs corner bedroom was used by a Duwamish Indian prostitute. One night, at exactly twelve-thirty, the young woman was brutally stabbed to death and cruelly mutilated. Her crazed lover's name, the article reported, was Manny.

In his home that night, the mystery resolved, ensconced in a recently installed easy chair, Henry awaited the haunted hour, knowing the weeping would be more faded still, as each night's occurrence had for some while grown by stages less severe. The murdered girl had needed someone to care enough to remember her sad plight, and Henry's caring quelled a degree of her suffering.

As he sat there in the dim light of a darkly shaded floor lamp, the art dealer felt a chill of realisation. He covered his mouth with the cup of his hand, pondering fretfully. It was true he had no fear of the ghost of the murdered prostitute; he pitied her poor troubled spirit, and would help her if he could. But what of the ghost of her murderer? He was there, too—and Manny's palpable malignancy was not to be doubted. Would he fade as his victim faded, or would soothing her sadness aggravate Manny's insanely jealous hostility?

Time would provide the answer, thought Henry, with deep unease.

Salvage

Chico Kidd

I'VE BEEN DREAMING ABOUT the Russian witch. In vivid, intimate, and disconcerting detail which my sleeping imagination insists on filling in.

But why now? I can't just say *why*. She's done her level best to seduce me more than once, and if I'm honest I can't deny that I've been tempted. But I haven't seen Tatiana for over two years. And now, out of the blue, she's invaded my dreams.

Damn it.

* * * * *

When a man hits forty he's supposed to 've grown into something, isn't that right? Wisdom or maturity or at least some kind of settled existence.

Not starting a new life. Not learning how to live with ghosts every waking moment. And certainly not discovering you can summon the dead from their graves.

Three times my life's changed completely. First when I was fourteen and signed on the old *Inês de Castro*. Second, at twenty, when I killed a man with murder in his eyes and rape in his heart. And third, a few months shy of forty, when my employer summoned a demon which sucked out his life and soul. And took out my left eye while it was about it. Leaving me a free man, but with wall-to-wall phantoms.

I've had nearly three years of that and I don't think I'll ever get used to it.

So there you have it. Brief history of Luís da Silva, master mariner and necromancer. As autobiographies go, not exactly run-of-the-mill. But some things haven't changed, thank God, and I say that as a man who's not sure he even believes in God any more. I'm still married to the woman mad Aldo had in his sights when I put my knife in him. And still the owner and skipper of a three-masted barque called *Isabella*. Fast as a tea-clipper, and beautiful.

Yes, the days of sail are over, I know. I know the economics of it, *obrigadinho*. But as long as there are some romantics wanting to travel by the four winds, I can make a living. Not a hugely prosperous one, to be truthful. Maintaining and crewing a sailing ship is a bit like haemorrhaging money sometimes. But as long as it lasts, I'm my own master. And I'd sacrifice a lot for that, because I know what the other side of the coin is like.

Still, if it wasn't for the ghosts, things'd be pretty close to perfect. Unfortunately it's damn near impossible to be free of them. There are very few places that aren't stuffed to bursting with the bloody things. Walking down some streets in Lisbon feels like being in thick fog. And I can't even escape them at sea. Ha. I say even, as if we humans haven't been losing the fight with old Neptune's realm for thousands of years. The oceans are full of the ghosts of ships, and some of them are things you wouldn't want to approach too closely. Shades can't do you any harm—or at least if they can, I haven't found out how yet—but I for one don't really need reminding of the many ways the sea can kill you.

One place has no ghosts. In my bed at home, I'm free of phantoms. In my bed at home, there is Emilia, and there isn't a ghost in the world that can take my mind away from my wife. I'm not saying I don't sleep well at sea. Though like any sailor I learnt the art of catnapping long ago, so I'm ready to come awake in an instant at any time. Time was when I could even do that after a night drinking on shore. I don't know if I could do that these days.

Be honest, da Silva. Couldn't drink that much and stay vertical at the age of forty-three.

Anyway, the ghosts don't disturb my rest, although *Isabella* passes through phantom ships from time to time. Much as I have to do, myself, with the dead of Lisbon. And every other city. It'd be nice if I could take as little notice of them as my ship does. *Certo*. Also be nice if I could come into a fortune. But I don't have any long-lost rich relatives, as far as I know. Though of course if I *did* know of any, they wouldn't be lost any more, would they? On the whole I'm more likely to find a treasure-ship.

Which, let me tell you, isn't everything it's cracked up to be.

* * * * *

We were a few days out of Belém—the one in Brazil, that is—bound for New York. The Caribbean's a bit too unhealthy for my taste, not that I've ever been sickly. Doesn't go with the job. I've even managed to avoid going down with malaria, quite a feat considering the Venetian did most of his business in places where the mosquitoes outnumber the humans fifty to one. Hide like an elephant, that's me. On the other hand, having an iron constitution doesn't make me complacent. I've got no wish to sample yellow fever. But strangely enough it's not uppermost in my mind at the moment. Ha. I wonder why that is.

Of course I was expecting something to happen. These days I can't put out of port without some kind of weirdness jumping out spoiling for a fight. *Meu Deus*, I can't venture out of my front door without it, sometimes.

That *Isabella*'s passengers to Belém *hadn't* turned out to be a family of vampires or sorcerers made me all the more suspicious. An uneventful trip across the Atlantic, now how rare is that?

Of course it's always when you've almost talked yourself into believing nothing will go wrong that—as Harris puts it—it ups and bites you in the ass.

Not that everyone else on board isn't also waiting for something to happen. They don't see the ghosts, of course, and they haven't got my Third's super-senses, either. Doesn't mean the buggers haven't got a healthy imagination.

'Pinto and Angelotti reckon they saw a mermaid last night,' he informed me a couple of days ago.

'A mermaid,' I repeated, raising an eyebrow. 'Pull the other one, Harris.'

Harris gave me a lopsided grin. 'I'm a werewolf. What'cha gonna do?'

Which is fair comment. Who the hell am I to say there aren't such things as mermaids? Haven't actually seen the fur sprouting, but you can't argue with two hundred and fifty pounds of wolf where Harris used to be. Especially when it calls you skipper.

'Fine,' I said. 'As long as they don't decide to go chasing after 'em.'

Harris stared over the rail, possibly looking for mermaids of his own. 'Nah,' he answered. 'Not those two.'

Knowing them, I agreed with him.

* * * * *

Tatiana Dimitrovna Andropova is her name. Our paths first crossed in Marseille, about ten years ago. Where she tried to kill me.

I really wish our relationship had stayed on that footing. Would've made things a lot simpler. But at least she's safely in London now and our paths don't cross. Or didn't, till she started invading my dreams.

Now I know that, whatever I say next, I'm going to lose. If I go on about my wife, you'll conclude I've got something to hide. And if I go on about Tatiana—you'll still conclude I've got something to hide. Heads I lose, tails I lose. So I won't hide it. I *do* find the Russian witch attractive. Damned attractive. If I'd met her before I was married, I wouldn't have resisted.

But I've never cheated on Emilia, and I don't intend to.

Though you wouldn't know it from the damn dreams.

* * * * *

Since I was asleep at the time, I didn't see whether we passed a ghost ship. Might've realised sooner if I had. As it was, I came awake in a virulent crimson dawn, after a bunch of dreams I didn't want, to find Harris's hand on my shoulder. He jumped back as I sat bolt upright in my bunk and swore at him. Held out his hands placatingly.

'What is it, Harris?' I asked, easing the kinks out of my shoulders before hunting for my cheroots. A yawn caught me unawares, and I glared at my third mate. 'And what have you done to the sky?'

'Nothing that ain't been there since yesterday, I reckon,' he replied morosely, squinting at it and taking out his cigarettes. Morose is something Harris is extremely good at. I suppose turning furry every month would tend to sour your sense of humour a bit. Not to mention putting a bit of a damper on your social life, too, I expect. And the moon'll be full in three nights, which always makes him grumpy.

Então, I have to agree that the weather's been weird. But sail the seven seas for long enough and nothing ought to surprise you.

This particular weirdness was a thundery feel to the air and what felt like damn near a hundred percent humidity. I could hardly have been wetter if I'd gone in after the mermaids. Yesterday the sea was a nasty, greasy, leaden shade and in a decidedly odd mood. Opening into troughs, swirling and eddying, all a *trouxe-mouxe*. Spurting up little waterspouts for no good reason, without any sign of a cyclone anywhere. And the barometer had gone crazy as well. The only explanation I could come up with was an underwater earthquake. Or even a volcano, who knows? Which is what I put in *Isabella*'s log.

Now, however, it had done something more while I was asleep. Spewed up something very strange. Though not, it seemed, supernatural.

A little reluctantly, I got out of bed and pulled my trousers on. The air felt less humid, but it was still pretty warm, and from the dampness of da Silva the night had been bloody hot. When I went on deck, it was already hot enough to burn my feet. I'd left the eyepatch off again. You don't wear one in conditions like these, not unless you want to grow mould under it. And I don't particularly want to end up looking like something out of one of Zé's pulp magazines, *obrigadinho*. The scar's nasty enough on its own.

Most of the crew were gawping over the side, but a few scuttled off guiltily when they spotted me. Nothing like the sudden appearance of the Old Man to make you remember what you were supposed to be doing. The others weren't so lucky. I barked at them, which made 'em move. Martinet, who, me?

I held out my hand for a telescope. 'All right, Harris, what kind of dead whale have you dragged me out of bed to look at?' A welcome bit of a breeze dried the sweat on my skin. Didn't stop me feeling grubby and itchy. Need a shave. I dragged a hand over my chin absently, and took a closer look at what the ocean had disgorged.

A derelict. Dredged off the seabed, I suppose, by the seismic rumbles that played havoc with yesterday's weather. Though *meu Deus*, it was hardly recognisable as a ship. A shapeless sodden hulk covered in weed and all the other stuff that attaches to wood at the bottom of the ocean. Last time I saw anything like that it *was* on the bottom of the ocean. A shiver ran down my back in sympathy for her drowned crew. Wrecks are always like that. Because in most cases, they're not just dead ships. They're tombs.

There was a kind of scummy film on the water all round the hulk, as if it were leaking something noxious, but strangely enough it didn't smell particularly bad. At least, not from where I was standing. I would've said she was downwind, but there wasn't any wind to be down of.

Harris lit a cigarette, and sucked so hard on it it turned into half a tube of ash in one drag. 'Some old windjammer, I guess,' he observed. I raised an eyebrow. Sometimes he's as bad as a bloody Englishman when it comes to pointing out the obvious. I nodded, and bit down on the cheroot I was smoking. What I needed was coffee. I handed the glass back and headed for the galley to get some. No, I don't employ a steward. João can provision the ship perfectly well, and I've no intention of employing someone else to shave me. Not at sea, anyway. I prefer the da Silva throat in one piece. Thank heavens for the safety razor.

My Third followed me, decidedly skittish. Which isn't a word I'd normally think of using to describe someone the size of Harris. I smiled to myself. But I made him wait till I'd drunk a mug before asking casually 'Want to take a look, then?'

He bared his teeth at me. As near as he ever gets to a grin. 'Deserting the ship, skipper?' he asked innocently.

All right, I suppose I deserved that. I lit up a cheroot and blew smoke at him. 'Any more insubordination, Harris, and you don't get to go.' Though he took about as much notice of that as my son would.

Merda. As if the thought summoned him, here's Zé at my elbow, burbling excitedly. I overrode it without listening. 'No, you can't go,' I told him.

'But——'

'Zézinho.' He scowled ferociously. He doesn't like being turned into a diminutive. Though if I could put half the threat into it that Emilia does into saying 'José' he might listen to me occasionally. Ha. The day I become President of Portugal. 'Haven't you got something you should be doing? And if you haven't, I'll find you something.' The watch had just changed, which is the only reason the young villain's out of bed.

Zé realised that he wasn't going to get anywhere, and stumped off huffily. Having him as a 'prentice on my ship is almost as harrowing as—well, as *not* having him where I can keep a watch on him. I sighed, and ran a hand over my hair. Decided a wash and a shave might help. So I sent Harris off to rustle up a crew for the gig and went below.

You may think I was being naïve, but it never even occurred to me that there was anything uncanny about the hulk. There was no sign of her ghost, but all that meant was that she'd shifted around a goodish bit after she'd gone down. Not unusual.

By the time I'd run a razor over my face and a wet cloth over the da Silva hide, the weather had taken a turn for the better. Nice contrast to yesterday. Calm sea, light breeze. Glass rising. Going to be a hot day. I felt a twinge of honest excitement as we neared the derelict. Harris gave a long low whistle.

'That tub's *real* old,' he muttered, pointing out the obvious again. I rolled my eye, but didn't comment. As we approached, I caught a whiff of rank stink for the first time. The weed covering the hulk had suddenly discovered air, and started to ferment. It was pretty bloody foul.

Harris and I scrambled aboard, more curious than the crew. The instant I set foot on the rotten deck, my neck started to crawl. I exchanged a glance with the mate, wondering whether he felt it too. From his expression, no question. The atmosphere on the wreck felt—I can only describe it as deadly. Yet I also had the peculiar sense, don't ask me why, that it wasn't the ship herself that meant us harm. Rather, there was something about the manner of her death that resonated. I can't put it any clearer than that. But it terrified me. I knew that if I outstayed my welcome by as much as a minute, something would be unforgiving. Though I had no idea what.

We cleared away some of the vegetation with boat-hooks, and found something that might've been a gun-port. I called to Angelotti and Pinto to follow us. Their reward for mermaid-spotting. They didn't seem to like the idea very much. I caught Pinto crossing himself. Superstitious folk, sailors.

For a wonder, I could still make out lanyards and deadeyes in the rigging, but everything was pretty much covered with weeds and slime and shells. The timber underfoot looked odd, and at first I couldn't figure out why. Then I looked a little closer and found that it was charred. My neck gave another prickle. Fire on a wooden ship. The very worst thing of all.

Then Angelotti trod in something that sent up a noxious cloud and made him cough and swear. Then Pinto, not to be outdone, slipped on an extra-slimy patch of weed and did an acrobatic bicycle kick before landing on his arse. I raised an eyebrow at Harris. Hadn't meant to bring the vaudeville troupe along with me.

'Let's have a look in the stern-cabins,' I said, lighting up a cheroot in the hope of overriding the worsening stink. And I didn't particularly want to spend any more time on the hulk than I had to. I'd scratched that particular itch enough. Some are easier to relieve than others. More urgently, something that could surface so suddenly could sink again just as easily without much notice. 'Put your backs into it, you two.'

I picked up my boat-hook again and tackled another pile of weed. Lead by example, da Silva. A dozen crabs scuttled out, and a moment later I uncovered a fish. It flopped on the deck helplessly, and I kicked it out of the way. It didn't look worth bothering with. Even Angelotti, who'll eat anything, turned his nose up at it. Though he probably thought it was a demonic fish or something. I was expecting giant squid myself by this time, at the very least, but the biggest thing we turned up was a rather scrawny octopus. Pinto, less fussy than Angelotti, bagged that.

More charring on the deck. Enemy action, I suppose. But something about it was odd. I started to mention it to Harris, but he swore suddenly, making me forget what I was going to say. I turned to see him staring indignantly at a broken knife-blade. Raised an eyebrow.

'Some of this junk's like stone.' Most of the wreck's timber was eaten away by teredos and suchlike, but it seemed some of it had gone the other way and got itself petrified. Seen it on wrecks on the sea bed. Where this hulk's been sitting for God knows how long.

As I opened my mouth to answer, the deck shifted underfoot enough to make me swear and catch my balance. Which means, it shifted a lot. Spend as long at sea as I have and you do that sort of thing in your sleep. I realised what the hissing I'd been hearing had to be. '*Merda.*'

The Third got it at the same time. 'Jesus up the mast. The holds must be full o' gas.' He screwed up his face, though I don't know whether his sense of smell is really any keener than anyone else's when he's not covered in fur. On the other hand two hundred years of rotting weed has a right to stink to high heaven. 'Shipfarts,' he added. I ignored this, as beneath my dignity.

'Better shift our arses, Harris, she's probably about to go down again.' But I was reluctant to leave empty-handed. Though what I thought we might find, I don't know. Da Silva, intrepid explorer.

Sweat was trickling down my face. I wiped it out of my eye. 'Come on, let's get a move on.' We set to again, Pinto and Angelotti casting nervous glances over their shoulders when they thought I wasn't looking. The stench grew worse. And the sun got hotter. And the derelict kept on lurching like a man with too much rum inside him.

By the time we penetrated as far as the great cabin beyond the quarterdeck we were all soaked with sweat. Even I could smell myself. I was glad I hadn't put a clean shirt on. Questioning, in fact, why I'd bothered to put one on at all.

Beside me, Harris wiped his arm across his forehead and jerked his head in the direction of Pinto and Angelotti. I nodded, and sent them back to join the other two in the gig. They'd been jittery enough even before we found the remains of a skeleton under a carronade on the quarterdeck. We'd got no work at all out of 'em after that, and Angelotti's praying was getting on my nerves. The bones themselves were too tangled up in weed to do anything about them. Not that I was too worried. They'd lain at the bottom of the sea for a century and a half or more. And funerals are for the living, not the dead. Certainly not the long dead.

Inside the cabin, the windows were so green with weed that the dim light made it seem as if the ship was still underwater. There wasn't much to see, though. Some broken rubbish, the remains of furniture. Deep slime, probably rotted cloth—curtains and upholstery, I suppose. Corroded cannons, barely recognisable. And, finally, something to show for our trip. A sea-chest. Judging from how light it was, a watertight one, too. It was crusted with shells and muck, but with luck something inside it might've survived.

As long as it's not anything like what was in the last stranger's chest I took on board. But most likely it once held ship's papers—probably still did.

I grinned at Harris, who was eyeing it with deep suspicion. Can't blame him. Though things that come out of mysterious boxes usually have *my* name on them, for some reason. I scratched my eyebrow.

'Skipper,' he said, and I realised he wasn't worried about the chest so much as the gassy hissing. Which had suddenly got much louder. Ha. Our little jaunt wouldn't be much use to anyone if I let the wreck sink under me.

'Time we were off this tub.' As I spoke the hulk lurched even more violently, and Harris clutched at a slimy bulkhead for support, cursing as his fingers slid off it.

'You're not wrong, skipper,' he agreed, frowning at his hand before dragging it down his trouser-leg.

We hoisted the chest between us—it wasn't heavy, just awkward. As we were leaving the cabin someone shouted from the gig. Made me jump. Da Silva, starting at shadows. And it was only then that I realised. What would you expect to find on a ship that went down with all hands? I turned my head to stare at Harris.

'There aren't any ghosts,' I exclaimed.

Before he could reply, the derelict gave a tremendous shudder. Which drove any speculation out of my head. By the time Harris and I got the chest to the side the damn ship was gurgling like a whale with indigestion. Stinking as bad, too. By then the stench had made even me feel a bit queasy. The crew of the gig didn't need any prompting to pull like maniacs to get away from the hulk as soon as we got our find on board.

The wreck, having scared us off, remained obstinately afloat for hours. I would've sunk her if I could, because she was a menace to shipping. But she was far too saturated to burn. So all I could do was note her position to report later.

Isabella resumed course, and I turned my attention to the chest. I couldn't think of any legitimate reason to banish Zé, so I had him under my feet. Not to mention a fair number of other spectators. All hoping for treasure, no doubt. Though I'd already warned 'em that the thing weighed too little to hold anything much in the way of bullion.

Zé, milking it for every last drop: 'D'you think this one's got a dead wizard's hand in it too?'

'I'll set it on you if there is,' I muttered, darkly. Didn't quell him. Didn't think it would.

Harris reappeared laden with tools, having apparently plundered the carpenter's stores. The bolts and hasps, however, put up a spirited resistance.

'Someone didn't want us to get into this darn box,' he grumbled, chiselling and cursing. I watched him. Lit another cheroot. I suppose I've got better things to do. But the skipper's entitled to be curious, no? And the weather didn't look about to pull any more nasty tricks. *Isabella* was practically steering herself. With a little help from—I looked round—Kirby.

One final thump, and the box was open. We all peered in. Amazingly, it *had* stayed watertight all those years. But there wasn't much to show for our efforts. Just a handful of coins, not a doubloon among 'em. And an ironbound book, only a little rusty.

This seemed to excite Zé more than anyone. I practically had to fight him off as I opened it. 'Zé, get your head out of the way before I thump it.'

He ignored me, reaching out a hand. I slapped it away, and he gave me an aggrieved look. 'It might tell us the ship's *name*.'

Yes, thank you, I'd worked that out for myself. Unless it was something other than the log, of course. I didn't want it to be anything other than the log. Nervous, da Silva? Well, I think I've got good reason to be suspicious of things in boxes.

But at first I thought we weren't even going to find a name. The pages at both ends were stained and crumbling, and even when you got further in the ink had all run and turned the pages a dirty grey without leaving anything recognisable as writing.

'Go a bit further,' urged Zé, impatiently. I was tempted to hand the whole thing over to him, but instead I merely pushed him out of the way again and went on prising the pages apart with my penknife.

At length we found some legible script. Though *legible* is pushing it a bit. It was cramped and crabbed and worse than mine on a bad day. We all pored over it for a while, trying to puzzle something out. Anything.

'I reckon that says HMS,' Harris decided finally, placing a large forefinger on the page. I looked at it dubiously. Gave up, and moved my gaze starboard a degree.

'Does that look like *Bellatrix* to you?' I asked.

'HMS *Bellatrix*,' exclaimed Zé. 'Got to be a warship with a name like that!'

'Yeah,' agreed Harris. 'Limey navy name, all right.'

We agreed the scrawl could be *Bellatrix*. A little later we discovered she'd been a forty-eight gun frigate. This was exciting, at least to Zé. My son's eyes filled with pirates and Spanish ships laden with gold.

'Maybe she sank in a battle,' he said eagerly. 'With a treasure-galleon. Maybe the Spaniard's still down there.'

We smiled indulgently at his fantasies.

However, by that time I—well, I wasn't exactly tired of it, but it looked as though that was all we were going to get out of the derelict. So I decided we'd spent enough time on it. *Certo*, life on board ship can get monotonous. At least on a routine voyage. And you welcome a bit of relief occasionally. But we'd had the exciting bit, and deciphering eighteenth century English isn't my idea of an interesting way to spend an afternoon.

As I somehow thought, it wasn't Zé's, either. *Não me diga*. So I told him to take the book to Ashley. Don't know how much the man knows about history, though most of the time I'm convinced he thinks he's Admiral Nelson reincarnated. He'd run his watch like a Royal Navy battleship if I gave him half a chance. Even for an Englishman he's stiff-necked. I used to wonder why he stays with this motley crew and her even more motley skipper. Then I found he'd managed to acquire himself a mistress in Lisbon. Amazing. Probably makes her salute the flag before—— Well, you get the idea.

Zé took the book gingerly. I expect he thinks Ashley will rope him in to help. My son apparently didn't realise at first that apprenticeship involves studying, and my First is a devil for that. Plus the instant he found out that Zé's inherited this knack I have for languages, he started turning everything into an English lesson.

Somehow, though, I don't think he was the one who taught him some of the English swearwords the boy's picked up. Can't even blame Harris for that. He had a fairly extensive vocabulary even before the Third signed on.

Hell. Must've got them from me, then.

Então, you meet some strange things sailing the seven seas, and the oddest thing about that one was the total lack of ghosts. Even the skeleton hadn't raised a flicker.

But I've got other things to occupy my mind. If I need to look for the uncanny all I have to do is think about my dreams, and I can live without that, *obrigadinho*. No, my concerns are all mundane for once.

Mermaids, I didn't even consider.

They were on Harris's mind, however. He's as determined to find a supernatural explanation for this as I am *not* to. All right, so I don't want to see what's under my nose. I don't want to see ghosts, either, or call them out of their graves. And the absence of 'em on *Bellatrix* was a bonus, if you ask me.

'Whaddya make of that, skipper?' he asked me, squinting in the sun and patting his pockets for matches. At least I assumed that's what he was looking for, since he had an unlit cigarette sticking out of his mouth. Full marks for deduction there, da Silva. I handed him my matches, and he nodded a thank you and lit up. Handed the box back and raised his eyebrows at me inquiringly. I hadn't answered his question.

'Nada,' I said with a shrug.

'I just kinda thought it was all a bit too pat.' He shaded his eyes with one hand and looked sceptical. 'A wreck, a box, a log? Just happened to rise off of the seabed as we came by? See what I mean?'

Yes, I know. No such things as coincidences. But, just this once, it hasn't involved something trying to kill me. Yet. So until and unless it does, I'm going to ignore it.

Harris, on the other hand, won't leave it alone. 'Any idea what those two bozos might've seen? I ain't buying mermaids, but I reckon they musta seen something.' I sighed, and shook my head. It was damned hot.

'You know what they're like.' I ran a hand through my hair. Damp. 'Could've been anything.' He nodded.

'Yeah, but I never would've figured 'em for that much imagination.'

'Well, what if they did?' I asked irritably. Fed up with this as a topic of conversation, but Harris isn't going to leave it until he's got where he wants. More like a bloody terrier than a wolf. 'Have *you* seen anything?'

He didn't reply at once, and I frowned at him. Let him do it in his own time, da Silva, you know it'll be quicker in the long run. I occupied the time lighting a smoke.

At last he answered slowly, 'You know how you always see shapes in clouds.' It didn't sound like a question, but I nodded anyway. 'Well, I been seeing 'em in the water, in the shadows—everywhere. And I know there's nothing there.'

'Seeing what, Harris?' His reply made me blink in surprise.

'Women,' he said, morosely.

Merda. Tatiana. Is it affecting everyone? *Meu Deus*, the whole crew thinking of women at the same time. More than they usually do. Now there's a chilling thought.

I exchanged a glance with Harris. Saw him thinking exactly the same thing. Opened my mouth to speak.

And Zé came barrelling along, face scarlet with eagerness. Sometimes his enthusiasm's downright embarrassing. Was I like that, at thirteen?

'*Bellatrix* was sunk by a sea-monster!' he blurted out at the top of his lungs. Shout a bit louder, Zé, I don't think they heard you in Trinidad. Heads turned, grinning.

Well, whatever I was expecting, it wasn't that. I rolled my eye at Harris and put a hand on my son's shoulder. Somehow, I can't see some damned Englishman writing as his ship goes down 'We are being sunk by a sea-monster.' No, wait. Yes, I can. If Ashley was in that situation, that's exactly what he'd be doing. Ha.

'Calm down,' I said to Zé, trying to sound stern. Which had about as much effect as telling Harris not to grow fur when the moon gets full. He ducked his head, but I'm not sure whether he was nodding or trying to move away from threatened hair-ruffling. Mind you, if his hair's as damp and clammy as mine, he's in no danger. 'Now, what's all this about sea-monsters?'

'I'm not making it up!' Never said he was. I raised an eyebrow. 'It's all in the log! Her captain was called Captain Jarvis and she was a forty-eight gun frigate and she *had* sunk a Spaniard'—triumphantly—'called the *Vera Cruz*, but she got badly shot up.' He paused, but it was only to draw a breath. Then he was off again, at a rate of knots. 'And they were heading back to port for a refit when they hit bad weather and then——'

'They met a sea-serpent,' I finished sceptically. Double standards, who, me? I got a scornful face in return.

'Not a *sea-serpent*,' Zé corrected me, like a schoolmaster with an extra-stupid pupil. 'You should come and look, even Sr Ashley thinks it's interesting.'

I turned to Harris, who was trying not to laugh, and pointed my cheroot at him threateningly. He threw his cigarette-butt into the sea and put one finger to his lips.

'Not a word, skipper,' he said.

Five minutes later I was reading Ashley's transcription of *Bellatrix*'s final log entries. Since his handwriting is worse than mine I'd probably have done better trying to decipher the original. The frigate'd had a hard time, all right. I read about shipping water and plugging shot-holes. Falling glass, shortening sail. And then things started to get worse.

Ashley peered over my shoulder. Zé's obviously right—the First's intrigued. He's never said a word about anything that's happened in the last three years. But then neither has anyone else. And they all know perfectly well what happens to Harris every month.

The English captain didn't describe the sea-monster. Might've been English reticence. Or possibly the thing was too horrible to describe. Now there's a pleasant thought. But Zé was right about that as well—it wasn't a sea-serpent. Nothing so predictable. Jarvis called it 'that which came out of the ocean' and said it had 'so terrible an aspect that the very ship seemed to shudder with fright, and shake herself apart'.

Merda. If that means what I think it does, we're in trouble. Or I am. Make it the latter. I scratched my eyebrow, not liking my thoughts one bit.

Here's the thing. Ships have ghosts, much like human beings. My theory, for what it's worth, is that the shades that throng the streets of Lisbon and every other city in the world are reflections of people when they were alive. They linger where they died, growing fainter as the years go by. Likewise with ships. So *Bellatrix*'s phantom will be wherever she went down. And so will all her crew's. That's why there were none on board. They didn't die in that place.

Those everyday shades aren't the kind of ghost you can talk to. *They* have to be called out of their graves. With people, on land at least, that's not usually the same place unless the fellow keeled over from a heart attack in the cemetery. But with ships, it is.

If a ship has a ghost you can summon.

It'll be easy to find out, because the skipper of the *Bellatrix* had noted down her position when the thing out of the sea first appeared.

Accept it, da Silva, there *are* no such things as coincidences.

'Will you want a change of course, captain?' Ashley asked.

Então, I'd prefer if Captain Jarvis had noted where the Spaniard had gone down, and all I had in my sights was sunken treasure. But no. Life always hands you the sea-monster rather than the bullion.

As Harris says, ain't it a bitch.

I nodded reluctantly, and Zé looked up at me wide-eyed. Ashley saluted—he does that—and went on his way.

'Are we going to—*papai*, what are we going to do?' Zé, mystified. Not surprising, since I don't know myself. I rubbed my scar.

'We'll find out when we get there,' I said unguardedly. Candour winning over tact there. My son grinned at me. 'What?'

He shuffled his feet and hunched his shoulders. I think it signified approval of having a father with unusual talents.

Could be entirely wrong, of course.

Turned out that *Bellatrix* had gone down not half a day's sail away. Our heading had taken us nearer to Jarvis's coordinates. Another coincidence, you think? And so we were, or rather I was, looking at her ghost the same evening. It wasn't anything like I'd expected. Which was, naturally, something that looked like the ship before she went down.

Should know by now that you never get what you expect. Damn it.

We were a few minutes into the second dog-watch. The sun was almost down, the sky had that utter clarity you get at that hour, in those latitudes. There was virtually no wind; it had died away. The sea was almost black. It looked like wrinkled wet silk.

And sure enough, the semi-transparent shade of a frigate rode the waves. I looked at her, scratching my eyebrow thoughtfully.

I could've called her captain easily enough, though I didn't want to. I didn't even need to know his full name. Like calls to like, after all. But I'd come to the conclusion that summoning the ship's ghost made more sense. Captain Jarvis hadn't known what it was that attacked them. And I was pretty sure that it was the spirit of the *Bellatrix* that was kicking up a fuss.

So I leaned over the rail and said softly 'Ahoy the *Bellatrix*.' Resignedly. Although it's not the same as dragging someone out of his grave. It's a hell of a lot bigger, for one thing. But it doesn't make me feel like a damned slaver. I know what slavery's like. The Venetian owned me, just as surely as if he'd bought me, for nineteen years. When I call a ghost I feel as if I'm no better than he was. Because they *have* to do what you say.

There was a split second of absolute silence, and then a burst of shockingly fierce wind blew straight in my face, so strong it made my eye water. I glanced up automatically at the sails, but the strange gust hadn't touched them. It was just for me.

Then I looked back at the ocean to find it bulging upwards. A little bit like a waterspout forming. The column of sea rose until its top was level with my face, and then it started to sculpt itself. Into the shape of a woman.

It wasn't, as I instantly dreaded, Tatiana's. It—she—looked like an Amazon. Well, you can't fault the logic. A woman, a warrior. Bellatrix.

Granted, she was thirty feet tall. But easier to talk to than something shaped like a ship. I suppose.

In the past three years or so I've met demons and witches and gods, sorcerers dead and alive, soul-eaters, golems, and the walking dead. Not to mention a couple of werewolves. None of 'em scared me as much as Tatiana Dimitrovna, and none of 'em were more pleased to see me than the ghost of a frigate.

'You came,' she said to me. Her voice was huge like the sea, like great horns, like wind in the rigging.

'As you see,' I answered, rubbing my scar. Trying for nonchalance. If that's possible, under the circumstances.

'Do not worry.' A ghost reassuring *me*? That's novel. 'A willing listener, though bound to your will, is no slave.'

Nice to know. I lit a cheroot.

The question being, of course, in this case: who's the one doing the summoning? I haven't forgotten what old Mohan Das said, eighteen months or so ago. *They know you*, he told me. *Your sight and your actions mark you, and they will recognise you.*

But then, he also said *You are not alone.*

I haven't decided yet whether or not that's a reassuring thought.

Então, da Silva, get on with it. Cut, as Harris says, to the chase. 'What,' I asked, 'do you want me to do?'

The watery form shivered and shuddered. She had currents, like the ocean she was made from. The effect was unsettling, to say the least. I must've sucked in a breath or something—whatever it was, she noticed.

'A moment,' she said, and sank back into the ocean. Only to reappear a moment later in front of me, rising out of the deck and ending up slightly smaller. A mere six feet or so.

They always go for taller. Don't tell me they're above things like vanity. And I end up with a crick in my neck.

What I'm not getting is information. 'Well?' I prompted.

'We have waited a long time for someone like you,' she said. And *that* doesn't reassure me at all. Or surprise me, either. I don't think anything can surprise me, these days. 'Something dwells in the seas hereabouts. It slept for a long time, and that was as it should be. But it was woken by blood and gold when we sank *Vera Cruz*. It is old, ancient. And it is hungry.'

A shiver ran down my back, despite the lingering heat. The daylight was almost gone now, but the figure in front of me glowed with faint phosphorescence. Then the moon rose out of the sea and laid a trail of broken yellow light over the waves and over the ghost. Her eyes, though, glittered deep inside.

'What is it?' What was so awful that Captain Jarvis couldn't describe it? It gnawed at me, like toothache. The skipper of a Royal Navy frigate had to be used to horrors. *That which came out of the ocean.* Not a promising turn of phrase.

Bellatrix's ghost looked wistful. If a six-foot woman made out of seawater can look wistful, that is. 'That one was only the harbinger, captain. It was to that which followed as a breeze is to a typhoon.'

Merda. So maybe there are still some things that can surprise me.

I took a long drag on my cheroot and exhaled slowly. Have to ask the question, of course. 'And what was that?'

'The Devourer,' came the reply.

Nice. The names these things have. Still, nothing if not descriptive. Not that I expect them to be called João or Ricardo, though that might be a good move now I come to think of it. Doesn't have the same grace or promise as Henriques the Navigator, but João the Devourer has a certain ring to it, no?

'The Devourer,' I repeated, on a sigh, wiping a trickle of sweat off my temple before it ran into my eye. 'What does it devour?'

'Everything,' answered Bellatrix, implacably.

Oh. Not anything as simple as—say—souls, then. I finished my cheroot, and threw the end into the ocean.

'I do not know,' the ship's ghost went on, 'if my crew's spirits are still in its belly after all these years, or whether it, itself, is a portal, in which case they are surely lost. But, captain, they deserve better. I held them as dear as your ship does you and your crew. And I loved my captain, though he never knew it or would even have understood.'

Talk. They all love it. Witches and sorcerers, and apparently ship-spirits. Do I need to know this? Everyone who's ever set foot on a ship knows they *have* spirits. Wouldn't have figured them as great thinkers, though. Certainly not philosophers.

'What do you expect me to do?' I asked.

'Arm yourself,' Bellatrix said, and it wasn't exactly a reply. It was a warning. I whipped out my knife, whirling round as I did so. Missing an eye is not helpful in a fight. Especially when it's your left eye and you're left-handed.

I've been making too many damned assumptions this trip. Ought to know better, da Silva. Assuming that the hulk's resurrection was just a trick of the ocean. That *Bellatrix*'s spirit would look like a ship. And that 'that which came out' would be something like old Rodrigues's army of the drowned.

It wasn't, of course, anything like that at all. And it didn't really come out of the sea, either. Though you could understand how someone might think it did. Where else *could* anything come from, when there's no land anywhere in sight?

Thing looks more like a scorpion than anything else. Though I'm not an expert. Lots of legs, insecty body, tail curved over the back. Head, triangular with huge faceted eyes. But it also came with an upright torso complete with arms. Insect-leg arms that ended in hands, holding a sword. Now there's a surprise.

Did I mention it was also as tall as Bellatrix?

Apparently it was headed for her, too. Makes a change. Usually the damn things've got da Silva in their sights. Unfortunately, I don't think it makes any difference this time. I'll still have to fight it. Bellatrix may look like a warrior, but she's a ghost. Not substantial. On the other hand, a demon might be able to kill a ghost. Oh yes, I think that's what this thing is. I've been through the options, and that's the most likely one.

Hell, it's the only one.

'This is not the harbinger,' said Bellatrix worriedly. Not what I want to hear. 'I do not know whence it came. Or why it is here, now.' I did my best to ignore this. Pay attention to the thing with the sword.

Então, da Silva. It's got more limbs than you, but I bet it's not very bright. And like all of these things, it probably won't like silver worth a damn. Hell, even Harris doesn't like it, and he's on my side. Makes it a pain in the arse trying to pay him sometimes.

Lop off a limb or two, then, and we might even things out a bit.

I stepped in front of Bellatrix and extended my knife to arm's length. Sure enough, the scorpion demon backed off. Wish I'd known about that three-and-a-half-years ago in Venice. I went up against that rat-demon with an ordinary steel knife: it hardly slowed the thing. It was Tatiana Dimitrovna who suggested getting a blade with silver in the mix. I'm grateful to her for that. If nothing else.

Should also remember demons aren't big on finesse. This one swung its great sword round in an arc that might've done some damage if I'd been anywhere near it. But I was ducking before it even started, and rammed the knife into its middle. Nasty yellow stuff squirted out. Don't want any of that on my hands, thank you very much.

'Captain, 'ware behind!' Bellatrix suddenly screamed, which startled me so much I was turning in reflex before she got the words out. Just as well. I'm not quick enough to swivel like that. When I saw what was coming I dropped to the deck and rolled. And the monstrous stinger on the end of its tail slammed into the boards where I'd been standing and stuck there.

Using my own momentum I finished the roll with a knife-stroke that severed the trapped scorpion-sting. And bounced back to my feet.

The damn thing started flailing its tail around, of course, spraying its foul juices all over the place.

'Captain, you *must* kill it,' Bellatrix said, in a more normal voice. I dodged another wild stroke and went for its sword-arm. The blade bounced off it, and I beat a hasty retreat.

'What the hell d'you think I'm trying to do?'

'It has wounded your ship,' she wailed, as if she was the one hurt. 'Only killing it will cure her.' I tried hacking at a limb, and the same thing happened. Must've been bloody lucky with the tail. I did some quick fancy footwork and dodged it again. Think, da Silva. Thing's like an insect. Joints must be the bits to go for.

Then I slipped in some of its horrible bodily fluids and fell on my arse.

Bellatrix stepped between me and the demon and took the swordstroke that would have skewered me.

Merda. I was supposed to prevent that. I scrambled to my feet, furious, and took a flying leap at the demon, aiming for its neck.

Did that right. The knife slipped in sweetly and I put all my weight behind it and lopped off the thing's head. It collapsed, thrashing. I turned to see Bellatrix dissolving slowly, whatever power that held the water in woman-shape broken.

She smiled as she sank into the boards. 'We are in good hands. I am content.'

The demon gave a final twitch, and fell into dust on the deck. I leaned against the rail to catch my breath. Wiped the sweat off my face with my sleeve. And wondered when the 'harbinger' would turn up.

I didn't even get a chance to light up a smoke.

Slowly, a dead sea-mist was gathering over the water's surface. But it was nothing like any sea-mist I've ever seen. There was a greasy, slimy sheen to it and it looked somehow thicker than normal fog. As if it had substance.

And it was crawling up the side of my ship. I had a certain and horrible conviction that if it got on deck it would overwhelm *Isabella* entirely.

Então, I'm pretty certain that's not something I want. Though I don't know what to do about it. It doesn't look like something I can fight with a knife.

Then I remembered the strange charring on *Bellatrix*'s deck. 'Harris!' I bellowed.

A tendril of mist poked itself through the rail. I slashed at it with my knife, and it cringed back. So silver works. But there's too damn much of the stuff for that to be a solution.

My Third arrived at a dead run and stopped short with a comical expression on his face. If he asks me what it is I'll kill him first.

'I'll get a torch,' he said, understanding instantly, and pounded off again. I went on slicing at the fingers of mist. They lingered for a few seconds once severed, coiling and uncoiling. I *really* didn't want them to touch me, so I found myself doing a little dance to avoid them. Entertaining for any one watching. Not much fun for me.

The creeping mist, I noticed suddenly, had an odd, musty smell. Lunging to slice at it again, I realised that it wasn't mist at all. Slow on the uptake there, da Silva. Of course it isn't. What it put me in mind of was mould, the thick white sort. The picture my mind presented me with, of *Isabella* coated inches, feet deep in the stuff, made me shudder. No wonder the Englishman hadn't wanted to describe it.

Where's Harris with that torch? Fire is the worst fear of every sailor on a wooden ship. But now it's the lesser of two evils. Damn it.

Sweat ran into my eye, and I raised my right hand to brush it away while lopping off another tendril. A stray blob of the bloody fungus-stuff landed on the back of my hand, sending a stab of agony lancing up my arm. The pain was unbelievable. I let my attention lapse from slashing at the creeping stuff—without stopping the slashing, naturally—and saw that it was visibly eating into my flesh.

'Better see to that, skipper,' came Harris's voice from my blind side, and I smelled burning pitch. He hove into view and started attacking the mist-fungus with his makeshift torch. I dropped my knife with a clatter. Fumbled my flask of holy water out of my pocket. My other hand was shaking, and I was soaked in sweat. I wondered dimly whether the holy water would work on something like this. Of course it will, I told myself angrily, what d'you call that stuff if not *un*holy?

It burned almost as badly as the fungus-stuff. I swear I saw steam rise off my hand. But thank God the pain dropped to a bearable level. All the same, when I bent to retrieve my knife I nearly passed out. I steadied myself on the rail. There was a bitter, acrid stench on the air now, and I realised that Harris wasn't the only one burning the stuff away. He'd enlisted Benjamin and another half-dozen of the more level-headed crewmen to help. Smart work, Harris.

Swearing at the pain, I dug a handkerchief out of my pocket and wrapped it round my bleeding hand. Raised my knife again and turned back to see that Harris and his firemen had cleared most of the foul fungus-stuff away. Nice job.

But how the hell do you follow that?

Don't worry about it, da Silva. You'll find out soon enough, I expect.

I found out.

Two nights ago, I'd been asleep when the hulk of the *Bellatrix* surfaced. I'd assumed her ghost would look the way she had in life. Now the last thing I expected was to find that what killed her . . . looked like a ship.

To be fair, I'm pretty sure it wasn't. That it could've looked like anything it wanted. But it sure as hell gave a good impression of it. I clutched the rail, my throat dry, my right hand absurdly painful. Watched the tops of her masts break surface, followed by the royals streaming water, the t'gallants and the topsails, jibs, foresail, mainsail. The bowsprit sliced up out of the sea, and then the deck shrugging off half the ocean. All in perfect silence, and all black: sails, masts, hull. Everything pitch-black, but glimmering with a sickly hectic phosphoresence. And I knew, beyond all possibility of doubt, that it was evil and unhuman and inimical. My back prickled. I wanted to shake myself, like a dog.

That wasn't the worst of it, though. As the black ship rose—and rose, and rose, looming over *Isabella* like one of the big Horn four-posters over a schooner—I saw her sides were ridiculously lined with portholes. And every single one had anguished human faces crammed up against it. As if the thing was full beyond comprehension with the drowned.

And as if that wasn't bad enough, I could hear them. A confused screaming and shouting that somehow wasn't quite human any more. As if they'd gone past the end of endurance and come out the other side . . . other. Changed, beyond all possibility of redemption.

It seemed *Bellatrix* was going to be out of luck. And, apparently, *Isabella*.

High above me, on the black ship's mighty fo'c'sle, someone laughed. Or something. It was the most chilling sound I've ever heard, monstrous. Put me in mind of an iron dungeon door clanging in a great void. I tipped my head up, suddenly angry past all description. Who, or what, is her master? What—since this is a pattern that seems to repeat itself, these days—will I have to fight to save my ship?

I realised, somewhat belatedly and almost too late, how close the black ship was. Made a leap for the wheel, yelling 'Get the helm over!' to Garvão. Grabbed hold and added my weight to his. *Isabella* responded, too slow, too slow, it was almost upon us, then my ship turned, the sails flapped loose, the black ship slid by. Far too close for comfort. Someone swore. I glanced at Garvão. His face was wet, and paler than it had any right to be.

'Keep your eye on that damned thing,' I said hoarsely.

'*Certo, senhor capitão,*' he answered. His voice shook. He looked as if he might faint. *Meu Deus*, do I have to steer the bloody ship as well?

Yes, probably. I'm the one who's supposed to be fighting things like this, after all. Or so old Mohan Das implied. I grinned mirthlessly at Garvão, who probably thought I'd finally gone completely insane, and relieved him of the helm. Might as well be in control, anyway. My scar was itching, but I didn't have time to scratch it.

The black ship was on the other tack already. Mighty fast for something that size. Or it would've been, if it'd been of this world. I put *Isabella* next to the wind and gained some distance, thinking furiously.

When I saw the Devourer looked like a ship and not the Titan Adamastor, I'd expected some hellish pirate to come and challenge me. Seems not. Wrong again, da Silva. Why not stop trying to guess what's going to happen? Almost never right. Should be fine as long as I don't want to go into the fortune-telling business.

Looks as if the plan's even less subtle. Ramming *Isabella* seems to be the order of the day. Then, presumably, devouring at leisure. And *meu Deus*, the bloody thing's big enough to turn us into matchwood.

Well, fighting someone bigger and nastier's never bothered me much before. At least the black ship doesn't seem to have a set of matching black cannons.

Only one thing to remember if you want to beat someone bigger. And that's that there are no rules.

So, be sneaky.

Keeping a careful watch on the monster ship, I shouted for Harris. He came panting up, still carrying his torch.

'You okay, skipper?' Harris wiped his sweating face with his hand. I raised an eyebrow at him. Do I look it?

'Just wonderful,' I said sourly. 'Have you got rid of that fungus stuff?'

'Just about. They're clearing the last bits now. It don't like fire, that's for sure, not one little bit. Whatcha gonna do about that thing, though?'

They always assume I've got a plan. I lowered my voice, though I've no idea whether that'll do any good. 'I don't think that thing will like fire either,' I said softly. 'So d'you think you can throw that onto her?'

A slow grin spread over Harris's face. 'Sure thing, skipper. Easier'n hitting a spittoon at ten paces.'

'It's turning.' He nodded. The black ship bore down on us. 'Now,' I shouted. Harris flung the torch, I hauled the wheel hard over. I saw the fire glow brighter as it spun through the air, felt the wind of the Devourer's passage as we slid past her.

Before it landed, though, the flame winked out. Didn't fizzle or falter and die. Just went out, like an electric light being turned off. I swore, and took a moment to scratch my scar. Harris spat over the rail in disgust.

'Bastard musta seen it coming,' he muttered, angrily. 'You want me to take another crack at it, skipper?'

I shook my head. 'No. But you can get me another of those. Only don't light it.' The Third raised his eyebrows. I bared my teeth. 'If we can't set that thing on fire from here, I'm going to board it and burn it.'

'Jesus on the mizzen royal footrope.' Harris sucked in air through his teeth. 'How the hell are you gonna manage that?'

Didn't answer that. Because I'm not sure how to. I ran a hand over my chin. Can't even remember the last time I shaved. Must've been this morning, but that seems like years ago. 'Think you can keep on dodging, if I give you the helm?'

Harris looked affronted. 'Sure.'

'Then fetch Angelotti and put an eyepatch on him.' That got me a grim smile.

'Yeah, if anyone's looking, that'll fool 'em from a distance. You wanna donate maybe a coat as well?'

'No, thanks,' I said. 'D'you see me wearing a coat?' You can have too much verisimilitude. And I really don't want something that smells like Angelotti inhabiting my clothes. Fastidious, who, me? Try spending a few months at sea. I dodged the black ship again, *Isabella* responding sweetly. The vast dark hull slid by. The mad dead faces screamed through the portholes.

'Go,' I told Harris.

I'd've preferred to take him with me. But he's the only man on board whose reactions I trust against that thing.

* * * * *

This does *not* feel like a good idea. I'm a forty-three-year-old man with one eye. And I'm about to—— Oh, stop thinking about it, da Silva. Just get on and do it.

So here I am, grapple in sweaty hand. Watching the monstrous bulk of the Devourer bearing down on *Isabella*. I clamped down hard on the bit of my mind that was screaming *This is impossible, you're an idiot*.

Waited till the last possible moment, then threw. The hook bit, I launched myself into space, Harris put the helm over, and Isabella swung away to safety in the nick of time. Truth is, I wouldn't trust anyone else's reactions to do that, either.

My momentum slammed me hard into the side of the black ship, driving the breath out of me. It gave slightly. Which made me nervous. Nervouser. Had it *felt* the impact? Or the grappling hook snagging it?

No time to worry about it. I started to climb, bracing my feet against the thing that so obviously wasn't a ship and trying to breathe evenly. My hands were sweating so much I thought they'd slide off the rope, and the right one still hurt like the devil. My head was pounding madly, and it wasn't with exertion.

Nothing happened. When I got up to the deck, there was nothing there. Nada. Up close, it only vaguely mimicked a ship. But the surface was dry and brittle and punky, like wormy wood. It looked as if it'd burn like tinder. Good.

First I unsheathed my knife and stuck it in my belt where I could get at it quickly. And, *oxalá*, not slice through the belt if I needed it. Bit of a hindrance in a fight, trousers round your ankles. Though on the other hand your opponent'd probably be laughing so hard you could kill him before he recovered.

After that, I unslung the torch from my back and took out my matches. Glanced quickly around to see if anything looked particularly inflammable. Not really. Better just get it lit and trust to luck. I struck a match. It went out. I muttered a curse. Sweat ran down my face.

Holding the torch near the pitch-soaked end, I tried again. The matchhead broke off and flared briefly before fizzling out.

Damn it. I tried a third, holding the torch between it and what I have to call the deck. The brand caught light, flames licking swiftly round it, and I drove it into the softish surface before it could go out as well.

It caught. Little blue flames ran out from it. Turned into big flames. The Devourer shuddered. Time to make yourself scarce, da Silva.

Only I couldn't. My feet were stuck. I looked down, my back as cold as ice. They were mired an inch deep in the deck.

Around me the fire crackled merrily. I'd been right about it not liking fire. Unfortunately I don't go well with fire, either.

Two choices. Well, only one, really. I pulled out of my seaboots. Doesn't matter what the deck-stuff does to my feet. Got to be better than fried captain. I ran to the side, trying to avoid the tacky feel of it, and jumped overboard.

Seemed to fall an awful long way before I hit the sea. And went down an awful long way after that.

Well, I can swim, though I don't suppose I'd win any prizes for style. Most sailors can't. Most sailors look at you as if you'd asked if they eat babies, if you ask that question. Don't ask me what they think they're supposed to do if they go overboard. Drop straight to the bottom and run like buggery for the shore, I suppose.

Feels like *I'm* going to hit bottom soon, at this rate. My ears'll burst if I go any deeper. Not to mention my lungs. I kicked upwards. No way of telling how far down I was. Never been diving in the dark.

A moment later I broke surface. Took a huge gulp of air and promptly started coughing. Smoke. Good. I trod water so I could watch the Devourer burning.

And also coming straight at me. Not so good. I started swimming *Isabella*-wards, but she had to tack to dodge the monster-ship again. Again, not so good. Ha. Nice work, da Silva. Why not set light to the bloody thing and make it even more dangerous?

Merda. I started taking deep breaths. Three will have to do. I filled my lungs, and dived again. Have to hope the bastard doesn't draw worth a damn.

Didn't get my back broken by its hull, so probably not. Leaves me with a bit of a problem, though. Now the Devourer's between me and my ship, and it could take all night to burn. And both of 'em could be ten miles away by morning.

Unfortunately, I'm not as good a swimmer as all that. And I'm getting tired. 'Getting' is a relative term. I was weary before I jumped into the sea. The acrid burning smell reminded me how much I wanted a smoke. Perverse, but there you are.

Something bumped me from behind, making my heart turn somersaults. I choked on a mouthful of the Caribbean I'd inadvertently sucked in, and started to cough again. Damn it. I turned, treading water. Found, instead of the expected shark, a piece of driftwood. Which I eyed suspiciously. It floated, despite being so soggy you could've used it as a sponge. It gave me a chance to rest and take stock. It didn't have *Bellatrix*'s name carved on it, but what do *you* think?

Isabella was tacking back round towards me, her course—or Harris's, though I did remember what the ghost of *Bellatrix* had said about her captain—describing a circle. The Devourer sat low in the water, burning with a sullen gleam, very much reduced in bulk. It was still relentlessly trying to pursue my ship, but its manœuverability looked almost zero. Even as I watched, it settled lower into the ocean. I had a momentary twinge of fear that something that size would suck me under when it went to the bottom, but realised almost at once that there wasn't much danger of that. It wasn't real, after all. Not in any corporeal sense.

Had enough swimming. I struck out towards *Isabella*, and Harris fished me out of the sea about ten minutes later.

'You took your damn time,' I grumbled.

'Was out dancing with your new friend.' He held out my cheroots, and I took one and lit it gratefully. Sucked in smoke. Beautiful.

'How'd that work out for you?'

Harris shrugged. 'Bit too hot for comfort,' he said.

Hot, yes. 'You could say that.'

He shot me an odd look. 'Mind telling me what you're grinning about, skipper?'

I wasn't grinning. I was looking thoughtful. 'Maybe one day.' Don't want to stretch credibility too far. And I think telling him that my English grandmother, my father's mother, was called Dorothea Jarvis . . . stretches coincidence further than it ever should be stretched.

But then I've always said there are no such things as coincidences.

Beyond the River

Joel Lane

I T'S A SURPRISINGLY LONG WAY from London to Devon: a tilted line across the map of England, from the wealthy South-East to the poorer South-West. The landscape becomes more stark and elemental the further you go. It took me three hours to drive to Exeter on a warm September afternoon, the setting sun ahead of me painting the edges of rock that showed through the hillsides. The fires of late summer had left blackened patches on the rusting wheatfields. I drove through run-down little towns too far from the coast to benefit from tourism. At last, the silver gleam of the Dart estuary was in sight. I could smell the rich odours of marine salt and river mud, faintly tinged with the chemical traces of industry.

Beside my road atlas on the passenger seat was a page from an A–Z map, with the road I was looking for circled in red. Underneath both was a hardback copy of a children's book: *The Secret Dance* by Susanne Perry. The front cover was a colour version of one of the interior illustrations, showing a forest in twilight. The trees were ancient, their branches twisted into bizarre shapes. Living things were just visible among the trees and in the tangled undergrowth: a few squirrels, two owls, a fox—and many cats, whose eyes glowed a deep undersea green. The copy was a first edition. I'd had it for thirty years; it had been a present from my parents on my fifth birthday.

The Perry house was set back from the road, behind a tall privet hedge. The front garden was full of roses: tangled, overgrown bushes with heavy blood-red flowers. The appearance of neglect surprised me; Susanne had sounded calm and relaxed on the phone, but perhaps the stress of the last year had got to her. I was here to interview her for the *Observer*, and expected she'd have things to say about her former publisher. But I wanted to tell the readers that she'd risen above the corporate nightmare: the world of her imagination couldn't be touched by business. That was what I wanted to see.

Wind chimes rang behind the panelled door. Susanne opened it. She was taller than I'd expected, and was wearing a blue-black dress that made her appear willowy rather than skinny. Her loose dark hair was flecked with grey, rather like Patti Smith's on a recent *Later With Jools Holland*. She looked no more than fifty, but her eyes were older. She grasped my hand with her long, narrow fingers. 'Hello there. Julie, isn't it? Do come in.'

The house was decorated in tasteful shades of dark green and auburn, with abstract pictures and carvings that might have come from Italy or Spain. Susanne led me through into the living-room, whose window overlooked the river. You couldn't hear the boats go by, but you could see them. The back garden was mostly long grass and weeds. Susanne made coffee, and we sat on her green couch at the end of the room. Her writing-desk faced the window; there was a small electronic typewriter on it, but no sign of a computer.

'Beautiful house,' I said. 'How long have you lived here?' As far as I knew, she lived alone. There'd been a marriage in the past, but no children.

'I was born here. It was my parents' house. I inherited it when my mother died, and moved back in. I used to travel quite a lot, but lately this is all I need. I like living close to an estuary. Where the river becomes something else, the movement flowing into what doesn't change.' She said this as casually as if she were talking about the availability of parking spaces at the local supermarket.

'Are there any forests nearby?' I asked. 'I didn't see one when I was driving here.'

She laughed. 'You have to know where to look.'

I wondered about asking her to sign my battered copy of *The Secret Dance*. Maybe later, at the end. She was probably sick of maudlin fans trying to relive their childhood. I wanted to appreciate the person she was now.

'How do you want to do the interview?' I said. 'I can show you the questions and let you think about them before we talk, or we can just start chatting and see how that goes. I'd like to get a photograph as well, if you're happy with that.'

'Fine. Let's start there. Maybe by the window?' I fished my Nikon digital camera from my bag, then stood back so I could photograph Susanne with the river-boats as background rather than the forsaken garden. She ran her delicate fingers through her hair. Her face took on a lost, haunted expression, as if she were dreaming with her eyes open. I took three shots.

Afterwards, it took her a few minutes to come back from whatever thoughts she'd given herself up to. She sipped her coffee quietly, her eyes closed. Then she smiled at me. 'Would you like something to eat? I can have some dinner ready in half an hour. Be easier to talk over a glass of wine.'

'That'd be lovely,' I said. 'If you're sure.'

'It's nice to have someone here. I haven't felt like company in a while.' She led me into the kitchen and prepared a light, elegant meal of grilled salmon with fennel and toasted ciabatta bread. I admired the tapestry that hung on the wall opposite the stove: an undersea scene of fish swimming through tangled weeds, coral, and the drifting hair of mermaids. It reminded me of Susanne's illustrations, though she always drew forest scenes since her books were set in a forest world.

We ate at a small table in the living-room, and shared a bottle of Chablis. I reckoned I could get away with two glasses if I wasn't driving for a couple of hours. And to be honest, I hadn't felt like company in a while either. It was nice, I thought, to share a drink with someone who didn't have an agenda, whether business or personal. The light dimmed in the bay window, and the small oil-lamps on the mantelpiece filled the room with trembling strands of light.

And she told me about the Forest of Scriffle. The imaginary twilight realm Susanne had developed as a background for the dreams, mysteries, and visions that she had wanted to explore as a young writer. The forest tales began as picture-books with text and illustrations on alternate pages, and ended as short novels with a few pages of artwork. Like Tove Jansson, she had always drawn her own illustrations. The forest had grown over time, becoming more complex and more strangely populated.

'Did you read that interview with Simon Maxwell-Hoare in the *Sunday Times*?' she asked. I nodded. Maxwell-Hoare was the Managing Director of Neotechnic, the edutainment and educommerce publishing company that was trying to sue Susanne for breach of contract. He had asserted that 'Susanne Perry is incapable of understanding the needs of her readership.' The interviewer might have pointed out that, as the executive publisher of the magazine *Children As a Market*, Maxwell-Hoare viewed the cultural needs of children primarily in terms of their need for Neotechnic's products. But he hadn't.

Susanne drained her glass and refilled it. 'The thing that infuriates me most about what he said is that the whole idea of the Forest of Scriffle was always quite commercial. But it gave me a peg on which I could hang my ideas about faith and imagination. Behind the dancing cats and the nervous squirrels and the world-weary owls were themes drawn from Wicca and nature worship. But I expect you know that.'

'I think I did even as a child,' I said. 'The pictures suggested something more than just a bunch of cute little animals. The patterns, the swirling effects. Things going on in the background that you couldn't quite make out.'

'In the seventies, some teachers said my books were a bad influence. They'd lead people to take drugs.' Her eyes widened. 'Which I never did, of course.' I suspected she was being ironic, but wasn't sure. 'But whatever I was putting into the books, Neotechnic didn't want any of it. They wanted the new books to be like papier mâché: the surface repeated all the way through. I was supposed to let Marketing decide on the content. My job was simply to write and draw what they told me.'

The grilled fish was rich and crisp. I relaxed, drank some wine, and kept the dictaphone supplied with miniature tapes as Susanne told me her story. Part of me was still five years old, dreaming with my eyes open, running with the little lost creatures through the ancient shadows of the Forest of Scriffle.

'I started writing those stories when I was a student at Bristol University. My lecture notes were annotated with little silhouettes of cats and distorted trees. I searched the university library for books of folk tales, and wrote a dissertation on archetypal themes in the tales of Hans Christian Andersen. By the end of my final year, I'd written an early draft of *The Secret Dance*. And drawn most of the pictures.

'Then I got a job in a Bristol museum. I kept putting the book away, then taking it out and doing more work on it. Eventually I had a typed draft with a set of pen-and-ink illustrations. I sent it to Dunwich Books because they were my favourite children's publisher. Once I'd sent the book off, I decided to put my youth behind me and never write or draw again. Then I got a letter from their editor, Judith Williams, saying they wanted to publish the book.

'They had a wonderful office building near Scarborough, full of pictures and book covers. Judith and I became good friends. She encouraged me to write more complex stories, aimed at slightly older children, so that my readership could grow into the series. *The Sleepless Forest* took me three years to write and illustrate, while I drifted from one museum or art gallery job to another. Then I met a teacher called Steven who was taking a group of kids round a dinosaur exhibition. We got a flat together, and got married a year later.

'When the third book, *Shadows That Dream*, won a literary award and became a bestseller, I was able to give up my job. By now I had an agent, Roanne Smith, who kept me busy with school visits and readings. Felicity Kendal read *Shadows That Dream* on the BBC's *Jackanory* programme. I had an offer from Puffin Books, but I wanted to stay with Dunwich—or at least with Judith. She was the only person who really understood the Forest of Scriffle. I did a painting of her in the forest, surrounded by cats. It stayed on the wall of her office until . . . the end.

'Steven was never comfortable with my success. He didn't mind me writing my little books and doing my little sketches, but the fact that I was earning more than him made him angry. Things were different then. He wrote a novel for teenagers but couldn't sell it, and things began to sour between us. Maybe if we'd had children it would have been different. Anyway, he met someone else.

'Then my father became ill and died. I was spending a lot of time here, which meant I was reliving things just as they began to slip beyond my reach. Do you know what I mean? The Forest of Scriffle became an escape for me, but also a place where I could try and make sense of things. That's why *The Moon*

Cats was a darker book. I was trying to help children see that life can't always be a happy thing. It didn't do as well as the third book, but I was proud of it.

'I wrote three more books in ten years, then decided that was enough. Dunwich Books kept them in print, and I was making enough money to live on. When Roanne retired, I didn't look for another agent. I suppose I didn't feel confident about writing another Forest of Scriffle book. I started working on an adult novel, a historical novel set in this region, but I still haven't finished it. People are harder to understand than cats. I drew some cards for Dunwich to print as merchandise, but that was all. Until the year before last.'

By now, we had finished the meal and drained the bottle of Chablis. I thanked Susanne for her hospitality, and changed the tape in the dictaphone. She disappeared into the kitchen, then returned with blueberries, ice cream, and coffee. The daylight was fading in the window, and I could see the lights on the river boats floating beyond the tangled shadows of the garden. The coffee was strong; its bitterness filtered through me as Susanne resumed her story.

'I'm sure you know most of it. Dunwich Books was bought out by Neotechnic, an American publishing corporation. They had to close their offices and move to the Neotechnic building in Telford. Have you been to Telford?' I shook my head. 'It's a new town, all shopping malls and identical streets, nothing built before 1980. Judith hated it. Then, after six months, they announced a "restructure". Dunwich Books would cease to exist as an imprint, and its line would be absorbed into the Neotechnic list of children's fiction.

'Judith was called into a meeting to discuss her future. She told me about it a few days later. At that time, Simon Maxwell-Hoare was the Marketing Director, not the MD. But he completely controlled the meeting. It all revolved around him. Judith was asked to explain her publishing programme. She got out about three sentences before he said: "There's no market for fancy books." Judith tried to talk about the reputation of the Dunwich Books list, its status in the field, and he cut her off again: "I call a spade a shovel, dear. I don't give a shit about literary awards. This meeting has five objectives: increase profit, increase our market share, increase the visibility of the Neotechnic brand, reduce overheads, and increase profit again. I don't see that you have much to contribute." The MD sat there like Buddha and said nothing.

'A month later, Judith and two other Dunwich editors were made redundant. Neotechnic put out a press release expressing regret that the extremely tough market had made this measure necessary. If Judith had stayed in children's publishing I would have tried to move with her, but she decided to take early retirement. She and her husband moved to France. Meanwhile, Neotechnic sent me nothing except a royalty statement and a subscription form for their magazine *Children As a Market*.

'Then I got a personal letter from Maxwell-Hoare, introducing himself as the new Managing Director and claiming to be a lifelong fan of children's fiction. He wanted me to come in and discuss the relaunching of the seven Forest of Scriffle novels in a new edition. As I recall, he said: "The Scriffle series is a key product within the Neotechnic brand, and we look forward to increasing its market share." He wanted me to write a new book in the series.

'I wrote back asking them to release me from my contract. That provoked a much less friendly letter informing me that Neotechnic would block any attempt by other publishers to reissue my work. It was their way or nothing. Of course, I should have got another agent. Or at least a solicitor. But I lost my nerve. This was just after my mother's death, and I was moving back here. I was very low, and short of money. Somehow I convinced myself that writing a new book would be good for me.

'So we had a lunch meeting at the only restaurant in Telford. There was Maxwell-Hoare, and the new Marketing Director, and the head of the design department. And Sally Black, my new editor, the only woman in the executive management team. Her contribution to the meeting was to smile and agree with everything that Maxwell-Hoare said. I recalled that Judith had mentioned Sally Black, but I can't quote her comments for legal reasons.

'It wasn't a very memorable meeting. Maxwell-Hoare informed me that he called a spade a shovel. Then he spouted some incomprehensible crap about market penetration and brand visibility. One of the phrases he used was "old wine in new bottles". I wish I'd paid closer attention, but I'd had a couple of glasses of real wine and wasn't at my sharpest. So when he said that I'd be working with Sally and the design team to make sure the new book did well for Neotechnic, I didn't ask what changes they had in mind.

'The next day, the contract arrived. It looked normal enough. There was a mention of touching up some of the old covers to give them more impact, and I thought that sounded quite reasonable. To be honest, I just wanted to get back into the Forest of Scriffle. I realised that ideas for an eighth book had been creeping around my head for years, waiting for me to notice them. I wrote the first draft of *Trees Never Forget* in about three months, and sent it to Sally Black.

'Then I was sent proofs of the new edition of *The Secret Dance*. That was a shock. They'd broken up paragraphs, replaced longer or less modern words with simpler ones, and introduced a hundred or so typing errors. Every illustration now had a small version of the Neotechnic logo in one corner. You know, that distorted N in a circle. The one on the cover was red on black; the others were grey on black.

'I sent the proofs back to Sally covered with corrections, and said I wasn't happy about the logos. When the new edition came out, hardly any of my corrections had been done and the logos were still there. I phoned Sally, and she said it wasn't cost-effective to make so many changes. "It won't affect sales." I said I had never agreed for the earlier books to be re-edited. She said:

"You can't expect us to publish them unless they're appropriate for today's market." I hung up the phone.

'A week later, my manuscript came back with Sally's comments. She started by saying that the language was too difficult for today's young readers. She wanted it "rationalised" in line with the changes she was already making to my other books. And she insisted that I use American spellings, in line with Neotechnic's house style. Then she started on the story itself. She felt the hints of nature mysticism and Celtic magic were inappropriate for a mostly Christian readership. She wanted the cats to be friendlier and less mysterious, so that children could "identify" with them. She didn't like the territorial hedgehogs or the sinister grass snakes. And she wanted me to mention a little blue dog, in order to tie into another Neotechnic product.

'A letter from the Marketing Director was attached. He wanted the illustrations simplified, made more "accessible", with more cats and fewer animals that the readers might not recognise. He wanted the little tie-in dog added at least three times, and shown in blue on the cover. A scanned image of said pooch was enclosed. Finally, he wanted the Neotechnic logo drawn into the forest background in every illustration.

'What could I do? I wrote to Maxwell-Hoare, saying that these demands were a violation of my rights as an author and a corruption of the relationship I had built up with my readers. I got a letter from the Neotechnic company lawyer, telling me that I had to comply with their demands; otherwise, my contract would be null and void. So I tore up the contract and sent them the pieces. I got another letter from the company lawyer, serving notice of legal action for breach of contract. The story got out, and here we are.'

It was dark outside by now. Susanne looked at me as if I had come with the bailiffs. I wanted to hug her, but didn't know whether that was appropriate. I rubbed my forehead nervously. 'I'm really sorry,' I said. 'It sounds like you've been shafted. But that's corporate publishing for you.'

Susanne raised her eyebrows in mock surprise, then smiled. Her eyes looked terribly weary. 'Julie, would you like some more wine? Or a drop of brandy? It's getting late, and you're welcome to crash out in my spare room. It's a long drive in the middle of the night.'

Ordinarily, I would have suspected an attempt at seduction. Especially as I'd put on a nice outfit for the interview. But my spider-senses weren't picking up any such vibes from Susanne. At the same time, her tone was too level for this to be simple helpfulness. She had an agenda, but I didn't think it was sexual.

So I accepted the offer of more wine. Susanne found a bottle of Chianti, and put on a Dr John CD to murmur darkly in the background. She drew the curtains, but left a window open. We sat and chatted for a while about subjects of mutual interest: modern art, blues, cats, Paris. I complained about the sexism of male journalists. Then she asked me: 'Would you like to visit the Forest of Scriffle?'

'Er . . . pardon?' What metaphor was this? Was she offering me a joint, or a folder of her illustrations?

'I mean it literally.' She wasn't smiling now. 'It's not far away. Like I said, you have to know where to look.'

'Where is it?' I asked, still mystified.

'Beyond the river. We can walk there.'

The full moon cast delicate shadows from the trees outside Susanne's house. At the end of the road, a footpath led between two tall hedges. She led me through a gap in a steel fence, and down a precarious slope to the river bank. It was the kind of route I imagined a cat might follow.

'I found the way when I was seven,' she said. 'I've been coming here ever since. But I think it might not be here much longer. I want to share it with someone while I still can.' The bank was overgrown, and I could see a factory wall on the other side. Susanne paused.

'Look.'

She was pointing down to the water's edge. The river was a dark skinless muscle with threads of moonlight. Just where the grass ended and the river-mud began, I could see two stone steps. The water smelt brackish. Susanne gripped my hand and pulled me forward. I felt a sudden, overwhelming sense of strangeness, as when you develop a fever or get caught between sleep and waking. I didn't think about my clothes, or my inability to swim. I just followed.

The steps led down under the water. It didn't feel cold, just a little more dense than the night air. Even breathing wasn't difficult: my chest just seemed to fill with air and exhale thin white plumes through the dark water. Fish or eels slid around my ankles. I walked for some time, holding Susanne's thin hand. It was much darker down here. Then she paused, reaching forward. Her drifting hair touched my face. She moved on, and we began to climb another flight of stone steps.

The moon's reflection shimmered on the water surface just above our heads. My foot slipped on river-weed, but Susanne drew me on. The surface broke, then healed below us. We stood dripping on the mossy bank. And there, just a few yards in front of us, was the Forest of Scriffle. The trees were silhouetted in the moonlight, their twigs as intricately patterned as mediaeval carvings. Drifts of dead leaves rustled in the night breeze.

I stepped forward, open-mouthed with wonder. My nostrils filled with scents of wood and leaf-mould, ferns and decay. But Susanne didn't move. I glanced at her and saw the growing terror in her face. 'What's wrong?'

'I don't now. It's not the same. This time of year, the leaves should all be on the trees.' She walked slowly forward. I followed her. Close up, I could see that the trunks were streaked with decay. The branches looked grey and brittle.

'What's happened to it?' Susanne said. 'The trees are all dead. And I can't hear the birds. At night there should be owls hooting, doves calling. It's silent.'

Then something came towards us out of the dark undergrowth. It reached a clearing and stood in the moonlight, uncertain. A black cat. It was sniffing the air, but didn't seem to see us. Susanne walked slowly towards it, reaching out a hand. 'Hello, little one. How are you? Where are your friends?' Then she stopped. 'Oh, no.'

The cat was blind. Its eyes were blank sockets. Its fur was patchy, and its ribs were visible through the taut skin. Susanne dropped to her knees and stroked the cat's neck. 'My God, what's wrong with you? What's happened here—' Then she screamed. I saw her rise to her feet and beat her hand violently against the trunk of the nearest tree. Some of the dead bark flaked away at her touch.

I went to comfort Susanne, but she backed away from me. The cat was lying on its side, no longer moving. I knelt to examine it. In the moonlight, I could see things moving through its fur. Crawling rounded shapes, like bugs or lice. Each one had a raised marking that glowed faintly with a terrible light of its own. A shape like a twisted letter N, red on black.

Now that I had seen them, I became aware that they were on the trees also. And on the dead leaves beneath my feet. And on a dead owl that was lying within my reach, its beak stretched open to receive the night. They were everywhere in the forest, infesting every living thing, leaving nothing but grey brittle remains and silence. The rustling I could hear was the lice, hunting restlessly through the dead vegetation in search of something further to eat.

Then another sound reached me. A living sound. It was Susanne, weeping. I couldn't see her at first, wondered if the forest had claimed her for its own. Then I found her crouched behind the dead hair of a willow tree. In one hand she was holding the clean-picked skeleton of a leaf. I pulled her to her feet, held her until she stopped shaking. Her tears were cold against my cheek.

'We have to get out of here,' I said. She didn't respond. 'Come on. There's nothing to stay for.'

'There's nothing to go back to either.'

'You know that's not true.' I gripped her hand and led her back towards the river. Behind us, I could hear the sound of dead trees creaking, breaking, and falling into the mounds of dead leaves. But something was calling to us through the night, from beyond the river. A heron.

Somehow we made it back the way we had come. The moon was lower in the sky, and it was colder than before. As we reached the house, Susanne began to shiver violently. She was pulling at her sleeves, checking them for signs of infection. I held both her hands, made her look at my face. 'Come on. Let's go inside.'

As I'd expected, Susanne seemed calmer indoors. She poured us both a large brandy, drank hers in a slow painful gulp. Then she walked up to the bathroom and closed the door behind her. I sat on the couch, drank my brandy, and reflected that I hadn't asked Susanne to sign my copy of *The Secret Dance*. It didn't seem appropriate just now.

To my relief, Susanne emerged after a while. She was wearing a dark green dressing-gown, and her hair was wet. I poured her another brandy. She sat on the couch for a while, lost in thought. Then she said: 'I have to go back there.'

'What for? You can't save the cats.'

'No, but I can burn them. Like a cremation. The wind will scatter the ashes in the river.'

I shook my head. 'There's no point, Susanne. If you go back, the forest will trap you. You'll die there. Your life is here.'

She looked at me then, and her eyes were full of ashes. 'What makes you so sure?'

'Because when things die, they don't stay the same. They rot. They become less than they were.' I could feel a bitterness in my throat like nausea as I spoke. 'You can't go back like that. No one can.'

Susanne didn't say anything more. She finished her glass, then pointed to mine. I shook my head. She spread a thin duvet and a few cushions over the couch, then went upstairs. I turned off the light and spent a sleepless night on the couch, imagining that I could feel dead leaves dropping onto my face.

In the morning Susanne was brisk and efficient, making breakfast and filling a flask with coffee to help me get through the long drive home. We didn't talk about the midnight trip. I never did get that book signed.

The feature article came out a week later. I'd glossed over most of the Neotechnic business, focusing on Susanne's earlier career and the enduring magic of the Forest of Scriffle. She sent me a card at my work address. On the front was an original sketch, showing two cats walking along a river bank by the light of a full moon. Inside was the message: *To Julie, a moon cat who keeps her feet on the ground. With love from Susanne.* Soon after that, Neotechnic dropped the lawsuit and stopped reprinting her books.

We've been in touch occasionally since then—phone calls, an exchange of Christmas cards—but she hasn't invited me to go back. I like to think that she's able to keep the river between herself and the ruin of her dreams. Sometimes I remember her smile, and it warms me. But sometimes I wake up shaking in the night, clawing at my skin, and nothing can take away the image in my head: an army of sleek black and red lice, working efficiently to pick the bones of a cat.

Only Sleeping

Peter Bell

> In the darkness be thou near me
> Keep me safe til morning light.
> *Childhood Prayer*

IT WAS THE LONG DARK CORRIDOR in the boarding house, amongst other things, that made Robert not look forward to going on holiday with his parents to the Isle of Man again.

For two whole weeks at the beginning of August every year the factory released his father from annual servitude, and as far back as he could remember Robert and his younger brother Jeff had regularly participated in the seaside summer pilgrimage. They had visited various resorts, all so depressingly similar that he could scarcely recall the names of the dreary places. That, at least, had been the case until now, when they proposed, against all tradition, to revisit the scene of last year's holiday.

It had been the first time they had visited an island. The vast expanse of the sea journey, gulls circling the ship with plaintive expectant calls, and the mysterious imperceptible approach from over the horizon of the emerald cliffs and hills had struck sympathetic chords in his imagination. The first few days had been genuinely enjoyable.

That, however, had been before the footsteps on the landing, the landing by the long dark corridor.

As he lay awake the night before the unavoidable return to the scene of his unease, he couldn't stop thinking of that awful house across the Irish Sea. In a final act of brave defiance he chose to challenge the shocking memories head-on, utilising a technique he often found helpful in ridding himself of the residue of a nightmare: he would reconstruct in cold precise detail and exact sequence the whole unpleasant drama, retrace it thoroughly in his mind, hoping thereby to execute something in the manner of an exorcism. . . .

The taxi from the pier drove along the two-mile arc of Douglas Bay before climbing up Summer Hill to the boarding house in Onchan. The sweeping terraces of tall hotels that curved around the bay spoke of better times. Though most still wore a superficial air of affluence, here and there a crumbling discoloured façade and the occasional unsightly gap made Robert think of a once fine set of teeth beginning to decay. High up on the cliffs, beyond the Palace Ballroom's dome, the pure white battlements and turrets of the Falcon Cliff Hotel vaguely reminded him of a poster in his classroom of mad Ludwig's castle in Bavaria. The Isle of Man, however, in contrast to the drab resorts they'd visited in recent years, still seemed to be making an effort to look festive and respectable. That at least was how he felt until, alighting from the taxi, he beheld looming before him the boarding house that would be his home for two long weeks.

The name, Sunny Bank, had conjured up an image of a pleasant homely cottage with roses rambling over a rustic wooden porch, but the house before him stood tall and grey upon a corner, long terraces extending on either side into an infinite tedium of look-alike holiday villas. Whilst most of these were fronted by colourful, well-kept gardens, exuding the gaiety of a seaside holiday, Sunny Bank, in insolent defiance of its name, was heavily shrouded behind a screen of unkempt sycamores and a riotous uncut privet hedge. He recalled the nauseating heavy scent of the privet blossom in the humid heat, embodying depression. Pangs of dismay overcame him as he contemplated the passage of a fortnight in this grim abode.

His immediate apprehensions, though, were somewhat mitigated by the light-hearted demeanour of their hosts. Mr and Mrs Moore were in their sixties; he a rotund, sun-tanned, bearded figure, reminding Robert of a small and friendly bear; she, grey-haired and tall with ruddy cheeks, an absent-minded air, and an appealing high pitched laugh. She had a crazy sense of humour, too, which she delighted in bouncing off the boys. Jeff seemed nonplussed at first when he was told by Mrs Moore that he would get pigs' feet for breakfast. This was to be her bantering refrain throughout the holiday whenever they enquired about the menu.

Their genial hostess, talking unceasingly, immediately showed them round. The hallway, lightened by a stained glass window on the stairs ahead, managed to avoid appearing too lugubrious, despite the usual guest house *bric-à-brac*. The wholesome dining-room opened off a corridor to the left, culminating in the kitchen and the living quarters of the Moores. The lounge, opening to the right, was bright and airy, with two bay windows, one on each side of the corner of the house. In contrast to the usual atmosphere imparted by such places, it did not summon up the unwelcome image of a dentist's waiting-room.

There was a youngish couple in the lounge, reading in the still bright sunshine of the afternoon. They had their backs towards the new arrivals but briefly turned in acknowledgement as the family stepped into the room. The man looked pale and tense, like someone suffering from a migraine, and his manner was perfunctory; he had the distant air of someone with trouble on his mind. She, raven-haired and beautiful in profile, was more effusive in her greeting, smiling broadly as she slowly turned her head and held Robert in a long and curious regard. Full-faced, however, her beauty was seriously flawed by an odd asymmetry of features, and there was misery in her hollow eyes. Her steady penetrating gaze made Robert feel naked and uncomfortable, and he was mightily relieved to depart. As they did so, Mrs Moore was whispering to his mother.

'Mr and Mrs Dennison. Alex and Maria,' she was saying. 'Maria was born in Russia. You should hear her accent; lovely! Like Marlene Dietrich, or someone. Her baby died earlier in the year and they've come away to help get over things. Very sad! We sometimes hear her crying in the night. They sleep just down the corridor.'

The corridor that Mrs Moore was referring to was reached by going up five steps left from a small landing on the staircase ahead. The main flight also turned up from here, reversing direction and leading to a broader landing above the hall, and this is where she led them first. A window overlooked the front garden, or, more exactly, what could be seen of it through the dense shading of the sycamores. On either side doors opened on to bedrooms. Above the lounge was the room where his parents were to sleep. With its pink and white-patterned paper, and windows in two walls, it looked instantly agreeable.

This was not the case, however, with the room across the landing, the one destined for the boys, which was much less prepossessing. Mrs Moore's repeated reference to it as 'the master bedroom' seemed as much an effort to apologise for its uninviting aspect as to banter with the children. Perhaps it was the fading of the old green floral wallpaper that made everything so depressing, while the fluttering density of the leaves outside the single narrow window reduced the light to a dim and intermittent flicker. The room felt overcrowded. One of the beds, which Robert commandeered, was flush against the window. The other, too commodious really for a single person, let alone a child, was very close to the entrance, and there was not a lot of space to get around its foot, especially as a dressing-table and a huge oak wardrobe flanked the facing wall. And he didn't like the way the loose brass doorknob sometimes went through several revolutions before it would engage the catch.

He was relieved, however, that his bedroom wasn't off the long dark corridor, near the room where the Russian guest could, apparently, be heard 'crying in the night'. The corridor didn't have a light, though there was a switch sealed up with masking tape, and the sole illumination was provided when a room was opened. All of these were on the left, and why no one had made a window in the right hand wall seemed inexplicable. The first bedroom off the corridor was occupied by the Moores, and it adjoined his own. Beyond was the room occupied by the Dennisons. The corridor seemed longer than it really was, no doubt something to do with the lack of light, and he could not quite equate the geometry of the upper floor with the size and layout of the space below. It felt horribly cut off, and it crossed his mind, even as his reason rejected the absurdity of the idea, that it would be easy and very awful to get trapped there. Any relief at having quarters separate from the dreary passage, though, was quickly dashed as Mrs Moore explained to them the position of the toilet—at the very end of the long, dark corridor.

'You've got a long, long walk,' she laughed, 'if you drink too much before you go to bed. So! Tread carefully in the dark!'

In the dark! He wouldn't like to go down there in the middle of the night, not at any price. He had no wish to hear the sound of mournful tears reverberating in the darkness.

Initially the novelty of the island holiday pushed such unwholesome thoughts into the background. But, as the nights proceeded, Robert's sleep became disturbed, strewn with unpleasant dreams difficult to recall on awakening, connected in some eerie way with the long dark corridor and Mrs Dennison.

The real trouble began at the weekend.

It was at the fading of a particularly mellow day, as they ambled leisurely from Douglas Promenade up to Onchan Head. The sun had dropped behind the hills and, as the sea-front illuminations came on, the bay became a luminescent golden crescent. Across the shimmering waters the lighthouse on the opposite headland was sending out with complex regularity insistent beams of light. It was quieter here than down in Douglas, the silence broken only by the distant sounds across the sands and the rasping passage of a tramcar on the Manx Electric Railway. They were looking down upon a rocky cove strewn with pebbles and seaweed, separate from the main sweep of the shore. A faded wooden sign guarded a concrete stairway that crumbled down the cliff to the strand below: PORT JACK—BEWARE!

Jeff scuttled down, the others following reluctantly. The steps were not quite so bad as they looked from up above, but there could be no doubt they needed care. Care was required on the beach as well, where one false move on slimy rocks could mean a broken ankle, and there were dire warnings about high tides. The cove was attractive in its own way but, isolated as it was from the distant swirl of coloured lights and the carnival sounds of the promenade, it felt a bit too lonely to be comfortable, and, in the evening shadows, rather dismal.

ONLY SLEEPING

There was only one other person, way over near the water's edge beyond a wall of large sharp rocks, a woman, it appeared. Odd as it seemed, Robert at first had the impression that it was Mrs Dennison. But this could clearly not be so, as he had seen their fellow lodger not half an hour before, slumped listlessly with her husband before the television. Whoever it was seemed to be crouching, burrowing in the shale. Her face was partly hidden by flowing tresses of unkempt hair, and there was something about the angle of the neck that didn't look quite right. It was difficult to be sure in the fading light, but the occasional glimpse of pale and ravaged features suggested not so much old age as premature wasting, no doubt the product of some bitter ailment. She seemed to be distressed. A harmless beachcomber, no doubt, but she conveyed an air of weirdness that reached coldly out to Robert.

No one else appeared to have noticed their twilight companion, and for reasons he could not explain he felt unwilling to elicit confirmation. Despite the cacophony with which his family heralded their progress along the beach, the huddled figure carried on its secret task undisturbed, seemingly oblivious to the presence in the cove of other people. Its mysterious movements continued unabated against the backdrop of the waves, now surging and falling more boisterously upon the rocks in the turning of the tide and the chilly rising wind.

The light was fading fast as they turned to go, the illuminations along the distant curving promenade now holding unopposed dominion over land and sea. The enclosing hills' silhouette was etched against a pink-flecked sky. East, beyond the bay's confines, the flickering orb of some nameless star hung above the dim horizon. The ill-clad family, dressed to suit the vanishing summer heat, shivered in the ever cooling breeze as they hastened precariously across the seaweed-covered cobbles towards the old stone staircase. Trailing at the rear, Robert took a last reluctant look behind. He tried to tell himself it was just the dying light that made the figure seem now to be standing upright, its crazy-angled pallid face staring at him. As he scaled the precipitous unstable steps, gripping the rusting handrail, he wondered how so obviously infirm a figure could negotiate the route back in the twilight, let alone the dark.

That night Robert slept more uneasily than ever, waking with a shout from a horrible, forgotten dream. It was still pitch black. He had an overwhelming urge to visit the toilet, a fate he had thus far managed to avoid. But there was no alternative: he would have to brave the perils of the long dark corridor. The terrifying beachcomber stalked his consciousness, a white face leering at him from a twisted neck; so much more shocking in the emptiness of the night. Maybe his father had been right: it had been a mistake to bring on holiday that book of ghost stories.

'Jeff, are you awake?' he called, but the sound of continued heavy breathing offered mute and categorical response, throwing into sharp relief the night's lonely well of silence. He stumbled round the foot of the bed. The shifting movement was just his dim reflection in the mirror, and it must have been a loose coat-hanger in the wardrobe that made him jump; but the hideous proximity of the ugly carved door, as he squeezed himself past its swollen bulk, conjured up all manner of terrifying explanations.

His hand was struggling with the recalcitrant doorknob when he heard outside a chilling sound, coming, as far as he could judge, from the stairwell. Determined footsteps had reached the turning near the corridor. The ominous treads halted and an interminable brooding silence prevailed. He froze, afraid to risk any sound that might give a signal to whatever loitered beyond the door. As he listened, heart in mouth, he persuaded himself that it was only the peculiar noises one often heard in a large old house at night as its beams and rafters settled in the falling temperature before the dawn.

But what in Heaven's name was that? Was it footsteps padding stealthily? Along the corridor? Down the steps and up the next short flight to his room? About to seize the loose door-handle? He listened in an agony of fear. For one awful second he thought he heard the handle turning. But there was nothing but the wind; and, beyond, the awesome vacancy of the early morning hours.

Eventually the imperative of nature triumphed. The corridor proved even darker than expected; the gloom felt positively tangible, and it was hot and stuffy, as if the heat of the day had been unable to dissipate in the ill-ventilated passage. The sobbing from the room next to the bathroom was no less harrowing for being indistinct, and he shuddered at the memory of the gaunt and haggard visage with its hollow eyes and ghastly smile. For, if truth be known, Mrs Dennison, gazing at him every morning in the breakfast room, was starting to bother him; and she was looking more and more wasted as each day passed. He'd even heard his mother talking about her deterioration in whispered tones of concern to Mrs Moore.

The corridor seemed even longer on his way back. His own foot creaking on a loose floorboard outside his bedroom brought his heart into his mouth, and for a dreadful moment he was certain that the door-handle had jammed completely, exiling him on the tenebrous landing. Behind him, yawning like a horrible expectant mouth, was the black vacancy of the deep stairwell. He couldn't rid himself of a wild and terrible sensation that there was something out there in the shadows. The house, cluttered and confined as it had seemed during the day, now felt like a monstrous cavern with crevices and corners where who knows what could hide. He gasped with relief as he shut the door against the fearsome terrors of the night.

In the purity of the summer morn, the gulls' insistent invitations shrilling outside, he tried to put his night-time fears into perspective. Fancy getting upset about that woman on the beach! That was why he felt so scared. And reading those ghost stories! What was that tale about an old farmhouse in Cornwall where an ancient crone crawled out of a slimy pond? And there was another one—something about children with no hearts and too-long fingernails, but he hadn't dared finish it.

It was, then, somewhat disconcerting when Mrs Moore at breakfast leaned over, nearly whispering, and said, 'I hope you weren't disturbed last night by the ghost.'

She was wearing a funny smile. Her head was bending closer and she was glancing back, surreptitiously, towards the door. Her voice was even lower; she was almost miming: 'Bill sometimes stays up late. When he's been to the club. He has a little tipple when he gets in. Falls asleep in the chair and comes to bed at all hours"

Robert breathed a sigh of relief. Only Mr Moore! Going to bed, drunk, at some unholy hour of the morning!

And there matters might have rested, had it not been for the visit to the old fun fair on Onchan Head. Robert's heart wasn't really in it; he was, as his mother put it, 'not feeling himself'. His throat was sore and he was overwhelmed by the lassitude and despondency prefiguring a cold. And he'd overheard Mrs Moore describe the fair as 'seedy and run-down'. It was with a prodigious sense of apathy, therefore, that he boarded the electric tram on the promenade and suffered the twisting, screeching movement of the antiquated vehicle as it trundled ponderously up towards the skeletal roller coaster and mournful clustered buildings, incongruously advertised in twenty-five-foot high illuminated letters on the headland as 'White City'.

Mrs Moore had certainly not been guilty of exaggeration: 'derelict' seemed closer to the truth than 'seedy and run-down'. But its uninviting atmosphere did not seem to have deterred customers. There were numerous visitors milling round, no doubt enticed like Robert's family away from the shore by the cooler, duller weather. Raucous youths stalked about. High-pitched female laughter echoed from a crowded arcade, blurred by thumping pop music. Long-haired men lazed in studded leather jackets outside an evil-smelling cafeteria. And there, entering the café, were Mr and Mrs Dennison. They appeared to be engaged in a quarrel. He could hear the Russian's broken accent, raised in strident petulance. Her husband wore a cowed look. And there could be no mistake: Mrs Dennison was now shuffling along with a pronounced uneven gait; she looked more haggard than ever. He noticed for the first time how tall she was for a woman. Robert was glad the family was behind them, outside the range of her awful roving gaze.

The attractions available at White City hardly seemed commensurate with the extent of patronage on that dismal day. Apart from a ramshackle roller coaster, the yawning death's head of the Ghost Train, the 'Las Vegas' amusement arcade, and several other dubious offerings, White City seemed to consist mainly of single-storey shuttered buildings, fallen into disuse, and a filthy public toilet which Robert had the misfortune to have to patronise. All in all it was an unsavoury, pathetic place, and not a little sinister in its uneasy balance between gaiety and decay. Only the cold unseasonable weather, surely, could have driven people from the freedom of the beaches to this forlorn and misbegotten outpost on the headland? High up above, the clacking wheels and screaming voices as the roller coaster car plunged down sounded like a skeleton wailing and rattling its bones in grim celebration of the dereliction of White City.

A desultory half-an-hour at 'Las Vegas' had passed, when Robert expressed a desire to go home. But his father, irked no doubt by the poor return on his investments, turned upon his son, savaging him with sarcasm.

'So you want to leave already, do you?' he said, smiling his meanest smile. 'I know what's the matter with you. Scared to go on that Ghost Train, eh? It's all those creepy stories you've been reading!'

Robert, if truth be told, didn't like the idea one little bit. What was that shocking tale he'd read last night about a man who met a terrifying companion on a ghost train? To deflect his father's barbs he declared, 'Not that rubbish! I'm going on the roller coaster!'

The prospect, actually, was almost as uninviting. Towering above, the pleasure-ride appeared nothing more than a flimsy wooden structure, its red and white paint peeling badly. Hadn't there been a horrific accident on the one at New Brighton? It had been in the newspapers and even on the television news. The *Liverpool Echo* had told how a thirteen-year-old girl had been 'catapulted to her death'. It had been forced to close down. His knees felt shaky as he gallantly marched towards the booking office, coins at the ready. He wondered whether to change his mind. But there wasn't really any choice: it was the roller coaster or the Ghost Train.

As the flimsy car climbed precariously, Robert quickly gained a bird's eye view of the fairground, and soon the wider aspect of the island opened up. The boat from Liverpool was turning into Douglas Bay. Across the sea the jagged hills of Cumberland rose up darkly, artificially near. You could even see the atomic power station on the coast, belching steam; it wasn't blowing up, was it? He could just glimpse, beyond Snaefell's pylon-crowned summit, the distant shape of Scotland. The motorcyclists were toy-town figurines, departing noisily on tiny silver bikes. The giant fangs of the Ghost Train's exit disgorged laughing teenage girls, accompanied by an eerie siren sound presumably meant to represent the wailing of a banshee.

As the car dived headlong, he half expected to be catapulted to his death. But sheer momentum seemed to keep it on the rails, swinging it up the next incline, then round the upper level of the figure-eight at breakneck speed. As the car careened down the central decline, towards the crossover, it lurched horribly. He suppressed a rising urgency to scream—only girls did that! They always did it on the roller coaster. How Dad would laugh! He thought for one awful moment, as he careered madly through the lower levels of the rickety latticework, that there was someone on the track ahead, but it must have been an optical illusion, for when he raced past, looping underneath the main incline, there was no one there. The ride seemed interminable, but at last the car came rattling home. Then he recalled the sign: 'Two rides for the price of one'. Already the car was starting its hellish journey up the first incline again, away from the world of Lilliput below.

As he neared the apex for a second time, there was a jarring motion and suddenly the car faltered. Underneath, the chain-like mechanism had stuttered into silence. Vertigo possessed him. In the distant fair below the movement of the people did not suggest awareness of anything unusual. He was stranded in this frightful eyrie, above the world of safety, and it was as he strove to accommodate this unpalatable fact that he became aware of the figure underneath.

At first he assumed it must be a repairman, something to do with the roller coaster's failure; but it was swiftly evident, even from his elevated distance, that this could not be so. The figure was dressed like no repairman Robert had ever seen; and it struck some eerily familiar chord. With a shocking sense of *déjà vu*, the evening at Port Jack came swirling back. The same inexplicable linkage of impressions raced across his mind: that it was Mrs Dennison, but a Mrs Dennison so utterly wasted that it was difficult to believe she could be this side of the grave. Simultaneously, the absurdity of this proposition confronted him, as he recalled his recent sighting of her. Though clearly in declining health, he didn't think she could so rapidly have departed this life! He laughed to reassure himself, but his laughter was short-lived, for whatever it was that prowled below was, horribly and obviously, straining to peer upwards between the latticework at the vehicle's terrified occupant. Like the figure on the shore, its neck was twisted at a crazy angle. Its wasted face, chalk white in the filtering rays of sunshine now cutting through the clouds like a spotlight, stared up at its lone audience like some phantom addressing the gallery in a stage play. And it seemed to be grinning, but grinning more widely than he'd ever seen anyone grin; and he, and he alone, was the object of its malevolent regard.

Mercifully, as in the breaking of a spell, the mute machinery leapt back into life, dragging the car over the apex, projecting it on its hell-ride round the creaking track. With choking terror he anticipated the swirling fall across the centre, down to ground level, near to the territory of the dreaded watcher. With the reluctant eagerness of fear he scanned the suspect area as he passed, but if the awful thing was still about he must have been travelling too fast to see. At last, with grateful relief, he zoomed in along the home stretch, into the haven of the terminus.

That night, half-listening for sounds beyond the door, Robert relived the day's strange events. A figure he had surely seen, and he was convinced it was the Port Jack witch. But reason told him there must be some other explanation. Maybe it was, after all, Mrs Dennison somehow straying onto the scene. But scarcely for a moment could this idea be tolerated; it was, if possible, even more preposterous. What on earth would she be doing down there? Presumably the ride was securely fenced off from trespassers. And anyway, he had just seen her with his own eyes, more infirm than ever, lurching unsteadily along. No, it was all nonsense. He must have imagined it.

But the awful mystery denied him sleep for ages. And somewhere in the distance, he was sure, was a mournful crying; it was not a pleasant sound. Then, just as he was dozing off, he heard what he hoped was a suitably inebriated Mr Moore on his way to bed. But the footsteps, he was sure, weren't ascending from downstairs, but from the direction of the dreadful corridor. The steps were moving softly, slowly, and purposefully, stair by stair, with irregularly paced intervals of silence as their unseen owner paused. The pauses were even more frightening than the steps, conjuring up an image of deliberative planning and cool listening malice. Were they going up the steps to the corridor, as Mr Moore's footsteps ought by rights to do? Or were they coming down? Coming down from the corridor and turning? Turning up to Robert's room?

They didn't sound anything like Mr Moore's footsteps either, shod or barefoot; more like the padding of an animal. But an animal that knew its business! And was that scratching that he heard? There wasn't any household cat, as he recalled, and the presence sounded too substantial. Anyway, a cat wouldn't make the banister creak. But which banister? The one going down the stairs, or—God forbid! There was the unmistakeable crack as the wobbly board outside his room yielded to the pressure of the footsteps. They appeared to halt right outside the door. He awaited, with beating heart, the awkward revolutions of the broken doorknob. But there was nothing—only the ominous silence of the night.

Next morning, their final day, he was late for breakfast. As he dressed he sharply told himself that it could only have been Mr Moore. He just hadn't heard him until he reached the turning on the stairs. He must have been trying to tread quietly to avoid waking guests, that was all. And he'd turned the wrong way up on account of having had a 'tipple'. Drunks always made mistakes. He laughed too loudly to himself. Only Mr Moore!

His family had already finished breakfast as he sat down at the table, his father glaring; and soon he had the dreaded Russian and her harassed husband as his sole companions in the dining-room. It made him feel self-conscious and uneasy. He didn't, in all honesty, like Mrs Dennison one little bit; he found her altogether strange. This no doubt accounted for her habitation of his dreams. There were quite enough odd things happening in this hateful house without this denizen from the long dark corridor adding to them.

As on previous occasions, she seemed overly interested in his presence, levelling a broad complicit smile at him every time he raised his eyes from the scrambled eggs; there was something almost indecent in her steady scrutiny. She was visibly more wasted; and her hair, flashing strands of grey in the sunlight, was in bizarre disarray. Her husband, as usual, sat impassive and morose; there was little talk between them. He wore a hunted expression, his eyes darting left and right, anywhere but towards Robert. He looked paler than ever.

Robert tried to avoid her eye, but it was difficult across the broad expanse of the breakfast tables; he felt vulnerable, naked. He could sense her baleful gaze even without looking at her. He hoped she wouldn't try to touch him as she left the room. She'd started doing that these last few days, and cuddling him as if he were a baby. Just because she'd lost her own! He didn't like her funny foreign accent either, the one that Mrs Moore called 'lovely'; he could hardly understand a word she said. And he didn't like the incongruity between the smiling lips and the haggard lines about the eyes, or the ghastly asymmetry of her features, now worsened by a nervous tic in her jaw. And, day by day it seemed, the pallor of her face was becoming more and more pronounced, the greying of her raven hair more blemishing, the dark hollows round her eyes more and more profound chasms. He had no wish to be embraced by this crier in the night.

Anxious to escape the desolation of the tragic woman's smile, and to avert the prospect of a cold embrace, he abandoned the remnants of his breakfast. Hurrying back to his room, he almost collided with his mother and Mrs Moore, who was engaged in a long monologue of complaint concerning her husband's laziness about the household.

'Take today, for example. Bill's left me to do the cleaning *and* go to the shops! And he's got the car as well! Went off yesterday to his brother's place in Ramsey and won't be back till evening. Golf! An excuse for doing nothing but lounge about in the sun all day, if you ask me. You don't see me with a suntan like Bill's got, slaving away indoors all the time.'

Robert shivered. So it couldn't have been Mr Moore after all. Then what on earth could it have been? Perhaps he had been dreaming. Since dreaming often took the guise, with astonishing exactitude, of the waking state, how could he be sure he hadn't dreamt the whole thing? His imagination had certainly been running riot of late. A nightmare it must have been. What were the alternatives?

A ghostly presence? Nonsense. No such thing. They were only stories in that terrible book. Dad was right—a load of old rubbish!

Who else would be creeping round the house at night? Certainly not his parents; he'd have heard them leave their room. Mrs Moore? But he distinctly recalled her shifting in her creaking bed beyond the wall. . . .

That only left the Dennisons!

His stomach churned as he grasped the awful logic of the explanation. Mrs Dennison didn't sleep at night. He'd heard her himself, weeping in the hours before the dawn. An insomniac, perhaps she padded round the house alone late at night after everyone had gone to bed. And she did have a funny way of walking—that was why the footsteps always sounded so uneven. And was it just insomnia? What was that story he was reading on the beach the other day about a boy who visited a friend who lived with a terrifying aunt? Hadn't that ghastly woman walked the house at night, spreading fear and terror? He shivered as he tried not to remember what had happened in the tale. Mrs Dennison was fascinated by him and liked to touch him. Maybe last night the fearsome guest had been lurking on the far side of his bedroom door, wondering whether to come in and smile her tortured smile at him; or cuddle him; or worse!

Revulsion towards his fellow lodger surged furiously in his breast, the recognition of her own miserable plight only serving to enhance the horror of her importunity. As long as he'd been able to interpret things as the product of a feverish imagination running wild, it had been possible to rationalise his terror, but now he had this fearful harridan from Russia to consider. In one sense this should have been grounds for comfort, for it explained everything in terms of human agency. And the woman did deserve some sympathy from what he'd heard, even if she did behave in a peculiar way, wandering the house at all hours and crying like a lost soul in torment, when all decent people were in bed, seizing hold of him, pinioning him with her monstrous smile. He wished, though, he hadn't seen the scratch-marks in the varnish on the banister as he made his hasty exit from his room that morning, marks she must have made by embedding in the woodwork the imprint of her long red-painted nails as she sneaked up to his door. To think he could have stumbled on her in the long dark corridor if he'd risked again the folly of a trip to the toilet; and been grabbed by her in the dark! Now wild horses wouldn't drag him down that loathsome tunnel outside her lair. He was relieved it was the final day at Sunny Bank; he only wished he didn't have to face another night within its spectral shadows.

The palest hints of dawn were in the sky when he found himself awake. At first he couldn't think where he was; all he was aware of was a feeling of impending dread. The awesome lodger sprung uncomfortably into his mind. Was it her hideous presence that he sensed? He lay in the pregnant darkness, starting at the slightest creak. The bumping sound was just the landing window knocking in the rising wind. There were lulls, long lulls, when it was absolutely quiet.

But there was no point denying it: he was listening out for something . . . expecting something . . . something terrible . . . something that scratched and padded . . . something awful out beyond the door. . . .

And, dear God, there it was! Awkward, slow and irregular, beginning at the stair-turning, like some ungainly cripple clambering on hands and knees . . . but this was not on hands and knees . . . the banister was creaking, the banister with the scratch marks . . . and was that a sound of long sharp fingernails screeching on the polished wood? He wanted to call out to Jeff, but that might only goad the stealthy creeper on the stairs. It struck him how confined the room was, especially from his perspective by the window, should an unwelcome presence materialise on the threshold. It flashed across his mind that he might unlock the window and test the feasibility of a leap into the garden, but he didn't dare take his eyes from the dimly illuminated door and its defective handle.

Then, horror of horrors, came the familiar snap as a footstep reached the loose floorboard. There was one more heavy tread, terrifying in its finality. Whoever or whatever was responsible was now lurking on the threshold. Crouched, stooped or strutting on hind-legs, it was all the same—abomination was awaiting. But would it merely wait? He was stricken motionless, petrified in abject horror. Pray God, it wouldn't touch the door-handle!

The door-handle! The door-handle that was faulty! The door-handle that went through several revolutions before it would engage the catch . . . was revolving and engaging!

He must have fainted when he screamed: the next thing that he knew was the light on in his room, his father angrily demanding what the noise was all about. Robert's incoherent, halting efforts to describe events did not elicit sympathy. And he was vividly aware that, even had he been sufficiently composed to articulate his explanation, an account of padding footsteps, scratch-marks, and a predatory lodger hardly carried conviction, except as the fantasia of a nightmare.

Their return to the island did not begin auspiciously. It was abundantly clear, as *The Lady of Man* launched upon her gloomy odyssey into the storm-wracked River Mersey, that it was going to be a rough crossing. The contrast to his maiden voyage, with its magic summoning of sun-lit hills from over the horizon, could hardly have been more pronounced. The island was virtually invisible behind sea-level cloud until they buffeted past the lighthouse on Douglas Head. The booming of the foghorn, dour and muffled, fell like a leaden weight upon his soul, presaging menace indefinable. A cold dank blanket hung everywhere as the exhausted family, pale-faced and irritable, queued outside the terminal for a cab. Robert didn't like it when he heard a local sailor call the mist, in almost reverential tones, 'Mona's Shroud'.

Shafts of hazy sunlight were percolating the cloud banks as the taxi reached the boarding house. Robert felt confused at first, for the aspect of Sunny Bank seemed somehow changed. Then he realised: the sycamores had been felled. The house, divested of its shadowy protection, looked much more wholesome; a multitude of August colours graced the garden. But, in striking contrast to this welcome renaissance of her property, the door was answered by a Mrs Moore looking ten years older. The gaiety of her smile had gone; her expression now looked forced. Deep lines furrowed her once rosy face and she had noticeably lost weight. He could tell from his mother's expression that she too was shocked at the ravaged demeanour of their hostess. An explanation was soon forthcoming.

'Bill died last month,' she gasped through her sobs. 'Sudden, like. A heart attack. I didn't like to tell you on the phone in case it put you off. The doctor said it was because he drank!'

His mother's commiseration was swept aside by the cataract of tears accompanying their hostess's revelation. And there was more to come. Mrs Moore was hesitating, as if considering whether to reveal more; tension and reluctance quivered round her lips.

'And—well—er—I suppose I ought to tell you; that is, if you haven't heard already,' she stammered, as if still unsure. 'You remember that young couple, you know, the Russian girl, poor soul? Mrs Dennison? Well . . .'

She was pausing once again, restrained by second thoughts; she was glancing at the boys. Her voice was fading to a harsh whisper, cold and awe-stricken, the fear in her eyes monumental and infectious. There was a terror in her silent sibilance that no amount of shouting or histrionic drama could invoke. A chill passed over Robert's spine even before the words came stumbling from her mouth.

'One night—not long after you left—she just got up, while her husband was asleep, poor man . . . you know she suffered from insomnia? And they found her in the morning . . . dead! At the bottom of those treacherous old steps down at Port Jack. Everyone thought she'd fallen, but they found a note. Suicide! Broke every bone in her body. And her neck—clean snapped through! One of the policemen that found her fainted when he saw what was left of her face.'

Mrs Moore sat down shakily upon the hall chair, bereft of the power of speech for some moments.

'She used to have these fits, poor girl,' she sobbed, 'when she'd cry and cry about the baby. Only six months old!'

There was a further tearful pause; then she continued, 'She's buried in the churchyard across the road. You know, St Ninian's? But the vicar wasn't keen; what with it being suicide, like. And not being a member of the parish either. But her husband wanted her to stay on the island.'

And then, her voice lowering almost to a whisper, she said, 'So they had to lay her in unconsecrated ground. Reverend Cavanagh insisted. It's just behind the back of the church, near the shed where they keep the spades and things. Just a mound with a little stump of a cross, poor girl!'

Robert went cold all over. 'Unconsecrated ground'. Wasn't that a phrase they used in ghost stories? He remembered the graveyard. They'd used it as a short cut to the golf course. He hadn't liked it, with its snub-nosed mildewed angels peering with terrifying vacancy through the brambles, its deadly-nightshade thickets and the looming Viking crosses blocking the horizon.

Mrs Moore was shifting to more material concerns. 'And it wasn't good for business,' she burbled. 'Word got round this summer that she'd killed herself in the house, if you please—you know how rumours start—and business had been getting bad enough anyway, what with young people going to Spain nowadays. And we'd just started doing a facelift on the house. Cut down those horrid trees! It got Bill in a real bad mood. Cursing and swearing something awful about the poor lass. Said she'd probably killed the baby herself and that was why she'd . . . you know. . . .'

One consequence of the disordered *status quo* at Sunny Bank was that the boys would not be staying in the dreaded 'master bedroom' again. It had been the last due for redecoration, when Mr Moore had died. Where, then, would they be sleeping? His parents had the same room. That only left the long dark corridor. A chill embraced him; already they were stepping up into its loathsome recesses. Despite the newly painted walls, it seemed as black as ever, and the facelift had evidently not included repair of the electric light. With mounting apprehension he realised, as Mrs Moore marched ahead, that she was leading them to the very end, to the room where he had heard the night-time strains of muffled tears, the room where the crier in the night had taken her decision to make an end of everything.

That night, as he climbed the stairs to bed, all his anxieties came tumbling back. As he passed the flight up to their previous room, its vacancy reached out like an unseen presence to envelop him. He tried his best not to look that way, but a brief involuntary glance caught uncertain shadows. He didn't like to touch the banisters, remembering the scratch marks. The corridor had certainly lost nothing of its power to terrify. As he plunged into its Stygian gloom it seemed even longer than he remembered. He wasn't looking forward to sleeping in the very bed, maybe, where the deceased had arisen for her final journey to oblivion.

Huddling down, he listened enviously to his brother snoring. He heard his parents shout 'goodnight' to Mrs Moore, and she herself visited the bathroom; the flushing made the water pipes above the ceiling wail and shudder like the damned. Occasionally a car went past. Down the street a dog was barking. Once there was a sound of shouting youths. But soon the silence, broken only by the muffled boom of the foghorn, proclaimed the lateness of the hour.

Then he heard the crying. It seemed to be coming from a distance, yet all around, indefinable. The more he listened the nearer it became, and now he was sure it was outside in the garden. The thought of the Russian woman's ghost coming back to haunt a scene of previous unhappiness leapt into his mind. Unconsecrated ground! He wanted to get up and look out of the window but didn't dare. He had no wish to see a shattered figure with a twisted neck coming up the garden steps, with a face too awful to behold.

But was it a woman? More like a baby yowling, a baby with a cracking, broken voice. Then there was another voice, low at first, almost inaudible, then rising in a long drawn out menacing crescendo, higher-pitched, and—there was no other way to put it—much more redolent of evil. The voices, if such a word could be used, seemed engaged in an inarticulate demented dialogue, with a hideous suggestion of controversy barely stopping short of strife, and it went on for a long time. As he listened, frozen, to this ghastly altercation, he wanted to block his ears, but curiosity triumphed over terror. Suddenly the tension broke, the fearful colloquy erupting into snarling scuffling violence, and a shocking indeterminate noise in the garden.

Cats! He should have known. It was always happening in Liverpool, in the back street where he lived. He'd somehow not expected it in bourgeois-land, as if the cats, bourgeois-like, would keep their feuds discreetly to themselves. People always said fighting cats sounded just like babies, that they had voices almost human. But the only thing, he thought, as he drifted off to sleep, was that at least one of the voices hadn't sounded human at all.

A horrified Robert learned next day that, instead of going for a swim in Douglas Bay, they were going up to Howstrake golf course on the headland, a journey that would inevitably mean a passage through the old churchyard. Worse still, his delaying tactics proving unavailing, his family left the house impatiently before him, leaving him to brave the cemetery, with its unconsecrated ground, alone.

Rooks were wheeling round the misty spire as he entered the jaws of the narrow, mossy alley leading to the graveyard. A mournful, incessant croaking and a wild fluttering were the only sounds to cut the morning haze. A watery sun was climbing through the lofty pines to the right, bathing the macabre monuments ahead in a pale diaphanous gold. The remnants of a heavy dew still dripped from unkempt shrubberies, catching jewels of light. The screeching gate led him first past recent graves, densely packed, glistening in the sunshine like a too-white set of new false teeth. Black- and golden-lettered epitaphs leapt out, incongruously optimistic. The flag-stoned path was older than the graves, lethal in its slipperiness.

A rotting wooden gate led through a second wall, and now he found himself in the old part of the burial ground, where grim green stones hid under canopies of rampant laurel, guzzling the brightness of the day. Some of the tombs were massive, too massive for the human scale, and surrounded by rusting iron fences. He wondered with a shudder what on earth they were supposed to be hemming in. The pebbledash over one grave near the path had cracked six inches wide. 'Only Sleeping', read the crumbling lettering on the head-stone. He felt relieved, once past the yawning gap, that no unearthly claw had seized his ankle.

The scratching on his neck was only holly; if he hadn't been in such a rush then he'd have looked where he was going. Black cypress sentinels and blood-red yews crowded in, blocking his way, and the cawing of the rooks sounded somehow different. Weird statues, winged or hooded, faces ravaged by weather, age, or worse, loomed horribly, trying to cut him off. Something dark and shapeless was pacing him in the undergrowth, but the small grey mangy cat without a tail that stumbled out in front of him only bared its teeth and hissed.

It must have been because he started running that he mistook the way. Instead of reaching the main gate on the far side near the Groudle Road, which a straight line should have guaranteed, he found himself before St Ninian's, towering above the cypresses in all its ponderous religious gloom. Already he could see the woodshed, guarding the frontier of the unconsecrated ground. Some hundred yards beyond, so near and yet so far away, were the high Viking crosses by the exit. But to get there would mean passing near the awful woman's final resting place—if resting was the word for whatever happened in unconsecrated ground. But going back, assuming he could find the way, would involve wandering again amongst the gloating statues and the caged-in tombs, not to speak of braving the passage of the ankle-snatcher's crumbling abode.

A quick dash was the only answer. Straight past the graveyard shed, eyes averted, then down the line of escape to the sanctuary of the Groudle Road. He summoned up the remnants of his courage and hurried on his anxious way, eyes fixed straight ahead upon the monolithic crosses. The tapping that he thought he heard wasn't coming from the locked up shed, it was only overhanging branches; but it distracted him sufficiently to foil his poise. For less than a fraction of a second his eyes betrayed him, and scanned with fearful curiosity the rough wasteland beyond the church. He tore his gaze away with sufficient speed to make uncertain just what it was he thought he saw.

As he made his precipitate exodus, stumbling headlong on the green-slimed flags, he tried to tell himself that all he'd glimpsed—he could hear the echo of Mrs Moore's hushed tones—was 'just a mound with a little stump of a cross'.

Returning late that afternoon, bad news awaited. A grim-faced Mrs Moore commandeered them in the hall. A water pipe had burst, bringing down the ceiling in the boys' new room. Repairs would be needed, and they would have to be relocated in their old quarters. Panic rose within him. *Not that room!* He could feel the slackness and reluctance of the door-knob, hear its tentative frustrated revolutions. Padding footsteps and a creaking floorboard echoed in his head, and he could hear, like a squeaky piece of chalk on a blackboard, the sound of fingernails rasping up and down a polished banister.

'You must be getting that cold Jeff's got,' his mother said. 'You do look rather pale.' She turned to Mrs Moore, saying, 'It's really gone to Jeff's chest. I was going to suggest he slept with us, but it doesn't seem fair to leave Robert all alone in that miserable room. Especially if he's going down with a cold as well.'

'In the quarantine ward!' laughed Mrs Moore. 'It won't be so bad once it's been aired.'

But the room was even worse than Robert remembered. It was as if the stripping of the paper had revealed the awful chamber in its true and shocking colours. The cold bare walls made him think of a derelict house or the stark unfriendly surrounds of some impoverished institution. The naked drabness was enhanced by the absence of any curtains. A pale moon tried to penetrate the grey scudding midnight clouds, casting doubtful shadows. The cyclopean wardrobe loomed, and the landing window thumped. His brother's fevered snoring sounded like an angry tethered beast. He hid within the womb of the blankets.

He seemed to lie awake for hours as the after-midnight emptiness settled like a shroud upon the world of the living. He tried to think of the pleasant things they'd done that day, but couldn't rid his mind of the graveyard. He tried counting sheep and must have dozed, for he jumped alert as he saw them leaping over a stumpy cross into a shallow grave. He tried hard not to think of what it was he thought he might have seen beyond the church.

He'd almost forgotten over the previous year what Mrs Dennison looked like, but now the Russian's face hovered before him with a dreadful crystal clarity. Appalling visions stalked him as he pressed his tired eyes into the pillow: the haggard eyes and ghastly smile; the clutching and the cuddling; the long, red-painted claws; the muffled wailing down the corridor; the broken babbling English. . . .

He must, eventually, have drifted off into a troubled sleep, for he awoke suddenly, beset by panic; an evil dream lingered in his mind, and he had a sense of something very wrong in the room.

The sequence of the nightmare, if nightmare it was, unravelled before his consciousness: a crooked figure moving with a see-saw motion across the road from the church; twisting with repulsive gait up the garden steps; a wan grinning face tilting up towards the window; an awkward yet deliberate plodding up the staircase, with a creaking and a scratching at the handrail, its abominable approach slow but inevitable; a long deadly silence; then the cracking of a loose floorboard and a hideous crescendo of grating metal as the temperamental door-knob was torn from its moorings by an over-eager, too-strong hand . . . and then a sense of stark, unalloyed menace . . . *the sense of stark, unalloyed menace that now enveloped the room.* . . .

Robert strained his eyes in the dim and insufficient light, beyond his brother's bed, towards the door. Jeff's harsh uneven breathing, horrible though it sounded, seemed to symbolise normality. As his vision gradually found focus in the deeper wells of darkness he realised with a galloping surge of terror *that the door into the room was standing three-quarters open.*

There was, as far as he could see, no presence in the room. But what in Heaven's name, then, was waiting outside on the landing? Was it, whatever it was, biding its time, watching him from the shadows? Anticipating in grisly satisfaction the certainty of conquest? Ready to dart into the room and seize hold of him, or worse?

In his panic there was only one thing he could think to do, useless as it was. Arising from his own, he climbed into his brother's gargantuan bed. Jeff was lying on the far side by the door, hunched beneath the covers, breathing uneasily. Robert burrowed under the blankets, turning his back upon his bedmate so as not to face the appalling vacuity of the doorway that he could still feel gaping. He felt his brother stirring, turning over sluggishly towards him, murmuring.

It was as his companion's arms stretched out to cuddle up to him that two dreadful revelations came to Robert.

The dim orb of light glimpsed upon the floor as he huddled in with his brother was indeed a loose brass doorknob torn from its moorings.

And beyond, in his parents' room, came a faint, familiar sound, ghastly in its wrongful context: above his father's angry muttering and the consoling tones of his mother, he could distinctly hear the voice, unmistakable in its petulance, of Jeff tearfully complaining that he felt so scared he couldn't get to sleep.

The last thing Robert saw, as the palest fingers of the dawn caressed the room, was a crumbling asymmetric face, lolling on a twisted neck, leering over him in grinning exultation.

Early the following morning Inspector Kneen, of the Douglas Bay Constabulary, knew he could forget about the weekend's golf; it was promising to be the busiest day in the annals of Manx crime. At 7.11 a.m., a distraught Mr Cavanagh arrived in person with a wild tale of an opened grave and a missing corpse; the first case of body snatching in the history of the island, his whisky breath declared, and, Holy Mother of God! it had to happen at St Ninian's! At 7.43 an incoherent call from a woman with a Liverpool accent eventually established that a twelve-year-old boy had mysteriously disappeared from a boarding house in Onchan. Minutes later came the third ill-omened tidings, and Inspector Kneen didn't take long in putting two and two together. Squadron Leader Rose, summer resident at the Crescent Hotel, had been forced to abandon his early morning bathe in the waters of Port Jack after finding the hideously disfigured body of a boy at the foot of the cliff.

For the second time in a year PC Jones fainted when he saw what was left of the corpse's face. What upset him most was not so much the missing throat and the talon-like scores in the flesh, but the uncanny way in which the twisted neck and lolling head so closely mimicked the injuries of last year's victim. And worse was to follow: in the evening twilight, scene-of-crime officers from the mainland unearthed on the pebbled shore the remains of a six-month-old baby, its tiny skull twisted back-to-front, almost severed from its spine, its face distorted in a hideous asymmetric smile.

You Should Have to Live with Yourself

Cathy Sahu

POLTERGEIST (German, 'noisy ghost'): A mostly playful and mischievous but sometimes malicious and baneful spirit which haunts a particular dwelling place and manifests its presence by manipulating (moving, hiding, throwing) household goods and furniture. In the case of the Doppelgänger (German, 'double-goer'), can take the form of a family member, servant, etc. (*see also* DOPPELGÄNGER) . . .

B*ONG BONG, BONG BONG.* The front doorbell was ringing. 'Hey, Barbara! Someone at the door!' Kelty bellowed, and kept on typing. He was on a roll:

> The typical poltergeist haunting generally passes from the initial stage of fright to a honeymoon period of amusement and even boasting and exhibition by the family to neighbours and friends; then on to annoyance, irritation, and finally, grudging tolerance. Poltergeists are notoriously difficult to get rid of but very easy to raise. The following incantation . . .

Bong bong, bong bong. That bell again—that silly bell, unbelievably pretentious for a tract home of this size. *The woman has no taste,* Kelty thought irritably. He ran a grimy hand through his too-long, greasy hair, and yelled again, 'The door! Someone at the door!' all the while drumming at the keyboard:

> The following incantation, accompanied by the proper offerings and candle burnings as described in the beginning of this chapter, will certainly give satisfactory results even to the novice.

'Ha ha ha,' said Kelty cheerlessly. 'To the novice, maybe—not to me. But, as they say: those who can, do; those who can't, write about it. Hell's bells, where is that woman? Barbara! SOMEONE AT THE *DOOR!*' he fairly shrieked.

Barbara Widgway, several years farther into middle age than Kelty but still trim and attractive, thought she heard someone calling her above the roar of the vacuum.

For some time she ignored it—she just wanted to finish this little corner *here*—but finally, reluctantly, she switched off her high-powered, commercial-grade upright, and heard now, rather too clearly, her lodger, Kelty, yelling from his back room that someone was at the door.

She sighed, untied her apron and head scarf, folded them, and put them away in their proper drawer in the dining-room, then went to answer the bell, which had rung once again in the meantime with the pretty chime Barbara had chosen so many years ago, while her husband was still alive, and which it still gave her pleasure to hear: four precise, discreet tones: *bong bong, bong bong.*

She paused before the mirror, took her clip-on earrings out of her pocket, put them on; checked her hair, and opened the front door.

The girl on the porch had already started back down the steps, but she turned and came up again with an embarrassed little laugh.

'Good morning, Ma'am,' she said. She was quite young, in her early twenties perhaps, slender but with a bit of a bulging tummy. Her dress was modest and well-ironed, her hair well-combed, so when she introduced herself as Jennifer, and timidly asked to come in and show her a new line of cleaning products, Barbara agreed to at least have a look.

'I have to warn you, though,' she said, ushering the girl to the sofa, 'I probably won't buy anything. I have just about every cleaning product known to man.'

'Oh, please, don't worry about that!' said Jennifer. 'It's so nice of you just to let me in. You're the first person who has so far.' Then, as if thinking she shouldn't have admitted that, she blushed, and hastened to add, 'What a lovely home! and immaculately kept!'

'Thank you, dear,' said Barbara, in a complacent voice that rendered unnecessary the addition of *That's what everybody says.*

The company Jennifer worked for was a sort of mix between Avon and Amway, and sold every type of beauty and cleaning aid a woman could want. There was a pudgy little catalogue, a copy of which Barbara accepted, and then several demonstrations of unique products just newly invented by a team of cutting-edge scientists who, one was almost led to think, were brilliant enough to work for NASA, but had decided they could do more good for humanity by intellectually bulking up the cosmetics industry.

In between, Jennifer, who was something of a talker, let on that she was twenty-four, had a baby at home that her husband was currently watching (along with the football game on TV), and another baby on the way; that this was her very first week on the job; that she was hoping to make enough extra money to buy a second car; and that maybe, if she were as successful as her Senior Sales Partner predicted, she just might win a Disney vacation, this being the prize for the Top New Salesgirl of the Western Region. Since there were four tickets, and neither of the babies counted yet, they could also bring along the grandparents. . . .

'I wouldn't count my chickens before they're hatched,' commented Barbara wryly.

'Oh, of course not.' Jennifer recalled herself nervously. 'Ahem. Now, I know you will want to see this,' she said, obviously lapsing into a memorised spiel. 'Our scientists have just come up with it: Magic Pol-Away, a new fingernail polish remover without the icky smell of the old ones. Don't you just hate that smell? I sure do . . .' As she spoke, she hastily took out a sample vial and twisted at the cap, which seemed to be stuck. 'Oh, dear,' she said, twisting harder—and instantaneously dropping it on the sleek surface of Barbara's Louis Quinze coffee table.

There! She caught it up before it could spill. But then, amazingly, and undoubtedly out of sheer terror at the look on Barbara's face, she dropped it again. And now Louis's veneer was splattered all over with Magic Pol-Away.

'Oh no!' Jennifer cried, frozen while Barbara whipped a cleaning rag out of her pocket and started mopping the gooey stuff up.

'Look what you've done!' Barbara burst out. 'My beautiful coffee table!'

Jennifer, trying to help, only managed to knock the vial onto the floor, where it immediately began to bond with the deep pile of Barbara's oyster wall-to-wall. 'I have something that will clean that up, somewhere!' Jennifer cried, leaving the vial to drip on the rug as she rooted frantically around in her samples case.

That was it. Barbara let the girl have a piece of her mind, all the while wiping and blotting. 'You little dummy!' she cried. 'How dare you come into my house and do something like this!'

Jennifer stopped rooting and started crying, which only irritated Barbara further. 'I didn't ask you to come in here!' she scolded. 'Did I ask you to come in and make a mess on my rug?'

Kelty, hearing the commotion, ambled out to see what was going on. 'Aw, leave her alone,' he said, seeing the company's name on the girl's sample case and extrapolating what had happened from there.

Barbara, bending over the carpet, glared up at him angrily.

'I'm so sorry, really I am!' Jennifer cried, hastily throwing all her materials back into the case.

'Sorry won't clean my carpet!' Barbara replied, scrubbing angrily.

Kelty opened the front door and, taking the girl by the arm, gently led her out. 'Here,' he said, taking a twenty dollar bill out of his wallet. 'Take this.'

YOU SHOULD HAVE TO LIVE WITH YOURSELF

The girl protested, but he thrust the money into her hand.
'Just take it, and run along now. And don't worry, everything'll be fine.'

'What did you give that girl out there?' Barbara asked, standing in the doorway of Kelty's room, arms akimbo.

She had finally finished cleaning up after the morning's fiasco. Thanks to her quick thinking, the spills were only barely visible, but the rug and table would never be the same, and grief made her voice sharp.

Kelty tried to ignore her. He had been running over the Poltergeist Raising Incantation, South Apennine Method, just to make sure he'd written it out right. The proper candles were lit on his desk, the correct herbs were simmering in the brazier, and, wand in hand, he was intoning, '*Asknaz shintab florund, mirabind zinder . . .*'

'Oh, please,' said Barbara witheringly. 'You know what I mean. You gave her money, didn't you?'

'. . . *triundum mohum*. Oh! spirit great or small, betwixt the light and dark; I, Kelty, thy master, call upon thee . . .'

'I can't believe your gall. Here you are, behind on your rent, and you're giving money away.'

'. . . that here shall be thy dwelling place until otherwise spoken. Welcome thou . . .'

'Can't you knock that off for a minute? I'm talking to you!'

'. . . seeing, saying, speaking double, here shalt dwell for weal or trouble!' Kelty thundered dramatically. Then he paused, arms raised, shifting his eyes over the room.

'What are you looking for?' demanded Barbara.

'Nothing,' Kelty sighed, putting down his wand. 'Nothing at all. I told you, I'll pay you on the fifteenth, when I get the final cheque for *Strange Brews*.' He snuffed out the candles and the brazier, then wiped his eyeglasses on his dirty cardigan.

'I don't know why anyone would pay money for the nonsense you write,' said Barbara. 'It's a very strange way for a grown man to earn a living, that's all I can say. Spells and mumbo-jumbo, and none of them work, of course. Haven't your readers figured that out by now?'

Ouch, thought Kelty, *that one hurt*. 'How is that your business,' he asked sweetly, 'as long as you get your money on the fifteenth?'

'Because you owe it to me *now*. And how in the world do you think I feel about you giving money to that girl who ruined my furniture——'

Kelty knew better than to reply. It was impossible to concentrate on his work while she stood there haranguing him, but he began typing again, not wanting to admit that she was getting to him.

'—and keeping this place like a pigsty,' she was saying. 'Expecting me to clean up after you. Really, you should have to live with yourself!' She started picking up some clothes draped over the bookshelf.

'I've never asked you to pick up after me, and don't touch any of my personal belongings, *please*.' He muttered an incantation designed to drive away noxious pests.

And oddly, now, she lapsed into silence.

Had the incantation worked? Was there yet hope that she might walk away and leave him in blessed peace? Kelty threw a glance from the corner of his eye. She was standing, looking into a small plastic bag he had absent-mindedly left there atop a pile of books. On the outside of the bag were printed the words 'Patrick's Pet Palace.' Oh oh.

'What's this?' she asked, drawing another bag out of the first one. 'Wood shavings? Litter?' Her voice became hard. 'Are you keeping some sort of animal in here?'

'Only a pair of white mice,' he said casually, and brought the wire cage out from behind his desk—no use in trying to hide it now. 'For a piece I'm writing on the transmigration of souls. Why mice, you might ask? Well, they live, and die, and breed at such an astonishing rate——'

'Just answer me one thing,' said Barbara, raising a finger to stop him. 'In our rental agreement, is there a clause about pets? And let me point out also: doesn't that agreement say, No Pets Allowed?'

'Well, I took that to mean, as any reasonable person would, cats and dogs and ponies, not two tiny furballs in a cage.'

'Doesn't it say, NO PETS ALLOWED?'

Kelty sighed, massaging his eyes with his hands. 'Yes.'

'Do you think it's fair to me to bring something like this into my home? If you were me, how would you feel?'

'I wouldn't mind.'

'Oh, of course not! You wouldn't mind the mess, and the rule-breaking, and not being paid your rent money. . . . I thought you said there were two mice in here?'

'Yes.'

'I only see one.'

'I'm sure there were two——'

'Kelty!' Barbara cried. 'The cage door is open!'

'Let me tell you something, Kelty—you should have to live with yourself!'

After an hour spent crawling around, looking for the escaped mouse, they finally found it under the bed in a half-empty bag of potato chips. Barbara had been nagging the whole time, and now, as Kelty sat at his desk, staring at the reunited rodents in the cage in front of him, she was still going on. Perhaps she was trying for a record.

'Really, you should!' Barbara continued. She was shaking out his bedspread.

He had told her not to make the bed, but she was doing it anyway. 'You should have to live with yourself! And then you'd see what it's like!' She looked at him hard, as if she were saying something new that needed time to sink in.

Perhaps it was the pitying look on the faces of the mice. At any rate, something inside Kelty finally snapped.

'If I've heard that once,' he said, 'I've heard it a thousand times. But today's the one that broke the camel's back.' He stood up, facing her, tired, droopy, baggy-faced. 'Barbara, you and I go back a long way. You were lonely after your husband passed away, and when I first moved in, you were good to me. Those were happy times, and I thank you for them.'

She stared at him suspiciously. 'I'm not going to——' she began.

He raised a hand to silence her. 'We used to be friends, and more. But the last few years, you seem to have tired of my society, and I, too . . . well, I know I'm not tidy, I know my writing hasn't paid off the way we both hoped it would, that I drink too much—so many other things. But, believe it or not, you're not perfect, either.'

'Well!' Barbara cried. 'If you think I'm going to stand here and listen to any more of this——'

'The time is ripe for a parting of the ways,' Kelty overspoke her. 'My mice, and my mess, and myself will find another abode.'

'You?' Barbara snorted. 'Where will you go? You can't afford to move.'

'I've got friends,' Kelty said. 'I'll find a corner of a floor somewhere. And you, I'm sure, will get along just fine without me. You don't really need the extra money, and no boarder could ever meet your stringent expectations. I certainly can't. So, I shall be packing my things, preparatory to moving out this very night. In the meantime . . . please leave my room!'

Barbara, speechless with shock and anger, did just that.

That night, she was alone in the house for the first time in years—a strange feeling, but she would get used to it. More, she would learn to like it. She was determined to.

The question was, how she had managed to put up with him all these years—with his slovenliness, his lack of presentability?

Another boarder might be neater, but would undoubtedly have other faults that were just as irritating. No, she was better off alone.

Now, determined to enjoy herself, she sat in robe and slippers, with a bowl of popcorn, a glass of diet cola, and a packet of pre-moistened hand wipes, in front of the Old Movie Channel.

She loved these old shows—everyone so well dressed and well-mannered, the story lines so clear and predictable. You always knew who the Good Girl was by the way she dressed: stylish, but conservatively, while the Bad Girl always wore too much jewellery.

And tonight there would be no Kelty coming in, making sarcastic comments about her taste in movies.

Yes, it was a little strange, knowing he wasn't there, not hearing the occasional cough, chuckle, or shuffling of papers from his room. She felt a pang of regret that she hadn't allowed him to leave a phone number and address where he could be contacted, in case she—well, of course she wouldn't want to get hold of him! If anyone called or sent mail here, he could just pick up the message himself. Let him find out what life was like without her.

Right before leaving, he had said he wanted to 'part friends.' She knew what he had really wanted—an invitation back! If he had apologized, she might have offered it. But he didn't apologize, and now he was just going to have to sleep in the bed he had made—or left unmade, more appropriately.

Doris Day, in a fuzzy pink babydoll nightie, was standing on a pink bed and giving Rock Hudson a piece of her mind over a pink princess phone when Barbara realized she was nodding off. She got up, turned off the TV, and brought the popcorn bowl into the kitchen. She rinsed it, squirted a little dishwashing soap into it, scrubbed it, rinsed it again, and left it to dry on the rubber drain mat. Then she ran the water and the popcorn kernels down the garbage disposal, washed her hands, wiped them with a dishtowel, and threw the dishtowel into the laundry basket. She looked into the laundry basket and counted: three items in there; when it got to five, she would do the wash.

She climbed the stairs to bed, went through her night-time rituals, and, lying neatly tucked into bed, saw by the bedside clock that it was 11.15. Thinking of how she would tackle the cleaning of Kelty's room tomorrow, she fell asleep.

Only to wake up, off and on, repeatedly. There were strange sounds from all over the house—things bumping around downstairs, sounds of floorboards creaking. Even water flowing through the pipes, though she knew nothing had been left on. Undoubtedly, these were sounds the house made every night. She was just noticing them now because she was alone.

She nodded off, then woke again with a start—somewhere downstairs a door had closed. Surely there was someone down there? Breathless, she listened for many minutes without moving a muscle, but there was no other sound.

Heart in mouth, she went downstairs and made a search of the house. Of course, everything was in order, the doors and windows locked up tight, the way she had left them.

She turned on the patio lights and the light over the driveway, then fixed herself a hot toddy, cleaned up after herself, and went back up to bed. After drinking the toddy and flipping through *House Beautiful* for a few minutes, she nodded off and, thankfully, didn't wake up again.

The next morning she felt a little groggy, and if her alarm hadn't awakened her at the customary 7.30 a.m., she might have slept in an hour longer. But there was Kelty's room to scrub down—better not to put that off. Who knew what kind of mess awaited her there?

She was already downstairs and cleaning up after her toast and coffee when she realized that she had forgotten the toddy glass that she had been drinking from the night before—it was still upstairs. She went up to get it but was surprised to find it not on the bedside table, or anywhere else nearby. She looked under the bed, thinking she might have knocked it off somehow, but it was simply nowhere in sight.

Now, this was odd. Barbara sat down on the edge of the bed and thought—it annoyed her when things just disappeared like that; she prided herself on her faultless application of the rule, A Place for Everything, and Everything in Its Place. Still, here was the toddy glass missing. Was it possible that she had already taken it down, either last night or this morning? She had definitely been feeling heavy-headed before her coffee.

Oh, well. She was feeling much better now, and the morning fog outside, that had contributed, perhaps, to her mental haziness, had lifted and the sun was shining. After washing up the rest of the breakfast things, she put the radio on—it was playing a medley of Broadway show tunes—and got out the bucket, brushes, and cleaning rags she'd need for her assault on Kelty's room. She licked her lips when she thought about those windows. She had been dying to give them a thorough scrubbing since last winter, and to give the place a good airing out, after all that candle smoke, not to mention Kelty's strange-smelling cigars.

It was with something very like disappointment that she found, once she threw open the curtains and took a good look, that the room was really not in very bad shape at all. The windows were quite clean, actually, and Kelty had dusted and even vacuumed before he left.

Well! All along she had begged him to be a little neater, and he hadn't lifted a finger until the day he was moving out. Undoubtedly he had meant to make some sort of point. Mean-spirited, she called it.

She picked up a corner of one of the curtains and sniffed. Nothing! No hint of smoke or soot or even dust. And the walls? They were clean also. Even the hair oil stain above the bedstead that had annoyed her so much was gone, scrubbed off completely.

Barbara sighed brightly. Clean, everything clean already! What a relief. Less work for her, and now she could attend to the rest of the house.

But, upon inspection, the rest of the house turned out spotless too. Of course it was—the house couldn't have got dirty in one day. Everything, everywhere was neat and clean around her, and now she could settle down for some much-needed rest and relaxation. After fourteen years of Kelty, anyone would need a vacation!

Slowly she carried the bucket and rags back to the hall closet. As hard as it was to imagine Kelty cleaning his room, here was evidence for it: someone besides herself had definitely been in here, rearranging things. The box of rags was on a shelf farther down, the sponges farther up. And the whisk brooms were now bundled all together, though Barbara normally kept them separated according to size. She rearranged things the way they should be.

Then she sat down in her neat little den and switched on the television to the Shoppe-at-Home Network. They had been advertising a pretty set of patio furniture that she had been thinking of buying, but right now a nice, well-dressed man, rather bouncy for his advanced age, was getting very excited about a smokeless fryer. Despite his enthusiasm, Barbara remained sceptical, and found her mind wandering to Kelty, and whether he had found a place to sleep last night. Perhaps he had had to sleep in his car. Well, that wasn't her worry, thank goodness. He was free to wander; she didn't own him.

Many years had gone by since she and he had been on anything more than business terms with each other, yet now she found herself remembering when he first came to stay; how glad she had been to have a man in the house again, and though he could never have measured up to her Frank, of course, there had been a time when she had found Kelty's bohemian ways attractive. Funny how you forgot those things! His easy-going manner, his sense of humour were qualities she had once admired. How had things changed between them? Familiarity had bred contempt, she supposed, on her part as well as his.

And now he had left, thinking he'd find a better place, where people would appreciate him! Where, far from expecting any type of civilised behavior, they would see his slovenliness as an aspect of his artistic personality, and indulge his bad habits—for a time at least. That sort of thing got old very quickly. Kelty would find out soon enough that other women would be even less tolerant of his piggishness than she was. Let him find out for himself how good he had had it here.

Irritably, Barbara got up and started wiping the already spotless wainscoting.

'I do like a man who smokes cigars,' said Garnet, regarding Kelty across the length of her small and very cluttered kitchen table. 'Put the ashes anywhere, it makes no nevermind to me.'

She had offered him asylum for as long as he needed to stay. Kelty, who had been looking around for an ashtray, now knocked the ashes onto his breakfast plate, where they stuck to the yellow remains of his sunny side up egg.

'Don't let me interrupt your routine, Garnet,' he said. 'I don't want to be any more of an imposition——'

'You're no imposition! And I have no routine.'

She continued to stare at him, chin cupped in hand. A bit unnerved, he asked, 'But surely you have something planned for today.'

'Oh, I have a few things up my sleeve, but nothing it would do to talk about.'

He thought it better to leave that one up in the air. After a time she added,

'If you talk about things, they don't work out. You shouldn't talk, you shouldn't even *think*.'

'Is that the philosophy upon which your success is based?' He was only half joking. Garnet was a much more accomplished practitioner of the Art than he, and perhaps it did have something to do with her attitude.

'Oh, yes.'

'I don't know how well that would work for me,' Kelty said. 'It's important for a writer to be explicit—to have an outline.'

'Yes, of course, but that's your trouble. You write about magick, but you're too intellectually engaged to perform it properly. That incantation you were talking about—for raising poltergeists?'

'Yes.'

'Well, you said yourself that nothing happened.'

'Nothing ever happens. Well, almost never. A few times I've been able to do simple spells. And once, when I was a kid, I started a fire.'

'Now, that's not easy. That's very difficult. Tell me about that.'

'There's not much to tell. I had this book with the fire lighting spell in it. A cousin and I made a pile of sticks and leaves. He was a real annoying guy—kept harassing me about how stupid this was, and how there was no such thing as magick. I didn't believe there was, either, at the time, but I really wanted to shut his mouth. And I did—the fire lit.'

'How nice for you!'

Kelty breathed out cigar smoke thoughtfully. 'Of course, it blew my mind. I've spent the last forty years trying to find out just what happened that day, though I've had little luck since then, with fire starting or anything else. . . . My cousin finally decided the bonfire had been lit by supernatural means—spontaneous combustion or something. Maybe he was right.'

'Or maybe,' said Garnet, 'it was your resonant emotion.'

Kelty looked questioning, and she continued: 'People always think we witches get our powers from an alignment with moral forces, either good or evil. But the source of our success is really emotion—strong emotion. Some people find it in anger, some in pity, some in the desire to dominate. You might find it in annoyance.'

Kelty laughed out loud. 'In that case, the poltergeist incantation should have worked! My landlady was standing there, annoying the heck out of me while I was doing it.'

'How do you know it didn't work?' asked Garnet with a slow smile.

Now it was Kelty's turn to stare.

The week went by, and Barbara thought she was going crazy.

Although there were other things in her life—the women's clubs, the bowling league, volunteering at the Red Cross—her primary occupation had always been that of housewife. She loved her home, loved decorating and cleaning it, entertaining in it. She was a bit nervous by nature, and whenever anything was bothering her, she found scrubbing or mopping or polishing helped ease her mind. It might not make sense to people like Kelty, but she always felt that, if her house was neat and in order, everything else in her life would fall into place, too, sooner or later.

Ever since Kelty left, the need to keep busy was especially strong. His going had left a gap in her schedule and, though it was hard to admit, in her affections, too.

And yet, no matter where she looked, she couldn't find anything to clean! Nothing needed cleaning. Certainly, since Kelty had moved out, there was less laundry and fewer dirty dishes. She had expected that. But there should have been other things—the settling of dust, the tarnishing of silver plate, the falling of leaves from the neighbour's tree onto her driveway. Every morning she searched, but could find no dust, no tarnish, no leaves.

And there were other things, like the laundry. The night that Kelty left, there had been three items in the downstairs linen hamper—Barbara remembered counting them quite clearly. Then, in the course of the day, she had thrown a few more things in—another dish towel and the two rags used on the wainscoting and on the chair rungs, though they weren't really dirty at all—that should have made six. But, when she looked in the hamper that evening, there were only three pieces of linen in it—the ones she had put in that day. Either she had miscounted the day before, or she had done the laundry herself and forgotten about it, or someone else had snuck in and taken them out during the night. All three alternatives seemed equally ridiculous. She couldn't figure it out! and yet it certainly wasn't anything to call the police about.

At night, she always took a hot toddy now, while she watched TV. And, though it helped to knock her out a bit, she had rather unpleasant dreams, always about the house, and vanishing messes. And there was always someone in the background, someone angry, who was blaming her for something, she didn't know what.

On Friday it was her turn to host the garden club. She decided to have the girls out on the patio, and was depressed, upon looking things over beforehand, to find that even the grass seemed to have stopped growing.

'The place is gorgeous! as spotless as ever,' Pat Ingersol said, inspecting her terra cotta pots, under which not a speck of mud or humus lay. 'You could eat off of these bricks! I can't seem to keep my patio neat, no matter what. While I'm sweeping up under one plant, another is dropping its leaves. And my house is worse!'

'I could come over and help,' said Barbara. 'Really, I'd love to!' She had continued to protest until she realized they were all looking at her as if she had two heads.

The girls were cheerful and noisy, as usual. Afterwards, she had taken the dishes into the kitchen, and then gone out to walk a few of them to their cars, light-hearted from the good company and also because, to be strictly truthful, a few of the girls were quite pigs and there would be a lot of crumbs and other mess to attend to. The whole patio might even need scrubbing down.

But while she and Pat were chatting about roses, Marie and Carmen had gone back to use the little girls' room. Or so they said—they were gone quite a long time and Barbara could have cried when she saw what they had really done: cleaned up! Washed the dishes, wiped the counters, even swept all the cheese and cracker crumbs off the patio. You would never have known anyone had been there.

It was all too much. Alone in her shining home again, Barbara wept as if her heart would break.

Finally, as the sun set, she got up and mixed herself a screwdriver: she hadn't much appetite and the orange juice, at least, was nutritious. While she was making it, the phone rang, and so unnerved was she at the sudden trill in the middle of such silence that she dropped the glass on the floor and broke it.

She started to pick the shards up, but the phone kept ringing, so she finally gave up and ran to answer it. It was old Mrs Cantor, reminding her of the Red Cross meeting next Tuesday at ten, and asking if she could come early to help set up the coffee urn and cookies. 'What's the matter, dear? You don't sound quite like your usual, chirpy self,' said Mrs Cantor. 'Are you taking good care of your health?'

Barbara, touched, assured the octogenarian that she was fine. She hung up, went back smiling to the kitchen—and found that the glass on the floor had been removed, the spilt orange juice mopped up, and a new glass with vodka and orange juice left sitting on the counter, centred neatly over a cocktail napkin.

Feeling faint, she looked down at her hand—there was a little cut, right on her finger, new, from the broken glass. It was proof that this was not a matter of forgetfulness on her part—a glass really had fallen on the floor. Nor could the garden club girls be the culprits this time, nor Kelty.

Either someone was in the house playing tricks on her, or she was really going crazy.

She checked the kitchen garbage pail. Yes, there were the pieces of broken glass, and several crumpled paper towels.

She stood thinking, her finger dripping blood spots, disregarded, onto the floor.

Then she picked up the second glass of orange juice and vodka, held it over the floor, and slowly, deliberately loosened her grip. The glass slid from her fingers onto the floor, shattering on the hard tiles.

Leaving it there, she went into the cupboard and took out the tin of flour. She took off the lid, tossed it on the floor, then sprinkled the flour all over the counters and sink. Next, she took a few eggs out of the refrigerator, and threw them splat against the cabinets. Took out peanut butter, and grape jelly for good measure, smeared them both all over the kitchen table. Sprinkled a bag of dry spaghetti over that, and a box of corn flakes.

In the living-room, she ripped open three pillows and swung them around until everything was covered with feathers and batting. Took the dishes out of the china cabinet, rearranged them in complicated stacks on the dining-room table; sprinkled salt and pepper over them.

She burnt newspaper in the fireplace, and smeared the ashes over the mirror above.

In the den, she turned the TV around backwards, tore up a magazine and threw the pages all over, took from the cupboard a couple of board games and three packs of cards and tossed them up into the air. They scattered over everything.

After similar sabotage in the bathroom and Kelty's room, Barbara went back to the kitchen, got the bottle of vodka and one more glass, and carried them up to bed.

'I don't know why you're so worried,' said Garnet. 'It's not like she'll be able to sue you or anything.'

At the cluttered little kitchen table (Garnet, like the serial inhabitants of ancient Troy, seemed to live in layers), they sat now over a very strange seafood concoction that Garnet had whipped up, and that Kelty had secretly dubbed 'Low Tide at Three Mile Island'. The conversation continued about the poltergeist spell.

'It just seems like a dirty trick to play,' he continued. 'If it did work, I mean.'

'From the way you describe things, it would serve her right,' replied Garnet, spooning up something grey and limp.

'You don't understand this woman and how she is about her house,' continued Kelty. 'She would go mad if there were something loose there, throwing furniture around and breaking her little knick-knacks.'

'Teach her to be less materialistic,' said Garnet between chews.

Kelty pushed back his bowl. 'I think I should go over there tonight and make sure everything's all right.'

'Well, it's up to you,' said Garnet slowly, putting down her spoon. 'However, as you know, these polts are easy to call forth, but very difficult to send away.'

Kelty thought. 'Would it be invisible?'

'No, probably not. Just hard to catch sight of. But still, it's something that could go very bad, unless you do it just right.'

Kelty had stood up, and now he paused, looking down upon Garnet's badly parted mop of hair.

She looked up at him coyly. 'You would need my help.'

'I suppose I would,' admitted Kelty.

'And I don't feel up to it right now. I have to be in the right mood, you know.'

Kelty considered this, then asked, 'When do you think you'll be in the right mood?'

'I have no idea,' said Garnet. 'It's sort of like cooking for me—I have to feel *inspired*—my resonant emotion being the creative or gestative urge.' She pushed her empty bowl away. 'My, that hit the spot,' she said cheerily. 'And now, how about some oxblood cheesecake? It's really good, you'll be surprised.'

Kelty sighed and sat back down again.

It had been only five-thirty when Barbara had gone up to her bedroom; now it was past midnight. She had drunk quite a bit—enough to nod off a few times but not enough to forget about what she had done downstairs and how she would have to, sooner or later, go back down again to see what, if anything, had happened in her absence.

Enough time had passed now, certainly.

She had left the bedside radio on for comfort and company. Now, she switched it off and sat listening. The house was quiet.

She got out of bed, put on her robe and tied it, ran her hands through her hair a few times. She found her slippers, put them on. Opened the door to the bedroom, stood listening again for a moment, then proceeded noiselessly downstairs. She stopped three steps from the bottom and switched on the light.

It was dreadful to look at, but wonderfully heartening at the same time—the living-room, in a complete mess, just as she had left it. Feathers, batting scattered over the oyster shell carpeting. Smeared mirror. And, on the dining-room table close by, the dishes stacked exactly the way she had left them.

In the kitchen she ran her eyes joyfully over the sticky table, the mucky counter, the floor littered with glass and clotted with goo.

Oh, what a relief! There was certainly nothing wrong with her, or the house, either. It was all some sort of mix-up—a weird series of coincidences that had misled her into thinking that something bizarre was going on. Oh what joy, to be reassured that everything was back to normal—*had* been normal, in fact, the whole time.

And, best of all, now she really did have a big cleaning job on her hands.

'I'll let it go until tomorrow morning,' Barbara said aloud cheerfully. It was close to one in the morning now—what kind of neat freak would be cleaning at this time of night?

She turned to go back to the stairs—and realized that she just couldn't do it. She just couldn't leave the house in such a state. She wouldn't be able to sleep, knowing that such a mess was downstairs.

'No,' Barbara said, 'if it takes me all night, I'm going to get this house back into shape. Other people might be able to live in a pigpen, but not me!

I'm just not made that way.' She went to her cleaning cupboard, took out the bucket and the whole box of rags.

She would start in the kitchen, and work from the ceiling to the floor. She had filled the bucket with soapy water and was just dipping her rag in when she heard a noise in the TV room.

It frightened her more in regards to her sanity than as a physical threat. The sound itself was not in the least disturbing or unusual—it was only that of the carpet sweeper going back and forth, back and forth over the TV room rug. And now she heard a voice too, like the voice she had been hearing in her dreams: annoyed and querulous.

The voice stopped, and so did the carpet sweeper. But soon again now she heard footsteps, and the hallway cabinet opening and closing. Barbara put down the rag, carefully climbed off the stepstool—her knees were shaking but she held on to the counter tight—slowly walked into the TV room, and switched on the lamp.

There was no one there. But the TV room was perfectly clean.

No board games, no cards on the floor or over her easy chair. The TV was turned around, the way it was supposed to be. And the magazine pages were neatly piled together on the table.

And from farther back in the house, down the dark hallway, the sound of that voice again, complaining and petulant. Barbara followed it. It seemed to be coming from Kelty's room but, as Barbara approached, it stopped.

Standing in the doorway of Kelty's room, she felt for the wall switch, and turned on the overhead light. Nothing but the usual contents of the room met her eyes. She went in, stood in the middle of the room, under the light. No one was there. But everything was, once again, clean, straight, tidy.

But just then the door, which she had thrown open, pushed to a little, and behind it, in the corner, she saw a figure. A figure smaller somewhat than herself, but very familiar nonetheless—wearing neat little clogs on her feet that looked just like hers, and a head scarf like hers, and the type of tailored blouse and slacks she favoured. The figure had its back to her—it was bent over and sweeping something up in the corner with one of Barbara's whisk brooms. And it was talking to itself, in a piping, nagging voice:

'Look at this! What a mess. Certain people should live in a pigsty, they really should. And expecting me to clean up after them——'

Barbara stood and stared as the creature straightened up, turned around, and fastened its little eyes on her. The two of them stood, staring at each other under the shadowy glare of the overhead light, for a full minute. Barbara, with a swoony bafflement, realized she was looking into a caricature of her own face. Except for scale, and a certain obnoxious exaggeration of feature, she and this neat but sour-looking little lady were mirror images.

'Finally!' the tiny woman said in a singularly unpleasant tone of voice that

Barbara would have liked to think was nothing like her own. 'Decided to drag yourself out of bed? After I've got most of it cleaned up, of course.'

The little woman leaned down to her work again, sweeping furiously. 'But you don't mind the mess, do you? It doesn't bother you. Just leave everything where you drop it! Someone else will clean it up!' She straightened, turning to Barbara with righteous anger. 'Do I look like your servant? Do I?'

Barbara backed off as the little doppelgänger came at her, arms familiarly akimbo, pushing its mirror face into hers and delivering a non-stop torrent of abuse. Finally, feeling she'd go crazy if she heard another word, Barbara dodged and ran out of the room, escaping from the sight of that face—but not the sound of that voice, which shrilled all the louder, and in such familiar accents, after her:

'*You should have to live with yourself, that's what! You should have to live with yourself!*'

The Sunken Garden

John Whitbourn

I WANTED TO TAKE HER AWAY before all the madness began. Which is a bit ironic really, given what happened. Especially when you consider my actual words. 'Let's slip away for a few days,' I said, 'before we're trapped.'

I think there's a malevolent scriptwriter above us, putting words in our mouths for us to trip over later. For a laugh.

That wasn't always my belief. Far from it. Such sentiments wouldn't have seemed right from the pulpit each Sunday. It's what I affirm now, though: 'Firmly and truly,' as the hymn says.

Courtesy of a loving family, a head-spinning schedule of anniversary celebrations was planned, culminating in the 'surprise gift' of a week in Minorca. However, their supposedly street-wise generation lacks the attention to detail instilled in us by a World War. The travel agent had *my* name when she rang up about a change in flight times.

'What holiday?' I said. 'News to me!'

The girl twigged instantly. 'Oh shit!' she exclaimed, and then 'Sorry, Reverend.' I think she meant about spoiling things rather than the industrial language.

Still, it's the thought that counts. We never let on to the family.

Don't get me wrong. It's not that we weren't grateful for the impending carnival of revelry. I'm sure our sons and daughters and their spouses (and bevy of ex-spouses—because they'd all been very 'civilised' about the splits) put a lot of time and trouble—and pounds—into it. We'd have worn a fixed grin whatever was arranged.

It was simply that we—or maybe I—fancied catching our breath beforehand; to convert what was coming into a *savoured* pleasure. And once conceived, that idea just seemed . . . right. Golden weddings aren't exactly ten-a-penny at the best of times. On the contrary; in today's world of serial monogamy and vows-taken-lightly they're an endangered species. Ours might be one of the last our stricken culture sees, and therefore not an event to be entered into 'unadvisedly, lightly, or wantonly, but reverently, discreetly, advisedly, soberly, and in the fear of God; duly considering the causes for which Matrimony was ordained', to borrow from our Anglican brethren's (criminally neglected) Book of Common Prayer.

Once you phrase it like that, there's little need for debate.

So I visited the Internet (because I'm no Luddite: my grandchildren called me 'techno-grandad') and booked us a weekend at a hotel near Stratford. The wife, a retired drama teacher, likes Shakespeare. I'm not so sure. Some of his sonnets are positively indecent. You realise they're written to a beautiful boy, don't you? Also, some of the plays shouldn't be handed over to a child, unsupervised.

Anyhow, Stratford-on-Avon leaped from the screen to my eyes. The hotel website was user-friendly, and blessedly accurate. The place proved to be clean and airy and generally . . . nice. A nineteenth century manor house, now part of a national chain. All other things aside, I'd recommend the place to you. If I were composing this some years from now when I shall be nothing but bitterness, I might even supply its full name and address. Just be thankful for my mercy.

Everything went swimmingly, from taxi there right through to evening meal. Afterwards, I rang senior son from reception to say we'd absconded but would be back shortly and not to worry. We're having a wonderful time—pass it on. Wish you were here, see you soon.

Two untruths, but only the first deliberate.

Next day, well fed, well rested, I went to explore while my wife still dozed. I do not sleep so well as her—one of the myriad pains of encroaching old age. Therefore, saying my morning prayers in the hotel grounds, post a full English breakfast, seemed a good use of wakefulness, as well as one of the little treats of life. I understand that Judaic theology believes each soul called before the Throne of Judgement must account for every—permitted—pleasure missed.

There was a back garden with a paved path leading to an ornamental pond. Mock-classical statuary was dotted about in hedge alcoves. I should imagine it wasn't so different in layout from when a family lived there more than a century before—all corseted lawns and herbaceous borders. The business that ran the place had a reputation for catering to the classier end of the market, rather than sales reps. The England meets Greece-and-Rome effect was presumably part of the image.

When I got there, in no hurry, the pond proved to be shallow and time hallowed. A silent Neptune-fountain rose from the centre. I walked round its circular avenue. Fish darted about in a few feet of greenish water, living careless, innocent lives—or so we're assured.

It was going to be a sunny day. Possibly even hot. Ideal for a lazy day in Stratford while my lady-wife sight-saw and I browsed bookshops. A spot of light lunch, maybe even a cream tea, and then back to the hotel for another grand repast. Food becomes more, not less, important to you as the years go by, you know. Other 'treats' aren't so readily available any more.

The good omens buoyed me up; I was inspired to bravery and exploration. So, when the lawn ended in a wall and shrubbery, I went further.

The wall had a gate in it—and what else are gates for? The worst that could happen was a groundsman saying, 'Sorry, sir, this bit's private.'

Not so. Beyond was more lawn, apparently open to all, with a sundial in its middle. Well maintained if not exactly well frequented. A fence at the further end marked, I assumed, the conclusion of hotel property.

Wrong again. I didn't need to venture the gate in the low fence to see that there was more. A set of steps descended steeply into an archetype Victorian sunken garden. It was a wilderness now, but an oval path still cleaved round the perimeter. Ionic type pillars and yet more cod-classical statuary peeped out of the jungle like a miniature lost city.

I saw no reason why not. And how many things, from the Garden of Eden onwards, have gone wrong for mankind due to that same reckless spirit?

The gate was creaky but co-operative; the steps intact. I descended.

Down below had a micro-climate of its own. The morning sun had not yet penetrated and night's chill remained. Damp in the air was made heavier yet by the perfume of massed vegetation, some of it rotting.

I tested the patina on the nearest bust. My finger left a moist smear like a snail trail on the brow of a Roman emperor.

Any beauty that might have detained me had left soon after the last gardener many years ago. A quick stroll round the circuit of the path would finish me with here forever.

Halfway round, the sky fell down on me. I had never felt such desolation. All colour fled out of the world and life, swirling away through my feet like water from a bath.

I could barely lift my face. Tears streaked it for the first time since boyhood. Yet lift it I did. That tiny movement took more courage than forcing myself ashore at Sword Beach on D-Day.

To find nothing. I stood in no especial place. Just another portion of path like any other. No statue loomed over me, no pitfall threatened. Nothing to justify feeling so utterly *lost*.

Yet there *was* power here. I had plugged into it the same as sticking wet fingers in the mains. It had noticed me for an instant before—praise be—passing on. Just space enough for the flicking open of a malign eye.

Never before in a long life with its fair share of sloughs had I considered suicide—until then. Though it was summer for the rest of the world, I was in

THE SUNKEN GARDEN

winter and shivering. The rational part of me, clambering to reclaim the steering wheel, said I must be going down with something bad.

Yet what sickness was there so 'bad' as to still the breeze and silence the birds? Alerted by an awful silence save for my heaving breath, I listened for them, but both were gone.

I certainly would be sick, sick as a dog, if I stayed. Aged legs became youthful again to propel me out of that abysmal place.

Nothing could induce me to retrace my steps, but through desperate eyes I saw a means of escape at the sunken garden's far end. The fence atop the high bank was pierced by a door.

The only way up to it was via a slope; out of the question in normal circumstances. Yet I took it like a teenager, ruining the knees of a new pair of slacks, and roughly took the apparent virginity of the door latch.

I found myself beside a busy road, gasping and paper-pale. Doubtless I looked a ghastly sight to the motorists streaking by. What was with that old boy wobbling on his heels where pedestrians weren't meant to be?

I didn't care. Right then I loved that fume-soaked, litter-strewn bit of kerb like I loved my own fireside. Like I loved my dear lady wife.

I was reassured. The world was like this—and increasingly so. *This* was reality. And reality—however degraded—seemed sweet.

I made my way back to the hotel hugging the untrodden fringes of motorway and roundabouts. Drivers peeped their horns at me. En route I decided not to believe it. Or rather I *preferred* not to believe it. Once back, I told my wife I'd got lost in a maze of strange streets. And fallen. Which was true enough, sort of.

At dinner that night we met a delightful couple from Yorkshire—very level-headed and down to earth. Plain speaking types, but good company. I'm ashamed to say they were ideal for my purpose.

Over a brandy (my first since VE Day) at the bar afterwards I mentioned the sunken garden to him. In fact, I skillfully reeled him in, like an angler playing a fish, though I say it myself. I hinted at enough of my adventure to make it a challenge to him without ever being explicit. A man of the cloth learns much about humanity in the course of his vocation—and not all of it to the species' credit. Accordingly, the temptation to tug upon people's strings is a sore trial. I succumbed to it.

I crave the reader's forgiveness. I was still shaken—shaken to the core. Core values were part of that shaking.

And the next morning they both went there, as I knew they would, with him leading. I watched from our window, skulking behind the net curtain.

When they returned they were no longer so friendly. I 'happened' to meet them in the lobby. They were heading for the bar.

'Why did you send us down there?' she demanded of me. Her face was drawn, his dotted with sweat.

'Shut up,' he told her. 'Just bloody well leave it, woman. I need a drink!'

I wasn't invited to join him, nor did we dine together that night. In fact they cut us dead. My wife thought that very odd.

So it wasn't just imagination, or leastways not just mine. I didn't know whether to be pleased or pained.

On the way to bed I cornered the manageress at the reception desk. Her type of job teaches insight just as much as the ministry. Subtleties in my face must have told a tale.

'Are you enjoying your stay, Reverend? Is there anything wrong?'

'No, not at all.' My voice was mock sunny. 'Except that I noticed your sunken garden today. I was wondering why you don't make more of it. In the brochure, perhaps. . . .'

'It's just an overgrown plot,' she said firmly—and so betrayed her own reply. 'A weed trap. Our maintenance contract doesn't include it. Why d'you ask? Did you go in? I hope you didn't fall. . . . No, we've never thought of restoring it. Oh, I tell a lie. I did ask our local handyman to clear the worst bits once, so it wouldn't be such an eyesore. He refused. He left. . . . Me? Two years as manager and two before that as assistant. . . . Yes, I went to look at it once, when I first arrived. Just from the top of the steps: just a glance. . . . No, never actually *in* there. This place keeps me far too busy. Are you sure you didn't trip over . . . No? Good.'

Her fears of being sued and all the associated paperwork receded. Then the small part of her not yet owned by the business could peek out its wan face.

'It's just a jungle,' she repeated, almost wheedling. 'There's nothing down there—is there?'

I must have been mad. Except that I know I wasn't. I was *famed* for my sanity. Doubtless my *Methodist Recorder* obituary and funeral oration touched upon my renowned rationality.

So what then drove me on? What self destructive urge led my feet to visit that place again? There was the open door before me of just checking out as per booking and driving off. I could have gone and forgotten—eventually.

My theory—which I've had ample time to hone—is that a lifetime of careful virtue isn't natural. Though I was not conscious of it, the human part of me was *bored*. Bored unto death. Nature—human nature—will out, whatever straitjackets we strap round it. A coiled up spring sprung, and propelled me to the sunken garden.

Or maybe it was just simple curiosity. The sort of laudable spirit that spurred men out of the caves and towards the stars.

Or fascination with the opposition. I'd devoted my life to one faction alone. It's natural to develop an interest in your opponent. Perhaps I secretly speculated whether *He* was actually as awesome as was said.

Take your pick of explanations—each equally likely. I no longer care.

THE SUNKEN GARDEN

It was late afternoon. We were leaving. The weekend had not been a success, for she knew I was out of sorts. Even in light and airy Stratford, amongst all the cultural homage, the sunken garden was with me. I carried its cloud on my back and in my head. The knowledge would not leave me that *there* occupied the same planet as Anne Hathaway's Cottage and the pub where I picked at an excellent ploughman's lunch. I lied to my wife and said that I felt feverish. With five decades of unbroken honesty behind me she simply accepted my words.

Her concern was characteristically unselfish: there was the imminent anniversary to gear up for. She wanted me at my best for it—for my sake. I took her proffered paracetamols.

We almost escaped. The bags were stowed in the boot, my navigator had the AA downloaded route resting in her lap. Then I lied again.

'Actually, darling, I think I left my driving gloves in the lobby. I'll only be a minute. . . .'

They were snug in my blazer pocket, and pressed against me like thirty pieces of silver as I walked.

Reception was empty, but there was a pair of teenagers canoodling in the bar area. Today I found that reassuring rather than shocking. At least there'd be witnesses to my whereabouts—just in case.

It didn't look as if the sundial lawn had been trod at all that day. Most guests had 'better' things to do than appreciate God's creation. Less than half, in my estimation, were actually married to one another. Likewise, I'd observed that the television in our room offered no fewer than four 'adult channels' for a small additional fee. Accordingly, someone immune to such 'attractions' could be alone in the great outdoors. I reached the sunken garden, doubtless unseen, and teetered on the edge.

I checked. There were birds in the sky, wending homewards (as I should be doing), but they were distant. Or silent. Imagination made me manufacture an anticipatory quiet seeping out of *there*.

A hesitation at the gate, but only a slight one. Anything more would call into question what I believed and based my life upon. And what I believed, in my innocence, was that there was a protecting power over me, stronger than anything the enemy could manifest.

Down below were pockets from which last night's frost had never fled. The grass to which I descended was crisp beneath my brogues. It provided the only sound.

Once round the path was my intent. To justify myself and prove all sorts of things. That there should be nothing was the maximum result. For it all to have been naught but fancy, so that I could enjoy a celebration before the celebrations.

My fingerprint was still upon the Roman Emperor, overlaid by a fresh patina of dew or stone-sweat. Proof of some sort. I *had* been here other than in nightmare. I had left my mark.

And now to take my leave. I brushed jostling foliage aside and rounded the far end. The scrapes left by my scrambling feet still scarred the bank. Up above the door swung loose just as I'd left it.

Which should have permitted traffic noise to invade. Surely the motorway beyond never slept. . . .

But my breath was all I could hear. I tried to regulate it. Alas, the pounding of my heart was beyond control.

Before me the sunken garden waited like an adventure. There was only me and it in the world, and above us only sky. Which is becoming my dark suspicion.

I stepped—no, *strode*—forward.

All the statues smirked simultaneously, animate for a fleeting second. Eyes flared red with borrowed vitality and . . . something . . . saw through them. Just so that I would *know*. That little was ample.

I'd seen some spirit older than I, older even than my mayfly civilization and faith. Something with roots back into a past I couldn't conceive—nor would ever want to.

Everything in every history book I'd read, or even in the Book of my religion, was as one transient lifespan compared to the life I glimpsed then. It was confident of the future, too, the far far future—and it *knew* it.

The garden was more sunken than hitherto. It had a lower level that I should certainly have recalled—and *certainly* should recall descending into. A mirror image of the one above. Yet there I stood.

Adrenaline coursed through me like a train. I looked wildly round.

Steps led up to the higher strata, but my way was blocked. I was not alone.

The figures were insubstantial. Men and women: faded shadows of what had once been, dressed in clothes of every era. Regency gowns and lace, Victorian top hats and watch-chains. Even some wartime uniforms.

The doleful procession did not just pass me by, it passed *through* me.

They left a great cold behind. Not the sort to raise goosebumps, but frostbite of the soul. God alone knew how many times they'd trodden that path. What else was there for the poor devils to do?

But that did not explain their anger, nor their looks full of hatred for me. Once kindly faces were now twisted.

I raced for the way out, but was thwarted. A glass ceiling barred me from the upper level. The dread place of mere minutes ago now beckoned like Paradise itself.

Neither of those locations were options. Not for me. Not now. I recognized that like swallowing lead. One was visible, the other hoped for, but both prohibited. Even the slightest step to either was forbidden.

So, all that was left for me was to turn and take in my new home—and eternal destination. I somehow knew its master would introduce himself sooner or later.

Before that, though, my wife 'found' me, along with the rest of the search party. The manageress and two hotel porters held torches but wouldn't enter in.

She did, though. Brave heart! I called and called to the soles of her shoes directly above me, but of course she couldn't hear.

It touched her: that much I saw. Yet only the externals applied, unable to get under the skin. My wife shivered, but no more.

I now see with exquisite clarity that she is—or was—a *good* person. Whatever ran the sunken garden could find no purchase on her. She was a greased pole to its talons.

Whereas I was hooked, heart and soul. Now, what did that say about me?

Watching her retreating back was a wrenching pain like no other. Or so I deluded myself in my innocence. However, it proved a pinprick compared to what came soon after. But concerning that it's best you know nothing.

I often wonder what she did about the Golden Wedding gala. I'm promised all eternity to ponder on it.

Apparently, the first few centuries are the worst.

Survivors

Edward P. Crandall

ONE OF THE THINGS THAT LEFT such a vivid impression on me that spring day in 1985 when I sat in Mrs Hara's living-room, drinking her tea and listening to her tell her story, was her voice. I can still hear the warm timbre she proudly maintained until her eighty-second year, and the slight wavering, barely noticeable, that had snuck into it, indicating the deterioration and decay that would slowly, over the year following our first and only meeting, draw the life out of her like a blood sample into a syringe and finally give her peace.

I say 'give her peace', but the fact is I am not sure that death and what she found there was peaceful for Mrs Hara. It is this thought that keeps me up at night sometimes, especially in early August when the heat lays thick like a woollen blanket over the land, pressing down with palpable weight on the chest, and the breezes that occasionally blow through the open windows are hot and disappointing. On those nights, I usually give up and light a cigarette in the dark. I take long drags and gaze at the inky landscape beyond my house in the country, and then I look up at the ebony sky sprinkled with stars. I never look around the room, and I never walk around the house on those nights. I look only at the vastness of the landscape and the night sky outside. Later you will understand why.

The *Nishi Nihon Newspaper*, the main editorial offices of which are located in the southern Japanese city of Fukuoka, hired me right out of college in 1976 as a cub reporter. I spent the first year doing manual sorts of jobs, writing out the long lists of birth and death announcements, help wanted columns, and other sections of the want ads. Then I was on the police beat in one of the centres of the city, the Nakasu section, where the drinking and entertainment establishments—which means whorehouses—were located. It was the nastiest section of town, and that made the work exhausting but enlightening at the same time. I learned in those two years that people can be self-destructive in a great many, and a creative number of, ways. I spent another year working in the grey world of the City Hall, where I was the junior reporter on a team of two. This experience, short as it was, showed me how people can live their lives in a listless routine that drags on numbly until retirement. After that, I was transferred to the culture desk, where I remained for several years until I finally became a desk editor. It was while I was on the culture desk that I met Mrs Hara.

The newspaper was planning a special feature on the fortieth anniversary of the bombings of Hiroshima and Nagasaki. In addition to our regular work, reporters were given responsibility for one part of the special issue, depending on their areas of expertise. Interviews, background research, photography; all these necessary jobs were divided among a team of reporters drafted from various desks of the newspaper.

I was put in charge of two interviews. One of them was a medical doctor whose father, since deceased, was one of the Japanese doctors who treated many of the radiation sickness cases that appeared in the years after the bombing. The man I interviewed had done groundbreaking research that built on his father's work on the effective treatment of radiation sickness, and he was now involved in the care of the many bomb victims who, now elderly, had developed cancers and other problems in their old age. I saw his clinic, spoke with some of his patients and staff, and talked for several hours over the course of two days with the doctor himself. Much of the conversation was technical, but he was very good about making it understandable to the layman. It was an interesting, if routine, interview.

The other one was Mrs Hara. She was a survivor of the bombing. Mrs Hara and her husband and daughter lived on the slope of one of Nagasaki's many hills, their house nestled in among many others of the same wood, rush, and paper construction that one still sees in the country in Japan to this day. The neighbourhood was completely demolished in the bombing. Her husband had been a factory worker at the Mitsubishi Arms Factory's Ohashi Plant in Nagasaki, where they had been born and grew up. He had been making machine parts for Japanese Imperial Navy ships for years and was killed when the factory building was flattened by the nuclear blast on August 9, 1945. Since before the war Mrs Hara had been working in the wholesale fish market along the waterfront of Nagasaki Bay. Her brother was a fisherman, and through this connection she found a place doing mainly clean-up chores with a group of other local women. Due to the war effort, the operations of the market were scaled back quite a bit. Many of the younger generation of fishermen were drafted or had volunteered, and with the constant threat of U.S. conventional bombings and other worries, the navy had restricted fishing to essentially subsistence levels. Thus, there were days when she wasn't needed at work during that last summer of the war. She and her husband had a daughter who had been fifteen years old in 1945 but had been spending the summer with relatives in the nearby city of Kumamoto, considered safer than the port of Nagasaki.

Mrs Hara had been forty-two at the time of the bombing of Nagasaki, where she lived still, which made her eighty-two when I met her that May afternoon in 1985. I spent the morning driving from my house in the suburbs of Fukuoka city south to Nagasaki. The drive along highways and country roads was pleasant, and the weather was clear, sunny, and warm. I had my camera and several rolls of film in a bag on the front seat beside me, a tape recorder, and a briefcase filled with notebooks and what little background information we had on Mrs Hara. She had been chosen mainly for her ordinariness. Her name was on the membership list of a survivors' support group and she was one of several people who agreed to be interviewed when we had contacted her over the phone several weeks before.

I had an early lunch at around 11.30 at a roadside McDonald's just outside Nagasaki city, and then continued into the city and through its winding streets to the neighbourhood where Mrs Hara lived. It was, to my surprise, the very neighbourhood where she had lived in 1945, though of course it had been completely rebuilt long ago. Still, all of the houses in the area were of wood and paper and roof tiles. Many were large two-storey homes, but most were the smaller, more modest one-storey style. I manoeuvred my car through the narrow streets and had to stop to ask an old man walking by where exactly the house was. Then, after a few more turns, I found it, parked right up against another relatively new looking car already in the driveway, went up the short walkway, and rang the doorbell.

'Coming!' a bright female voice called out from within the house. It sounded too young to be Mrs Hara, and, sure enough, the woman who answered the door turned out to be her daughter.

'You must be Mr Mori from the newspaper. I am Yuko Uesugi. My mother has been looking forward to meeting you.' She bowed and asked me to come into the house. Mrs Uesugi was a youthful looking woman who, at the age of fifty-five, had managed to retain a brightness in her eyes that indicated a mind that was still capable of childlike wonderment. She was dressed in dark slacks and a tasteful blouse of yellow. She wore no jewellery other than her wedding band and a watch. Her hair was shoulder-length and slightly wavy. She spoke in an even and slow voice.

'I have been looking forward to meeting your mother as well. Her experiences are a very personal part of our national history, and I am happy that she has given me and the newspaper this opportunity to share her story with our readers.'

Mrs Uesugi, which was apparently her married name, looked at me squarely but not coldly. 'My mother hopes for peace more than anything else. She doesn't particularly have an interest in history, and doesn't, I think, see her experiences in that way. She just wants somehow to make sure no one ever suffers as she did. And does.' Her eyes softened and she smiled. 'Please. Come into the living-room and make yourself at home.'

I followed her down a short corridor and into a room about ten by twenty feet, the floor of which was covered in *tatami* mats. There was a Buddhist altar set into an alcove in the far wall. A black and white photo of a man in his forties, whom I assumed to be Mrs Hara's deceased husband, hung above the altar. I knelt before the altar, lit a candle and a stick of incense, and took a set of prayer beads from a small stand to my right. I lightly struck a bowl shaped bell with a wooden rod made for that purpose, pressed my hands together, and offered a prayer. The scent of the incense swirled languidly around my face.

Mrs Uesugi had been behind me praying, and as I extinguished the candle with a wave of my hand and turned, she stood up, invited me to take a seat at the table in the centre of the room, and left down the corridor just outside the door. The room contained the low solid wood table where I was seated, and a chest along one wall that looked antique with its deep-grained wood and decorative metal joint braces. On the chest was a long cloth of red and blue silk and on top of this was a blue and white china bowl in which a thick and healthy looking plant was growing. Soft light filtered in through the white paper shades on the window behind me. In another alcove next to the altar, a work of calligraphy hung above another pretty white bowl bearing a strong lined landscape drawn in blue.

Mrs Uesugi returned a few minutes later with a teapot and cups on a tray, sat down opposite me, and poured out two cups of tea.

'How was your drive down, Mr Mori?'

'Oh, it was fine. It's a nice day for a drive. And the directions you gave me were excellent. I had no trouble at all.'

She smiled and offered me a cup of tea. 'I visit my mother a few days a week when I can. I live nearby, and I have not been working for some years now, so I try to help out with things as much as possible. She doesn't take care of herself as well as she should, you know.' We sipped our tea. It was light, yet aromatic and almost sweet.

'Well, I am glad that you are here. Your mother may feel more comfortable with someone from the family here during the interview.' This was a lie. It was my experience that people tended to speak much more guardedly when in the presence of others, especially family members. 'And perhaps you wouldn't mind adding some of your own memories and experiences. It would make for an even more interesting account, I think.'

Mrs Uesugi momentarily averted her eyes. 'Well, that is quite nice of you, but I really don't think anything I could say would be of much interest. Besides, I have to be leaving soon. I am meeting some friends for a meeting of an organization I belong to.'

'That is a shame. But still, it is nice that we could meet and talk like this.' I took another sip of tea. 'The tea is very good.' I smiled.

'I am glad you like it. It is from Ureshino, to the north in Saga Prefecture. Mother likes it the best.'

I was about to say something when the sliding *shoji* door to the room opened and Mrs Uesugi jumped up to help her mother to a place at the table. Mrs Hara was a small woman with very thin hair that was streaked, almost in thick stripes, with grey. She walked slowly and deliberately, as if it were hazardous, and in fact it probably was. She wore a white blouse and dark slacks and she had put on make-up. She limped, I noticed, and she seemed to favour her left side. In fact, she kept her face angled slightly towards my left, as if hiding the right side of her face. She sat down heavily, letting her weight drop of its own accord the last centimeter.

'I am very glad to meet you, Mr Mori.' She studied my face intently. 'My, you are young.'

'It is my pleasure to meet you. I can't thank you enough for agreeing to meet me and talk with me.'

She continued studying my face as if she were waiting for me to finish. 'I am thirty-one, ma'am.'

Her voice, as I have said, impressed me. It was steady and firm, unlike her gait. It was not at all overpowering or intimidating; it simply had an irresistible presence. She spoke with the local cadence and diction, but somehow seemed to transcend this particular place.

'I see you have met my daughter. She is such a help to me. Most of my neighbours and friends are gone, you know. Oh, the new people here are nice enough. The Nishikawa family across the street are lovely people. The little girl is so sweet. She visits me sometimes on her way home from school. I have never before in my life seen such a small girl eat so many tangerines.'

'Mother attends exercise classes at the community centre, and meetings of the bombing survivors group as well. I tell her to stay active, and I am glad that she does go out sometimes. Still, I worry. . . .'

'Oh, you worry too much, I think. But I am glad that you come by to see me so often.'

Mrs Uesugi finished fixing another cup of tea and set it down for her mother. 'Would you like any more, Mr Mori?'

'Oh, no. I am fine, thank you.' I now saw why Mrs Hara had favoured the left side of her face. As she turned her head slightly to stretch a bit, I could see that she had the thick, fibrous scar tissue of severe burns all along the right side of her neck and up to her cheek. As she reached for her teacup, I saw that both of her hands were similarly deformed. Her fingers were unnaturally stiff and it was obvious that even such a small, simple movement took a great deal of effort to accomplish successfully.

'Mother has never talked about what happened to her to anyone outside the family, Mr Mori.' She looked sidelong at her mother. 'I am sure she hasn't told us everything that happened then. I was not in Nagasaki when the bomb was dropped. I was away at the time.'

'Thank God you were, Yuko. We sent you to your aunt's so that you could stay safe, and safe you were. Yes, you were. Look at you now——'

'But mother, you could have come with me. How many times have I said that to you? We all should have gone.'

'You know your father couldn't. You know how it was. Soldiers everywhere. Plus, your father wouldn't have gone even if I had suggested it. Please, we don't need to go over this now, especially . . .' Mrs Hara and her daughter seemed to drift off in their thoughts, their memories. Mrs Uesugi was fighting tears. Just a bit, but fighting all the same.

This was one of the only times, perhaps the *only* time, when I felt that I was intruding, that I had no right to be there listening to this conversation, that journalism had a limit and I had crossed it. These people shared fear, the kind of fear it is difficult to imagine, but they also shared a very particular form of dread. I think it is the dread of death that becomes so real, so much a part of your daily routine and thoughts, that it expands, enlarges, becomes so heavy and unwieldy that it eventually folds in upon itself—bends under the sheer weight of its intolerability—until you come to terms with death. And after that it settles down with you comfortably, and for some people perhaps never leaves. This is something far beyond the merely personal or private. This is something, I thought that day, that is so much a part of one's very existence as an individual that no one should have the right to see it. Some things cannot bear witness.

But Mrs Hara seemed undaunted by such thoughts, if she even had them at all. She patted her daughter's hand with one of her own, and her daughter in turn used her free hand to pat her mother's soothing hand. It was a gesture that seemed plain enough, but I know I didn't understand what passed between them.

'You would like to hear about the bombing, Mr Mori?' said Mrs Hara. 'So, I will tell you.'

I got out my notebook and pen, suddenly remembering why I had come, though now doubtful about it. She started by giving me the background of where she and her husband worked at the time, and other necessary details, and then got to the day of the bombing itself.

'It happened in the morning, late in the morning. We had heard that Hiroshima had been bombed a few days before, but we didn't know the extent of it; we certainly didn't know anything about atomic bombs. No one knew.

'Yuko's father had gone to work at the factory, as usual, but I wasn't needed at the fish market that day. I was at home working around the house. It was a clean-up day, when everyone in the neighbourhood would get together and walk along the street pulling weeds and cleaning up garbage and things. Of course, so many people had gone away to relatives where they felt safer, and so many of the young men had gone to war, that there were only a few housewives and the older folk doing the work. But those of us left had tried to keep up the old routines, make sure somehow that life was continuing on as close to normally as we could get ourselves to believe.

'Mr and Mrs Shimada from next door were walking with me, talking, making me laugh now and then. Our family had known theirs for years. Mrs Shimada was my source of information. She always knew who had a little extra cabbage to spare, who might have had a bigger or nicer piece of fish, who had just opened a long-buried jar of pickled radish. Everything was so scarce, you know, in those days. But even the Shimada's rabbits always had something to eat. Three fat little brown things, so cute. And Mr Shimada always seemed able to find another litre of diesel fuel to run the generator we had for electric power in the neighbourhood. To this day, I can't imagine where he got it. He almost never spoke, Mr Shimada did. Though he was seventy-three, he would just work and work, and once in a while stand up straight, take off his straw hat, and rub his bald head with a towel. He always wore tan pants, a stained white t-shirt, and black rubber boots. He would go off once in a while and come back with fuel, or firewood, or something else useful.

'We had just finished up and I was back home, doing some little chores in front of the house. Watering, tidying up. As I recall a truck came by, a truck filled with soldiers. Young, energetic boys, faces filled with excitement and fear. They looked so dashing. Their eyes were so clear, fearful as they were, and their faces so fresh. Ah, that's why it is so hard to see them afterwards, how they looked, to see what happened to them . . .' She trailed off in mid-sentence, lost in the thought.

'Mother, you——'

'I'm fine. Really.' Mrs Hara looked up at her daughter. 'Shouldn't you be going now?'

'Oh, you're right. Look at the time. But mother, how can I go, with you here putting yourself through this?'

'I am not putting myself through anything that I wasn't perfectly aware I would be putting myself through, dear. Now, don't worry about me. You do what you have to do, and I will do what I have to do. I am certainly not a baby.'

Mrs Uesugi patted her mother's hand again, obviously giving up. 'It was nice meeting you, Mr Mori.' She rose and looked down at her mother. 'And mother, please take it easy.'

'I will. You drive carefully now.'

Mrs Uesugi bowed slightly to me, and left the room swiftly.

Mrs Hara sat silently for a while. I didn't feel I could break the silence comfortably, so I sat there with her, listening to the breeze blow gently against the paper shade on the window. In the room, the aroma of tea mixed with a faint hint of cedar wood was carried on the slight breeze. After a while, Mrs Hara looked at me again and took a deep breath.

'I know exactly what I am getting myself into. You will see in time, Mr

Mori, what I mean. For now just listen.' I saw her raise an eyebrow just slightly. 'You might want to turn your machine on, too.' She pointed with twisted fingers to my tape-recorder. I checked the tape and pressed the record and play buttons simultaneously, setting it moving.

'I was squatting down behind a low concrete block wall at the edge of the property in front of the house, pushing a trowel into the ground. I was going to plant some bean plants. Had them laid out on the ground beside me, little stalks, you know. That was when the bomb exploded. Well, the bomb went off and first there was a flash, like a huge overwhelming camera flash, and then time stopped. It was frozen, I guess; I don't know how to say it. But it seemed frozen in that instant. I couldn't hear anything at all; there was no sound. But the air was thick with something, electric in a way. I don't know what to call it, maybe like electricity, perhaps like electricity was in the air. But that is ridiculous, I know. I just don't know how to say it.

'Anyway, the air moved a little, like a breeze was coming up the hill. It does that sometimes, you know. The breezes blow up the hill, and sometimes they are very cool off the water. Well, it was like that. But then the breeze seemed too strong, a bit, just a bit. And then——' She paused. Her lips were trembling. Her eyes were becoming thick with welling tears. 'Well, then I could hear a roar, oh . . . like an earthquake; no, more like a typhoon I guess. A terrible roar that scared me, and I remember sort of balling myself up tight while squatting there, just before the wind came and blew everything around me down. Yes, Mr Mori, that is how it happened. A roaring wind came, and it tore up trees and threw carts and wagons around and blew the houses down. They just blew away, Mr Mori. And it was so hot, oh, like everything was burning. Everything was burning as it flew through the air above me.

'That wall is what saved me, that low concrete wall. I don't know why but it didn't get blown down. Maybe it was too low, I don't know. But it had these triangular openings, like decorations, about two-thirds of the way up, and it was through those that I was burned. Oh, it hurt so much, Mr Mori. I can't tell you. And like many things that happened that day, the pain hasn't gone away. So many things that happened that day are still with me now.

'I was knocked down by the force of the blast, I guess. I just found myself on the ground after a while. I don't know how long I had been there. But I got myself up into a sort of sitting position, looked around, and I saw that . . . that . . . well, everything was gone. There was a town around me a minute or so ago, and then there wasn't. It was as simple as that. Where the town had been was wreckage. Just wreckage. Down the hill it was worse, and from a distance off to my left a huge cloud, a terrible brown and white thing, was rising into the air, so high into the air. I couldn't bear to look at it. So, I looked towards where the Shimadas' house had been, but of course there was nothing left. But in the middle of the rubble, something was moving. I tried to get up slowly, hurting everywhere, and found that I couldn't. I couldn't stand, couldn't walk;

I was still too stunned. I sat there watching the spot where I had seen movement, and slowly, so slowly, Mr Shimada pulled himself up to a sitting position. His clothes were mostly gone; burned away. He was bleeding everywhere. It was horrible. But then he turned, so that he was facing me directly, and . . . and . . .'

She started to sob uncontrollably and buried her face in her hands. I didn't see any tissues in the room, and the tea was gone, so I got up and went into the kitchen. There I found some tissues and I got a glass of water. I brought both back to her and set them on the table. She just sobbed for a short while, and I urged her to drink some water after a few minutes. She did. Then she wiped her eyes.

'I am sorry, Mr Mori. I didn't mean to cry.'

'I can't imagine how horrible it was for you.'

'No, Mr Mori,' she said, slightly recovering, 'you can't. But you will.' I didn't know what she could have meant, at the time.

'You see, Mr Shimada must have been sitting at the table in his living-room with the right side of his body facing the direction of the blast. I say this because when he turned to face me, I could see that the entire right side of his face had been burned away. Completely. I was looking at a person who had a normal left side of his face and a bare skull on his right. There was no skin, no muscle, no eye in the black socket. Nothing. But the horrible, the most terrible thing . . .' She started to cry again at this point, more gently than before. 'The most terrible thing, you see, was that he was still alive. He was groping towards me, stretching out his right hand, itself just bone with bits of flesh hanging off. And then he fell down, dead I suppose. I never checked to see if he actually died then, but I simply hold on to the hope that he was dead because to think that he lived for even a moment beyond that is too much to bear. Too much to bear.'

I didn't know what to say. What *could* I say? Anything would have sounded stupid, and how could words soothe what this woman was feeling, what she had been feeling ever since the day she was reliving for me now? I gradually began to loathe myself for coming, for making her tell me these things and thus experience them again. And what made me feel physically sick was that I planned to write her story down and share it with the thousands of people who read the newspaper.

'Well, I sat there for a while just numb,' she continued. 'I didn't know what to do. And I hurt all over; my whole body, head to toe. My hands were bleeding and burned. So was my face and neck. After some time passed I got up finally and started to walk slowly down the hill. It was like walking in hell, Mr Mori. Dead people were everywhere. And the dead were not just . . . they, well, they were black and shrunken, some of them, others torn apart, and the pieces were everywhere. Here and there people were still moving. They weren't dead yet, just burned it seemed. Trees were broken, pieces of things from people's houses were laying all around: dishes, cups, papers, broken pieces of furniture, half-burnt blankets. The ground was black and smoking and the air was heavy. And there was no sound. It was silence all around. Unreal. Like a nightmare.

'I walked along and I saw a girl lying up against a low stone wall. She wasn't so badly burned, at least as far as I could see. She was crying. Crying was the first sound that broke the eerie, unreal silence. Crying. So, I bent down and took her hand and I said "Don't cry, I'm here. We'll be all right." She had wide, scared eyes, eyes beyond pain and fear. Her hair was all messy, but I could see that it was long and luxurious. She was maybe seven or eight. Then I looked at her belly. It was black. And below that, her legs . . . one of her legs was gone and the other was shrivelled and twisted and charred. She clung to my hand desperately, gasping shallow, pitiful breaths. She looked at me and said, "Momma, I'm dying." I cradled her head in my lap and held her hand until it went loose in mine. It didn't take long, thankfully. I guess it was just a few minutes until she slipped away.

'There was more, Mr Mori. I saw more that morning and afternoon. I walked past the burned shell of a school building, the books and pieces of furniture black and smoking all around, the pieces of the school children and the teachers black and smoking among them. I saw trucks overturned and still on fire, their gas tanks pouring thick, acrid smoke into the air, the drivers bloody and torn apart. There were people impaled by pipes, people ripped in half, people bleeding and throwing up into rancid pools of water and oil here and there. As I got down the hill it was getting worse. You know, I was walking towards what they now call ground zero, vaguely towards the tower of smoke that had risen into the sky. But even I knew that it would be folly to walk towards that thing, that horror. So, I went around it, keeping it to my right, and as I walked I saw more horrors, more burned bodies, more faces blasted flat with their eyes staring with unspeakable pain and overwhelming destruction. Dead, blank eyes that had seen far too much in just a moment.

'I stopped by a river and realized that I was thirsty. So many other people were there too, drinking, trying to wash their wounds. I bent down to drink and saw my reflection in the water. It was not so bad, really, except for my neck and part of my cheek.' She now consciously showed me the burned parts of her neck and face that I had glimpsed earlier. 'I have these scars now, so painful, you know. I can't move my fingers, and my neck hurts all the time. The exercises help, though. The people at the rehabilitation centre are quite nice. The one nurse is a bulldog. Tough as nails, keeps me at it no matter what . . . .' She trailed off again, seeming to lose her focus, and we sat there for a short time while she was somewhere else. Then, suddenly, she came back.

'Well, after a while, I don't know how long, a truck came by with doctors and nurses and other people, and a group of us were brought to a tent that was being used as a hospital. They treated my burns. Others were worse than me, of course. There was constant wailing and crying in there. So much pain. So many people died there, too. So many.

'And that is my story, Mr Mori. Do you have any questions?'

I fumbled for words. I was still trying to deal with all she had said. She had taken me by surprise by ending so abruptly, and I hadn't had a chance to form in my mind how I wanted to follow-up. I finally decided, after rejecting a few other options, on bringing her into the present for a while, and seeing how she would reflect. 'I wonder, Mrs Hara, how the distance of time has affected your view of what happened. I mean, when you look back now, so many years later, does it seem somehow different to you—almost, as they say, like it happened to someone else?'

'Oh, I see what you mean. The doctors at the rehabilitation clinic sometimes ask me things like that. They seem so learned, trying to help me, trying to make sense of it all.' She leaned in towards me, gazed at me, and let her voice—her steady, knowing voice—work its way into me. 'But the fact is, Mr Mori, there is no distance between that day and today. You see, I am still having the experience.'

'Still . . . ? You mean that you relive it in your dreams, or——'

'No, I mean that in fact, quite literally, I continue to have the experience. And not in my dreams or in my imagination. In reality, here. Even right now.'

'Right now? You mean that by telling me the story you——'

'No, that is not what I mean.' She smiled, and gazed at me with her steady eyes, forced her voice into every pore of my body. 'Would you be so kind as to turn around and look at the corner of the room behind you and to the right?'

I felt a wave crawl across my skin, as if thousands of ants had run just under its surface. But I also felt ridiculous. I felt that my story and even my guilt at having intruded to get it, at having invaded privacies not meant to be invaded, were all a crude irony. She was obviously crazy if she thought there could be anything behind me that I would see. But her eyes, and her voice especially, told me that she wasn't crazy.

Slowly, I turned towards my right, looking over my shoulder as I shifted my body so that it faced the direction she had indicated. With the passing of time, the light had changed in the room, and the corner was in shadow. At first, I saw nothing but the shadow. But as I gazed at it, the dark seemed to have a form, the rough form of a person. And the more I looked, the clearer it became. I could make out a head, shoulders, torso. It seemed to be seated on the *tatami* in the corner. It raised its head and regarded me blankly. There was no face. I turned and looked back at Mrs Hara.

'This is Mrs Shimada. Remember I told you that her husband had been sitting with his right side facing the blast? Mrs Shimada had been sitting facing it, it would seem. Well, you have a look and tell me if she was or not.'

I looked back and saw that the face of the form had peeked out from the shadow that it was in or that it was made of. I gasped. The lower jaw and mouth were those of an elderly woman, but, above that, the nose and eyes were gone, burned away so that bare skull was where they had been. Black sockets stared out at me, above them bare white skull, smudged with dark patches of carbon, where the forehead and hairline should have been. And above that was hair twirling wildly in all directions. I noticed the aroma of burning human flesh. The apparition sat there, regarding me silently with a black emptiness. Its clothing was torn and hanging in shreds from its shoulders, the pale, unreal flesh beneath hanging as well, bone visible here and there. The blood was not red; it was more of a pink, washed out, faraway colour. The apparition did not move; it made no sound. It simply sat. I heard Mrs Hara's voice from behind me.

'Mr Mori, they are with me, all of them. The ones I saw, the ones I don't remember seeing. They are all still with me. Ghosts, you may call them, I don't know. . . . Survivors in a way, I suppose. But they are here, now. The shredded, melted, torn apart people still oozing blood and pus. They are here in this house. They are in the dark places, behind closed doors, poking their bleeding eyeballs out from behind boxes in the kitchen cabinets. Sometimes they just stand in a corner of a room, looking, watching. Everywhere in the house I find them. Or pieces of them from time to time. A hand under a pillow. A shock of hair lying on the kitchen table.

'The first few years after the bombing, I saw nothing unusual. But, oh, maybe five or six years later—yes, about that—I saw the first one. I thought I was going mad, and so I told no one, of course. I saw them in the house, standing on street corners, looking at me as I shopped down the road in the grocer's. And after three years of seeing them, I began to notice their pattern. I see them each year beginning just after New Year's, and they are all here by the anniversary of the bombing. Droves of them. Oh, around the anniversary, there are more of them than there are of us. The strange thing, though, is that from August tenth to December I hardly ever see one. Perhaps they relive the shock and devastation of the blast and are paralyzed or something. I don't know.' She took a deep breath.

'But there is more. Come with me, would you?'

Mrs Hara got up slowly and with difficulty. I ran around to her and steadied her as she got to her feet. She took my arm affectionately and led me down the hallway. There were no lights on in the house, and the sunlight filtered in weakly, casting pale shadows. She led me to her room, and to a far wall against which stood another large bureau. She took a small lacquered hand mirror down and held it so that I could not see the reflection. She glanced at me over her shoulder. 'Just remember, Mr Mori, it was you who wanted to know what the bombing did to me.' And she looked in the mirror.

I saw in the reflection a black, charred face. One eyeball lay useless against the cheek, blood dripping from the socket. The hair was all burned away. Long, deep cracks in the blackened, shrivelled skin oozed with thick viscous white fluid. But through all this ruin and deformity, the face was still recognizable as Mrs Hara's. It was too much to bear.

'Do you——?'

'Yes, I see it, Mr Mori. Of course, I see it. It is me, after all. Or what I could've been, or what I will be. I try not to think about it much these days. I see this from time to time. Well, after spring and through the summer mostly. Until August tenth, that is. I have my daughter do my make-up for me when she visits. I couldn't do it myself, you know, looking like this. And what difference could a little makeup make on this face, eh?'

I found I couldn't laugh at her joke.

I didn't write up her interview for our special anniversary issue of the bombing. I told my editor she turned out to be a kook, that her story was a rambling, nonsensical, half-imagined thing. Of course, I didn't tell him any of the actual things she had said. I made up something on the spot, and though he was disappointed, he agreed not to run the interview. I ended up interviewing someone else and publishing that story.

She died a year later of cancer. Since the day I met her, I have often thought about her story, and the strange experience I had in her house. I think about it more and more these days especially. They are not ghosts, exactly, I think. I believe that, whatever they are, they exist in a special reality that may have been created by the tremendous power of the bomb. But the bomb also seems to have created yet another reality, the one in which Mrs Hara was killed. These realities coexist with the one in which we live now and in which Mrs Hara survived. Why it is that only some people—though the only one I know of is Mrs Hara—can see them, I don't know.

But in the last few months—and this is years after I met Mrs Hara—the shadows in my house seem to have taken on a more defined shape. And just last week, at the end of July, I opened the closet in my bedroom to get a new sheet for the bed and I found an arm, bloody and black, lying there among the linen in the drawer. I turned away and when I looked again, it was gone. Then, a few days later, when I woke up in the heat, I saw the figure of a soldier standing at the foot of my bed. His clothing was tattered, and his face . . . well, I won't talk about his face.

I don't know why she decided to tell me her story, and what she was able to see. Perhaps it was something she had to do before she died, something she had to share with another person. As I have observed so often and noted above, the people closest to you are sometimes the very ones you cannot talk to. Maybe the fact that I was a stranger made it easier to talk about.

Was it the power of Mrs Hara telling me her story that made them visible to me? Were they always visible to me, if only I had known to look? I don't know. But they are the reason I keep my gaze at the black mountains in the distance or at the stars overhead when I wake up at night. I don't dare look around my dark room. Who knows what figure will be standing there on an August night, unaware that it was blasted apart in a moment, unaware that it occupies a space not meant to be occupied? Do they see me as I sit with my back to the room? Do they see anyone at all when they appear in grocery stores and supermarkets, on street corners, and probably in cars and in forests and in telephone booths? If they do see us, I wonder what they think of us. I wonder if we look as ghastly to them as they do to us.

Inside William James

Steve Rasnic Tem

WILLIAM JAMES? *Time to wake up, honey.*
    He did not really believe it was his mother speaking to him. He knew what people said about him, but he had more sense than that. He didn't always remember things right, but he still had all his marbles. He smiled because that was a joke. He had a big cloth bag full of marbles under his bed that he traded with, always fair about it but still trying to get the better deal. If anybody needed proof he was no dummy, all they had to do was watch the way he traded those marbles.
    Out in the big world nobody paid attention to such things as marbles and trades and William James. Out in the big world folks had bigger fish to fry, and they weren't sharing those fish with the likes of William James. The younger kids were the only ones cared about trading marbles with old William James. The only ones. He wouldn't cheat the younger kids. Not that he'd ever cheated anybody, but even if he felt he had to cheat somebody for something real important—to save the world maybe, big world and little world and all the places people and fishes lived—he still wouldn't cheat one of those little kids, kids what had to be protected from the bad traders in the world.
    But he'd still try to get himself the better deal because that was what trading was all about. Not too better, not to take the other people's marbles he didn't deserve, especially not the little kidses.
    You've been sleeping too long, William James.
    But William James knew there was no such thing as sleeping too long. Bed

was a good place, maybe the best place, and nobody had the right to ask you to leave it unless they were your mother.

That wasn't his mother's voice but he pretended it might be. That didn't make him a little kid, did it? But it sure made him sad. Sure, he got to talk to his mother some way or other most every day, but it wasn't the same since she was dead. She got tired easy and didn't want to talk too much. Being dead, William James decided, took a lot out of you.

William James . . .

His eyes opened up like butterflies, a few flying away at a time. He couldn't stop them—you couldn't catch every butterfly that came around. They were like nervous people who didn't know how to behave, so they did what they worried on, and didn't think about if it was wrong or not.

The woman had a big face, not nervous at all, and not like his mother's face.

'Hey, Nurse Bossy,' he said to the face.

'Hey, William James. Time for breakfast.' She smiled. Nurse Bossy was what he called her, but it was kind of a joke. She told him what to do, all right, and he didn't much like that, but she could be pretty nice about it, saying things that sometimes made him smile. And he had known her as long as he'd been here. He loved her.

'Do I have to Nurse Bossy?'

'You have to eat, child! If you don't eat you die.'

William James nodded. He couldn't argue with that, but he didn't like her talking about things he didn't like thinking about. He didn't want to talk anymore.

She stood by while he got dressed, just in case he made a mistake. But he almost never did. He was the last one to the breakfast table but that usually happened no matter how fast he went.

He did what he always did when he first sat down: looked around to see if there was anybody he didn't know. Sometimes there would be somebody new and he'd have to get up and go shake their hand just because that's the kind of person he was. Or maybe wanted to be. He couldn't remember. The nurses always said it was 'a nice gesture', but sometimes they had to calm a new person down when William James went over and grabbed their hand like that.

He didn't think there was anybody new just then so he started to dig into his eggs and sausage—sometimes he made the eggs smile and stuck the sausage in like a big C-gar, but when he was really hungry time was a wasting and the food was for eating not for making faces up at you.

And then he saw the new face.

The new face came right out of the big freezer door like he'd been on skiing vacation and sat down at the next table across from William James and stared at William like he was one of those fancy fruit cups they had for breakfast on extra special occasions when lots of visitors came.

William James didn't know exactly who it was, but he sure knew what it was—he'd seen that kind so many times before. The face all grey and the hair burned off, big patches on the skin dark like wet leaves been run over by a car a hundred hundred times. He didn't like this kind of new at all, so he tried to look down at his breakfast, follow the stripes in the bacon back and forth and around where it curled into the burned part. He tried to pretend the new one in the eating room was a lamp with the bulb burned out, just waiting to be taken out to the trash.

Didn't work.

After a while he looked back up at the new one, stared it right in the ugly, and stuck his tongue out.

The new one stuck his own tongue right back at him, and it was like a bone spoon full of black ashes and it made William James shake all over, like he was looking into a bad dream mirror. At himself.

William James got out of the chair and walked right over to the new one, spilling a few of the other people who lived there out onto the floor, where they whimpered or bawled or threw up, depending on what they were best at that day. 'You ain't me!' he yelled at the bad ash face. 'But give here,' he said, throwing his arm right up to the ugly burnt nose, 'shake!'

Bad Ash Face just stared, and William James could see then that even the man's eyeballs were burned. That made him swallow some, but he still held his hand steady as he could. 'Go on, take it! It's a nice gesture.'

And when the Ash Face wouldn't, William James tried to grab the new one's hand and make him shake hands. And felt his own hand tingle, like a little bit of the skin on his fingers was peeling back, and then his hand went through all that ash and skin and came out the other side.

William James felt other hands then, on his back and shoulders, a couple on his sides, pulling him back and down to the floor. He tried to fight his way free, swinging and punching people he didn't really want to hurt, but didn't feel he could choose not to, either.

'William James, what's come over you?' That was Nurse Bossy—Nurse Betty—right behind him and he made himself not hurt her.

'Tell me he ain't me!' he cried, pulling his arm loose enough to point. 'And tell *him* that, too.'

But the Ugly Ash Face was already mostly gone. Just a smear of sooty skin here and there like something on a dirty old window. And then that little bit cleaned off, and there was nothing.

* * * * *

Nurse Betty was terribly sorry but she had to ask him to stay in his room that night. He was real sorry too, for scaring everybody the way he did. There wasn't a mirror in the room, but the dresser was pretty shiny, and if he put the lamp on it just right he could see his reflection pretty good.

He had some scars all right, but nothing like that Ugly Ash Face. His were small and smooth and here and there, like somebody had taken a giant eraser to his face and tried to rub out the lines.

* * * * *

William James. William James? Time to get up now—haven't you slept long enough?

William James didn't know how to answer a question like that; he just kept his eyes shut so he could think about it for a while. Inside William James things were all stirred up. People were moving in and out of houses and there were boxes everywhere, going on trucks and being carried inside, shoved around on the floor and stacked in the backs of closets. The cars on the street were old and broken down, so everywhere people were walking. Then the sky got bright enough to turn the houses orange, and everywhere inside William James people were walking with their heads on fire, even the younger kids, and they didn't even know it, walking around like giant burning matches.

'Hey, Nurse Bossy,' he said, opening his eyes.

'Time for breakfast, William James. Do you feel well enough to come down to the dining room, or do you think it best that you stay in your room a while longer?'

William James closed his eyes to think. That was the longest question anyone had asked him in a very long time. He sat down in the middle of the street to think about it. He didn't worry about any cars coming and running him over because none of the cars were running.

The sun was falling down out of the sky a few blocks away. A couple of houses caught fire and nearby a car or two exploded. The sirens came but they forgot their fire engines and all the firemen that usually rode on the fire engines' backs. So the sirens just stood out in the street and screamed at the burning houses. By the time they were done screaming the sun had finished its burning and the sky was black. The street lights came on but the sky was still like shiny coal with fireflies resting here and resting there, burning themselves on and burning themselves off.

People were walking through the yards and walking through the streets, all of them going someplace where the light was the brightest. So William James got up to follow, thinking that whenever a lot of people go to one place there's always food, and William James was hungry enough to eat anything, even if it wasn't cooked right, even if it was burnt.

But then he saw Ugly Ash Face, who smiled at him and waved, then came over and tried to shake William James' hand. But the worst thing was that Ugly Ash Face wasn't so ugly right then, and William James recognized him as a neighbour who used to live down the street from him.

William James tried to turn around then, but there were so many people pushing their way into that house he couldn't turn against them. Before he knew it he was inside, and practically everybody was making a nice gesture, shaking his hand and telling him what a lucky young man he was.

And there was his mother, all shiny like a Bluebird in her favourite party dress. She had little brownies with red hearts on them she was handing out, and everybody was saying how yummy yummy yummy they were, but when she handed one to William James he just couldn't eat it. He couldn't bite into one of those bright red hearts.

Don't get him too fat before the wedding, Maria! the man on William's right said, taking a brownie in his burning hand, the chocolate melting across his fingers, the red icing dripping to the floor. *Then his pretty bride won't want him!* The man laughed, the inside of his mouth vanishing into flame, the fire burning up through the skull and escaping where the nose used to be.

William James ran out of the room, up the stairs to where he knew his room, his bed must be. He jerked open his bedroom door and the first thing he saw were his marbles scattered across the floor. He hadn't thought about his marbles in years, he hadn't played with them since he was a little fellow, but he'd kept them special in a fancy cloth bag his mother had made for him, tucked up under the bed against the wall.

Now they were scattered everywhere, eyes and jewels and little round jellyfish, on the floor with the light dying inside them.

And on the bed lay his fiancée Elise, her pretty gown in disarray, still holding on to his brother Carlos, crying and telling William James not to be angry with her, that she had been feeling a little sick and Carlos was just helping her, after all they would be family soon, but still holding on to Carlos as if she didn't know what else to do.

But William James could no longer look at Elise and his brother, so his eyes found something else to look at: the marbles everywhere, and the dying light flickering inside them, and his eyes seeking the source of that flicker found the candles he'd bought placed in every corner of the room, the candles he had told his brother about, all their different smells like being inside a burning flower shop, the candles he'd planned to load into his car for his wedding night, when he would put them around their marriage bed, hundreds of flames and smells for his beloved Elise.

He gazed at his brother Carlos, who stared back with those not-sorry eyes. Who was not stupid. Who knew he would be caught like this, in his brother's bed, with his brother's candles, his brother's fiancée. It was only Elise who might not have fully understood, Elise who had been stupid, but never as stupid as William James himself.

William James could feel the anger charging his muscles like electricity; his fists curled on their own, tight enough to cause him pain. He looked away from Carlos and Elise, determined that he would not step towards them, and looked at the candles instead, the ones he'd picked and bought from every place he knew that sold candles, their combined scents so thick and heavy now they smelled like layers of garbage. He swung a forearm into the dozen or so on his desk, and those in turn toppled dozens more. Unable to stop himself, even after his shirt caught fire, he waded swinging into the tiers of candles, dancing through the flames, his legs kicking into heat and his lungs ragged and rough with smoke. Now and then he felt their hands on him trying to stop him, but they gave up right away, and he was dancing alone. In some distant place inside him William James could hear the last of their singing: his mother, the rest of his family, friends and neighbours, Elise.

William James . . . William James . . .

Nurse Betty showed him a worried person's face, and others were there with angry faces and faces that didn't care either way. They helped him up and sat him in a chair, and one of the doctors checked him over and after he said what he had to say everybody but Nurse Betty left him there.

'You'll be okay for breakfast, won't you William James?'

William James nodded. 'No trouble,' he said, and busied himself getting dressed with Nurse Betty watching him. For a little bit he was confused with his socks until Nurse Betty took them away and got them started for him. He felt embarrassed, but grateful to her just the same.

Breakfast was almost over by the time he got to the dining room, but they fed him anyway. Most of the other residents had left—he could hear one of them crying out in the hallway and figured it must be Jimmy.

He looked around at all the new faces. Some of them he had seen once or twice the past few months, but others were new new, and had never been here before. Some of them looked like women from the old neighbourhood. Some of them looked like men he'd known all his life. Ashen hair and blasted skin, now they all looked his kin. Some of them nodded his way, then looked back down at their hands. They smelled like smoke and garbage. They were his mother's friends, and all had come to his party.

William . . . William James . . .

His mother's breath was like a warm candle. It tickled the inside of his throat. William James opened his mouth and waited for his mother to come out.

Someone Across the Way

Steve Duffy

IT WAS LATE, GONE MIDNIGHT, when Gary first became aware of the lighted window in the house across the way. By day the view was dull, quintessential shabby-urban rental: concrete backyards pierced by weeds, scrubby grass patches worn to mud by tethered dogs, the flat roofs of dilapidated garage blocks, phone lines sagging from the weight of lifeless conversations. He must have stared out at it a thousand times or more during the ten years he'd been at that address: vacantly, after shaving, maybe, or when turning from the blank computer screen in irritable exhaustion, but he couldn't remember a lighted window over there ever having caught his eye just so. Funny, the way things stood out sometimes.

That night he was fidgety, restless, wandering from room to room without bothering to turn the lights on, wanting to be doing something, he didn't know what, knowing only it was too late, somehow, in some way he couldn't quite explain; too late. In the back room the curtains, as always, were open; just as they were in the sparsely furnished attic room across the way, except that there the lights were on.

Or a light: a table lamp in the lower left-hand corner of the window. Its brightness was sharp, clear, practically unshielded—at first he thought it was a bare bulb, but once he'd taken his army surplus field-glasses from their case, he saw it was a brass reproduction oil lamp with a frosted-glass chimney, the kind of thing you'd get from the catalogue back in the 1970s. They'd had one at home when he was a child. For a moment Gary paused there in the dark—he still hadn't turned on the light in his own room. Squinting through the field-glasses made him feel at once absurd and slightly seedy, like some middle-aged voyeur too shy to pick an occupied window through which to stare. He paused for a moment before lifting the glasses again. Blurry darkness swung through his field of vision, then he focused on the warm yellow rectangle of the lighted window. Which was now no longer unoccupied.

Someone was sitting with his back to the lamp, facing across the room towards something on the right—Gary couldn't see what it was. The man (it was a man, he could see that much) had on a faded green polo shirt which seemed familiar somehow; he was dark-haired, neither young nor particularly old. It was hard to see his face; he was sitting sideways on to the window, slightly silhouetted by the table lamp. Also he was wearing spectacles, which caught the illumination from behind and glinted slightly.

Perhaps he was watching television? There was no bluish flicker in the room; and surely the table lamp behind him would have reflected uncomfortably on the screen? And there was something about his posture—still and correct, back upright, head straight—that seemed almost excessively formal in one merely watching TV.

Gary put down the field-glasses. This was ridiculous. Was this what he'd turned into? Alison had been right: clearly he did need to get out more. He was about to go through to the kitchen, make some coffee he really didn't need, when in putting his field-glasses away he happened to glance up at the window one last time, and saw that the man across the way had got up from his chair.

Without thinking Gary took up the glasses again, refocused on the far window. The man was crossing the room to a place just fractionally outside Gary's line of sight. Someone else seemed to be waiting there, standing on the very brink of visibility—he tried squinting, looking through one eye only, playing with the focus, but nothing really helped. Just the hint of green that was the man's back—and were they bare arms, raised to embrace; the suggestion of bodies, maybe, coming together?

Frowning, Gary shifted from one side to another, tried to peer around the edge of the window-frame, but from his vantage point it was impossible. Branches obscured the line of sight, the eaves of the intervening buildings nibbled into his field of vision. He had to make do with just the peripheral view, rippled out of shape in the old window-glass and difficult to interpret, stray glimpses growing shaky as his hands grew tired of holding the heavy Red Army glasses.

Something about the composition of the scene looked wrong: awkward, stagy almost. Wasn't it about time one or the other of them moved back into view? Wasn't it just a trifle coincidental for them to be staying *out* of view of the window that way? A vision came to Gary of kids in the playground, standing in a corner and wrapping themselves in their own arms so that from behind it looked as if they were smooching. *Was* there someone else in the room? Or was it only an optical illusion, the oldest trick in the book?

In which case, why on earth would the man be doing such a thing? Maybe it was some sort of confused cry for attention; after all, only if he knew he had an audience would it make sense——

Gary snatched the glasses away from his face and stepped back hastily from the window. He hadn't been seen, had he? The neighbours already looked at him as if he'd done away with Alison in an acid-bath, or buried her in the cellar: to be tagged as the local peeping-tom was the last thing he needed. Mobs of villagers with burning torches: the monster at bay up in the windmill. He looked around. His room was dark, the other lighted: surely it wasn't possible for someone across the way to look out across street and backyard and see into an unlit window? Decisively, he set the glasses down on top of a pile of cardboard boxes. Enough. No point in taking risks.

After putting the kettle on—still in the dark, there was a street light whose light came through the kitchen window and it was enough to see by—Gary went into the back room to close the curtains. It was not a thing he normally bothered with, but this time he thought it might be for the best. In attempting to free the curtains on their stiff runners, he looked out, again without consciously meaning to.

There was the man, back in his chair by the table lamp. There was still no definite sign of anyone else in the room; except that now the man seemed to be talking, addressing that part of the room Gary couldn't see into. His head was cocked slightly up, as if to the face of a person standing before him; from time to time he would raise his hands, gesturing without heat or animation. He might have been describing some object, small and compact, he had once held and examined.

Irritably, Gary fiddled with the knurled focusing wheel on his glasses. It was no good: not even with the best glasses Communism could bequeath him would he be able to see around corners. All that *was* visible in the rest of the room was a large sideboard on the back wall, and above it a poster, unframed. More out of frustration than through any genuine interest, he inspected the sideboard. There were books lined up on the top of it, as if on a shelf: if he altered the focus ever so slightly, he could just about make out some of the individual spines. And guess what? there on the end of the row was one he actually recognized, a largish slip-cased hardback with a thick orange-and-blue spine. It stood out among the others: up to a month ago, it had stood out on Gary's own shelf. Coincidentally, he'd taken a copy of that book to the second-hand shop just recently. Alongside it was a smaller, chunkier volume, some sort of reference work, he supposed. In fact—he tried to concentrate, to bring back memories of shape and detail—didn't it look rather like an encyclopaedia he'd once owned when he was younger? Undeniably, it did.

Above the eyepieces of the field-glasses, Gary's eyebrows came together in a frown of curiosity. Was it possible? Were these books what he'd naturally assumed them to be, mere duplicates of popular titles he'd once owned? Or, more spookily, were they actually *the same books*, his very own copies? Rationally speaking, the first book at least might well be the same copy he'd just recently sold. There was nothing to stop anyone from visiting the local second-hand shop and buying it, was there? But the other one, the encyclopaedia; Gary knew he'd owned that book as a child, it was probably still stored in the loft of his parents' house. Clearly it couldn't be the same book—even though that shabby torn-and-taped spine did seem very familiar.

Remember, he told himself, scanning along the rest of the row, one person's interests might quite easily be more or less the same as another's, especially in a city the size of London. 'More or less' being the operative qualifier—but wait. There was another title he recognized, an American short-story anthology you couldn't readily get in the U.K.; and there was another; and another. In fact, the more he looked, the more Gary was prepared to swear that he'd owned, at some time or another, practically all the books on top of the sideboard. He'd sold them, or given them to charity shops; loaned them to friends he'd subsequently fallen out with, or left them on the Tube or whatever; and now here they were, in the room across the way, the property of the man in the chair——

Who was unmoving again, relapsed into that perfect, almost autistic stillness, backlit by the table lamp—shit! No! Gary nearly bit his tongue as the connection clicked in, with all the formal elegance of advanced paranoia. The table lamp, the one his parents had owned when he was a child. If those were his books, then that was the table lamp. Samey-same.

Could it be? Of course not. Okay, yes, it was a *similar* lamp, but there were hundreds, thousands, of the same model knocking around, weren't there? Everyone had them, once upon a time: six hundred Green Shield stamps, or whatever. This was crazy. Gary twitched the glasses away from the lamp, unwilling now to let his gaze settle on the man in the chair. There was the wardrobe, and behind it the poster; which, he realized with a shock that nearly made him drop the field-glasses, was the exact same poster he'd had on the wall of his bedroom, twenty years before. Bought, he remembered, on a college trip to Brussels, and treasured for its rarity: an inexpensive repro of *The Threatened Assassin*, unframed, curling slightly at one corner; instantly recognizable.

Apprehensively Gary directed the glasses back towards the man in the chair. As he centred him in the lenses, the signifiers fell one by one into place: short, dark hair; heavy, thickset build; spectacles; that faded green polo shirt. . . . Before Gary could bring himself to do much more than acknowledge the dreadful possibility (but that in itself was more than enough, was in fact altogether *too much*, thank you very kindly), the man turned away from the window, reached towards the lamp, and the light went out.

At once the room disappeared. Gary swung the field-glasses this way and that: nothing but darkness, impenetrable shadows, and above them the orange fuzz of the night-time city sky. He tried looking without the glasses; saw only the dull, imprecise bulk of unlit buildings, trees trapping the street lights in an impenetrable web of branches. With a clammy, plunging sensation like vertigo he stumbled through to the bedroom at the front of the house, yanked the curtains shut, switched the light on. He spent the best part of five minutes strewing the contents of wardrobe and drawers across the bed, until he was forced to the conclusion that at some point or another—when, he couldn't remember, and he should remember, he *should*—he must have thrown out the baggy green polo shirt he used to mow the lawn in.

He looked up from the jumble of clothing and caught sight of himself in the mirror, kneeling by the bed, face pale, eyes wide and saucer-round behind his spectacles, there beside the bedside reading lamp. How had he failed to recognize him, the man across the way? It was just like looking in a mirror, no more, no less.

* * * * *

After a mostly sleepless night, Gary got up with the first light and went into the back room determined to confront whatever hallucination he'd imagined the night before. *Things always look different in the daylight,* he told himself; and peering out of the window now he acknowledged the truth in that old cliché. Looking from his room on the second floor, it was clear to see why he'd never before noticed the house across the way. There was the backyard of his own building, and those of the houses in the next street; then between two of those houses a gap, the space between two sloping roofs, part-filled by a bare-branched tree; and there, in amongst the branches, barely visible unless you knew what you were looking for, the gable window, greyly commonplace and humdrum, of a house across the next street. The field-glasses, still focused to the correct range from the night before, isolated it, brought it up close, but revealed no further detail: the sun rising behind the house made it hard to pick up much in the shadow, except that the curtains were now drawn shut.

He spent the time it took to run his bath (and a little more besides) searching through his books, shelf after shelf, pile upon pile, all the cardboard boxes under desks and in corners, looking for this or that title he thought he'd seen over there in the room last night. The fact he couldn't find any of them didn't in itself prove anything, he knew; still, he would have been oddly relieved to find just one of the books, and he didn't.

Of course, he'd known he wouldn't, really; though the books in his flat ran well into the thousands, still he knew the contents of any given stack or shelf to a pretty fair degree of certainty. As Alison had pointed out, memorizing their positions had more or less taken the place of reading them. It had been Alison who'd nagged at him to clear out a few boxes-full for the charity shops; this just before she'd cleared out herself, the inevitable end of their fraught cohabitation. From there, it sometimes seemed, it had been a scarily straightforward progression to holes in his underpants and eating out of cans.

Still clammy from his tepid bath, he put on an overcoat and went to buy milk from the shop on the corner. It was a brisk sharp day in late autumn, and a thin wind stirred through the tree-lined terraced streets of bedsitland: pages torn from tabloid rags and voided lottery scratchcards blew around his feet as he paused, irresolute, at the corner of his road. Why not have a look, anyway? What harm could it do? Passing the corner shop, he walked to the end of the block and stood at the corner of the street parallel to his. There, six or seven down on the right, was the house with the top-floor gable window from the night before.

It was a large Victorian town house, split up, like most of the others on the street, into flats. In lieu of a front garden it had a thinly gravelled area, on which a rusty car, its windows smashed, its bonnet gaping, had been abandoned in the lee of an overflowing skip. At the side of the house stone steps led up to a covered porch; alongside the open door were six or seven separate bell-pushes. A white sign screwed on to the glossy seagreen tiles of the porch identified the premises as a Kinship Halfway House, maintained (however little evidence there might be of any actual maintenance about the place) with the support of the local council.

Standing in the driveway, Gary looked up at the front of the house. Most of the windows were curtained against the daylight, and probably stayed that way twenty-four-seven; in the others, cheap dusty dreamcatchers competed for space with stickers for local radio stations and, in one case, a set of blinking Christmas fairy lights. From where he stood he could see little of the gable window on the top floor that concerned him most.

A giggle caught his attention; looking back towards the porch he saw a wasted black-haired girl in a dirty towelling dressing-gown, watching him with a fixity he couldn't help but find slightly creepy. As their eyes met she giggled again, one hand raised in a bony fist to her mouth; on the whole, he decided, 'halfway' was a pretty optimistic estimate of her distance from the norms of everyday social interaction. Clearly, she was one of those unfortunate borderline cases, not quite damaged enough to draw down support, not quite intact enough for comfort, no more prospect in life than to attain the status of a statistic. He tried not to look as the dressing-gown blew open a little in the breeze; for her part, she made no attempt to cover the exposed portions of her scrawny body, staring instead at him with a gappy, unnervingly rigid grin.

Satisfied, if that was the word, for the time being, Gary backed away from the house. Head averted, eyes lowered, he was ideally placed to notice the little tide of rubbish spilling from an overturned wheelie-bin on to the gravel driveway; to spot, tucked away in the jetsam and trash, a common enough (yet in the context infinitely significant) item—a small marble-index notebook, just like the ones he used to write in when he was a teenager.

Heedless of the girl in the doorway, he stooped down to the rubbish, salvaged the notebook from amongst the empty cider bottles and the medical waste. Brushing the muck from its marbled boards, he saw the brand-name, and recognized it instantly; recognized too the red fabric spine, the cream lining on the inside cover, the red double margin of each blue-ruled sheet. Almost scared to look inside, Gary slipped the notebook into the pocket of his coat and strode away quickly, down the street and round the corner. The morning sun had gone behind clouds, and there was a sudden chill in the air.

Outside the corner shop he took the book from his pocket. Breathing deeply, he opened a page at random, half-knowing what he'd find, half-afraid to validate that intuition. There it was, just as he'd feared: line after line of the minuscule fountain-pen scrawl he'd affected in his adolescence, unindented, one never-ending paragraph bursting with the raw prolixity and incontinence of youth. Page after page: his handwriting, his thoughts, his guts spilled out in smudged blue ink.

He clapped the book shut, swayed for a moment on his heels, his head a kicked beehive of doubt and incredulity. When the shopkeeper dropped an empty milk crate on the pavement behind him, he let out a sudden involuntary yelp, like a kicked dog. The man moved the crate into its place by the shop door, staring at Gary as if he'd seen a ghost.

Back in his flat, Gary was at the rear window within seconds. The curtains of the window in the halfway house were still drawn closed; they remained that way until late into the evening, when on what might have been his fiftieth inspection he found the lamp lit and the man sitting there beside it in his high-backed easy chair.

Doggedly, yet with a feeling of aversion he could almost taste, Gary took up his field-glasses and surveyed the tableau of the lighted window. There was his poster; there, his old books; there, the brass lamp his mother had bought with Green Shield stamps back in 1973. And there *he* was—this other, this pretender to Gary's cast-off ephemera—sitting like a statue, gazing across the room. What was he looking at? Gary wondered. What in that Spartan cell of a place might contrive to keep his attention? Besides the sideboard, there appeared to be little or nothing by way of furniture in the room; it had the look of somewhere only recently occupied, or perhaps of somewhere in the process of being vacated.

Frustrated, Gary tried another tack. He retreated temporarily to the front room, where he felt he could probably risk a light. There he picked up the notebook he'd retrieved from the rubbish and studied it more closely. It was his handwriting, certainly; but had he really written all this drivel? These histrionic pronouncements, these shallow aperçus . . . riffling through the pages of adolescent dreck, at last he found something he could fix on and remember.

It was a diary account, in rather more detail than seemed either chivalrous or wholly warranted, of the long-delayed occasion on which he'd finally, after years of close encounters and fruitless skirmishes, lost his virginity: a fumbling drink-fuelled rendezvous between himself and an incapacitated fresher called

Emily, one boozy blacked-out night after a party in the student halls of residence. Emily; God help us. In the morning she'd said nothing except *no* and *gerroff me knickers willyer*; she'd blanked him for the rest of the term, and moved back to Bolton at Christmas.

Bad enough; but that was by no means the worst of it. If only. Reading through his own overheated testimony, Gary was appalled to discover that all the more blatantly salacious extracts—each rapt lubricious description of form or action—had been underlined in thin wavering ballpoint: two or three times in some places, depending on the intensity of the particular act or sensation being described. After one particularly purple passage, the unknown annotator (Gary felt his face go first of all scarlet, then drain entirely of blood) had added a set of exclamation marks, and the comment *ha ha ha*.

Gary hurled the book across the room; went and picked it up, then chucked it away again. What was going on, for Christ's sake? Face the facts: someone, some stranger across the way, might well have bought a few of his discarded books from the local charity shops. He might own a poster he'd once owned; it wasn't impossible. He might even, come to that, happen to look something like him. But the notebook: how could his private notebook from over twenty years ago have turned up in the rubbish outside the stranger's house?

He knew where all his stuff was, or so he'd thought. Most of the morning he'd spent going through the contents of every cupboard, every drawer, and now the place looked even more than usually as if a bomb had hit it. He'd found some of his notebooks, each with the date carefully inscribed on the flyleaf; there were gaps in the inventory, though, and he couldn't for the life of him remember what had become of the missing volumes.

Had he thrown them away? Out of the question: he still had the cinema tickets from when he'd been to see *Star Wars*, and *that* was back in school, for God's sake. Had Alison chucked them out? Quite possibly; but even if she had, the problem remained: how did they get into the rubbish bin of the halfway house? Probably only one person, Gary reflected bitterly, knew the answer to *that* one.

Back at the window, the pretender (as Gary was beginning to think of him) remained seated, waiting in that maddeningly tranquil way of his for God alone knew what. Fiercely he trained the field-glasses on him, and was surprised to see that he was no longer wearing his—Gary's—old green polo shirt. For a moment this seemed unequivocally a Good Thing, until he recognized the pretender's latest item of attire as a grey Lonsdale sweatshirt he'd left in the changing rooms of the Finsbury Park swimming baths fourteen, maybe fifteen years previously. Cursing under his breath, as if afraid the other might hear him over all that distance, he concentrated on the bright image in the window of the halfway house, missing nothing, taking it all in, thinking what to do next. Somewhere round the half-hour mark of his vigil, he was rewarded with a movement; the pretender was getting to his feet.

He crossed to the right-hand side of the room, out of the line of sight. Gary swore again, softly as before; but soon the pretender was back in his high-backed chair and once more adopting his serene seated posture. But no: it was not the same. His hands moved, he cocked his head slightly to one side: again he seemed to be talking to, or at least responding to the presence of, someone else in the room, and again Gary couldn't see across to where that person might be standing. On an impulse, he hurried through to the bathroom, where there was another, higher window he thought might do the trick.

It worked, after a fashion; though he had to stand on the very edge of the bath and lean dangerously across to his left to be able to reach the small propped-open high window. Once he settled his elbows and raised the glasses to his eyes, he was rewarded with a slightly different perspective of the room across the way. Unfortunately, it still didn't show him what he wanted to see; he could, however, make out some fresh details of the room. On the bare board floor behind the chair was a mattress with sheets and blankets; while he couldn't exactly say he recognised it *per se*, it bore an uncomfortable—in every sense of the word—resemblance to the sleeping arrangements in his very first London bedsit, the coal-cellar basement room on Knollys Road in Streatham. This was getting ridiculous. Was there any area of his life that hadn't been colonised by this usurper?

Teetering on the edge of the bathtub, Gary strained for a view of the pretender. Where had he gone? Was there someone in the room with him? Both questions were answered in dramatic fashion. All of a sudden, Gary saw two bodies—one all too familiar in his old grey Lonsdale, the other thin, white, naked, unmistakably the girl from the doorway that morning—hurtle through his field of vision, the girl first, the man hard after her. They collapsed together on to the mattress, his considerable bulk dropping full-force onto her skinny bones. The jolt of their impact must have knocked over the lamp on the nearby table, because the next thing he knew, the light went out, and Gary nearly went sprawling himself into the empty tub.

Thinking about it afterwards, as he sat in the dark by the back-room window with a cup of coffee, field-glasses at the ready should the lights go on again, the encounter he'd just witnessed took on a slightly disturbing quality. There had been a force in their collision, the pretender and the girl, a kind of desperation which had taken him aback. While it had been some time since Gary had felt even a hint of the momentum that sheer physical passion was capable of generating, he could dredge up enough of a memory of it to feel fairly sure that what he'd seen in the flat across the way had gone beyond simple fun and games. It was the contrast, as much as anything, between the customary Zen-like composure of the pretender, and the sheer violence with which he'd piled onto the mattress. More martial-arts than passion, it just didn't look good: it looked scary. And then there was the girl.

With the first stirrings of a morbid, narrowly bounded sort of arousal,

Gary considered the girl. How she'd gawked at him from the doorway that morning, grinning inanely; how her dirty towelling dressing-gown had blown apart in the wind, exposing the fishbelly whiteness of her flesh. . . . It had, after all, been quite a long time now since Alison, and it felt considerably longer from where he was sitting: all alone in a box-room, spying through binoculars on some loser in a halfway house getting extra-physical with Miss Care In The Community. Had it come to this? he asked himself. Was there really no hope? What else (he had to ask himself) had the pretender commandeered that Gary hadn't really finished with yet?

For so long incapable of feeling very much of anything, Gary was strangely thrilled to realize that he was taking it all rather personally—that he was in fact developing a distinct personal animus towards his magpie doppelgänger in the halfway house. Not only was there the matter of simple justice, he told himself, of taking back what was rightfully his, reclaiming all the jumbled discards which had somehow found their way across into the stranger's room. For the first time now the concept was starting to take shape in his head of something more—of damages, of reparation; the idea that this intolerable infringement on his existence ought, in some way, to be punished. There in the junkyard clutter of his dark back room, Gary began to understand the necessity of having a plan of action, something to take the fight across the way.

* * * * *

By morning, Gary had his plan worked out. Dawn found him sitting on a bench in the next street, opposite and a little down from the halfway house, smoking his slightly queasy way through a pack of Marlboro Lites—he'd given them up six years previously at Alison's insistence, but felt under the circumstances that they were just another aspect of his past life he might as well reappropriate, before the pretender beat him to it. This was the start of Phase Two: Gary strikes back. Action, not reaction.

Like a patient in the terminal ward coming out from under morphine to face another day, the halfway house yawned into a vague and fuzzy wakefulness. Here and there a curtain slid back, a window opened, the brimming contents of an ashtray were tipped out on to the gravel below, an ashy grey confetti. Only when the milkman and the postman and the community nurses and the care workers had come and gone, and half-a-dozen or so of the house's inhabitants (the skinny girl not amongst them) had wandered off out to haunt the shopping precinct for the day, did Gary get up from the bench and make his move.

Over-casually, he crossed the street and sloped up to the door of the halfway house. There were half-a-dozen bells to push, each with a name alongside; except for the top bell, where the name had been obliterated in a frenzy of biro scribble. Gary hoped it wouldn't be necessary to ring any of them in order to gain access; he had a cover story prepared, which cast him as a man from the council who'd come about the fire regulations, but he didn't need it. The front door swung open to his touch, admitting him into the dark hallway.

Inside, everything that wasn't nicotine yellow was chocolate brown, from the stair carpet to the bare light bulbs. Every door on every landing seemed to have been kicked in, scorched as if by blowlamps, wrenched half away from its jamb before being mended with the scruffiest, most ill-matching piece of hardboard in the builder's yard; but that was fine. What mattered most to Gary was that none of them should open as he crept past. He made it as far as the third turn of the stair before someone—he thought it was a woman, but he couldn't be sure—stuck her head round a door and coughed messily before enquiring, 'Seen him, have yer?'

A woman, yes, but so old that it really didn't make much of a practical difference. She was looking in his general direction, but not at him, which left him free to stare: the top half of her clothing appeared to be a poncho arrangement of quilts and blankets, while the bottom looked suspiciously like bin-bags. He was about to try out his man-from-the-council cover story, but she cut across his hesitancy: 'Never helped me, did he, down the tunnels? The rotten little bleeder—I know his sort, I seen 'em in the war, din' I? Oh yes. There he goes with his eye out—what?' She stopped, and looked at him more closely. 'Mister bleedin' Bingo? Eh? What you want, then?' Before he could answer she slammed the door shut. From behind it was plainly audible one last dismissive disyllable: 'Arsehole'. For a moment Gary thought of some of the things he might have said; found none of them covered it, really, and carried on up to the top floor.

Here, in the narrowing space beneath the eaves, there was only one door, at the head of the stairs. The top-floor light bulb had been removed, and there were no windows on the landing. Above the door to the top flat was a rectangle of safety glass, wired and frosted, a hint of the daylight outside. Gary tiptoed up to the door, bent to the keyhole. A glimpse of bare wall; no more. He breathed heavily for a moment or two, as much from nervous tension as from climbing the stairs, then tried, very gently, the doorknob. It turned in his hand, and before he knew it the door was open an inch. A thick sour stink came through, cutting the communal reek with its leaden basenote of stale nicotine: the smell of old dog-ends, all the cigarettes he'd smoked in a lifetime, never mind that morning on the bench. He swallowed, and pushed the door open wide.

What would he have done if the pretender had been there? The easy chair was the first thing he saw through the opened door, but its regular occupant was nowhere to be seen. Heart thumping like a cross-country runner's, Gary slipped inside the room and closed the door behind him, trying not to make a noise. A voice inside said, *You've done it now*; he ignored it. At this stage, he knew exactly what he was doing, or so he told himself as he quickly cased the joint.

There was another room beyond, a door in the far wall: a bathroom, he supposed, since the mattress on the floor suggested there was no separate bedroom. Bathroom it was, he saw when he peeked round the door: no one there, just the bare grimy fittings, toilet and bath, and a musty smell of damp. The bath in particular seemed to be in something of a state; still nauseous from his chain-smoking session on the bench, he didn't feel like looking too closely. Anyway, there was enough in the front room to keep him occupied.

On close examination, it was even worse than he'd thought. Yes, the poster was his; there was the price, in francs, pencilled on the back, bottom corner on the left. Yes, those were his books; some even had his name inside, stamped in violet ink with his old John Bull home-printing kit. There was his polo shirt, balled up in a corner, smelling unpleasantly; even the rusty old water-stain on the mattress looked familiar. But worse than that—the easy chair, he realised with an abrupt return of his vertigo, was the Parker Knoll rocker they'd had in the lounge when he was seven or eight.

He'd broken it in a game with the next-door kid, kneeling on the seat facing backwards and pretending to ride it like a cowboy on his horse: he remembered his father shouting at him, then carrying it through to the shed for mending. It had been patched up after a fashion, but it never rocked again: crippled in the springs and callipered with metal brackets, it remained in the shed, testament to his father's rudimentary DIY skills. Yet here it was, the pretender's *pièce de resistance* pulled out of nowhere, his dad's rough repairs setting it aside from all others.

This latest discovery left Gary speechless, poleaxed with the sheer surreal horror of it all, able to do nothing except flop down in the offending chair. Sickly, he wondered just how far the pretender was prepared to go with this relentless annexing of his past. How many more surprises could the sparsely furnished flat conceivably hold? Part of the answer came when he let his eyes rest on the sideboard on the back wall, the one with the books on top. Three drawers in the middle, a cupboard either end, the piped 1920s moulding knocked off one corner; it was the one that had belonged to Gary's grandparents, of course, the little retirement flat in Harlow. Shocked into submission, Gary stared at it emptily for a while before the memory started to come through. Something about the cupboards? Yes, that was it. God, yes.

The cupboard on the right: more than thirty years ago, that right-hand cupboard had held particularly unpleasant associations for him. When he was very small, a toddler still, his grandmother had bought him a toy lion, an ugly thing, not in the least cute or cuddly. The mere sight of it had sent the infant Gary into a paroxysm of screaming, and the lion had been hastily thrust inside the cupboard, where it remained for the next few years. But Nana was never one to take a hint: each time Gary's parents dropped him off there for the day, she would bring out the lion hopefully, each time with the inevitable result— the tears, the screams, the tantrums, the smacked bottom, and no treat.

For one reason and another, it took Gary a good ten minutes to get up and look inside the cupboard. If the lion had been in there—who knows? Surely he'd worked up the courage to sneak it out and burn it, back when he was ten or so . . . but there was no lion. Instead, there was a pile of miscellaneous junk, some of which, as he'd come to expect by now, looked unpleasantly familiar. Suppressing a slight gag-instinct, Gary emptied it all out on to the floor and began to sort through it. Before long he was wishing he'd left it where it was.

Here were the rest of his missing notebooks: some annotated in the same malicious style as the one he'd found outside in the rubbish, others illustrated with the kind of gynaecological line-drawings more commonly associated with the gents' bathroom. Here, a bundle of mail in a shoebox: letters he'd received, the dear-Johns of traumatised girlfriends, long-suffering creditors of his affections; letters, more worryingly, he'd written himself, sealed with meretricious kisses, damp with expedient tears, rank with the fever-stink of desperation. Please, I'm sorry, let's give it one last chance, hey, let's stay friends, you vicious bitch, hope your fucking dog dies—*no*! He hadn't written *that*. . . ? Distractedly, he stuffed the letters under the mattress.

Back in the cupboard, horrors proliferated. Here was a pair of his childhood NHS spectacles, left lens shattered from when Fatty Quantick had pushed him over in the playground. Here was the dog-eared playground copy of *Razzle* his mother had found underneath his bed. Here were photo-booth snaps dating back twenty years and more, all acne and dissatisfaction, bad hair days without number fixed in fading film. Here were the pair of panties he'd stolen from the lingerie drawer of his best mate's fiancée. Here—no. Enough. He shoved the lot back in the sideboard and fell, sweating, into the easy chair.

It had always been a comfortable chair, even after it lost its rock. Remember, too, he'd spent the last two nights awake, on watch at the window; be that as it may, it still wasn't his intention to fall asleep, there in the very lair of his quarry. But fall asleep he did, slipping by degrees into a jittery fugue of uneasy dreams, truncated only by the nag of his bladder and the realization, as he threshed into consciousness, that it was already coming on dusk.

How long had he been asleep? Too long. Sick and unrefreshed, he struggled to his feet in the gathering dimness of the slope-ceilinged room. Suppose the pretender had come back, had found him there? What would have happened? Stupid, stupid, stupid; but first he had to take care of his bursting bladder.

It was dimmer still in the bathroom, where the tiny window was high and begrimed and the sixty-watt bulb fizzed briefly and popped as he pulled on its cord. There was just enough light to take care of his most pressing need; after that, he splashed water on his hands in the sink and looked around for something to dry them on. There were no towels in the bathroom; no toilet paper, and come to that no toothbrush or soap that he could see. Wagging his damp hands in front of him like a magician about to make passes, Gary stood there helplessly for a moment; then his attention was caught once more by the mess in the bottom of the bath. A saying of Alison's came incongruously into his mind: *that's not dust, that's topsoil.* . . . Whatever it was, there was lots of it, and seemingly it came in more than one sort. He bent over, straining to see in the gloom. Was that——

Gary came bolt upright, as one by one the various constituent elements of the muck in the bathtub revealed themselves. *Hair*, he thought, his own follicles rising on the back of his neck, *hair, that's the clue right there. Loads of it, down that end—work out the hair part of it, and you've got the rest.*

Like a cat retreating in disgust from its own mess in the litter-tray, he took several frozen steps back, eyes fixed on the bathtub; shuffled sideways till he reached the open door, slammed it hard behind him. After a minute or two of deep breathing, back braced against the door, he edged over to the sideboard, keeping his back to the wall all the time. Eyes all over the room, he felt with one hand for the children's encyclopaedia (*his* encyclopaedia), fished it out from among the rest of the books (*his* books), and scuttled over to the window.

There in the last of the daylight he flicked through the pages of the encyclopaedia, looking, looking—there it was. The entry he'd remembered, the one that had made such an impact on him as a kid. Like a learner-reader's, his lips moved and he traced the lines with his finger as he read:

> A WHOLE NEW YOU: Though Mummy makes sure your sheets are kept clean and freshly laundered, did you know that each night as you sleep, you shed thousands of tiny flakes from your skin—the *epidermis*? Like your hair and your fingernails, your skin is renewing itself all the time, and the dead tissue from the outside drops off in pieces so small you can hardly see them. A snake does this all at once (there's a picture of a snakeskin on page 96) and you do it too—only gradually, a few little scales at a time. But it all adds up: just look how much of yourself you'll cast off over the course of your life, as every seven years you grow *an entirely new body*!

And there was the drawing that had lurked in the back of his mind down all the years, only to leap out again as he leant over the bathtub. A beaming cartoon man, naked and sexless, hands spread out in inexplicable pride, standing alongside a pile of cartoon dust, a great sifted mound of sloughed skin-flakes towering above his head. *Here I am*, he seemed to be saying: Gary imagined the cheerful speech bubble popping into existence above his head. *Here I am—all of me.* . . .

Just like in the bathtub. The hair had been the giveaway, clumps and mats of it like seaweed at low tide. Once he recognised that, once he acknowledged its greying wiry wave as his own, then the rest followed on inexorably. That sludgy mess, like the mud that washes round the seaweed? Epidermal shed; year upon year of it. Those shrapnel shards, down the end where the taps were? Nail-parings, brittle and yellow. Those whitish porcelain fragments, in amongst the hair? Gary ran his tongue round the inside of his bone-dry mouth, feeling gaps and cavities, the dead plastic of his dental plate.

He swallowed uncomfortably. Slowly he set the book down on the table by the smashed lamp. Straightening up again, he happened to look out of the window. Across the way, a light was on. Due to the unfamiliarity of his vantage point, it was some time before he realized that it was the light in his own back room. Silhouetted against the pallid glow was a figure standing at the window, hands braced either side of the frame: Gary didn't need his Red Army field-glasses to make out who it was.

* * * * *

He pelted down the ill-lit stairwell, heedless of the threadbare carpet underfoot, of the clattering echoes he raised. Someone was in the way as he skidded round the last corner, possibly the old woman from earlier; he pushed his way past and out of the front door, went hurtling across the street and around the block into his own road. There, he spent an agitated minute or two in the porch of his house trying to get his keys out before realizing that the front door was already open, left on the latch.

Had he left it like that? It was a thing he never did; some of the other tenants used to, sometimes, but he'd always snick it shut behind them once they were through the gate. It just wasn't safe, not in the city, not these days. Out of habit, he slipped the latch back to the locked position. Certain that the much-deferred final confrontation was here at last, Gary crept up the stairs to his flat, where another unpleasant surprise awaited him: another open door. More nervous now than ever, he pushed it wide and tiptoed up the last few stairs.

The smell alerted him first, put him on his guard before he dared feel for the switch and risk a light. All through the flat was the thick invasive stink of wet paint; the bulb in the hall, when he turned it on, hung bare from the ceiling, stripped of its Japanese paper-lantern shade. The walls, once a warm and welcoming pink, were now covered in a fresh coat of forbidding white. Underfoot, there were only dusty boards, all the carpets taken up. The pictures on the wall, the coats on their hangers, shoes and shoe-rack alike; all of them nowhere to be seen.

Gary bit his knuckle, blinking back tears of anger and bafflement. Moving with excruciating slowness on the creaky floorboards, he stole through into the back room, where the light was already switched on. There was nothing there—no books, no boxes, no furniture of any kind. Likewise, no sign of the pretender.

In every room it was the same. All his belongings had been cleared out, and the painters had followed on after, leaving each room a white featureless cell with its shiny black pane of uncurtained window-glass. Gary sank to his knees on the floorboards, moaning and sobbing as the mounting panic possessed him. What had happened to him? What was there left now of his life? Eyes stinging with abject tears, he got blindly to his feet, stumbled back into the boxroom and over to the window where he'd first looked out and seen his pretender, his arch-enemy. His foot caught something, kicked it across the bare boards. Wiping his eyes, he looked down. There were his field-glasses, come to rest against a painter's tray and roller.

It seemed almost like a mocking sort of invitation. Still sobbing, Gary picked up the glasses. He brushed away his tears and focused on the room across the way. There was the lighted window of the terrible top-floor flat. And there was the silhouette of the pretender, hands braced against the window frame—just as he'd appeared only minutes earlier, standing exactly where Gary was now.

Feet hammering on the bare floorboards, he charged through the empty flat, slamming first the inside, then the outside door shut behind him. Too late, he realised what he'd done, tried to put his shoulder in the way of the front door—no good. He tried his key: it ground uselessly against the keyhole, wouldn't even fit in. They'd changed it, of course. Locked out. No time to waste, though. Feeling as if his clenched and labouring heart might burst against his ribs, splat like an overripe windfall on concrete, he sprinted round the corner, right up to the halfway house—

—where the front door was bolted shut against him. He beat on it with his open palms, then with both fists: it rattled on its hinges, but wouldn't give way. He didn't recognize his own voice at first, mistook it for one of the chorus that yelled and snarled and gibbered at him from inside the halfway house; but when he heard the wail of sirens approaching he stopped, stood stock still in the porch, and heard himself shrieking inarticulately, one bestial howl after another.

He choked back the screams, teeth drawing blood from his tongue. The police sirens were much louder now, much closer, almost on him. It did not occur to him to stay: to tell the police what had happened, to take them round his stripped and ransacked flat, to explain to them that up there in the attic room was the man they *really* wanted, the true culprit, the thief of his very existence. None of this crossed his mind, then or afterwards; instead, he dropped down quickly from the porch steps, crept back out into the street, then ran in the shadow of the trees to a place on the corner where he could still see the driveway of the halfway house.

The police arrived, two officers who got out of their car and shone torches round the undergrowth in a desultory manner, clearly going through the motions. From his hiding place at the end of the street Gary could hear voices: someone, the old woman from the stairs, was directing them to search the premises more fully—'Take up the manhole covers, get the bleeder before 'e goes to ground down there'—and the police were telling her to go inside and lock the doors. Wistfully, almost, Gary watched as the police car drove away, and silence settled once more on the suburban street. Walking back now to the bench opposite the halfway house, he could see curtains drawing shut on the darkness and the panic outside, cosy lamplit windows rich with the promise of warmth, food, and shelter, charms against the chilly autumn evening. With a sigh, he sat down on the bench. Up on the top floor, the lights were on, but from down in the street he could see nothing of the attic room. He drew the collar of his overcoat tight against the brisk wind now springing up along the street. It was going to be a long night.

A long night, and a cold one, and most of all lonely, more lonely than he could ever have imagined. After an hour or two on the bench, staring up at the lighted window, Gary went and tried the front door of the halfway house again, quietly this time, without banging or shouting. Still locked. He pushed a few of the doorbells, but no one answered. He wandered off around the corner to the next street and his own house—could he call it that any more, though, really?—and fumbled uselessly with the lock. No good. He searched through his pockets for his mobile phone: the charge had run out, and all his contacts, including Alison's new number, were lost to him. A handful of change, some notes stuffed in his back pocket: that was all there was.

He passed some time in a café off down the high street, nursing a cold cup of tea until nine o'clock when the thickset proprietor stood with folded arms and unblinking stare by the door and saw him off the premises. There was a McDonald's open nearby, but it was full of teenagers pushing each other and shouting abuse. He walked on down the deserted high street: past pubs belching warm breaths of beer and cigarettes, past deserted amusement arcades where the bright and strident machines clanged and chattered to each other, past chip shops and kebab joints white-tiled like hospital morgues, their jaded staff leaning on the counter, staring into the darkness that lay beyond.

Buses grumbled by, fewer and fewer as the evening grew late; cars with custom trims and pumping bass bins went slamming past into the muffling maze of ring roads and intersections, the bellow of their passing deadened to a far-off headache throb. Street light passed him on to street light; junction, to junction. Obedient to the street's dictates, he plodded on, uncaring now, numb from the piercing cold and from the sheer magnitude of his defeat. At some point or other, hours gone by into the night, he found himself on open ground, leaning shivering in a bus shelter up on a hill with a view over the city. He looked out across the midnight sprawl of the capital, looked for something to hold on to in all that rambling vastness of secular solitudes; saw only his own face, ashen in the shelter-glass, drained of all meaning, and began weeping, very quietly, for all he had lost. After a while he pushed himself upright and started slowly, heavily to retrace his steps.

* * * * *

When he woke, the first thing he saw made him shut his eyes again very quickly. Grimacing, he opened them again, but the offending image had not gone away. At some point in the night a dog—call it Dog A—had wandered up to the bench on which he'd slept and chosen the stretch of pavement directly beneath his head on which to evacuate its bowels. Some time after, another dog—Dog B, surely, please God, not Dog A again—had come upon the fresh evacuate, tried unsuccessfully to consume it, and vomited the whole mess out again half-masticated. All this within a foot or so of his head, as he lay on the bench outside the halfway house. How had he managed to sleep through that?

Everything in him, skullbone to ankles, groaned as he tried to get up. Involuntarily, he grunted in pain; hoarse and parched, he sounded like the crows that flapped and jostled in the conker-trees above his head. He leant on the bench for a while, stooped over like an old man, until his stiff tendons allowed him to stand upright. He peered through gummy eyes at the halfway house; to his unspeakable relief, the front door was propped open again.

He'd made it back to the bench some time in the absolute pit of the night. There, he'd waited, cold and exhausted, for some sign of life in the slumbering block, some latecomer or early riser, but there had been nothing. Only the light in the attic window, high and unreachable. The last thing he remembered, he'd been staring up at the light: if truth be told, he found it hard to remember much of anything before that. How had he got here?

Now, he shuffled forward into the street, heading across the way to the halfway house. A car swerved round him, horn blatting out a raucous double-pump of warning; he paid it no mind. Only the doorway mattered now; only inside. Climbing the stone steps to the porch, slipping inside the building, he hardly noticed the doors that opened, then closed again hastily at his approach; dragging his feet up each successive flight of stairs, he never heard the muttering of voices in the stairwell down below, the whispers along the landings. Somehow, he made it to the top floor, where the door to the attic room stood open just a chink. Heedless of who or what might be waiting inside, Gary tottered forwards. The door yielded to the pressure of his outstretched hands, and he was inside the room.

He drank greedily from the tap at the bathroom sink, splashing the chlorine water over his reddened, frost-nipped face, not bothering to look over his shoulder at the bath and its contents. Back in the living-room, he collapsed on to the mattress, groaning afresh as his bones slammed down on the flattened springs. For a while he just lay there, exhausted, sapped of all volition. Rolling over on to his side he winced as a hard object dug into his ribs. There, in amongst the clammy sheets, were his old Red Army field-glasses from across the way.

Inured by now to any development, he crawled across the floor on his hands and knees, propped himself up against the window sill, fumbled the glasses to his eyes. There was his old house across the way; there, he saw, was the pretender, standing in the back-room window, every inch the king of the castle. Blinking away the last of his sleep-crustiness, squinting into watery focus, he saw without surprise that the room was once more furnished. All his old belongings had been returned, put back into place, only tidier now, more tastefully arranged. There was an air of domestication about the place, a woman's touch——

And naturally there she was, Alison; moving into view alongside the pretender, resting a hand on his shoulder, snuggling close as he slipped an arm around her waist. She looked happy; happier than she'd been in a long time, Gary guessed, happier than he could ever remember, certainly. But he could remember so little . . . already they seemed like strangers there in the room across the way, the dark-haired man with the smiling girl at his side, the happy couple, captured for a moment in a stray glimpse through a city window.

Gary nodded slowly, bleakly, and lowered the field-glasses. Behind him the door to the room creaked open. With an effort he turned around, still on his knees. There in the doorway was the skinny girl, wearing the same dirty bathrobe she'd had on the day before—or was it the day before that? How many days now? It was no use; he couldn't remember. The girl's mouth was stretched in a rictus grin, but in her eyes there was only a terrible, mushy vacancy as she let the robe slip from her shoulders and fall at her bare feet. Underneath she was naked, horribly emaciated, great bruises livid against the pasty whiteness of her skin, the random tattooing of trackmarks and contusions, the map of her fragility.

Still grinning, she edged around the wall, never once taking her eyes off him. When she reached the mattress, she giggled vacuously, then sank to her haunches, holding out her sticklike arms in an unmistakable gesture of invitation. Gary stared back at her, mouth slack, then became aware he was still holding something. He looked for quite a long time at the field-glasses without seeming to take in their nature, let alone their purpose. Shaking his head slightly, he let them drop to the floor. Dimly recollecting what he had been about to do just a moment ago, he shuffled forward on his knees across thin crunching shards from the field-glasses, from the shattered chimney of the table lamp, on into the skeleton embrace of the mad girl.

The Cross Talk

Rick Kennett

ONLY LATER DID IT COME BACK to him with any significance that the telephone rang that afternoon with an odd, flat sound. Not its normal tone.

Half asleep on the couch, Jeff sat up, a twinge of middle-age backache making itself known in his lower spine as he swung his legs to the floor.

'Lucy! Lucy?'

There was no answer from anywhere in the house and the phone was still ringing.

'What's the use of being married if you have to answer the phone yourself,' Jeff muttered. He shuffled across to the other side of the living-room, picked up the receiver. 'Hello?'

Nothing. Not even the honey bee drone of the dial tone.

He hung up, grumbling, then leaned through the lounge door. 'Lucy?' Jeff frowned. 'Where is she?' He clucked his tongue, suddenly remembering. 'Of course. Her shopping spree. Brian's coming home tonight.'

If Jeff was being honest with himself he had to admit he wasn't entirely looking forward to meeting again with his estranged son. He'd left the house two years ago, parting on bad terms with his father. 'You never take the time to understand me.'

Jeff had never actually uttered the word *disappointment*, but he'd come close to it. 'You never do what I tell you,' had been his reoccurring phrase that had finally pushed Brian away. Now a reunion, brokered by Lucy, the mother, the wife, who had always tried to see both sides. Though she would often tell Jeff that Brian was not a child anymore. 'You can't tell him how to live.'

Brian was nineteen now——

No, must be nearer twenty.

—yet despite misgivings Jeff was curious as to what his son's independence had wrought. Had he made anything of himself? Was he still as stubborn as he had been or was he more amenable now?

Jeff turned around and was once more heading for the couch when the phone started again. He glared at it, waiting for it to stop. But it kept ringing, that odd, flat sound. Not its normal ring. Jeff shrugged and picked up the receiver again.

'Hello?'

No answer.

'Hell-o!'

Still nothing. He was about to drop the receiver back into its cradle when a faraway voice said, 'Dad.'

Jeff pressed the receiver close to his ear. 'Brian? Brian, is that you?'

'Dad? Dad?' The voice grew louder. 'Yes, it's me. It's Brian.'

Two years away and he didn't sound any different from the day he left.

In a voice cracked with emotion Jeff said, 'Hello, son. How have you been?'

'Dad, I need your advice.'

Jeff hesitated. He didn't know how to answer. His independent son was asking his advice. 'About what?' he asked carefully.

'Dad, I want to know which way to go.'

'Which way to go? I don't quite——'

'I need to know whether I should go on or go back.'

'Go on or go back? Brian, you're not making sense.'

'I don't know how to express it. I'd like to go back.'

'Go back?' said Jeff incredulously.

'Yes.'

'Absolutely not!'

'But Dad, I want to . . . and yet, now that I'm here it seems wrong somehow.'

'Where's *here*?' said Jeff with some of the old annoyance with his son coming back into his voice. It was then that he heard that other sound on the line: an echoing babble, unintelligible and faint in the background, as if Brian were calling from a crowded, noisy hall. 'Brian, I don't understand. Are you in some sort of trouble?'

'No. No trouble.'

'Then where are you?'

'On the highway . . . I'm on the highway.'

'All right. Now tell me what's happened.'

'No time to explain——'

'You're still the same, aren't you? Everything I tell you you gainsay.'

'No . . . no time . . . no time.' The voice was fading again, as if to underline that there was no time. 'Please, Dad. I'll do what you say. You were right . . .

you were right . . . but I need to know now: should I go on or should I go back?'

'You'll listen to me for once?'

'Yes! Yes!'

'Go on.'

'Okay, Dad, I will go on.'

'You know, Brian, your mother and I really want to see you——' Jeff stopped, aware he was now talking to silence. The background sounds, the faraway babble had cut off suddenly, without even the click of a receiver being hung up.

Brian's was a closed coffin funeral. His highway accident had smashed him up very badly, though had not killed him outright. He had lingered.

'I said go on,' Jeff whispered to himself at the graveside. Lucy, crying mother's tears, never understood what he meant by this; and her husband, never forgiving, never explained.

Phones make him nervous now. He still waits for one to ring again with that odd, flat sound, not its normal tone.

The Belfries

Paul Finch

THE FIRST TIME STELLA REALISED there was something odd about the new housing estate was the second night of her residence in it.

She sat up in bed, still fuddled with sleep, but staring at the thinly curtained window. Little light shone through, as no street lamps had been erected yet. Her digital alarm clock gave a faint neon glow—2.15. Beside her, Matt stirred, muttering in his sleep. He turned over under the duvet. Stella considered waking him, but then thought better. He had a long drive ahead. The last thing she wanted, three weeks into their marriage, was to make his already difficult job even harder. Especially over something like this . . . a suggestion of a scream, which had ceased the moment she'd opened her eyes.

'Probably a nightmare,' he'd mumble. 'Go back to sleep.'

He'd be right of course. But that didn't stop Stella putting her robe on and making her way downstairs. In the hall, she negotiated the various boxes and packing cases still waiting to be opened, and stepped outside.

It was mid-July, but the skies over southern England were crystal-clear and speckled with stars. For that reason, it was slightly colder than usual, though Wiltshire in summer was rarely cold in the way a northerner like Stella would understand the term.

The silence in the cul-de-sac was total. There was no passing rumble of late-night traffic, no clatter of fallen milk bottles as cats needled past, no raucous chuckles as clubbers wound their way home. The other houses were dark and lifeless. Handsome though they were, built in the country-cottage style with white coving and fake black beams, not one of them as yet was tenanted. Dusty shadows bulged in their putty-smeared windows.

Stella wondered again about the scream. It had been a woman—of that she was certain—and a woman not just in terror, but in pain. Agony even.

Stella remembered the shrill, wavering tone . . . prolonged, it seemed, for minutes. No movie scream, that. Raw, gutsy, real.

Of course, that was nonsense. It had to be. Yawning, she turned and went back into the house. As far as she knew, Monkton Bassett was the nearest town, and that was four miles distant. There was nobody close enough for her to have heard them scream. And even if there was, what did it have to do with her?

* * * * *

Breakfast was the usual chaotic affair.

Their gleaming new kitchen had looked wonderful and spacious in the show home, but Matt and Stella had wasted no time cluttering it with their own stuff, and two days into their occupancy it was already a mess: the sink was stocked with dirty crockery; toast crumbs and butter smears covered the worktops; shreds of packaging paper littered the tiled floor.

'Be nice to have a morning paper, wouldn't it,' Matt said, drinking tea as he combed his thick, dark hair.

As always when he was on the road, he looked immaculate, his suit smartly fitted and razor-sharp. Miraculously, considering that he was late and rushing, he'd avoided dripping marmalade onto his florid tie. It was this sort of fastidiousness which made him so good at his job.

'Be nice to have a newsagent,' said Stella, sliding more bread into the toaster. 'I've never seen a place with as few amenities.'

Matt brushed a few imaginary motes of dust from his lapels. 'I wouldn't worry. Everything'll be up and running in no time. You'll see.'

She handed him his case, pecking him on the lips. 'I don't know why they're taking so long. Every house is built.'

He smiled that warm smile of his, hazel eyes twinkling, then leaned down and kissed her properly. 'Bit out of town, that's all,' he said. 'Don't worry. They're queuing up to move to this part of the country. Be a smashing place to live in a few months.'

Stella nodded. She accepted that, of course. Wiltshire was possibly England's most scenic county, all rolling downs and green woods, not to mention the home of fascinating attractions like Avebury and Stonehenge. Even new housing estates, like this one, were built in the rural style to complement the verdant havens surrounding them. What more could she want . . . a Manchester lass, who'd spent her entire girlhood in tower-block land?

Outside, Matt put his briefcase in the boot of his Peugeot, then took his jacket off and hung it in the back, straightening out any creases. Stella watched him. He was a software salesman by trade and regularly travelled the length of the country. She'd known that long before he'd proposed to her, but the point of moving down south had been to bring him closer to the majority of his customers. Thus far, it hadn't seemed to reduce the amount of time he was spending away.

'When are you back?' she asked.

He considered. 'Sevenish. Not much later. Be all right?'

She nodded. 'Plenty to do here, 'til I get a job.'

Matt shook his head admonishingly. 'Stell . . . I've told you, I don't want you to get a job. It's not as if we need you to. Just stay here and enjoy yourself.'

She nodded again, wondering if he realised exactly what he was saying when he told her that. A moment later he'd gone, the Peugeot vanishing around the corner in a cloud of builders' dust. Stella stayed where she was for a moment, thinking how glad she'd be to see one or two hardhats now, even if she was only clad in a short robe and had her long red hair down past her shoulders. She could put up with more than wolf-whistles, she thought, so long as it meant she wouldn't be on her own all day.

Still . . . it was important to get things in perspective. She had a lovely new four-bedroom home, a handsome husband pulling in 40K a year, and a summer of relative leisure ahead. The sky was pebble-blue, birds sang, the neat lawns in front of the houses were an impossible green. What did she have to feel down about?

Five minutes later, she was back inside and had changed into sneakers, jeans, and a paint-stained sweatshirt. She pinned her hair up, put the kettle on, and sat down to consult the day's itinerary. There were still ornaments to place, clothes to unpack, bedrooms to decorate.

Before she did any of that, however, she called her mother in Manchester. The phone rang out a few times, then it was answered.

'Hello?' said a familiar, sing-song voice.

A tear came to Stella's eye, the way it had the morning after their wedding, when it had suddenly struck her that the happy home-life she'd enjoyed for twenty-four years was over.

'Hi, it's me.'

'Stella! Now then, how was France . . .'

Before Stella could reply, her mother's voice began to fade. A fuzzing of static replaced it, then the line went dead. Stella gazed at the receiver. She dialled again. The second time, her mother's number was engaged . . . the old dear was probably still on the line. Stella hung up and waited. The third time she called, the phone rang out and was promptly answered, only for another ferocious crackle to intervene and the connection to break.

Irritated, she banged the receiver down. Matt had forewarned her that new houses always looked amazing, but that much of this was cosmetic and that there were usually as many problems with them as there were with old ones. They'd have to grin and bear it. Stella was willing to, but she'd never expected this. It made her feel even more isolated.

Determined not to be beaten, she finished her tea and made her way upstairs to the first of the spare bedrooms, the second largest. She wasn't pregnant yet, but she'd already made her mind up that this would be the nursery. She hadn't wanted to tempt fate by purchasing children's wallpaper, so she'd opted for something neutral; flower patterns in pastel shades. She surveyed the four blank walls for a moment, sizing them up. Before her, the trestle was already laid out, the paste mixed.

Stella rolled her sleeves back and got to it.

Considering she had no prior experience of decorating, it went surprisingly well, and by noon she had two walls covered. She stood back, pleased; no wrinkles could be seen, the joins were almost invisible.

Deciding she owed herself some lunch, she popped into the bathroom to wash her hands, then went down to the kitchen. A plate of sandwiches was waiting in the fridge. She was just taking it out, when she sensed movement. Startled, Stella looked round and saw a figure flit past the side window, as if walking towards the rear garden. It had looked like a young woman with a pony-tail, carrying a shoulder-bag. Stella glanced out through the main window into the garden proper, expecting the visitor to appear. Then the doorbell rang.

She couldn't believe it. No one at all, then suddenly people were everywhere!

She hurried down the hall and opened the front door on a prim-looking middle-aged lady, dressed in a kilt and grey sweater, her hair thickly curled and silver-rinsed.

'How do you do,' said the lady, with a pleasant smile. 'I'm Mrs Mimms, Margaret. I thought I'd introduce myself and welcome you to the neighbourhood.'

'Oh . . .' For a moment Stella was lost for words. Five minutes ago, she'd have been delighted to find that somebody was living close by, but now she was distracted by the knowledge that they had a trespasser.

'Well . . . I'm really pleased . . .' she stammered. 'Look . . . do you mind hanging on, just for a sec?'

Still beaming, Mrs Mimms stood back as Stella stepped out and walked quickly around the side of the house. A high slatted fence separated their property from the one next door. It also enclosed the garden, which was a large grassed area, perhaps thirty metres by forty. There was no other way out of it. Whoever the girl with the pony-tail was, she'd still be down there.

Which was odd. Because she wasn't.

Stella stood at the corner of the deserted lawn. After a moment, she ventured forwards, wondering if the girl was hiding. Not that there was any place to hide. A wooden shed occupied one corner, but as far as Stella knew, Matt kept it locked. She checked all the same—it was. Glancing in through its dusty window, she saw only plant-pots and garden tools.

She turned, baffled. Had the girl climbed over a fence? Was that possible in such a short time? Stella set off back. Maybe Mrs Mimms would have an answer.

'I'm terribly sorry about that,' she began, as she rounded the front of the house. 'You didn't have anyone with you, by any chance . . .'

Her words tailed off. Mrs Mimms was no longer there. Perplexed, Stella walked to the end of the drive. There was no sign of anyone, either up or down the cul-de-sac. It was always possible she'd offended the neighbour, she supposed. But that seemed unlikely. In any case, what had the elderly lady done, sprinted back to her house?

Stella went indoors. She stood in the hallway, deliberating. If people were playing games with her, she decided crossly, they'd better watch out. But somehow she didn't think it was that. For one thing, she hadn't been here long enough to make any enemies.

Then she heard something upstairs. Stella froze. She glanced up, listening intently.

There it was again . . . a faint, almost furtive rustle, as if someone was going through paperwork and trying to be quiet about it. A chill ran down her spine. One thing she hadn't considered was the possibility that mysterious, vanishing Mrs Mimms had invited herself in.

'Hallo?' Stella said, warily ascending. 'Mrs Mimms? Is that you?'

Paper rustled again, this time loudly. Stella imagined pages turning. She began to wonder if she or Matt had left anything out which might be of interest to an intruder: a photograph album, a ledger of accounts?

'Hallo?' she said again. 'Who's up there?'

Still there was no reply. Stella reached the top of the stairs. To her right lay the master bedroom, the secondary bedroom—which Matt intended to use as a study—and the box-room. To her left lay the nursery and the bathroom. From where she stood, Stella couldn't see into any one of them, but all was still. No shadows flickered in doorways, nothing had been moved. She held her ground, uncertain, frightened. The silence seemed to grip her.

'Mrs Mimms?' she said again. 'Are you up here?'

Paper crackled furiously. Stella jumped. It had come from the rooms on the left—to be precise, the nursery. Before she knew what she was doing, she was rushing towards it. Stella's blood was up. They had no right. . . .

She burst in, but the shout on her lips died. As she stood there, in the otherwise empty room, another sheet of wallpaper ungummed itself and rustled noisily to the floorboards. Downstairs, the phone began to ring.

Stella had seen the funny side before she reached it, and was still nervously tittering when she answered.

'Everything all right?' Matt asked. He sounded far away. Traffic roared all around him.

'Yeah,' she replied, glad to hear his voice. 'Just me being daft. I thought someone had come in.'

'What!'

'No . . . it's nothing. I made a mistake.'

'Oh . . . right.' He didn't sound convinced. 'Er, look love . . . I'm going to be a bit later than I thought.'

That sobered her. 'Oh.'

'It's nothing too serious,' he said. 'I've got to go on to Newport. There's another job on. Probably take me 'til about six. Should be home for nine.'

'Fine,' she said, trying to keep the disappointment out of her voice.

'Sure everything's all right?'

'Course. What could be wrong? The phone seems to be working again . . . that's something.'

'Why, what was the matter with the phone?'

'I called mum earlier. Couldn't get through.'

Matt sounded puzzled. 'Give her another buzz. I had no problem, and I'm on the mobile.'

'I will.'

'So . . . I'll see you later, okay?'

'See you,' she said.

'Love you, babes.'

'Love you too.'

After she'd hung up, Stella did try her mother again. Once more the call was answered quickly; once more the sweet old voice was lost in a storm of static. Seconds later, the line went dead. Stella considered calling the operator, but finally decided against it. Matt had got through all right . . . it had to be her mother's phone that was on the blink.

Stella ate a desultory lunch, and in the afternoon decided to do some unpacking. After her abysmal decorating efforts, it seemed the safest option.

The day they'd moved in, the haulage team had humped a lot of gear into the garage and left it there. It hadn't been the ideal thing, but the alternative would have been to render the house's already chock-a-block corridors impassable. It had never been the intention, however, to make the garage into a lumber-room, so that seemed the best place to start. Stella entered by the internal connecting door, but found it dark and stuffy in there, so she opened the main garage door and dragged a couple of boxes out onto the drive.

She was sorting through their contents when she heard the first strains of music. Initially, she barely noticed. Then, suddenly, it registered. She glanced up. By the sounds of it, somebody was playing a radio. Workmen probably. That was good, Stella thought. Yes, that was definitely good. Happier, she continued to pick through the box. She even recognised the song. It pre-dated her, but she'd heard it from time to time. It was a piece by that now-extinct New Wave band, Siouxie and the Banshees; an old Beatles number rehashed—'Dear Prudence'. Something to do with psychosis. Not very pleasant, but at least it was a sign of life.

The same track, however, continued to play for what seemed like the rest of the afternoon. Stella only noticed this after about half an hour. She stood up, brushed herself down, and listened curiously. Whoever it was, they were clearly a Siouxie fan. This was . . . what, the fifth or sixth time it had now been on? She walked to the end of the drive, and only then did the music begin to fade. Eventually, it fell silent.

As before, the cul-de-sac lay empty. From what Stella could see of the adjoining street, that too was deserted.

* * * * *

Matt was home that evening earlier than expected, which after the day his wife had had, was more than a bonus. For dinner, they ate pork in sweet sauce with green vegetables. Matt opened a bottle of chilled Chardonnay. He was in a good mood.

'I don't know what you mean,' he said, laughing. 'There's nothing weird about this place.'

'After everything I've told you that's happened?'

'There'll be a perfectly rational explanation,' he replied, tucking into his meal. 'There always is.'

Irritated, Stella laid down her cutlery. 'All right then . . . how big would you say this estate was?'

'I don't know . . . a few square miles at least.'

She nodded. 'Exactly. It's massive, isn't it?'

'Okay, it's massive. So what?'

'You don't think it unnatural there's no one living on it at all except us?'

'Why?'

'What do you mean "why"?' she said. 'These are supposed to be desirable executive properties, in the most beautiful corner of the West Country!'

Matt dabbed his lips with his napkin. 'That doesn't mean anything. There always has to be a first person to move in. It's not as if we've been here very long.'

Stella had to concede that point. 'I just feel so marooned,' she finally said.

'Get out of it,' he replied. 'You've said yourself there are people knocking around.'

'Yeah . . . they've been a real comfort so far, haven't they?'

'Look,' he said, 'if it's really bothering you, why don't you pop in to see the sales agent in the office? Ask them what the score is . . . you know, when are there some new families moving in.'

Stella shrugged. 'It's not worth that.'

Matt finished his meal. 'It's up to you, of course, only . . . I might as well tell you, I'm away for two days from tomorrow.'

She sat back and gazed at him. 'Thanks for breaking it to me gently.'

'It's a bit sudden, I know,' he said. 'But there's a job up north and no one else to cover it. Sorry, love.'

Stella knew there was no point in making an issue of it. Matt's career was everything to them at that moment. As well as this brand new home, it had also bought them a sumptuous honeymoon in Provence, and the way he racked up bonuses, it promised even more. There was an emotional side to it as well.

Matt was a Londoner by origin. It was during a sales trip to Manchester that he'd first met Stella. She couldn't thank his job enough for that. Just so long, of course, as he didn't meet anyone else. Not that she expected this from a lovely guy like Matt.

'You'll be away overnight then?' she asked.

''Fraid so.'

She could tell his regret was genuine. She leaned over the table and kissed him. 'Just keep up the good work.'

* * * * *

Matt left before seven to get a good start, and Stella busied herself around the house for two hours before setting off for a morning stroll. She didn't intend to walk over to the sales office, which was located beside the main entrance to the estate, on its far eastern boundary, but that was eventually the route she took. All the way there, she saw no one. House-front after house-front . . . in all cases, the small lawns were neatly cropped, the token flower-beds freshly weeded. Yet no cars occupied any of the drives; no curtains were visible behind windows.

At length, Stella reached the office. It was built into what would eventually be the double-garage to the first of three clearly defined show homes. A row of flagpoles stood in front of it. To one side there was a huge billboard bearing the building firm's slogan and telephone number, and the name of this particular development: 'The Belfries'.

She entered through a sliding door with hanging baskets to either side, profusions of blooms pouring out of them. The interior was done in cream and hung with water-colours depicting the many styles of housing available here. In the centre there was a desk and telephone, with an empty swivel-chair behind. Stella resolved to wait, knowing that sales negotiators often nipped into the show houses to use the kitchen facilities.

'Hallo dear,' said a voice.

Stella turned sharply. She hadn't even heard the woman come in.

'Hallo,' she said in return. For a second, she didn't know what else to say.

As if appreciating this, the woman sidled around her and settled into the swivel chair. According to the plastic badge on her blue silk lapel, her name was Enid.

Enid was not the tidiest person Stella had seen in a sales job. Her bleached blonde hair hung in limp curls, the make-up she wore on her wizened face was clumsily applied; her lipstick too glossy, her eye-shadow too heavy. The blue tunic was crumpled and unbuttoned.

'How can I help you?' she asked.

'Er . . .' Stella felt herself blush. 'Well, actually, I already live on the estate.'

'I know you do, dear, I know you do.'

'Oh, right.' Stella laughed. 'Well . . . I was just wondering, it seems like a silly question I suppose, but . . . is there anybody else here apart from ourselves? On the estate, I mean?'

Enid frowned. 'Why do you ask?'

Stella shrugged. 'It seems so quiet.'

'But that's its main selling point. The peace and quiet.'

'Yes, but not this quiet, surely?'

'You mean you're a little bit lonely?' Enid said understandingly.

'A little bit, I suppose, yes.'

Enid nodded. 'Not to worry. It might come as a surprise, but there are already others on the estate. And the way things are going, there'll be lots more. Lots.'

The woman said this with great enthusiasm, which left Stella even more bewildered. 'Oh . . . I didn't know. I mean, I've hardly seen anyone yet.'

'Well you won't, dear,' said Enid. 'It's the commuter belt, you see. Monkton Bassett is the nearest town and it's four miles away. Not even a bus route set up yet.'

'I know,' Stella replied glumly.

'You could always walk there, of course.' Enid added this afterthought with all seriousness. 'A healthy young woman like you. Glorious countryside on the way. Absolutely glorious. I only wish I could pop down there myself.'

* * * * *

Even for as healthy a young woman as Stella, who did aerobics and was planning to join a local gym the moment they got settled in, a four-mile hike to Monkton Bassett was out of the question. Not because she didn't fancy the exertion, but because she didn't want to find herself on some lonely country road after dark. The thought of visiting the town grew on her, though. At least there'd be shops to look in, people to talk to. Later that morning, she changed into a t-shirt and denim cut-offs, then dug her old bicycle out of the garage. It was rusty and squeaked, but it would make a nice change. Stella hadn't cycled anywhere in six years.

She wheeled the old machine to the end of the drive and was about to mount up when she spotted something. At the entrance to the cul-de-sac, a yellow football was sitting in the middle of the road. She pedalled over to it. It was of old, beaten leather, but fully inflated and in good condition; not the sort of thing to be left lying around. She glanced about. As always, the many avenues were bare of life.

Shrugging, she cycled away. It was scarcely her problem. When she was about sixty yards off, however, she looked back and saw a small blond-haired boy standing in the road watching her. He was in shorts, a white jumper, and blue Wellingtons. He was also holding the football under his arm. When Stella looked again, he'd gone.

She pressed on, putting it from her mind. A few moments later, she'd left the estate and was on her way towards Monkton Bassett. One thing she couldn't deny about this place: as Enid had said, it was glorious. The closest thing to rusticity in the urban sprawl of Greater Manchester had been the wild moors of Heyden and Saddleworth; great sweeps of rock-strewn heather, hard to get up to and even harder to get down from. This was altogether gentler. For half an hour, she followed shady lanes through vast breaks of larch and alder-wood, beyond which lay a rolling downland, quilt-worked with crops and pasture. Here and there, the road dipped between hedgerows thick with leaf and brier, splashed all the way with vivid colours, the blues and pinks of forget-me-not, the orange of apricots, the reds of wild strawberries.

Monkton Bassett was a pleasant market town, typical of England's shire counties. Tudor-fronted pubs faced onto tight, cobbled squares, where backpackers haggled with stallholders for bric-à-brac, and beefy men, red-faced and stripped to their shirtsleeves, sat jovially together, consuming ploughman's lunches and pints of frothing ale. Wherever you walked, there were narrow, meandering sidestreets, filled with craft shops, coffee bars, booksellers. Many roofs were thatched, many passages arched and hung with ivy. There was a constant gabble of rural English voices.

Stella idled about at her leisure. Just being in company lifted her spirits. At lunchtime, she strolled into a beer-garden and treated herself to chicken and chips and half a cider, which in this part of the country was the real thing— Scrumpy Jack, served ice-cold and filled with apple slices. Later on, she bought herself an area guidebook. It was late afternoon when she slipped into a brasserie for a cream tea. Under low oak-beams, she leafed through her new purchase, and only then did it strike her what an eccentric region she and her husband had moved to.

Beyond the Salisbury Plain, it was said, in a village called Odstock, a succession of churchwardens had died violently through the curse of a Gypsy queen. In Salisbury itself, legends persisted that a child bishop had once presided over the district; a statue in the cathedral allegedly represented him. Silbury Hill was a vast mound of earth, raised by human hands in neolithic times for no known reason. Then there were the great henges, the hillside figures, the giants' graves, the ancient temples denoting convergence points for ley-lines, the many scenes of witchcraft and haunting. The list went on . . . fascinating, and all so local.

'Miss?' someone said.

Stella glanced up. A waitress in a pinafore was standing there.

Stella smiled. 'Another tea please.'

'Sorry miss. We're closing now. We close at five.'

'Oh.' Stella looked at her watch. She hadn't realised she'd been there so long. 'Oh . . . right.'

When she stepped outside, she found the day had cooled. In the eastern sky, shreds of salmon cloud suggested the morrow would be just as fine. For now, though, there was only the brewing dusk and the long cycle-ride back to The Belfries.

It took her the best part of two hours, and there were more uphill stretches than she remembered. As she pedalled slowly onto the estate, her calves ached. The hard saddle was a killing pressure beneath her buttocks. She glanced sideways at the sales office as she passed it. It was locked; there was no sign of Enid.

Stella wove her way through an empty maze of roads, feeling progressively more uncomfortable. She now knew there were other people here—she'd seen them—but once again, there was no sign of life when she most wanted it.

The house, when she let herself in, was cold and still. A minor relief, however, was the light of a single message flashing on the telephone answering-machine. Stella hit the playback button, then hobbled around the lounge, drawing curtains, switching lamps on.

'Stella . . . it's me,' said a distant voice.

It was her mother.

'I was waiting for you to call back . . .' And slowly, inevitably, the message faded into static.

Stella could have wept with frustration; but, determined to be strong, she went upstairs and ran herself a hot bath. At least there was nothing wrong with the plumbing. Later on, more relaxed, she put on her robe, tied her hair in a towel, and wandered down to curl up in front of the TV. Outside, night had fallen. And on The Belfries it really was night. Stella resolved not to even glance at the black veil beyond the window.

A few seconds later, though, light blazed there. Despite herself, she jumped to her feet. Headlamps. A car was pulling up. Stella yanked the drapes aside. To her disbelieving joy, she saw Matt's Peugeot drawing slowly along the kerb. She even saw Matt behind the wheel. He was steering carefully, peering out through the side window as if looking for something.

She dashed out into the hall, unchained the front door, and ran onto the drive. The first thing that struck her was how dark and quiet it was . . . had he switched his lights and engine off?

No. Apparently.

Because then she saw him back at the entrance to the cul-de-sac. His Peugeot was turning onto the next street. Wildly, she hared after it. Had the silly buffoon forgotten where he lived? She almost laughed. Anything was possible in this place.

When she got to the corner, though, there was no sign of Matt or his car down any of the adjoining streets. Stella stood there for several moments, her smile gradually waning.

When she got back indoors, she made sure to lock everything, then went straight up to bed. Sleep evaded her, however. She tossed and turned for what seemed like hours. At about two o'clock, the music started.

Stella sat stiffly up. It was the same song from before—'Dear Prudence', with all its eerie tones and vocals. For a moment she was helpless, shivering. At length, though, she climbed from the bed. It was coming from somewhere outside. At the rear perhaps. Slowly, Stella made her way to the back bedroom. Light was shining into it. She approached the window.

Beyond the garden, on the other side of the fence, there was a similar house to their own. Stella had assumed it empty. Now she realised she'd been wrong. In its upstairs window, a light was showing. And in that light there was a figure. A very distinct figure. The girl from before, the one with the pony-tail and shoulder-bag. Even now, she still held that bag. But hey . . . since when was that a crime?

Stella backed away. When she climbed under her duvet again she was less worried. Two mysteries solved, it seemed: first of all the music—its source was now obvious; secondly, the figure walking past the house the other morning— the shoulder-bag girl taking a short cut.

The spooky music droned on for another hour, but Stella was now oblivious to it. It implied another human presence, and just at the moment that was all she wanted. The last thing she remembered thinking was that in the morning she'd go and call on the shoulder-bag girl.

*****

It wasn't hard to find the right house. At least, Stella assumed it was the right house. It was one of many similar detached homes in another empty street, but when she knocked on the front door, it creaked open.

Stella waited on the step, a nervous smile on her face. 'Hallo?' she said. 'Anyone home?'

Slowly, however, it dawned on her that the hallway was uncarpeted, as were the stairs. The walls were bare plaster, the light fittings just nests of disconnected wires. With a sinking feeling, she ventured inside. The lounge was completely unfurnished. Where some future occupant might install an ornate gas-fire, there was now a breezeblock hearth with builder's chalk marks around it. She walked through to the kitchen, finding the brand-new units untouched, still sheathed in polythene.

By the time she'd ascended to the upper floor, Stella was trembling. She knew what she'd find—more empty rooms, dusty, strewn with wood-shavings. She wasn't wrong. The room where she'd spotted the girl was the most barren. Its bulb socket was empty, despite the fact she'd seen a light on the night before. Stella doubted there'd even be any power to switch a light on with.

She retreated to the top of the stairs. The silence was numbing. On all sides, entrances to rooms gaped. The front door seemed a long way away. Stella descended slowly towards it, but from somewhere above, woodwork creaked . . . loudly, as if under a ponderous footfall. Stella began to run, scrambling down the remaining few stairs, but always the door seemed further away. There were vast regions in this house . . . even now, she realised, something was hurtling towards her from its farthest corner, something determined to intercept her before she escaped.

She burst out from the front door with a scream, and threw herself onto the lawn, gasping. Seconds passed before she was able to clamber to her feet and lurch to the pavement. Behind her, the house sat quietly, its windows blank eyes reflecting the morning light. Crying to herself, but also enraged that she'd reacted the way she had, Stella staggered around the corner into her own cul-de-sac. She'd call Matt and tell him to get home immediately. Okay, the phone was dicky, but so far he'd been able to contact her and . . .

She stopped in her tracks. In the circular section of road at the far end of the cul-de-sac, there was a woman. A woman with long dark hair, wearing high heels and a green cocktail dress—sexy, figure-hugging, split to the thigh. More baffling still, she appeared to be lost. She was turning slowly, as if in a daze. Stella found herself rooted to the spot. She knew there was something wrong before the woman even looked at her, but when the woman did . . .

Stella thought she was going to collapse. Even from this distance, forty yards or so, she could recognise the results of savage brutalisation: the black and blue flesh, the smashed nose and mouth, the dried bloodstains all down the front of that slinky dress.

Clapping a hand to her mouth, Stella reeled towards her open front door. Before she knew what she was doing, she'd blundered inside, grabbed up the phone, and dialed nine-nine-nine. Miraculously, she got through, but even then it was minutes before she could make the CAD operators understand what was going on, and longer before she was able to give them directions to a housing estate so new it wasn't even on the police maps yet.

Only then could she totter into the bathroom and vomit violently. The room spun around her as she leaned over the bowl. After that, she slumped into a corner, feeling horribly faint. Unconsciousness . . . unconsciousness would be a solution. She could let this horror wash over her then.

Stella may well have fallen unconscious. The next thing she knew, someone was knocking insistently on the front door. At first she held back, fearful that it might be the injured woman, but the bulky shapes of uniformed figures were visible through the door's frosted-glass panel and, when she glanced around the curtain, Stella saw two police patrol vehicles.

* * * * *

Whether they believed her or not, she wasn't sure, but they made a thorough search of the area. There was no sign of any woman in a green dress, but Stella couldn't fault the officers for their efforts. They drove up and down the estate for twenty minutes. A plain-clothes man even arrived, introducing himself as Detective Sergeant Blackwood. He was young and slim, with a head of brown curls and a smooth, surprisingly innocent face.

'You couldn't have made a mistake, could you?' he wondered, as she sat on the sofa, sipping the tea he'd made for them both. Another police van went past the window. 'I mean, we've got the dogs out there now and even they haven't found anything.'

Stella chuckled bitterly. 'That figures. Things have a tendency to vanish round here.'

'How long have you been here?' he asked.

'Less than a week. Seems like a lifetime.'

'I can imagine. Can't have been much fun on your own.'

'Tell me about it.'

'I'll make sure the lads give the place plenty of attention now that I know you're here.'

The cop's concern seemed genuine, but Stella knew that soon he'd be gone again and she'd be left behind. 'What about the woman?' she asked. 'I didn't imagine her. She could be lying hurt somewhere. She was in a terrible state.'

Blackwood made a helpless gesture. 'We can only look. As yet, no one's reported any kind of assault or accident.'

Then something occurred to Stella. 'The little blond boy!' she said. 'He plays around here. He might have seen something?'

Again, Blackwood shrugged. 'At the moment, there's no one around at all. Believe me, we've searched.'

Stella sipped her tea. 'I know that feeling.'

* * * * *

Matt was home mid-evening, visibly tired. He listened in silence as she poured out the events of the last two days, then went upstairs to take a shower.

'So who do the police think she was?' he asked, as he towelled his tall, muscular frame.

'They don't know,' Stella replied, seated on the bed.

He shook his head. 'Bloody marvellous, isn't it. They're not exactly rushed off their feet in this part of the country, and they can't even sort something like this out. Did no one else see her?'

His wife looked up at him. 'Matt . . . how many times do I have to say it, there's nobody else here. Nobody at all.' Her voice became tearful. 'God knows how long it's going to take to fill up. I hate it already.'

'You don't hate it,' he said, rubbing his hair dry.

'How do you know? You've hardly been here.'

He sat beside her. 'I know. And I'm sorry.'

'I want to move.'

'What?'

'You heard. I want to move.'

He stared at her, stunned. 'Already? We'd lose a fortune.'

She shook her head. 'I don't care.'

'Stell . . . you've got to be realistic about this. We'd have mortgage penalties to pay, we'd lose all our moving fees.'

'I still don't care.'

Matt put a gentle arm around her shoulders. 'Look, you're upset. And it's understandable after today. But . . . try and think things through for a minute. Look at it this way: it's the first time you've lived away from home, which is always a choker. And I've not been around much, which has hardly helped. In a couple of months' time, when you've got used to it, none of this'll bother you. You'll look back on it and laugh. Honestly.'

She listened. Matt was ten years her senior, and as well as a looker, and a font of wisdom, he was also a ruggedly reassuring presence. When they'd first got engaged, she'd been fond of telling all her shop-girl friends how he'd literally swept her off her feet. If anyone had a solution to these problems, it would be Matt.

'How about if I try and get some time off over the next few days?' he said. 'I mean, there're no more overnighters coming up, but what if I try to take some holiday time as well?'

'That would help,' she said.

He smiled. 'I thought it might. Come here. . . .'

* * * * *

An hour later, Stella put her jeans and sweater on and wandered downstairs. That husband of hers was some lover. She wandered out to his car to bring in his briefcase and overnight bag. A pale twilight was falling. Dreamy stuff, she thought . . . then she saw something which jolted her back to reality: on the dusty bodywork of the Peugeot, by the rear nearside door, there was a handprint.

A smeared bloody handprint.

Unable to stop herself, Stella screamed.

Matt appeared, now in his tracksuit. She hurled herself into his arms, pointing at the car, gabbling that the woman must still be around somewhere, that she was actually hanging around the house, oh Jesus, oh Lord . . .

Then Stella was back inside, back on the telephone, wildly hammering out nine-nine-nine. It rang for what seemed like ages, but no sooner had someone answered it than Matt materialised beside her, snatched the receiver, and slammed his hand down on the cradle.

'What the hell's the matter with you?' he hissed.

Stella backed away. 'What? What?'

'Have you gone bloody barmy?'

She shook her head, lost for words. 'But . . . the car . . . on the car . . .'

'What's wrong with the sodding car?' he snapped.

She took him by the elbow and steered him out onto the drive. With a shaking finger she pointed at the stain on the vehicle's flank. It was a deadening moment when she realised that all she was looking at was a splatter of mud. She circled the Peugeot several times, but nowhere on its sleek form was there so much as a speck of red. She gazed again at the mud . . . no matter how hard she tried, she couldn't visualise it as a hand-print.

'I think you're in shock,' Matt said irritably, wandering back indoors.

That night, as they lay in bed together, having hardly spoken all evening, Stella heard the music again. She turned onto her front and jammed a pillow over her ears. It was all in her mind, she told herself, frightened tears filling her screwed-shut eyes. Ignore it and it would go away.

But it didn't.

The next morning, after a sulky breakfast, she stood by the lounge window, watching her husband set off for work without even waving to her. Eventually, she turned and surveyed the lounge. There was still a mess. She'd neglected things over the last couple of days, she thought. Not that she could face it now. She went upstairs and got dressed. She was in the bathroom when there came a thunderous knocking on the front door.

Stella walked to the top of the stairs and looked down. An indistinct figure waited beyond the glass. It knocked again. After a second, she descended, fastened the safety-chain, then opened the door a couple of inches. Detective Sergeant Blackwood was on the step, a buff folder under his arm.

'Morning,' he said cheerfully, though his smile didn't reach his eyes. 'Can I come in?'

Stella admitted him, told him to take a seat in the lounge. She made them both coffee, then sat opposite. Blackwood was leafing through a sheaf of documents, some with photographs clipped to them.

'Is everything all right?' she finally asked.

He glanced up. 'Hard to say.'

'Oh?'

He dug a glossy from his file. 'Mrs Stevens, I don't want to show you this, but I think I have to.'

Stella felt a prickle of fear. 'I see.'

Blackwood cleared his throat. 'Er . . . the woman you saw yesterday. Could you describe her again?'

Stella cast her mind back. 'Black hair, longish. Quite shapely, so I suppose she was reasonably young. Wearing a green evening dress, split up one side.'

The detective nodded as he listened; then he handed the picture over. 'She didn't by any chance look like this? I hope it doesn't upset you.'

It wasn't the worst thing Stella had ever seen, but it wasn't far off. It showed the corpse of a violated woman. She was lying, knees bent and legs spread, on a rubble-strewn concrete surface. Her high heels were scuffed and broken, her green cocktail dress torn up past her waist. Her groin, clearly minus underwear, was a mass of clotted blood. Splayed black hair concealed her face.

Stella handed the image back. 'It does look like her,' she said, chilled.

Again, the cop nodded. 'Well . . . this picture was taken in Aberdeen.'

'Aberdeen?'

'The night before last,' he added.

Stella felt a surge of relief. 'Oh . . . well, it can't have been her then?'

'No, I suppose not,' he said. 'Her name was Maureen McNickell. She was a working-girl, as if you couldn't tell. She was raped, then battered to death.'

Stella shook her head. 'As I say, it couldn't be the one I saw. That was yesterday morning.'

Blackwood mused on this.

'Have you found the little blond lad yet?' she wondered.

He shrugged. 'No. We're not likely to either. According to the agent down at the sales office, you and your husband are the only people living here.'

Stella looked up sharply. 'Well, that's not what she told me. Anyway, I've met other people. One came round here to introduce herself . . .'

Blackwood gazed at her.

'I'm telling you,' Stella insisted. 'They're lying to one of the two of us.'

* * * * *

They drove to the sales office together, in Blackwood's car. Once there, however, the woman Enid was nowhere to be found. Instead, a young man with sandy hair and glasses was taking an enquiry on the telephone. He indicated that he wouldn't be long. They sat down to wait. Stella couldn't help noticing how different the young man's uniform was from the one worn by the woman. His tunic was green rather than blue. His lapel bore no name badge.

'Hi,' he finally said, hanging up. 'Andy Wilson.' He glanced at the detective. 'Inspector Blackwood, isn't it?'

'Sergeant.'

'Oh yeah . . . sergeant. Well, what can I do you for?'

'Where's Enid?' Stella asked him.

Wilson kept smiling. 'Sorry, who's Enid?'

'She works here. Or so she told me.'

He shook his head. 'I'm the only agent on this site.'

'There's never been anyone here called Enid?' Stella asked.

'Not as far as I'm aware.' He tried to make light of it. 'I don't think I've ever met anyone called Enid.'

Now Blackwood cut in: 'This woman . . . Enid, told Mrs Stevens there were other families living on the estate.'

'There will be soon,' Wilson replied, looking pleased. 'I'm starting to get enquiries.'

'But there's no one else at the moment?'

The salesman shook his head.

'No one called Mimms?' Stella wondered.

'No.'

'No one with a little blond boy . . . like the one I've seen playing with his football?'

'No.' Wilson was finally getting agitated. 'No one. I've told you.'

Blackwood rose to his feet. 'Then I think we've wasted enough of your time, sir.' He opened the door. 'Mrs Stevens . . .'

'Just a minute . . .' she began, but the cop gripped her by the arm.

'No! *You* just a minute!' He propelled her outside. 'Get in the car.'

Bewildered, Stella did as she was told. Blackwood jumped into the driver's seat. They roared around in a tight circle, then drove off the estate at high speed, leaving Wilson watching through the office window.

'I'm not sure what game you're playing, Mrs Stevens, but I'm going to find out right now,' the cop said.

'Where are we going?' Stella demanded.

'Where do you think?'

'Wait a minute . . . am I under arrest?'

'You bet,' he snapped.

* * * * *

In actual fact, Stella wasn't under arrest. When they reached the police station, no charge-office procedures were followed, no caution given. She was left in a side interview room, and even provided with tea in a paper cup, which she angrily ignored.

When Blackwood eventually reappeared, he did so in company with another detective, a much older man with collar-length silver hair and a deeply lined face. For a moment, the two cops stood in the doorway, staring at Stella as if wondering what to make of her. At length, the sergeant approached and laid out three rows of snapshots on the table. The first were classroom portraits, depicting a variety of smiling youngsters; the second were holiday pictures, showing middle-aged, grandmotherly types; the third row was of hard-faced younger women—most of these photos looked like police mugshots.

'Recognise anyone?' Blackwood asked.

Stella stared at the pictures. After a careful moment she was able to select four. The first was of a blond schoolboy who might or might not be the lad she'd seen with the ball; the second two were from the central row, and clearly portrayed Mrs Mimms and Enid; the fourth came from among the younger women—it looked very much like the shoulder-bag girl.

When she'd set them aside, Blackwood turned to the other cop. Their expressions were impossible to read, but the sergeant seemed to have paled a little. A moment later he turned back to Stella. 'Would you consent to having your fingerprints taken?'

'Why?' she asked, now seriously frightened.

'Just answer the question, Mrs Stevens.'

'I suppose so, but why?'

'How about providing a DNA sample?' His eyes were fixed intently on her.

'Well . . . yes,' she said. 'If it'll help.'

'In which case,' said the older policeman, speaking for the first time, 'I'm sure there's no need.'

And without another word, he left.

Stella and Blackwood gazed at each other. The sergeant wore a confused frown. 'Thanks for your help,' he finally said. 'I'll run you home.'

As they drove back to The Belfries, a surreal calm lay on the surrounding fields. Scarcely a bird was moving. At last, Stella could take no more. 'You owe me some sort of explanation!' she blurted out.

Blackwood nodded. 'If I had one, I'd give it to you.'

'You'll have to do better than that.'

He sighed. 'That was Detective Superintendent Peake you saw back there.'

'Polite chap, wasn't he.'

'He's got a lot on his plate.'

She snorted. 'Haven't we all.'

'Not as much as him. He's handling the south-west arm of a nationwide enquiry that's on at the moment.'

'So?'

Blackwood struggled to find the right words. 'Well . . . I didn't mean to get you involved, but it was sort of unavoidable.' He glanced at her, still puzzled. 'It was the little lad with the football that started me thinking. Not to mention Enid, Mrs Mimms. . . .'

'I don't understand,' said Stella.

'We haven't made a big thing out of this,' he went on, 'because we don't need hoax confessions coming in. But . . . well, there've been five murders around the country which we're starting to think are linked.'

Stella looked slowly round at him. It took several seconds for what he was implying to strike home. 'You're not telling me I've been seeing ghosts?'

'I don't know,' he admitted. 'It's almost too odd.'

'What actually happened?' she asked.

'Six months ago in Exeter, a prostitute called Joanne Selby was garroted with the strap of her own shoulder-bag. She'd been raped first.'

Stella closed her eyes in horror.

'Three weeks later,' he added, 'Margaret Mimms, a secretary in Lancashire, was dragged into an alley on her way home. She was raped, then battered to death. A month later, the killer struck again . . . this time in the Midlands. Enid Taylor was an assistant at a travel agency. She was murdered in a park in West Bromwich. On that occasion, a little boy was also killed . . . beaten 'til his skull cracked. He'd been playing with a football nearby. Chances are he saw something, so the killer took him out.'

Stella's heart drummed inside her.

'The Aberdeen prostitute's the latest one,' Blackwood said. 'She must be. The similarities are too great to be coincidental. Especially now.'

'Now?'

He looked sidelong at her. 'The modern police service doesn't shy away from any method if it gets results, Mrs Stevens. This wouldn't be the first time we'd used a medium to make ground in a murder hunt.'

Stella shook her head. 'I'm no medium.'

'You sure?'

'It's never happened before.'

The sergeant seemed vaguely embarrassed about his knowledge on the subject. 'Maybe that's because you were in the wrong place. The West Country's unlike anywhere else. There's a rich history of folklore here. Certain spots are supposed to have . . . well, power.'

Stella thought about the stone circles, the ley lines. As she'd grown fond of saying to herself, anything was possible in a place like this.

They drove on, stopping only at a newsagent's so that Stella could buy a paper and read the story for herself. Ten minutes later, they were back on the estate. Blackwood dropped her off, asking her to contact them if there was anything else suspicious.

She nodded, then went indoors. Once she'd put the kettle on, she began to leaf through the newspaper. It wasn't hard to find a reference to the Aberdeen murder.

Lorry Driver's Shock Discovery

Beneath the lurid headline were two grainy photographs, one showing the crime-scene, taped off and with a tarpaulin tent in the middle of it. The other was the victim as she'd been in her youth: short black hair, startling blue eyes. A pretty school-leaver, with a glittering future ahead of her . . . or so she'd thought. Thus far, Stella noted, the police tactic of playing dumb had worked. Nowhere in the grim story did the panic-inducing phrase 'serial killer' appear.

Tea and paper in hand, she made her way back into the lounge. Glancing through the window, however, she was stopped by the sight of a yellow football on the front lawn. Immediately, she dropped everything and dashed outside . . . just in time to see a diminutive figure disappearing round the side of the house.

Stella followed. 'Wait!' she called. 'Please wait!'

On entering the rear garden, she saw the boy in a far corner, next to the potting shed. He was standing perfectly still, with his back turned. There was a heavy, almost blanketing silence. Stella took a step forward. From this close range, she could see that the child's jumper was streaked with brownish stains, that the blond mop on top of his head was a sticky, crimson mess.

'I have to talk to you,' she said in a quavering voice. 'Look . . . it's very important. I need to know what's happening here.'

From somewhere beyond the house, an engine rumbled. Stella glanced over her shoulder. She wanted to call out to Matt, to get him round here as quickly as possible, but something stopped her. She looked wildly back to the boy . . . and, inevitably, he'd gone.

'No . . . no!' she stammered, hurrying forwards. 'No!'

Then she halted. Where the boy had been standing, there was a metal bucket. Warily, she approached it. There were reddish stains around its rim. Glancing inside, she saw an old cloth. This too was blotched red.

She knew instantly what she was looking at. Blood. Human blood. A Scottish prostitute's blood, in fact. Stella recalled the handprint on the flank of the car, which Matt had been adamant was not there. She knew it had been. And now she knew why five minutes later there'd been no trace of it. She gazed at the bucket, a creeping numbness in her bones.

The son of a bitch had worked quickly.

But not quickly enough.

He obviously hadn't had time to conceal this evidence. Presumably he'd then forgotten about it.

Stella sensed the eyes upon her. She knew without needing to see for herself that she was being watched. She could picture their mournful figures in the upper-floor windows of the surrounding houses: Margaret Mimms; Enid Taylor; Joanne Selby.

Like an automaton, Stella made her way back to the front of the house. She virtually sleepwalked. Her mind was a fog of fear and uncertainty. She barely noticed the Peugeot parked on the drive.

Matt was inside, in the lounge, standing in front of the television, checking news items on the Ceefax service. He gave her a big, cat-like grin. 'Hi.'

'Hi,' she said. 'Home early then?'

'Not really. It's nearly six.'

'Oh. I didn't notice.'

'You all right?' he asked curiously.

'Yeah.' She tried to smile. 'Got a lot on my mind.'

'Anything I can share?'

'No, no,' she said, edging towards the kitchen. 'Women's stuff.'

'Ah.' Matt nodded. He spotted the newspaper on the sofa and swooped it up. 'Been out, I see.'

'Er . . . yeah. So, what do you fancy for tea?'

'Wondered if you wanted to eat out?' he replied.

'That'd be nice,' Stella said, moving on into the kitchen, where she stood by the sink.

She glanced sideways at a rack of knives. They were brand new and virtually unused, each one razor-sharp. She wondered if she should pick one up, conceal it on her person. She wondered if that would be sensible, if Matt might notice. But surely there was no need? Surely Matt wouldn't hurt her? Not her Matt?

The realisation of what she was thinking left her queasy. Suddenly she had to lean on the draining-board. Only then, after several nauseous seconds, did it strike her how quiet things had gone in the other room. Well, why not? Matt was reading the newspaper.

The newspaper.

Which she'd inadvertently left open on the story of the Aberdeen slaying.

Stella went rigid. The shock passed through her like a spear. Hardly daring to breathe, she glanced again at the knives. Then at the back door. She turned round.

Matt was standing directly behind her. He punched her in the head with explosive force.

* * * * *

When Stella came back to consciousness, she was lying on her front on the garage's cement floor, hog-tied. Her wrists were bound to her ankles with thick wrappings of duct tape. Matt had backed the car in behind her. He'd opened the boot and was now loading it with a shovel, rolls of canvas, and a coil of rope.

'You bitch!' he spat, when he saw she'd woken. He was ashen-faced, and wore a disgusted expression. 'This is all your fault. There I was, a happily married man, with a nice house, a good job, and a pleasing hobby. And then you have to screw it all up by sticking your nose in!'

There was a frenzied wildness in his eyes. 'I never wanted this, Stella. There was no need for it. I never brought any of it home with me. There was no reason for you to get involved, but you just had to, didn't you. Well, now you're going to pay the price. And a hell of a bloody price it'll be!'

'Matt . . . just, just wait a minute . . .'

'Shut up, bitch!' he screamed. 'Don't make it harder on yourself.'

He was a like a thing demented, clattering wildly about the garage. In no way did this person resemble the Matt Stevens whom Stella had married.

'I'll have to do you differently, of course,' he told her, now throwing a sack of tools into the boot as well. 'I'm not sure how yet. Maybe I'll peel you. Or saw you up. I might soak you in petrol and set fire to you.'

Dizzy, agonized with cramp, Stella gave a choked sob.

'It's got to be different,' he added. 'I can't risk the law connecting you to the others. You realise that, don't you?' He seemed genuinely interested in her answer.

'Matt . . . please, for God's sake!'

With a howl of rage he was down on his knees beside her. 'No! For my sake, Stella! For my sake, for a change! You bloody women, with your female problems and your times of the month and your neuroses! You think you're so special. Well I don't. To me you're just playthings. Toys to be used, abused, and thrown away when I'm finished with you. I'll teach you a lesson.' He banged her head on the hard floor. 'It'll be a lesson you'll never forget. A lesson none of you bitches will forget!'

Jumping back to his feet, he slammed the boot closed. 'You waltz in here, you make my life hard, you try to get me in trouble. All you care about is yourself. You're going to pay. Bloody hell, are you going to pay!'

Again, his voice had risen to a scream. Grabbing her by the hair, he hauled her round the corner of the car. Stella shrieked, only for the maniac to slap a piece of duct tape across her lips, with such force that it loosened her two front teeth. Coppery blood filled Stella's mouth.

'Be warned,' he snarled into her ear, 'the harder you make it, the worse I'll torture you.'

Then he wrenched open the car's rear nearside door, picked her up like a rag doll, and thrust her into the back seat. A second later, he'd jumped behind the wheel, jammed the keys into the ignition, and switched on. The tape deck came alive and filled the car with Siouxie, at deafening volume: 'Dear Prudence'.

With reckless speed, the madman then accelerated out of the garage and down the drive, swinging wildly into the cul-de-sac. Immediately, though, he hit the brakes.

'What the hell is this bitch doing?' he shrieked.

Stella craned her neck up. Between the two front seats, framed in the windshield, she saw a woman in a figure-hugging green dress, standing in the middle of the road; she was turning slowly to face them. Matt swerved, tyres squealing. The woman was now looking directly at them. Her face was pulped fruit, caked in blackened gore. Two startling blue eyes gazed out from the ruined flesh.

Bellowing like a bull, Matt lost control. The next thing Stella knew, they'd mounted the kerb and smashed head-on into the brick gate post of the house opposite. The front of the Peugeot went up and up. There was a grinding of metal. Shattered glass sprayed over her. The music ended in a screech of knotted tape.

Stella was thrown heavily against the offside door, which burst wide open. Then she was lying on the tarmac of a drive, her body a mass of sprains and twists. With a groan, Matt fell out beside her. Blood ran freely from a gash across his forehead.

Only a moment passed, though, before he'd climbed groggily to his feet. 'That God-damned Scots whore!' he blubbered, reaching into the pocket of the buckled driver's door, lifting out a long, curved tyre iron. 'She wants doing again? Well that's fine by me.'

Then his demented eyes fixed on his wife. He grinned wolfishly. 'But first . . . I'm going to bloody do you!'

If she'd been able to, Stella would have screamed hysterically. As it was, she could hardly breathe. Matt towered over her. He raised the brutal weapon high.

She shut her eyes, praying that it be quick. That, if it be anything, please Lord let it be quick . . .

There was a sharp, loud CRACK, like a firework detonating. Involuntarily, Stella flinched. Yet she felt no pain. Confused, she glanced up.

Matt had toppled backwards against the wrecked car, an amazed expression on his face. A spreading crimson stain was visible on his white shirt-front. With a clank, the tyre iron fell to the tarmac.

'Je—Jesus,' he muttered.

Then he fell too, slumping down over his wife.

Stella heard feet approaching. She couldn't turn to look, but she imagined the Aberdeen woman, all bloody and bedraggled, coming slowly over the road in her rotting dress and broken high heels. After Matt's mania, it would be a positive respite.

Needless to say, the new arrival was someone else entirely. He was a young man, dressed in boots, dark blue overalls, and a dark blue beret. In his leather-gloved hands he clutched a smoking semi-automatic rifle. Other similarly clad men were emerging from drives along the cul-de-sac. With them, armed with a revolver and wearing a black baseball cap with chequered banding, was Detective Sergeant Blackwood.

He hurried forwards, holstering his gun, hunkering down and tearing Stella loose from her bonds. He looked seriously shocked. 'What can I say?' he stammered. 'Apart from . . . sorry? Truth is, I thought you might be involved. Another Myra Hindley, if you know what I mean.'

Slowly, with great care, he helped her to her feet. 'We staked your place out . . . thought you might both try to split. Jesus, it's a good job we did.'

Five minutes later, he'd assisted her back into the house. An ambulance was on the way, he said. Almost as an afterthought, he went and switched the kettle on. Outside, there was commotion. Police vehicles seemed to be everywhere. A group of older men in suits, Detective Superintendent Peake in their midst, were standing around Matt's stiffening body.

To Stella it was a dream. Vague, unreal images swirled about her. When the telephone suddenly rang, she hardly heard it. She groped blindly out, lifting the receiver to her ear only slowly.

'Stella? That you, darling?'

'Yes mum, it's me,' she said quietly. Tears sprang into her eyes. 'Yes, I can hear you all right now. I can hear you . . .'

Crazy Little Thing Called Love

John Pelan

IT WAS AS DARK AS THE SMOKE from a peat-fire inside The Smoking Leg. As no one was playing darts or pool, the lights by the boards and tables were turned down. A solitary drinker sat at a corner whispering conspiratorially to the glass of whatever it was that he was imbibing. Four workers from the nearby construction project were busily downing their beers with the desperation of men who know they have only minutes to get back on the job-site. My friend Ian was nonchalantly chopping limes in anticipation of a busier time at happy-hour.

The advantages of taking a late lunch are many, not least of which is the relative quiet that comes over most neighbourhood pubs in mid-afternoon. Why I initially chose to visit The Smoking Leg is hardly a mystery: I was intrigued that anyone would name their pub after an obscure story by John Metcalfe. I was amused to find that, while the day bartender was indeed a reader of Metcalfe (as well as a number of other authors of supernatural fiction), the owner had chosen the name for a considerably more grotesque reason, which I'll relate some other time. Still, it tickled me to think that an occasional passer-by might be reminded of, or at least introduced to, the obscure British author as a result of the pub's odd name.

Pete Byrne had been a career mail carrier and had invested a goodly portion of his salary in the stock of local firms. As these firms included Microsoft, Starbucks, Amazon.com, and several bio-tech companies, he wound up doing rather well for himself. In any event, when Pete's career with the U.S. Postal Service drew to a close, his stock portfolio had swelled. With his new found wealth he opted to buy an old café and refurbish it completely. Pete preferred to work in his oddly named establishment on the weekends when it was busiest, leaving the day-shift to my friend Ian and the nights to a rather dour young woman named Vanessa, who also maintained his books and ledgers.

I'd met Ian on my first visit to the place and remarked on the name of the establishment as he handed me a cup of the vilest, blackest coffee I'd ever encountered. He smiled and said, 'It's from a story by Metcalfe, you know. . . .' At that point I knew I'd run into someone that I could chat with, though I was later to find that an enthusiasm for weird fiction was just one of Ian's interests. He supported his major expenses through his music, compositions that range from ethereal electronic sounds to far grimmer industrial noise. Next time you're in a music store look at the labels on some of the better known European bands' CDs—you'll be surprised how often the name Fleurmal shows up in the credits.

Musical composition was Ian's predominant interest, and one that paid the majority of his expenses. His other passion was 'finding out things', something that a bartender is certainly in a unique position to do. So it was that he came to take the day shift at Pete Byrne's oddly named pub, and I became somewhat of a regular. . . .

I climbed onto a barstool and nodded towards the lone drinker in the corner. 'Busy afternoon?'

Ian chuckled and placed a cup of gelatinous coffee in front of me. 'You ever talk to Curly?'

'Well, no, but I suppose the old guy has a story or two to tell, now that you mention it.'

'Oh, indeed he does. You might be surprised that the "old guy" is maybe two or three years older than you are. You're what, forty-one, forty-two?' I nodded, and he went on. 'Yeah, Curly's just a bit shy of forty-five.'

I couldn't help but stare at the mumbling figure in the corner. The man's hair was a dirty grey, and his posture suggested such a degree of weariness that merely raising his glass to take a drink must have called for a marshalling of all his strength. What I could see of his face was the sort of grey translucence that you see on the very old or very ill: the wrinkles were etched deeply enough that I could make them out from where I sat.

Ian looked at me for a moment, taking in my reaction. 'I don't know exactly what his story is, but I'm sure he's seen something, something that he can only hide from in alcohol. Here, why don't you put some music on, it's far too quiet in here.'

I let the jukebox swallow up two dollars and pressed buttons at random. The Smoking Leg has possibly the most eclectic music selection of any bar I've ever visited. Johnny Cash next to David Bowie, the Waterboys alongside Sisters of Mercy, Tangerine Dream and Hank Williams. You get the idea.

As I took my seat a selection from Queen began playing—the late Freddie

Mercury extolling the quirks of 'A Crazy Little Thing Called Love'. Ian put the limes away and remarked, 'Funny that you should play that. I was just going to tell you about one of those odd things that you write about from time to time. I don't recall if you've told me whether or not you've ever seen a ghost?'

I paused, relishing the bite of the caffeine. 'No, I've never seen a ghost, and quite frankly, I don't know anyone who has. At least anyone I'd consider reliable. . . .' I inclined my head meaningfully towards the man at the table.

'People tell me all sorts of things, you know. A lot of folk drink to celebrate the extraordinary, and a lot more drink because they're in fear of it. Do you remember Darren who used to come in here about three or four in the afternoon, the guy we called "The Birdman"?'

'Oh, the computer guy! The one who would come in with the mynah bird on his shoulder, like some sort of geek version of Baretta.'

'Yep, that's the guy. Would you consider him reliable?'

I thought about the man in question: a social misfit with far too much money and time on his hands, he was one of the Seattle nouveau riche created by an outburst of paranoia on the part of Microsoft. Darren had owned a small software company where he was pursuing some sort of interface with what later became known as the Internet. Whatever sort of project it was that he was working on, the Goliath in Redmond gave him a considerable amount of money and stock to stop working on it.

Darren was a millionaire at twenty-seven without having to do anything else in life except not work at the one thing he was good at. Consequently he spent a good deal of time in bars or indulging in expensive hobbies. You'd have thought that women (at least opportunistic ones) would have flocked to him like IRS agents to a lottery-winner, but not so—Darren's general geekiness was just too off-putting, and it wasn't as if was very interested in the opposite sex. He certainly wasn't gay, either; just sort of asexual, like the whole subject was somehow disinteresting, if not actually unpleasant to him.

The mynah bird was the only lasting legacy of the numerous expensive hobbies that he picked up and discarded, as readily as another person would change their shoes. Were it anyone else sitting in a bar drinking expensive scotch with an exotic bird perched on his shoulder, he'd be the life of the party until closing time. Not Darren. Would-be acquaintances were caught in a conversation that readily turned from his remarkable pet to jabbering about bits and bytes—and that would soon send them scurrying off in search of other company.

'You don't mean to tell me The Birdman saw a ghost? I'd think the only ghosts he might ever encounter would be in chat rooms.'

Ian took the guy in the corner another drink and sat down. 'No, Darren didn't see a ghost, but he certainly felt one. . . . This is what happened, as best as I can piece it together from what he told me the last couple of times I saw him.'

* * * * *

'Darren came in one night after he'd moved from his condo downtown to an actual house over in Redmond. You know the area, a scattering of pre-Depression houses here and there between the cubicle cities and the Microsoft campus? Well, rather than continue staying in Seattle I guess he wanted the rub of being in proximity to the company that had made him wealthy. On the other hand, perhaps he just needed more space to store all the accumulated debris of his various short-term enthusiasms; in any event he'd landed one of these big old barn-like places with six bedrooms and two-and-a-half baths, and hadn't been in here since he'd moved.

'Darren didn't look quite right, not that he ever seemed the picture of health, not with his pasty-pale skin and hair that looked like he washed it once every two weeks. But there was a look about him as though he were actually ill, as though there were a sort of cancer eating away at him from deep inside. And for the first time in two years, he didn't have the bird with him.

'He sat right there, next to where you're sitting, and asked me to pour him four fingers of Southern Comfort. He seemed like a man in need of a strong drink, and if he got too messed up I could always pour him into a cab and send him home. It's not like he couldn't afford a taxi—so I got him his drink and asked if anything was the matter.

'"Well, after I moved, strange things started happening, and now I don't know what I can do about it." He paused long enough to slam the rest of his drink and motioned for a refill.

'"You know my mynah bird Gorshin imitates whatever he's around? Like when I bring him in here and he starts making noises like the pool balls clicking against each other, or the darts thunking into the board?"

'"Sure, that's what mynah birds do, they're pretty smart as birds go: very aware of their surroundings. . . ."

'"Exactly, maybe not so much 'smart' as they just seem to notice things. Just like cats and dogs will set up a howl at things we don't see, mynah birds seem to notice everything, and their imitation of sounds is just sort of part of that. Anyway, here's what happened after I moved in to the house. . . ."

* * * * *

'"The house is on a stretch of about four acres just north-east of Redmond; part of the area is still farm country and this place is no exception. It's close enough to town that you can be anywhere you need to be within twenty minutes or so, yet far enough off the main roads that if you had a mind to you could go days without seeing anyone. I was glad enough to get out of the city, but I did miss the old hangouts, and this place in particular. The first few days I was at the house I spent most of the time calling the phone company from my cellphone, trying to get my modem lines and telephone running.

'"As I said, the place is damned old, but the last owner had replaced all the ancient wiring with circuit breakers, and even added a back-up generator, so that once I had all the utilities turned on, I was all set. I took a walk around the place again, but other than a decrepit old barn, there really isn't much of interest to the property. The interior of the house is a little odd, in that most of the bedrooms seemed to have been sub-divided at some point into smaller rooms; as though perhaps a large family lived there at one time.

'"It was listed as six bedrooms, but four of them were sub-divided into smaller units. I guess I could truthfully say that I have a ten-bedroom house, but that would only work if the small rooms were for the Seven Dwarfs or kids.

'"I didn't really care about that, as the one master bedroom was certainly large enough; and as far as I was concerned the smaller rooms would just be for storing stuff anyway. The main floor had a huge living-room and a study where I had all of my equipment set up. I put Gorshin's cage in there too; although once he got acclimated he could have the run of the house.

'"I suppose it was a week or so before the weird stuff began. You probably know that I'm not really supposed to be involved with anything that smacks of software development. Well, as I know you won't say anything, I'll admit that I fudge on that a little bit from time to time—mostly pretty innocuous stuff, like gaming, just enough to sort of keep my hand in and chat with people with the same background. . . . Anyway, I was on-line helping a friend with some bugs he was trying to excise, when I had the strangest feeling of someone standing behind me. It was more than just a feeling of someone in the room; it was as though there was a faint shadow on my screen coming from between the computer and the floor lamp.

'"I turned around, expecting God knows what, and saw . . . nothing. The room was empty, of course. It was then that I noticed Gorshin peering intently at a spot just by the door. As I watched, it seemed he tilted his head as though watching someone leaving the room and walking down the hallway. Pretty creepy. In spite of myself I got up and looked down the hall—of course there was nothing there.

'"Over the next few weeks I had the sensation again: once when I was heading into town I could feel that someone was watching me from inside the house—from one of the bedrooms. I almost went back inside to investigate, but decided that was crazy. Guess I should mention that I have state-of-the-art motion detectors throughout the whole house and on the grounds; it's really not possible that anyone could get in without my being aware of it.

'"Anyway, a few weeks ago things changed. Whatever was in the house seemed to be watching me constantly. I saw nothing, but from time to time I would feel a soft touch on my cheek, as though someone had stroked it with a feather, or a draught had blown across the back of my neck. Other times I would be cognizant of being watched, and I would see Gorshin peering intently at the doorway, as though there were someone standing there about to come into the room. I didn't know if I was losing my mind or what. It got to the point that I didn't want to stay home, but what was I going to do? The place cost a fortune! I couldn't turn around and sell so quickly, I'd lose thousands.

'"I'd started dating a woman I'd known from back when I had the company, and I totally blew that on the third date. We'd gone to her place the second date, and so it was time to visit my place. Maybe I'm no real lady's man or anything like that, but I've never had any kind of problems in the bedroom. Until that night. It started as soon as we went upstairs. Gorshin started shrieking something awful. I put the night-cloth over his cage and locked the door, figuring that he'd settle down and go to sleep.

'"We went upstairs and put some music on, and Gorshin started shrieking again. At the same time I had the feeling that someone else was in the room, and that that someone was angry. It was awful. The feeling was so strong that I couldn't, uh, perform, and ended up claiming that the wine got to me. I don't know why, but I felt as though I should take Jill home, and stay there. We ended up having a terrible fight: she thought I was trying to get rid of her, that I didn't find her attractive. . . . Well, what the hell was I supposed to tell her? That I thought something awful might happen if she stayed?

'"We drove back to her place and she stormed in, slamming the door in my face. I went home and puttered about for a while before returning to the bedroom. I don't know why I'm telling you this, but I've got to tell somebody or I'll go crazy. The presence, whatever it is, came into my bed. . . . It's a woman, no mistake about that, and it wants to be with me. And, God help me, Ian; in some ways I like it. . . ."

'I had to pour myself a drink after he told me that. I didn't know what to say. Either the living in isolation and fooling around with computers all day had unhinged his mind, or he'd been drinking somewhere else before he came in here. He finished his drink, asked for another, and had me call him a cab. I didn't see him again for a couple of weeks, and when I did things had apparently got much, much worse.

'He came in here late on a Thursday afternoon, and seemed completely rattled.

'"Ian, I don't know who else I can tell this to. I told you about the strange things that have been happening since I bought the house. . . . Well, I spent most of today talking to the police. . . . You see, they wanted to charge me with murder."

'I frowned as he downed half his drink before going on; it was obvious that it would be taxi-time again when he left today.

'"Murder? You?" I couldn't see it, not in a million years.

'"Well, they finally admitted that I'm not a suspect. I was having dinner when it happened, and a dozen people were at the restaurant, all of whom can swear they saw me. The horrible thing is that the poor girl was coming over to see me. And she died. Died for no reason at all."

'"Maybe you'd better start at the beginning; this isn't making a lot of sense."

'"It was Jill. She was coming over to patch things up, I guess. I think *She* strangled Jill. She's awfully jealous. I don't know if I told you that she killed

Gorshin a couple of weeks ago. I guess I was paying too much attention to the bird for her liking. . . . I don't know what to do; I'm afraid to go home, and at the same time I'm afraid not to."

'He went on like that for an hour or so, talking what seemed like nonsense. I started getting a little busy with the happy hour, and when I went over to take drinks to one of the tables he got up and raced out the door. I haven't seen him since.

'Well, this whole business got me curious enough to poke around a little bit at the County Office. Darren's house wasn't a large family estate, like he thought; it was something with a much more sinister history. . . .'

'What was it? You aren't going to tell me that there's a haunted house here in Redmond that no one's ever heard of?'

'Haunted? I don't know about that. I'm still somewhat of a sceptic when it comes to ghosts. I'm much more inclined to believe in the concept of a *genius loci* that is perhaps strongly influenced by events that take place in its presence. You're familiar with the concept behind poltergeists? That the poltergeist is some combination of psychic activity coupled with some sort of presence that's already there?'

I nodded, and he went on: 'I don't know that a human remnant has anything at all to do with this, but what I found out was that the property that Darren bought used to be a sort of a halfway house. . . . Seems that back in the fifties, as the mental health field was slowly coming out of the Dark Ages, the courts were looking at what to do with teenagers who were too disturbed and violent to be housed in regular facilities, but were too vulnerable to be locked up with the adults at Western State. Darren's house was one of these facilities. Matter of fact, it was the one that was involved in a scandal that set the whole programme of halfway houses and the like back a decade.

'The place was closed down after one of the nurses blew the whistle on the staff for horribly violating the public trust and the trust of their charges. One of the residents in particular is noteworthy. An eighteen-year-old girl, violently psychotic, and apparently a nymphomaniac, hanged herself shortly after the investigation. It seems the staff had been taking advantage of her in all the ways that you might imagine for months. Tragic as it is, that's probably the closest to any sort of positive attention that she'd ever received. I couldn't find out anything really specific about her juvenile record, other than that there was a murder in the background.'

I couldn't help but shudder. 'So maybe the ghost of this poor insane girl is haunting the place and is infatuated with Darren?'

Ian lit a cigarette. 'That would be a pretty prosaic way of looking at it—as well as acknowledging the existence of ghosts. The only problem I have with that idea is, that if we allow for one ghost, then where are all the others? It may be just as disturbing, but imagine: if the concept of a *genius loci* feeding on nearby impressions is valid, what sort of thing would be created by the years of madness and sexual energy released at that house? Imagine the *thing*—ghost, or *genius loci*, or whatever you want to call it—sitting there festering all these years until someone with sufficient vulnerability to establish some sort of unholy rapport with it comes along. Hell, we're all broken and twisted in some way: you're an ex-drunk who hangs out in bars and doesn't drink; I'm so obsessed with my composing that I took this job just to keep me from hiding in my condo and quietly going mad. We're all "touched", as they say, in one way or another . . . but Darren? Here was a man who was so unsuited to dealing with people that he spent his whole adult life locked away from the real world as much as possible, surrounded by machines. How can a psyche like that have any sort of defence against the sort of thing we're talking about?'

I felt that if there was ever a good time for four fingers of Bushmill's this would be it; but the urge passed, and I asked, 'So you haven't heard from him since the murder? Shouldn't we maybe try and get him out of there?'

Ian sighed. 'The mind's a pretty funny thing. Whatever is at that house up in Redmond, and whether or not it actually killed Darren's bird and that woman, or if they're just two awful and unrelated accidents, I don't know. Whatever the case, when he left here, there was no doubt in my mind that Darren was rushing home to be with whatever it is that he believes is waiting for him. I said that I hadn't seen him since, but I didn't mention that he called once. . . .'

'Really? What did he have to say? Did he decide to sell and get out of there?'

'No, not all. Quite the reverse, in fact. He did say that he likely wouldn't be back in, and thanked me for listening to him. He mentioned that he really didn't see any reason why he'd ever have to leave the house again, said he had everything he needs there.'

I could see that. Darren had enough money to retreat from the outside world and just have his necessities (and luxuries) delivered to his front door if that's what he wanted. Still, I had to ask. 'Did he say anything about the ghost or presence, whatever it is?'

'Oh yes, that. . . . As far as I know, they're still together, happy after a fashion, I guess. . . .'

ns*Three Fingers,
One Thumb*

Stephen Volk

FRANKLY, I WASN'T TAKEN IN BY THE CASTLE. It looked fake. But of course, that was what it was all about. Fairytales. Make believe. *Fake.* Of course, it didn't matter. Our five-year-old, Elize, was completely spellbound, and that was what counted. This was her world. *Their* world. Children.

Stupid grown-ups, a thousand lollipop-lickers were thinking, rightly. *What do they know?*

It was the holiday we had promised ourselves for years, ever since Elize was born. The first year, Val seemed to be post-natally ill or morose most of the time and I was overworked or depressed—which was increasingly normal in my line of business. The second year, we were in the same stressful lethargy. By the time Elize was three, the idea of a holiday had evaporated—we'd got lazy with our lives. Then we both realized it was all part of the drawn-out grief which was sucking us down. Elize didn't save us from it, as we'd prayed, but buried us in it. Now was the time to get our lives in order, shake ourselves up. Or else.

I was headhunted by a firm in Swindon, a goodish leap in salary. It meant Val could stop part-timing and study something afresh—which she needed to do, badly. Something self-expressive, to let out that pernicious anger I could see burning inside her. Crass as ever, I decided that what we needed was a holiday before I started the new job. I booked four weeks in the States, with an Avis hire car we picked up in that microwave oven they call New Orleans (or rather, *Noo ORRlins*).

A year before Elize came on the scene, we had lost our first child. I had seen and heard him inside my wife's body, but he had only a fleeting glimpse of our world. After nine months in darkness, in a sea of vague, dimly-grasped sensations, Christopher died the first night he spent at home.

We'd worked so hard for him. As Val bulged and bloomed, our love for each other became almost uncontainable. Painting the nursery ready for the new arrival was an unbridled joy. We chose bright pom-pom circus colours, and that wallpaper with the endlessly repeated cartoon animal, big ears and black olive-shaped nose, trail of stars striping from a white gloved hand. We heard our kiddie's laughter in our mind as we smelled the drying paint, but it was never to be. Not in real life.

It was a dark house afterwards. The non-eye contact of friends begged us to try again. We were in two bubbles of horror and emptiness. The little we talked, we bandied self-accusations and guilt. All we saw in each other was a mirror screaming back at us the memory of that tiny being, lost from the moment it breathed air. We never said it, but we wished we could kill each other and say, 'There. All gone. All over.' I think the only thing that stopped us was Elize.

Elize was born, perfect, beautiful. She arrived like Pinocchio. Like we'd made a wish. She saved us, God bless her.

Val and I felt a natural trepidation bringing her home to that room. It was unchanged, of course. We couldn't even bear to repaint the furniture pink instead of blue. I don't think we had touched the door handle since the doctor came and knelt beside the cot that morning. I remember he joked about his cold stethoscope and I laughed. God above, how could I have laughed?

That night I dreamed of Christopher sleeping in the next bedroom, his inadequate breathing coming through the baby listening device.

When Elize awoke, crying, I went in and cuddled her to my chest. She stared around her wide-eyed at the cartoon animal, the animator-created buck teeth, bow tie, happy whiskered cheeks, duplicated on the wallpaper like some kind of saccharine but sinister modern-day hieroglyphics. I wondered what was going on behind my daughter's gleaming, bewildered, tear-filled eyes. I kissed her roasting cheeks.

The same cartoon animal stood there, in the flesh now, in sunlight, gloved hand raised, waving good-naturedly in big trousers. The fixed upturned snout, the clown shoes. He gave me the creeps, the way only images of enforced happiness always do: clowns, dolls. Who was inside? *Was* anybody inside? He held hands with the crowd. They loved him.

America the beautiful.

Land of make-believe. Where you can be anything—even sane. *Noo ORRlins.*

I bought a Diet Coke. I was dry as a rock.

Children chuckled and roared all round me. I took Elize on a ride and she clung to my body, terrified and screaming with pleasure. Fear and laughter beamed from her face and she was eager for more. But did she know real fear? Could she? She felt so fragile, like a trembling leaf.

Elf-like minions ran around ensuring the enchanted realm was litter-free. Fairies and frog princes paraded comically under the beating sun, half a world away from the Brothers Grimm. But for all its staggering banality, I found myself enjoying the place—the force-fed feel-good factor, the unembarrassed kitsch, the simple born-again faith in Goodness. It was forbidden here to be unhappy. Depression did not compute in Fairy Land. It didn't *exist*.

How could you fail to have a good time, when dragons in dungarees were dancing and playing banjos?

Val came back from the Haunted Wood to find me sitting on a large concrete ladybird. Before she stopped striding she was saying 'Where is she?' I couldn't see her eyes behind the Ray-Bans. The sun had reddened her nose. She said Elize had run ahead to meet me while she, Val, searched for the Ladies. I looked round stupidly. Val's head darted like a chicken's, she must be round somewhere, she can't be *far*, for God's *sake*. 'She's not here,' I said. She looked at me.

The earth, this pit, opened up.

Trying not to panic, we retraced Val's steps. The crowd was thicker. There were hundreds of kids like Elize—God, why didn't we dress her in polka-dots or a hat with great orange plumes or something instead of bloody blue jeans and a white fucking T-shirt? The heat and sudden activity started to slosh nausea—*NOR-sha*—round the pan of my skull, like someone panhandling for sense. I shoved Val in the direction of one of the elves, to get an announcement over the speakers. *Quickly!* Anything.

Oh, Jesus.

I ran after the parade, following the kazoo music. I trod on heels, side-stepped pigtails. I fought against the rapids of people. My eyes lost focus.

Maybe it was a mirage in the heat haze. I saw a familiar shape in the crowd, towering higher than the little kids—the enormous ears, black in silhouette, the round nose, the whiskers. A girl at his side. The cartoon-red lips in a fixed grin. I thought of the wallpaper in the house we'd long sold—the wallpaper peeling, faded, rotten, decayed.

'Elize!' I screamed, clawing through the crowd in pursuit. I tore at the jungle of T-shirts and Nikons, sun tans and shades.

But when I reached the merry-go-round, its bongo-drumming beating against my forehead—nobody was there.

Her name piped over the speakers. I ran to every ride we'd been on, every shop. I pulled little girls by the shoulder—never the right one. They were alarmed when they saw the tears running down my face.

I elbowed past Rumpelstiltskin. I smacked the head off a Dodo. I crossed rainbow bridge after rainbow bridge. The children's universe closed in on me with pirate parrots and Nutcracker toy soldiers and the Woman Who Lived in a Shoe.

Christopher, no! I was gibbering inside. *We loved you—we did love you! We will always love you!* I began calling for Elize again. The sound of her name seemed abstract now.

Dusk fell violently red. The crowd thinned. I wandered aimlessly. I lost all sense of time.

When it was dark, the elves swept the streets and *Make Three Wishes* played as some bulbous American cops arrived and my wife wept in my arms.

At 3.00 a.m. the cops wept too, when they found Elize, curled up like a foetus in the trash behind a pink-and-white striped cotton candy stall. The smell of burnt sugar was sickly in the air.

Now Val and I are dead again. We're walking and breathing but we're dead. Christopher knows that. He knows that there'll never be another child now, to take his jealously guarded place in our memories. And he knows that, when I identified my daughter's little broken body, though I'll never—*could* never—tell my wife, I saw the bruises on her poor, small neck.

Of three fingers, and one thumb.

Safety Clowns

Glen Hirshberg

'and
      the
            goat-footed
baloonMan   whistles
far
and
wee'

                      e.e. cummings

A S SOON AS I SPOTTED THE AD, I knew I'd found what I wanted. *Like being the Good Guy? Like happy faces? Safe driver? Safety Clown needs you.*

One phone call and thirty seconds later, I had an interview appointment for 5.45 the following morning with Jaybo, dispatcher, founder, and managing owner of the Safety Clown Ice Cream Truck Company. 'Bring your licence,' Jaybo half-shouted at me, voice hoarse as a carnival barker's, and hung up.

Replacing the phone, I lifted the red dry-erase marker out of its clip on the message board and made a tentative check next to item #7 on my mom's list: *Find USEFUL summer employment. Help people. Have stories to tell. Make enough to concentrate on school in the fall.* Then I sat down on the tiny lanai to watch the evening marine layer of fog roll in off the beach and fill the ravine between our condo complex and the horse racing track down the hill.

My condo complex. I still couldn't get used to it.

My mother had scrawled her final message board list for me in the middle of the night, three hours before I drove her to the hospice to die. That had been a little over a month ago, orphaning me on the eve of my twentieth birthday. She'd left me our one-and-a-half bedroom condo, enough cash to finish my sophomore year at San Diego State without taking any new loans or another job beyond my work-study at the library, and her cactus garden. 'No way even you can kill those,' she'd told me, touching her fingers one final time to the tiny prickles in each individual window box. It had taken me less than four weeks to prove her wrong.

The morning of my interview, I set the alarm for 4.45 but woke a little after three, prickly and unable to sleep any more. After this, the only undone item on her list would be #1: *Celebrate your birthday*. And it was a little late for that. So. No more mom lists. Nothing left to do for anyone but me. Already, I was certain I'd sell this place, maybe before September. And I'd slowly lose the memory of air-conditioners hissing in all the condos jammed up against ours. I'd forget 4.15 a.m. garbage trucks and dogs snarling through screen doors at the hot-air balloons climbing with the light to lift rich people into the sunrise.

But I probably wouldn't forget the summer afternoons playing skateboard tag with the thousand other kid residents in the alleys of our sprawling nowhere of town-home blocks, stealing each others' wish-pennies out of the fountain by the guard shack, and waiting for 3.30, when the ice cream trucks descended *en masse* and we engulfed them. Hours after the trucks left, the buzzing tinkle of their music stayed trapped in our ears, like the bubble of pool water you can't quite shake out.

This would be my farewell, not just fulfilment of my mother's wishes but tribute to her. To my father, too, although what I mostly remembered about him was the smell of the strawberry air-freshener he insisted my mother spray all around to hide his sick smell, even though it didn't, and the way he'd died, holding his wife's and his seven year-old son's hands in his surprisingly strong ones, croaking, 'God. Damn. I can feel myself going down.'

At breakfast, alone in my condo, I watched the marine layer through the open lanai door, hearing horses nickering as stable-hands led them to the beach. Right on time, I left, pointing my mother's battered blue Geo down the empty I-5 freeway. I kept the window down, and the fog buffeted my face as though I were piloting a speedboat. Jaybo's directions pointed me above 10th Street into a motionless neighbourhood of empty lots and warehouses. At that hour, even uphill and inland, mist streamed from the lampposts and chain link fences. Reaching C Street, I slowed, turned, and began creeping east, looking for a street number or sign. What I saw, mostly, were human-shaped humps curled under newspapers or garbage bags along the fencing. I was about to turn around when I spotted the hand-lettered poster board lashed by its corners to a post at the end of an otherwise deserted block:

SAFETY CLOWN.

Next to the letters, someone had drawn a primitive yellow sun, with pathetic first-grade rays pointing in too many directions, so that it looked more like a beetle. I parked, walked along the fence until I located an opening, and stepped through it.

I got maybe five steps into the lot before I stopped. Strands of fog brushed against my face and hands like a spider web I'd walked through. My shoulders crept up, my hands curled in my pockets, and I stood rooted, listening. Peering to my left, I confronted the dead headlights of five hulking white vans. I looked right and found five more vans facing me in a perfect line. No movement, no lights, no people anywhere.

I was in a parking lot, after all. Discovering actual vehicles parked there rated fairly low on the discomforting revelations scale. Except for what was sprouting from them.

Clinging to them?

I took a step back, realized that put me closer to the vans behind me, and checked them, too. Sure enough, giant cockroach-shaped shadows clung vertically to each sliding passenger door from top to bottom, spindle-legs folded underneath and laced through the handles, tiny heads jutting from between knobby, jointed shoulders. It was the fog—only the fog—that made them twitch, as though preparing to lift into the air like locusts.

'Hey Jaybo,' a voice called, surprisingly close behind me, and I turned again. From somewhere among the left-hand vans, a man had emerged. He had red hair, dark coveralls, a grease rag sliding around and between his fingers like a snake he was cradling.

The barker's voice I'd heard on the phone yesterday answered him. 'Yep?'

'Think our lucky newbee's here.'

'What's he look like?'

The guy in the coveralls flipped his grease rag onto his shoulder and stared me up and down. 'Kind of short. Too thin, like maybe he needs some ice cream. Good bones. I like him.'

A door clicked open towards the back of the lot, and another face peered out. This one was narrow, with bulbous green eyes and a mouth that hung a little open even at rest, like an eel's. 'Come on in,' Jaybo said, and retreated into the lighted space.

Why did I have to be here this early, anyway?

The manager's office proved to be a silver Airstream trailer lodged against the wall of a warehouse. Making my way there, I sensed shapes drifting behind windshields, cockroach shadows shivering as the vans rocked and the fog swept over them, and with a flash of disappointment I realized that these had to be the ice-cream trucks. I'd been hoping for the milkman-style vehicles that used to service us, with their bright blue stickers of Popsicle Rockets and Igloo Pies pasted unevenly all over the sides like Garbage Pail Kid stickers on a lunchbox. I wondered if these vans even played music.

Hand extended, I stepped into the trailer. 'Good morning, Mr Jaybo, I'm Max Wa——'

'Just Jaybo. You're not that short.'

Instead of accepting my offered shake, he waved one arm in the air between us. The arm had no hand on the end, or at least no fingers, ending in a bulging ball of red skin. I dropped my own hand awkwardly to my side.

'Thin, though.' He cocked his head. Up close, his eyes were almost yellow behind his filthy round glasses. Stubby silver hair studded his skull like pins in a cushion. 'Think you're going to love all kinds of things about this job.'

Except for a small stack of ledger paper and a pen cup full of cheap, chewed-on Bics, Jaybo's desk had nothing on it. On the wall behind him, he'd tacked a massive map of San Diego county, with snaky pink and blue lines criss-crossing it like veins. Other than the map and a green, steel file cabinet, the trailer's only adornment was an Al Italia calendar, two years out of date, opened to April and featuring a photograph of a woman with astonishingly long, silky brunette hair and a smooth-fitting stewardess uniform, smiling sweetly. The caption read, *Roma? Perfect.*

'You're Italian?' I asked as Jaybo settled behind the desk and dropped both hand and stump across it. There was nowhere for me to sit.

'If *she* is,' he said, smiled with his mouth still dangling open, and wiggled the fingers he had at me. 'Licence.'

I gave mine to him. He noted the details on his ledger. Remembering this was an interview—the whole morning had felt more like sleepwalking—I straightened, smoothing my checked shirt where it disappeared into the waist of my khakis.

'Like kids, Maxwell?'

'Always. Last summer I——'

'Like making people's days better? Giving them something to look forward to?'

'Sure.'

'You're hired. You'll train today with Randy. *Randy!*'

I shuffled in place. 'That's it?'

Jaybo turned slightly in his chair and winked, either at me or his Al Italia woman. 'I know trustworthy people when I meet them. And anyway'—he grinned, thumping his stump on the desktop—'you're going to love this job.'

The door of the Airstream burst open, and I turned to find the entry completely blotted out, as though some massive, magic beanstalk had sprouted there in the three minutes I'd been inside. The beanstalk bent forward, and an ordinary head popped under the top of the doorframe.

'Randy,' said Jaybo. 'This is Max. Make him one of us.'

Randy had neatly cropped brown hair with a few shoots of grey along the temples, slitty brown eyes, and a jaw so long I half-expected him to whinny. Inviting me out by inclining his head, Randy withdrew, revealing the foggy world once more as he stood to his full height.

He wasn't that big, out in the air. My head nearly reached his shoulders, which looked square and hard under a tight green camouflage t-shirt. So maybe 6′5″? 6′7″? If he stood with his legs together, I thought I could probably get my arms around his calves. Maybe even his knees.

Wordlessly, he lead me around back of the trailer towards the long cement warehouse that formed the property's northernmost boundary. He whistled quietly but expertly as he did so, with little trills and grace notes. After a few seconds, the tune registered, and I started laughing.

Randy swung that epic jaw towards me. 'Join in. I know you know it.' His voice had an odd, strangled quality, as if his throat were too narrow for the rest of him, like the barrel of a bassoon.

I did as he'd directed. '*She'll be coming 'round the mountain when she comes.*' Maybe the vans played music after all.

The warehouse door was metal and ribbed and freshly painted white. Still whistling, Randy beat on it with the heel of one huge hand, and it shuddered like a gong.

'C'mon, Monkey, open up, we got joy to spread.' The jaw swung my way again like the boom of a sailboat. 'Randy, by the way.'

'I'm Max.'

'Imax. Big Screen.'

I had no idea whether that was a non-sequitur or a nickname, but it made me laugh again. Randy pummelled the door some more, and it jerked and lifted off the ground on its chain. Freezing air spilled over our feet.

'Freezer,' I announced, instantly felt stupid, and so employed Mom's Law of Idiotic Comments: go one stupider. 'For the ice-cream.'

'Big Screen,' Randy said, and thumped me on the shoulder.

Inside, I found myself facing a desk made from a slab of wood and twenty or so stacked milk crates. This desk was as empty as Jaybo's except for a sleek black Thinkpad folded open. Behind the desk on a swivel chair sat the grease-rag guy who'd greeted me, wearing gloves now. Beyond him, ceiling-high stacks of cardboard boxes with clear stretch-plastic tops fell away in rows to the back of the warehouse and out to both side walls.

'How many, Randy-man?' said the guy at the desk. His rag lolled from the pocket of his work-shirt like a friendly, panting tongue.

'Feeling good today, Monkey. Thinking Big Screen here's going to bring me luck. Let's go twenty and twenty.'

Monkey shook his head and tapped the tab key on his keyboard. 'Going to put us all to shame. You're learning from the best, kid. All-time champ.'

Resuming his whistling, Randy marched past the desk, tousling Monkey's hair. At the first stack, Randy hunched, got his arms around the bottom box, and held there like a weightlifter preparing for a clean-and-jerk. Then he just stood up, no effort at all, and the boxes came off the ground and towered in his arms.

'God*damn*, Randy,' said a new voice from the entry, and I turned to find three new people lined up by Monkey's desk. The speaker had to be over seventy, long and thinner than I was in his grey denim jacket and red Urban Outfitters cap. Next to him stood a Chinese kid about my age, and behind them a yellow-haired forty-something woman in sneakers and a sundress.

'Morning, slow pokes,' Randy said, pointing towards another stack with his foot. 'Big Screen, grab me another five, would you, and bring them out front?'

'Must eat half of it himself,' the old guy muttered.

'He doesn't touch ice cream and you know it,' said the woman in the sundress, and Randy nudged her affectionately with his elbow as he strode past.

Under cover of the patter, I approached the nearest stack of boxes, slid my arms around the top five, and gasped. They were freezing. As soon as I lifted them, the crook of my elbow began to ache, and my fingers cramped. But at least they were lighter than I was expecting. I gazed through the clear plastic of the topmost box. There they were, in their garish orange and Kool Aid-red wrappers. *We'll be bringing Popsicle Rockets when we come...*

'Hey, Randy,' Monkey called as the big man reached the door. When Randy turned, Monkey tossed him a long white envelope, overstuffed and rubber-banded twice around. Without any sort of hitch or arm adjustment, Randy stretched out his fingers and snatched the envelope out of the air, pressing it against his tower of boxes. 'Might want to count that.'

The sound Randy made came as close to *pshaw* as anything I've heard an actual human attempt. He strode into the fog, and I hurried after him.

'See, Big Screen,' he said without turning around, 'we're all independent contractors. Great system. You pay for your product up front, in full, so the trick is buying only what you're going to sell. Jaybo gets thirty percent, Monkey gets five for keeping your van running smooth, and that's it. Rest is yours, in cash, free and clear.'

Even after he mentioned the vans, I somehow forgot about the cockroach things until we were halfway back to the front of the lot. The cold and the weight from the boxes seemed to have latched onto my ribs like pincers. When I remembered and looked up, the figures were where I'd left them, just hanging against the van doors the way spiders do when you stare at them.

Randy went right on talking. 'But see, the best thing about Sunshine Safety Clown, Jaybo's got the routes laid out for you. Long a route as you want, street by street, stop by stop. These are guaranteed sales, man. *Guaranteed.* You saw Jaybo's map?'

'And his girl,' I murmured, boxes starting to slip, eyes still flitting between vans.

'What girl?' Randy said, lowering into a squat and settling his boxes on the asphalt next to the front-most right-hand van.

'Guess we have different priorities.' I lowered my own boxes a little too fast. The bottom one thumped.

'Careful, Big Screen. You bought those, you know. All right, I'll open her up and let's feed her.'

Did I imagine him pausing for just a moment as he approached the van's side? His fingers drummed the thighs of his jeans, and his whistling ceased. Then he jammed his hand between those giant, spindly legs, twisted sideways as though tearing out a heart, and ripped open the van door.

He came back fast, whistling, and hoisted the top five boxes off his stack.

'Randy, what is that?'

'What?' he said. But he knew what I meant.

'On the side of the van.'

'He's . . . a friend. Load up, and I'll show you.'

For the next fifteen minutes, we arranged ice cream cases in the freezer bins that lined the inside walls of the back of the van. Around us, meanwhile, activity increased throughout the lot as more doors slid open and more ice cream disappeared into bins. Randy worked quickly. When we'd finished, he banged the bin lids shut, hopped out fast, and started around front.

'Close that door, will you?' he called over his shoulder.

If there'd been a way up front from where I was, I'd have used the inside handle. But the back of the van had been sealed off, probably to help maintain coolness, and so I had no choice but to hop down and face the bug thing.

Up close, it looked wooden. The fog had left a wet residue on its slats, and I could see splotches of coloured paint all up and down them. I remembered my mother taking me to the natural history museum in Balboa Park once to see newborn moths dangling from their burst cocoons, wings drying.

Randy stuck his head out the passenger window. 'Hurry up. Don't let the heat in.'

With a grunt I didn't realize was coming, I reached into the nest of slats, grasped the metal handle at their centre, and yanked. The door leapt onto its runners and swung closed with a click.

'Okay. Back up,' Randy said. 'Further.'

I could see him at the wheel, hand poised over the control panel. When he saw me looking, he nodded. 'Say hello,' he said, and pulled down hard.

For a second, the bug thing quivered on the pegs holding it to the van. Then it unfolded. First a leg, human-shaped, popped free of the nest and dropped earthward as though feeling for the ground. As soon as that one was fully extended, another fell. The legs had purple striping, as did the arms, which clicked open, pointing sideways. Finally, the head sprang up, tiny black eyes staring at me above a deflated balloon nose, wide red happy mouth.

Thinking that was it, I peeled myself off the neighbouring van where I'd been watching. Then the whole clown pivoted on its pegs and swung perpendicular to Randy's door. Its puffy marshmallow of a right hand pointed its little red STOP sign right at my heart.

I stepped around it to the passenger side window. 'That's for cars, right? So kids can cross the street?'

Randy nodded.

I grinned. 'It'd work on me.'

'Me, too.'

'Jaybo made those?'

Randy shook his head. 'Loubob.' When he saw my expression, he cocked his head in surprise. 'You know Loubob?'

Memory poured through me, of my father with his determined, trembling hands on the steering wheel as he drove us to Loubobland the night before Halloween, two months before he died. The last time I'd been in a car with him.

'Yeah,' I said. 'I mean, I've been there. The muffler men.'

'The muffler men,' said Randy, and nodded. 'Hop up.'

I did, remembering that long, silent drive east into the farmlands of Fallbrook, the sun pumping redness over the horizon as it sank behind us. I couldn't recall a single thing my father and I had said to each other. But I could still see Loubob's junkyard. He'd been a carnival skywheel technician, the story went, then a funhouse specialist, then a circus-truck mechanic, before retiring to sell off a career's worth of accumulated spare parts and create annual Halloween displays out of rusted mufflers and scrap metal and hand-built motors. His muffler men wrapped themselves around eucalyptus tree trunks as though trying to shinny up them, shambled from behind junk piles like prowling silver skeletons, dangled from overhead branches to bump shoulders with shrieking guests. My father had loved it.

When I'd buckled myself in, Randy released the lever on the control panel, and the Safety Clown clattered back into place against the side of the van. Randy blasted the horn. An answering blast followed almost immediately from deep in the lot. Over the next sixty seconds or so, blasts erupted from all the vehicles around us. But no one honked more than once, and when I'd come back to myself enough to glance at Randy, I found him counting silently.

Eight. Nine.

Before the tenth horn blast had died to echo, he punched the gear shift into drive and moved us out of the lot. My eyes flicked to the side mirror, where I saw the clown shuddering as the wind rushed over it, and beyond that, the rest of the vans falling into line in rhythmic succession.

'You always leave all together?'

Randy shrugged. 'Tradition. Team-building, you know?'

'Then shouldn't I have met the rest of the team?'

'They won't be selling your ice cream.'

We were headed, I realized, for the port, and for the first time the absurd hour made a sort of sense. The workers down here had been on all night, probably shifting huge crates inside cargo containers that trapped heat like ovens.

'So what are yours?' Randy said as we crossed the Pacific Coast Highway, angling between grunting eighteen-wheelers as we approached the docks. Between trucks and stacked crates and gantry cranes, I caught glimpses of big ships hulking in the fog, their steel siding so much more solid, somehow, than the glass-and-concrete structures perched on the land behind us.

'I'm sorry?'

'You said you guessed we have different priorities. I'm not sure I liked that. I want to know what yours are.'

Startled, I turned towards his enormous frame—a super-freighter to my weekend eight-footer—and decided on caution.

'Just . . . spread a little happiness,' I said. 'Get some myself. Make buttloads of money so I don't have to eat Top Ramen and bologna at the end of next semester. Maybe get laid for the first time since high school.'

'See?' He sounded almost defensive as he let the van glide to a stop in front of two forklifts and some more heavy machinery I had no name for. 'Happiness and money. Don't know about you, but I'm thinking I haven't had my share of either, yet.'

Reaching under his seat with both hands, he pulled up the first assault rifle I had ever sat beside. It was flat black and spindly except for the chamber, or whatever it was called, that ballooned off the back of the trigger area. The barrel pointed straight at me. Randy did something that made the whole thing click, swung the stock to his shoulder, and sighted down into the dash, then returned the rifle to its hiding place.

'Is that an Uzi?' I whispered.

'Not a Corps man, huh, Big Screen?'

'You were?'

'Six severely fucked up years. Wait here. I'll introduce you properly from your own van tomorrow.'

He opened his door and hopped down, assuming point position in the phalanx of van drivers that immediately formed around him. My eyes kept wandering from the phalanx to the shadows under Randy's seat to the Safety Clown crouching in the corner of the side mirror, right above the *Objects May Be Closer Than They Appear* warning. My father's ghost kept floating up in front of me, too, so it didn't occur to me that we hadn't reopened the back of the van or dug into any freezer bins until Randy returned, dropping a small, square cardboard box onto my lap.

'Count those, okay?' This time, he didn't even wait for his colleagues to reach their vehicles, and he didn't wave as we U-turned and blew by them. Seconds later, we were speeding north on the freeway.

I pried the duct tape off the top of the box. 'Seemed like you trusted Jaybo,' I said.

'That wasn't Jaybo.'

The box lid fell open, and I lifted out the topmost plastic baggie, zipped tight, packed with white powder that shifted when I pressed like confectioner's sugar. I knew what it was, though I'd never done any. Dazed, I started counting bags, got most of the way through, and looked up.

'How many?' Randy said. I could feel his eyes on me in the mirror.

Don't react, I thought. Don't react, don't react. '*This is fucking cocaine!*' Randy grinned. 'Appreciate the appraisal. But I need a count, there, Bubba.'

My brain scrambled back to the pier. I'd barely paid attention. I didn't even remember seeing anybody but Safety Clown drivers.

'Thirty-seven,' I said dully.

'You're sure?'

'Thirty-eight.'

'Positive?'

I nodded.

'Guess you're not going to find out what kind of gun this is yet.' The note of open disappointment in his voice drew my gaze, and my gaze made him laugh. 'Got ya.'

The next three hours passed in a blur. The marine layer had burned away, leaving a bottomless blue emptiness overhead. We stopped at two law offices and one dental practice in Sorrento Valley. By the time we reached the dentist's, I'd started getting nauseous and rolled my window down, which is how I got to hear the receptionist with the white, winking hair yell, 'Hey, Doc. Here comes the cavalry,' through the open office door.

Our next stop was Ripped Racquet and Health Gym, where a pony-tailed tai chi instructor halted the class he was conducting on the circle of grass fronting the building to stop Randy. 'Hey, guy, do the clown.'

'You're doing him just fine,' Randy answered, then gave the instructor what looked like a brotherly chuck on the shoulder of his robe as he breezed past. He was inside almost half an hour, and when he returned, he waved at me to pass him the cardboard box from the floor. He fished out three more baggies, tucking them carefully into the waistband of his jeans. 'Walk-up biz,' he said happily, and trotted back indoors.

From there, we cut over to the 101 and up the coast, stopping at Del Mar Plaza and the Quesadilla Shack five minutes from my condo door, where I laid myself flat on the front seat and told Randy I was known in this place. The real reason for my hiding had more to do with the number of dinners I'd eaten with my mom on the red picnic tables in the sand outside the Shack.

Randy gave me a long look, and the fear I should have been feeling all along finally prickled down my scalp. But all he did was pat my head. 'You should eat, Big Screen. I get so caught up doing this, I forget half the time. Doesn't mean you should. Want a *carne asada?*'

Just the thought made me gag. He came back ten minutes later with a Coke for me and nothing at all for himself.

'Okay,' he said. 'Ready for the good stuff?'

I leaned my head against the window and kept my eyes closed, and we drove a long time. When I finally opened my eyes again, we were juddering over a dirt road just a bit narrower than the van, crushing birds-of-paradise stalks on either side as we rumbled forward. Still nauseous, increasingly nervous, I scanned the fields and saw red and orange and blue flowers nodding in the wind we made like peasants at a passing lord, but no buildings anywhere. I thought of the poppy fields of Oz, the witch's voice and her green hand caressing her crystal ball. Randy downshifted, and I sat up straight as the van coasted to a stop.

No one on this planet knew where I'd gone today. Certainly no one other than the Safety Clown people had seen me arrive downtown. *Training*, Jaybo had called it. What if it was more of a test? And I had not accompanied Randy on a single sale.

'Get out,' he said quietly, and popped the locks on both our doors.

I did, considering bolting straight into the flowers. But I had little chance of outdistancing my companion. I watched him remove his not-Uzi from under his seat, step down, and swing his door shut.

'Listen,' I said. He was already halfway around the front of the van, using his gun machete-style to chop flowers out of his path. I'd meant to start pleading, but wound up standing still instead, gobbling up each tick of insect wing, every whisper of wind in the petals. I swear I could hear the sunlight falling.

Arriving beside me, Randy stared into the distance, dangling the rifle by the trigger-guard. For a few seconds, we stood. Above us, the blue yawned wider.

'So what do you think, Big Screen?' he finally said. 'Just you and me?' In one motion, he swept the rifle butt to his shoulder and fired five quick bursts into the sky, which swallowed them. Then he grinned. 'Better get that door open.'

Before I'd even unlocked my knees and gulped new air into my lungs, people sprang from the flowers like rousted pheasants in a whirl of dark skin and tattered straw hats and threadbare work shirts open to the waist. Several of them chirped enthusiastic greetings at Randy in Spanish as I stumbled back against the van. He chirped right back.

'Hurry up, Big Screen,' he barked, and I reached a trembling hand between clown slats and grabbed the handle and twisted. I was grateful I hadn't drunk any of the Coke from the Quesadilla Shack. If I'd had any liquid in me, I would just have pissed it all over my legs.

As soon as the door was open, Randy jumped in and threw back the nearest freezer lid. The field hands nuzzled closer to us like pups vying for suckling spots, though they avoided so much as nudging me. One, a boy of maybe twelve, met my eyes for a moment and murmured, '*Buenas dias.*' Several others nodded as they edged past. I climbed up next to Randy.

'*De nada*, Hector,' he was saying, handing a chocolate nut Drumstick to the nearest worker, whose spiky streak of dirt-grey goatee looked embedded in his skin like a vein of ore in rock. Hector handed Randy a dime and retreated to the back of the group, peeling eagerly at the paper wrapping.

Distribution to the whole group took less than five minutes, but Randy lingered another twenty, dangling his legs out the cabin door, talking only occasionally, smiling a lot. The workers clumped in groups of two or three, leaning on hoes and wolfing down Igloo Pies while gazing over the fields. Their dwellings, I realized, might well be hidden out here somewhere, along with any other family members who'd somehow made it this far and managed to find them. None of them spoke to me again, but every single one tipped his sombrero to Randy before melting away into the fields they tended. They left neither trash nor trace.

'This stuff sold for a dollar when I was ten,' I said. 'And that was ten years ago.' My voice sounded strained, shaky. Randy's rifle lay seemingly forgotten between freezer bins in the van behind us. I almost made a lunge for it. But I couldn't for the life of me figure what I'd do afterwards.

'Cost me a buck-twenty per,' Randy said. 'But see, I figure I can afford it. Starting tomorrow, you can make your own decisions. Beauty of being a Safety Clown, dude. Ain't no one going to know or care but you.'

Clambering inside, he collected his rifle, hunched to avoid banging his head, and began swatting freezer lids shut. He didn't seem thoughtful enough to be deciding whether to mow me down.

'Why not just give it to them?' I asked. 'The ice cream, I mean.'

Randy cocked his head. The gun remained tucked under one arm against his chest. 'You like insulting people, Big Screen?'

I gaped at him.

'Didn't think so. Remember, they don't know what it costs me.' He left me to slide the door shut again, and we rumbled out of the fields and returned to the coast.

Another two hours passed. We stopped at an antique shop and some accounting firms, a bowling alley, and a retirement home. At the latter, I finally emerged from the van. Partially, I did so because I thought I'd better. Partially, I wanted to get away from the freon I'd been breathing virtually non-stop for the past eight hours, and which by now had given me a sledgehammer headache. But also, I'd got curious. The experience in the flower fields had shaken something loose in me, and I could feel it rattling around as I stepped into the midday heat.

Randy had already been inside fifteen minutes. I wondered if he'd received the same joyful, personal greeting there that he had everywhere else we'd gone. Edging forward, I reached the sidewalk fronting the main entrance, where my progress was blocked by a bald, pink-skinned marvel of a man whose curvature of the spine kept his head roughly level with my navel. Jabbing the legs of his metal walker into the ground like climbing pitons, the man dragged himself towards the brightly lettered sign at the edge of the parking lot that read BEACH ACCESS. Below the words on the sign was the silhouette of a long-haired bathing beauty laid out flat with her breasts poking straight up in the air. The man didn't acknowledge me as he inched past, but he did remove the cherry lollipop from his mouth, and it hovered in front of his lips like the dot at the bottom of a kicked-over question mark. I thought about lifting him, ferrying him gently to the sand.

Only then did it occur to me that the man might well have hauled himself out here for Randy. *Help people*, my mother had commanded, since the day I first started working. But help them what? Which jobs, exactly, qualified, and who got to say?

By the time Randy returned, I'd stumbled back to my seat, more confused than scared for the moment, and the question-mark man was well on his way to the bathing beauties.

'Two-thirty yet?' Randy asked, though he was the one with the watch. He checked it. 'Right on.'

Leaving the coast, he drove us across the freeway, over El Camino Real and into the maze of white and salmon-pink condo communities and housing developments that had all but enclosed the eastern rim of North and San Diego counties during the course of my lifetime. Any one of them could have been mine. Blood beat against my temples and massed behind my forehead. I closed my eyes, caught an imaginary glimpse of my mother bent over her potted plants at the nursery where she'd worked, better paid and sunscreened than the workers in the flower fields but nearly as invisible, and opened my eyes again to find Randy's hand hurtling towards my chest.

I twisted aside, but he didn't seem to notice, just grabbed the knob on the dash that I'd assumed was a glove box handle. Now I realized there was no glove box. Randy twisted the knob to the right.

For one blissful moment, nothing happened. Then the air shattered into winking, tinkling shards of sound. My hands rose uselessly to my ears, then dropped again. The van slowed, stopped on the curve of a cul-de-sac, and Randy shouldered his door open, nearly banging his head on the ceiling as he jumped out and rubbed his hands together.

'Watch the master, Big Screen. Learn.' Striding around front, he stood with his hands on his hips, gazing into the yards like a gunslinger as the sound rained down on him. Then he bounded around the van, pulled open my door, flicked the lever on the control panel, and danced backward as the clown leapt off its stilts and started unfolding.

I staggered from the van as the first children of the entire day swept around the curve of the cul-de-sac on their skateboards and bore down on us. My ears finally filtered enough distortion for me to register the tune the van was blaring.

'"Classical Gas"?' I babbled, as Randy stepped carefully around the clown. It hung still now, STOP sign jabbed over the street.

'What about it?' Randy threw open the sliding door and began pulling up multiple bin lids.

To my amazement, I felt my lips slip upwards. 'I've got a friend who claims this is the only music on earth it's impossible to make a girl have an orgasm to.'

If my own smile surprised me, Randy's nearly blew me backward with its brightness. 'Wish I had enough experience or knowledge to challenge that statement. Always been kind of shy, myself. And lately, I've been too busy making money. My *man*, Joel.'

He stuck one huge hand past me, and the first skateboard kid to reach the van smacked it with his own. 'Pop Rocket, Randy,' the kid said, straightening the cargo shorts from which his watermelon-striped boxers billowed.

'Cherry, right?' Randy had already handed the kid the popsicle without waiting for an answer. 'What-up, Empire?'

The reasons for that nickname never revealed themselves to me. What became immediately apparent, though, was how much this second kid liked that Randy knew it. He gave his board a kick-hop and wrapped it in his arms and stood close to the van, looking proud, as Randy gave him his ice cream. By the time that group had departed, twelve more kids, ranging in age from maybe five to no younger than me, had emerged from houses or backyards or neighbouring streets. No one seemed to mind the racket roaring out of the rooftop speaker, and a few customers even turned their bodies and faces to it, arms outstretched, eyes closed, as though accepting a cooling blast from a garden hose. Every single person knew Randy's name, and he knew most of theirs.

'You Randy's new helper?' said a soft voice so close to my ear that I thought for a second it had come from inside me.

Turning, I found myself confronting a freckle-faced girl of maybe fifteen, with a yellow drugstore whiffle bat over her bare shoulder. Self-consciously, she wound the wild strands of her strawberry-blonde hair back into her scrunchy with sweaty fingers. Her eyes, green and soft as the squares of over-watered lawn fronting the houses of this block, never left mine.

Too much time passed, and I had no answer. I wanted to borrow her bat, dare her to try to pitch a ball past me. I also wanted her to stop flirting with me because she was too young and only adding to my anxiety. I thought of my mom peering down from the heaven she didn't believe in, and had to smother competing impulses to wave and whimper.

'You should be,' the girl finally said, in that same breathy voice. 'Hey, Randy.' From her pocket, she withdrew a wad of bills, palmed them, and passed

343

them into the van. Randy ducked inside and returned with a baggie, which disappeared into the girl's shorts pocket.

'Go easy, Carolina,' said Randy. 'Say hi to your sis.'

The girl wandered away, wiggling her bat once at both or neither of us.

I sat down on the curb under the Safety Clown's arm, and the sunlight dropped on my shoulders like ballast. For the first time, I let myself ask the question. *Could I do this? Did I want to?* It'd pay for next semester, all right. And it'd certainly qualify as a story to tell. Once the statute of limitations ran out.

We were close to an hour in that one cul-de-sac, then nearly two in the fire lane of the circular parking lot of a little league complex with four grassless fields that looked stripped bare like shaved cats. Kids just kept coming. Mostly, they bought ice cream. Every now and then, one or a little group would lurk until a lull came, then dart or sidle or just stride forward and pop $75 or sometimes an envelope into Randy's hands.

At one point, feeling oddly jealous as yet another group of kids clustered around and jabbered at him, I asked Randy, 'What happens if you're not sure?'

'What's that, Big Screen?'

'What if it's a kid you don't know? You wouldn't want to make a mistake.'

'Oh.' He turned to me, grinning. 'I've got a system.'

Not twenty minutes later, I got to see the system in action. The kid in question looked about eleven, despite the pimples peppering his forehead and leaning off the end of his nose. He hovered near the swing-set just off the parking lot, sweating and jumpy in his long-sleeved, webbed Spider-Man shirt. Finally, he came forward, eyes everywhere.

Randy glanced at me, mouthing *Watch this*. Then he stepped from the van to meet the kid, folding his arms across his cliff of a chest, and said, 'Yo, friend. What's your name?'

'Zach.'

'Yo, Zach. Did you need ice cream or . . . *ice cream*?'

I stared at Randy's back. He swung his head around and beamed proudly before returning full attention to his customer.

'*Ice cream*,' the kid said, flung $75 into Randy's hands, and fled with his treat.

Randy employed exactly the same technique a little later with a pale, teenaged girl with black lipstick and what appeared to be at least five different henna tattoos applied one on top of another on her bare ankles under her long skirt. The resulting mess looked like hieroglyphics, or a gang tag. When Randy asked his question, her mouth unhinged, as though he'd bonked her on the head. He gave her two Drumsticks for her dollar, called it his 'Welcome to Randy special,' and directed me to shut down the music and reel in the clown. I did both, leaned out the window to watch the clown fold, and nearly slammed into the scowling woman's face with my own.

She wore a navy blue button-up shirt, tight blue slacks, and, for a second, I thought she was a cop. She'd pulled her red hair back so tightly that the wrinkles in her forehead seemed to be splitting open. As I stared, gargling, trying to sort whether I was terrified or relieved, she banged my door with her hand, rattling the clown on its stilts. Beside me, I felt Randy settle into the driver's seat. Then his hand crossed my chest and pushed me gently back against the peeling vinyl.

'Ma'am. Something I can get you?' Randy asked.

'How about a brain?' the woman hissed. 'How about a conscience?'

'Now, ma'am, I'm sure you have both those things.'

The woman nearly spit in our faces, and my legs started shaking. Abruptly, my head jerked sideways, checking for Randy's other hand. It was on the steering wheel, not feeling around under his seat. And on his face was a smile gentler than any I'd seen all day.

'That's your natural colour, isn't it?' He didn't even turn the key in the ignition. 'Beautiful. Almost maroon.'

'Ever seen someone die, Mr Smarty-Arty Ice Cream Man? I have. When I was nine years old. Janitor at my school. Want to know why he died? Because some service asshole like you was parked in the fire lane and the ambulance couldn't get up the driveway.'

Randy made a *pop* with his cheeks. 'Right,' he said. 'Absolutely right. I'm sorry, and it won't happen again.'

The woman blinked, hand half-raised as though she might slap the van again. Instead, she shook her head and stalked off.

'Never understand it,' Randy murmured, starting the van. 'Why are moral people always so angry?' Pulling out of the lot, he glanced my way, saw me ramrod straight against the seat back with my legs still trembling together. 'Know many people like that, Big Screen?'

My tongue felt impossibly dry, as though it had been wrung. 'Um.' I put my hands on my legs, held them until they quieted. 'I think I thought I was one.'

'You?' Randy grinned. Then without warning he reached out and patted me on the head. 'Not you, Big Screen. You don't have it in you. And you don't treat people that way. Trust your buddy Big Randy.'

We stayed out four more hours. Around six, Randy began cruising family pizza restaurants, the multiplex lot just before the 7.30 shows, a 24-hour workout gym where he sold only ice cream (no *ice cream*) to exhausted soccer parents and desk-drones desperately stretching their bodies. Most of these people knew Randy's name, too.

Finally, a little after nine, on a residential street overlooking Moonlight Beach, Randy shut off the van, then turned to me. Out on the water, even the moon seemed to be burrowing a straight, white trail to his door.

'You haven't eaten a single goddamn thing, have you, Big Screen? I'm sorry about that.' Almost as an afterthought, his hands slipped under the seat between his legs and came up with the rifle.

My breath caught, but by this point I was too tired to hold it. 'You either,' I murmured, watching his hands.

'Yeah, but . . . You'll see. Tomorrow. There's this charge people give off when you're not judging them, just giving them what they want and letting them be. It's a physical thing, man. It's in their skin, and it's more filling than any food. I'm so charged, most days, I barely even sleep. Not to mention richer.'

It was true. I'd watched it happen all day. I wasn't sure anyone in my entire life had ever been as pleased to see me as Randy's customers were to see him. And he felt the same way.

The rifle slid into his lap, muzzle aimed just over my legs at the centre of the door. 'You'll be back?' His voice bore no apparent threat.

Eventually, when I'd said nothing for long enough, Randy nodded. 'You'll be back. You're the thoughtful sort. Like I said.'

'Does it ever bother you?' I asked.

Randy stared at me, and the moon lit him. 'Does what?'

Dropping the rifle back in its place, he drove us straight to the freeway and back downtown. He didn't turn on the radio or say another word. White and red reflections from the dashboard and passing cars flared in his skin like sparks.

In the lot, we found all the other vans not just parked but empty, clowns locked into cockroach position at their sides. A single low light burned in Jaybo's trailer. I wondered if he lived there, then why he would. He had to have plenty of money.

'Go home, Big Screen,' Randy told me as soon as he'd backed the van into its space at the head of the right-hand row. 'I've got to wipe out the bins and finish up. You get some food and sleep.'

I didn't argue. My head hurt, and a loneliness less specific—and therefore all the more suffocating—than any I'd experienced before crept into my chest and filled my lungs. And yet I found myself turning to Randy, who flashed me his blinding, affect-less smile. I thought he might burst into one last chorus. *We'll all have chicken and dumplings when she comes.* But he just smiled.

The only thing I could think to say was, 'Looks like we're last ones back.'

'Always. Going to give me a run, Big Screen?'

Slipping from my seat, I stood blinking on the pavement while the fast-cooling air pushed my grinding teeth apart and drove some of the deadness out. My fingertips began tingling, then stinging, as though I'd just come in from sledding. I was trying to remember where I'd parked my car—could it really have been earlier today?—when the door of Jaybo's Airstream opened and his goldfish eyes peered towards me. I froze.

'Max?' Out he came. His shorts had flowers on them. Maybe all Safety Clown employees slept here. In their vans. In the freezer bins, which doubled as coffins.

'You have a good time, son? Learn a lot?'

'Tired,' I managed, watching him, listening for any sign of Randy stepping out to trap me between them.

'Randy's a madman.' Jaybo smiled. 'No one expects you to work like that. But I thought you'd enjoy learning from the best. Like my clowns?'

I resisted the urge to look at one and shook my head.

Jaybo's smile got wider. 'Got to admit they're memorable, though. Knew they'd be our logo, our signature, as soon as I saw them.'

'Loubob's. Right?'

'You know Loubob's? See, I knew it, Max. No one comes to us by accident. I went there looking for belts and hoses for these babies.' He waved his stump at the vans. 'And there were the clowns just lying in a heap. I asked what they were, and he says, "*Project. Didn't work.*" Ever heard Loubob speak?'

I shook my head again, checked Randy's van, but saw no sign of him, just the passenger door hanging ajar. Jaybo took another step closer. 'Not many have. I got the whole lot for $50.'

To his left, at the very end of the row, one of the clowns had come open, or been left that way. In the shadows, at this distance, I couldn't see its face, but it was shivering like a scarecrow in the salty ocean breeze.

'See ya,' I heard myself say.

'Tomorrow. Right?'

Without answering, I turned, waiting for the rush of footsteps or flick of a rifle safety-catch, and started for the street. Just as I reached the gate I heard a thud from Randy's van, couldn't help turning, and found Randy's face filling the windshield. When he saw me looking, he pressed one gorilla-sized hand to the glass, fingers open. Waving. I got in my car and drove home.

I'd tiptoed halfway up the entry stairs before remembering it would take more than that to wake my mother. I made myself a tuna sandwich and ate a third of it, seeing Randy's last wave, his wide open grin. The condo felt even emptier than it had for the past month, even the ghost of my father's smell drained from the walls. My mother had left no smell, ghostly or otherwise. I crawled off to bed and miraculously slept until after four before bolting awake hyperventilating.

Flipping onto my stomach, I curled into myself like a caterpillar and managed, after ten minutes of total panic, to get myself calmed enough to start to think.

As far as I could tell, I had three choices. I could get up and join Jaybo and Randy and the gang spreading joy, ice cream, and *ice cream* throughout San Diego County, have a hundred or more people of all ages and types rush out to greet me by name whenever they saw me, and make more money in a couple of months than my mom had in any one decade of her life. I could call the police, pray they found and arrested all Sunshine Safety Clown employees, and then spend the rest of my days hoping none of them got out, ever. Or I could do neither, hide here in the fog with the horses, and hope Jaybo understood the absence of both me and the police as the don't-ask-don't-tell bargain I was offering.

Instead of choosing, I got sick.

For the first few hours, I figured I was faking it, or manufacturing it, anyway. Then, when the chills started, I dug around in my mother's bathroom, found a thermometer in the otherwise empty cosmetic drawer, and checked myself. I got a reading of 102, climbed back into bed, and stayed there two days.

No one called. No one knocked at the door. No one parked by the complex's sauna and played a blast of 'Classical Gas'. Around midnight of the second night, the phone rang, and I dragged myself out of bed. Passing my mother's doorway, I half-believed I could see her tucked into her usual corner in the king-sized bed she'd once shared with my father, not moving or breathing, as though she'd snuck out of her grave to get warm.

The fever, I realized, had gone. The hardwood floor felt cool on my feet, the air gentle against my itching legs. This was just the world, after all. Big, thoroughly mapped place to sell joy or buy it, hunt company or flee it, trust yourself or your friends or your instincts, stretch the hours as much as you could, and one day vanish.

Pulling my mother's door shut, I padded into the living-room and picked up the receiver just before the sixth ring, beating the answering machine. But on the other end I found only electrical hum and a distant clacking sound.

The next morning, I got up, broke eggs into a pan, and flipped on the pocket television on the counter for company. Then I stood, staring, wet yolk dripping from the end of my wooden spoon onto my mother's once-spotless hardwood floor.

Under a flashing banner that read *LIVE—BREAKING NEWS*, a camera scanned a downtown parking lot. Red and blue lights flashed and reflected in the windows of ten white vans, illuminating what looked like spatters of mud all over their metal sides and grilles.

'*Once again, a scene of incredible, despicable violence downtown this morning as police discover the apparent massacre and dismemberment of as many as fifteen employees of the Sunshine Safety Clown ice cream truck company. Police have long targeted the company as the key element in a major Southland drug trafficking ring, and department spokesmen confirm that this vicious mass slaying appears to be drug related. No additional specifics either about the trafficking ring or the nature and timing of the murders has been released as yet.*'

I put my hand down almost inside the frying pan, jerked back, and knocked egg everywhere. My eyes never left the screen.

'*We've had our eyes on these people for months,*' a police department spokesman was saying, as the camera prowled jerkily, restlessly behind him, capturing lights, an open van door, a helicopter overhead, body bags. More lights. '*Arrests were forthcoming. Imminent, in fact. We're disappointed and also, obviously, horrified.*'

An attack of this ferocity is unprecedented in this county. These people are savages, and they must be rooted out of our city.'

'Randy,' I whispered, surprised that I did.

Suddenly, I was bent forward, so close to the tiny screen that it seemed I could climb into it. I waited until the camera pulled back to scan the lot again.

Then I was out the door, not even buckling my sandals until I'd driven the Geo screeching out of the condo lot to the bottom of the hill to wait for the endless, stupid light at the lip of the freeway on-ramp. Traffic clogged the interstate, and I was nearly an hour getting downtown, but I don't remember thinking a single thing during all that time except that I was wrong. It was ridiculous. Juvenile. Wrong.

What I should have done was go to the police. Instead, I parked as close as I could to the temporary barriers the cops had erected, edged through the block-long crowd of gawkers, got the single glimpse I needed to confirm what the cameras had already shown me, then very nearly shoved people to the ground as I forced my way back out. My breath was a barbed thing, catching in the lining of my throat and tearing it. An older Hispanic woman in a yellow shawl threw her arm around me and made comforting shush-ing sounds. I shook her off.

What I'd seen was blood, all right, splashed all over the vans, coating the wheel wells and even some of the windows. I'd seen doors flung open, some wrenched half off their hinges. What I hadn't seen were clowns. Not a single one, anywhere. Just the wooden frames where they'd hung like bats to sleep off the daylight.

I drove around and around downtown in a sort of crazy circle, Hillcrest, India Street, Laurel, Broadway, South Street, the harbour, the Gaslamp, back again. They'd been taken off, obviously. Ripped free in the fray, or pried away by police for easier van access. This was just another deflection, like my two-day fever, from having to deal with my own culpability. Then I thought of muffler men peering around trees. And I remembered the midnight phone call I'd received last night. Sometime in the late afternoon, I stopped the car, wobbled into a payphone booth, dialled information, paid the extra fifty cents, and let the computer connect me.

The phone in Louboland's junkyard rang and rang. I let it, leaning my forehead against the sun-warmed glass, sensing the ocean scant blocks away, beating quietly underneath the boats and pilings.

Several seconds passed before I realized my call had been answered, that I was listening to silence. No one had spoken, but someone was there.

'The clowns,' I croaked.

The person on the other end grunted. 'I have nothing to say.'

'Just one question.' I was blurting the words, trying to fit them in before he hung up. 'The project.'

'What?'

'You told Jaybo the clowns were a failed project. I just want to know what it was.'

Silence. But no dial tone. I heard fumbling, for a match, maybe. Then a long, hitching breath. 'Neighbourhood watch,' Loubob said, and hung up.

That was five hours ago. Since then, I've been holed up in my mother's condo—it will never, could never be mine—thinking mostly about Randy. About his 'Coming 'Round the Mountain' whistle and his electric shock of joy-giving, his hand against the windshield as he waved goodbye. I hadn't been considering joining them, I thought. Not really. Not quite.

But I hadn't called the cops, either. Because I was scared, maybe. But mostly because I hadn't wanted to, wasn't so sure who was doing good, being useful, making lives easier. And I'd liked the way they were together, the Safety Clown family. And Randy. . . . I think Randy took me for his friend. Maybe I could have been.

So I'd let them be. And the clowns had come.

I've got the blinds thrown wide, but I can't see a blessed thing out there through the fog and dark. I keep the TV off, listening instead to the air-conditioning, wondering for the thousandth time if I was supposed to have called the police, and whether that would have saved anyone. Or me.

Tomorrow, maybe the next day, if no one comes, I'm going to have to get up. Maybe I'll go to the cops, and let them laugh. I've got to find another job if I'm going to go to school, have a life. But for now I'm staying right here, in what's left of the place I grew up in, holding my knees, while my ears strain for the clacking I heard on the phone two nights ago, the clatter of footless wooden legs on stairs that will tell me once and for all if what I do matters, and whether there's really such thing as a line, and whether I crossed it.

The Listener

Christopher Harman

WORD HAD SPREAD, Bentink had to assume, as he replaced the receiver, more bemused than flattered. He'd become aware of a low murmur accompanying his outline of the scope and aims of his book. After concluding with a lame, 'That's about it, really', it had been as if a needle had been dropped on a record. A minimally modulated voice, almost monotone, raised a little as if against the din of a pub crowd. Names and dates flew past. *Not now*, he'd thought, and it had been like wading against a strong current to say 'Can we meet? I haven't seen the place yet.' The bursar had poked his head around the door of Bentink's office and they'd signalled and mouthed at each other, and Bentink had been left with a computer disk, which he'd shut in his desk drawer along with his agonised fingers.

And during that distraction the telephone had gone dead; not even a dialling tone. There was a buzzing in his head, though; a name—Church Arms, Old Town; and a time, five-thirty.

Bentink rang his wife to tell her he'd be an hour or so late and why. She assented with a sigh. 'Don't get smashed like last time.' A television audience clapped and cheered his recent performance at the local Historical Society's fiftieth birthday do. Hardly smashed—he'd just mixed grape and grain stupidly. Home in time to throw up on the doorstep. But she was in tune with his mood, which Old Town at dusk on a Friday evening would do nothing to improve.

He didn't have great hopes of The Church Arms in any case. The older, quieter, quainter establishments he'd saved for last were proving a let-down, with varying combinations of unhelpful landlords, less than forthcoming regulars, and lacklustre beers. Until now he hadn't even heard of The Church Arms, and the chances of an outcry at its omission from *The Public Houses of Fishwood* would be surely nil.

Bentink cleared his desk in the university administration building, and after a leathery omelette in the Buttery, followed by ten gridlocked minutes in the city centre, he was on the road that descended to the Old Town district.

Copses of red lights stopped him every hundred yards for dribbles of crossways traffic. At every pedestrian crossing the green man flashed for fewer and fewer walkers, and finally nobody, as Bentink drummed his fingers on the wheel and stared balefully at the red light and Old Town below—a smudged fingerprint of cramped streets, mist, and shadows. Distant houses merged imperceptibly with hulks and cranes lining the sluggish estuary. Black fragments wheeled over the banquet of worms in the mudflats.

A church spire drew him, a motionless black flame amidst huddled dwellings. Here were no traffic lights, and for now at least no need of them in the absence of any car but Bentink's own.

He parked in a street of boarded shops and crumbling kerbs. Guided by the spire, Bentink entered an alley in a blackened terrace and emerged from darkness a moment later into a tight quadrangle of massive weed-fringed paving slabs. The light of a lonely iron street lamp failed to reach façades that were obstinately and oppressively black against the dirty pearl grey of the sky. None were as black as the spire that appeared out of scale, as if a pinnacle of rock had been transplanted from a pitiless mountain landscape. Access to the church was presumably provided via the black gape of a ginnel in a terrace containing three front doors and fewer windows. Above a door next to the ginnel a sign sticking out at right angles depicted a church set on a bed of white gravestones. Smoke clambered down from a chimney to the sagging roof. A deep-set window contained an ochre flickering.

Bentink's steps chattered and whispered back from the murk of walls and doorways as he crossed the square to the pub. Pushing through into the discreetly lit interior, a ghost of his breath vanished ahead of him

Weak blue light from the single small window didn't quite meet a flaky orange glow from two brass lamps set amidst mainly empty shelves behind the counter. The barman's lips moved in what Bentink took to be a welcome despite the fierce, rapt eyes. A black cowlick of hair sloped down to eyebrows like inked bristles of toothbrushes. Off-white shirtsleeves were rolled back from forearms too thin for the long black hairs that straggled in varying directions.

At an inquiring jerk of the barman's head, bristly eyebrows raised, Bentink asked for a pint of bitter and turned away to inspect the three others he'd belatedly noticed.

Beneath the window sat a figure in a shapeless coat belted arbitrarily at chest level with coarse rope. Grey and fissured like a brain, a woollen hat encompassed most of a nodding head. A mouth moved in a soundless mutter. Two others hunched, murmuring, the black beaks of their caps almost touching over the black disc of a table.

An impact on the bar top. 'On the house,' the barman said with a grin that went down at the corners and displayed a lower row of ale-hued teeth. He backed off, eyes darting between Bentink and the chunky, faceted glass as if it contained fireworks. Bentink thanked him with more surprise than pleasure. He said, straining for affability, 'Dark looking brew', words that too briefly put off bringing the glass to his lips. The barman encouraged Bentink the rest of the way with smiles, bobbing eyebrows, and vigorous enthusiastic nods. Overcoming an unprecedented reluctance when it came to alcohol, Bentink sipped.

Characterful, came to mind. Strong, smoky—it settled in cold coils inside him.

The figure beneath the window gave forth an old woman's cackle. The beaks turned slowly Bentink's way and back to their table. White spots in the black—dominoes, though none touched each other as Bentink had supposed the rules dictated. They were arranged rather in rows; grave plots came to mind, and with the church a stone's throw away that was hardly surprising. Wooden chairs and benches looked as uninviting as pews. An empty stall, whose back and sides were at head height, might have been cut from a superannuated pulpit.

The players discussed something in low murmurs. The woman, in similar tones, appeared to be reprimanding her mole-like hands, which were, Bentink now saw, bound in rosary beads. He recalled words that hadn't fully registered at the time on the telephone: 'Keep going till you get to the snug.'

'Keep going' suggested a trek, but the ground plan of the pub couldn't be that extensive. A wide, comparatively well-lit archway, adjacent to the back corner of the bar, looked promising.

'This way to the snug?' he said lightly, gesturing with his glass. The barman snapped a tea towel over his knobbly shoulder and, bowing deferentially—but not deeply enough to conceal his grin—he ushered Bentink onwards with a 'be my guest' sweep of his hand. This, or Bentink's half-serious inquiry, had elicited croaks in the dimness, fluttering sounds at the rumour of low beams.

Did they know his business here? A good idea to meet somewhere apart. He was in no mood for eavesdroppers, let alone intrusions from punters with their own testimonials. One source of information would suffice tonight. Beneath the arch he paused, ostensibly for another swallow of beer. He glanced back and was right—somebody had occupied the stall. White hair haloed a mumbling darkness that was looking full at him.

There was no evading that scrutiny, for the archway was only a few feet deep. It was more of a long narrow alcove than his notion of a snug. His reflection moved obscurely in the dark panelling of the back wall as he slipped behind a round, beaten copper table. In the end wall to his right, pale flames squirmed in a narrow fireplace above and to the left of which was a framed picture—a study in black but for a pale wedge in the bottom left.

Bentink felt framed himself by the arch, and with his immediate surroundings checked there was little option but to gaze passively out into the shadows of the main bar.

The stall was empty now, though how the man had exited silently on boards that had complained at Bentink's every step was a mystery. Not his contact then. He sipped, trying to disentangle relief from disappointment, then drank some more before pushing the glass away. If it was to last to the end of the encounter he needed to resist nervy drinking.

The muddy stew of voices Bentink blamed on the low ceiling, the boxy floorboards. The speakers were out of sight around the corner of the counter. A chuckling joined in; insanely self-absorbed, it bubbled along, almost—but never quite—becoming words. He isolated it to the stall. Hadn't the white haired one's murmurs implied another occupant concealed by the nearer side panel? Breaking his resolution Bentink reached for his glass, swigged, swallowed, let out his breath in an audible 'Aagh' from the back of his throat that nearly convinced him he wasn't uneasy. Strangers, be warned; mad folk present. But then the chuckling dimmed as if a wall had grown around it—and that suited Bentink fine.

He checked his watch: 5.15. He'd condemned himself to a quarter of an hour in which to feel edgy, and sense that those responsible for the low mutterings were aware of him, and listening for him and not each other. He placed his glass down soundlessly. The stall was silent now, but only pretending to be empty, he was sure. He got up and went to the fire that he'd noticed was recessed beyond plaster pillars built out from the walls. He found himself in a space that formed the crossbar of a T with the alcove he'd just left. Against the right hand end wall was a large, unevenly stuffed armchair. If this was the snug one chair was hardly sufficient.

The flames were like white tapes fluttering up from a vent, and he felt more movement than heat when he spread his fingers before them. It was a photograph in the picture frame; the black could have been a dank and dripping cave wall were it not for the dim outline of an arched window. The white wedge was sunlit gravel. Sticking out of the grass, and just discernible in the deep shadow, was a spade.

The darkness in the frame was becoming a hollow Bentink's gaze had to scramble out of. With an old-fashioned frown at his glass he flopped into the armchair. Better here, sheltered from prying eyes. A mouthful of beer chilled him. Most of a second sprayed through his fingers. Suppressing a cough with difficulty, he peered through tears.

If it had been a face checking him out, pinched to narrowness and multiplied in the facets of his glass, it had been and gone in a flash. He got up and poked his head around the corner. Nobody sat at the copper-topped table, and an accidental glance at the picture proved his examination had been careless.

There was the shadowed bulk of the nave, the window, and the spade—

and clasping the spade handle a hand. A figure, black against black, had thrust the blade into the grass or was about to pull it out.

Back in the chair Bentink felt short-changed. The drink was blunting his perceptions as well as loosening his limbs, but well-being eluded him. He sat up as a new voice came from the bar. He stopped patting his pockets for his notebook and relaxed again. Or tried to.

Though equally voluble, this was not his contact, who in any case would surely have sought him out immediately. The voice was frustratingly unclear. Not happy, Bentink reflected, trying for objectivity. A sudden fit of guffawing shocked him. At first he thought it was a reaction to what the voice was saying; not that he could make out anything himself. Other voices murmured on, ignoring both outpourings though surely not oblivious to them. The hoarse laughter didn't so much cease as fade away. If only the sour voice would follow it. If anything it was sounding nearer. Bentink deadened his breathing. He felt enclosed, cornered; then the opposite.

Space yawned behind him. He sprang to his feet in a thrill of panic that was almost immediately ridiculous. No witnesses, thank God. Not an abyss, but a gap of two or three yards separated the back of the chair from the wall. He couldn't think why it hadn't been apparent before.

Barstools were ranged before a narrow shelf on which were several glasses. Figures wandered in fog; at least, that was what the wallpaper, with its design of grey blotches on a white ground, wanted him to believe. The voice wandered too, searching for someone to buttonhole. *It's not going to be me*, Bentink decided.

The chair seemed enormous as he crept around it like a child past its bedtime.

He leaned against the shelf, took a sizeable gulp from his glass. They had been abandoned recently, the glasses, the stools—or so he presumed until he noticed dried smears on glass, dried rings on varnish. The light cast from a naked bulb ended abruptly at a proscenium affair to his left that marked the threshold of a neighbouring room. There was a farther unlit room and possibly more—like the beginning of a tunnel of receding mirrors, the effect only compromised by a distant light like a hint of dawn in a window.

A new, maudlin voice—close but muffled. The armchair was absorbing the sound. It was large enough to conceal an average sized man hunched small. The speaker must have secreted himself there whilst he'd been preoccupied with that tunnel of rooms. He couldn't think why it would be more than he could stand if a head rose above the back of the chair and turned to face him; so it was some relief, though not much, when the voice began to emanate from a sequence of other points. He couldn't pinpoint them, but they were threatening to converge with him at any moment. 'Keep going till you get to the snug.' This wasn't it: more than a corridor but less than a room. Bentink pushed away from the shelf and headed for darkness.

He'd lost the voice, and three or four paces would have taken him through the unlit room had he not stopped as someone moved momentarily parallel with him. He turned sharply, breathed again. A round mirror hovered in the darkness. He approached it, had to whirl about once more to scotch the absurdity of what he thought he'd seen reflected.

There were no seated figures, row upon row of them merging into complete shadow. Back to the mirror, now webbed with concentric and radiating metallic wisps. The bulls-eye abseiled on the end of a thread, then scuttled to the perimeter. Bentink's gaze rapidly circuited the dart-board for a more convincing answer than that of his vision not immediately measuring up to the darkness. The segmenting wires blurred in a swirling black, drawing him in. He tottered back, liquid slopping onto his hand—an 'it was me' admission. But with only a third of a pint gone he wouldn't allow it to be any more than part of the explanation. He pushed on between the next set of dark-stained pilasters.

He wasn't going to linger here either. A large rectangular object draped in grey took up most of the space. He edged by it, eyeing the blanket that covered only flatness. A table—not his fault if the name of the pub should suggest an altar, a tomb. And if the black brickwork within the third set of pillars were a dead end it would be no bad thing for him to be forced to return. That armchair would cease to bother him when he sat in it and waited—until last orders if necessary.

A closer look revealed the brickwork to be the far wall of a short passageway heading left to end at an opening, where another passageway went off at right angles. Through there was the source of the weak blue light that had drawn him. He was deciding whether or not to go on, when the image of the draped table behind him flashed so vividly he might have had eyes at the back of his head. Its likeness to a bed brought with it a groan, at once in his head, at his ear, and rooms away. Bones cracking as if someone stretched free of slumbers. A 'whumph' as covers were thrown back. Imagined sounds; he wouldn't believe them, and wheeling about before he could freeze to the spot, he didn't have to.

The darkness pulsed in time with his heart, but the blanket was in place. Before he could think about it he stooped, clutched a fold, and uncovered a corner, then with a flourish the whole surface.

Perished baize was black as mud. Disturbed dust motes danced gleefully, along with something larger. Avoiding his batting hands, negotiating his flinches, it chaotically orbited his head. Gone, though not at his insistence, perhaps tangled in his hair. Gingerly exploring with his fingers, he envisioned an entry for The Church Arms in his book. Yes, a blank page. Why not a *black* page: mysterious, post-modern, get the students scratching their heads. There was little to recommend so far. A dart-board without darts, a billiard table without cues or balls—and that was the least of it. The ale foisted on him was decidedly suspect, and as for the clientele. . . . The handful congregating where he'd left them had been joined by a number of others—at least on the evidence of that vague murky chorus.

Bentink replaced the blanket as he'd found it and stepped back into the passageway. He halted at the end to lift with his pen the barrier of a frayed, insect-spotted veil. He stepped through and watched the web rise dreamily through violet-grey light hanging in great dusty robes from a mullioned skylight. A stump of chimney leaned perilously over the glass.

Chimes drew his gaze down to the end of the passage, where a grandfather clock was set back behind an arched opening. It wouldn't have surprised him if the resemblance to a religious statue in a church alcove was intentional. The metallic after-sound buzzed to nothing. How many chimes had there been? The clock wasn't telling, other than to indicate with its stubbornly blank dial 'Look, no hands!' Did clocks chime the half-hour? Twenty-five past according to his own watch—which he wouldn't have credited but for the racing second hand.

The fluttering thing had found him again—a moth, as he'd suspected. From his wild misses it retreated haphazardly up towards the skylight, in which there was now no chimney visible, though he walked back and forth seeking a better angle.

Somebody on the roof? Gone now, but should he be an upright citizen and inform the landlord? For the moment at least he wasn't tempted to return through what he'd named the 'games rooms'. Like the graph of a precipitous decline, a crooked descending crack in the rough plaster wall pointed the way. A warm light gleamed on the clock's pendulum.

Turning left at the clock he found himself in a narrow room stretching to left and right. Bookshelves were bracketed to an end wall. Bent inquisitively from the top shelf, a jointed anglepoise lamp shone on three lower shelves. Each held a dozen or so books with dusty cloth bindings, some with ragged dustjackets. A collection started, or abandoned, Bentink guessed—or the remains of one after incremental borrowings and theft.

A sound; someone as curious as he, throwing back the blanket on the snooker table. But then a yawn or groan of misery heralded a new voice—a woman's. The voice was embittered, wretched, without hope. Bentink grabbed at a book: *Old Times in Old Town*. Offering comfort was unthinkable, and not merely because her misery sounded unassailable. Here was someone resigned to her lot and grimly, unintelligibly relishing the telling of it. He shook off a vision of hands grabbing his lapels, a face up too close. Wishing she'd take her troubles elsewhere seemed to work. The voice diminished suddenly as if its owner, or Bentink himself, were plummeting into a pit. 'Yes; go and drown your sorrows,' he whispered with a little gasp of satisfaction that sounded more like despair.

The dead silence that followed was barely preferable to the voice. Pressing on equated, in its lack of appeal, with the thought of retracing his steps. Forestalling a decision, he opened the book.

The tiny print didn't encourage reading. Bending the pages and rapidly flicking them from his thumb transformed letters to squirming grubs. At the brief shadow of a photograph he halted the pages.

Three figures in the foreground: a man in a shabby frock coat and scarf, a round-shouldered underfed youth, and an acid-faced woman in a shawl. Behind them figures followed forever a coffin carried out from the black edge of a church. Leaning on his spade at a respectful distance a gravedigger watched: mud-caked boots, drab white shirt, whiter hair kindled by the sun.

An involuntary recollection of the monologue over the telephone wires, Bentink thought at first. He listened hard. A conversation was hardly what he was hearing, unless the other voices that had re-emerged in greater strength were obscuring the quieter interjections of another party.

Shutting the book sent a bouquet of dust at his face. He sneezed, blinked dry eyes at his watch. The hands were an open beak, 5.30. 'Dead.' Flicking the watch face with his thumb, the second hand measured a few beats, then stopped. 'All right, dying then.' He re-shelved the book, suspecting his own would end up in similar forgotten corners; still, immortality of a kind.

It was surely well beyond half past. But if he hadn't unearthed the snug, yet at least his contact wasn't ahead waiting for him impatiently. The voice had dimmed. *Gone to relieve himself—or he's remembered to buy a drink*, Bentink thought. *He must know I'm here.* A bare minimum of five had noted his entry, and surely wouldn't hesitate to pass comment on the stranger in his office gear, his expectant manner signalling the fact that he was more than passing trade. Even now he couldn't help but hear himself the subject of a uniform insect hum of voices.

But that was going too far, and if not quite paranoia then evidence of an inflated ego. He wasn't that important. Neither was his book, if he was honest with himself.

He sat on a bench at the opposite end from the bookshelves and waited. Two inches of beer remained. When he tipped his glass to drink, the liquid moved viscously, like the artificial lava sea in one of those see-sawing glass cases. He peered fuzzily past his glass. The bookshelves appeared diminished, as if behind sheets of fly-spotted glass. The three lower shelves were three gapped and snaggle-toothed mouths on the point of smiling. Before him black-painted pilasters, dividing off this end of the room, rose to a dark ceiling beam like a gallows. A cold finger of air tested the flesh of his neck, prompting him to look right.

He was at the turn of an L. A window was the source of the draught; a red velvet curtain was shy of the ledge by a good three inches. Grey light seeped in. Beneath the window was a chair, the comfiest looking chair he'd ever seen, red plush, comforting wings curving round at head height. A storyteller's chair, complete with small round wooden table and not-so-comfortable-looking three-legged stool for the listener. Homely after what had gone before. Yes, snug, Bentink concluded, moving light as a balloon and dropping heavy as a sack of sticks into the chair. He'd kept going and the very voice that had suggested he do so was coming nearer—further proof, if it were needed, that this was the appointed meeting place.

Stealing across his mind, the phrase 'better late than never' seemed questionable as the beer floated him to his feet. It was small wonder the man ignored Bentink's extended hand. Unblinking, sustained eye contact with Bentink meant such a periphery was missed by a mile. Lowering himself onto the stool, the man was well into his stride, his cloudy yet intense voice as incomprehensible as it had been on the telephone. Bentink extracted his mini tape recorder from his jacket pocket. Technology wouldn't let him down.

'Hang on!' he begged, outwardly his brisk professional self, inwardly his consternation growing at the man's appearance as well as his own failure to understand.

Wrist and cheekbones pressed white and sharp against tautened skin. White hair and feathery side-whiskers rendered the face insubstantial at its margins. A white collarless shirt hung on the slenderest of frames.

Except nothing was as white as it should have been. Bentink stared up; the ceiling lampshade was a hideous mud-yellow tasselled thing, but where was the obstruction casting the man in shadow? But if the blank-eyed face talking at him was troubling, he could take comfort from its familiarity. The man who'd watched, then disappeared, from the stall had been his contact after all. But why the delay? More intriguing was the striking resemblance to the gravedigger in the book. Quite possibly related, though generations might separate them. He'd ask when the man stopped for breath, though understanding his reply might be another matter.

Flat northern English, he couldn't deny that. But the meaning constantly slipped away, like dust blown off a sheet of paper, leaving a faint, echoing residue of friendships and feuds, saints and villains, poverty, sickness . . .

'Do you mind if I . . .?' A second floundering jab with his finger found the record button. Downing the rest of the beer was like drinking shadow, and as tasteless. No other alcoholic beverage had affected him like this one—and rather than some acoustical quirk of the building, it was the beer making nonsense of the voices he'd heard tonight.

He swung his glass before the man. 'Speciality of the house?' Intended to sound unimpressed, his voice emerged querulously, words washing into each other much like the man's. Too dark, too rapid in the papery face, lips may have been shaping an answer, but other sounds encroached on Bentink's strained attention. They came from outside the window; beneath the curtain was a slow threshing of shadow. Bentink rose in the rocking room, turned unsteadily, swished back the curtain.

Tethered together by ropes of mist they worked their ways between the stones and crosses of the dismal graveyard. There was a bottleneck where they filed into the dark ginnel alongside the pub. It must have been a movement of the curtain that drew a skeletal old man in a flat cap and threadbare ankle-length coat to the window. His sunken jaw chewed . . . no, he was speaking. His eyes were chips of grey glass, sunken and immobile. He turned his whole body to scan the window, and even then Bentink wasn't certain the eyes had truly found him. He flung the curtain—holed and frayed, he now noticed—back into place.

'Who are they?' he asked, swaying, buttoning his suit with difficulty. The man's eyes followed him like a portrait's in a gallery. He'd splayed his fingers on the table and was drawing them back, each black-encrusted nail ploughing its own route through dust.

Bentink hit the 'off' button of his tape recorder. It didn't matter—he'd no intention of ever hearing this voice again. He panted like he'd run to the snug.

'I'll send you a copy. When it's done.' The route back to the street, tortuous but without diversions. 'Send it here, shall I?'

The man may have been saying they were taking a short cut through the churchyard, but his voice reverberated back on itself in grey echoes. *Don't you breathe? Yes—of course he does, and to even ask that means I really am drunk.* Shameful on the strength of one pint. He pocketed the tape recorder.

The many more voices inside the pub should have reassured him. Office workers interrupting the journey home, he thought at first; until it occurred to him Old Town wasn't on the way to anywhere but decrepit docks and miles of mud and hissing marram grass. They were locals, of course, supplemented by the ones cutting through the graveyard. They sounded a distance away, and of course were. He'd lost count of the intervening spaces between here and the front of the house. At the thought of pushing past so many he was overcome by a vertiginous self-consciousness.

And The Church Arms was still filling. Were none of them happy? Each voice added to the mulch of sound; he heard tones of complaint, fear, weariness, but listened in vain for a dialogue, shared laughter, the clinking of glasses. In his own glass a dry, dark sediment remained. There was an aftertaste like puddle water in his mouth. The draught from the graveyard was colder. He stuffed his trembling fingers into his pockets.

The voices, a multitude it seemed, were coming nearer, surely overflowing out of the main area. How would he get past them all? As things were he'd surely see the first at any moment. His eyes widened at that prospect. His heart blundered like a lost thing in the mist, and suddenly felt as cold and motionless as a stone slab. He'd have thought it had stopped entirely as he slumped back down into the chair, were it not that he still heard the man's voice, one woollen stitch in a tapestry of other voices. He didn't acknowledge Bentink's collapsed state. But the others, stepping into the alcove, surely would. *I don't feel at all well*, he rehearsed, though the voice in his head sounded more pleading than apologetic.

The confined space seemed to have a limitless capacity, for there seemed no end to them pushing and shunting against each other weightlessly.

Bentink watched and understood too well. *He's late because he's been spreading the word, and there were so many to tell—so many.*

The snug was dense with shadows and voices, and more were arriving. Listening was torment enough; worse was a dawning comprehension of what they were saying.

Biographical Notes

PETER BELL ('Only Sleeping') is a historian, teaching undergraduates in York, England. He has written a revisionist study of Neville Chamberlain, published by Macmillan. He is a contributor to *All Hallows* and *Wormwood*. Hailing from Liverpool, he is a great admirer of Ramsey Campbell's stories set within that city. Other favourite writers include Karl Edward Wagner, Robert Aickman, Terry Lamsley, and Joyce Carol Oates; and he admires for their sinister atmosphere the films of Alfred Hitchcock and Ingmar Bergman. 'Only Sleeping' was inspired by the childhood memory of unexplained disturbances heard at night in a boarding house on the Isle of Man, and by a fascination with the eeriness of fading holiday resorts.

SIMON BESTWICK ('Beneath the Sun') was born in 1974 and lives in the former Lancashire mining town of Swinton. When not working in a soul-destroying day job, he writes fiction, poetry, and drama, occasionally acts, goes to rock concerts, and generally pursues the delights of wine, women, and song (two of these with somewhat greater success than the third) while daydreaming of a life of ease, preferably on a rugged stretch of coastline or on an island in the Outer Hebrides. His first story collection, *A Hazy Shade of Winter*, was published by Ash-Tree Press in 2004. Simon writes: 'Reading a certain classic story, I loved it, but found it very different from what I'd visualised after hearing it discussed by friends. So I wrote down the scenario I'd imagined. "Beneath the Sun" is the result.'

RAMSEY CAMPBELL ('Breaking Up') is described by *The Oxford Companion to English Literature* as 'Britain's most respected living horror writer'. He has been given more awards than any other writer in the field, including the Grand Master Award of the World Horror Convention and the Lifetime Achievement Award of the Horror Writers Association. Among his novels are *The Face That Must Die*, *Incarnate*, *Midnight Sun*, *The Count of Eleven*, *Silent Children*, *The Darkest Part of the Woods*, *The Overnight*, and *Secret Stories*. Forthcoming are *The Communications* and *Spanked by Nuns*. His collections include *Waking Nightmares*, *Alone with the Horrors*, *Ghosts and Grisly Things*, and *Told by the Dead*, and his non-fiction is collected as *Ramsey Campbell, Probably*. His novels *The Nameless* and *Pact of the Fathers* have been filmed in Spain. Ramsey lives on Merseyside with his wife Jenny. He reviews films and DVDs weekly for BBC Radio Merseyside, and his pleasures include classical music, good food and wine, and whatever's in that pipe. Of 'Breaking Up', Ramsey writes: 'I'd already written one macabre tale about a mobile phone, and then it occurred to me that there could be another. I suspect all this is my mental preparation for owning one of the things.' Ramsey's web site is at *www.ramseycampbell.com.*

EDWARD P. CRANDALL ('Survivors') was born in 1964 in New Jersey. He has lived alternately in Japan and the United States since 1987, and currently works as a columnist and reporter for the *Saga Shimbun* newspaper, writing in the Japanese language. His Japanese language journalism has also been published in the *Nishi Nihon Shimbun* and the *Mainichi Shimbun,* and his English language non-fiction has appeared in the *Asahi Evening News.* This is his first published work of fiction. Edward writes: 'The germ of this story came from two experiences. First, I walk for an hour every morning starting at around 5.30. Through the fall and winter, it is still dark at that time of day. One morning as I wound my way through the narrow, poorly lit streets of my neighbourhood here in Japan, I got to thinking about ghosts and how they could be hiding in any one of the dark shadows in people's yards, just inside their gates, and behind trees. I started thinking about who those ghosts might have been and what, if anything, they might be thinking, if they were able to see me walking along the street. The other experience was a dream. I wrote the scene in the story of Mr Shimada's half-burned face and bony, scalded arm reaching out from the ruins of his bomb-flattened house just as I dreamed it, and worked out the details of the narrative, characters, etc. from there.'

STEVE DUFFY ('Someone Across the Way') has written short stories which have appeared in magazines including *All Hallows, Ghosts & Scholars, new genre, Darkness Rising,* and *Supernatural Tales.* Two collections of his work, both solo and collaborative, have been published by Ash-Tree Press; a third, *A Presence in the Room,* is in preparation. Steve's story for the earlier Ash-Tree Press anthology *Shadows and Silence,* 'The Rag-and-Bone Men', won an International Horror Guild award for the year 2000: should lightning strike twice, and the pattern thus established repeat itself, he thinks he could probably deal with that. About his story, Steve writes: 'There are two sorts of people in the world—those who see a lighted window in a strange house at night and are able to pass by *without* looking in, and all the rest of us. I expect the latter group will get the most out of this story.'

JOSEPH A. EZZO ('Vado Mori') is a professional archaeologist living in Tucson, Arizona, who got the idea for writing 'Vado Mori' while on leave as a visiting professor at Tsukuba University, Japan in 2001. His horror novel *Cold Raven Moon* will be published in early 2005 by Cyber-Pulp Books, and his contemporary thriller *Makai* is due in 2006 from Hellbound Books. He writes: 'The idea for "Vado Mori" came to me when I was accidentally diverted during an internet search, and ended up at a website dealing with the *danse macabre.* At the time I was doing research on patron saints for another story, and decided to put the two ideas together.'

PAUL FINCH ('The Belfries') is a full-time writer based in the U.K. He earns his bread and butter working in film and TV, but is no stranger to the short-story market, having had over two hundred tales published on both sides of the Atlantic. His first collection, *After Shocks* (Ash-Tree Press), won the British Fantasy Award for 2001, and his short novel *Cape Wrath* (Telos Books) made the final ballot for the Stoker Awards in 2002 and has since been optioned for movie development. Two more collections, *The Extremist* (Pendragon Press) and *Darker Ages* (Sarob Press) were published during 2004. The Brit horror movie *Spirit Trap,* which Paul co-authored, is due for release shortly, and he

BIOGRAPHICAL NOTES

is now writing two more scripts in the genre. Paul lives in Lancashire with his wife, Cathy, and his two children, Eleanor and Harry. Paul writes: '"The Belfries" was inspired by a house that we bought in 1994. As it turned out, we lived there very happily for six years, but the first few months were unnerving. The house was on a new estate which was empty of fellow residents. It's odd, but I found it more oppressive to be surrounded by silent houses than I ever would to be surrounded by silent woods.'

ADAM GOLASKI ('Weird Furka') is the horror fiction editor of *new genre* (*www.new-genre.com*). His fiction and poetry have been published in a number of journals, including *American Letters & Commentary*, *Hanging Loose*, *All Hallows*, *Supernatural Tales*, *LVNG*, and *eye-rhyme*. He lives in Missoula, Montana with his beautiful wife Zetta. Adam writes: 'With their children playing, my mother would ask other young mothers if they'd ever heard any true ghost stories. She discovered that many of them had first-hand experiences. My father is an amateur radio historian, so I grew up listening to radio shows. He and I learned that many radio stations created shows that were only meant for local broadcast. Some of those shows crop up from time to time, when attics and cellars are cleaned out.'

CHRISTOPHER HARMAN ('The Listener') lives in Preston, Lancashire. He has held a variety of jobs in the Lancashire County Library service and currently works in a hundred-year-old Carnegie building on the Fylde coast. His stories have been published in *All Hallows*, *Ghosts & Scholars*, *Dark Horizons*, *Electronic Enigmatic*, *Kimota*, *The Year's Best Fantasy and Horror*, and last, but not least, *The Doppelgänger Broadsheet*. In his spare time he writes, watches films, and sometimes heads for the nearest hills. Christopher has become an avid reader of science fiction after ignoring it for twenty years, but ghost stories, fantasy, and horror occupy most of his reading time. Of 'The Listener' he writes: 'The story was prompted by my experience of the kind of "blink and you miss it" pub that has a surprisingly extensive, and sometimes confusing, interior.'

MARK P. HENDERSON ('Rope Trick') is the pseudonym of a middle-aged British medical scientist who writes fiction when he thinks no one's looking. He's afraid that if the authorities discover how much he enjoys it they'll stop him doing it. He's published a lot of boring scientific stuff during the past three decades, but he can't help that—it's his job. He's published short stories as well, two of which have appeared in *All Hallows*. He now lives with his Scottish partner in Derbyshire in central England, a county rich in supernatural folklore, and divides his time among medical and scientific work, lecturing, walking in the local countryside, visiting his two daughters, and cooking. He previously lived and worked for many years in Scotland, the country that provides the setting for 'Rope Trick'. The author comments: '"Rope Trick" explores the reactions of intelligent present-day people to a situation that seems to deny explanation. It was written in response to a challenge. During a conversation with friends about the prerequisites for an effective supernatural story, I suggested that it would be possible to construct an effective, unnerving tale of suspense without any of the usual trappings: no dark shadows, no storms, no grim legends, no dead bodies or monsters, not even a creaking door. Most of my friends were sceptical, so a bet was placed—a bet I won.'

GLEN HIRSHBERG ('Safety Clowns') has won two International Horror Guild Awards and received four World Fantasy Award nominations. Both *The Two Sams*, a collection of ghost stories, and his first novel, *The Snowman's Children*, are published in the United States by Carroll & Graf. His fiction has appeared in numerous magazines and anthologies, including *The Mammoth Book of Best New Horror*, *Trampoline*, *The Year's Best Fantasy and Horror*, *Cemetery Dance*, *Dark Terrors 6*, and *The Dark*. The highly acclaimed 'Mr Dark's Carnival' appeared in Ash-Tree's earlier anthology *Shadows and Silence*. Glen lives in the Los Angeles area with his wife and children, and has just completed a new novel. As to the origins of 'Safety Clowns', Hirshberg will say only: 'A little too much of this story is true.'

RICK KENNETT ('The Cross Talk') was born in 1956 and has lived in Melbourne all his life (he hates to travel). His work has appeared in many magazines, and in anthologies such as *Strange Fruit*, *Terror Australis*, *Southern Blood*, and three 'Year's Best' volumes. Rick's books include *13: A Collection of Ghost Stories* and *No. 472 Cheyne Walk: Carnacki, the Untold Stories*, written with Chico Kidd. His interests include naval history and wandering through cemeteries—necrotourism. Rick notes: '"The Cross Talk" has its basis in the phenomenon of phone calls from the dead. Add to this the fact that communication is often prone to misunderstanding.'

CHICO KIDD ('Salvage') likes learning new things—sailing, canoeing, fencing, judo, Russian, Latin, French, and German, all before the age of eighteen. Then she gained a law degree, saw her first story published, and discovered what unemployment was like. Before she reached thirty she made a success in advertising, learnt to ride a horse, and to ring church bells (badly). She got married on her thirtieth birthday, and has since learnt to scuba dive, has studied Italian, Spanish, and Portuguese, had three books published, travelled to twenty-five countries, ridden elephants and camels, and run the London Marathon. There are still a lot more things she wants to do, and she still can't ride a bicycle. She can't write without music: fado opera, baroque. When it comes to art she will actively seek out Miró, Gauguin, Paula Rego, the Renaissance, and some of the Pre-Raphaelites. She loves Gaudí's architecture, but her favourite city is Lisbon. Writing influences that she can identify include M. R. James, Raymond Chandler, C. S. Forester, William Hope Hodgson, Rider Haggard, John Buchan, and Joss Whedon. Where Captain Luís da Silva came from she still doesn't know, but he's still going strong after sixteen long short stories (all published) and four novels (so far unpublished). Chico is four chapters into the fifth novel at the time of writing. Most of the da Silva tales, likewise, arrive unannounced. 'Salvage' is unusual in that the encounter with the derelict was suggested by an episode in *Odysseys and Oddities* by Captain Frank Shaw, who wrote a number of fascinating volumes of reminiscences and memoirs. 'Salvage', for those who take note of such things, takes place some time after 'Arkright's Tale' (in *No. 472 Cheyne Walk*) and 'The Dragon That Ate the Sun (which appeared in *Supernatural Tales* #6).

JOEL LANE ('Beyond the River') is the author of two novels, *From Blue To Black* and *The Blue Mask* (Serpent's Tail); a collection of short stories, *The Earth Wire* (Egerton Press); and two collections of poems, *The Edge of the Screen* and *Trouble in the Heartland* (Arc). He has edited an anthology of subterranean horror stories, *Beneath the Ground* (The Alchemy Press); and he and Steve Bishop have edited an anthology of crime and suspense stories, *Birmingham Noir* (Tindal Street Press). He is currently working on his third novel, *Midnight Blue*. Joel writes: '"Beyond the River" is a tribute to the genius of Tove Jansson. It's also a polemic on behalf of independent and creative publishing, and against the dead hand of corporate commerce.'

GARY McMAHON ('Out On a Limb') is an English writer who has placed stories with several magazines including *Fusing Horizons*, *Bare Bone*, *All Hallows*, *Supernatural Tales*,

BIOGRAPHICAL NOTES

Jupiter, Black Petals, Whispers of Wickedness, and *Midnight Street.* He has also sold tales to the anthologies *Poe's Progeny, Dark Sins and Desires Unveiled, U-nrestrained K-reations, Dark Highways, Potters Field, Maelstrom, Dark Elation,* and *Lunar Harvest.* His chapbook *Breaking Hearts* is available from D Press. Gary lives with his wife and son in West Yorkshire, and can be found at *www.GaryMcMahon.com.* Gary writes: '"Out On A Limb" was originally written as part of a planned anthology that was to be put together by the members of Ramsey Campbell's on-line message board. The anthology idea bit the dust, but the story has made its own way in the world, like a persistent child.'

REGGIE OLIVER ('The Devil's Number') has been a professional playwright, actor, and theatre director since 1975. He has worked in radio, television, films, and theatre, both in the West End and outside London. His plays include *Imaginary Lines,* which was first produced and directed by Alan Ayckbourn at Scarborough, and has since been translated into several languages; *Taking Liberties* (Wolsey, Ipswich); *Put Some Clothes On, Clarisse!* (Duchess Theatre, London); and *Winner Takes All,* most recently revived at the Orange Tree Theatre in 2000. His biography of Stella Gibbons, *Out of the Woodshed,* was published by Bloomsbury in 1998, and he is a contributor to the historical magazine *History Today.* He has written, and written about, ghost stories for such journals as *All Hallows, Supernatural Tales,* and *Weirdly Supernatural.* His IHG award-nominated volume of ghost stories, *The Dreams of Cardinal Vittorini,* was published in 2003, and a further volume, *The Complete Symphonies of Adolf Hitler,* is to be published in 2005. Reggie writes of 'The Devil's Number': 'As a biographer, I have often dreamed of finding a hitherto unknown manuscript by, or about, my chosen subject; but sometimes the dream is a nightmare.'

EDWARD PEARCE ('Jenny Gray's House') is a translator who lives in London but spends as much time as he can at his second home in a small Lincolnshire market town. His interests include reading, antiques, music, museums, galleries, walking, riding, and British History. He was inspired to begin writing ghost stories by the greatest of them all, M. R. James, whose stories he has read more times than he can remember. 'Jenny Gray's Farm' in Stonea, Cambridgeshire, provided the name and inspiration for that character in this story. As regards locations, Wakeford is Wisbech, Upper Marwell is Upwell combined with Friday Bridge, and the original of the cottage is in Broughton, all in Cambridgeshire.

JOHN PELAN ('Crazy Little Thing Called Love') is the editor of more than two dozen volumes of supernatural, horror, and mystery fiction. As an author, his stories have appeared in numerous venues, two novellas are forthcoming from Cemetery Dance Publications, and a collection of his ghostly tales is forthcoming from Ash-Tree Press. He is currently working with Mehitobel Wilson on a sequel to H. P. Lovecraft's 'The Whisperer in Darkness', involving Lothar Von Richtofen, FTL travel, and inter-stellar contact with the Great Race. John writes: 'Like most of the "Smoking Leg" stories, much of "Crazy Little Thing Called Love" was composed (mentally, if not on paper) at the Knarr Tavern and Murphy's Pub in Seattle. Neither establishment bears much resemblance to the pub in the stories, but literary inspiration often comes during a game of darts or pinball. The real genesis of the tale was a discussion long ago on the Usenet group alt.books.ghost-fiction with the late Johnny Eatman, Jim Rockhill, and some other regulars, where I declared my intention to write a really nasty modern version of "How Love Came to Professor Guildea". The story that resulted isn't really as much of a riff on Hichens as I'd intended back then, but I do feel that it turned out suitably nasty. I hope you agree. . . .'

BARBARA RODEN ('Northwest Passage') was born in Vancouver, British Columbia, and has been reading ghost stories since the age of seven, when she was given a copy of *More Tales to Tremble By* and introduced to the writing of, amongst others, H. R. Wakefield, William Hope Hodgson, Cynthia Asquith, and M. R. James. In her spare time she edits *All Hallows*, the award-winning journal of The Ghost Story Society. Although the exact setting of 'Northwest Passage' is not specified in the story, it is based on a real place, a cabin called The Lookout, which perches above a valley some miles southwest of Ashcroft, B.C., where the author lives with her husband Christopher and son Tim. Barbara's story stems from two fascinations: with Canadian legends like that of the Wendigo, and with the lives of Arctic explorers, those men who felt driven to leave civilization behind and seek—*something*—missing from their existence. In Franklin's day there was ample opportunity to make such a quest under the guise of filling in the blank spaces on the map; but now that those spaces have been filled, what becomes of such people? And what happens when such a person meets more than he bargained for? Thus was 'Northwest Passage' born, with an acknowledgement to the late, great Canadian folk singer Stan Rogers.

CATHY SAHU ('You Should Have to Live with Yourself') is a housewife with a background in nursing. She lives in Southern California with her husband and four children. Besides writing ghost stories and screenplays for amateur films, she studies Chinese. As a result, she has fallen rather behind in her housekeeping. The exemplary habits of Barbara in 'You Should Have to Live with Yourself' are based on those of the author's sister, Jeanie, who also loves ghost stories but somehow finds the time to keep even her patio so spotless it looks vacuumed. She is, however, not a nag: the inspiration for that less pleasant aspect of Barbara's personality must remain nameless.

JESSICA AMANDA SALMONSON ('The Weeping Manse'), when asked for a brief biographical note, replied: 'How 'bout: Jessica gardens on Puget Sound.' Well, that's true enough, but it ignores the fact that she has published many novels, short stories, and poems, chiefly in the area of fantasy and the supernatural. Her previous books include *What Did Miss Darrington See?*, *Tomoe Gozen*, *The Golden Naginata*, *The Encyclopaedia of the Amazons*, *The Eleventh Jaguarundi*, *A Silver Thread of Madness*, and *The Dark Tales*. It ignores, too, the fact that she is the recipient of a World Fantasy Award, Lambda Award, and Readercon Award. Jessica has edited volumes of stories by Julian Hawthorne, Marjorie Bowen, Thomas Burke, Alice Brown, Sarah Orne Jewett, Georgia Wood Pangborn, Harriet Prescott Spofford, and Mary Heaton Vorse for Ash-Tree Press, and her own collection, *The Deep Museum: Ghost Stories of a Melancholic*, was published by Ash-Tree in 2003. Of 'The Weeping Manse', she writes: 'It was inspired by an old Georgetown legend of Seattle and re-told with licence, but the majority of the particulars are frequently told 'round town as a "true" story. Another version of the legend adds a slain infant whose corpse is buried under the staircase. The specific mansion of the story today houses an arts cooperative, but its use has never been very stable, and it is apt to be something else altogether next year.'

BRIAN SHOWERS ('The Old Tailor and the Gaunt Man'), a native of Madison, Wisconsin, has lived in Dublin, Ireland since 2000. He graduated from the University of Wisconsin in 1999 with a degree in English Literature and Communication Arts. He

BIOGRAPHICAL NOTES

writes short stories and comic books, and is currently looking for a publisher for his book of literary walking tours through Gothic Dublin. Brian writes: '"The Old Tailor and the Gaunt Man" originated with a morbid thought I once had while walking through Mount Jerome cemetery in Dublin: Most people are buried in their Sunday best, but like flesh and bone, clothing deteriorates. So who do the dead go to when their suits need mending? It can only be a mixed blessing when such a customer comes a-knocking at your door. . . .'

MELANIE TEM ('Visits'). Melanie's solo novels are *Prodigal* (recipient of the Bram Stoker Award for Superior Achievement, First Novel), *Blood Moon*, *Wilding*, *Revenant*, *Desmodus*, *The Tides*, *Black River*, *Pioneer*, *Slain in the Spirit*, and *The Deceiver*. Collaborative novels are *Making Love* and *Witch-Light* with Nancy Holder and *Daughters* with Steve Rasnic Tem. The chapbook *The Man on the Ceiling*, written with Steve Rasnic Tem, won the 2001 Bram Stoker, International Horror Guild, and World Fantasy Awards. The award-winning multi-media CD-ROM *Imagination Box* was also a collaborative project with Steve Rasnic Tem. Melanie's short stories have appeared in anthologies, magazines, and in the collection *The Ice Downstream*. She has also published non-fiction articles and poetry. Recipient of a 2001–2 associateship from the Rocky Mountain Women's Institute, Tem is also writing plays. Her one-act *The Society for Lost Positives* has been produced in Denver, Salida, and Chicago. Also a social worker, Melanie lives in Denver with her husband, writer and editor Steve Rasnic Tem. They have four children and three granddaughters.

STEVE RASNIC TEM ('Inside William James') has had more than two hundred and fifty short stories published, in (among others) *Mike Shane Mystery*, *The Saint Magazine*, *New Mystery*, *Fantasy and Science Fiction*, *Asimov's*, *Twilight Zone*, *Cemetery Dance*, *Weird Tales*, *Hardboiled*, *Crimewave*, *New Crimes*, *Constable New Crimes*, *Year's Best Fantasy and Horror*, *Shadows*, and *Masters of Darkness*. A major collection of his short supernatural fiction, *The Far Side of the Lake*, was published by Ash-Tree Press in 2001.

DON TUMASONIS ('A Pace of Change') once spent many hours on the rocky heights, practising the infamous Whillans stance, cigarette butt on lips, wondering if his own notorious two-finger belays would hold his worried partner, a Nanda Devi summiteer. That last individual, although having gone bald from the well-known Tumasonis nonchalance, nonetheless survived and quit mountaineering, saying none of his Himalayan experiences had prepared him for those days with the author-to-be, who himself gave up climbing and smoking long ago for the marginally less dangerous pursuits of deep-sea diving and explaining to his wife the purchase of yet another book for their library. Regarding his story, he dares the reader to guess which of the book titles mentioned is fictive.

STEPHEN VOLK ('Three Fingers, One Thumb') is mainly known as a film and television screenwriter, with *Gothic*, *Ghostwatch*, and *Octane* among his credits. He is currently working on a big-screen adaptation of John Masefield's children's fantasy *The Box of Delights*, and his six-part paranormal drama series *Afterlife*, starring Lesley Sharp and Andrew Lincoln, will appear on ITV in 2005. Of his story, Steve writes: '"Three Fingers, One Thumb" came from the observation that we surround infants with relentlessly cheery cartoon characters which, to me—like clowns and ventriloquists' dolls—immediately evoke sinister, even malevolent, intent. Add to that my inherent suspicion of the enforced happy-clappiness of American theme parks, and the story virtually wrote itself.'

ACQUAINTED WITH THE NIGHT

JOHN WHITBOURN ('The Sunken Garden') is a former archaeologist now professing to be 'going straight'. He has had nine books published since winning the BBC Radio 4/Victor Gollancz 'First Fantasy Novel' prize with *A Dangerous Energy* back in 1991; these include: *To Build Jerusalem*, set in the same altered history where the Reformation failed and magic works; *Popes and Phantoms*, which 'wreaked stylish havoc' on Renaissance Italy; *The Royal Changeling* which likewise assaulted Stuart England, and was described as the first work of Jacobite fantasy fiction for several centuries; and, most recently, Simon & Schuster released the three volumes of his 'Downs-Lord' trilogy, concerning the establishment of empire in an alternative, monster-ridden England. John has also had numerous short stories published in the U.K., Canada, and the U.S.A., not least being two collections of his linked 'Binscombe Tales' ghost stories (*Binscombe Tales: Sinister Saxon Stories* and *More Binscombe Tales: Sinister Sutangli Stories* (Ash-Tree Press, 1998 and 1999)). Amongst other Millennial fears, people accordingly awaited *Yet More Bloody Binscombe Tales* in 2000—but that will never be (though sinister events surrounding a suppressed edition of *Binscombe Tales* are narrated in a new Binscombe 'tale', to be published in a new Ash-Tree volume of Whitbourn stories in 2005). He is also currently working on his 'Army-Faith & The Stronghold' young adult series. Readers of Ash-Tree anthologies will also be pleased to learn that John retains his day job as part-time military attaché at the Zulu Embassy in London. Of 'The Sunken Garden', John notes: 'I am indebted for the setting to a "true ghost stories" book—title and author alas forgotten—read long ago.' And if all of this doesn't tell you enough, insatiable thirst may be slaked at *www.btinternet.com/~john.whitbourn*

THE EDITORS:

BARBARA and CHRISTOPHER RODEN's long-time interest in the ghost story translated into the formation, in 1995, of Ash-Tree Press, which specializes in the publishing of classic supernatural fiction, old and new. In 1997 Ash-Tree Press won a World Fantasy Award, and in 2000 it was honoured with the special award of the Board of Trustees of the Horror Writers Association. Their involvement with the ghost story also extends to the day-to-day running of the Ghost Story Society, for which they edit a thrice-yearly journal, *All Hallows*, which won an International Horror Guild award for 2003.

Their second major interest is Sherlock Holmes and his creator, Sir Arthur Conan Doyle. Together they run the Arthur Conan Doyle Society (which Christopher founded in 1989), and edit its publication *ACD*. A second publishing imprint, Calabash Press, specialises in fiction and non-fiction related to both the great detective and his creator. Barbara became a Master Bootmaker (Canada's highest national Sherlockian award) in 1992, and was winner of the Derrick Murdoch Memorial Award of the Bootmakers of Toronto in 2002 for her regular 'A Bootmaker Out West' column in *Canadian Holmes*. Christopher had to wait until 2000 for his Master Bootmaker elevation, and was invested a Baker Street Irregular ('Sir Henry Baskerville') in 2002.

After establishing Ash-Tree Press in England, Barbara (a Canadian) and Christopher (born in England, but now a Canadian, too) moved to Canada. They now reside, with their seven-year-old son Timothy, in the small village of Ashcroft, British Columbia, 200 miles northeast of, and half-a-day away from, Vancouver. Their house is overrun by books, and submerged in paper.

ACQUAINTED WITH THE NIGHT

The first printing of the Ash-Tree Press edition of
Acquainted With the Night
was published on 10 December 2004
in a hardback edition of Four Hundred copies
and in an unlimited paperback edition.

Ash-Tree Press

Titles Published

1994
Lady Stanhope's Manuscript and Other Supernatural Tales (Card Covers)

1995
The Five Jars *by M. R. James*
The Alabaster Hand *by A. N. L. Munby*
Intruders: New Weird Tales *by A. M. Burrage*
They Return at Evening *by H. R. Wakefield*
Nine Ghosts *by R. H. Malden*

1996
Sleep No More *by L. T. C. Rolt*
Randalls Round *by Eleanor Scott*
Conference With the Dead: Tales of Supernatural Terror *by Terry Lamsley*
Forgotten Ghosts (Card Covers)
The Executor and Other Ghost Stories *by David G. Rowlands*
Old Man's Beard *by H. R. Wakefield*
Ghosts in the House *by A. C. and R. H. Benson*
A Book of Ghosts *by S. Baring-Gould*
The Occult Files of Francis Chard: Some Ghost Stories *by A. M. Burrage*

1997
In Ghostly Company *by Amyas Northcote*
Under the Crust *by Terry Lamsley*
Unholy Relics *by M. P. Dare*
Imagine a Man in a Box *by H. R. Wakefield*
The Rose of Death and Other Mysterious Delusions *by Julian Hawthorne*
Midnight Never Comes *edited by Barbara and Christopher Roden*
The Haunted Chair and Other Stories *by Richard Marsh*
Someone in the Room: Strange Tales Old and New *by A. M. Burrage*
Annual Macabre 1997 *edited by Jack Adrian*

1998
Binscombe Tales: Sinister Saxon Stories *by John Whitbourn*
Out of the Dark: Volume 1 *by Robert W. Chambers*
The Night Comes On *by Steve Duffy*
The Clock Strikes Twelve and Other Stories *by H. R. Wakefield*
Aylmer Vance: Ghost-Seer *by Alice and Claude Askew*
Twilight and Other Supernatural Romances *by Marjorie Bowen*
The Fellow Travellers and Other Stories *by Sheila Hodgson*
Nightmare Jack and Other Tales *by John Metcalfe*
The Black Reaper *by Bernard Capes*

The Terror by Night *by E. F. Benson*
Lady Ferry and Other Uncanny People *by Sarah Orne Jewett*
Annual Macabre 1998 *edited by Jack Adrian*
Nights of the Round Table *by Margery Lawrence*

1999
Six Ghost Stories *by T. G. Jackson*
Ghost Gleams *by W. J. Wintle*
The Night Wind Howls: Complete Supernatural Stories *by Frederick Cowles*
Binscombe Tales II: Sinister Sutangli Stories *by John Whitbourn*
Norton Vyse—Psychic *by Rose Champion de Crespigny*
The Terraces of Night *by Margery Lawrence*
Strayers from Sheol *by H. R. Wakefield*
The Wind at Midnight *by Georgia Wood Pangborn*
The Passenger *by E. F. Benson*
The Phantom Coach: Collected Ghost Stories *by Amelia B. Edwards*
Annual Macabre 1999 *edited by Jack Adrian*
The Talisman *by Jonathan Aycliffe*
Warning Whispers *by A. M. Burrage*

2000
Phantom Perfumes and Other Shades: Memories of *Ghost Stories* Magazine *edited by Mike Ashley*
The Horror on the Stair and Other Weird Tales *by Sir Arthur Quiller-Couch*
Dark Matters *by Terry Lamsley*
Reunion at Dawn and Other Uncollected Ghost Stories *by H. R. Wakefield*
The Cold Embrace and Other Ghost Stories *by Mary Elizabeth Braddon*
In the Dark *by E. Nesbit*
We've Been Waiting For You *by John Burke*
The Lady Wore Black and Other Weird Cat Tails *by Hugh B. Cave*
The Moonstone Mass and Others *by Harriet Prescott Spofford*
Summoning Knells and Other Inventions *by A. F. Kidd*
The Secrets of Dr Taverner *by Dion Fortune*
Annual Macabre 2000 *edited by Jack Adrian*
Shadows and Silence *edited by Barbara and Christopher Roden*

2001
Where Human Pathways End *by Shamus Frazer*
Mystic Voices *by Roger Pater*
The Golden Gong and Other Night-Pieces *by Thomas Burke*
After Shocks *by Paul Finch*
The Far Side of the Lake *by Steve Rasnic Tem*
The Shadow on the Blind and Other Ghost Stories *by Mrs Alfred Baldwin*
Mrs Amworth *by E. F. Benson*
A Pleasing Terror *by M. R. James*
The Floating Café *by Margery Lawrence*
Annual Macabre 2001 *edited by Jack Adrian*
The Five Quarters *by Steve Duffy and Ian Rodwell*
Couching at the Door *by D. K. Broster*

2002
The Invisible Eye *by Erckmann-Chatrian*
Hauntings *by Vernon Lee*
Sinister Romance *by Mary Heaton Vorse*
The Amazing Dreams of Andrew Latter *by Harold Begbie*
Not Exactly Ghosts: Collected Weird Tales *by Andrew Caldecott*
No. 472 Cheyne Walk; Carnacki: The Untold Stories *by A. F. Kidd and Rick Kennett*
Figures in Rain *by Chet Williamson*
Schalken the Painter and Others *by J. Sheridan Le Fanu*
Off the Sand Road *by Russell Kirk*
The Mirror and Other Strange Reflections *by Arthur Porges*
Annual Macabre 2002 *edited by Jack Adrian*

2003
Yesterday Knocks *by Noel Boston*
The Experiences of Flaxman Low *by Kate and Hesketh Prichard*
What Shadows We Pursue *by Russell Kirk*
The Face *by E. F. Benson*
The Basilisk and Other Tales of Dread *by R. Murray Gilchrist*
The Haunted Baronet and Others *by J. Sheridan Le Fanu*
Night Creatures *by Seabury Quinn*
The Empire of Death and Other Strange Stories *by Alice Brown*
The Casebook of Miles Pennoyer: Volume One *by Margery Lawrence*
The Deep Museum *by Jessica Amanda Salmonson*
Annual Macabre 2003 *edited by Jack Adrian*

2004
Tales of the Uneasy *by Violet Hunt*
The Devil of the Marsh and Other Stories *by H. B. Marriott Watson*
Dancing on Air and Other Stories *by Frances Oliver*
The Captain of the *Pole-Star*: Weird and Imaginative Fiction *by Arthur Conan Doyle*
A Hazy Shade of Winter *by Simon Bestwick*
The Nebuly Coat *by John Meade Falkner*
Satan's Circus *by Lady Eleanor Smith*
Acquainted With the Night *edited by Barbara Roden and Christopher Roden*

Titles in preparation
Sea Mist *by E. F. Benson*
The Watcher by the Threshold *by John Buchan*
The World, the Flesh, and the Devil: Fantastical Writings *by Gerald Kersh*

Ash-Tree Press Classic Macabre Paperbacks
The Door of the Unreal *by Gerald Biss*
The Ghost Pirates *by William Hope Hodgson*
Children of Epiphany *by Frances Oliver*

Ash-Tree Press New Century Macabre Paperbacks
Divinations of the Deep *by Matt Cardin*

Ash-Tree Press Vampire Classics Paperbacks
Vampires Overhead *by Alan Hyder*